Mario 4

Free Fall

Mario 4
Free Fall

by

George Hatcher

WARNING
ADULT MATTER

This book is intended for adults. Violence and sexual antics are not intended to be read by minors or sensitive readers. Mario is a work of fiction. All the people in Mario 4: Free Fall dwelled and died only in my imagination, soon to dwell in yours. Any resemblance to actual people should be apparent in your imagination too, when you read the book. The story is purely a product of my latest long, boring plane flights leading to flights of fantasy, the wild goose-chasing of a caffeine-free imagination (I watch my caffeine intake these days), and years of experience in wrongful death cases. Like Mario, I am still no lawyer. Unlike Mario, I do not employ nubile sex groupies, or toss people out of high rise buildings when they get on my nerves, no matter how much I might want to.

George and Molly 1968

My one and only Molly
It's all for you and only you.

Acknowledgements

Jody, always with your eyes open, keeping track of everything. Thank you for what you do.

Jorge Bouza, thanks for your rendition of Mario. You do great voice.

 If it were up to my collaborator and editor, Allie Bates, this book would be in edits for the next two years. I always have to pry my manuscripts out of her grip while she is still marking them up. Even after we're in print, she comes yelling after the delivery truck. On this book, the annoying refrain was "Are you certain you want to put in that footnote?" Thanks for the countless days and nights of high blood pressure and indigestion from nitpicking and arguing over things we agree on.

Works by George Hatcher

One Wilshire

Fiction by George Hatcher

Ambulance Chaser Series
Mario 1: Woman in Jeopardy
Mario 2: Coming of Age
Mario 3: Risky Business
Mario 4: Free Fall (2017)
Mario 5: Jack the Banker *[1] (2018)
Mario 6: Flyboy * (2018)

Independent Titles
Arabe (2018)

Pretty Face (2018)

CasaHatcherPress Pasadena

[1] Titles of pending books may change

Epigraph

He didn't like Mario. The big American was too sure of himself. It was bad enough that he knew Spanish, and that the lovely and sympathetic team of girls he surrounded himself with were any man's wet dream. There was something charismatic about him that connected with the families of victims. The families all loved him, but as far as he was concerned, the ambulance chaser was only annoying, cocksure and greedy. He hated how he had to work for every client he got, but the families followed the American like he was the fucking pied piper of plane crashes. Mario was an obstacle choking the pipeline of what was supposed to be a piece of cake operation. They were going to have to do something drastic to get him out of the way.

I swung my arm to the right, blind, and connected hard with somebody. I tangled my hand in his shirt, jerked hard. He fell in my direction and I tossed him across the hallway, his body slamming into a load-bearing column between wallpapered sections of the hall. He went down on his hands and knees, leaving a bloody spot on the pillar. I always told the girls that when they were attacked, their goal was to run to safety. But I'm not in danger of becoming a victim. I made a move toward him and felt a sharp pain in my back, once, twice. Someone moved behind me. Heavy tread, not one of the girls. There were two of them. Back in the hall, I kicked the door shut, yelling for the girls to lock the door. I whipped around and got a good look at a face that was swollen and bruised, but one I recognized as belonging to one of the apes I'd handled before. I looked for the gun I'd been shot with, expecting a .38 or something, but it was a dart gun. Their faces loomed strangely, like a view in a fisheye lens.

I said, "What the fuck?" Or at least I think I said it. The lights went out.

Chapter 1
January 7, 1975
LAX : The Adventure Begins

"The traffic was murder," I told the girl from American Airlines. LAX was a madhouse. The lines at all the ticket counters were long and chaotic, as if instead of ticket agents handing out plane tickets, Bob Barker was handing out cash for guesses on *The Price Is Right*. You wouldn't think January seventh would be so hectic. It wasn't a weekend and not a holiday. Soon I would be with ticket in hand, out in the wild blue yonder, checking out new horizons. I had said goodbye to everyone fifteen minutes before.

"Your flight closed ten minutes ago, Mr. Luna," the ticket girl said. She was tanned and blonde, with straight hair, perfect teeth, the epitome of a typical California girl. The American Airlines uniform didn't give much away about her figure.

"I only missed it because I was stuck in this line." It came out kind of like a snarl.

She tapped my hand, looking at her charts and papers. She had a phone to her ear and was talking to someone in booking. Except she *was* booking. She palmed the mouthpiece and said to me, "You missed your flight, but it looks like it was overbooked. Let's get you on the next flight and bump you up to first class for free. How about that?"

"I was supposed to be in first class, but it was overbooked," I said, keeping my temper in check.

Her shiny smile dimmed a little. "Let's see what we can do for you, then." Her cheery exterior looked a little brittle, as if she were about to crack and say what she really thought. "First class, plus a discount."

"I'm not built for economy seating."

She glanced from my toes to the top of my head.

"Oh my," she said. I swear she licked her lips. My sense of frustration evaporated, and I went into hot chick mode, and gave her a suggestive look. She didn't seem so brittle any more.

I winked at the California girl. Definitely a hot chick. "That works for me, unless the wait is until tomorrow."

"Two hours." She winked back.

I watched her as she finished up the call with booking, thinking of the last time I had fucked a blonde. From time to time, Pixie has been a blonde, but this girl was a natural, I was sure.

I am a former ambulance chaser, now real estate owner, and soon-to-be world traveler. If a male other than myself called me an ambulance chaser, I would probably slap him around. I wouldn't slap a girl around, but I'd still explain to her that I have never chased an ambulance. I don't work for anybody. I guess you could say I am an entrepreneur. I used to handle client development for a lawyer named Jake, but he was found murdered. Someone had been trying to kill me too, but I'd tossed him out of my high-rise apartment. It's not like my life is humdrum. I am currently recovering from being gunshot. I'm not working, and just taking advantage of this opportunity to get out of Los Angeles and see the world, or at least Europe.

This isn't something I'd tell my girls, but maybe I'm not just getting out to do a world tour for the heck of it. Maybe I'm feeling a little lost. Maybe I'm unsure of my next move, my next big project. That's new for me. I've never not known what to do, not since I was a kid. I sold my business, my contacts, practically my whole life, and what am I supposed to do now? Especially with all the people I have depending on me.

The switch to another flight gave me too much time to think and a little time to wander the airport. I passed a dozen phones and phone booths, but didn't pick one up. In fact, not calling to let everyone know exactly where I was felt very wild. The nature of my business has always meant I have to be plugged in, and this was my first step in being unplugged. I'd been taking it easy ever since that smarmy-ass Hugo Pliego shot me with a .38 a couple of months ago, but I had not been totally unreachable. I hit the gift shop, grabbed a handful of post cards and a newspaper, and headed for the coffee shop to while away the two hours. The coffee tasted like soapy dishwater, so it chilled in the cup while I looked over the classifieds, by habit. I circled things of interest, knowing I'd never pursue them. I was planning to be gone for a while. Six months, maybe a year. I needed a break from the city that killed Jake and tried to kill me. I gazed into the crowd thronging past. LAX is primo for people watching.

I have a long list of people I will miss: Aunt Carmen, who raised me; Jo, who used to work in an office for me for lawyers, and who later joined me in the field chasing cases, but who now manages my apartment buildings; Pixie, my childhood sweetheart, who grew up as a 'corner girl' and now works with Jo handling my tenants; Niley, the little sister of my dear friend Tanis, who is now raising her two children and the two that Tanis' death left as orphans, and who makes up the third of my trio of apartment managers; Cosmo, the karate-teacher father-figure who first hired me at ten to grow his client list; Harry, my first lawyer/mentor, who hired me at fourteen, and who died last year of a heart attack; Jake, who was murdered in cold blood, leaving me unaffiliated. I might even miss all of Los Angeles, and the hundreds of people who have come to me for help with their auto crash cases. Not every case has a happy ending, but many of them do.

The loudspeaker called out Air California. I couldn't hear the gate, but it wasn't mine, anyway. I checked the time; my diner stool had a good view of the clock, which was running five minutes behind my Rolex. Still an hour left to wait for my plane. I stared out into the crowd at a family that rushed by. A stocky man, petite wife, son and daughter. Hispanic family, dressed in their finest. The wife had a cane she wasn't using. At the announcement, they started running, all laughing, to make it to their plane. I didn't know them, but they had a familiar look. Who did they remind me of? I'd helped hundreds of families. Then I remembered: Carlos Hernandez. Hernandez had been rear-ended by a truck. The accident sent him and his wife to the hospital, leaving their ten-year-old daughter and nine-year-old son with no one at home to take care of them. A neighbor whose kids went to school with theirs took them in until Hernandez was released from the hospital, followed by his wife a week later. It had been a tough year for the family. He couldn't work, and it took almost a month for disability to kick in. His wife, who had worked part time, was not entitled to disability. I had helped them make ends meet, and eventually Carlos paid me back in small increments. It took a year for the case to settle. Though he would never be a hundred percent again, both parents recovered from their injuries. After attorney fees, they went home with a check for forty-six thousand dollars[1]. To get that much in compensation, the victim had to have an injury he'd be dealing with the rest of his life. I was at Jake's office when Carlos and his wife came in for their check.

"We're going to have a great Thanksgiving," Carlos said as he gave me a big hug. I hadn't seen them in a couple of years, but the kids would be older now than the ones running for their flight. They were out of sight.

I will not miss the IRS, who held an axe over my head for four years, or Terminal Island Prison, who had me for nine days, long enough to scar anyone for life.

I sent some postcards out from the airport. One to my team. One to my aunt. Wish you were here. Big picture of LAX on the back. I wish I could have mailed something to Harry, Jake, and Tanis, but there's no postal service to the great beyond.

---

[1] $46,000.00 in 1975 had the same buying power as $209,636.80 in 2017

The trip to New York took a little over six hours. I sat in first class and was very careful to sip rather than chug the wines they served and temper their effects with a snack. I was not going to have any hangovers. I had planned on snoozing through the over-the-water flight from New York to London, but the woman sitting next to me talked up a storm. I had no idea of her age, but she reminded me of Melina; this girl could talk, and I felt like listening. She introduced herself as Sami. She was pretty, with a fair complexion, reddish hair, and that translucent-looking English skin that looks like she'd been wandering around her whole life in a moist fog.

Sami's attire reminded me of Melina, too. Her expensive bellbottoms weren't just bellbottoms, if you know what I mean. Not that I know anything about women's clothes, but for the past year, I have been comparing Jo, Niley, and Pixie's department-store clothes to Melina's high-dollar designer purchases and hearing the girls yammer on about designers. I couldn't tell you who made what, but even I can see the difference in quality. Like Melina, this girl spent a bundle on clothes and shoes. I doubt anyone had offered her a first-class discount. She'd paid a bundle for the seat her shapely ass was sitting in, and that ass looked like it hadn't ever flown any other way.

She showed me her one-way ticket. I showed her mine.

"I live in London," she told me. She had come to New York to visit with her father who lived there, and to meet his fiancée. She said she lived in a flat.

"What's a flat?"

"We call apartments flats."

"Got it."

"After my mom died, I decided the house was not for me any longer, so I bought the flat." She smiled. "You need to come visit me."

"Thank you for the invitation. I may do that."

"How long are you going to be in London, and where are you staying?"

"Not sure how long in London, but I'm staying at the Mandarin."

"Nice hotel," Sami said.

"My friend Melina recommended it."

"I live ten minutes from there. Give me a call when you get settled. I'll give you the four-star treatment. Take you to all the sights. Show you the best nooks and crannies in London."

"I'll take you up on the invitation, for sure."

She pulled a pen out of her purse, grabbed my hand, and wrote her phone number on my palm with a bright red Flair.

This meeting was getting interesting. She didn't say and I didn't ask if there was a man in her life.

"So good looking, so tall," she said, "and you have such big hands." She stroked my hand, and I had to put my briefcase on my lap to conceal my reaction.

The plane landed. She surprised me with a kiss that was more passionate than casual, then we got separated in the crowd, and she disappeared into the airport. I didn't see if anyone came to meet her. I was glad that all I had with me was one carry-on so I didn't have to go to the baggage counter. I wondered if all the airports in Europe were as chaotic as Heathrow. I caught a taxi to the hotel.

London streets were packed, and the sidewalks were just as packed; taxis and buses ran everywhere I looked, and trains ran underground. After I was settled, I tried all of these modes of transport, but preferred walking to most places. In Piccadilly, I saw a couple of live musicals: *The Mousetrap* and a couple of others. It was neat that vendors sold ice cream during the one intermission. By the time the shows were over, I'd made friends with those sitting around me, mostly apologizing for being so damn tall. Everyone was friendly, but shows were just not for me.

Piccadilly didn't just have theatres. Bars, restaurants, and night clubs were full of people my age. Lots of girls in bright colors and short skirts. Piccadilly was a long walk from Knightsbridge where the hotel was located, but walking at a fast pace was great exercise. Twice when I found a female companion who seemed to be looking for company just as I was, we took a taxi from Piccadilly back to the hotel. Once there was a little whirlwind in front of the hotel, and when we encountered it, I discovered one of my new friends was going commando under her miniskirt. I don't think she was aware she'd flashed the world, but the doorman and I were equally appreciative. It was so cold that I always asked the girls if their leggings were warm enough, considering how short miniskirts were.

Once, weather convinced me not to walk, and I took a train to the hotel. I was standing in the aisle across from this hot chick with her lovely legs crossed. As I'd done with other girls, I asked if the leggings were warm enough. She showed me a big smile and said they were. Some random guy on the train thumped me on the back and said, "She's perfectly fine, and none of your damn business."

"Sorry," I said, "I was just curious."

I looked at her once more. Her smile was still there. I maneuvered past the big guy so I could stand on her other side.

There was a lot to take in, and no one to bounce my responses off of. I was accustomed to having Jo, Pixie, and Niley around me all the time, and Melina close by. It felt strange to be footloose by myself. If I interpreted that strangeness, I'd guess I'd say I was lonely.

This was just the beginning of my journey. Italy and the South of France would be there for the taking when I tired of London. I was feeling the lack of apparel, but as I'd planned all along, I dropped into the men's shops on Savile Row and laid out a bundle on top of the line menswear that would knock Melina's socks off. I looked forward to seeing her expression when she saw my booty. I'm accustomed to buying off the tall rack, when I can find clothing to fit. A lot of tailoring was involved in these new purchases, but I had nothing else to do; and I've never had clothes fit so well. Until recently, my attire consisted of jeans and a shirt worn out or tucked in, depending on what I was doing. If I was signing a case, I'd wear a sports jacket.

Here in London, I bought a couple of steamer trunks. I'd already filled one with new suits and shipped it home. I'm no clothes horse, but I planned to fill the other one with whatever I found on my travels. I'd heard a lot of good things about Italian tailors too.

I worked out in the hotel gym, but karate exercises tended to draw a crowd, so space became an issue. I learned quickly enough that I was better served keeping the karate in my room.

It was the dinner hour, and except for me, the gym was deserted. I was on the treadmill, sweating up a storm to pumped-in brisk dance music from some London radio station. A Eurasian girl walked thru. She was clearly a tourist, wearing sweats and carrying a book. I perked up, thinking there'd be company to sweat with, but she opened a door I'd been ignoring. I grabbed my towel, stepped off the treadmill, and went to the door she'd used. It had a big red sign: Guests Only. WET AREA. I don't know why I'd never noticed it before. In my head, I'd always assumed it was something janitorial.

I stepped through into a breezy tiled hall with high windows on one wall that would have been letting in sunlight if it had been day. At the far end, I could see a glass door and the heated indoor pool beyond and hear the echo of yelling and splashes. But what really caught my attention was the girl I'd followed in here. She was a slim little thing, slipping off her sweats and shoving them into a locker and stringing the key to a chain around her neck. She'd stripped down to the kind of bikini my aunt called "Band-Aids and string." She opened the glass door—not the one to the pool—and went inside. I walked up and tried to look in, but all I could see was a cloud of white, like London fog, and inside I heard a kind of hissing. I turned to the wall that had gym lockers. They were like the ones you'd see in school, but nice, painted in the hotel colors and topped with a sign: GUEST USE ONLY. They had little keys built in, like bus station lockers. I opened one and pulled off my sweatshirt, socks, and shoes and shoved them inside. I applied the key to the locker, and the little "occupied" sign came up. Behind me, the door opened and a waft of scalding steam whooshed over me.

I whipped around and came face to face with the little Eurasian girl looking like a boiled lobster. Her nose and cheeks were scarlet, damp hair was plastered all over her face, and her glasses were steamed over.

"Whew," she said in a British accent. "Too hot for my blood." She looked up at me. "Be a good chap and hold this. I'm Angela." She draped her towel over my arm and took off down the hall. I heard a splash and a squeal as she jumped in the pool. She was back in under a minute, sloshing back through the glass door, dripping wet, glasses and all, and carrying a strong scent of chlorine.

"Hi, Angela," I said. "I'm Mario."

"Thanks, Mario." She took back her towel and wiped off the glasses. "They have a nerve calling that pool heated, don't you think?"

She did not return to the steamy hell room, but disappeared behind the wooden door.

I stood there, not sure which door to take. I'm a curious man, so I stepped into the room with the steam, walked over to a big tile bench, and sat down, drenching my sweatpants.

"Fuck."

I jumped up. My pants were sopping.

I ran my finger along the wall. Drips streamed down my hand. Everything was soaked, even the tiled walls and ceiling. I took a deep breath, and my lungs filled up with what felt like boiling air. I started hacking. Something rumbled, a fresh blast of steam filled the room, and I shot out.

"Damn," I said to no one. I took a couple of breaths of normal air, recovering. By comparison, the hall now seemed cold as an ice box, and I well understood why after a couple of minutes in there, Angela had taken that dive in the pool. I didn't think the hotel would like my Santa Claus boxers as a bathing suit, so the pants stayed on, and I skipped the dip. I felt a little more prepared to try the second room. I opened the door.

"Shut the sauna door, Mario," Angela said. She was lying on her back on the top row, like toast under a broiler, except she was reading a book. "You're letting all the hot out."

I shut the door. It was a gentler, dry heat in here. I could get to like it. Three tiers of benches circling three walls, ringing the side with a wooden box and a bucket and ladle. The all-wooden room smelled of sandalwood and eucalyptus. Angela stepped down, grabbed the ladle, and poured the liquid into the box. It hissed. She dropped the ladle back in the bucket, crawled back up, straightened her towel, lay down on it again, and recommenced reading. There was nowhere long enough for me to stretch out. I sat on the bottom bench, wet sweats hissing. My legs got hot and the surface of the wood was too hot to lean on. I'd left my towel outside in the locker, so I sat upright while all the cold London winter melted out of me. I could grow to love a sauna. I didn't have Melina here, with her degree in shopping, so I decided to ask the concierge to procure me a couple of towels long enough for me to use in the wet area, now that I'd discovered it. I visited the steam room and sauna every day after that.

Two weeks after I'd checked into the hotel, I got a phone call from Sami.

"You haven't called me," she said.

"I've been taking in your city. And I washed my hand, so I lost your number."

"You're coming over for lunch. What's your favorite food?" Her commanding delivery reminded me of Melina.

"Steak. But I eat anything. No worries."

She drove up in a four-door Jaguar. It was sleek, shiny, hunter-green, and smelled like money.

"Nice Jag," I said.

We talked for a few minutes about our conflicting pronunciation of the word Jaguar as I adjusted the seat so my long legs could fit. Before she hit the gas, she leaned toward me and we kissed, the same kind of potential-filled kiss as on our parting. I stared at her great legs in that tiny miniskirt. All the girls in London were wearing them, but few wore them as well. I figured that with a just a little breeze, that fabric would ruffle and expose whatever was underneath. I told my dick to calm down and tried to think of something else.

"Where are we going?"

"Across from Hyde Park."

The hotel was next to Hyde Park, and her flat across the street from Hyde

Park was some three miles away. Hyde Park extended for miles more. The drive to her place took under ten minutes.

She led me off the elevator at the top floor of the twelve-story building and unlocked the door. Even at first glance, I could see the flat was huge.

"When you said flat, I pictured a small apartment," I said.

She laughed. "It's a penthouse, but here in London, it's still a flat." She took my hand. "Let me give you a quick tour so you feel comfy."

I stopped counting at five bedrooms. The master bedroom was enormous. It reminded me of a furniture showroom of what a bedroom was supposed to be like, only more so. The penthouse had a cedarwood sauna, steam room, a couple of small round tubs—one hot, one cold—and a doorless shower in a tiled room with a drain. I marveled, exercising my new expertise of steam and sauna. The set-up was nicer and cozier than what was at the hotel. When we got to the kitchen, we encountered servants. That was a first for me, while on a date. She introduced them.

"This is Crispin, my chef and houseman, and Ginger, my housekeeper."

Crispin was short-haired and sharp-featured. He seemed thin for a man who must do a certain amount of labor, and I would guess that he was in his thirties. Ginger was pale and freckled. She wasn't that tall, probably five and a half feet, strongly built, but not fat. Her hair was in a bun at the back of her head and mostly hidden under a sort of cap. Judging by the freckles and the name, she probably had red hair. Her eyes were pale, more gray than green, at least in this light.

I followed Sami to the living room, where we sat on a white sofa. I had never seen furnishings like this before, and tried not to gape or sound like a yokel. Sami was rich. Hell, she was loaded.

"I see you're well off."

"My mother was well-to-do. My father makes a good living, but not up to the standards my mom had been raised in."

"What does he do?"

"He's a plastic surgeon."

"I'll have to remember that in case I ever need a face lift."

She laughed.

"I remember you said you were visiting him in New York."

"He and his fiancée have an apartment in Manhattan and a house in the country."

The building wasn't new. Everything was polished, a mix of old and new that didn't feel very lived in.

"I take it you didn't grow up here?"

"The house I grew up in came down to me from my mother's parents. I'm lucky it wasn't entailed. It's much too big and outside the city, so I don't stay there much. I found this flat, spent a year or so fixing it up, and bought two one-bedroom flats on the third floor for Ginger and Crispin to live in."

"Convenient."

"Exactly."

"You got really good taste," I said. I had thought my place was a big deal, but this was totally above me. We're talking tall ceilings with gilt frescos, marble floors, rich fabrics over the windows, plush carpet a mile deep, and furnishings that were a mix of designer and antique. The street-level entrance to the lobby and the entrance from the parking garage had a couple of Johnsons working security.

She asked about Los Angeles. I told her a little, and finally she asked, "Are you married?"

"No, and never been."

She seemed pleased.

"What about you, Sami? Are you married?"

"Not married. I saw what happened to my parents and I just don't need it. Even growing up I knew there was conflict."

"No special person?"

"Anyone I date has to be special to me," she said. "But there's not just one."

"I feel the same way."

"In case you're wondering, I'm thirty-five," she said. "How about you?"

"You look twenty." I said, "I was born in New York, on New Years, 1948. So I'm going to be twenty-seven in eleven and a half months."

There was the smile again. No dimples like Niley. But she was adorable.

"Most people would just have said they were twenty-six. I'm almost a decade older than you."

"Could have fooled me. I thought you were twenty."

"Maybe we can do New Year's Eve on your birthday next year," she said.

"I have no idea where I'll be by New Years. If I'm still here, for sure."

The housekeeper came out and exchanged some kind of signal with Sami. Ginger was wearing a crisp-looking gray uniform out of the last century, with a white collar and white sleeves and a white cotton apron. It sent my mind off on a wild goose chase of seeing Sami in a French maid outfit. Ridiculous, since Sami's mini already bared more than a French maid outfit.

Sami stood. I followed suit, appreciating her legs again. She took my arm and led me into the dining room, where a huge porterhouse steak was put in front of me. Sami was served the same. No way was she going to fit that huge piece of meat in that great body. There was no room. The housekeeper carried around side dishes, first standing to Sami's left to show her the dishes, then serving each of us from the right. This formality reminded me of Melina too. Before the trip, Melina had talked me through how butlers served. This was England, and there were rules everywhere, some, apparently, breakable. Ginger was not a butler, and she didn't put the dishes on the sideboard, but on the table in easy reach. I was glad I hadn't grown up having to put up with all this pomp, but on a vacation, it was pretty cool.

"Thanks, Ginger," Sami said. "That will be all."

I went for the mushrooms twice. The corn on the cob was smothered in butter and clumsy to eat without the little cob holders Aunt Carmen had picked up at the dime store, but delicious. The dessert selection was on the sideboard and reminded me of fancy restaurants I had ended up in by mistake since I'd been in London. The brewed English tea was better than any I'd had in the states. I only drank tea back home because Melina insisted. Jo liked it, but I preferred coffee. This tea had a hefty caffeine kick, a buzz that promised to keep me from sleeping tonight. I was getting used to tea overall, but I still didn't love it.

"I have an extra bedroom back home," I said. "I use it as a home office. Why so many bedrooms?" If I had been home, I'd have said, "You only have one ass to sleep with." But I didn't think that would go over too well here.

"If and when I sell, the property should be worth more. When I get tired of looking at a bunch of unused beds, I can always convert a room to something else. Like a home office." She elbowed me and we both laughed.

She had a plate with a scoop of chocolate soufflé in front of her, with whipped cream on top. She dipped her spoon into it and took a bite.

"So what do you do? Are you a jetsetter?"

"Actually, I'm a doctor. A doctor first, and a jetsetter second."

Her answer took me by surprise. "You are way too beautiful to be a doctor."

Her smile flashed. Our eyes met. The tip of her tongue delicately traced her upper lip, and wiped away a trace of whipped cream. I felt like she was communicating something to me, but then she looked down. She dabbed her mouth with the linen napkin and replaced it on her lap.

"You're funny," she said. "I am a doctor without an office. I don't have a private practice, but I handle patients at Children's Hospital. It gives me the opportunity to stay keen at my profession. I try to be where I am needed."

"Your patients are very lucky."

"Thank you, Mario."

We walked over to a balcony overlooking the park. It was dusk out, and in the fading light, the hues of London were muted. I could see gardens and trees, paths cutting through the green, and people wandering on foot and by bicycle. Twelve floors up was too far to see details and too close to see the panorama of all London; but what I could see was trim and crisp and orderly. People here seemed to move slower than they did at home, but maybe that was just an illusion from up high. The noise of the busy street below was slightly muffled and sounded almost like music. The atmosphere was strange and exotic and added to the excitement of being here. I wanted to live like this. Someday.

Crispin had a fire going in the balcony fireplace. Without it, we would've been freezing.

"What do you do?"

I told her about my team back home. I left out the details that I had sold my business, and how dabbling in real estate was paying the bills for now. It took some explaining, but she finally got it.

"Exciting," she said. "You are so creative to do what you do. You must be really good to afford the Mandarin Hotel." She giggled. It was not a Pixie giggle, but it came out funny, and we both laughed.

"I've done well. I have no complaints."

"I have a friend, a lawyer with one of the giant insurance companies here in London. He defends insurance companies. I should introduce you. His name is Jason."

"Love to meet him. I work the other end. We go after the insurance company."

"I know. And you're in the United States. But who knows? He might have something interesting to say to you about the people on the opposite side of the table."

"Any friend of yours is a friend of mine."

I beamed. She beamed back.

Crispin set up a silver champagne urn with a bottle of Dom Pérignon. I knew from being around Melina how pricey that was in the US. After being in London for two weeks, I knew how much more costly that bottle would be in a restaurant. By the arrival of the second bottle, night had fallen. The sharp pinpricks of light below were far away, subdued by the distance, muzzled by night. The park had gone to mysterious darkness, broken here and there by park lights, but otherwise it was still and silent against the street's river of light and traffic that continued to surge in a steady current. Echoes of the vehicles and chatter of persons underneath us filtered up, enhancing the solitude of this balcony where we were now snugly sitting side by side.

I felt totally sober, but knew I couldn't be. I was drunk on her, as much as the champagne. Under candlelight and the fireplace, Sami looked too lovely to be real. The color of her skin, that English complexion of hers with wind-burned cheeks, glowed as if she were the source of light. Her eyes were as green as Hyde Park had been, and they glittered like crystal.

Ginger filled our glasses from the second bottle. Our flutes clicked and we sipped.

"You want to go in my bedroom and play doctor?"

I laughed.

"You probably say that to everyone."

She punched me in my stomach, reminding me of Jo.

"Ouch," we both said, simultaneously.

"You're like steel." She rubbed her hand. "I don't tell that to everyone."

"I'm not steel," I said, "just flesh and blood. And you do say that to everyone."

"Maybe," she said.

We were both laughing.

"I tell it only to those I want to fuck." She was still laughing.

I think I gasped. I didn't mean to, but I'd made a real effort to clean up my language for her. That was the last word I expected out of her mouth.

"Did I shock you?" she asked. Her smile dimmed. She'd moved her hand on to my chest and was running it up and down my abs. She stopped. She'd noticed the gunshot scars. I'm not vain, but hoped they didn't put her off. But then, I guess scars wouldn't bother a doctor.

"A warrior," she said.

Okay, the scars didn't bug her. I was a little relieved. In fact, they seemed to turn her on. She was fondling my abs. I started laughing.

"I'm not shocked. I'm glad to hear you guys use that language here too."

"Fuck is fuck in every language."

I picked her up and carried her into the master bedroom. Truth is, when I use those muscles, I still feel an ache where I'd been shot, but my recovery had been accelerated by a grueling workout schedule.

Going down the hall, I could have gotten lost, but the other doors were shut, and the light from her bedroom showed the path. More Dom Pérignon waited in an ice bucket on a serving tray, accompanied by a dish of strawberries and chocolates on shaved ice.

We stood naked, facing each other.

The taste of chocolate melted in my mouth.

"You're beautiful, Doctor Sami. I think I have a little fever that needs your attention."

The color in her cheeks turned from pink to scarlet. "I think I know how to cure what ails you." It appeared she was shy. It was charming.

She looked me up and down, and her gaze froze around my midsection. Her eyes got big. I got bigger.

"I had no idea, Mario. I should have known you would be huge. When I wrote my phone number on your hand, it was so big. But my goodness."

Under her eyes, I got bigger and harder.

"Is that a problem?" I asked.

She shook her head, no. "I want it all."

She grabbed my dick. And I'd thought she was shy. Clearly, I'd been mistaken. She pulled me to bed. I thought I was already hard, but the more she pulled, the harder I got.

"I told you I'd show you the best nooks and crannies in London," she panted. She was proving to be a woman of her word.

I spent at least ten minutes getting my tie right before I joined Sami in her dining room to breakfast from a buffet on the sideboard that put the hotel offerings to shame by comparison. Not that I wanted blood sausage or sweetbreads or what the English call bacon. I was happy with coffee and scrambled eggs. I felt a little sorry about all that wasted food, but maybe that went to Crispin and Ginger. I was feeling pretty good about the trip so far and planned to head back to the hotel to change into jeans.

Sami looked at me critically.

"That just won't do," she said.

"What?"

"You're wearing that great suit and a Windsor knot."

She reached for the tie I had tied so carefully and yanked it loose.

"It's a waste to have a fine suit and such a pedestrian knot. Do another one. Try the Eldredge or the Trinity or the Van Wijk."

Of course, I had no idea what she was talking about. Under her watchful gaze, I tied it again, as I'd had it before. She sighed, yanked it loose, and rang a little glass bell.

The door to the butler's pantry opened, and Ginger emerged.

"Yes, ma'am?"

"Stand up, Mario, and let Ginger show you how to tie the Eldredge."

Ginger was a pretty good teacher. She walked me through it twice, under Sami's critical eye.

"There are other knots too, but you should just use this one till you have it down. Then Ginger can teach you another."

I laughed. "Okay, I'll come over here for my tie lessons."

"Of course not," Sami said. "You must stay here as long as you're in London. I'd be insulted, otherwise."

I've never been a mooch in my life. I told her so when she insisted. But she wouldn't take no for an answer.

"You're not a mooch. You're a guest. No strings," she said. "You can go out. You can fuck around. Just stay here while you're in London. Please, Mario. With you here, I feel like the carnival has come to old London Town."

I'd never been compared to a carnival before. How does a red-blooded American man say no to that?

He doesn't.

Ginger drove me over to fetch my things from the hotel. I would have thought it would have been the chef, but she told me the houseman felt like playing chauffeur was beneath him. I could tell I was walking into a power struggle between Crispin and Ginger, but it wasn't alarming. It felt familiar, the way Jo and Pixie and Niley used to wrestle for preferred clients.

Sami was at the hospital when Ginger put me in a great guest room across from the master bedroom. She came home less than an hour after I arrived. We hugged like we had known each other forever.

"You know what's amazing?" I asked.

"What?"

"I didn't get a hangover. That's impossible."

She banged my stomach. "I expect you have a high metabolism. And look at you. You worked it off."

We laughed.

What I saved not paying for the Mandarin, I spent on more clothes. I had that new trunk to fill, and it was huge, as big as New Jersey. Sami liked to go out, and the clothes were essentials. I didn't need a tie, but I had to buy two more suits, a sport jacket, several interchangeable button-down shirts, and two pair of shoes. They all had the snob factor of being from Savile Row. When I got home, my suits would knock Cooke's out of the water. Sami and I shopped, clubbed, and hit all the high spots in London. We ate at Rules Restaurant at 35 Maiden Lane. Sami laughed when I told her their steak was almost as good as what was served at the Pacific Dining Car, but to give credit where credit is due, I don't think the Prince of Wales ever ate at PDC. London has a lot of drinking spots, and we visited pub after pub after pub. Buttoned-up Londoners open up a lot in a pub, but the pubs all shut down at eleven.

"PDC is open all night," I told Sami.

She changed the subject. "Jason is coming over for dinner. Remember the attorney friend I told you about?"

I remembered and pretended eagerness, though I didn't want him to intrude into my time with Sami. I mentally prepared for some guy getting possessive over her. Sami herself was a great personal connection. She was perfect. Didn't want to get serious but did want my company and my dick. I felt the same way. I wanted her lovemaking. She was a firecracker. In bed, I could not believe she was a doctor. Maybe she was good because she knew all about human bodies, but there was nothing clinical about our time in bed.

"My whole life has been about making connections." I assured her. "Bring him on."

Like me, Jason was tall with dark hair. He was wearing a suit that had come from Savile Row. We shook hands. It was almost like looking into a mirror. We were almost eye to eye. He was deeply tanned, like he'd come from a beach vacation, even looked a little bit Mexican. I am a little taller though. I guess Sami has a type.

Crispin and Ginger served up a storm of food. By their comments about who liked what, I could tell this was not Jason's first dinner here. He was on Sami's right, and I on her left, and since she was at the head of the table, that put Jason and me facing each other. It was civil. There were dishes I couldn't handle like mutton and pigeon, but I was polite about it. I noticed how Jason relished all the game and organ meats, and no one called attention to me waving Ginger away with one dish or another. The beef stew was fantastic. I caught Ginger's eye, so she brought seconds.

"Sami says you work for attorneys in personal injury," Jason said, making conversation between consumption of various small game birds.

"Yes," I said. "Client development."

"Only in America," Jason said with a chuckle. "There's money in automobile accidents?"

"Yes. There are more small cases than bigger cases, at least in my direction." I wasn't sure if I liked Jason. I was uncertain if he was mocking me. It was as clear as glass that he was very fond of Sami and she of him.

"How many cases do you provide the attorneys? What volume?"

"It's one firm. In a good month, three hundred or so plaintiffs, give or take a dozen or two."

Jason stopped eating. "Good God. Are you serious?"

I looked right at him, and smiled. He wasn't mocking now.

"Very serious. Figure an average of three persons in a car. It varies."

Sami nudged Jason and said proudly, "I told you this American friend of mine is very creative. He's got a gift."

I thought a moment about how she used gift.

"Thanks," I said.

"Does the firm handle anything other than car accidents?"

"Sure. Used to be a lot of green card work for immigrants. Whatever develops. A little workers' compensation. When an existing client needs civil litigation assistance, we accommodate them."

"Why aren't you a lawyer?" Jason asked.

"No time."

Sami and Jason laughed. He was as stiff as any Brit, but Jason's laugh was good-humored and engaging. I started warming to him.

We moved to the sitting area off the dining room. Over small talk and wine, Jason asked me if I ever handled an aviation case. Sami sat in the loveseat we had shared yesterday, but now she was with Jason. I sat across from them in a loveseat of my own, and covered my feeling of awkwardness by sipping the wine.

"No aviation," I replied. "But I could get interested."

"You have plane crashes in the states. I handle claims from here when they happen and we happen to be involved."

"You mean, when the insurance company you work for is involved?"

"Right," Jason said. "A plane is not insured by one company. The losses can be enormous, so it's insured by multiple companies. If there's a loss, the loss is split among the companies. Of course, the insurance companies in the consortium also split the premiums the airline pays."

"Of course," I said, as if I'd known this all along. I watched Jason drape his arm familiarly over Sami's shoulder.

"There is a lot of money to be made by lawyers who handle victims of plane crashes. In most cases, the victim is dead. The families of the victims get a lawyer and come after us."

"I see," I said. This was something I wanted to know more about. It sounded the same as car crashes, except that plane operators must have much deeper pockets than drivers. I encouraged Jason to talk.

Sami watched me. Every once in a while, when I looked her way, she would respond. She tilted her head, or smiled or grimaced, or winked a message directly to me. I didn't need to be a mind-reader to see things were heating up between Sami and her guest. She might be wishing me to perdition now for distracting Jason, but it was her fault she'd brought Jason here to get me interested in the topic. I wasn't going to let the opportunity pass.

I tried to recall the few plane crashes that I'd heard about in the US. There weren't many of them. It had never dawned on me that these were cases.

"I don't think we have many plane crashes."

"You have a lot of helicopter and small craft crashes. More than you realize. Even commercial airlines have small, non-fatal events fairly frequently. Most of their insurance coverage comes from here. I primarily work airline tragedies."

"Are there many airline crashes everywhere? Enough to be worth looking into?" It was a dumb question, but I wanted some idea of the numbers.

"More than you can imagine. No matter where they happen in the world, most of the insurance is written here in London. It is all highly regulated."

"So you handle a case, no matter where the case happened?"

"If we're the insurance carrier, either myself or another attorney would handle it, yes. There are many of us in aviation insurance, just as there are in automotive circles."

He kissed Sami on the cheek like it was something he couldn't resist. Sami kissed him back. She looked at me, sideways.

"Sorry to be imposing on you," I said. "Too many questions."

"Nonsense," Jason said. "It's a pleasure."

"One final question. I promise this is my last. If a case happens in Italy, or Spain, or somewhere else, can the attorney in the United States represent the client in Italy or Spain or somewhere else?"

"Good question. It's unlikely a US attorney would have a license to practice in other countries. He can't go to court in Italy on behalf of the client, but he can represent the client, and try to reach a settlement with the insurance carriers here in London. If that fails, he gets a local lawyer in Italy to file the case in Italian court."

I nodded.

"Mario." He used my name for the first time. "Most cases never go to court. If you are wondering if a lawyer in the US can do business in other countries representing victims on this side of the ocean, the answer is yes."

Again, I nodded my understanding. "Thank you, Jason."

"My pleasure," he repeated, before kissing Sami again.

"Excuse me," I said. I went to the restroom. When I came back, Sami and Jason were gone. I hadn't really meant to let Jason off the hook. I was still full of questions. I picked up my glass of wine and sat down on the loveseat, thinking about plane crashes. By all rights, I should be missing Sami, but I wasn't finished grilling Jason. I wished he would come back and talk more. Ginger appeared.

"Sami says she will see you in the morning."

We both knew where they'd gone, but like a dummy, I had to ask.

"Where did they go?"

Ginger didn't answer the question. She just looked at me. "She asked me to offer you a massage."

Ginger was a cutie, older than me, but I had no idea by how much. Seemed like everyone was older than me.

"A massage?" The idea took me by surprise.

"I'm good at it."

I was a little tipsy from the wine but that was no impediment. "Of course, I'll be happy to take you up on it."

Ginger said, "Give me twenty minutes. I will prep the spa and be back for you. You can steam or sauna, then shower. I'll massage you. I promise, you'll relax."

I was anything but tense. I had a flashback of Pixie and Jo and Niley giving me a massage, probably not the kind Ginger was talking about. Ginger seemed anxious to demonstrate her skills. Any distraction from the notion of Sami and Jason would be welcomed.

I walked down the hall and stood quietly. The lush carpeting and excess of fabric muted sound to a degree, but it was clear what was going on in Sami's bedroom. Sami was fucking Jason. I shrugged it off and retrieved my glass, sipping my wine until it was gone. I walked around the great room and looked at painting after painting on display. The hall was like a museum gallery.

Ginger reappeared looking much different. I hadn't noticed before that she had long hair, but now it was tied back in a russet ponytail that made her look younger than I'd thought. She had changed into some white lycra outfit, a cat suit like Melina might have worn on the rare instances she worked out with me. She was no Pixie, of course, no one was, but the lycra outlined some impressive curves. I followed her to the spa, and once there, I reached for my tie. She pushed my hands away, took off my tie, then my jacket and shirt. When I slipped off the slacks and shorts, she handed me a huge plush towel.

I walked into the hot steam room, bare-ass naked with a towel over my shoulder. There wasn't a whole lot of room, but I managed a few stretches that fit the space. I did some isometrics, and repeated a few moves, just enough to get my blood moving. I'd had enough experience now to know how to use a damp towel to ease breathing the steam. The heat and moisture of the air filled my lungs, and along with the alcohol, made me light-headed enough for me to feel like I was floating somewhere around the ceiling. I tossed down the towel and parked myself on it, bending my knees to fit on the bench. I hadn't doubled the towel, but it felt almost as thick as a mattress, the way it gave under me. Steam hissed. The fog spread, and the immaculate tiled space filled with the minty scent of eucalyptus. The feel of steam on my skin was delicious, the heat driving out every trace of winter. I stayed there as long as I could bear it, until I was desperate for a cooling off. The cool shower was a relief.

I stepped out.

"Sauna's ready too," Ginger said.

I considered the option and stepped back in the shower till I was chilled again, then hit the sauna. It was much smaller than the hotel sauna. I nearly went to sleep. I'd swear I could smell the wine evaporating.

This time when I emerged from the shower, Ginger started drying my wet skin. I stopped her. She couldn't help but notice the scars. The recent gunshot wound had healed, but it was only a few months old and was still an angry pink. She grimaced.

"I'm sorry," she said.

"It doesn't hurt."

The steam and sauna had cleared my head, and I was feeling good. I sat on the massage table while Ginger buzzed around me, repositioning oils and towels and who knows what else.

"Ready?"

I nodded. She flicked off the lights and repositioned my legs so that I was lying on my back. A good twenty candles were burning. They were scented, too, but I'd be hard put to say what the flavor was.

I know Pixie is a skilled masseuse, but Ginger's hands were outstanding. About fifteen minutes in, she asked if I liked it.

"It's wonderful."

"Tell me if I do anything uncomfortable," she said. "I probably should have said that first."

I opened my eyes to watch what I could see of her expertly working my neck and shoulders. She avoided the scars left by Hugo Pliego's gunshot and the older scars from when I'd been shot at a Los Angeles motel.

"Don't worry about hurting me," I assured her. "I'm good now."

Ginger ignored my directions and worked lightly around the scars.

I'm a big guy, and she was stronger than she looked. Eventually she flipped me onto my stomach. I shut my eyes, and my brain was hovering around the ceiling like I'd passed out, but I was still semi-conscious. I was relaxed, maybe even half asleep. My thoughts were nowhere at all, but my body had taken center stage, greedily absorbing a variety of sensations. Beneath me, I could feel a soft towel, plush and deep, cool linen sheets, Ginger's hands, strong and sure, stroking oil slick against my skin. I might have even fallen asleep, but I came aware when she began rubbing the oil from me with a towel. I felt little bites on my ass cheeks. A chuckle bubbled up from somewhere deep in my chest.

"I wasn't sure you were awake," Ginger said.

"Did Sami tell you to do that too?"

My face was still down on the table. Ginger whispered in my ear.

"She told me to take good care of you."

"And you always obey." I was just tossing conversation, but I was getting hard.

"I always obey."

Gently, she turned me over.

I felt her mouth and tongue. I thought of Melina, when she had told me she was going to give me a deep throat like in the movie. I thought of the thousand blow jobs Pixie had snuck to me in the secret dark. I thought about Ginger's obedience. Ginger said nothing. Her hands went under me and cupped my ass, one hand on each side, and she worked me to heights I had not yet had in London, not even with Sami. I am sure I screamed aloud.

She washed me right there on the table as I lay there drained and boneless, still shivering in response. Somehow, I got to my feet and looked around for my clothes, but they were gone. She must have gotten them when I was in the steam or shower. Several white cotton robes hung on hooks, and Ginger slid my arms into one of them, belted it, and led me to my room. I was in a somnambulant daze, and feeling like a happy sponge that had been wrung out of all its bubbles, but I still noticed Sami's bedroom door was shut.

Ginger closed my door as we walked in. I doubted Jason could equal for Sami what Ginger had done for me. Maybe if she was lucky, but that degree of satisfaction didn't happen every day.

My bed was already turned down. I sat on the comforter. Somehow, I was not surprised when Ginger tucked me in. She kissed me on the forehead.

"You're a beautiful man, Mr. Mario. Good night."

I heard something in her voice. Maybe it was instinct, but I didn't like the feeling she would be leaving unsatisfied. I reached for her arm. "Don't ever call me mister. I'm Mario to you." I sat up. I tugged till she was sitting on the side of the bed. I kissed her gently on the lips, felt her leaning into me. I pulled her across my lap. Her shoulder lay against my chest, cradled, her torso against me, her feet hanging off the bed. The long sweep of her bright hair fell across my chest. "Thank you, Ginger."

I felt a shiver run through her. I remembered everything Pixie had ever taught me about women. I remembered the time Melina had accused me of being selfish. I reached for the bedside lamp and flicked off the light.

"Ginger. Are you wanting? I can't leave a woman wanting." I whispered in her ear.

I freed the cloth band around her ponytail, and her hair cascaded down. She said nothing with words, perhaps restrained by her Britishness, but the way she reclined across me was language enough. She answered me with her body. I put my hand on her thigh, and when I moved to the center of her heat, she moved and shuddered against me, clutching me like her life depended on it.

Ginger left, moving silently into the night. I could not have been more satisfied. I didn't even think about aviation and the new doors opening up to me.

I'm sure I smiled the entire night, and I'm pretty sure I wasn't the only one.

Knocking woke me. I sat up in the pitch dark.

"Come in."

When the door opened, a stream of daylight flooded my room. A cheerful Sami walked in.

"I thought you may want to go out for lunch."

Sami sat on the bed and gave me a tiny kiss as my head went back down on the pillow.

"Lunch sounds great. What time is it?"

"Half past twelve."

"Twelve? As in half past noon?"

She laughed. "Yes. It's the blackout drapes. Want me to open?"

"Yes, please."

It took a minute or two for my eyes to adjust. I guess I was still on LA time.

"You'd never know that at home I get up at five in the morning to work out. My body doesn't know what time it is."

"How was your massage?"

I focused on Sami and sat up, my feet hanging over the side of the bed.

"Loved the massage. Ginger is very special. I promise your Jason didn't measure up to Ginger."

"Indeed," Sami agreed with a little laugh. "I'm jealous."

I put my arm around her. "I'm jealous too."

We both laughed. Neither of us was the least bit jealous.

"I'll shower and be ready in thirty minutes," I said.

"Okay, I'll be in the study."

"You don't work today?" I asked.

"Not on a Sunday. Besides, I only go in twice a week. It's only more if I have a special patient, but twice is the norm."

"What a great job."

She kissed me and got up. "I'm hungry. Hurry."

We had lunch at the Ritz. It was way too fancy, much fancier than the Mandarin. I ordered a steak.

"Sami, I totally appreciate your hospitality, but as welcome as you, Ginger, and Crispin make me feel, I'm uncomfortable. I don't want to wear out your hospitality."

Sami was quick to respond. "I love having you at the house. I want you to be comfortable. We're friends." Her hand took mine across the table. Melina used to say the same to me.

"Of course we're friends," I said. "Did Jason say anything about me staying here?"

She squeezed my hand. "I don't doubt that he wishes he could be a permanent guest."

"So why me and not him?"

"I don't know, really." She looked away and then back at me. "Maybe because he'd like to stake an exclusive claim. I don't know if that's what I want. You told me about Melina and your girls back home, so I know you understand. Anyway, the penthouse is lonely. I could fill the bedrooms with just a few phone calls, but not with company I want. You and I hardly know each other, but we understand one another. I want us to be good friends."

Three weeks later, I was in Milan with my steamer trunk half full of British menswear. It was a major pain in the ass. It didn't fit in any European cars, and it was like hauling around a pet elephant. I must have been out of my mind to think I was going to deal with this burden every day left in my European tour. I parked it in the hotel room, spent a day at an Italian designers' getting enough menswear to fill the damn thing, and after six days, when the tailors were done, shipped it home. I bought a normal suitcase, keeping in it only the minimal essentials.

Milan is a seat of fashion, and the home base of countless models. By day, they work the runways of all the famous designers, but they have little to do at night except hang out in clubs. It didn't take me long to make friends. At the clubs, I had a number of offers. I checked out of the hotel after seven days, having no idea where I was going to end up.

Chapter 2
February 16, 1975
Milan, Italy

Zara and Bella. They were the two French models who took me in.

Their apartment was tiny, my half of the weekly rent was cheap, and they made me feel welcome. The flat consisted of one bedroom with two full-size beds, a bathroom, a hot plate, and a percolator. After my stay with Sami, this was roughing it. Except for the lack of a real kitchen, it wasn't too far off from how I grew up. It's not like they needed a kitchen. We ate mostly at cafés.

When I needed money, Jo wired me a thousand dollars[2] by Western Union. It converted very nicely to lira. I drank more than ever, but only wine, which was better and cheaper than at home. Italians put away wine like it is water. My workouts were infrequent, but I did sit-ups, pushups, and quite a bit of walking. The first time I'd been shot, I drove myself like a demon till I was up to speed. Not this time. The scar was still sensitive, but it was my own fault from babying myself too much. If you call five hundred sit-ups babying myself, then I was babying myself. I did skimp on the aerobics. They say wine shows around the waist, but I wasn't going to let that happen.

Zara and Bella were from Paris. They had similar looks—fair skin and long straight hair—but they were not related. They looked like Twiggy's taller sisters,

---

[2] $1,000.00 in 1975 had the same buying power as $4,557.32 in 2017

eyes spiked with black lashes. They had a waifish quality. No idea what their hair color was—they changed it every week, and they usually matched, since they tended to work the same shows for designers who wanted girls with their particular look. It was a lot like a guy-fantasy of being with twins, except they weren't. Their first language was French, but both spoke fluent Italian. Luckily for me, their Spanish was better than their English. They called themselves starving models, working but were paid a pittance as far as I could tell. I never knew if they deliberately starved themselves for the camera and runway, or if they were actually hungry and could not afford to eat. Their bodies were slim, sometimes too slim. Certainly Zara and Bella had gorgeous bodies, but compared to Pixie, Jo, and Niley, they were downright gaunt. I warmed them by night, and they warmed me back. The second bed got little use, and after a few days, we rearranged the room and pushed them together to make a bigger bed. I'm accustomed to feeding my girls. I missed my peanut butter, but I browsed the local cuisine and left lots of food lying around: bread, cheese, pastries, street food. None of it went to waste. Aunt Carmen would have approved.

When I talked to Jo, it was always business. The apartments this and that. She took the assignment very seriously and was anxious to make the rentals more profitable, so I'd be happy with her work on my return. When I spoke to Niley, it was to assure her I was just fine. Pixie was a different story. She was on my ass from start to finish.

"What the fuck are you doing, boss? When are you coming home? I'm wearing out vibrators. One a week, at least."

Melina's conversation was filled with recommendations of where to go next, ending every conversation with "I miss you, friend. I really miss you." I told her I was staying with some lovely girls.

"You mean hot chicks, right? You going to use yourself up on them?"

"Yes, they're hot, but not as hot as you. And you know they don't take your place. Nobody could do that. Come see me," I said. "You promised."

"I'll try, I promise."

"Promising to try isn't promising to be here."

She laughed. "I can hear you pouting from six thousand miles away."

She was too busy with the markets to detour to Europe, but that was okay. I was learning some French and Italian, and Zara and Bella were filling the lonely spots. As much as I missed the girls back home, making new friends in Milan was an adventure. The heat was off. No one was pissed off at me or coming after me with a gun like back home. I often thought of the three humans I had been forced to kill to keep them from killing me. I still couldn't get over that asshole Hugo nursing all that rage.

She was a new acquaintance, but I called Sami at least twice a week.

"You're living with two models?"

"Zara and Bella, lovely girls."

"I'm jealous," Sami said.

"You're not jealous. Jason move in yet?"

"Okay, maybe not jealous, but I miss you. No, he didn't move in yet. Please come back."

"I miss you, too. Bet you he'll offer you a ring."

"Do you miss my body?"

"I'm still hot for Doctor Sami."

I had to be the luckiest man on earth. Sometimes I asked myself what I'd ever done to deserve everything I had going for me.

I spent a lot of time thinking about Jason and the aviation business seeds he had planted in my brain. If I went to aviation, I would need a lawyer to handle the cases I got. I wondered if Cooke would want them, but I still wasn't sure about working with Carson. I could always find a lawyer in England or Italy, but eventually I would have to go home. I would be starting completely over.

After a while, I realized I was getting too comfortable in Milan. I wasn't here to put down roots, but it was starting to feel that way. I gave Zara and Bella half the cash I had in my pocket and told them I was moving on. I wasn't sure if their tears were from losing me or my wallet. Maybe it was mean to think like that of them, but they had turned themselves over to me during my stay. I paid their way and saw that they ate. They washed my clothes and ironed even my boxers—models press everything. I lived in jeans in Milan, and it was strange to have ironed jeans. I never wore any of the Savile Row garb. No need to dress up. I was slumming and loved it.

At a train station in Milan, I made a long-distance call to Jo and arranged for her to wire money to me in Venice, Italy on April sixteenth. I heard myself tell her April, and I could hardly believe it had been four months.

"How exciting. Venice!"

Jo sounded happy for me. The train station was not a good place to talk, so I promised her I'd bring everyone up to date when I had a phone handy.

It was neat that I arrived at the Hotel Danicli via a water taxi. That's what they called the motor boat that brought me over from the train station. Staying at the hotel was going to be more expensive than Zara and Bella's cheap room, and much more than mooching off Sami, but I loved the hotel right on the lagoon. Going native was okay for a while, but I could dig the phone in the room and the prospect of room service.

Venice smells awful, but it is a wonderful city for a pedestrian. I walked tirelessly for hours. Everywhere I looked, there was beauty: the old buildings, the quaint boats, the statuary, the horizon, the canals, even the pigeons. The locals I ran into were shopkeepers and workers. The main population lived on the mainland. I mingled with tourists. Plenty of young ladies traveled with a girlfriend for safety, and some traveled alone just as I was. After about a week there, I was having coffee at an outdoor café when I met Fae. She was twenty-five, two years younger than I, and from Paris. I gave her some of my focaccia and shared a demitasse of the café's signature strong coffee. Her sandals were worn out and her bell bottoms had seen better days. I told myself that even if Fae hadn't been a stone-cold fox, I would have brought her to my room to soak in the bathtub, eat a good meal, and sleep in a comfortable bed. It wasn't about wanting sex. But she was a fox. We had a great time hanging around together, but we didn't understand each other at all.

She knew her way around Venice. She joined me in a tour of the Piazza San Marco. She scavenged day-old bread from the proprietor of an open-air café, and we fed it to the pigeons, which were everywhere.

I stopped off at the desk when we got to the hotel, checking for messages. The concierge, Rémi, handed me a couple of notes: one each from Sami and Jo. He was an older man, and dressed very well, as befit his job. Around the eyes, he reminded me a little of Harry. He had a warm manner that I always associate with Italians, unlike the exceedingly proper British concierge at the Mandarin. I asked for an extra room service menu. When he handed it to me, I said, "Merci," since I'd known he was French.

Rémi replied in French. "De rien."

Fae said, "Est-ce que vous êtes français?"

He said, "Marseillais."

She replied, "Moi aussi," laughed, and said, "Marseillaise."

That's where they lost me. He and Fae started chattering in French. I was mystified, and it must have shown on my face.

"We are both of us from the Marseilles." He had a big grin.

They chattered some more, and she pointed at the menu.

I looked at him expectantly.

"She recommends the sardines," he said with a big smile. "It's a traditional dish here. I agreed with her, it is probably the most delicious thing on the menu." I thanked him. My favorite so far had been pasta dishes with sausage and other meat and fish.

Back in the room, I saw that her backpack was empty of clothes. From our lame conversation, I was able to make out that she had sold everything but what she had on. All she had, literally, were the clothes on her back. She was in the bath when I snuck out with her bell bottoms and blouse and found a store where a saleslady was able to eyeball the battered pants and blouse to get the size right. I bought a couple of changes of clothes, excited about being in a position to help a transient who was down and out. When I got back, she was asleep in the tub. I knocked on the door to wake her, and when she stuck out her arm, I handed her the hotel bathrobe. It was huge on her, but fluffy and deep.

I had ordered the fish dish for her. They wheeled it in and put plates on a small round table. It was a fishy appetizer, not something I'd have eaten voluntarily, so I was glad I had ordered it only for her. If that was the best thing on the menu, I wasn't going to eat anything but breakfast here. However, there was also a wonderful crusty loaf of Italian bread, butter, and two coffees. She was charming and surprised, and she sat at the table in the bathrobe, for all the world looking like a queen and reminding me of Melina, somehow. After the servers left, she took off the robe and seemed perfectly content to be in the towel.

Her English was terrible, my fledgling French so-so. I drank coffee and watched as she ate slowly and savored every bite. I showed her one of the shirts I'd gotten; it made her laugh. It was a nice shirt. When I asked, "Pourquoi?" *Why?* she hopped up and spread the shirt across my torso, pointing out that the long sleeves barely came to my elbow and bared my abs and didn't come anywhere near reaching the breadth of my chest. She laughed some more, and I laughed with her. Against me, it looked like doll clothes.

Her laugh was like tinkling bells, with a rusty throatiness that sounded like it had been a long time since that sound came out of her. I wanted to hear more. When she was all laughed out, I took the shirt from her, and as she had done for me, held it to show her how well it was proportioned for her, not me. She caught on and burst into tears, then dived against my chest, getting my tee all wet. It took a good five minutes to get her smiling again, and it was with caution that I handed her the rest of her new clothes. This time she didn't cry. Her eyes got moist and she made some speech in rapid French that I could make neither head nor tail of.

"You owe me nothing," I said.

Her new clothes were a revelation. Fae was lovely, with a little bit of an overbite like Leslie Caron. Or maybe that was just me in my head, seeing her as a French girl. Her mouth was like a kiss. Her hair was as dark as Niley's and as long as Zara and Bella's, but it dried in a froth of dark, bouncy curls, and that turned out to be a reflection of her personality. We left the hotel room and watched some glassblowers, then we went to a street market, where I got her a new pair of hand-made Italian leather sandals. I wagged my finger at her when I got them, but the shoes set off her waterworks again. She put them on right away. We fed the pigeons more scavenged bread scraps and took a ride on a gondola. We had walked the day away. It was late in the evening, and I took her to eat Italian. Fantastic pasta was everywhere, better than anything back home. In a candlelit café, we ate like hungry horses, but she was smaller even than Niley, and she filled up fast. Our conversation was funny. Between her broken English and my way-out French that she kept scratching her head over, no one else could have figured out what we were saying to each other. I wanted to ask what had brought her to this point, but even the proverbial "How did a nice girl like you end up in a place like this?" was beyond the reach of my French. Her manners and mannerisms were more like Sami's than Pixie's, so I had a feeling she had come from money. I knew there was a story there and wanted desperately to know it. We walked back to the hotel, pointing at things of common interest and talking, after a fashion.

I had housekeeping bring a rollaway bed to the room. Fae looked at me, puzzled.

"Why? You no like?"

"I do like you, but I don't want you to think I did this for you because I planned on taking you to bed with me."

It was so hard to get that across with gestures and broken language. I'm not sure she understood. I think her feelings were wounded, but she went to bed on the rollaway. I crashed on my bed. Sometime during the night, the bed linens moved, and I found Fae snuggling her fine naked ass under the covers against me as I pretended to be sleeping. I made no moves.

Overnight turned into a week, and Fae was still there. I would have moved on but I liked being with her, even more than with Zara and Bella. A couple times a day, we managed to encounter Rémi, who was happy to translate for us our most recent confusion. I asked him how to tell her she owed me nothing. She said she already owed me more than she could repay. Rémi sighed over us and called us lovebirds. Friday came.

I had tickets, and I had to move on. I dreaded telling Fae the news.

"Please tell Fae I am leaving for Rome in the morning."

I stared at Fae as she listened to the translation. Her eyes were downcast, but she raised them to my face. She smiled at me and gave me a thumbs up. It was the first smile of hers that I did not believe.

"Tell her that I'm worried about her staying in Venice alone. I want to help her get back home. She can come with me. Hell, she can stay with me. Make her understand."

I grabbed both her hands.

I half understood what she told the concierge to tell me, more from her expressions than her language. I was getting pretty good at reading her, in spite of the language barrier.

I watched their faces. There was more than a mere translation. I could tell that they were arguing. I saw frustration on Rémi's face, and stubbornness on Fae's. I believe that Rémi was trying to encourage her to stay with me, and not getting very far doing it.

"Fae says if you can take her to Rome, she will go on her own from there. She's not ready to go back home."

My frustration mounted. "Tell her she can stay with me." But before he translated, she squeezed my hand.

She said with great intensity, "I be okay, Mario."

The next day we caught a train. I had misgivings all the way, and I wondered if I should have cancelled my ticket. In four hours, we were in Rome. I got an Italian newspaper to send home to the girls to show where I was. The date on the paper was May first.

"You stay with me," I said.

"Okay. Tonight, Mario." Fae gave me a thumbs up.

I checked into the Inn at the Spanish Steps. Melina's recommendation. Once we were settled, we took a very long walk. The cobblestone streets were a workout, but they got the kinks out after four hours on the train. So many people walking and shopping, countless shops. I forced her to let me buy her a couple of great-looking shorts and three blouses. Piecemeal, store by store, I cajoled and got her a pair of jeans that were made to show off her fine ass, more shorts, and underwear. She would be all set for the coming summer. I bought her a light canvas duffle bag to hold her new things. Our final stop before dinner was a shoe store.

"Mario, no, please."

I pushed her into two pairs of sandals, better walking shoes than what I got her in Venice, and a pair of soft canvas shoes like Keds sold back home in the US. We had dinner in a quaint restaurant that served Italian and Western food. I had a hamburger and fries, because I was starting to miss normal food. Our conversation was incomprehensible chatter, but we drank wine, ate, and laughed a lot. I wasn't sure I could let Fae go. She was good company, but she was also cute and fragile, and I worried about her. It was more than her pouty lip, bouncy curls, and vivid personality. She wasn't like Sami, with a home and money; she wasn't like Zara and Bella, who had each other and a profession and community they loved. She was alone in a strange country. I was afraid that some asshole would take her and abuse her. How would she defend herself? How had she defended herself before I found her? I didn't know what had landed her here, or even if she'd been abused. I didn't know if she'd left a bad situation in France, or if she'd tell me even if she knew the words.

We had been doing more than just sleeping together for that week in Venice. In Rome, sex was different. We tried positions that were new to us. It went on for hours. It was slow and wonderful. Our night was filled with passionate kisses. We fell into a deep sleep, satiated and probably engaged. I went to sleep thinking Fae was going to stick around.

In the morning, I woke alone. Fae was gone.

Chapter 3
Spring and Summer 1975
Adrift

If we had been in Venice, I'd have gone to Rémi. He cared about Fae, and would have moved heaven and earth to find her. The concierge at the Inn at the Spanish Steps was formal and polite and had never noticed her. His small black eyes narrowed at me. His foot tapped, and he was impatient for me to leave so he could go about his business. I cursed myself for not giving her my contact information. If only I'd slipped money into her backpack in the night. I'd never given her money, because I was afraid she would take it as a sign to leave, and that was the last thing I wanted her to do. My mistake was not finding someone to tell her I was asking her to stay with me. I would never get a chance to see her wear the new clothes I had bought her. At least I had done that. I am a light sleeper. Why didn't I wake up when she slipped away? I went out for breakfast, looked for her, and when I came back, I asked the front desk. No one remembered her.

I walked around the city and saw her on every street corner, every sidewalk, in the profile of every girl I passed. But she was gone. I visited the Vatican and lit a candle for everyone back home and for Tanis, Harry, and Jake, who had moved on to the next world. I felt a great sadness for everything that would not be. I lit a candle for Fae. I prayed for God to watch over her and to help her find her way home. Everything is possible in God's hands, but I still saw her everywhere.

Mid-May, I traveled to Naples and Capri, making friends everywhere I went. It's not so hard to do when you use public transportation and talk to people, join tour groups, and sit at communal tables. During my ten days in Naples, I hooked up with a pretty chick named Natalia, originally from Romania. Her hair was a blunt-cut pageboy that swung when she moved. She had broody eyebrows, wide Slavic cheekbones, and hair that exactly matched her narrow, wide-set brown eyes. Her mouth was wide too, and usually lipsticked in a burgundy red that matched her wine. We met in a bar where she frequently went to satisfy a strong appetite for the local vintage. Her story was that she lived with her parents in Napoli, that she was twenty and between jobs. I took her home with me to the hotel where I was staying, and she stayed with me. I wasn't sure where she really came from or if she really lived with her parents, but I know I never saw her sober.

"Where did you learn English?"

"Some in school, some by talking to tourists here in Naples."

"You are so hot," I said.

"And you so tall and handsome."

She painted her toenails every morning, wearing nothing but a smile. I don't know if it is a talent that is useful, but she could balance a wine-glass any-where. I would lie on the bed, and watch her sitting on a chair, one foot on the floor, the other bent so she could reach her nails, glass impossibly perched on her knee. I'd wait for it to fall, but it never did.

Natalia knew Capri and was happy to guide me around the island. She knew everyone at every bar, and they knew her, but during the day, she took me to a nude beach where we spent hours on the sand and swimming in the surf. She buried me in sand except for my face and teased me until my erection poked through the sand. Natalia and everyone around went wild with laughter. She used my Kodak Instamatic to take pictures.

On our last night together, our outdoor table was lit by a candle. She sat across from me and thanked me over dinner.

"You have been fantastic company," I told her.

She drank her wine and licked her lips. She wasn't a subtle sort of girl, more like Pixie than Sami. I doubted her parent story but didn't hold it against her.

"What else is fantastic?"

I was going to say Capri, but I knew that was not what she wanted to hear. "Sex with you is out of this world. Watching you lather and soap your body in the shower has been a turn-on. And watching you paint your nails." I thought about mentioning how she could drink me under the table, but wasn't sure she would appreciate it. Pixie would have thought it was a hoot, though.

"Whoever you end up marrying will be a very lucky woman."

"Not going to happen anytime soon," I said. "I enjoyed being with you."

"I feel the same about you, Mario. As long as I live, I will never forget your flagpole sticking out of the sand."

I joined her in laughter.

We took the ferry back to Naples, and she accompanied me to the train.

"Call me collect, whenever you want." I gave her my card. I thought about Fae out there in the world, alone, unprotected, and broke. I slipped four hundred dollars[3] into her purse.

I waved at her as the train pulled out to Monaco.

Now, every time I hear a whistle blow, I remember Fae alone in Rome and again wish I had given her a way to reach me.

On May twenty-fifth, I got to Monaco, beautiful and boring, with lots of boats. The big palace where royalty lived overlooked the city. All the roads led to the palace, and everywhere I went smelled like the filthy rich. The luxury of my hotel was off the chart. I was alone and didn't need the fancy room, but I checked in anyway. I didn't want to buy, wear, or haul around a tuxedo, so I didn't visit the casino across the street. There was still plenty of room in my new suitcase, but I

---

[3] $400.00 in 1975 had the same buying power as $1,822.93 in 2017

was slowly filling it with gifts for the girls.

I did a lot of walking. I saw the changing of the guard, which happens daily around noon, but once was enough for me. I only found one sandy beach, but there, the girl-watching was worth it. Nothing in Monaco spoke to me, so I rented a car. Back at home, American cars were huge, but every vehicle in Europe was too small. I squeezed into an Audi, and, crunched as I was, I drove to Cannes, arriving for the last few days of May. Cannes was not boring.

I decided to stay two days. That extended to four days because I found a short-haired cutie, Roxanne Miles, from New York. She was about my age and had just undergone a divorce. We were staying at the same seaside hotel. We met on the beach and escalated quickly to her hotel room. Sometimes we hit her bed and other times my bed. She seemed sex-starved. Put that appetite together with a guy like me who walks around with an erection, and we made a perfect couple. We were both moving targets. Roxanne didn't want to go with me to the nude beach, so I went alone. I'd already had practice in Capri. After about two hours on the sand, I made friends with a number of nudies. It was too bad sex in public wasn't allowed. No one buried me in the sand, but I went happily back to the hotel and shared some more time with Roxanne.

I got to Nice on June second. I stayed in Nice for two nights and made friends with a looker who said to call her Lola but told me that was not her name. She was hot, younger than me, and she invited me to her room across the street from the bar I met her in. I tried to give her money, and she refused it. The fake name made me curious. She wore a wedding ring and made no effort to hide it.

"I should pay you, big boy. You know how to please a woman." I left her with a big smile on her pretty face. It was a great memory to take back home. By the fifth, I was in Saint-Tropez, France, another place designed to separate wealthy tourists from their money. The people I ran into were from all over the globe, but only two were from the States, and they were paunchy old men. Everything was expensive. If I had been with someone, I wouldn't mind spending, but alone, nothing was worth the price tag. I'd done my share of burning cash at the Hotel de

Paris in Monaco. In Saint-Tropez, Spanish Ava made my first night memorable. She was hanging out at the hotel bar with two girls from Germany who reminded me of a couple of badly aged Zaras and Bellas. The sex was good, but I really appreciated speaking and hearing Spanish. On the second night, I shared my bed with Emma and Ela, also from Spain but not from Madrid where Ava was from. Two-for-one sex, plus the Spanish bonus. I wondered if the trip was wearing on me, because I was so glad to have someone to talk to, but the feeling passed. I moved on.

By June eighth, I was in Marseilles. Part of me was looking for Fae. I wished I'd understood more of her speech, because I'd have known where to look for her. I started off in a marina filled with small boats and huge yachts and listened to a skinny young guy rattle off (in four languages) about how Marseilles was a jumping-off point to the Mediterranean and its gorgeous beaches. I passed on the boat ride but stayed at the Marina and took a walking tour around the beautiful city.

This sounds stupid, but there are a lot of French people in Marseilles. I missed Jo, Pixie, Niley, and Melina more than I could express. Not sure how to explain how the feelings were different, but they were. I was in love with all my girls back home. Maybe being on this vacation was fun, but at times it was just lonely. I found myself swimming in a sea of strangers.

I was coming out of a bar when I ran into a pretty girl. She was tall and curvy, and something about her struck me as familiar. She wasn't Spanish.

"Mister, I go with you to hotel. Twenty American for an hour or forty American for all night."

In broken English, she introduced herself as Sunny. She was clean and dressed in a cheap cotton sundress. I normally don't look for pay for play, but she had a pretty face. No, that wasn't it at all. She reminded me of Pixie.

"You want money now or later?"

"After."

We walked over to my hotel, not one of the better ones I've been in, but not a cheap joint, either. We were walking up to the elevator, one of those old ones that had a metal lever you had to operate manually to close. The bellhop ran up and stopped me, said I had to see the desk clerk. The bellhop was just a kid, so I let him off. Sunny hunkered back while I went to the desk.

"The woman is not registered to the room."

Something about the way he said "the woman" made the hair stand up on the back of my neck. I could have squashed him like a bug, but I got a grip on my temper. I guess Sunny was known to the proprietors. She didn't look at all like a hooker, and it pissed me off that this jerk had the balls to tell me I couldn't take her up. I gave him a ten spot American and he was suddenly my best friend and waived the need to register. Maybe shaking down horny guys was his sideline.

We didn't say anything in the elevator or until we got into the room. I had the feeling she was embarrassed, but I wasn't sure.

"Where did you get the name Sunny?"

She shrugged. "I like that name. From the song."

It took a moment for me to remember the ten-year-old song by Bobby Hebb. "I always liked that song."

Sunny gave me the best deep throat ever, during which she hummed the song she had named herself after. I handed her forty dollars, after which she walked with me back to the bar. I had another beer with her and got up from the table where we were sitting. I paid the waitress and handed Sunny a hundred[4].

She seemed startled and said, "Mister, you already pay me for the night."

"The night is yours, Sunny, but thank you. You are very special."

I don't know if it was my compliment or the money, but when I left her, she was beaming.

By the eleventh of June, I was in Paris. I had read a lot of travel brochures about Paris and it had been one of my major destinations.

There was nothing in Paris I didn't love. It was always awake. On my first night, I went home with two girls I met at a club. The next day, I checked out of my hotel. Simone worked in a bakery, and Junon worked in a government office.

---

[4] $100.00 in 1975 had the same buying power as $455.73 in 2017

Like Zara and Bella, they liked having me around. My first night there, I paid a half share of their monthly rent. I saved a bundle not having to pay a hotel, and the social benefits were obvious. Plus, the flat had a phone.

Having a phone meant I could arrange communication. I started calling home at specific dates at seven in the evening Los Angeles time. Instead of making a bunch of separate calls, Pixie, Jo, and Niley would each be on an extension. Back in January, the calls from Sami's back to Los Angeles had been only for a few minutes, but now that it was June, we'd talk for an hour or longer. There was no hiding that I was getting homesick, and there was so much to catch up on.

During one of those calls, Jo said that Cooke had been paying me the ten grand a month that I had really not expected him to pay. He only owed it if Carson was matching the volume I had when I turned everything over; but it would have been easy for Cooke to claim that the case numbers were way below what he expected. He had made six payments. There were six more to go. That money alone paid for my trip, plus expenses back home. And as far as the rental income was concerned, there was no pressure on Jo. The mortgages were all covered, and the rental income that came in monthly was gravy.

"The vacancy factor across all the buildings is only five percent," Niley said.

"Vacancy factor when we took it from the management company was four times that," Jo boasted.

"You are magnificent, and I love you all. My aunt must be delighted with these figures."

"She is," Jo said. "But you must take after her, because she's pushing for zero vacancies."

I laughed with them.

"Come home, babe, for reals," Pixie said. "I know you're getting all sorts of head over there, but homemade is always best. I promise."

"I just got hard," I admitted.

"Yeah, you been gone too long, sweets," Jo said.

Even Niley complained. "Mario, isn't it time? Don't you miss us?"

"I miss you terribly."

I didn't always catch Melina at home. Sometimes I called back a couple of times, guessing what market she might be in. When I did connect, she was the only one who encouraged me to stick it out until I was ready for my return to reality. Melina admitted she'd stayed away for six months. I was approaching that mark and had barely explored Paris.

"I do miss you, friend."

"I miss you too, even here in Paris."

"How often do you fuck?"

"I forget how plain-spoken you are."

"How else can I ask? Answer the damn question."

I mentally ran through all the girls I'd been with since I'd been in Europe. It was a lot. "Every day. Gotta get off. You know how I am."

She mumbled something. I thought I heard a man's voice on her end and listened intently. I felt a surge of jealousy.

"Are you there? Did we get cut off?" she asked.

"No, I'm here, baby," I replied. "I was just trying to hear if that was Carson in your bed."

"Asshole," she said.

"But when I do fuck, I think of you."

"Fucker," she said. "Do you ever call the chickadee you're fucking by my name?"

"You know I do." That was a lie. But every night, I imagined Melina somewhere in the picture.

"Lying fucker. Maybe it's time you come home after all. I'm getting hot just talking about sex with you."

"And I have a hard on that's about to make a hole in my jeans." I told her about getting buried in the sand at the nude beach. She demanded pictures. We laughed all the way through the rest of the conversation, but I was starting to think she was right about coming home.

Even though my reality was a fantasy, I thought about banging Simone while I was with Junon or the other way around. I was always pretending I was with Jo, Pixie, or Niley. One time Junon and I broke the small wooden table in the kitchen when she was bent over it and I was behind her, my chest leaned forward on her back. I had to run out to buy a new table. We laughed for days about it.

Simone was from Amsterdam but had been in Paris for years. For a woman, she was kind of tall. She didn't quite look me in the eye, but she nearly did, and she had that Nordic look. Icy blue eyes, blond hair, a thin but substantial nose. She never wore makeup but always had flour on her clothes, somewhere. Though she was feminine, pale, and pretty, she had broad shoulders. I didn't believe Junon's claims that she was as strong as an ox until I saw her in action at work. She claimed the bakery she worked in would have closed long ago if not for her. I went there frequently and watched her behind the counter in a white chef's uniform, not just filling the bakery case and doing the baking, but also hauling hundred-pound bags of flour and sugar, cast iron cookware, and supplies. The bakery was in a primo location, with lots of foot traffic just off the Champs Elysees, one of the principal streets in Paris where the Arc de Triomphe was situated. If it had been in Los Angeles, I'd have bought it in a heartbeat. The glass cases were full of flaky pastry and there was a line from when they opened in the morning till when they closed around four p.m. when the shelves were bare. They didn't even have chairs, only tall tables where people stood and scarfed down pastries and coffee. Simone's boss had died some time ago, and his widow was an absentee owner more interested in moving to the country than keeping the business going. I gave Simone two grand US[5] to buy the bakery, with only a promise that I would own half of the business. I opened a personal bank account in Paris where she would deposit my share of the profits every month. The night the sale was finalized, I bought Dom Pérignon, then Simone and Junon and I tore up the sheets. I still think of

---

[5] $2,000.00 in 1975 had the same buying power as $9,303.74 in 2017

Simone as the best-smelling woman, ever. She smelled like French pastry. Junon was smaller and rounder, and possibly the most cheerful person I've ever met. She had a dimple in both cheeks and smiled all of the time, even when she was sleeping. The celebratory champagne had reminded me of Sami and unfinished business with Jason.

Junon quit the office job and started working at the bakery full time. They were elated. I stayed in Paris another month after Simone took over. I spent many mornings eating breakfast in bed with Junon and Simone, both showing me the right way to eat a croissant. You're supposed to rip off a little morsel and butter it, then pop it into your mouth, one buttered crumble at a time. It was delicious and wonderful, and that's not even going into all the crumbs that got licked up that fell where they wanted to. I had to start jogging before I turned into a croissant myself. I didn't know anyone in Paris with a gym or a treadmill.

A proper business person would have asked what the projection was of how much I'd make each month. I didn't ask. I figured that every once in a while, you got to give back and not always to just the people you know. If Simone never paid me a dime, it would be okay. I would know that I had helped her get on her feet. It was just what Harry had done for me. Had Harry not given me a huge bankroll before I knew I'd need it, I'd never have made it as far as I have.

"You got a winner," I told Simone. She'd already improved the business, now that she was able to make any changes she said she'd been wanting to.

"We got a winner, partner," she replied.

London was right across the channel, only ninety-three miles from Calais.

"I'm going to London," I told Jo on the phone. It was around the end of July. "The next time you hear from me, I'll be calling from London."

London
August 1, 1975
Dear Jo, Pixie, and Niley,
     I'm writing this while squeezed behind the steering wheel of my tiny rented car. Check out the picture on the postcard. It's in front of Hyde Park, across the street from where I'm staying. We hear about Europe, but the distances are mind-boggling. As the crow flies from Calais to London, it's only as far as it is from LA to Big Bear Lake in San Bernardino County. I said goodbye to Junon and Simone, put my things in a rental car, and was off for Calais and the ferry. I planned to check into the Mandarin, but when I called from Calais to give Sami fair warning, she said that if I didn't come right over from the airport, she'd bribe her way into my room and cut my balls off while I slept. I wasn't going to risk that. I didn't tell her I was driving in. If I had, she might have talked me out of it. I wrote this far on the ferry and will finish up when I get to Sami's.
     For such a short distance, it was a grueling, long drive. The weather was awful, the streets were mystifying. I won't repeat the drive to London again. I'll chalk it up as a learning experience. I didn't even think about how terrible parking is in London, though I enjoyed the ferry ride across the channel. It rained the whole way. I'm dropping this postcard off in a red post office box. The public mailboxes look more like big red pipes than what we have back home.
     Love you all,
     Mario

It wasn't home, but a feeling of familiarity hit me when I got to the twelve-story building where Sami lived. I circled the block seventeen times before I found a spot to put the car in and walked through a downpour to the entrance.

Sami, Crispin, and Ginger met me at the door as I came out of the elevator at the penthouse. Sami greeted me like she'd known and missed me for years, instead of this being my second trip to London. Crispin, bless his well-paid heart, went out to the car in the pouring rain to retrieve my suitcase. Ginger blushed when she saw me, and I remembered that massage, and afterwards.

Ten minutes after I walked in, Sami and I were undressing each other in her bedroom.

"I missed you, Sami."

"I missed you too. I'm sure you regret doing that drive from Paris."

"Paris to Calais was not bad. Dover to London was fucking terrible, but now I know."

After we christened the bed, and a chair, I wondered aloud if that mink carpet on the floor was big enough and long enough for me to lie down on. It was. The two of us tried it out and ended up there, with her on top. Doctor Sami knew where all my buttons were, and after she made some direct hints about eating pussy, guided me to her buttons as well.

Ginger served us a light dinner in the bedroom. I winked at her, but with Sami there, she was seriously into her housekeeper role and kept a sober expression. She didn't wink back, but I felt the vibes from her. As great as the sex with Sami was, she wasn't why I had returned to London. I had come because aviation was the logical progression in my line of work. It had been working on my brain ever since Jason had brought it to my attention. Thanks to Sami, aviation was the new direction I would be taking, but I needed to know more before I launched into it.

"I will be flying home soon. I need to talk to Jason again before I go."

"You like the aviation idea, don't you?"

"I am leaning in that direction. I left home with no idea what I was going to do next, but now, it just seems the logical thing to do."

"It will be no problem. Jason is dear to me. He will do whatever I ask."

"I don't need him to do anything. I just want to talk. He's smart in this area as anyone I could ever find. I just need to feed off his brain a little more."

Jason came over two nights later, for dinner.

"Cutting it short, are you?" Jason asked. "I hear you're catching a flight to the States tomorrow."

"It's in the works," I said. I was ready to go home, except for this last conversation with Jason.

"Not if I have anything to do with it," Sami said.

Crispin cooked his heart out. Ginger was on hand to bring in platter after platter of different food for everyone else, but she brought in a rib-eye steak for me, and I was content. I wondered how Jason managed to put away so much food without being fat; but he was very fit.

Jason and Sami teased me for my American taste buds, but I didn't mind. The teasing made me feel more at home. They asked about my wanderings. Sami had already told Jason everything I'd already shared with her, which was why Jason seemed really interested in my roommates in Milan and Paris.

"You stayed with two girls, twice?" He wanted to know the details of the living arrangements. I assured him that they lived up to any fantasy he could imagine.

Sami applauded my helping Simone with the bakery. Jason frowned and told me I should have done the paperwork to secure my investment. He offered to assist in that matter. He wasn't licensed to work in France, but when he said he networked cases with a firm in Paris, I laughed. He sounded like me. I told the story about Fae in Venice and how she had disappeared in Rome, no doubt to free me from what she believed was a responsibility that I didn't need.

"I feel guilty that I didn't try harder to find her. Maybe I could have found a way to help her get on her feet." Talking about my failure to find her made me feel down. I told them about Natalia in Naples and when I was done with the short story about her, Sami said, "I can tell you got attached to that one too."

"Attached to all of them and none," I said.

The aviation discussion waited all through dinner. After dessert and port, Jason opened the door.

"Sami says you have questions. Ask me anything you want."

I declined port and accepted coffee because I wanted to remember every word I heard tonight.

A tray of fruit and cheese waited on the table, as well as an array of pastries similar to those from Simone's bakery. I broke off a small piece and put it in my mouth; it wasn't half as good as those I'd left behind in Paris. The pastry melted in my mouth, embraced the coffee, and did a dance on my tongue. I could only imagine how it would have been with Simone's.

"Since you opened my eyes, I've been following the news. As you said, crashes are happening all the time all over the world."

We were seated as before, Sami and Jason on a loveseat across from me. Sami was quiet, her hand on Jason's thigh, the other holding a glass of champagne. I wondered what Ginger would be doing tonight and suppressed a smile.

"If there is a plane crash here in the UK or Paris, and I fly over here to speak with the families of those who died, am I breaking any laws?"

"You're not a lawyer. I'd say that as long as you keep it smooth and non-solicitous, you'll be fine."

"So I sign a family in Paris, take the retainer to Los Angeles. The lawyer there puts the airline on notice just as we put the defendant of an auto accident on notice. The airline turns the matter over to their insurance company that may or may not involve you at all."

"Correct."

"And chances are we probably will never have a case of yours because there are so many insurance carriers, but you never know."

"In a car accident, the lawyer sends the insurance carrier all the damage documents that include the car repairs or replacement, medical bills, loss of income when there is loss of earnings, and anything else that shows damage to the client. Is that the way it works with an aviation case?"

"Exactly. Very important is a history of the victim's employment or self-employment. Let's say that a person is thirty-five when he dies in the crash. He has about thirty years of life expectancy at that point. Very broadly speaking, if he's making ten thousand a year, then his loss of income is three hundred thousand dollars.[6] Then there is a possibility of pain and suffering damages, loss of consortium, etc."

"And if we don't settle, then the lawyer in Los Angeles gets a lawyer in the country where the tragedy happened and files the case in court?"

"It's a bit more complicated. There is an international treaty that protects the airline for damages a passenger or passenger's family can collect. I'll give that treaty to you and when you read it you will understand. Basically, you got it. It's

---

[6] $300,000.00 in 1975 had the same buying power as $1,367,196.53 in 2017

like a car accident, only with a possible bigger recovery since in most cases you are dealing with loss of life. A death in a plane can result in millions to the family. It just depends on who died. The country of residence of the decedent can make a difference as well. You also need to get around the treaty. A number of things are spelled out there."

I had no clue what attorney would be interested, but I knew I could sell it. I wasn't just thinking about the attorney fees or how much I would make on a case. I would be looking for the maximum compensation for the people who trusted me enough to sign a retainer with the attorney I recommended. I was eager to get home and get started.

"You said a minute ago a case can be worth millions. I am guessing that is on the high end. Do you have any idea of what a case can normally settle for? A range, maybe?"

Jason had already explained this, but I needed more clarity.

"Compensation varies," he said. "Each person's loss of income is unique, so compensation is unique. A thirty-year-old factory worker does not have the same loss of income as a thirty-year-old attorney. The attorney's family should get a lot more than the factory worker based on their earnings and earnings capacity."

I understood pretty well, although I didn't look forward to tackling the treaty. I would get to that on my own. I needed to find an attorney already well-versed in cases like those Jason was telling me about.

"The treaty is in place to protect the airline operator and assure that a claim does not exceed a certain amount. However, there are ways around this compensation cap."

Ginger made another pass with the coffee. She faced me for a moment, and when I saw her wink, my heart beat faster. I had plenty to look forward to tonight.

The next morning, I almost ran into Sami and Jason coming from the sauna but ducked back into my bedroom before they saw me. They'd both been wrapped in towels, and I saw for myself that Jason was pretty fit. He probably had some favorite sport like tennis or soccer. I waited till after Jason left to head for breakfast, but Sami waylaid me. Except for last night, when Jason had stayed over, I'd slept in Sami's bed and not in my guest room.

"Today is too soon," Sami said.

"Last time we talked, my travel agent was working on tickets for today," I said, sitting up in bed with a tray filled with enough breakfast goodies to hold us until lunch. I fed strawberries to Sami and she fed me grapes. By now, we knew each other's preferences.

"Unacceptable," she said.

"You remind me of Melina back home. She's bossy too."

Sami moved my coffee cup beside hers on the glass-topped end table. She slipped me another grape from the tray. All that remained were the crumbs of a couple of croissants and some assorted fruit. I gave her a strawberry. The linen napkins were balled up, and the silverware lay in the corner of the tray bearing traces of butter and jam.

"I'm jealous," Sami pouted.

"No, you're not."

A picture of Melina flashed in my head. I did miss her, even now next to this very beautiful lady. Hell, I missed Pixie, Jo, and Niley, too. I missed my whole life back home. I was ready for home.

"Mario, stay longer. We'll have fun. We have lots of places to go that you haven't been. Please."

"I've been gone so long," I said, hesitating. Telling Sami no to anything was hard. She asked for sex, but I wanted sex as much as she did, so that didn't count. She never wanted anything else.

"If you stay, I'll make it worth your while."

"How?"

Sami flashed me a provocative grin, and tossed the tray aside. It struck the carpeted floor with a clatter. The gesture was a little alarming. She dove on top of me, kissing me fiercely. She trailed kisses down my face, my chin, the hollow of my neck. I tried to move inside her, but she pushed out of reach and shook her head.

"Stay."

"Baby," I said.

She teased some more. I grabbed her hips and pulled her down on me. She gyrated, but kept out of reach. I couldn't take any more.

She handed me the phone and crouched over me, on her knees, with her arms crossed stubbornly.

I dialed.

"Had an emergency," I told the travel agent. "Change the tickets." I tried to sound like myself, but Sami was still teasing me, and I felt like a bottle rocket about to go off.

I tossed the phone in the general direction of the receiver. Sami reached over and hung it up.

She grinned triumphantly and, with a flex of her hips, mounted me. We came to a furious conclusion.

Maybe I am a totally pussy-whipped dummy. Everyone should be so lucky.

On August twenty-fifth, I was headed home.

I knew that Jo, Pixie, and Niley were picking me up at the airport. They were at the gate, waiting as I came out of the jet bridge. I spotted them right away, and they were the most welcome sight. Pixie had changed her hair again: blonde, Faye Dunaway in *Chinatown*. Niley had a tan and was in a skinny tee and tiny shorts that were painted on; she had gold streaks in her dark hair that reminded me of her sister. How do I describe Niley's tan? It was a light glossy finish. Jo looked exactly the same, with her chin-length hair, perfect suit, and stilettos. I'd never heard such squeals and hugs. Not in public anyway. They hugged me all at once, and I felt a great rush of happiness.

We walked through the airport in an awkward mass, the girls all chattering at once. It was great to be home. LAX felt like my own back yard, though the instant I stepped out of the doors, the August heat nearly knocked me off my feet.

Niley was leading the way, and she pointed to a car pulling up. Pixie was on one side and Jo on the other. They navigated me to the car. The door opened and I was hit by a welcome blast of icy air conditioning. What I didn't know was that inside the Mercedes limousine, Melina was aboard, nor that Johnson would be driving, outfitted as a chauffeur. I found myself in the back seat, surrounded by the people I missed the most. I gave Melina a three-minute hug and four-minute kiss. The rest of the world disappeared and it was just the two of us. Halfway through the kiss, I realized the girls were cheering and catcalling, so I toned it down.

Melina handed me a glass of champagne, which they all encouraged me to gulp down. I complied and handed back the empty glass.

"So how is everyone? What's been going on? Why the limo?" I asked.

"We're fine and about to be better; what's going on is that we've all been working. The limo belongs to Melina, and look who she hired to drive," Jo said.

"Johnson, good to see you," I said. Johnson had been on the apartment security team when I was attacked last year. He had been a good friend as well. He'd always called me boss and bossman, before anyone else did. When it started, it had been banter, but more and more these days, everyone was calling me boss. Though I understood the landlord's reasoning, I hated that management had entirely replaced the security guards after the breach. I'd asked the girls to find him, since I had the idea of hiring him myself, but it looked like Melina had gotten to him first. Gotta love her.

"Bossman, welcome home."

Pixie giggled and went for my buttons.

Melina said, "Take it slow, Johnson, and don't look back."

She slid the window closed.

"Yes, Miss Melina." I heard the warm Johnson laugh that I hadn't realized I'd missed.

"Help, Johnson!" I raised my voice.

Chapter 4
August 26, 1975
Homecoming

He didn't answer, but I knew by his chuckle that he'd heard me.

It's a good thing that the windows of the car were tinted. By the time Johnson had pulled away from the terminal curb, I was stripped of all my clothes, and Melina was astride me, wearing nothing but a gold necklace and earrings. Everyone had glasses of champagne but me, as my hands were full. The girls alternated giving me sips straight from their mouths. Melina rode me hard through an orgasm and back again, then I was able to last through Pixie, Jo, then Niley. I've never heard so much laughter for so long. How do I say how it feels to have four naked women all over me in a moving car? I felt like I was one of Willy Wonka's Everlasting Gobstoppers—the candy that you can suck forever and never gets any smaller. I don't know where we drove, nor how long it took, but it was a hell of a ride. All I know is that we did not go straight home.

The drive continued until the girls and I were worn out. After Niley's final gasp, and my own, Melina knocked at the glass, the signal for Johnson to get us to the apartment. Then it was a race to get dressed, sort of. Niley couldn't find her shirt and had to wear mine. Jo lost one of her shoes, and just for the hell of it, Pixie didn't put her bra back on. Melina was perfectly put together except for her hair, which was sticking up oddly. No one mentioned it.

Johnson made the familiar turn and pulled to a stop. Jo was by the door, and she got it open. We all piled out, first Jo, then me, and Pixie, Niley, and Melina; and we ran in, in laughing disarray. Security greeted us with a smile. So did Tito Lopez, the front door man who had replaced Johnson.

Tito was about my age, Cuban, and dark skinned. He was like a jitterbug. When he spoke, the words were like lyrics of a song. I had met him a few times after I'd gotten out of the hospital, but hadn't really gotten to know him yet. He seemed to be a nice guy.

"Glad to have you back, Mr. Luna."

"It's good to be home," I told him. And it was true.

I opened the apartment door to someone else's living room suite. I stepped back out, checking the number. I'd never seen that furniture before. It was just for effect; I knew perfectly well that I was back in my old apartment on Melina's floor. Someone had been shopping. It was a sweet gesture, as most of my stuff had been trashed when Hugo tried to kill me and only managed to kill my apartment. A leather sofa I'd never seen before faced my television. It looked expensive, like something Brigitte Bardot or Catherine Deneuve would be posing on, in white fur or black silk. And there was a little plaque on the wall: Casa Luna.

Hugo had plunged through the living room window and shot me (not in that order). When I'd come home from the hospital after four weeks, the apartment management had already relocated all my things and fired my man Johnson. Johnson was a loss to the building, but I was glad Melina had hired him. As for the furniture, at the time, I hadn't bothered to have anything replaced, though everything in the den had been left bloody and slashed by Hugo's knives. This living room suite was one I'd never seen. I knew it was my place because the weapons cabinet was there.

"Melina did it all," Jo said. "She's got such great taste. Except we came up with the name, Casa Luna. We remembered. We let Melina hire someone to make it frame-able."

"She wouldn't let Jo reimburse her," Niley said.

"You owe me zero." Melina hugged me. "I love you, Cuz."

"I'm paying you for this," I said firmly. "We'll deal with it later."

"We hung up all your new stuff," Pixie said. "Everything from the trunks that you shipped home is in your closet."

I went straight into the kitchen and came out with a jar of peanut butter and a spoon.

"You can't believe how much I missed this." I unscrewed the jar and savored a mouthful. "Best stuff ever. Europe doesn't know what it's missing."

I sat on the couch for the first time. I noticed that the leather felt soft as butter and it sat at a good height for a tall man; for once, my knees were not around my ears. I put the jar down on a marble-topped coffee table I'd never seen before. After a second, I picked up the peanut butter jar and moved it to a marble coaster that I'd also never seen before. Melina sat down next to me.

"I remember when I came back from Europe after being gone for as many months as you've been gone, I felt good. Mind you, I had no one greeting me. And my apartment was practically empty and in total disarray. That was about five minutes before we met."

I hugged her.

"I feel good, really good."

I got up and hugged Jo, Pixie, and Niley all at once. Melina remained seated and watched, then applauded us.

"Picture perfect," Melina said with a big smile.

You wouldn't think that wine and peanut butter would be a good combination, but under the right circumstances, peanut butter goes with everything. The five of us drank wine in the living room. The team asked a million questions, and I think I answered a million and one. Melina stuck around, never mentioning how busy she was. I knew her hands were full. She had four markets open that I knew of. I'd have to ask if she'd opened another while I'd been gone.

"How are the apartments coming along?"

The girls got excited and launched into a saga of what had been going on with my real estate investments for the past eight months. I could tell by their en-thusiasm that the venture had been going well. But I put my hand up to stop them. I already knew it was good because I talked to them so often on the telephone.

"I hope you're ready for a change," I said.

Chapter 5
August 27, 1975
Aviation Takes Off

Jo looked faintly irritated: furrowed brow, mouth stubbornly pursed, hands fisted at her side. I knew she'd thrown herself wholeheartedly into management. Of all of us, she was the least flexible. She wasn't crazy about change, but I knew once she heard the plan, she'd be on board.

"We're going back into PI," I said.

Jo looked instantly relieved.

"We're going to work plane crashes. Get your passports in order. And I mean right away."

"What?" Pixie sat down, looking confused.

"If you prefer to stay on apartment management and not dive in with me on this, you can. No pressure."

"You must be loco, boss." Pixie dove at me. I was sitting on the sofa next to Melina, and the impact rolled the three of us into a pile on the rug. We stood up laughing, but I pushed the girls to the couch and started walking. Pacing sometimes frees up my mouth.

"I met an insurance lawyer in London who brought me up to speed. Plane crashes happen all over the world, and there are families who need representation." I explained to them everything that Jason had told me.

"We're in!" Pixie yelled so excitedly that Melina started laughing. "Let's go for it!"

"I think Pixie speaks for all of us on that count." Jo glanced at Niley, who nodded.

"We're going to travel?"

"I'm not kidding about the passports," I said.

They asked the same million questions I had asked Jason. I went to my carry-on and unzipped it, pulling out the envelope that Jason had given me. From it, I extracted my copy of the Warsaw Convention and handed it to Jo.

"Convention for the unification of certain rules relating to international carriage by air, signed at Warsaw on 12 October 1928," she read aloud, looking perplexed. "That's a hell of a title, boss."

"Make copies for everyone," I said. "This is our new bible, and we're going to learn it backward and forward. It's complicated, but not that long. I've read it. It's written in legalese and it protects the airlines, but a good lawyer will know how to work around this. I'll check with Oscar to see if there are other protocols we have to follow."

"Send me a copy," Melina said to Jo, in her lawyer voice. Melina had sunk her passion and expertise into her string of Mexican markets, but I could always see when she switched into lawyer mode. "I'll read it and give you feedback if you need it."

"Is that lawyer you?" asked Niley.

Melina laughed. "I don't practice," she said.

"Doesn't practice because she's already perfect," I said.

Melina elbowed me in the side. "Quit trying to butter me up. Niley's right to wonder. What lawyer are you going to send aviation cases to? Who handles aviation cases?"

"Not sure yet," I admitted.

Jo was already skimming the Warsaw Convention, but she asked, "What about the apartments?"

"Pick a good management company," I said. "You kids know all about that now."

"We sure the fuck do."

"And we're good at it."

"First, I need to find a lawyer who wants to handle aviation cases. Truth is, if I had a bunch of clients right now, I wouldn't even know what retainer to use."

"Oscar Cooke has been paying like clockwork. Seems like a real standup guy," Jo said. "Why not him?"

"For sure, I'm going to hit him up." I wasn't sure I wanted to be close to Carson.

Melina leaned forward, toying with her glass of wine. "You'll find someone. I bet there's as much competition as in car crashes, but it's a big world. Hungry lawyers are everywhere. Plane crashes are everywhere. I read about a terrible one last month."

"Eastern Airlines, July, New York. Or did you mean Air Maroc, on August third?" I asked. I was already psyched to go after it, but I wasn't prepared. I didn't want my first go in this new arena to end up a fiasco. I wanted to hit the ground running.

"Either one, we're in," Jo said. "Anything you want, boss. We're there."

Every day since I got home, I'd done a full workout. For the first few days, they could have used pictures of me on a Geritol commercial. I was moving like Arte Johnson's Tyrone F. Horneigh character after a hard night of chasing Gladys around the park bench. I hurt like hell, a well-deserved pain thanks to my slacking off. Sit-ups, pushups, and a little bit of walking can make you look buff, but not actually be buff enough to handle a karate workout unscathed. I knew I had to get over to Cosmo's again for a couple days a week to get back where I should be, but I wasn't going there until I could make it through a normal workout without a pain hangover. It took four days to adjust to the time change and about that long for the pain to turn into normal day-after stiffness.

I'd never called Carson to check on how my old cases were going. I'd never communicated with him about the arrangement where Cooke got my contact list, with Carson working my contacts for future cases. I only hoped the clients were being taken care of.

I met Cooke at the restaurant on top of his office building. I was in one of my English three-piece suits, a pair of alligator Italian shoes, and I had tied one of my new ties in one of the new knots I'd learned. I remembered when we'd been here before, and I'd been so impressed. It was no less impressive, but the trip to Europe had given me perspective. It was as fine as it had ever been, but I was less dazzled.

"Looking good, my boy."

"Likewise, Oz. Good to see you."

I ordered wine with my meal. He seemed surprised.

"You must have a PI mill by now. How is Carson doing?"

"I'm very proud of Carson," Oz said.

He was no longer complaining about Carson's lack of incentive, nor of his being slow. I suppose that meant that he was making good use of my contacts.

"We're doing well. The volume does not quite match what yours used to be, but as you know, I've been sending ten grand every month as we agreed. Overall, it has been a good arrangement for me."

I knew he had to be getting a ton of cases, unless Carson was sending some somewhere else. But that was none of my business. I picked up the wine and swirled it in my glass. The dark burgundy caught light from the restaurant's sconces, and it smelled like the night in London when Ginger had made spaghetti, and Sami and I had gotten wine and sauce over a perfectly fine set of sheets. The burgundy reminded me of Sami, who reminded me of Jason, who reminded me of aviation. If Oscar was interested, I wouldn't have to put feelers out for a new lawyer. I took a deep breath. It was now or never. I picked now.

"Oscar, I have what I believe could be a good deal for you. I want to pass it by you before I go elsewhere. You get first shot, if you're interested."

I saw no physical reaction, but my second sense caught his excitement. He nodded for me to go ahead. We were each eating rare strip steaks. He sliced into his and speared the bite with his fork. I did the same, but I was too excited to eat.

"How would you like to handle aviation cases?"

"There's a lot of money in aviation cases. I'm interested," he said. He put down his fork and looked me in the eye. I could see my excitement was contagious. "Flying is my thing. I never told you. There would be no reason to bring it up." He swallowed a laugh. "I'm a pilot. For years, I had a twin-engine Cessna to play with. Last year, I got a Learjet, and I'm checked out in it."

"Checked out?"

"In other words, I can fly the plane. I need a second pilot, but I can do it. Flying is my thing."

"I'm impressed you have your own jet and can fly it yourself. I can dig it." Now my going into aviation seemed more than a coincidence. How did I not know this before? "The aviation business I am referring to involves commercial airliners."

"I know that." Oscar gestured with his fork. "I can hire an aviation attorney. No big deal. I expanded my office to accommodate the PI business you turned over to me. I know right where our new aviation guy will go. Corner office. Great view."

I clinked glasses with him. "You got the space. If you have an aviation attorney, all you need are the cases."

Cooke asked, "Where is the business coming from?" I could see him trying to think of US crash cases.

"I'm looking outside the United States."

I shared Jason's explanation of how we could work it and the likelihood of settling. "Of course, you're the ace. Your take on handling cases will be the right one."

"The aviation attorney I hire will know what to do. You make a good point about taking the cases in hopes we can just settle them. Interesting."

"Does interesting mean that you're interested?"

"We have some kinks to work out, but I'm in. Great idea. New pastures. Green ones." He paused. "Will you use your team to get the business?"

I nodded. "Of course. And I don't want any percentages. I want a set amount for each case I sign up. I don't want to be stuck again waiting for a bonus when each case settles. You know how much I lost when Jake died."

"I have no intention of dying any time soon," Cooke laughed. "We'll come to an understanding. Figure it out, and we'll work it out." His laugh was engaging. I laughed with him.

I knew it wasn't a done deal yet. We were still setting the stage. My team would have to learn the new business, but we had a good foundation to build on. We certainly had experience with the families of victims, and knew our end of the ropes and knots of wrongful death cases.

Cooke sent me the draft of a retainer to use. The cover letter promised the retainer would be translated to the language of the family interested in retaining us. The last paragraph stated that "Our firm will reimburse you for expenses and services rendered in conjunction with signing a family of a decedent/victim of an air tragedy."

A few days passed. The girls had gone to the library to search out recent accidents. They brought home stacks of newspaper and journal articles, which I was studying. It was morbid to be sitting around waiting for an accident to happen, though we'd had to do the same with car accidents. I figure that once we had cases, Cooke would push for maximum compensation for the families. I hoped that he was already working on getting an aviation attorney to handle the department. I was confident I would get the volume, but the wait made me anxious.

It was after midnight when I dialed Jason's office. In London, he was eight hours ahead.

"I hope this isn't a bad time," I said.

"Call me anytime."

I had one of the newspaper articles in front of me. The accident had happened during the last week of July.

"There was a bad crash in New York a couple months ago. Do you know how I can get a list of passengers and addresses?"

"The manifest is usually published in newspapers after the families are notified. A private investigator is also a good option."

"That's good to know," I said. I made a note to tell the girls.

"I may be able to find something. That was Eastern Airlines. It's not our case, but I may be able to get something for you."

Two days later, Jason called me back.

"I mailed you the manifest, and I've checked the names of those families that have engaged a lawyer."

My heart raced with excitement.

"When you get this list, copy it in your own handwriting and destroy the original. This is between us."

The list took five days to arrive.

For eight months, I'd been starved of my most familiar cuisine. I'd never run into a Mexican restaurant in Europe or London. Spanish food was nothing like Mexican food, though you'd think that it would be. The girls brought in Mexican food from Barragan's Restaurant on Sunset Boulevard. Since I'd been back, I couldn't get enough of it. The table was covered in the usual tacos, enchiladas, and Mexican rice, but also fajitas, machaca, ropa vieja, steak picado, salsa, guacamole, and enough fresh tortilla chips to make even Pixie happy. After we ate, we worked and grazed.

I handed Jason's list over to Jo. On a yellow pad, Jo recorded details of the families who had not yet engaged a lawyer. There were families from New Orleans where the plane had originated, and some in New York. Of those, I looked especially for Latin names, since in car crash cases that had been our "in."

"You copied the whole list?" I asked Jo.

"Every word."

"Okay. Your list is the master copy," I said. I balled up the paper and walked into the kitchen.

Jo grabbed my arm. "What are you doing?"

"Keeping a promise," I told her. "You copied it all, right?"

"Yes, but you know I like to keep originals."

"Not this one. Your copy is the original."

I walked into my kitchen. The girls filed in behind me, watching as I put the ball of paper on the gas burner of my stove and lit it. In moments, it was a weightless bit of black ash. When Jo sponged it into the sink, it dissolved into nothing and ran down the drain.

"Promise kept," I said. "Let's get started."

Two families from Puerto Rico had been aboard, one Texan on the ground had been injured, and one man in a pickup had been killed.

"That English guy is a fabulous connection," Jo said.

"He said the newspaper would publish the manifest. His notations on who has a lawyer have to come from a connection of his. It's not his case."

"Boss, when can I fly to London and suck him as payback?" Pixie asked.

Niley gasped as if she were shocked. Jo kept on writing. I didn't know if she was kidding or not. I didn't know how Sami would feel about it, so I didn't answer. I changed the subject.

"Let's get some practice on this local crash."

"Local?"

"Local, as in the US."

The information operator gave the name and number of three private investigators in Puerto Rico.

I talked to all three and settled on Juan Reyes, who had the best rates and the longest experience. My team clustered around me, trying to listen in when I called him back.

"I have an address for two plane passengers who died in a recent airline tragedy here in the United States. I need you to get me a phone number for their family. Can you do this?"

"Yes, sure, Mr. Luna."

"You said you charge twenty dollars per hour and take care of your own auto expenses?"

"Si."

"Tell the family that an assistant for an attorney in Los Angeles wants to speak with the head of the family. Get permission for me to call them."

"Can do."

"After I hang up, I will run over to Western Union and send you two hundred dollars.[7] That's ten hours of your time in advance. Just remember that this family lost loved ones less than two months ago. You need to be soft and sympathetic with them, Juan. You got it? Cover this, and I'll know who to call whenever I need a man in Puerto Rico."

"Got it, Mr. Luna."

"I'm going to give you to my assistant, Jo."

Jo, who was standing by my side, gave me a thumbs up and grabbed her yellow pad.

"Give her your information. Give me your full name and I'll send you the money within an hour. And you can call me Mario."

The girls could tell the call was positive, because I was smiling ear to ear. I handed the phone to Jo. I felt like I'd hit the jackpot, and I hadn't even gotten on a plane yet.

Melina had been hanging out with me, but she took off for the Montebello Market. The girls and I drove over to Western Union on Flower Street, a venue that was within walking distance from the apartment. I wired the retainer.

The girls and I had moved to the den and were sitting on the new sofa.

---

[7] $200.00 in 1975 had the same buying power as $911.46 in 2017

The television was on, muted, and music from the stereo filled the room.

"Why are you paying him in advance?" Niley asked. "Isn't it a risk that he'll just run off with your money?"

"Sure, it's a risk, but not much of one. He's looking at the possibility of more easy work coming in. This has got to be easier than other private investigator work. Trailing cheating husbands and wives, sitting outside of motels, researching a crime, tracking down stolen property. He probably won't have to look very far. There were probably obituaries for the victims in their local paper."

Jo added, "The money is incentive to take care of business right away, and to know Mario is for real."

"Of course," Niley agreed. "I should know that."

"Never be afraid to ask," I told Niley.

Pixie had stretched out on the chaise with a pillow over her head. She wasn't asleep. She was tapping her feet in rhythm to the music. Salsa.

"Then I have a question," Jo said. "What drove you to call information in Puerto Rico, just like that?" She snapped her fingers. "And to ask for an investigator?"

"Jason."

"The guy who sent us the list?"

"He made some suggestions for our next steps."

"Good deal," Jo said. "Sounds like he knows the ropes of..." She struck a pose like she was scratching her head, thinking of the right word. "...plane chasing."

I rolled my eyes, but I could see she wanted to tell me something.

Jo continued with a frown on her face. "You think he knows the ropes as well as Pixie knows the ropes? About apartment management, I mean."

Pixie hopped up. The pillow went flying and would have knocked over the wine bottle if I hadn't caught it right before impact. She crossed her arms over her chest and got a familiar obstinate look in her eye.

"What's up, Jo? Spit it out. I can see you got a story in you."

"I'm no rat, but did you hear yet what Pixie did to the tenant?"

My first thought was that she sucked him into submission, but maybe I'd better not go leaping to conclusions. With Pixie, anything was possible.

"Better tell me," I said. "Pixie?"

She didn't pretend not to know what Jo was talking about. This was obviously a sore subject between them. "A fucker's rent is due. I forget his name. Let's call him Asshole. It fits. Asshole keeps hanging up. Asshole won't talk to me. I need reinforcements. So, I go over to Hollenbeck and pick me up a homey so big he hardly fits in the passenger seat."

Pixie loved being the center of attention as she was right now, and she made the most of it. She illustrated her story with big facial expressions, gestures, and body language. She pretended to climb into a car too small for her. It reminded me of me in the passenger side of Melina's Corvette.

"I drive Homey over to the building. By the time we reach the third floor, where Asshole lives, Homey is pissed big time about the stairs."

She pantomimed being a big guy climbing up steps. "I knock on the door."

She knocked on the table to illustrate her point. Once. Twice. Three times. "No answer. Homey bangs on the door."

She slammed her fist on the table a couple of times. The pictures in the room clattered. The wine glasses on the table shivered and bounced.

"Asshole comes running. Opens the door. He takes a look at Homey and at me and says, 'What?'

'The rent, Asshole,' I tell him. 'Pay up or get the fuck out.'

He says, 'There's a process to evict people.'

I say, 'I'd rather have the rent than evict you.'

Asshole goes on ranting. 'You can't just come over here and strong-arm me. I got rights. I got—' Homey doesn't let him finish his sentence. He grabs Asshole by the shirt, pulls him off his feet for a whole minute. Homey says, 'See here, candyass, I don't like you and I don't like your stairs. Pay the stone-cold fox her money, or I'm gonna dropkick you down to the basement.' Asshole raises both hands in surrender and begs to pay. 'I got the rent, give me a minute.' Homey puts his big foot in the door to keep it from shutting. Asshole comes back with the green. Homey points to me." Pixie licked her finger and pantomimed handing over dollar after dollar.

All of us applauded. Pixie took a bow.

"Then what happened?" I asked.

"I give Homey a ten spot and drop him off at the park where I found him."

Applause came from all of us again. Pixie stood up and took a second bow.

"Did you give Homey any favors?" asked Jo.

"Nope. He's way too big for me, and I don't mean his verga! And I don't think he's had a bath since Abraham Lincoln was president." Pixie giggled.

"It's a great story," I said. Jo was right to get this out in the open. I was thinking that an untrained Pixie was a lawsuit waiting to happen. It wasn't her fault. I'd thrown them into the deep end of this management business without any coaching. I didn't have to worry about Jo. She'd worked in lawyers' offices for years. But Pixie was a whole other story. I tried to broach the subject without putting her on the defensive. Eight months she'd been out there, doing stuff like this. There might already be lawsuits I didn't know about. "Doll, we do work for lawyers. We know better. We can't go strong-arming our tenants. Besides, we'll be out of management very soon. You know that could have been dangerous."

Pixie wouldn't let go. "Dangerous for that asshole. Only for him."

I could see Jo shaking her head. Her expression told me they must have had this conversation before. Pixie isn't always good at listening, and her solutions aren't the kind of answers that Andy Griffith would approve of.

I was sitting. I stretched out my arm so Pixie'd come hug me, and she did.

I was in a deep sleep when the phone started to ring. During my trip, I'd been weaned from phones in general, and from five a.m. phone calls in specific. I picked up my illuminated clock to read the time and almost knocked the phone and the clock into the wastebasket. Okay, I did toss the clock, but I pulled it out right away.

I sat up, switched on the light, and reached for the phone.

"Yes."

"Mario, this is Juan. Sorry to call so early. The matriarca of the dentist's family you sent me to is waiting for your call. I left her thirty minutes ago."

"Great work, Juan."

I scribbled down the name and phone number Juan gave me. He said they had been very nice to him and offered him coffee.

"I'll call you in a little while."

I splashed my face with water to wake myself up and stared at myself in the mirror for a couple of seconds. The guy in the mirror looked tired, out of shape, and unkempt. The hair looked like the lawn in the neighborhood you call about when it needs to be mowed, and it went perfectly with the unshaven face. The long lapse in working left me feeling a little insecure. I'd talked to thousands of referrals, but never about a plane, and never in Puerto Rico. I scrubbed at my face with the towel and gave myself a thumbs up and a huge, fake, beaming smile. That was better. Still sleepy and out of shape, but now I looked excited and happy. This was going to be the beginning of a whole new challenge. I practiced the conversation in my head and started the percolator, then I ran back to my room. I'd been out of the loop for a long time, but this is what I did best. I might only have one shot at keeping Mrs. Beltran on the telephone.

"Señora Beltran?" I said.

She answered in English.

"This is she. Is this Mr. Luna?"

It was like the old days. I fell into the familiar pattern.

"Yes, Mrs. Beltran. Please call me Mario. First of all, please accept my deepest condolences for your loss."

"Thank you, Mario."

"Mrs. Beltran, if you already have a lawyer representing you, we can end this call right now. It would not be appropriate that I talk to you without your attorney present."

"No, I don't have a lawyer."

Jason's information had been right. I gave myself a thumbs up in the mirror.

"Mrs. Beltran, I'm not a lawyer, but I consult for a very powerful attorney in Los Angeles named Oscar Cooke. Are you up to discussing this with me right now?"

"Yes," replied Mrs. Beltran. "I've had calls from local attorneys, but I have not spoken to any of them. When the investigator came this morning and told me about you being from Los Angeles and interested in this case, I was impressed that someone from so far away wanted to speak to me."

"Of course we are interested," I said. "Mrs. Beltran—"

"Call me Bertha," she said.

I wiggled my toes in delight. I did a little dance.

The call went on for at least thirty minutes. Normally I would not have kept a prospective client on the phone that long, but I needed to be certain that Mrs. Beltran was interested in retaining Cooke. I outlined the terms in the retainer.

It was too early to call the girls. I drove over to Cosmo's and used my key to get in. I lucked out that there was no six a.m. class. By the time Cosmo arrived at eight, I was done. I was so out of shape, it was embarrassing.

"Cosmo, I missed you."

"I miss you too, Mario. How's the gunshot wound healing?"

Cosmo hugged me carefully, as if he were afraid I'd break. When we'd met when I was ten, I'd already been inches taller. Now I towered over him.

"It's good. Not sensitive anymore."

He wagged his index finger at my face and said, "No full contact. Don't hit that spot for another four months. A year has to go by to really heal."

"I got it, my friend."

"You need to tell me about your trip."

"I will, I promise, but another day." I gathered my workout garb. "I have an appointment."

I got lucky on my car phone and reached the mobile operator on the first try. She connected me to Jo at home.

"I'll see you three in two hours. Bring everything you can find on the plane crash."

"Sure thing, boss. Did you hear from Puerto Rico?"

"Juan did good. I talked to the widow. I think she likes me. She told me to call her at two our time, and she'll tell me if she's going to sign with us."

"I can't believe it!" Jo screamed.

"Neither can I," I said. "But we're not out of the woods yet."

At half past nine, I was out of the shower, dressed, and sitting behind my desk at home on the line with Oscar Cooke.

"Eastern crash, New York. I may have the widow of a thirty-four-year-old dentist with a ten-year-old daughter in Puerto Rico."

"Wonderful." I could hear in his voice that Cooke was jazzed. His excitement reminded me of Jake.

"I have a call with the widow at two."

"Let me know how it goes."

Jo and the girls were still handling management issues. We hadn't pinned down a management company yet, but Jo dug up everything the library had on the plane crash: copies of magazine articles, newspaper articles, and some legal-looking reports. I was surprised by how much there was, but much of it was duplicate information, and some of it conflicted. I wanted to look over everything so I could be informed before I talked to Bertha Beltran. Jo punched holes in everything on the Beltrans and put it in a notebook so I could flip through it and use it for reference. I called Juan to thank him. He told me I was entitled to a couple more hours, but I let him know we were straight until I needed more work.

I tried reaching an investigator to help with the Texas family, but I got busy signals, ringing phones, and investigators who weren't interested. I wouldn't need an investigator if I had the contact information of the Texas family, but I didn't have that yet. These frustrating efforts filled the hours till I could call Mrs. Beltran back.

By the time the operator put me through, I was ten minutes late.

Mrs. Beltran didn't hesitate. "I discussed this with the family. We'd like to meet you. I believe I want to sign with you." Magic words. I wanted to dance around with the phone, but I held steady. If the girls saw my solo victory dance, I'd never hear the end of it. I might have whooped once or twice. The girls whooped too, but I covered the receiver.

"Jo," I said, "put me through to Oz. Looks like we're going to Puerto Rico." I stood up and did a little dance around the room with Pixie and Niley and, after she handed me the phone, Jo.

Oscar Cooke's secretary must have been waiting for the call. I got through his gatekeepers in record time. I didn't even have time to untangle the cord.

"Oz, here's the deal. I need ten grand for expenses with no guarantee that I will sign the family in Puerto Rico. But if I do sign them, we have a dentist who is yours. He had a good income, a wife, and the daughter. She's the only child."

"You're learning fast."

I didn't remind him I had been in client development for over a decade. The only difference so far was that my former clients' vehicles weren't designed to leave the ground.

"If I come back with two retainers, I want thirty thousand dollars.[8] I don't need a bonus or a promise of anything when the case settles. If I get any other cases out of this crash, we'll negotiate just like on this one. What do you say?"

"You don't leave room to negotiate, kid, but I'm hungry for this type of case. You got ten without strings and thirty if you come through. I'm in."

As much as I wanted to take my team with me to Puerto Rico, it just wasn't practical. They were still handling apartment management issues. No one had passports yet—not that a passport was necessary for Puerto Rico—and all of them

---

[8] $30,000.00 in 1975 had the same buying power as $136,719.65 in 2017

were snowed under. I extracted a promise from Jo to keep Pixie from doing anything that would get us arrested, then I went to the airport alone. Los Angeles to Miami, then from there to Puerto Rico.

It was going to be a short trip. I left my car at the airport.

Juan met me at the airport in Puerto Rico. He was thirty, a rugged dude, born in Puerto Rico, with blue eyes and dark tan skin. He was good-looking, like an actor out of a movie, but what do I know about how good-looking a guy is?

"Thanks for coming to get me," I said, managing to squeeze in his VW bug.

"No problem," Juan said. "Sorry about the car. I didn't realize how tall you are. Do you mind if I practice my English with you?"

"Car is fine, Juan. And you can practice your English with me if I can practice my Spanish with you."

"Eh, but your Spanish is perfect," he said.

I wanted Juan to go with me to the Beltran residence where I was to meet Bertha Beltran and her family. Juan had opened the door for me. I wanted to see him in action with the client.

At first we just made conversation.

"Is it always this hot here?"

"Yes, always hot."

I asked why he'd gotten into private investigation.

"Used to be a cop. *La Uniformada*, as we say here," he said. "Too many guns. But me, I am a peaceful man. So now I just investigate."

He told me a little about finding the family. His eagerness reminded me of the hours I'd wasted trying and failing to find an investigator in Texas.

"How busy are you?"

"Not busy at all. Business is so bad I think of going back to the uniform."

"If you went to Texas for me, do you think you can find a family?"

Juan took his eyes off the road and focused at me. I grabbed the steering wheel.

"I am good at what I do, Mario. I have my ways."

I steered. "Eyes on the road, Juan. I believe you."

Bertha Beltran trusted me from the start. It was almost overwhelming how much she trusted in me, a total stranger from halfway across the world. Before she signed, she made me feel at home, fed me coffee and a homemade *arroz con dulce*, coconut rice pudding. After she signed, she showed me pictures of her husband and daughter. She and her daughter had very nice teeth.

Four hours later, I checked into my hotel to call home. I invited Juan up with me, and he sat at the table in my room, nursing his coffee as Jo answered.

"I need details," I said. I hadn't brought all of the news articles on the accident, just the notebook Jo had put together on the Puerto Rican family. "Call me back in thirty minutes with all the details you can find on the family of the man who died on the ground when the plane crashed on the approach to the New York airport."

I still had no details on Durango except what had been on Jason's original list: he'd been living in New York but was from Dallas, had no lawyer, and he had been killed on the ground by the plane crash. Jo called me back to tell me that the flight manifest published in the *Dallas Morning News* was different from Jason's list, and that she'd had no luck finding a Texas investigator.

"Good work with Mrs. Beltran," I told Juan as I sat down and poured myself some coffee. "We had no luck finding a local private investigator. Would you be able to handle finding this family in Texas?" I pointed out the name on the list in front of me. "Is this enough for you to go on?"

"Sure," he said. So I hired Juan to go that afternoon to Dallas, Texas to find the family of Gil Durango, the deceased truck driver who'd been killed on the ground.

I had a night to kill before my flight. I was jazzed about signing the case and thrilled Juan was on his way to Texas for me. The excitement just naturally channels into my all-consuming sex drive. I went down to the lobby bar. It was packed. I ordered wine and sat on a bar stool. Three sips into the wine, a dark, pretty girl squeezed between me and the next guy. She was young, probably younger than me.

"A booth is more comfortable," she said. Her teeth were white, her eyes dark, her hair nearly black.

"A booth it is," I agreed.

I walked behind her and got a good look at that fine ass and tiny waist. I was horny, but that had nothing to do with my eyes appreciating her feminine aspects. Ten minutes later, we were in my room, clothes off, and her mouth was taking in my erection. I held on for at least an hour.

"Are you sure you don't want anything else?"

I stood up from the chair, lifting her as I stood. Her legs wrapped around my waist and I gave her a big hug. "Thank you," I said. "I'm good now."

I handed her a hundred-dollar bill. She was gone in a heartbeat, and I slept like a baby. In the morning, I took a taxi to the airport and thought about the young fox who had never given me her name.

As I waited for the plane to Miami, a small crowd formed at the gate. All the people with tickets were sitting in a boxed-off area close to the entry to the jet bridge. A dark-haired man sitting beside me was looking through a newspaper. He looked at his watch and offered the paper to the attractive woman sitting next to him. She didn't want it. They were both about thirty years old, in jeans and with five little kids in tow. They were clearly a couple. They were all dressed in blue, looking like a family out of a magazine.

He offered me the paper.

"No thanks," I said.

The kids were quietly roughhousing and laughing among themselves.

"Yours?" I asked, indicating the kids.

"Yes," he said. He was so happy, so proud. I felt a little envy.

We talked for a while. They were on their way to Miami on vacation. He had a business in Puerto Rico, but I didn't ask for details. Before we boarded the plane, he gathered his family and handed me a camera. They posed for a picture, and I took several of them, with kids posing dramatically in different positions. Their oldest couldn't have been more than seven. When we boarded, I went into my single seat in first class, and they bustled toward the back of the plane. I never saw them again.

In Miami, I had a two-hour layover before the flight to Los Angeles. I walked around the airport and thought how aviation cases differ from traffic accidents. It was certainly more lethal—and more lucrative. I had earned a cool thirty thousand dollars plus ten thousand[9] minus my expenses. I would have had complete confidence in Jake if he'd been alive, but couldn't help worrying if Oscar Cooke could handle this aviation case and others that might follow. Would he know what he was doing in this aviation business? He certainly wasn't Jason, who worked aviation every single day. And he wasn't Jake. From the looks of it, Cooke was not hurting for cash, and he didn't get that way by being stupid. I hoped for the best.

Flying out of Miami, I had a window seat. As soon as I sat down, I fell into a deep sleep that lasted all the way to Los Angeles. I didn't even notice who was sitting next to me. When I got home, it was midnight. I was too well-rested, and to convince my body it was time for bed, I ran the stairs a dozen times, the way I used to, got out of breath and all I earned was a stitch in my side. I walked back down to my apartment and took my time in the shower.

It was always good to be home. When you travel a lot, there's something to be said for the familiar: good water pressure, a showerhead of an appropriate height, plenty of hot water, and your own familiar soap. When I came out of the shower, who was there but Melina, wearing nothing but a smile.

"Get in the shower with me," she said. "I've had a long day and I need to wash it all away while you watch."

"My pleasure," I said, walking in behind her. "I'll wash your hair."

The soap melted to nothing, but we didn't turn off the water. Melina turned to face me, stepping close, so that her feet rested on top of mine. She looked

---

[9] $40,000.00 in 1975 had the same buying power as $182,292.87 in 2017

up into my eyes through a latticework of water drops hanging from her lashes. Hunger intensified the tension in her face. I kissed her, ran my hands down her shoulder and the sleek line of her back, jerking her closer. She made a wordless groan. The sponge she was holding splashed to the tiles, and she wrapped her arms around my neck. She stood on one leg, the other wrapped around my hip. My hands slid down her lathered body to her cheeks, and I cupped them, lifting her ass just high enough that I could reach her. Her hand moved between our bodies, guiding me inside. I heard her gasp at my entry. She was hot and deep, and the feeling was beyond exquisite. She flung her head back, and her animal cries urged me deeper, higher. She was slippery and hard to hold, but she hung on with one arm firmly latched over my shoulder; her free hand slid over my ribs and up my chest. Her hands met around the back of my neck, gripping each other, holding her own weight as her other leg wrapped around me. The move freed me. I was able to spread my legs and brace myself, and I found a corner to buttress against, which loaned my thrusts greater support and constancy. Her hips twisted and flexed and pushed against me, demanding more. And I gave more, avid, rhythmic, giving, taking. We rocked. I stepped back, braced hard against the shower wall, the thudding water pounding, flowing over both of us. Her legs, her arms wrapped tight around me. The tempo of our blood joined, our pulse and bodies rising in concert. Mouths pushed together, tongues as wild as the hammering of our bodies. Friction. The rise and fall hurled us beyond the pinnacle. We erupted in a frenzy. Up, over, beyond. The pace eased and resonated, echoed, and quieted to stillness. I felt the tiles behind me and beneath my feet. Back to earth.

We soaped each other again, rinsed, and stepped out of the shower in silence. I reached for a towel. Our hands met. We focused on each other, blotted and rubbed our bodies dry.

We headed toward the bedroom. Melina had been at work. The lamp was off, but a dozen candles burned, lighting the room in amber. The sheets were folded back. Two stacks of pillows rested against the headboard, one for each of us, propping us up. I sat on the bed and Melina ran into the other room. She returned bearing peanut butter and pistachio ice cream and a couple of spoons. She sat beside me against her own nest of pillows. We feasted, then set aside the food.

"I missed you, Mario."

Something was different tonight. She rarely used my name. It was always "friend" or "Cuz."

"I missed you too," I said.

We shoved aside the extra pillows and, lying flat, looked up at our images in the mirror above the bed. Our eyes met in the glass. The candles flickered, and we wavered in the yellow light.

"Where have you been all my life?"

"Mario, I think I love you."

I loved her too. Surely she knew that. But I did not know what to think. Melina usually avoided outpouring of emotion, preferring her freedom. I had to ask. "Are we still friends?"

"Yes, we're friends, but I love you."

In the night, I found myself still locked in an embrace, but when I woke at five, Melina was gone. I felt a rush of disappointment, and maybe a little relief. I still did not know what to do about her profession of love. There was no time to wallow in it. I rose. I worked out and showered. When I stepped out of the bathroom, the smell of coffee and toast greeted me. Melina was back. My heart leapt with happiness.

"You were gone. I thought you would be in bed with me this morning." I kissed the top of her head and sat at the dinette beside her. "I want more nights together. I want waking together in the morning in your arms."

She poured me coffee.

"You wish," she said, biting a piece of her toast. "One day at a time, Mario. I think it hurts your girls to share you. I don't want to hurt anyone."

"I like it when you call me Mario. More intimate than Cuz."

"Cuz is us, and us alone," she said. "Nobody else rescued me from a burning car, or snuck into the hospital pretending to be my cousin. I have no other family than you, Cuz."

"This morning, why did you leave?"

"Mario." She said my name, like she was testing how much I liked it, but she didn't answer the question.

I smiled.

A thoughtful look crossed her face. She spoke carefully. "I got sentimental last night."

"You said you love me. Did you mean it?"

She set her cup down. "You're the only family I have. The only person I really trust. Of course I love you."

"Of course," I said, kissing her lightly on the lips. "I love you too."

Another kiss. More toast.

I told her about the family I'd seen at the airport.

"Do you want a family?"

"No," I said, "but for a moment there at the airport, it got me to think-ing."

She looked at her watch. "We must pick up this conversation again. I'm going out to the Hacienda Heights store. Traffic is a mess going that way."

Then she was gone. I was alone again.

Three days after I got home, Juan called from Dallas, Texas.

"What's up, man?" I asked.

Chapter 6
September 1975
Case-hopping: Dallas, Puerto Rico, New Orleans, and London for fun

"Durango had a wife and two kids living here in Dallas. He also had a girl-friend that he lived with for the past three years. He has a kid with her too."

"Did you get a chance to talk to the wife?" The wife would probably have the best case, but I wasn't sure. We'd had car crash cases like this. Children were always valid heirs.

"I talked to both of them. I figure you want to talk to both of them, too. You should meet them personally."

"I can do that, but I can't just barge in. They have to want to talk to me."

"They will want to by the time you are here. I promise."

"Juan, are you sure?"

"I'm sure."

"Call me in three hours, and I'll give you the time I'll be there."

I waited for confirmation from Juan. He didn't say anything. Seconds passed.

"There's more."

"Spit it out."

"Wife and girlfriend are broke. They're all living in the same house. They could use cash. They need money for food." Juan sounded a little freaked out. I didn't know if it was over their financial situation or the wife-and-girlfriend situation. As a private investigator, surely he'd seen something like this before. I certainly had, but then I've dealt with thousands of cases.

I let it pass. "I can't believe no one from the insurance company has contacted them."

"All I know is they are broke. If you bring cash, you sign them."

"I'm not buying the case, Juan."

"I don't know what you mean 'buy case,' but I call you in three hours."

Jo was working in my office, sorting through some of the tenant records. She looked up as I walked in and took a seat at my desk.

"How's the plane case going?"

"Durango has a wife and a girlfriend and two sets of kids in Dallas, all cohabiting," I said. "I need to fly there tomorrow."

"I'll get your tickets," she said.

On the other line, I called to thank Jason for sending me that list.

"I know London is eight hours ahead, and it's late there. I can call you back if you are tied up or asleep."

"Not asleep, not tied up. Thinking about heading over to Sami's. How can I help you?"

"Knowing who didn't have representation let me cut to the chase. It was an enormous help."

I mentioned the wife and girlfriend; he confirmed that offspring would be legal heirs. If there were problems, they could be decided in court. It was the same as a personal injury case that turned into a wrongful death. We'd hunted out the heirs.

"There might not be the usual conflicts, though," I said. "The wife and girlfriend are living together."

Jason found that amusing. He laughed loud enough that Jo heard him across the room.

When Juan called, I confirmed that I'd secured a flight to Dallas and would be arriving tomorrow.

"I need the marriage certificate and birth certificates of the kids, including the girlfriend's kid. We will make copies. Let them know I'm bringing some cash to show we're for real. We will need these documents to prove they are eligible for compensation."

Finally, I called Cooke and explained the family situation Gil Durango had left behind.

"I figure I need to give the wife and girlfriend a couple thousand each as an advance that you get back when this case settles; and I need five thousand for expenses."

"So far, so good," said Cooke.

"I have trouble putting a number on the decedent. I don't know what he did for a living. He drove a truck as a sideline, but there was more. Not sure what to do, but I'm open for suggestions."

"I'll give you your seven-point-five grand no matter what."

"Make it ten and I won't up it, even if he turns out to be a doctor."

Cooke laughed. Considering I was twisting him, I was a little surprised. I highly doubted Durango was a doctor who drove a truck on the weekend. I didn't think a doctor would leave behind women in financial distress.

"You got it, Mario. Ten grand it is."

"Are you pleased with the Puerto Rico cases?"

"Elated. Go get Texas."

"Be there tomorrow morning," I replied and hung up. I turned to Jo.

"Coming with me to Dallas?"

She shook her head. "No way, José. I'm swamped. Niley and I are winding down the apartment transfer to the new management company. Take Pixie."

When I woke at five for my workout, it was to the smell of coffee. Pixie had stayed the night so that we could get an early start. She was in the kitchen, ready to leave.

The last thing that I remembered from last night had been Pixie astride me after her massage left me boneless and relaxed.

"Did you sleep?"

"Yep, I sure did. Showered, too."

I could see that for myself. Her hair was still wet. It was still cut like Faye Dunaway in *Chinatown*, but she'd dyed it cherry red. Her lips matched her hair and shoes. "I dig that hair color," I said. "You should get some wigs so you don't mess up your hair with the hair color changes you do."

"Boss, thanks for the compliment and the advice."

I didn't need to ask if the red was a wig because I'd checked last night, and it was all Pixie.

"I got you packed with four days' worth of clothes, in case it takes longer than you expect."

I kissed her and wiped the lipstick off my mouth with a napkin. "You're my treasure."

"You're my treasure, boss," she said and looked at her watch. It had a red band. "I'll have toast ready to go when you're done."

I cut the workout to a half hour, then took my coffee to the bathroom to shave and shower. Two hours later, I parked my car at the airport. We walked across the street to check in for our flight to Dallas.

Pixie's first time on a plane had been when we flew to San Francisco to see Pélon in San Quentin. I let her take the window seat. She snapped her seat belt over her miniskirt and leaned over to whisper in my ear. "I'm so fucking excited, I've come three times in the last five minutes."

My reply was a smile. My left hand tapped her upper thigh. She shivered. Her lips returned to my ear.

"Boss, you just made me come again."

She pulled away, collapsing against the seat with a little gasp. Our eyes met. We exchanged smiles. Pixie's smile was gone an hour later. When the ride became very bumpy over Arizona, Pixie turned as white as a sheet. She had a death grip on my hand. I didn't let it go for at least thirty minutes. The plane bucked and heaved. Items fell and rolled around on the floor. The stewardesses had secured a beverage cart and were buckled in. A small tin of juice rolled up and down the aisle unimpeded. The captain came on the speaker and assured everyone that it was just a touch of weather, and we would be through the turbulence soon.

"Jo and Niley won't have anyone to sign for my death," Pixie whispered. "I got no one but Lainey and Aunt Carmen."

"You are not going to die," I assured her.

"What do you know?" she said sarcastically. "We're on a plane flying to sign the family of someone who died in a plane crash."

What she said made me think of my own family. The only blood relative I had on the face of the earth was Aunt Carmen. I thought of Melina, whose mother had died while Melina was just a girl, her death followed by that of her father, and finally her aunt. She called me Cuz, but she really had no one at all.

We arrived none the worse for wear.

Juan picked us up at the airport in a rented sedan. I introduced him to Pixie.

"Don't let this go to your head," Pixie said as she shook his hand, "but you are one good-looking stud."

Juan's dark skin blushed a shade only slightly less red that than Pixie's current hair. He looked her up and down. "You not so bad yourself."

We went straight to the widow Durango's house, where the girlfriend and her two-year-old were also living. The widow had two children, a five- and six-year-old. The widow signed retainers for herself and her children. The girlfriend signed for her son.

"I want it to be clear that your attorney will try to get you some compensation, for you personally, but it's a long shot. For your son, it's hands down."

"I understand," the girlfriend said.

Mrs. Durango and girlfriend Durango showed me stacks of invoices. I could tell from their living arrangement that their financial situations were teetering on desperation. The neighborhood wasn't too bad, their clothes weren't threadbare, and the kids weren't barefoot, but the affordable house they were renting was a big old rattletrap in need of extensive repair. There was less in the refrigerator than there had been in Niley's when I took her under my wing. I advanced the widow two thousand dollars that she would pay back when she received her settlement. I gave the girlfriend a thousand dollars.[10]

The widow and girlfriend hugged Pixie and me. I'm underplaying it here. They were crying their eyes out, and with the kids all standing around like skinny little scarecrows. I felt good that I had arrived in time to save them from having to stand in a soup line, but I was pissed off at the insurance carriers that they had made no attempt to help this family. The insurance carriers hadn't helped in Puerto Rico either, but at least that family hadn't been on the verge of starvation. While we were saying our goodbyes, I gave Juan a twenty, and he went out and grabbed burgers, fries, and shakes for all of them. They fell on it like it was solid gold sirloin steak. I got a little choked up.

We never had to check into the hotel. Juan took us back to the airport.

"A man with that many dependents should have a plan. He left then high and dry."

"It's not like he was planning to have a plane land on him," Pixie said.

The two of them argued all the way to the airport. Before he let us out, Juan said he was leaving in the morning for Puerto Rico. We got lucky finding a flight. An hour later, we were on a plane to Los Angeles.

I'm always ready to have sex with the right girl or girls, but especially when my emotions are at a spike or in a nosedive. Either I'm really happy, excited, or down and out. On the plane, I wanted to take Pixie right there. Maybe Pixie sensed what I was feeling. Nothing was said, but when we landed in LA, we walked to the car, stashed the suitcases in the trunk, and two minutes later, we took a wild ride in the back seat, right there in the parking garage. It was way too fast but way too good. Sometimes the best sex is on impulse. Caught up in hysterical laughter,

---

[10] $1,000.00 in 1975 had the same buying power as $4,557.32 in 2017

we moved to the front seats without using the doors, a piece of cake for Pixie, but not so easy for me. It was temperate for mid-September, but the windows were fogged from the heat we generated.

"You deserve more than the back seat," I said. "I should have waited."

She thumped my arm. "Boss, don't be nutty, and don't apologize. I needed that as much as you did. Maybe more." Then she added, "You got to keep a box of Kleenex in this car already." We laughed even more.

I drove out of the parking lot, trying to concentrate on the traffic.

"It was so fucking good," she said.

Pixie was able to get the mobile operator on my car phone to connect her to Jo. She turned on the speaker, and we talked at once, both of us giving her the news of the case. Then we got lucky again and caught the mobile operator, and a minute later we were talking to Niley.

Over the next few days, the girls and I combed the list for other families we could approach. I called Juan in Puerto Rico.

"Do you feel like going to New Orleans?"

"Okay, yes, I go anywhere you tell me."

"Total long shot. Looks like a family of four. Three were slightly injured, and one died. The last name is Latin, family name Toro. Luis and Kamila, Kamila was his wife. Luis survived. I don't have the kids' names. My information is that they are Puerto Rican, but live in New Orleans."

"I take all information from Jo and I work on it."

Cooke's firm had several conference rooms. One was a huge room with bookcases filled with law books, a couple of leather-bound chairs, reading lamps, and a table. In his personal office, Oscar had his own library cabinets lining one wall, with nothing on the shelves but books on law. I remembered the office toys that Jake had left me, and how what he called 'objects of art' were scattered among the books. Cooke's shelves were grander and fancier and held only books. When

I arrived at his office, he was reading a hardback book at least five inches thick, part of a leather-bound set. He put it away when I came in and was very glad to see me, especially when I presented him with a stack of pages.

He accepted the retainers and backup documents like they were the Nobel Peace Prize.

I knew he was glad to see me, but I had more in mind than paperwork.

"I need to find a 727 pilot hungry enough to come to my apartment and give the girls and me lessons on everything to do with an airplane. I want him to bring pictures and go over all the different parts of a plane, especially parts that can fail and cause a plane to crash."

Cooke clipped his cigar and lit it. His eyes were on me, thoughtful. I knew he was proud of his pilot's license, and counted a number of pilots among his friends, but I didn't know if he knew anyone who flew big commercial planes.

Cooke nodded his head. The tip of his cigar burned brightly as he inhaled, then the color dimmed. "I've interviewed several aviation lawyers, but I've not been impressed yet. I'll find a 727 pilot, and when you suck up everything he knows about the 727, I'll get you another expert for the next plane of interest."

"Great, Oz."

"I'll pay for the lessons," Cooke offered. "Tape it, and give me a copy, and I'll benefit from his expertise, too. Two birds with one stone."

"Good move," I said.

Cooke took out his pen. He chewed and sucked on his cigar, and said, "You are absolutely certain that you aren't going to come back later to complain that I took advantage of you by not giving you a piece of the fees?"

"I told you already, Oz, I learned my lesson. I can't enforce a deal for a cut of the attorney fees. I can't expect what I can't enforce. I'll take my front money and run. What you get at the end, you deserve."

Cooke put the pen to the check. The office was so quiet that I heard the scratching of his nib and the crackling of his burning cigar. He handed me the check.

"When I make a deal, you never have to worry about me changing it or crying that I got fucked."

We shook hands. I took out my wallet and slid the check inside.

"Whatever you say, Mario."

Cooke called me back that same afternoon.

"I've got your man," Cooke said. "Even better than a pilot. He is a fantastic trial lawyer as long as he stays sober. He was apparently not a good husband when he was drunk. Not being sober cost him his marriage and a number of good jobs. But he knows planes. I'm thinking of hiring him to come on board and work aviation."

The pilot Cooke hired was a fifty-four-year-old aviation attorney named Tom Jones, just like the entertainer. I invited him to the apartment to meet the team.

Jo, Pixie, and Niley bustled around like it was going to be a party instead of a class. Pixie began putting out wine glasses until I put my foot down.

"Anything you want, but no wine, no beer, no booze. He's got a problem with liquor."

Pixie switched to water glasses and loaded up the serving cart with soft drinks and mineral waters. Niley came in, loaded down with a couple of appetizer and dessert trays from one of Melina's markets.

I suppose because Cooke hired him, I was expecting someone shinier than life, exuding overconfidence and new money, but the instant Tom Jones walked into my apartment, embracing me and the girls, I could see he was not standing above us nor on ceremony. On our first meeting, he felt like an old friend. He was tall and trim, clean-shaven, with a short dusting of graying hair with a friendly sort of face. His eyes impressed me most. Round and warm and empathetic. They positively twinkled with soft friendliness, but he was a keen wit cloaked in civility, a blade in its sheath. He was a former Air Force pilot, and he knew everything there was to know about any commercial aircraft using up air space. A minute after I met Tom, I knew we would become good friends. He knew what he'd been hired to do, but I still told him what I wanted.

"We're not looking to become aircraft mechanics, but we need to know what we're talking about. I know what a car engine looks like and the spark plugs, carburetor, radiator, and the battery. We need to know what makes a plane work, and what makes it fail. We need to be as comfortable with that knowledge as I am about what makes a car go, or not go. Families will ask questions. We should be able to answer them."

He promised to bring us up to speed on the Boeing 727 that Eastern Airlines lost in the New York tragedy.

We sat around my dining room table. The trays from Melina's market were center stage, plus our usual goodies were available: ice cream and peanut butter. Soda, mineral water, coffee, and tea were on the cart.

Tom had brought a box of loose black-and-white eight-by-tens, pictures of the 727 in production and the finished product. The finished product was a shell.

"The seats, seat belts, engines, and all electronic components come from outside vendors and are installed in the aircraft that Boeing manufactures. Let's go through them."

Tom was patient. He spoke slowly and checked our faces for comprehension, or its lack. He began with the preplanning of the plane and talked us through its completion and entry into service. He talked us through the plane's assembly line in the plant. He then pulled out a photo of the Eastern Airlines crash in New York. He talked about debris fields, and the specific procedures investigators followed as they examined all the facts and evidence to figure out what had happened. He mentioned US planes and briefly mentioned international planes and the Warsaw treaty. He promised to talk more about Warsaw, but said we could hold off on that until we were working an international crash.

"After a plane crash, the evidence is pieced together to find the cause. They actually collect the parts and try to put it together. That is not always possible, but every effort is made. A plane doesn't just crash. There has to be a reason."

"What if something goes wrong?" Jo asked.

"If a component fails, and there is proof that it was something specific, say, the altimeter, then we sue the manufacturer of the altimeter. The operator, Eastern in this crash you are working, will have to pay the passengers' families. It doesn't end there; at least, it doesn't end there if I'm handling the case. I hire experts to comb the official reports, looking for the failed component. If there is evidence, bang, we sue."

He went on for a couple of hours, and after he went home, Pixie brought out the wine. The girls and I came up with a list of questions to ask him the next time we met.

I called Oscar. "Oz, I have good vibes about Tom Jones. I hope you hire him to work the aviation cases."

"Way ahead of you, I hired him before I sent him over to give you the first lesson."

"Good news!" I said.

Juan opened the door to the family in New Orleans. I was able to go there and talk to Luis Toro, who had lost his wife Kamila in the crash. Luis and his two children had been injured seriously enough to hospitalize them for a week. I didn't sign Toro the first trip. When he called to say that he was ready to sign with us, I went back a second time.

It is strange how similar and how different these family crises are. The Durango women in Texas had pulled together to fill the hole left by the death in their family. Toro was at a loss without his wife. She'd been the one to deal with the house and kids, but his family had pulled together, grandparents and aunts joining forces to keep Toro's household going. She hadn't been the breadwinner, and I didn't know what the actuarial tables would say about her value, but it had taken the combined efforts of half a dozen family members to try to take Kamila's place; and it was clear they weren't succeeding. I saw the outpouring of grief and chaos in their home, and wondered what would come of them all; but at least I knew I was going to be able to help them a little.

Because we had come into the accident so late, I thought the cases we had already signed were all we were going to get from this tragedy. Cooke was happy with what we had, and so was Tom Jones. I was happy that Cooke had hired Tom to handle the aviation cases.

I was considering recent crashes, especially now that we had a management company running the properties, and the girls were pretty much out of real estate. Jo was back in my office, fiddling with aviation documentation, and answered the phone when my real estate broker called about "...a fantastic deal in Monterey Park. A complex with two hundred apartments, up for grabs. The heirs were in a bitter battle."

I hadn't been looking for more properties, but I wasn't doing anything else, and his enthusiasm was catching. I drove by and took a look. I drove by three times in one day. The complex was for sale at one million dollars. The next day, I walked the grounds. I was seduced by the idea of what a fantastic opportunity it was. If I came up with two hundred thousand dollars for the down payment, it would leave me with a little over one hundred thousand in the bank. My CPA checked the figures.

"Mario, you need to buy this. Maybe we can find a way to get the sellers to accept the down payment as prepaid interest, and that way you can write it all off this year. I don't understand how it hasn't sold already. You can't build this for what they are asking or anywhere near it."

"I have to buy it as is, where is, no inspections. I got zero protection."

My conservative CPA said, "I would do it."

I offered nine hundred thousand, but that was rejected immediately. They wouldn't budge on the million dollars. I was consumed by my desire to buy the complex. If it followed through like my other buildings with a low vacancy factor, my net cash flow would be fantastic.

Pixie let it slip that I was looking at the property, and that the first offer had been rejected. During Sunday dinner at her house, Aunt Carmen offered me fifty thousand she had stashed.

"Auntie, I love you for offering. I have the money for the down payment. I'm okay."

"You will need money to fix up the apartments so you can rent them. It's not just about buying the building."

"I have really good cash flow from the other apartments. There's enough to get this building in shape, if we do it one apartment at a time as we have done before."

"If you need the money, it's here."

"I'll come knocking if I need it."

My CPA and my real estate broker were geniuses. Within two weeks, by October, I was approved by the mortgage company for an eight hundred thousand dollar loan. [11]

Melina had gotten us the credit line for the market back when I had few assets to list. She was also a whiz; she knew how to manipulate the banker, and she did it when it was necessary.

I called the stockbroker Melina had introduced me to. I had started with twenty-five thousand, and after a while, I invested just under a hundred thousand. It had grown to two hundred ten thousand. I had done as well as Melina had predicted. I sold everything but my original investment, putting me back to where I had started. I figured I needed that money as a cushion. When escrow closed, I did my customary admiration of the complex from all possible angles. The team and Aunt Carmen joined me, and we did the group admiration thing; then we met with the management company taking care of my other buildings. They were extremely excited about the new purchase. I rolled out the plan we had for gradually refurbishing the apartments. I was still pretty excited over the purchase when we went back to my apartment. The girls intended to head home but drew straws over who was filing some of the sale papers first. Jo went home with the short straw.

---

[11] $800,000.00 in 1975 had the same buying power as $3,645,857.42 in 2017

The phone was ringing when we went in, and Pixie dashed in to answer.

"It's some guy," she said. "I could just eat up his accent. He's... English." She did her best British accent on the last word.

"Jason," I said, taking the phone. "What's up?"

Pixie squealed, "Jason, Jason, Jason, I could just eat you up!" I had to cover the phone, hustle her out of the office, and shut the door. I could hear her on the other side, going on to Niley about Jason's accent.

"I got a lead for you. A 747 out of Texas dropped an engine and rained fire on the fringes of Guatemala City. It wiped out a slummy adobe neighborhood on the outskirts of town. Many homes were destroyed. Eleven deaths and three times that many injured."

"I haven't heard a thing about it." I felt the familiar excitement build. "I'm on it."

Pixie opened the door, peeked in, and mouthed at me, "Should I tell Jo to come in?"

I shook my head. "Go home, but tell her to make it an early morning." When I took my hand off the mouthpiece, Jason was still talking.

"I don't have a list for you, but you won't need it. Just get there. It won't be my case, but it will be handled out of the UK, so you're good."

"Jason, you're too good to me. I promise, I will be there soon to thank you."

"I know Sami misses you. I look forward to your coming."

When I hung up, I couldn't help wondering why a person in Jason's position would call me from London to give me a lead.

I sent Pixie downstairs for a paper. The *LA Times* had only a tiny article about the event tucked into a back page. I'd never have known it was there. Had it not been for Jason's heads-up, we would not be getting tickets for a plane headed to Guatemala.

The next day, we met Tom in his office at Cooke's firm and got a quick briefing on the plane. He gave us some materials to look over on the flight, then,

Jo, Pixie, Niley, and I took a plane headed to Guatemala City. Juan did the foot-work for me, and provided a selection of guides. From his vetted list, I hired a driver and car to take us to the area, and to stay with us as our guide. I didn't need him for protection, and I didn't need him to translate, because Guatemalan Span-ish is quite close to Mexican Spanish, but it was good to have a local who knew the roads, and we needed a car.

"I can't believe we're here, boss," Pixie kept saying, overwhelmed by her first time out of the country.

The road from the airport started off comparable to roads in the US, but worsened. Everyone in Guatemala City knew where the accident had occurred. It was not a good area of town, but it was a very big deal. Some of the city sections we went through were sketchy, but our driver had no difficulty finding the district we were looking for on the city outskirts. As the neighborhoods degraded and we approached the accident site, I was reminded of the drive from Dover to London. The "scenic" route is often more scenic than it's worth.

We were excited to be in Guatemala and on this case, but the drive to the accident site was worth its weight in headaches. Our driver, José, was polite and deferential to us, even with Pixie, who kept laughing in hysterics every time she goaded him with another "no way, José", but he got aggressive with his fellow locals as we drew closer to the accident site. He yelled out of the window, made rude gestures, and sometimes dispersed crowds that blocked us by acting like he was going to run over the whole crowd. Each time he did something we should be ap-palled by, he turned to me in the front seat and said, "Sorry, boss."

I was getting used to the 'boss' handle. More and more, I was addressed that way. With our driver, it was probably because I was paying him, but others called me "boss" spontaneously. Maybe I've just been dressing like a boss. Today, a three-piece suit would not have been appropriate.

Pixie chattered and picked on the driver all the way from the airport. Our driver blushed, and got flustered in response. I could tell he liked the attention of a pretty girl, though he never stepped out of his role. Pixie had such an impulsive personality; I wasn't alarmed, but I was prepared to tell her to get a grip on herself before we approached the families. She hardly seemed to notice the worsening neighborhoods, but as we got close to the scene of the accident, to her credit, she was overwhelmed and silenced herself. We had reached an impoverished neighborhood, incrementally worse than anything in Los Angeles.

"I can't believe people live like this." Pixie looked at José and said, "Sorry, José."

"No offense taken," he responded in Spanish.

By the time we reached the scene of the accident, it had been almost forty-eight hours from when we left home. Arranging transportation in Guatemala City and getting some rest had gulped up a chunk of these hours. We stopped at a hotel five miles from the site, and I got us a couple of connecting rooms. I carried our bags into the hotel and nearly collided with a tired young maid who was putting towels in my room. She introduced herself as Selina, and said to ask her if we needed anything.

The driver got us to the devastation, and we spent thirty minutes or so there. I had been passing out dollars to the residents milling near the accident site. We connected with one family that had escaped the impact of the airplane engine and the fire; they took us around to locate families who had suffered casualties.

"It looks like a war zone," Jo said. "It reminds me of pictures 'Nando sent me of Vietnam."

Niley said nothing, but she looked shocked. All three of the girls were crying.

I'd seen fires, but I could not imagine what the area had been like before. The demolition was like an earthquake had hit. It looked bad. The walls of many adobe homes that were damaged were still standing, more or less, but the roofs were gone. Evidence and the stink of fire was everywhere. Everything that could burn had turned to ash, though there were skeletons remaining that once had been furniture or appliances.

"Pictures," I said. I passed out the cameras. Jo had the Polaroid, Pixie had an Instamatic, and Niley had a thirty-five millimeter. We walked around and talked to people and stayed in sight of each other. I'd read enough about crashes at this point. Although Jones told me that the authorities immediately roped off the crash site area to preserve evidence and no one was allowed in, no such precautions had been taken. Maybe Guatemala hadn't gotten the memo. There were a couple of officials there, and a number of volunteers. I attached myself to a talkative local official and walked around with him. He gave me a copy of his list of names of victims. That thirty minutes proved to be more than enough time. I had made connections with a couple of officials who could give me news. The girls were quiet as we returned to our base at the hotel.

"We're here to help," I reminded the girls as we approached our new digs. I talked with them a little about how we were going to meet survivors. The pretty maid I'd run into, Selina, was still making her rounds.

"Dollar bills go a long way here," I told the girls. "We need to meet the neighbors of the victims and see if we can find the names and locations of surviving family members. Use bigger bills when you have to. I haven't yet met someone so shy they didn't take the green from my hand."

The maid approached us tentatively. She was young, but had a careworn look that struck me as familiar.

"Mr. Luna," Selina said, making me feel like I was a million years old. "I've heard what you're doing here. My husband and I live in the area you are talking about." She introduced me to her husband, Modesto Zacapa.

The Zacapas' home had just escaped the impact and fire. He was a little man, probably my own age, but he was thin and slight, with muscles like beef jerky. He worked as a laborer. I already knew his wife cleaned rooms at the hotel where we were staying. Modesto took me around to locate families who had suffered losses. Pixie, Niley, and Jo paired off with neighbors, who helped them locate relatives. Again, we worked relatively close to each other, all working the same method, cash in hand.

In the ten days we were in the country, we covered a lot of ground. After we'd signed a couple of families, we moved to a hotel near the hospital and spent much of our time there.

In the PI business, after a car accident, especially one with serious injuries, it was common to run into an insurance adjustor at the hospital trying to settle a case before the victim signed with a lawyer. So far, this did not seem to be how an aviation case was handled. I couldn't believe how none of the insurance carriers were around. The engine and its hundreds of pieces were still scattered throughout the neighborhood. If I were the insurance carrier, I'd have been there the next day, making good. And for sure, I'd have the mess cleaned up immediately after it was documented. If the insurance guys had been there, my team and I would not have the opportunity to sign the families we got signed during the trip. They never showed. All I knew was that Tom Jones had retainers printed in English with Spanish translations, and we put the documents to good use.

Jason had said there were eleven deaths. When we got home twelve days later, I had retainers for thirteen deaths and twenty-four injured persons. Some of the injured had succumbed, and the initial count had been off, anyway. The trip back also took forty-eight hours, although it seemed shorter coming back.

Even Pixie had been overwhelmed with exhaustion. She slept on the way back, even through turbulence. We were still tired on arrival. We circled the airport and had a smooth landing. The captain's announcement that we were here took forever, but finally we were allowed to disembark. I stood in the aisle, reached overhead, and retrieved the girls' carry-ons. They were in front of me as we exited; I came out of the plane through the jet bridge behind them.

I don't have an alternative name, but I've always thought "gate" was a bad name for it. Sure, each "gate" was really a gated area with two sections; one was for those entering the plane, and the other for exiting. The exiting side was always lined with families, boyfriends and girlfriends, spouses, and loved ones coming to pick up relatives who had just flown in. It was an eager, frantic crowd I always walked through, oblivious, since I frequently drove myself to the airport and returned in the same way. Today, I was surprised to see Melina, busy, impatient

Melina, patiently waiting for us.

"You actually came out here to get us," I said, picking her up, kissing her. "Are you figuring we're going to do it in the back of your car again?" I laughed.

"No sex today," she said. "No time. Have to get back. I called Tom Jones and he told me when you were arriving." She hugged Jo, Pixie, and Niley as she spoke.

"Thanks for coming out." I put my arm around her. We gathered our luggage and walked out of the terminal to find Johnson waiting. He opened the door for us. The girls gave him a quick pat on the hand as they got in.

"I am so tired," Pixie said.

"We all are," Jo agreed.

When we arrived at Bunker Towers, the girls didn't even come in. They got their keys from the doorman and headed to their cars.

Melina and I stepped into the elevator with a kiss that started on the ground floor. Either it was just hitting second gear when we hit our floor, or we were both falling asleep. I'm not sure which. I led her to my door, but Melina leaned in the direction of her place.

"Shower," she mumbled.

I took that to mean she wanted to shower at her own place after her long day at work. It wasn't even dinner time, but she usually goes in when it is still dark. She tends to be a workaholic. It takes a lot for her to be too tired to talk. I guess she was as exhausted as I was.

We could have ended up in a tug of war to convince her not to go, but the thought took too much energy. I walked her to her door. She unlocked it and stepped inside.

"Thanks, Cuz, for picking us up."

"No thanks needed. I missed you a lot."

"Ditto," I said.

Once I was home in my own place, I refused to surrender to my exhaustion. I was still running on leftover adrenaline fumes. I felt like an archeologist returning home triumphantly with my piles of treasure after covering a new territory. Jason had been my guide. I called him before I even kicked off my shoes. Actually, I sat on my couch, took off my shoes and socks, and stripped down to my underwear while we were talking.

"Jason, I don't know how to thank you." I gave him the rundown of our success, and sprawled out on the couch.

"All I ask is that you never mention me," he said.

"Of course not, but I owe you, Jason. I need to find a way to repay you for all you've done for me."

"Come to London," he said. "We'll have dinner. You owe me nothing."

"I promise I will be there."

After talking to Jason, I had to call Sami. He would certainly tell her we'd talked.

Ginger answered. It took only a few moments for Sami to pick up the phone, and five minutes for me to squeeze a word in edgewise.

"Jason has been fantastic with me."

"I'm happy you're happy," she said.

"I'm delighted. I owe you, Sami. I owe you both."

"Come visit at least for a few days. Get on a plane."

"Get my guest room ready," I teased her. "I'm wiped out from this trip I just took, not even sure why." I damn well knew why; I hadn't stopped running in Guatemala, and I hadn't slept.

"Your guest room is my bed. I miss you, big boy. I miss your big boy." She laughed.

"Is that all you miss?"

"I want to play doctor with you," she said with laughter.

The instant I hung up, exhaustion hit, again. I barely made it through a shower. When I came out, Melina was there, in one of my tees. It hung on her like a dress. Her hair was wet from her own shower and pulled back into a ponytail, her face still damp and squeaky clean.

"You look about twelve years old," I said.

"Gee, I knew there was a reason I liked you," she said, yawning.

I staggered to the bed. She curled up behind me and spooned. Best sleep I ever had, or at least I think it probably was. I don't remember a thing. I crashed for twelve hours straight. It was four in the morning when I woke up alone. Nothing remained of Melina but the dent in her pillow, which spelled like her shampoo. I lingered in bed a while, drinking in her fragrance.

I worked out, burning the extra hour in exercise. After a shower, I knocked on Melina's door, but there was no answer. On the way out, Tito told me Miss Melina had gone to work already, so I went to the Pacific Dining Car alone, at seven, for breakfast. I had missed my routine reading of the classified ads. I scanned the entire paper, page by page, for airplane crashes. There wasn't very much at all, good news for us in the USA, but not so great for my developing a process of discovering aviation accidents. Tom had advised me that foreign aviation cases were good, partly because there was always a crash somewhere. The case could settle before we had to go find a lawyer to file a lawsuit in the country where the crash occurred. His training opened a part of my brain that I didn't know was there. The girls were also soaking it up.

After I left PDC, I made a package deal with Cooke on the Guatemala case. He gave me a flat hundred thousand[12] that included all my expenses. For me, it was a lot of money all at one time, but it would be a much bigger deal for him. Tom Jones was delighted to get the case.

I called the girls to meet me at PDC for dinner. I arrived early and gave my friend Maurice, the headwaiter, a little bonus. By now, since I'd done this several times already, he knew the drill. He rallied his troops. He and his waiters served up a top-notch dinner with seven courses. After dessert, I gave the girls each

---

12 $100,000.00 in 1975 had the same buying power as $455,732.18 in 2017

a five-thousand-dollar bonus. They were thrilled and excited, full of food, and their arms were full of packages of leftovers that would hold them for several days. Everyone was happy till I said to take some time off.

Jo was the first to speak up.

"I don't want time off," she said. "We're just getting started."

Niley, who never complained, said, "I agree. I slept for twelve hours last night, and now I'm ready to work."

Pixie just glared at me. It was the first time since I had given up my referral list to Cooke that I told the girls to go home, spend time with their kids. Anger was not the response I'd anticipated. I tried to explain it to them in another way.

"Work on what?" I asked. "We don't have a case. Aviation isn't going to keep us as constantly busy as car accidents used to. We are on standby for a big plane crash. We just had three great cases from the Eastern crash, and now look what we brought home from Guatemala. This is the calm before the next storm. Babies, we're on call."

Jo looked mollified. "That's a little better," she said. "I can live with being on call."

Pixie and Niley looked like they were still thinking about it. I turned to them. "Go find a boyfriend or something. I've been hoarding up your life. I'm sorry if I've prevented you from being with your kids and taken you out of circulation. Working aviation cases will give you more time now, probably a lot more time than working the apartment buildings, taking calls all the time and running out to meet a plumber or a manager. Be happy, please."

"Fuck you, boss." Pixie had the least amount of emotional control. She'd always had a hair trigger on her emotions and was quick to stand up to me. "If I wanted a boyfriend, I'd have one." She actually started crying.

"I don't need a fucking boyfriend," Niley added.

Jo looked at me like I'd shot her best friend, but then, I was probably her best friend, so maybe not. I wanted to explain, but they all stormed out. It was not the best meeting. Niley never talked that way unless she was kidding, but today she wasn't kidding. She was pissed or hurt or offended or some other emotion that was beyond me.

After the disastrous meeting, I reimbursed my sock, replacing the cash I had taken to Guatemala, and banked what was left.

I had no clue what to buy for a person who had everything, but I went to Robinsons Department Store and gave it a good try. I bought Jason a gold money clip with a twenty-dollar gold piece. For Sami, I bought Joy and Taboo perfumes. The saleslady assured me that the fragrances were extremely popular. I handled the bottle of Joy, and it reminded me of Tanis. I would not tell that to Sami. I bought Crispin a great-looking sweater at Brooks Brothers, and from Bullocks, a sweater for Ginger.

It took me thirty minutes to pack a suitcase, and the bulkiest things I had, I put on: a long overcoat, scarf, and hat. It was the first of November, unseasonably cold in Los Angeles, but I knew London would be freezing.

I drove myself to the airport and left my car. I had an open return ticket. All I needed to do is was call American Airlines for date availability and a seat in first class. Simple stuff. I didn't need a travel agent anymore.

On the two-hour layover in New York, I called Aunt Carmen.

"Auntie, I promise to visit you soon as I get back," I told her. "I have to make a quick business trip. I gave the girls some days off, but they never heard of the word 'vacation.' They don't even know I'm here."

"You just got back from Guatemala!"

"I know, Auntie, I know."

I called Sami to tell her I was taking a taxi from the airport. After I caught the plane from New York to London, I settled in for the flight, but I was still agitated over Pixie, Jo, and Niley.

Fuck it. I give the girls time off with full pay, a five-thousand-dollar bonus, and instead of enjoying it, they get pissed off because I suggest getting a boyfriend.

I slept on the plane, but only a little. As excited as I was over getting to see Sami again, I was anxious over the girls, wondering if I'd done the right thing.

I was really troubled by leaving with my relationships in a mess and not fully understanding why they exploded.

I took the elevator to the penthouse.

Sami was as gorgeous as ever. I picked her up so our lips met.

"Take me to bed," she said. "I need you right now. I just want to hold you and you hold me and run those big hands of yours all over my body. I want you to pinch my nipples and finger me." She took two of my fingers and sucked on them, playfully laughing.

Sami liked words. In bed, she'd tell me what to say to her. She'd have me say, "You've got such a great ass," or "I love your pussy," or "Love the way you fuck." What turned me on was not what I told her. It was her response. She'd go wild.

Life in the big penthouse with Sami was like a version of paradise. On this trip, I didn't feel like a mooch. I was comfortable and appreciative, especially since Sami said she wasn't going to the hospital to work during my entire stay.

"Tell me you're going to stay for a long time."

"Let's play it by ear. I'm on call. If an interesting case pops up, I might have to take off unexpectedly."

"No, don't say that." She clutched at me.

"I have a team back home depending on me and a business that will need my attention, just as your patients need yours." I squeezed her tighter. "I'm here right now. Let's enjoy it. I love being here with you."

"I love to hear you say that."

"Do you prefer I tell you that or the dirty talk?"

"Both."

The first morning in London, I called my apartment. Sure enough, Jo was there and so were Niley and Pixie. I talked to the three of them at the same time.

"Do you have any idea how fucking worried we've been?" Pixie was pissed.

"How could you not tell us?" asked Niley.

"Even your Aunt Carmen doesn't know where you are." Jo had called her, but Aunt Carmen hadn't shared.

"I figured by the way you stormed away, you guys wrote me off."

Pixie was crying. "Don't pull that bullshit. We were about to call the cops. We thought someone had gotten to you, hurt you, or killed you."

I felt like a heel.

"I'm sorry. I didn't plan the trip. I just packed and left."

"You should have told us."

"You're right, I should have called you guys, I'm sorry. I'll call back in a few days. You don't have to camp out at my apartment unless you really want to be there. Go spend time with your families."

Everything was fine. We were all on the same wavelength until I opened my big mouth again and mentioned they should start dating.

They hung up on me. Inside whatever controls my feelings and desires, I didn't want them to find boyfriends. I wanted them and I didn't want to share them. The problem is that I know that, being who I am, wanting them to be mine was not fair to them. I loved them with all my heart. I loved them more than I would love a sister or brother, though I have neither. When you love someone else that much, you don't eat up their best years of their life with no personal future at the end of the day.

Jason came to Sami's for dinner. He greeted me with a big hug, and I responded in kind. We lingered at the dinner table for more than two hours. The food was grand and the conversation grander. Crispin had the fireplace roaring, a necessity on a November evening. We sat on the balcony.

Sami sat between us. We drank way too much Cristal champagne.

I was a little high, and felt great. I figured that Sami and Jason would escape to the master bedroom as they usually did. I was looking forward to a steam, a massage by Ginger, maybe with a happy ending. I felt a shiver of anticipation.

Jason left for the restroom. Sami put her arm around the back of my neck, and her lips to my ear.

"Jason wants to watch."

I'm such a dummy. I didn't catch on right away.

"Watch?"

"Watch us." It was that hot whisper that made it clear. I could feel her lips on my ear.

It's a good thing that candles hide blushes.

"He likes to watch. He's not gay. He's not after you."

Sami had a funny laugh when she was tipsy, and she was definitely tipsy.

"Are you sure?" I reached for my glass and took a hundred-dollar gulp of Cristal.

"You don't have to, if you don't want to."

She pulled back and looked at me with those hungry eyes of hers. She nipped a spot on my neck, and I felt my cock jump in response. Then her lips were against my ear again. She might have nibbled my ear lobe. Her lips were warm and soft. My cock pulsed.

"I wish you'd say yes. It sounds exciting to me, to think someone is watching me get fucked by a beautiful man like you. Isn't that hot?"

"I've been to bed with four girls, but never a guy."

"He just watches. And you're not going to bed with him."

"He's a voyeur then?"

"No questions," she whispered.

My cock was all for it. My mind was all over the place. Melina had told me she used to frequent orgies, but we never went to one. I had never been to one, unless you counted the girls and me. But that wasn't an orgy. It just happened. Even if Jason was a voyeur, and I wasn't shy, I wasn't an exhibitionist. This was him watching. As much as I owed him, big time, that didn't factor in. What mattered to me is that it turned Sami on. She got another glass or two of champagne down me. It wasn't a lot of time and I wasn't using that time to make a decision. My brain was in neutral, and my cock was in overdrive. She led me to the bedroom. I coasted along behind her. The master bedroom was lit up with candles, but the room was still dim. Jason was sunk so low into an upholstered chair that I hardly noticed he was there until he stood up.

Sami was cool as could be. So was Jason. I wondered if they'd done this before. He walked over to Sami and undressed her. I didn't want him undressing me. I don't know if that was in his head at all, but I undressed myself, slipping out of everything, leaving it in a pile on the floor while Jason was still nuzzling her neck and slipping off her blouse. They were so easy over it that I decided that Sami and Jason had done this before. Jason took his tie and jacket off and returned to the chair he'd been in without removing the rest of his clothes.

For the first five minutes, I felt awkward. I wondered if Jason expected this as payback, but the champagne kept me from thinking too clearly or too much.

Sami lay on her back, slim and curvy and welcoming. She looked up at me, smiled, and spread her legs. The shadows curled around her body, making her look mysterious and inaccessible. I got in bed and explored her body. I touched her. I was already excited, but felt my excitement mount. I teased till she was voracious, squirming in need. When I embraced her, she was as soft and sweet and warm, as I was hard and ready. She burst around me like fireworks, or a flower; I couldn't say. But I teased her again till she was gloriously impatient and ready. For two hours, I kept her nearly at the pinnacle of her excitement between several quick climaxes. She gave and I demanded more. I focused on Sami, on her breath, her passion, her heartbeat, her hungry lips. I had to stop her a couple of times, but I managed to hold back. Jason had a ringside seat, but I never heard or noticed him except that he moaned when either of us moaned. Maybe someone watching was a turn-on for Sami, but it got better for me when I forgot he was there. Goblets of Cristal were out, and I never noticed when Jason filled them. I won't deny the Cristal helped erase him from the room, at least for me. Every twenty minutes or so, we stopped to sip and then got at it again. Sami had amazing stamina and a remarkable appetite for sex. As for me, it was one of those nights when, even at rest, I was up and hard as a bat.

The Cristal found its mark. I stopped thinking about Jason. I knew Sami's preferences and talked dirty to her as she liked, at her whispered command. It had never been my thing, but in the moment, the sensation of being a slave obeying my mistress' commands made me more excited. In my head, I came close to asking for permission to come. I could not have said that aloud with Jason in the room, and did not. I took a bathroom break to relieve myself of all that champagne, and when I returned, Jason was gone. Sami had her arms extended, beckoning for me to return. I slid right in.

After we woke up, I followed Sami to my old bedroom across the hall. I did not have a headache or any signs of a hangover. My suitcase had been parked there already.

"Much better," Sami said. "Fresh linens. We should have done this last night."

"Your linen was fresh last night," I reminded her. "And Ginger's already changed your sheets."

"True."

We destroyed Ginger's work and snogged in the fresh bed. Snogging, my new word. I kissed her.

"I slept like a baby," I said.

"I didn't sleep. I sat on the bed and watched you sleep."

"Liar," I said.

We laughed.

"If I wasn't so old, I'd ask you to marry me, Mario." She didn't laugh.

"You're not old. Where did you get that idea?"

"I'm afraid to do the math, but I figure nine years older than you, at least."

I didn't inquire about the marriage thing. She'd said something like it on my last visit. But I did tickle her into hysteria. Then she rolled on top of me. I was inside her, her breasts against my chest, her lips kissing my face.

Sometimes it felt bizarre to me how much alike Sami and Melina were, though they had never met, and lived an ocean apart in different countries, with completely different histories. Their ages, taste, and mannerisms were close. Melina had said she loved me though, and Sami didn't say that. Sami and I had sex again, and Sami fell asleep. I sat awake. It was perverse of me, but when I should have been thinking of Sami, my mind was on Melina. I know she was all about her independence, but I wondered how she felt about my having all these women. I had been jealous as hell when she'd been with Carson. In fact, in the past, when Jo had had 'Nando, and Pixie had had other men, I'd never been jealous.

After breakfast in bed, we walked to the spa. The steam was just the right temperature. The jets in the spa were whirling, and the sauna was set to medium toast. We went from place to place, sharing the moment.

The aroma of eucalyptus hovered in steam so heavy we could barely see each other. I fancied I could feel the poisons seeping out of me. On a shared towel on the marble slab, I kissed her left shoulder. She took my hand and lifted it to her lips.

"I shouldn't ask, but you and Jason, is it just a one-time thing?"

"Jason and I have fucked for years. He's special to me and I am special to him. I guess you could say it's a one-night-at-a-time thing."

We took a cooling shower, dried each other off, and wrapped up in towels. Ginger approached. I was glad to see her, but a little less so when I saw she was leading in a couple of strangers. She introduced a cute chick as Olivia, and a stocky young man as Liam, both dressed in sweats. "She's your masseuse, Mister Mario, and Liam is here for Miss Sami."

"Doctor, so good to see you again. Thank you for asking Ginger to call me," Liam said. I wanted to talk to Ginger, but with all this formality, it didn't seem appropriate.

"Sami, you didn't tell me we were going to get massages. This is a treat."

The two massage tables were set up about six feet apart from each other. I dropped my towel and lay on one and Sami lay on the other. The masseurs set to work as Ginger lit candles and incense all around the tables, then excused herself with a promise to check on us every thirty minutes.

Olivia was working out the kinks in my neck. "You have great hands," I told her.

"Thank you, Mister Mario."

I could not see what was going on with Sami, but judging from the sounds coming out of her, apparently it was good.

"Delicious," Sami said after about ten minutes.

"Olivia, can you dig the size of his package?" Sami asked.

"I dig it," Olivia said. "Haven't seen a tallywacker this size. I'll get to it."

I started laughing, then realized what Olivia was promising.

Olivia whispered in my ear, "I'm anxious to see Tally when he gets hard."

That turned me on instantly.

By the time we showered at six, the entire day had been spent in steamy luxury, and I do mean spent. I was neither jealous nor envious of Sami. She had whatever pleasures she had. I thanked her for her generosity with me.

When we went out that night, Ginger drove us in a black Rolls Royce.

We were settled in the back seat. I wondered aloud, "I never saw this car before. Did you just get it?"

"I have five cars."

I was surprised.

Sami turned to look at me. The night was dark, and the light in the car dim and indirect. Brighter lights skipped past. Traffic. Headlights shined on us inside, and skittered past. I could see her clearly, in flashes. We clicked champagne glasses.

"You need to buy two more cars."

"What on earth for?"

"Seven days in a week. You only have five days covered."

Sami laughed. So did Ginger. I heard her through the open partition.

"What else do you do?" I asked Ginger.

"You name it, Ginger does it. Ginger is the best," Sami answered for her.

"Thank you, Doctor Sami."

Ginger pulled up in front of the restaurant. She was outfitted like a chauffeur, and hopped out of the car to open the door, sidewalk-side. Sami got out. I slid over and exited right behind her.

"We will be here for at least one hour," Sami said. "Maybe an hour and a half."

It was one of those places where the light is dim, and candles burn in the center of each table. Aunt Carmen was wary of places like that. She doesn't like it when you can't see what you're being served. The thought made me chuckle. The tablecloths were cotton or linen, but not checkered red and white as they might be back home.

"What's funny?" Sami asked.

I explained to her, and she laughed too.

"In some places, that's probably a good idea."

They brought food. English food, and rather tasteless. I was thinking how I could use some jalapeños, when Sami said something.

I looked up and said, "What?"

"Come live with me. We can have so much fun. We can travel the world. We can do anything you want, and everything you've ever dreamed. I could get a private plane so we could travel without having to use the airlines." She warmed to her topic. "We could make a list of everything possible and just go mad on it."

My jaw gaped open. I snapped it shut. "You gotta have five hundred guys who'd give their right nut for a chance like that. And Jason is crazy about you."

"The five hundred are dead bores. Neither Jason nor I are looking for a permanent relationship. We dine out. We have fun. We fuck. That's it."

I shook my head. "I've seen how he looks at you. One of these days, you'll be getting married."

"Not for me," she said.

I didn't believe her, but I didn't say so.

"My family left me too much money. Marriage can get very complicated with that kind of money. The money and my mother being older than my father fucked up their marriage. But you're different. You're not clingy, and you don't care if I am as free as you are. I love being with you. And I love your..." her voice dropped to a loud whisper, "...tallywacker."

She laughed and so did I.

"I'm flattered by your offer," I explained, "but I'd make a lousy partner. And really, we hardly know each other. I've stayed at your house, but we've really only met a couple of times."

I enjoyed my time with Sami. She was fun and entertaining, but I didn't feel for her as I would for someone I'd want to be with all the time. I didn't feel about her the way I felt about my team and Melina back home. I could never leave them. Besides, the loss of Harry and Jake taught me that nothing was forever.

"You would never have to work again." Sami wouldn't let up. "I have enough money for many lifetimes. Tell me you'll think about it."

I reached across the table and took her hand.

"We come from different worlds, Sami. And we really hardly know each other." I kept my tone even. I was feeling a little uncomfortable about her intensity. I had been blindsided by this, and the one thing I knew for certain was that I wasn't about to turn into a gigolo.

"Different is what makes it fun. Unknown is what makes it exciting. Tell me you'll think about it."

"Brat," I said. "I just did."

She laughed. "Think harder," she said, a little wildly.

"You're a spoiled brat, and I don't take orders from anybody. I'd be pissed off at you the first time you commanded me to do anything but come, and you'd blow your top the first time I said no."

"I'm not spoiled. I just want to be with you. The penthouse vibrates with action when you're in it. Didn't you like Olivia?"

"She does great massage. Did you like Liam?"

"I always enjoy Liam. He gets all the right spots. We could have people pamper us every day, forever."

"Sami, that doesn't even sound tempting to me. I'm not a toy you can take out of its box whenever you get bored. I have a life. And if I moved in, it would really hurt Jason." I knew I couldn't do it. I smiled at her to soften the blow, but I'm not sure she was even hearing me.

"I get a lot of pampering from Liam, Olivia, and others, but it's more fun when I have someone I like there with me, like today."

Sami was eating a shrimp cocktail ever so slowly. She'd take a nibble, then talk away. I had finished mine in a minute or two. Melina had told me she loved me, then played it down. Sami was just promising a good time. I don't think love was in the picture.

"What are you thinking about?"

I couldn't tell her I'd been thinking of Melina, so I lied. "About how beautiful you are." Sami's nose was sharp and narrow; she was pale in an English way, with cheeks that were habitually windblown and pink. It's true that she had her own brand of beauty. But then, so did Melina. So did Pixie and Jo and Niley. I really wanted to be home with them now. Why did I keep leaving? Even I didn't know. I sure as hell loved coming home.

"You are so sweet, so nice to me all the time." She paused. "And the way you make love to me, it's so wonderful. I just got a chill thinking about it." She shivered, and touched my leg under the table.

"And I just got hard," I said. Olivia had touched me, and her caresses made me hard while I was just lying there, doing nothing. Sami was molding me into a total sex freak. I was freaky enough on my own.

I was looking at Sami. I should have been feeling the moment, but instead I was thinking how everyone had always been nice to her. She'd never gone without. She'd never known hardship, and she never would. It just wasn't part of her world. I was contemplating how many layers away from hardship she was, when a huge explosion somewhere made walls shiver and glass crack.

The candle on the table quivered. The pools of melted wax flickered wildly with reflected light. Something shook the restaurant, impact or air pressure rattling the booths and tables and glasses. The electric lights blinked and went out.

"What was that?" I jumped to my feet.

The lights came on again. I saw Sami was standing also, along with everyone in the restaurant. The nervous buzz of restaurant patrons hummed indistinctly, but I didn't hear anyone's voice in particular. I think if we had been in Los Angeles, we'd have headed for the closest earthquake safety zone, but this was London. We all sat down. Sami and I exchanged a word or two, but Ginger rushed in, out of breath.

"We should go," Ginger said. "There was an explosion down the street. It jolted the Rolls like you wouldn't believe. Must be close by."

"What about the check?"

"They know me," Sami said. "Let's get the hell out."

Ginger led us through the crowd inside, then the chaos outside, and a street over, where she'd stashed the car. We were silent as we concentrated on getting away, but once we were in the car, I had questions.

"After something like this, how do you know where to go and not to go?"

"This has been going on for years. This is the closest it's ever been to me. It's the IRA business, all political," Sami said. "But you can't just stay home, afraid. Lucky for us, no one knows the ins and outs of London like Ginger."

I reached for the corked Cristal bottle we had started on our way from the house and poured it in the glasses we'd left on the console.

I clicked clinked her glass. "*Salud*, beautiful."

We gulped it like a whiskey shot.

"I hope no one was hurt—or worse," I said.

"Hope for the best."

I poured more champagne.

We were sitting right up next to each other on the slick leather seat, lights off, traffic heavy. Passing cars and London's many lights provided just enough light for us to see each other.

Sami pushed the button to shut the partition. The glass moved.

"Ginger, I don't want you to hear me," Sami said

The sound of Ginger's laugh was cut off as the glass snapped shut.

"You have a choice," Sami said. "Fuck me with this." She squeezed my hard on. "Or," she took my right hand. "This."

I moved my hand between her legs and found her wet. She flexed her hips to rub against me. I took my hand away, and she grabbed it with both of hers, trying to put it back where it had been.

"You're not getting off as easy as that," I said, unzipping my pants.

I turned towards her. She curled her legs and rested them on top of mine. Our lips touched. In this new position, my free hand again found her. My fingers pressed inside, then I replaced my fingers with my cock. I couldn't really move, but then, I didn't have to. She went wild, twisting, pushing her body against the probing so I could go deeper. It's a good thing the partition was closed, and music roaring in the front seat, or Ginger would have gotten an earful. Just outside the windows of the car, traffic was mayhem. Through the night, a fire burned, smoke poured into the sky, people screamed, and bobbies directed traffic. Sami and I were getting off on each other.

We had two other dinners with Jason at the house. There was no voyeur encore, and Jason made no mention about that night. At both dinners, Jason answered every question I threw at him about aviation cases, and there were a lot of questions. He and Sami left me and went to the master bedroom. Ginger and I had a repeat performance, which was great for both of us.

As much as I enjoyed living on the wild side in London, it wasn't home. It was what I enjoyed, but not what I loved. I was more than ready to return to my apartment in Los Angeles, and the women I had left behind.

Eight days later, I was in the car in the drop-off lane in front of the airport, and Sami was driving.

She was back on what was turning into her favorite topic.

"Tell me you'll consider my offer?"

As many times as I had already told her I wasn't ready to move to London to shack up with her and let her look after me, she had not seemed to hear it. I wondered if I needed to cool my jets to get the point across, but I didn't want to hurt her.

Flying across the Atlantic, I had time to think. Melina and Sami were both rich, and both control freaks. They were funny and fun to be with. Melina was married to her job and seemed to be afraid of her own feelings. Sami was probably part of the aristocracy; she was Lady something or other. I didn't know or care about the complexity of her social standing. She gave me more time, and had some kinks in her wiring that might not be compatible with mine. Sami's real life was a fantasy. Her being a doctor was another compartment in her life that was real but separate. Not that Melina was an angel. She'd been to orgies, screwed Carson to persuade him to help her off someone in prison, and claimed she screwed some California official to get a concealed weapon permit. As a human being, she was far more vulnerable than Sami.

I didn't tell the girls I was on the way. My car in the airport parking lot was waiting for me. It had gotten filthy sitting there for the duration of my trip. I pulled up to the Bunker Towers, and tossed Tito the keys.

I had bought more suits, but had shipped them home. I hadn't gone for fittings. Sami had just called the tailor to come to me. The one suitcase I left with was all I brought back. Tito reached for it. I put my hand up, stopping him.

"Tito, I got it. But maybe you could get someone to wash this thing, please?" I pointed at my dirty car.

I handed him a couple of bills.

"You got it, Señor Luna." He bowed.

"Tito, you don't need to bow, and don't call me Mr. Luna."

"Yes sir, Mr. Luna." He bowed again.

My apartment was immaculate. The girls had been there working; I saw notes and stacks of work in my office, and items posted on the bulletin board. I saw two stacks, one pristine before and a rumpled after, the newspapers I subscribed to, neatly folded, and a basket of mimeos of plane crash articles, all tiny mentions of small crashes from the aforementioned newsprint. They kept everything tidy whenever they were there. And my housekeeper came in three times a week, even when I was gone.

I smiled when I saw the basics were in the refrigerator. Jo would have handled that, even though she had no clue when I was coming back. I'd missed them all terribly. There was a good chance they were going to still be upset with me. I was too tired to deal with it.

I was tired and I needed to get myself together. I was suffering jet lag, and not sure of the day. I had to check the current newspaper to see it was Friday, November 14, 1975.

The only person I called was my aunt. I caught her at home.

"I'm back. Are you okay?"

She was a little sassy.

"The question is are you okay? You're the one that's been halfway across the world. Again."

We talked for a few minutes. The instant I told her how tired I was, she cut it short and told me to get to bed. I didn't call the girls.

Chapter 7
October 1975
Lull

"Boss, you piss me off," Pixie said when she came in. "You been here two days."

"You are so mean, boss," Jo said. "Not telling us you were home."

"Nothing from you?" I turned to Niley.

"Fink!"

The girls were a sight for sore eyes. Jo had cut her hair into a bob and left all her suits hanging in her closet. She showed up all in black, like a Bond girl or Audrey Hepburn in that beatnik scene from *Sabrina*. Long-sleeved black turtleneck with a black fur collar. Tight black pants. The stilettos were sitting by the door, but I could see she was wearing black stockings. Pixie was in a mini that wasn't much more than a long, belted shirt, which clashed violently with her bright red hair. She was all pink and orange and green stripes, orange tights, clunky orange heels in a pile by the door. Her feet were bare, and each of her toenails was painted a different pink or orange. Niley was in a plain white tee and beat up jeans. She left her stilettos in the shoe pile and went to my closet. She came back wearing a pair of foot slippers. That is, giant slippers shaped like bare feet.

"I was tired," I told them. "I came in, hit the bed, and didn't get out of it for two days."

Hearing me say it out loud stirred up round two of the vent. Thirty minutes and a bottle of red later, I was smothered with hugs and kisses.

"Boss, you can really put that vino away," Jo said.

"In Europe, wine is safer than the water. It doesn't bother me anymore, but I try to keep it moderate." Moderate? I don't think so. I put away Sami's Cristal like it was water.

"And how's the English lady doing? Did she leave anything for us?" Pixie asked.

"Sami wants me to quit everything and come live with her. She wants me to be her kept man." I was laughing. "Tempting offer."

The girls got totally silent.

I picked up the empty bottle, carried it to the kitchen, rinsed it out, and put it on the counter against the wall. Pixie took them home. She and her daughter dripped wax on them and used them as candleholders. By now, they probably had a million of them. I came back and joined them. They were still at the table, and not silent anymore.

"She wants to break up our family here?"

"I couldn't do that," I said. "I tried to let her down gently, but she had trouble hearing me. She knows it's not happening. Sami knows all about you three and Melina. She invited you to come with me some time."

"Cool," Niley said. "Is she the jealous type?"

"Not a chance. She's a lot like Melina."

"We saw Melina several times when we were here. She popped in a couple of times to see if you were back."

Melina. I didn't mention that the two days I'd been home had been in my bed, mostly with Melina. She'd left for work twice, but joined me as soon as she was back. All that bedtime hadn't been spent sleeping. If I said anything about it, there'd be a round three of ranting.

"When are we getting back to work?" Jo asked.

"We're waiting," I replied.

"So we just sit on our asses waiting for a plane crash? We've been poring over newspapers. I'm going to have to get reading glasses, or else go blind."

"Pixie, we want big cases. They don't have to be aviation cases. We deserve the time off, so fuck it. You guys are getting paid. Relax. Be cool."

"It's not the money," Niley said. "Okay, it's not just the money. I'm anxious to get out and get busy."

"I can't go out and invent a plane crash, and I'm not going to pray for one either."

"Of course not," Jo said. "Sorry, boss. We're just anxious and hate taking money from you every week and not doing anything for it."

"When the next crash happens, you'll make up for it. Don't sweat the small stuff."

The girls unpacked me and put everything that wasn't washable in a bag for the dry cleaners.

"Boss, you didn't bring us any gifts from London. What the fuck?"

"Pixie, the big stores where I shopped during my first trip are targets for terrorists running around London. Sami suggested I not do too much shopping."

The girls looked pretty upset over the mention of terrorists.

"I was kidding, boss. Fuck, you're home. That's the biggest gift of all."

She dove at me and kissed my lips, her fingers digging into my lapels.

"I didn't know they had that kind of problem in London," Jo said.

"Next time you look over London newspapers, see what it says about the IRA."

"Will do."

"Scary," Niley said. "Thank God you got back unharmed."

I considered not telling them, but Jo put out fresh, hot tortilla chips, salsa, and guac, Pixie started massaging my feet, and Niley opened another bottle of red. Before I knew it, I was halfway through the story of the pub that had been bombed down the street while we were having dinner. That just made them hug me more. It was good to be home. They wanted to hear more about Ginger and her chauffeur suit. I told them all about Ginger. Almost all.

Over the next few days, during breakfast, I read the *LA Times*, looking for plane crashes. Nothing. I perused the classifieds and came across something interesting and circled it.

Train car filled with toys, at least 75% undamaged.

I called and found it had been an insurance claim. I bought the contents for five thousand dollars[13] and donated it to the Salvation Army but let the girls handle the logistics to keep them busy. The toys were in pretty good shape, and only needed minor repairs that the volunteers were able to handle. Five hundred kids who would have had nothing would be getting something this Christmas. One of the seniors there asked for my schedule because they wanted to give me an award.

The next day, on the way home from the Pantry, I was beeped. When I got home, I returned the call. It was Oscar.

"Mario, I haven't seen a case from you in a long time. Did you retire?"

For Oscar, a week was a long time.

"Not a chance," I replied. "Just got back from a pleasure trip to London. Still recovering. How is Carson doing?"

"He's good. We're good. Very busy."

"Be sure you take care of those clients. I know them all."

Oscar chuckled. "I take care of them. Get some business over here. I need the big stuff."

"Don't we all?"

Juan checked in every week from Puerto Rico. When I was in London, Jo had taken his calls.

"Glad you're back, boss. You got anything for me?"

"Hang in there. We'll get something," I assured him. "I'm sending you five hundred[14] today by Western Union."

"It's okay, boss."

---

[13] $5,000.00 in 1975 had the same buying power as $23,259.34 in 2017.

[14] $500.00 in 1975 had the same buying power as $2,278.66 in 2017

"If you were okay, you wouldn't be calling. Jo will give you the pickup ID number later today."

"Thank you, boss."

On November twenty-first, I got a call from Jason. He opened with a couple of minutes of small talk about my trip, then casually said, "You may not have heard about this one."

"I'm all ears," I said. I wanted him to dispense with the small talk and get straight to the business, but Jason was too polite for that. There'd been a crash in Venezuela.

As soon as I hung up, I called Juan. He set off for Caracas, Venezuela, where an airliner had crashed, killing seventy-seven people. Because the plane was manufactured in the United States, Tom Jones said it would make for a better case, but even if it hadn't been, we'd be heading to Caracas to try and sign the families of victims. I knew that the operator of the airline was insured in the UK.

Juan proved again that he was a good front man. After two days, he called early, around seven. I had already breakfasted and returned home, anxious for his call.

"Many families are in a hotel in Caracas where the airline put them while they recover the bodies. I am staying in a hotel across the street and already making friends. Get ready."

"We've been packed since you left Puerto Rico." We weren't packed, but we were ready. The girls had already made arrangements for their kids.

"Okay. You have confidence in Juan."

"For sure, my friend."

"I didn't get vaccinations in Puerto Rico. Had to do at airport here. Better you get in Los Angeles."

I called Tom, and he prepared some materials for us on the plane involved. Niley picked it up. We planned to look over it on the flight. My passport and vaccinations were already straight, but the day before Thanksgiving, the girls were in my car on the way to the vaccination clinic Jo found. By noon, the girls had been poked and given proof of vaccinations.

I spent Thanksgiving Day at my aunt's house with Pixie and Lainey. Jo and Niley had their own Thanksgiving dinner together with their kids and Jo's mom. We were all anxious and ready to go, but had decided to wait until after the holiday. Late Thanksgiving night, the girls brought their suitcases to my apartment and parked their cars in my apartment lot. We sat around waiting for Juan's phone call. We would be flying to Miami, just as I had done when I went to Puerto Rico. From Miami, the next leg was direct to Caracas.

Tom Jones prepared the retainers as before, in English and Spanish. He'd put in details about the crash where necessary on the retainer forms, and told me he would be working on improving the language of the retainer contract with each case.

"We're all ready, and don't even know for sure the families will want to see us." Jo was fidgety. She's great at juggling a dozen things at once, but not so good at doing nothing or twiddling her thumbs.

"Be positive. We only need one family to invite us. Then no one can say we're over there soliciting."

"But we are soliciting." Pixie grinned.

"Shut up," Jo said. "You know what Mario means."

Pixie gave us all the finger. "Everyone is so jumpy. I was kidding. Chill out."

Hours later, we were all in bed. No one was feeling sleepy or sexy or in the usual post-Thanksgiving coma. We were all fully awake and as wound up as if we'd each drunk a pot of espresso. We were sitting in the dark, yakking about nothing, practicing talking aviation in Spanish, and waiting for the call. I was resigned that it wouldn't ring till morning. Venezuela was four hours ahead. But then, the phone rang. It startled us. It startled me. I knocked the phone off the hook while I grabbed it. Niley was on that side of the bed and got down to pick the base of the phone off the floor.

"Boss, I have eight families that want to talk," Juan said very calmly.

We were the opposite of calm. Pixie let out a whoop. We all leaped out of bed. Jo got on the phone with the airline. We got into our travel clothes and were off to LAX to catch the first available flight to Miami.

It took twenty-four hours for us to land in Caracas.

From his hotel room, Juan arranged us a car so it was waiting at the airport. The driver, Yaz, spoke English and Spanish and was very talkative, informative, and opinionated. He spoke in English. The girls responded in Spanish.

"Your Spanish is very good," Yaz said. "Are you sure you're Americans?"

He bragged to us of the city's population of over two million; and, without knowing yet it was our objective, mentioned the plane crash from the week before.

"The pilots, may they rest in peace, but how can they be so stupid as to crash into a mountain right after taking off?"

Since we'd all been taking instruction from Tom Jones, we were full of answers, though Yaz had surely meant the statement rhetorically. He had no idea he was in the car with a bunch of fledgling aviation experts. He got an earful.

"They might have had instrument problems, like the altimeter may have failed. Pilots might have gotten dizzy. They call it... they call it..."

"Spatial disorientation," Niley interjected.

Jo nodded. "It's hard to know what happened right away if the pilots didn't say something specific to air traffic control."

"They have eyes," Yaz said. "Or had eyes." He pointed to the green rise ahead of us. "They should have seen the mountain!"

"There is that." Pixie nodded, squinting at the mountain. "Hard to miss."

"Clouds," Jo said, counting off on her fingers obvious reasons a pilot might not see an obstacle. "Fog. Rain. Night. Headlight failure, instrument failure—"

"Let's not jump to conclusions," I said, more to the girls than to Yaz. "It doesn't matter what happened. The families of the passengers have to be paid."

"And that's what we're going to do," Pixie said.

The driver was listening to us, but we weren't saying anything that wasn't public knowledge.

"The pilots are dead and not here to tell their side of the story. Investigations sometimes blame the pilots when they can't figure out another cause. Be careful what you say or agree to in front of the families, or anyone, for that matter." I nodded my head toward Yaz, whose eyes were on the road. It was a good thing, too, since Caracas was a busy city, and the traffic was as bad as anywhere I've seen. Niley slapped her hand over her mouth and looked appalled. I could see she was trying to think if she'd said something out of line. I almost laughed aloud at the expression on her face.

"Got it, boss," Jo said.

"Of course. Whatcha think? We're beginners?" Pixie said in a stream of giggles.

"I'm a beginner, but they won't hear it from me," Niley said.

Jo had reserved a suite with connecting rooms, so it was like a two-bedroom apartment. Their room had two double beds. I'd offered to get a rollaway or the use of the sleeper-couch in my living room, but they said they preferred switching up each night who was doubling up with Pixie. The main suite where I was parked had multiple bathrooms, a living room, dining area, and a great balcony overlooking the busy streets below. It was a tall building, but not so tall that it gave a sweeping view of the city. We'd seen plenty of Caracas on the way here; the city had a lot of skyscrapers like many modern cities, but there were many older, smaller buildings. Mountains dominated the landscape. I was on the balcony, checking out the view, when Juan arrived.

"The families are in a hotel ten minutes from here. The families I have talked to are expecting you in the morning."

"Good," I said. "Have you seen any competition?"

"Two local lawyers are roaming the hotel and talking to the families. Both are from the same firm. Gustavo Martino and Lario Flores. They've seen me around but haven't said a word."

"Good work. It's good we have the rest of today to settle in."

Juan brought with him a shopping bag filled with local newspapers and magazines that had stories about the crash. I knew from experience there were more detailed accounts in the local magazines than had hit any English publications.

"Put them on the table," I said. "I need a shower, and I'll be back with you."

That night, we turned in early. The girls said goodnight and walked through the connecting doors to their own rooms and beds. Jo doubled back to grab a couple of the articles. She gave me a kiss on top of the head.

"You okay, sweets?" she asked.

"Never better."

She grabbed another magazine. "Reading material," she said, and shut the door, leaving me alone with my thoughts.

I crashed on the king-sized bed, too tired to think about being alone. As I was dozing off, I was dimly aware of a soft body that got under the covers with me and snuggled. When the sun through the window woke me, Pixie was asleep on the pillow next to mine. She looked so comfortable, I hated to wake her, but there was work to be done. There had been no sex last night, but I had slept well. Whether it was a snuggle, a scratch, a fondle, or a massage, Pixie read me like a book.

We took a taxi to the families' hotel. While I was engaged with the taxi driver, the girls had taken a few steps toward the building and were talking among themselves.

"Not good," Jo said to me as I approached. She pointed out the armed soldiers in green fatigues who stood at the entrance of the hotel where the families were staying. No one was getting in without a good reason.

"Hang right here," I said to my team. I walked around the big building, looking for an officer with stripes. I found one better, with three bars. I tried asking for entrance, speaking to him in English, which he seemed not to understand, then Spanish, which he did.

"What business do you have inside?"

He looked over my team standing fifty feet or so away, outside the entrance. What he saw was that the girls were all wearing suits that looked professional, in conservative shades of blue and gray. Jo had on something in a pinstripe fabric that looked very expensive. Pixie still had her Faye Dunaway hair from *Chinatown* and was wearing a professional-type jacket that was cut shorter than a man's would have been and was fitted tightly to her waist. Underneath was a cummerbund that was bright red and so small she looked like she might break in half, and a slim skirt, cut longer than the ones she usually wore back home, though it was still above her knee. Niley had no jacket, but a fitted woman's vest and tie over a crisp button-down shirt that completely bared her arms, as November in Caracas had highs in the eighties; she was wearing one of Jo's favorite pencil skirts that was very narrow and slit up the side, revealing a peek at long legs in black stockings.

I pulled out a neatly folded hundred-dollar bill.

"Please take no offense," I said. "We have what could be very important business with eight of the families who have requested to see me."

I slipped him the bill.

He asked no more questions, but his English miraculously returned. He jerked his head toward my team.

"I'll walk you to the lobby. Follow me."

Once we were in the lobby, the officer left.

I had no idea entrance would be so easy. I was feeling great relief, and could have just collapsed somewhere. Juan saw us and greeted us warmly. His welcome felt good, especially after my false show of confidence. The girls had taken it in stride, though, with no clue how close we'd come to being locked out.

"How the hell you been getting in here?" I asked Juan.

"I show my investigator badge from Puerto Rico. It works fine."

I patted him on the back.

"You do great work, Juan. I'm happy you are on my team."

"Okay, boss, I happy too." His Spanish is flawless, but Juan always practiced his English with us. In English, he tended to speak in the present tense, and skip some verbs. Good English, really. Pixie called it street English, but it was better than street English. Juan pointed at two big, suited guys across the lobby. "The lawyers I tell you about. I don't know who is Gustavo and who is Lario."

I wasn't sure if we should meet with the families all at once or individually, so I asked what they wanted to do. The family consensus was that we should see them together, so we met them in a conference room that Jo rented at the front desk. Room service provided us ongoing beverage service and snacks. The hotel set up a table where my team—Juan, Jo, Pixie, and Niley—sat behind me, facing eight families. The twenty-six individuals in attendance sat in rows on folding chairs. They had grouped themselves so it was easy to pick out the families. I approached the lectern, a small mahogany box resting on one of the conference tables; it had a tilted top for a speaker's notes. I had no notes. I tapped the microphone, and it squeaked shrilly. It was a small room, and I chose not to use the microphone. I spoke in Spanish, looking directly at the families closest to me.

Renzo Ramiro was an older man, and seemed to have gotten the nod of approval to speak for the group. He had thick, dark hair turning silver around the edges. His face was creased with pain; his voice was so deep, resonant, and passionate, it was easy to see how the families had chosen him to be their spokesperson. He wore glasses, a plain cotton shirt, and an air of gravity you would expect from a man who had just lost a daughter.

"We have talked to your investigator, and to attorneys with offices here in the city, but still we have many questions no one has answered. Juan says you can answer some of them."

"Of course," I said. "We don't know everything, but I will answer everything I can. First of all, please accept our deepest condolences for the loss of your loved ones. The attorneys in Los Angeles that I am speaking on behalf of, and my team here, and I are tremendously sorry. We can only imagine how devastated you must feel. We are here for you. If there was room at this hotel, I would be staying here, but my hotel is only minutes away."

Tissue boxes were passed around. I waited as the families composed themselves.

"As Juan has told you, I am not an attorney. I realize you don't know me or my team, but I want you to get to know us. We are not here to sell you anything. We are here to help you through. Call us advocates of fair and just compensation for families of victims who have lost loved ones in aviation tragedies. I know that is a lot of words. It just means we are here to help, and we are here to help only you. Not the plane manufacturers, not the airlines, not the insurers. We have experience with cases that face huge companies like the insurance carriers, and the airline in this case. I am a consultant to attorneys in Los Angeles who specialize in wrongful death cases, and I have been doing client development for personal injury and wrongful death cases for many years. If you honor us by allowing us to represent you, you should know that the key attorney who will handle this case is not only a lawyer, he is also a pilot who flew fighter jets in the US Air Force. He has been checked out to fly huge cargo planes and aircraft like the plane in this tragedy. So he understands what goes wrong. He will understand the accident reports, because he knows the subject inside and out, not only as a pilot, but also as a lawyer."

I could tell the family members understood that. Some of them exchanged quiet comments among themselves.

"The important thing for you to remember is that you need to get an attorney. When you do, be sure that the attorney you hire is an aviation specialist, and one familiar with international law. It doesn't matter if you retain the lawyers I can introduce you to or if you get someone else. The plane crashed here, but its point of origin was out of the country."

Whispers buzzed from my audience. Questioning faces turned to Ramiro.

"Why a lawyer?"

"That's a good question," I responded to Ramiro, but I knew I was answering them all. "You must know that the airline has already hired lawyers. Their insurance companies have also hired attorneys. You have just undergone what is probably the worst tragedy in your lives, and in the face of this arena of legal experts, you are vulnerable. Chances are you are not at your best. After this terrible tragedy, when you are so defenseless and sensitive, being unprotected by a lawyer would leave you exposed. Also, you need a lawyer who understands international law as it applies to planes. There are treaties involved with planes that cross international lines, and the questions of law can get very tricky."

I saw nods of approval. I snuck a look at my team, all alert, and looking compassionately at the families. I had told them not to look away, and not to stare at just one family member, to be attentive and receptive. This was the first time we had ever had a meeting like this, and they were doing well.

"If we could get you your people back, we would. But that miracle is not available to us. No amount of money will ever give you back the loved ones that were taken away from you last week."

I heard crying in the audience, and paused for a moment.

"In a few days, there will be funerals. After you have put your loved ones to rest, we can talk more thoroughly about how we handle this type of case. I know you have questions. We will do everything we can to answer any questions you have; but out of respect to you and your loved ones, I will not make this a long presentation."

The vibes I felt coming from the families were good.

I took a drink of water.

"The accident happened in Venezuela, but the insurance companies that will pay for this tragedy are located in England. The lawyers I will talk to you about are in Los Angeles, California. Chances are that this case will settle without having to go to court. If it is necessary to file these cases in the courts, either here in Venezuela or in the United States, where the plane was manufactured, the attorneys you will retain through me have the financial means to fight these giants to the fullest."

I took another drink of water. Room service attendants were making their way through the room. The families were loosening up. They were accepting coffee and other beverages.

"It is good to be here in front of you, meeting with you together. In the days to come, being in a group like this may lend you strength. It does not take away your individuality. You should know each of you is unique. Every case is a different case. Each person in this accident was a different age, had a different occupation, a different history. How much compensation will be paid to you will have a great deal to do with how old your loved one was, what he or she did for a living, and how many family members were left behind. These things will have a great deal to do with how much compensation will be paid to you. We will get into this in detail at a later time, after the funerals."

My team was flanking me on both sides. I looked at them, left and right. It was time to sum up.

"Thank you so very much for meeting with me tonight. I will be here if you want to come up to talk to me privately, or we can let this go for now until after the funerals."

"I have a question," a man said, getting up. He was younger than Ramiro, and looked both sad and angry. I sympathized with him. If I had lost someone on that plane, I would be angrier and louder than he was. The woman beside him put her hand up as if to stop him.

"Of course," I said.

"Why do we need a lawyer in the United States?"

"You don't need a lawyer in the United States. You just need a lawyer that has aviation experience."

The man had a surprised look on his face. He sat down. "Thank you."

Another man got up. "What if there is a problem, and nothing is paid by the insurance company?"

"That is unlikely because of that international treaty I was talking about. There are obligations that are laid out that the airline must fulfill. However, if that were to somehow happen, you would pay our attorneys nothing. The contract you will be asked to sign to retain the American lawyers is in English and Spanish. It is very clear and easy to understand. The American lawyer gets a percentage of what is collected for you. If nothing is collected, you owe nothing."

I wanted to cut it short. It was disrespectful to get into the money and the retainer too deeply until after the funerals. But the group kept on coming up with questions.

At last, we came away from the table to mingle with the families one-on-one as they drank coffee and snacked on cakes. Juan didn't stick around. He left when we mixed with the crowd. The families ate and talked and began to feel comfortable with us. When they left for their rooms, we exchanged hugs rather than handshakes.

Tom Jones advised me on the phone every day.

I told him the arrangement with the hotel. "Our eight families all lived in Caracas or within thirty minutes of the city. The airline is allowing them to stay at the hotel so they could be with other families, at least until the funerals."

Tom said, "Even here in the states, the airline rents a hotel or hotels where all the families come to stay during the recovery of bodies and to be given updates on any preliminary findings about the investigation of what caused the crash. It is easier to communicate to everyone if they are all in one place."

"I've gotten in, but it's hard to do. And I'm not the only one working the families."

"Anyone from the US there?"

"I haven't a clue. The only lawyers giving me competition I can see are from Caracas. There are two of them I've seen around, but I haven't met them."

I got a call from Ramiro. He was still stiff with me and calling me Mr. Luna, though I kept insisting on Mario.

Ramiro said, "We need to see where the crash occurred. Can you work on this with the airline company? I already talked to them, but all they tell me is that the only roads up to the site were made by their contractor and are not suitable for cars or buses to travel on."

"Of course," I said. "But this is probably an insurance issue."

I called Jo to the main suite. She whistled for the others. They sat fairly quietly for them. Jo handed out magazines and got them all reading the various Spanish articles about the crash. Meanwhile, I called Tom Jones and discussed the issue with him.

"It is very common for families to be taken to the crash scene when possible. I can understand that in a mountainous area, it is close to impossible if there are no roads."

"How about a helicopter?" I asked.

Jones thought it might be a workable option.

I had the hotel operator connect me with Jason's home number. It was late in London, but normal decorum was out the window where he was concerned.

"Jason, I hope I didn't wake you. I need your input." I explained that some of the families wanted to see the crash site. I told him about the terrain there and what I had learned.

"If I were handling this case, I'd give you a hard time about paying for helicopters to take the families up there. It's just not practical. If it was a place where you could take everyone in buses, we do that all the time. I don't think you're going to get the insurance carrier to spring two pence for that."

The conversation drifted away from the case and spent five minutes going nowhere in British small talk. I sent my best to Sami, in case he saw her before my next call.

"Give her a squeeze and a kiss for me."

"Count on it," replied Jason.

I hung up the phone. The girls were watching me like hawks, magazines open on their laps. Pixie's magazine was upside down.

"What?"

"You really know this guy good," Jo said.

"Yes."

"How good?" asked Pixie.

"He's become a good friend."

"How good a friend?" asked Niley.

"What is this? An interrogation?"

The girls backed off. They knew me too well, and guessed something was up. I wasn't about to tell them he'd watched me have sex with Sami. That was in the past, anyway.

Jo reached over and flipped Pixie's magazine so she could read it. She said, "So I need to find a helicopter or two for an entire day to shuttle the families who want to see the crash site. Who is going to pay?"

"I'm sure I'll be stuck paying, but it may not cost that much. We're in Venezuela, not Los Angeles."

Jo nodded.

"What about the wreckage? What if there are still bodies out there? What if there are parts of bodies?" Niley asked.

"Dreadful," Pixie said, looking aghast.

"Good thinking," I told Niley.

I called Juan.

"Find me a helicopter. I want to fly over the crash site tomorrow. Can you do that?"

Jo gave me a thumbs up. She pulled out her little book of lists and scratched something down. I'm guessing she was taking "FIND HELICOPTER" off her list.

"For how many?"

"Probably just me."

Pixie whacked me on the head.

"Strike that," I said. "Okay, for all of us."

"Okay, boss, I work on it."

When Juan confirmed that we had a helicopter for tomorrow, I had him invite Ramiro.

Ramiro called back.

"There are more families who want to see. It's not just me."

"I'm arranging the helicopter now, but we need to take a look first. We have to see if the site is clear of anything that may offend a family member."

Ramiro made a sharp noise and was silent for a moment. He sounded to me like he might have been crying. His daughter had been one of the bodies recovered from the wreckage.

"If it is too much for you, you don't have to come with us."

"No. You are right, of course. I did not think. I will be there."

"Juan will pick you up." I had not wanted to mention body parts specifically, but that was what I was worried about. He'd obviously come to that thought on his own. I'd already noticed that in countries other than the United States, many of the photos released to papers and magazines were more grisly than our media permitted. I didn't trust any of the photos of the site, anyway. I had to see for myself.

At ten in the morning, we were on the heliport on the top floor of our hotel. We'd heard the helicopter when it came in for a landing. It was a noisy mother.

"Oh my God, it's huge. I'm going to come!" Pixie clapped her hands.

I took a hard look at the Sikorsky. The ten-passenger helicopter was way too big for our needs today, but at least it had been available.

Juan appeared with Ramiro, who was grim and pensive. I expected he was thinking of his daughter. For once, Pixie had the good sense to hold her tongue.

Jo's silence was another thing entirely. It occurred to me that she might be afraid. I boarded, then reached for her hand as she climbed the stairs. She cast an uneasy smile in my direction.

"I hope this guy can fly," she whispered. "I've been reading way too much about helicopter crashes lately. They're a lot more common than airliners."

"You can stay here if you want," I whispered back. "There's no need to put yourself through this if you're afraid."

"And miss this? Never."

Twenty minutes later, we were above the crash site with no place to land.

The pilot had to hover high to avoid disturbing the workers below. Huge trucks and tractors were removing the wreckage. The trucks were so big that they must have traveled on roads; but that was not a point I could quibble over, if there was no official transport we could get to the site.

Niley was by the window, and Ramiro sat between her and Jo. As the helicopter hovered, Niley got up and gave the window view to Ramiro. I gave Niley a covert thumbs up for her kindness and saw Ramiro's eyes were filled with tears. Jo had her arm around his shoulders and Niley was on her feet behind him, whispering in his ear. Pixie was sitting next to me with a box of tissues. She took one for herself and handed the rest over to Jo. Niley blotted Ramiro's eyes.

As far as we could tell from our vantage points, the news accounts that all the bodies had been recovered were correct. What remained was wreckage we could not make out very well, at least not from the height we were flying at.

Juan cleared his throat and said, "The crews have been down there for ten days."

Ramiro agreed that there was nothing gruesome to be seen that would offend anyone. The families would still be affected by what they would see below. Ramiro was deeply moved, though I am afraid all he felt was pain. He had his hand clutched over his heart, and I think he whispered his daughter's name aloud. I know he prayed. The girls and I were quiet. The helicopter certainly drowned out the sound of Ramiro's voice, but I felt like God heard what he was saying, anyway.

Back at the hotel, Tom Jones called me.

"I talked to the airline attorney. He refuses to have the airline pay for the families to helicopter over the site."

"We went there today." I explained the circumstance. "Thanks for trying, Tom. I'm going to cover it."

I had not brought a black suit, and the girls had brought nothing in black. It was not difficult to find appropriate clothes. A week after we arrived, we attended funerals for twenty-one decedents whose remains had been released to the families. We did not mingle, though each of our potential families came over and greeted us, thanking us for coming. We kept our distance. We didn't want to be a distraction.

Ramiro pointed out the two attorneys from Caracas who were there. I had noticed them, but we'd been doing a good job of ignoring each other all week.

"You see the people they're with?" Ramiro asked.

I nodded. "I don't recognize them."

"I believe those are workers from their office," Ramiro said.

When we were leaving, and we were in the parking lot near the cars, I saw that none of the families were around, but the local lawyers were. I walked over to them and introduced myself. I extended my hand.

Neither of them extended their hand to me. Assholes. I was reminded briefly of Hugo, the former competitor who had tried to kill me several times and ended his life doing a back flip out the window of my high-rise. Of course, Hugo had hidden his animosity until he was standing with a gun in my face. At least these guys were open in their hostility. There can be a lot of competition in this line of work.

I spoke to them in Spanish.

"If you find this case is more than you can handle, contact me. We can make a deal so that my attorneys handle the case for you. We'll work out something." I gave them a polite smile and walked off.

Okay, I was a total snob. I dropped two of my business cards on the ground in front of them and walked away.

The bigger asshole cussed at me in Spanish. I didn't turn but raised my arm overhead and gave them the finger. I was angrier at myself than at them. Pissed off because I'd been there over a week, and they had never made a move to come talk to me. Not a single overture from them, but here I went to them, and came away with my tail between my legs. I wanted to go back there and slap them around. Fortunately, the girls were watching, which put me on better behavior.

The families who had funerals left the hotel that night.

The day after the funeral, we engaged the same pilot and helicopter to make three trips. Ramiro and the other twenty-five family members decided among themselves who would fill up the ten spots on each of the three flights. Ramiro rode every time, acting like a guide.

News travels fast. The morning after helicopter day, I was still in bed and heard the phone ring.

The girls were using one of the rooms in my suite as our office. I stretched and heard Jo answer.

A second later, she poked her head in my room. Her message got me out of bed in a hurry.

"The front desk says a big group of people is waiting for you downstairs."

I took the fastest shower in recorded history, then the girls and I came down to find more than sixty additional family members waiting for us, with Ramiro at their helm. They all wanted an opportunity to visit the crash site.

"Be right back," Jo said. She ran upstairs to arrange a deal with the helicopter company for three days' rental.

"Good thing we brought that extra money from my sock," I told the girls.

The meetings with families were now held at my hotel. I had some meetings with one family, and sometimes with three families or more. We were busy from early morning till late at night, getting retainers signed left and right. It was like a dream for me.

On our tenth day there, I held the phone as Jo counted retainers for fifty-one decedents.

"Unbelievable!" Tom Jones said during our daily phone call.

I heard Oscar's voice. "Mario, you are the fucking best!"

I was still on the suite phone, and laughing as the girls danced around me.

"We aren't done yet. I think we're going to get some more. I just don't want to push too hard. Not sure how many families these local attorneys have. The local attorneys don't like me very much. Oz, you are going to owe me big time!"

I had no idea what payment to expect from Oscar, but what the fuck. We'd deal with that later. The girls and I had talked about it, and although in front of them, I had projected confidence, in my heart of hearts, I was overwhelmed to have come to a strange country and secured the trust of so many family members.

Oscar had faith in me, and I had faith in Tom Jones. He knew this business. As time passed, I found myself respecting him more and more. I believed he would do his best, and that meant maximizing the compensation for each family we signed.

I called room service and asked for their top vintage. They recommended a red wine from Argentina. When I ordered three bottles, the girls cheered. I guess we all knew we had a celebration on the way. We had not had alcohol or sex since we arrived.

We polished off two bottles and hit my bed.

If you never been in bed with three wild ladies, there are no words I have to explain it. It certainly wasn't the first time, but it always felt like it was, to me. It had been ages since we'd all gotten together. It was a different experience to be at this hotel, though after ten days, even a hotel can start feeling familiar. We had no candles, but there was enough light to see in the dark. I was so very hard, and felt like I could fuck all night. That night, the girls got it in their head that they wouldn't stop till I'd come with each of them. The girls are hella competitive with each other when they want to be. Who am I to complain?

Fantasy is a crazy thing. I had my three, but I guess fantasy is always about who isn't there; pictures of Melina and Sami flashed in my head. I enjoyed Sami, and love Melina, but Jo, Pixie, and Niley were also special to me. They labored next to me, were with me at my beck and call. Even a family couldn't be as close as we were. And family sure as hell didn't roll around and fuck the way we did.

It was midnight. We were still going.

Pixie said, "Do you hear that knocking?"

Jo groaned. I heard her say, "Don't stop."

"You're hearing things," Niley said. Niley was astride me, and it was all I could do to hold still. Pixie and Jo were kind of busy doing something to each other.

I hadn't had my first orgasm, but at Pixie's insistence, I stopped. We all stopped moving and heard nothing but silence, maybe some hotel noises. Niley wiggled her hips, and I groaned aloud. We moved again.

Pixie said, "Be still. There it goes again."

I heard it then. A definite knock at the door.

With all the moans and groans and laughter, it was a wonder that we heard it.

"Maybe it's room service."

"What the fuck? We didn't order anything else," I said.

"I'll get it." Pixie walked out of the bedroom bare-ass naked.

"Grab a robe," Jo yelled.

The light went on in the living room. Niley had moved to peek out the bedroom door, and then got back in the bed. I was between Jo and Niley. Our hands were all over each other when we heard Pixie scream.

I jumped over Niley on my left and landed on my feet next to the bed.

In seconds, a big gorilla stepped into the bedroom. Jo and Niley screamed. He had one hand over Pixie's mouth, and the other held a gun against Pixie's head. He stepped out of the doorway, revealing a second gorilla behind him.

One of them spoke Spanish. "Dress, Mario. You're coming with us." He had a gun too, and it was pointing at me.

"Fuck you," I said.

"I don't think so," gorilla number two said in Spanish. "Maybe you want to see the blood of this little girl all over the room."

"Let her go."

I was contemplating my next move when Pixie bit the gorilla's hand. He slammed her to the floor and kicked her.

I saw this and got furious. I was ready to kill this motherfucker, but two guns were now aimed at me and the girls behind me.

One of the gorillas flicked the switch, and the bedroom lights came on.

My dick went down. Shit like guns and brutality can do that. It sure as hell killed the buzz from the wine.

Gorilla number two saw my boxers on the floor and kicked them and my jeans over to me.

"Cover your fucking ass," he said.

I slipped on the boxers and my jeans. The two assholes were ten feet from me. I only needed to be a little closer to wreak some damage.

"Are you okay, Pixie?" I asked in English. She was on the floor, curled up in a ball. She sat up and crawled toward the bedroom door. I could see she was hurt. A trail of blood leaked from the side of her mouth. I didn't know if it was hers or the guy she'd bitten.

"I'm okay, Mario. Don't do anything stupid, okay?"

"What the fuck you want?" Niley screamed in Spanish.

"I want to fuck you," said one of the gorillas.

"Fuck you," Jo said.

"We come back and fuck all three of you," said the other. He kicked at the corner of Pixie's robe and whistled. Pixie made no effort to cover herself, but glared at him. He wasn't looking at her face.

"No shoes," one of them said to me.

I wanted to thank him. He didn't know what was coming with me barefoot.

"You can't just go with them," Jo said.

"I haven't got much choice." I grinned at her. Not that I felt like laughing, but I wanted to give her confidence.

I took a step towards them. We were out of the bedroom, and into the main room of the suite. That's when Pixie lunged at the leg of the guy who was ogling her.

Both gorillas were looking at her. She threw them both off guard just long enough for me to kick gorilla one in the solar plexus. The gun went flying off in one direction; he went flying in the other, slammed hard into the wall, and then hit the floor. Hard. In passing, I snatched the gun from gorilla two.

Gorilla one was on the floor, struggling for breath. Pixie hopped up and kicked him a couple of times, not that she did any harm. The other one wanted his gun back. I had to convince him of the error of his ways. I slammed his face with the heel of my hand. Maybe more than once. Okay, it was a bunch of times, really fast. I heard teeth crunch, and his nose. Blood flowed. I got the other gun off the floor and gave them both to Jo. Jo stood up, both guns trained on the intruders in the general vicinity of their crotches. She looked awful comfortable with those guns. I was a little surprised.

"I know it's tempting, but better aim at the widest point," I said.

"Sure thing, sweets," she said, raising the angle of the guns toward the center of each guy's chest. "Did I ever mention to you that 'Nando used to like to go shooting? He was a sharpshooter, back in the day. Taught me everything he knew."

Both intruders were pretty helpless.

Pixie was holding on to her stomach, and Niley was a shivering lump on the bed. Calamity Jane was busy, but she was also the only other one standing.

"Jo, open the door," I said.

Jo managed to keep both guns pointing at our unwanted guests as she got the door open.

I pulled the bleeder by his hair and threw him out in the hallway, then came back for the second one.

Jo kicked the door closed. She put the guns on the end table.

"I'm getting our robes," she told Niley. Niley mumbled something back. Her voice was shaking.

"Hey, Jo," I said.

"Yeah?"

"When we get back home, let's go shooting sometime."

She walked into her rooms, laughing. I called the front desk. We heard a commotion in the hall. Within minutes, an army of police stormed the corridor.

The intruders were handcuffed right where they lay on the carpeted hallway. Jo put on her robe before she handed the guns to the local cops and ran a hot bath for Pixie to soak in.

The hotel manager was off duty, but he was at my door thirty minutes later to apologize. He promised a full investigation, and to do something with my hotel bill. He offered to send Pixie to a doctor. Pixie declined.

I remembered the intruder I had thrown out the window of my apartment. Security is worthless, everywhere.

Pixie insisted that the kick wasn't that bad. There was a bruise, but she endured Jo's mothering and came back from her bath filled with good humor. We polished off the third bottle of wine.

"Things happen," I told the girls. "I'm so very sorry. It seems like trouble follows me no matter where I go."

"Mario, don't be silly. This could have happened at home."

"It has happened before. Too many times."

"I'm sorry." I wished there was a magic word I could say to undo things, but of course there never was.

It was my turn to shower. We had decided not to leave Pixie alone, and were going one by one. I had absolutely no evidence on my body that I had been a fight. I was lucky, but felt terrible for Pixie, and worried that she was injured worse than she was letting on. Niley seemed to have recovered, but I knew she had to be thinking how her sister had been shot by someone gunning for me. She didn't show it when she came in the bedroom, wrapped in a towel. And Jo was a rock. She'd taken me by surprise with the Calamity Jane routine. She moved to stand between Pixie and Niley, with her arms draped over their shoulders.

"We're not going to let a couple of dick-weasel fuckwits come between us, are we?"

Pixie let out a little laugh. "Peckerheads."

"Bastards," Niley said.

Pixie looked at Niley in concern. "We gotta work on your vocabulary."

Jo cleared her throat. "Where were we?"

Pixie dived across me, snugging on one side. Jo climbed in more sedately, but not by much.

"I'll tell you," Niley said, dropping her towel. "I was in the middle. I had Mario."

"Bring it on, sister," Pixie said.

I woke up when Jo opened the door for room service. Three trays were rolled into the dining room. The servers set up the dining room table with an assortment of Western-style breakfast foods and some popular Venezuelan dishes normally served for lunch.

The girls wore hotel robes. I was in my boxers.

"No question that last night was intended as a message to scare me away from here," I said, chewing away. "Maybe it was those fucking lawyers behind it."

"Has to be something like that," Niley said.

"Yes, but you don't know for sure who did it. Maybe it was a lawyer that wants in and didn't get in at all, like that loser Hugo," Pixie said, with her mouth full.

"Scary goons, those two," Jo said.

"I was thinking they were more gorilla than goon. Big and fat," I said. "Without the guns, they were nothing." I put down the cheese-filled arepa I was holding and stared at Pixie.

"Pix, you did great. Had you not distracted them, I'm not sure what my move would have been. Are you hurting at all?" I asked.

Pixie smiled. "I'm fine."

I know we're both halfway through our twenties, but she grew up hard, and her eyes had seen so much more than most people our age. She looked like a little girl this morning, with her hair in two high little pigtails, and a ring of milk around her lips.

"Maybe we should pack and leave," Niley suggested.

"No fucking way," Jo said.

I looked at Jo.

"And you," I said to Jo. "Fucking Calamity Jane."

Jo laughed.

"If you're worried, Niley, you can go home. In fact, maybe the three of you should leave. You can take the retainers we have to the office. I'll stay here with Juan for a little longer to see if the families thinking about it may sign."

"I'm not going home by myself," Niley said, a little uncertainly, "and I'm not leaving any of you."

"Of course not," Pixie said, reaching over and patting Niley's hand. "We're staying. All of us."

"Of course," Niley said.

"I'm going to eat you tonight," Pixie promised.

"Stop it," I said. "Let's plan the day."

"That's what I was doing," Pixie said.

Niley turned the color of the red guava paste in the pastry she'd just finished.

Juan called. Ramiro was on the way with two families. It was eight in the morning. Jo barely had time to arrange for a conference room. We decided to have room service in attendance.

The two decedents were represented by nine family members who came with Juan and Ramiro. Most of them were milling outside the room we were using.

Ramiro said, "Lupe and Sonja lost their husbands. They signed contracts with the local attorneys, but they want to change to the lawyer in the Los Angeles."

I wanted to say ouch, but managed to keep my mouth shut. Poaching is not something I do, but when clients leave another firm to come to me on their own, how could I turn them away? People change their mind. It just happens. This happened sometimes with my car cases, but this wasn't a car case. If the local attorneys turned out to be the two jerks who wouldn't even shake hands with me, it could be a dangerous move. Especially if they were the ones behind the gorillas.

We were standing in the doorway to the conference room. I moved aside, and Juan escorted in the two widows and showed them to a seat. No one sat down yet. We all were looking, measuring each other. I shook Lupe's hand.

Lupe was older. Her hair was curly, touched with gray, and cut short. She was dressed very well, with expensive pearls around her neck and ears, and gold bangles on one arm. The bangles were similar to some I'd bought for my aunt last Christmas, and they had been very expensive. She was wearing a scent, too, one I didn't recognize. It smelled like money.

Sonja was younger and much less well-off. She seemed a little anxious, but also was determined and decisive. Definitely a college girl. As I shook her hand and leaned in, the only scent I detected was some fruity shampoo. Her only jewelry was a plain gold wedding ring on her left hand. She wore her dark hair long and straight, parted down the middle. Her clothes were those of a co-ed: well-worn jeans, a sleeveless cotton shirt, canvas tennis shoes. Both the jeans and shirt and even her tennis shoes and shoelaces looked like they'd been dyed black. She was thin, except around her middle. I realized she was expecting. The baby would be good for her case. I pictured her walking into a courtroom a year or two from now, a baby in her arms.

Jo and Niley shook hands as well. Pixie touched Ramiro's hand and smiled at him, then took both of Juan's hands in her own and smiled at him. Pixie had to be in pain, but she was hiding it well. My first thought was that she was incorrigible, but then she took Juan's left hand, and Sonja's right, forming a little chain of connection. I have to admit that Pixie's behavior is often unfathomable. Her formal manners are not good and her curses would make a sailor blush. But she has a physical perception, some kind of kinesthetic awareness that cuts through to the heart of matters.

"What is the name of the firm you signed with?"

They confirmed it was Gustavo and Lario. I worried that there would be repercussions.

"Do they know you want to dismiss them?"

"Not a word from them since I signed the contract," said Sonja.

"Same with me," Lupe said.

"In the United States, you have the right to change lawyers. I don't know what the law is here about contracts."

"I don't know the law either," said Ramiro, "but these two families don't want them. They want you."

I could hardly turn them away. I looked at Sonja and Lupe.

"Are you sure you want to sign with my attorneys?"

Sonja nodded immediately. She was a girl who knew what she wanted. Lupe hesitated. She had the air of someone new to making decisions. I was guessing in her life, her husband had made all of their decisions. It could be a problem, but it turned out not to be. She nodded too.

Pixie let go of Juan to hand each of the ladies a tissue. Both were openly crying. She was still holding hands with Sonja but let go as Juan pulled out the chairs for the widows to sit. Niley, Jo, and I took our seats across the table from them. I don't like to be standing over a client while they are making decisions. It is too intimidating a posture.

Pixie, still standing, moved behind both widows. She put a hand on each of their shoulders and leaned forward, her head level with theirs, and touched her cheek first to Sonja's cheek on her left, then Lupe's on her right. Lupe seemed startled, but her left hand grabbed hold of Pixie's fingers like a lifeline.

I turned to Jo. "Sign them up."

"My pleasure," Jo replied in Spanish.

Pixie and Niley chatted with the two widows like they were family.

"I'd like my brother-in-law to be here," Sonja said.

I asked Lupe if she wanted us to bring anyone in, and she nodded, asking for Rudolpho. Ramiro brought in two young men, one who was Lupe's grown son, and the other who was Sonja's husband's elder brother. Both were family members who had encouraged this change of lawyers. I got up and stepped aside to confer briefly with Ramiro and Juan as Jo filled out the retainer forms, then I took information about the decedents and heirs. The whole process took a little over an hour. I stepped out to the lobby and the hotel operator put a call in for me to Tom Jones.

"They want to jump ship and go with us," I told him.

"Fuck yes. Sign them," Tom said. "We'll give the lawyers something for their time if they raise a lot of fuss. It's only been a few days. What the fuck could they have done to earn any fees? You sign them. I'll work it out when you get back with the retainers. What do you know about them so far?"

"Lupe looks like her husband might have been a professional. She seems well-to-do, and has several grown children. Sophia is college-age, and expecting. I don't know yet if there are more children. No idea of her husband's income yet."

"Fantastic work."

"There's something else." I hesitated. I really didn't want to bring it up, but it was something I ought to mention. "Last night, a couple of thugs paid a visit to my hotel room. It wasn't anything I couldn't handle. I booted them into the hall. The local cops collected them and hauled them away. I have absolutely no proof who sent these apes, but I have a gut feeling that it's the attorneys who represent these two families. I bet they are pissed that I'm getting so many of the families."

"Trust your gut. I trust your street smarts. Be careful. Maybe it's time to wrap it up," Tom said.

"I have families on the fence who are thinking about signing. I want to give them a few more days to make up their minds. Who knows? I may get more families."

"Be sure you call in tomorrow. I'll bring Oscar up to speed."

"Tell him not to worry about me." I chuckled. "It is the girls' welfare I am worried about." I'd have to keep them right next to me for whatever time we remained here.

"Give me the name of the two attorneys you suspect and the name of their firm."

"Gustavo and Lario."

I gave him what little information I had on them and returned to the conference room, where the widows had already signed the retainers.

I felt better, except when thoughts of last night snuck in my head. Karma can be a bitch. I only worried about the girls getting hurt in the crossfire. As for me, I was ready.

I went to the desk and asked if they knew what the police had done with our attackers. They didn't know. I made a mental note to have Jo look into it. I hoped they'd locked up those guys and thrown away the key.

We had ordered room service and had salads at the girls' table. Afterwards, we settled into my dining room that we were using as an office. Niley turned on the television and switched through the four channels on the hotel TV.

"Hold it there," Jo said. "That's from a novel."

"That thing you did in the conference room this morning. It was a great move," I told Pixie. "Getting on their side of the table so they didn't feel alone and outnumbered. How did you know?"

Pixie shrugged. "They were hurting," she said.

I wanted to ask her more, but the phone rang.

I had to get up to reach the phone closest to me, which was across the small room on an end table. It was annoying that the cord was short, tethering me the sofa bed. I missed the extra-long cords I had on my home lines. I picked up, expecting it to be Tom, but instead, someone on the line began yelling at the top of his lungs, before I even got the speaker to my ear.

He yelled furiously in rapid-fire Spanish. I held the phone slightly away from my ear, smiling across the room at Jo, who was watching with curiosity. I gave her a thumbs up and she returned to doing whatever she had been doing. If the room's television hadn't been blaring out an episode of the *Doña Bárbara* series, the girls would have heard, for sure.

"You fucking Americans. You come to our country and bribe our poor families with money and helicopter rides to get signatures on contracts that give you permission to rob them of their compensation. It isn't enough that you already have most of the families. Now you are taking clients away from my partner and me. You are a greedy son of a bitch. I will not let you get away with this."

I did not get a word in. The fucker hung up on me. I could feel my ears go hot, which probably meant I was flushed, and revealing my anger. I turned away, facing a window, so the girls could only see my back, and tried to get calm.

"Sure, thanks," I said to the empty line, and I hung up the phone.

I waited for them to ask about the phone business, but they didn't. I realized I wasn't sure who had called, Lario or Gustavo. For that matter, someone may have called on their behalf. The fucker ranting his lunatic head off had never given his name.

We had dinner in one of the hotel restaurants, La Vista, which was located on the top floor. It was a very high-end eatery, and many of the diners were dressed up. We were in denim. The girls wore jeans well, all having what I call a fine jeans ass.

Our round table was set against the wall, with windows wrapped around us, showcasing a panoramic view of the nightscape. The smaller, older buildings disappeared in the dark. Yellow headlights stopped and started along the busy streets, and the taller buildings glittered white. The restaurant view was more spectacular than the one from our room, even better than the balcony.

I ordered the Argentinian wine we had drunk the night before. Before the food arrived, we went through three bottles. Except for my attack of conscience because I don't like to keep secrets from the girls, I think we were all feeling good. I never mentioned the call I had gotten. Why should I let the girls suffer more anxiety? They didn't act or behave apprehensive, but they had to be after that scare the night before.

I was forcibly reminded of Hugo's attempts on my life. After the call, I was more certain than ever that the apes who attacked us had been sent by Lario and Gustavo. The thing that I found perplexing was that they had wanted me to go with them. If it was a warning that was intended, then they could have warned me and been done with it. One ape would still have his teeth and nose, and possibly Pixie would not have been tossed on the floor and kicked.

"A fuck for your thoughts," Niley said.

"Make it two."

"Three," the girls all chimed in, and looked at me expectantly.

No way was I saying what I was thinking.

"Jo, check up on what the police did with our visitors from yesterday. I'd like to know if they're in jail."

"Can do," she said. A shadow passed over her face. "You're not worried about them, are you?"

I didn't want to lie. "It can't hurt to keep track of them."

"Ditto that," Pixie said.

I changed the subject. "We need to start thinking of going home soon. We've gotten what we're going to get. I don't want to take cases away from those two jerks. We wouldn't do it back home with car cases, and we're not doing it here."

"We're ready when you are, boss," Jo said.

"I'll give these families who are thinking about it another couple days max, but in the meantime, let's wind it down. Let's check on available flights."

The girls brightened. Maybe they were getting homesick and hadn't let on.

Jo used the room key to my suite. I held the door open for the girls to walk in before me. Just as I followed the girls in, the hair on my arms stood up. Halfway in, I could feel someone there. I smelled beer breath, sweat, and aftershave that wasn't mine.

I swung my arm to the right, blind, and connected hard with somebody. I tangled my hand in his shirt, jerked hard. He fell in my direction and I tossed him across the hallway, his body slamming into a load-bearing column between wallpapered sections of the hall. He went down on his hands and knees, leaving a bloody spot on the pillar. I always told the girls that when they were attacked, their goal was to run to safety. But I'm not in danger of becoming a victim. I made a move toward him and felt a sharp pain in my back, once, twice. Someone moved behind me. Heavy tread, not one of the girls. There were two of them. Back in the hall, I kicked the door shut, yelling for the girls to lock the door. I whipped around and got a good look at a face that was swollen and bruised, but one I recognized as belonging to one of the apes I'd handled before. I looked for the gun I'd been shot with, expecting a .38 or something, but it was a dart gun. Their faces loomed strangely, like a view in a fisheye lens.

I said, "What the fuck?" Or at least I think I said it. The lights went out.

Chapter 8
December 1975
Storm

Everything was dark, but I knew I wasn't in the hotel hall. The hall didn't vibrate like the floor of a plane. I was definitely in flight on the floor of a small aircraft. I squeezed my eyes open. Pitch black. Face felt like raw hamburger. I could feel the vibration of the propellers, hear the roar of the engines. I tried moving, but pain and dark washed over me and took me out.

I woke up to being hauled around and in pain. I staggered into a roundhouse kick and heard someone yell in pain before I passed out. No idea who it was. Dizzying light. Couldn't keep my eyes open, then I was tossed into a vehicle. More movement, voices, but couldn't make sense of the words. Passage of time, dim awareness of wakening several times, someone dragging me with a hard grip under each arm. Awake again, dragged across somewhere with fresh breeze and bright light. Awake again, listening to a loud voice speaking Spanish. Cold, hard surface beneath me. No one was touching me, holding me up, or dragging me. I held very still. My mind was registering a lot of things. I wasn't in the hotel. I wasn't in a plane. I was not in a car. I was in a dimly lit room in a building, with no idea of the time or place. I barely flexed a muscle, and my whole body clenched in pain. Every part of me hurt like hell. I didn't even try to open my eyes. The apes were standing above me, talking. No, yelling. They were arguing. I heard two, no, three voices. Tried to make sense of them.

"Fraco! Fredo! How much do you think he's worth looking like this? You fucking imbeciles!"

"Patrón, he knocked my teeth out. I was just giving him back some of what he gave me." I recognized his voice. Ape one. The one I had dubbed Toothless. I'd done some damage to his dental work at the hotel.

"They will want to see him. Look at his eyes. I should shoot you!"

"Patrón, I'm sorry."

I recognized that voice as belonging to the second ape. I didn't recognize the voice of their patrón. I wanted to move, but they were still standing around me. The pain was intense.

I felt a foot nudge me, and as I was rolled to my side, I tried moving my hands, but they were bound, dead weight. I thought I might pass out from the agony. Maybe I even did. I don't know. Now I was on my side, facing a wall. I squinted, and I could barely see it. The concrete floor reeked of urine. I didn't know if it was mine. They were still talking. Their boss wanted them to untie me.

"Patrón, we can't untie him. This man is an animal. He'll kill us."

"That's your problem. Get him cleaned up. Feed him. I'll be back, and he better look good enough for the pictures I need to take of him. He looks half dead. He better not get all dead."

The voice of the man talking came closer. I lay perfectly still.

"Get him off the floor and on the cot. He's still out. That fucking elephant trank you shot him with works for days on a human. Take advantage and get him cleaned up."

"It's been four days since we got him. I don't believe he's unconscious anymore."

"So what? You prefer I shoot you and bury you with him?"

"No, Patrón. I'll keep the door locked, and one of us will have a gun on him."

"Have you given him water?"

"Patrón, *si, seguro que si.* Four or five times a day and more."

I heard the patrón grunt. Whoever he was, these apes seemed fearful of him.

"Have Valita get you beef steaks from my freezer and apply to his face, especially his eyes. When I get back, he better be on his feet and ready for pictures."

"Whatever you say, Patrón."

"You better not kill him or hurt him, pendejos."

"Of course not. We understand. When will you return from Caracas, Patrón?"

"A week, maybe ten days, maybe before. Don't fail me!"

Who was this guy holding me for ransom? Was it one of the lawyers? I heard footsteps, and someone left. Maybe they all left. It was awfully quiet. It must have been all of them. I was alone. For a while, I lay still, waiting for the apes to make their move. My mouth was a desert. I remembered the wine I'd had with the girls. So thirsty. I couldn't remember anyone giving me water, but after four days, I suppose I'd be dead of dehydration if I hadn't had water. The only muscles I moved were my eyelids, and even they hurt. I opened my eyes, and found myself on my side, still facing the wall. My hands were tied painfully behind my back, useless. My feet were tied. I ran my tongue over my teeth. No gaps or breaks. From this view, the room was a concrete box. Concrete floor, concrete wall. I didn't know if it was day or night. I tried to be positive. At someone's funeral, I had heard some priest say every day was a gift. But if that was true, then today was coal.

My bound hands under me were numb. This position on my side was killing me but only slightly better than on my back. I rolled forward to my stomach. The air was muggy with a strong smell of coffee. The concrete was cool beneath me. By bracing myself against the wall, I managed to inch to a sitting position. Once I was sitting up, I saw a cot in front of me with a thin mattress like something out of a prison. From the corner I was in to the far wall was a long distance. I was in an empty warehouse, maybe sixty thousand square feet. High ceilings. A couple of florescent tubes built into the ceiling were off. A row of small windows near the roofline provided light, and the beams that came through were so bright they looked solid. When I tried looking at them, I had to shut my eyes. A small shaving mirror was tacked to the wall across the way, along with a wall clock. The security door to my left opened. I had been leaning against the wall, but straightened up.

That's how the gorillas found me when they walked in.

When they saw I had moved, that I was conscious, they took their guns out and pointed them in my direction.

"Go ahead. Shoot me so your patrón castrates you! Wrong, he's not going to castrate you. He's going to bury you with me, so I can beat you both for eternity."

"If you pull anything, we will hurt you without putting any marks on you. Patrón will never know." They walked slowly toward me.

"How are the girls? You didn't hurt them, did you?"

"Ah, the girls," Toothless said, nastily.

"*Cállate, carajo* Fraco! Shut the fuck up," Fredo snarled at his partner. "If you get him started, I'll beat your ass."

"Tell me about the girls, and just maybe I'll let you live for a few more days."

Toothless laughed nastily.

Fredo said, "The girls we didn't bother. You give us trouble or pull any of that fancy fighting on us, and the girls will pay for it."

"Touch them, and for sure I will kill you."

They laughed.

Toothless was still pretty battered. His face was varying shades of purple. I hadn't hit his eyes, but I'd obviously broken his nose. That causes black eyes like his, when the swelling goes down and the colors worsen before they get better.

"We are going to untie you, and you have this huge place all to yourself. Outside is a shower and a toilet. As long as you keep your fucking hands to yourself, we will not hurt you."

"Yeah," Toothless said. "You aren't worth much if you look dead. And you stink. You're going outside for a shower."

"Motherfucker!" I was seething.

"You want to remain tied, or what?"

I caved. "Untie me."

Toothless held a gun to my head. The other cut me loose. He was creaking around like an old man, so I had done some damage to him too. The stench of urine was terrible, and it was mine. As bad as it was, I was glad at least it wasn't from somebody else. My hands and feet were so numb I could barely stand. They got on either side and hooked me under the arms, dragging me outside. I remembered them doing this before.

The heat hit me immediately. The sun baked straight through my shirt like a broiler. I looked back and saw that the warehouse I'd been housed in looked like it was made of solid concrete. A couple of main houses were off in the distance. The area was surrounded by a wall of tropical trees and foliage thick enough to call it a jungle. The sky was a sharp blue with bright light that was cutting straight through to my skull. I smelled the output of a gas combustion engine, but more than that, I smelled green. A different green from a mowed lawn. Trees. In the distance, a dog barked.

I could hear birds. The buildings weren't like anything I'd seen in Caracas. More like ranch houses, only bigger, lots of timber and stucco and tile. I heard a distant motor power up, but it didn't sound like a car. More like a compressor. The clearing also included a landing strip. I couldn't tell how long it was. Too many trees.

"Get this straight. Any funny moves or whatever it is you do, I will shoot you. And don't think about running. The only thing between here and Caracas are snakes and hungry wild animals waiting to feed on you."

I wanted to taunt him, but didn't take the opportunity. I had to wait until I was capable of some of those funny moves he was referring to.

Pipes emerged from a rusted pump to a couple of houses on the property, and one hose went to the outdoor shower that was my destination, probably twenty feet from the building I'd been housed in. I heard the pump motor kick in and smelled gasoline from the compressor powering it. A couple of distant gas generators hooked up to somewhere unseen kicked in. The bright light hurt my eyes, and I moved my unbound hands to shade them. I was bruised. When I touched my face, it felt strange. Swollen. Eyes were practically swelled shut. My hands were useless. I don't know how long I'd been tied. Even washed out from the sunshine, I could tell they were purple. I flexed them to get the blood moving.

I was glad to see the outdoor shower, even as primitive as it was. That was a tropical forest out there. I was really in the boondocks. I had a memory of lying on the floor of a plane. Maybe someone had poured some water in my mouth. I wasn't sure. The apes were crouched by the pump, trying to figure something out.

"Take your clothes off and get in the shower."

I struggled to get the clothes off. I couldn't manage the buttons.

The sun was burning down, and my back and the top of my head were steaming hot. My whole body was hot. I was overdressed. In heat like this, being naked would be overdressed. I fondly remembered my air conditioning at home. My fingers were awkward.

"Did you understand? Take off your clothes and get in the fucking shower. We sure as hell aren't washing you."

"Sure thing, Toothless," I said back. Toothless, the one called Fraco, snarled at me. I laughed.

I looked up and saw a woman staring at me. I had not noticed her approach. It was too bright for me to make out her features. She could have been any age. She was of average height, not as tall as the girls at home, but she had a shapely silhouette. She reached up and undid my buttons. My hands fell to my sides.

"Thanks," I said, in English.

She made a tsk tsk noise and grabbed one of my hands, turning it over, looking at the marks the ropes had left on my arms. She muttered something. I think it was 'pendejos.'

"Look out for him, Valita. He's dangerous. He'll bust your ass," they said.

"Mind your own business," she said. "I do my job. You worry about yours."

"I wouldn't hurt a woman," I told her.

She shrugged, not seeming to care one way or another.

"You got a toilet I can use? *Los servicios*?"

She pointed to a battered-looking portable toilet some distance away, in this clearing but well away from the buildings, and close to the edge of the forest-line. It had once been blue, but the sun had bleached parts of it to some paler color. I staggered toward it, a long walk in the shape I was in, and used it. While I was inside, one of the apes yelled, "We're watching you. If you run, we get to play target practice." When I came out, the gorillas yelled at the woman to back off from me. They cussed at her, and she cussed back. She didn't seem to like them any more than I did, but then, even their boss didn't seem to hold them in esteem.

She helped me pull off the shirt but backed off to let me unfasten my jeans. I kicked them off. I was going commando, but my nakedness didn't seem to phase her.

I still couldn't make out her features, but after the outhouse, she smelled pretty good. She took my jeans and shirt.

"I will wash for you and bring back," she said. "Patrón wants you to be clean."

She handed me a bar of Ivory soap that reminded me of when I was growing up. Aunt Carmen used it to wash clothes that she didn't put in the washing machine.

She walked off, holding the clothes like they were rotted road kill covered in dog vomit. I was a little embarrassed at their condition. When I turned to inspect the shower, I caught her staring at my naked body.

The water came from a hose connected to a rusty, gas-generated pump that looked a hundred years old. The shower was hung with a camouflage-patterned shower curtain affixed to a circular rod, and reminded me of the outdoor showerhead at the YMCA in LA, where they made you shower before they let you in the pool. I stepped inside, expecting bare earth or mud, but there was a base made of wooden slats over a bed of sand. The showerhead was a couple of inches under seven feet, so I fit below it.

The showerhead arched from a seven-foot tall pipe supported by a wooden frame that stopped halfway up the pipe. I turned a lever, and then the faucet, and got the water running. Warm water came out, and gradually got freezing cold, pumping directly from some underground well. It could not have felt any better. I stood in the spray and drank my fill, letting the water numb my burning face. The water tasted strongly of minerals, but it was cold and wet. I might end up with Montezuma's revenge, but it was better than dying of thirst. The spray stung as it hit my torn skin, but it carried away the heat and eased my swollen eyes. I used that bar of soap as though it was the expensive stuff that Sami kept in the bathroom of my guest room in her home. I lathered up twice. After who knows how many days spent unconscious in my own filth, I needed it. The cool water got me as comfortable as I could be under the circumstances. I wasn't coming out until someone came to get me.

The woman returned, and yelled in Spanish, "This is for you."

I turned off the water. There was a discolored tin dish clumsily drilled into the wood for the soap, but I wasn't leaving it for anyone else to use. I stashed the Ivory under a corner of the wooden slats, and left the shower reluctantly. She handed me a pair of khaki cut-offs and headed back where she had come from.

"Thanks, Valita."

She looked startled that I used her name, but did not reply.

I put on the shorts. They were short, worn, and tattered, but otherwise fit. I was dripping wet but could feel the water steam off me as I stood there. No need for a towel. I already wanted to return to the flowing cold water.

My hands were feeling better, almost like normal. My feet felt intact. I needed to plan an escape, but Toothless and Fredo didn't give me much time to get my bearings. They herded me back into the concrete prison and left. The wrought-iron gate clanged and rattled as they locked it. When they were out of sight, I put both hands on the bars and shook them, hard. It was impregnable, and I was without tools, and saw no way to dismantle it. I headed for the far side of the warehouse to examine my face in the five-inch shaving mirror. I could not see my whole face at once. Probably a good thing. My eyes looked like Joe Frazier's after he lost the World Heavyweight title to George Foreman. I looked like I'd gone a round with Sugar Ray Leonard. My nose wasn't broken, and there was no split lip, but my eyes were like two squashed blueberry muffins. I was looking grizzled and in need of a razor.

The iron entry was close to where the cot was located. The door was not solid but an ironwork concoction of curved bars like a gate, a dead-bolted entrance intended to keep persons out or property in. It was wrapped with a heavy chain and secured with two padlocks. The only way in or out was this wide single gate. The windows were about twenty feet straight up.

That first night, I was startled after it got dark, when a kid called me to the gate. He handed me a steaming cup of coffee through the iron bars, three quart-sized jugs of water, and three pieces of pan dulce. From somewhere behind him, I heard a low growl, disembodied in the night.

"Provecho," the kid said and started to walk away.

"Gracias, kid. What's your name?"

"Salazaar. They call me Ratón," he said, disappearing in the darkness.

In and outside of the warehouse was pitch black, except I could make out some light from some distant houses across the compound. I could hear a distant generator, and every so often the generator near the well kicked on. The warehouse light switches were on the wall by the door, but I preferred the dark, where I could see out and not be seen.

Cosmo had not taught me any tricks to open padlocks and cut chains. I parked my ass right next to the gate, drank the hot coffee, and ate the three pieces of pastry. It was a real treat. I never heard or saw the apes. I made my way to the bed, and after a long delay, finally went to sleep on the bare mattress. I was as secure in that warehouse as they believed I was.

Any time I wasn't locked behind that gate, a gun was on me. I could measure the passage of time by my facial hair, although since I'd never actually cultivated a beard before, I had no prior notion of the growth rate, except it was pretty fast. I had a good start on a beard. Valita had cleaned and pressed my clothes and returned them to me. I thanked her for them, but stashed them under the cot, and lived in the cut-offs. I took them off in the shower and washed them with the Ivory soap, rinsed them, then put them back on wet. They dried quickly and helped me keep cool. Inside the warehouse, it wasn't unbearable, as long as I sat on the cool concrete.

Valita or Ratón brought me food. They were usually accompanied by a huge, fearsome German shepherd, which my jailors avoided. I could tell the dog hated my captors as much as I did; but he didn't like me much better. Toothless and Fredo were the only ones to let me out for the outhouse. In the morning, Valita handed me a piece of steak for my face. She held the meat to my eyes, showing how I should apply it, and for how long. It was very cold, no doubt right out of a freezer just as the Patrón had said. I lay down and applied it to my eyes, wondering if it would actually help. It was disgusting, but until it defrosted, it made a decent ice pack, at least until the sweltering temperature made it too warm.

Each day had a routine. At lunch, Valita brought coffee, a bowl of beans, some kind of stew, and a couple of quart-sized milk jugs freshly filled with well water. That was when I saw the dog in the daylight for the first time. He really was huge. He had long hair for a shepherd and was mostly black with touches of tan on his tail and lower legs. His eyes were black and intense, constantly at attention. He was on guard, watching for something, eager to go after it. His teeth leapt into a ready snarl at the smallest provocation. He was angry at anyone who dared come near Valita or Ratón. He did not like Valita coming so close to the gate that held me in.

"Stay back," she said. "He bites." I hung back as far as I could, and the dog attacked the gate in frustration that he could not get at me. She called him Lobo, chided him, told him to back off, and gingerly handed me my meal. The dog also accompanied Ratón, so I saw him several times a day. Several meals passed before he would accept the bits of food I saved for him; but by the time I was getting frozen meat twice a day to put on my face, Lobo and I were pretty good friends. He had no objection to disposing of defrosted steak.

The first day, I passed on Valita's stew but chugged down all the water and asked for more. I hung on to the coffee till it was room temperature and drank it down. It was bitter and so robust it didn't need a cup. It could have stood on its own. Venezuelan coffee, I guess. Four times a day, Toothless and Fredo trained guns on me as they walked me to the outhouse.

Being kidnapped is dull business. I was bored with nothing to do. During the day, I jogged around the warehouse. Jogging was never my thing, but there was little else to do. I came up with different workouts, but it was a while before I could attempt them. On the first day, after a mere three sit-ups, my face ached and I was drenched in sweat.

Every chance I got, I took a shower. I usually managed four showers daily, as long as I could keep from antagonizing my jailers too much. It wasn't just for the cleanliness, though that was a factor. It was hot, and I got ripe. It was also tactical. When I was outside, I would scan the area for whatever was happening. Look at the landing strip for a plane or chopper. Look at the houses for signs of activity. Check out what the laborers were doing, building, cleaning, whatever. They were too far away from where I was for me to get a good look at them or them at me. Twice a day when Valita or Ratón brought food, I was as polite as humanly possible. I also cultivated my acquaintance with Lobo. If I ever got loose, I didn't want him to gnaw off my leg.

I noticed Ratón and Valita's accents were different from the lawyers', and even from the guards'. They were clearly locals. Ratón was a talkative boy, and he made conversation with me.

"Valita told me your name for Fraco," Ratón said. "I told the workers." He grinned.

The nickname stuck, and everyone was now calling Fraco 'Toothless,' which I found very entertaining.

After a few days, even Valita smiled at me and carried on short conversations. When Valita smiled, it was like a light shining in a dark room; but I gathered she did not often have anything to smile about. She didn't warn me about Lobo anymore. I started off finicky and wary of whatever meat might be in those stews, but after days of only beans, I took to eating whatever she brought. Valita added a night snack, so I got something to eat three times a day, plus she started adding extra fruit, guava or mango and sometimes both.

Valita was not cute. Little girls and puppies and kittens are cute. Valita had an elemental look to her. She was primitive, and powerful, and womanly. She had full lips, and eyes so deep I could fall into them. A woman like that belonged to someone. I wondered who. Although Ratón was nice to me, it was Valita's visits I looked forward to. I am a fucking flirt. I guess it wouldn't surprise anyone that even in my present situation, I was flirting with Valita. I got this way-out feeling that maybe she was also flirting with me.

"You should be healing faster," she said. "You are not putting the meat on right."

She instructed me time and again how to apply the frozen steak. I suppose it stayed frozen longer than ice cubes in an ice pack, but I don't know how much good it did.

"I'll try harder," I said with good humor. I didn't tell her that, on the first day, I'd passed out with the steak on my face or that I wished I could cook the fucker and eat it.

In this heat, water was a big thing. Each time she came with food, Valita brought a couple quart milk jugs of well water. I'd always know when she was coming because I could hear her using the hose to fill the jugs. I squirrelled away the jugs, and would take them with me on outhouse trips and fill them from the hose. After a few days, I had half a dozen of them. The water wasn't just for drinking; it was for keeping cool. On every outhouse trip, after I filled the jugs with well water,

I stood in the shower as long as they would let me. I was glad the warehouse had no john, because I lived for the trips outside. If they came to let me out and I still had water stashed, no problem. I'd empty it, pouring what was left over my head. It went lukewarm after half an hour, anyway, so I was always clattering around, re-filling every chance I got. I must have sweated out most of it, because otherwise I'd be peeing all the time. When one of the workmen left a bucket in the vicinity of the warehouse, I snagged it. I didn't bring it inside, because I knew my jailors. A piss bucket would be an excuse for them to quit escorting me outside. I angled the bucket in range of the gate. If they were late and I had to go, I could always aim outside for the bucket.

Toothless unlocked the gate. I headed for the outhouse, my arms full of water jars, my jailers trailing as usual. I heard them talking behind me, something I normally ignored, but it was a hailstorm of cussing. I turned to look toward the house for the source of their disturbance and saw Lobo bounding in our direction like some saber-toothed canine out of prehistory. I dropped the jars on the grass. I froze, not knowing what he would do. He'd never seen me not behind a gate. I wouldn't say exactly that I was afraid. I just didn't want to harm the dog my only two friends held in such high esteem. He launched himself from yards away. His mouth was open, his tongue lolling out, his heavy, wavy coat flapping in a breeze of his own making, his ears back, teeth poised. He put his feet up, nailing me in my solar plexus like he'd been taking karate from Cosmo. Rammed me at full speed. He and I were both on two feet, eye to eye. Lobo dug his claws into my shoulders, and got busy covering my face with slobber. Toothless and Fredo, had their guns trained not on me, but the dog. They went from sheer terror to humor. Hell, they were laughing their asses off. They came up to gloat. Came too close for Lobo, who sensed them coming and looked over his shoulder. Lobo changed his demeanor. I swear that dog inhaled, his teeth popped out, and he grew a foot. He made a one-eighty-degree turn. His ears were perked, his tail arched back and stiff, and his fur stood out like he was inflated more than his recommended PSI. His bridgework gleamed like some zoo-kept predator. He growled. He snarled. He glanced back at me, then put himself between me and them. Gave me the kind of look Aunt Carmen used to, when the bus took a turn too fast, and she'd put her arm over me so I didn't go flying off the seat. When he looked at me, I could read him just as clear as any human. It was "Hey man, no worries. I got this. I'm opening a can of whoop-ass on these yahoos."

Toothless and Fredo took a few steps back. They were about to shit themselves. Lobo crouched and advanced a little more for every step they took back, till they were against the wall of the warehouse. I could have walked away, but I still didn't have transportation.

Toothless said, "Shoot it!"

Fredo yelled back, "You shoot it!"

"I'm not gonna be the one who kills the *jefa's* dog."

My jailers had a dilemma.

I didn't get to see their solution, because Ratón was there. He walked up casually, put his hand out to me. Good grip for a kid. He was stronger than he looked, but didn't try to squeeze my hand off.

"You okay?"

I nodded.

He dimpled up, then hid his grin, and called Lobo in a sharp voice.

"Come. Sit."

Lobo stepped beside Ratón, gave me a lick on the arm, and sat.

I told Ratón, "I'm guessing he doesn't like a break in his supply chain of raw beef."

"Nah, he likes you."

He turned toward the house. Lobo gave me a glance again, like "Sorry, dude. Catch you later," and followed.

Toothless waited till he was far enough away, and yelled at Ratón's back, "Get that man-eater out of here before I shoot him."

I turned around, used the outhouse, then came back to gather up the water bottles to fill them, following up with a shower that was twice as long as usual. Toothless and Fredo didn't say a word.

A week or so later, they had their revenge. I stepped in the shower and saw something move on the wooden slats. A coiled snake, ready to spring. I didn't know what kind of fucking snake it was, but I knew from their laughter that the apes had put it there. I almost jumped out of my skin, but in a single move, I hit the ground and grabbed the snake by its head. It was a long snake that swung as I gripped it. I was double thankful in that moment; first and foremost for Cosmo's training that kept my reflexes sharp, and second for Pélon's brother who had been a snake nut, and had taught all the neighborhood boys the safe way to hold a snake. Not that my aunt thought there was a right way, after I'd done my share of scaring her with whatever constrictor was living at Pélon's. As a kid, I'd been no angel and had suffered the smacks from the Sunday school nuns' rulers, and I had callouses on my knees from crawling up the church aisles to give penance to prove it.

Once I had him, I wasn't scared. I ran out of the shower with it in hand. I ran at the two apes that were about twenty feet away from the shower. They looked at me like I was Death himself. They were transfixed with terror and forgot for a second entirely about their guns. Their eyes got big, and their jaws dropped. The snake's mouth gaped open, fangs and tongue working. I came close to shoving the snake in Toothless' face, but when Fredo cocked his gun, I tossed the snake vaguely toward the wild vegetation. I could have snapped it like a rope and its neck would have broken. But now at least one of us was getting away. It took off making tracks from the three of us, into the jungle. It had already disappeared by the time Fredo remembered he had a gun, and he pointed it toward the jungle and fired a couple of times, swearing.

"It was a joke," Toothless said, laughing.

The shots had drawn the attention of some of the workers, and a couple of them came running to the clearing we were in. Most of them looked like they were indigenous Indians, probably living in the huts they had built themselves on the far perimeter of the clearing.

"Snake!" Toothless yelled. "*Una serpiente.*" And they all went back to what they were doing.

"I should kill you both." I said.

I went back to the shower, bare-ass naked, dick swinging. Valita was watching from afar. I was sure I felt her smile touch me.

That night, Valita brought me the coffee, water, and pan dulce. It was dark, but I could see her smile as she handed me what she had brought. I tossed Lobo his piece of defrosted steak, and he wagged his tail before bolting it down and lying down on the path.

"I brought you papaya and pears," she said, handing me the fruit.

"Valita, thank you."

"You are very brave, mister."

"My name is Mario."

"You speak perfect Spanish. Where are you from?" she asked.

"California."

The bars were not in parallel like jail bars, but they served the same purpose: keeping me inside. I gripped the bars and shook the door. It did not budge. She touched my hand. I snapped to attention. My heart raced, and my skin hungered. My body felt like a woman had not touched me for years.

"You are so young and handsome. You must be very rich."

"I'm not rich," I said. "I was working in Caracas and they got me with a tranquilizer gun."

"If you are not rich, I don't understand why you were brought here. I'm sorry for talking about this." She started to walk away.

"Valita. I know you can get in big trouble, but please trust me, I would never say anything to jeopardize you. Tell me what you know of your bosses."

She took the few steps back to the iron door that separated us. "You are different," she said. "I never say more than one or two words to others who are brought here. Most are older and are so scared. They won't eat, they cry and yell all day long." I pictured what she described. It pained me to think of the innocents that had been here before, no doubt unable to defend themselves.

I took my chances. "Are there two patróns or just one?" My suspicions ran high that it was the lawyers.

"Two," she said. "I must go. We talk more tomorrow."

She was on the verge of telling me more. I reached for her, and she took my hand, kissed my palm. "Mister, they will skin me alive if they know I talk about them."

"Trust me," I repeated. I gently pulled her to the gate and our lips met. "Valita, gracias."

"*Eres muy macho,*" she whispered. She called Lobo to her side, then disappeared into the dark.

In the morning, Toothless unlocked the door for me so I could walk to the outhouse. I stopped and looked down on him from my superior height. He put the gun under my chin. I grabbed his arm and twisted him around, leaving him bent at a painful angle. I took the gun away from him and shifted him into a headlock, casually, with one arm free. I pointed the gun at Fredo.

It was Fredo's turn to piss in his pants. The gun he held on me was shaking.

"If you ever pull that snake thing on me again, I will kill you. If you pull anything like it again, I will kill you. Do you fucking understand?"

Toothless was mute and passive in my chokehold. He couldn't answer. Fredo was stunned, and his gun was pointing at me. He didn't answer.

I pointed the gun back at him. Aimed straight between his eyes so he would get the message. I knew I could take both of them down at any time. Now they knew it too. It wasn't the smartest thing I could have done, tactically, but it sure felt good. I didn't have a way out, so there was no point in doing more. It wasn't the guards that made this prison, but the jungle.

Toothless made a little jerk like he was trying to get away. I jerked right back, letting him know he better behave.

Fredo said, "It won't happen again."

"You too," I told Toothless. I saw his mouth move silently.

"It won't happen again."

I shoved Toothless in Fredo's direction. Toothless coughed. He should be happy he was breathing.

"Put your fucking gun down," I said.

"You put the gun down," Fredo said.

I focused on his eyes, his facial expression, and his body language. He wasn't going to shoot.

I put the gun I was holding in Toothless' hand. He was still coughing, trying to get air in his lungs. I thumped him on the back. He grasped the gun and yanked.

"Chump," I said, then looked at Fredo, still holding the gun. "Pussy!"

I walked toward the outhouse. If I got shot, it wouldn't be the first time. I was fed up. I wanted to strangle them both, but with no way out, what would be the point?

I took my shower. No taunting. Neither had any of their usual stupid things to say. They were silent. Their guns were holstered.

I walked back to the warehouse ahead of them. No guns were drawn.

Once I was locked behind the gate, Toothless got close to the bars, his face contorted.

"You touch me again, I will kill you," he said. "And if Patrón gets pissed, I kill him too."

It was my turn to laugh.

Fredo slapped Toothless. It was not hard, but it was a slap just the same. "You are not fast enough to kill him." He pointed in my direction. "Accept it." Fredo looked from Toothless to me through the bars. He grinned and said, "The Patróns will kill you. We won't have to."

"Bring the motherfucker on."

Fredo had just confirmed what Valita told me. He didn't say patrón. He said patróns. There *were* two. My bet it was the Caracas lawyers.

Both apes walked away.

Afterwards, Ratón brought me two jugs of water and a pillow that he pushed through the bars. I gave Lobo his snack. I wasn't getting beefsteak facials any more, but Lobo didn't hold it against me. I scratched his head. He wagged his tail. He ate anything I offered him except fruit. Ratón and I exchanged smiles, but not a word.

It was dark when I awoke to the sound of the gate rattling. Valita.

"Mister, I have your food."

I jumped out of bed and took the few steps to where she was standing outside.

Lobo lay down by the gate. I bent down and rubbed his head with my fingertips, then reached for the food.

"Good night," she said, handing me the big mug of hot coffee, followed by the pan dulce, two jugs of water, two oranges, and two mangos. She handed me a sheet.

"Put this over the mattress, maybe you be more comfortable."

"Gracias, Valita. Ratón brought me a pillow. All the comforts of home. When I get out of here, I will not forget your kindness."

I extended my arm out and caressed her face. She didn't pull back.

"You are so strong," she said, taking my hand that caressed her face. "I saw what you did with the snake." She laughed softly. "I hate those two."

"I hate them too," I agreed. "I don't want you to get in trouble for talking to me too much."

"They are down there at the bunkhouse with the other workers, drinking. They figure you are not going anywhere with this big chain and lock."

"Valita, are the two patróns lawyers in Caracas?"

"Lario Flores and Gustavo Martino," she said very calmly.

"They are lawyers. Why would they be in the business of kidnapping?"

"For the money. Why else? And who would ever suspect a lawyer?"

"I just wanted to confirm it."

"You said you were in Caracas doing business when you were taken. What kind of business? Drugs?"

"No drugs. There was a plane crash. Many people died. I was in Caracas to offer them legal assistance by American lawyers I work with in Los Angeles. Lario and Gustavo were also after the families of those who died, but I signed many families. Some families that had agreed to be represented by Lario and Gustavo came to me and I accepted their cases and took them away from the patróns."

Valita's eyes widened. "I understand now. No difference. Now you are here. They will want money. Even if the family pays, I don't know anyone before who lived." She took my hand. "I don't want you to disappear like the others."

"We will talk tomorrow." I pulled her to the bar and our lips found each other. I touched her tongue with mine. I felt her shiver.

"*Buenas noches,*" I said. "*Gracias por todo.*"

"You're welcome." She let go of my hand and started to walk away, but turned around. I could barely see her face. "I don't want them to hurt you, or worse—kill you."

"That makes two of us," I said.

Ratón brought me food in the morning.

"Valita will bring you more, later."

"Thanks, Ratón. Have you got a minute?"

He nodded.

"How far is Caracas from here, or from the nearest town?"

He stared at me. "Valita says I can trust you. Is that true?"

"I swear to you it is true. You can trust me."

He looked up like there was an invisible map in front of him. He carried a couple of dishes, and they rattled a little as he answered. "It is about 150 kilometers to Caracas. In harvest season, the coffee beans are taken by truck down a narrow road cut through the jungle. Best way to get here is by airplane or helicopter. Don't try it on foot. They will catch you and kill you faster."

No doubt Valita and Ratón were tight. I couldn't believe the kid was leveling with me like this. I pushed it.

"I see jungle, but I also see farmland. What do they grow?"

"It's a coffee plantation. The patróns have two big homes on the other side of the compound. They come during harvest, and when weather is good. Valita works for Pátron Lario. She's the housekeeper. Not much for her to do when he is not here," Ratón said. "She is the lucky one. Maybe lucky. He likes her. He does not…respect her, but he likes her very much."

I knew what he meant by that. It made me angry, but there was nothing I could do about it, at least not yet.

"When is harvest season?"

"Harvest is October through January, but the season runs late this year. Only maintenance now. There are forty hands all the time. During harvest, there are more than two hundred." Talking so much made him nervous. "I better leave." He looked around cautiously. "Say nothing. They would kill me, or just as bad— I would lose my job."

"Thank you," I said, extending my hand. His hand met mine.

"Being killed is as bad as losing your job?"

"It is the same thing. There is no place else to work around here. I have my mother and siblings to take care of. If I don't work, my family starves."

When Valita came that night, I didn't mention my conversation with Ratón, but she did.

"Ratón said you talked about the patróns and asked how far to Caracas."

"Yes, I need to figure how to get out of here."

"I left here twice," she said. "During harvest, I got in one of the trucks and rode all the way to Caracas. My freedom didn't last long. Patrón Lario had me found and returned here."

"I'm sorry," I said.

"So am I," she said with acceptance.

"Does this happen often here? Having a prisoner being held for ransom?"

"Never during harvest. This warehouse is to store the coffee until it is transported."

"Do you have any idea what happens to the people that are brought here?"

Valita hesitated. "Only rumor. Not sure anyone really knows."

"What is the rumor?"

"Are you sure you want to know?" She grasped my hand.

"I want to know."

"The rumor is that after the ransom is paid or not, the person is killed here, burned, and the ashes are scattered during the night."

"No question then. I have to get out of here," I said with a little amusement that seemed to surprise her.

"You are not scared?"

"I'm not scared," I said. Melina would have said "I'm only scared of what I don't see coming." I don't think much would surprise me at this point. Valita had just told me what to expect. "Thanks to you and Ratón, I am seeing the future with some clarity. I can plan."

"I can help you, but if I'm caught, I'm dead, and Ratón would be suspect too."

"Is Ratón related to you, or are you––"

She interrupted me. "Ratón is a little boy. A brave young man, but I'm too old for him. He's my only friend here."

In the morning, when Ratón showed up with my food and drinks, I asked, "Why are you being nice to me?"

"Because you're nice with me, and Valita likes you," he replied. "I heard what you did to those two, taking the gun away, beating up Toothless, and then handing him the gun back. You are very brave, Señor."

He was telling me the same thing as Valita. I was probably as scared as any of them, but maybe a little better at seeming brave. Karate doesn't defend against bullets.

"Ratón, a few questions. I promise, just a few, and you don't have to answer." I smiled, trying to seem harmless, and led with a harmless question. "How old are you?"

"Fifteen."

"You are a grown man, Ratón. Your parents must be very proud of you."

He nodded and blushed a little under his tan.

"Do the people go home after the patróns get their ransom?"

Ratón looked me in the eyes. He swallowed. "I don't know for sure. I think they kill them. We all think they burn them, and scatter the ashes. Valita told me you asked her this too."

I smiled. I was so cool, like you wouldn't believe, though my heart sank. I could get free at any time, but I had to wait until there was transportation I could use. I had no idea when that would be.

"Thanks, my friend. I owe you."

"Mister, please don't say anything. Please."

I extended my hand as before, and we shook.

"You can trust me, Ratón."

I paced. I began my usual jog around the building. I spent half the day jogging and in calisthenics, wondering if contact had been made by the kidnappers. Who was there to contact? How much were they demanding? I felt my temper rise. I hate feeling fucking helpless. I'd already spent days worrying about the girls. I couldn't trust a word the apes had said. I wondered if these assholes might have them held up somewhere. I told myself that it wouldn't make sense to hurt the girls. They were the link the kidnappers had to getting money.

Venezuela was hot. This jungle was just this side of Dante's Inferno. Inside the concrete building, it was marginally cooler than outdoors. Concrete, for the most part, stays cool, except that the sun streaming in was like lava. The plastic mattress was no longer as sticky and miserable now that I had a sheet and pillow, but during the day, when I wasn't working out, I could lie down on the cool floor and douse myself with water.

At least I didn't feel completely alone anymore. Valita and Ratón were a font of information. And, for sure, I had the hots for Valita.

I had no gear to work out with, but I wasn't limited to jogging, or walking handstands. I did a lot of isometrics and pushing against the wall. I tried weird stuff, like doing a handstand, then pushups from the ground while I was in the handstand. Two handed. One handed. It was like bench pressing my body weight. The shaving mirror showed my face still looked like shit. The lower half of my face was starting to bear a resemblance to Fidel Castro. But at least I was feeling better.

Tropical fruit is great, but I missed refrigeration, air conditioning, and peanut butter. I would just push myself, tell myself to work out until the next shower. When my jailors showed up, they'd ask what I'd been doing to get so sweaty. I would just shrug, and say how hot it is.

I couldn't get Jo, Pixie, and Niley out of my mind. I wanted confirmation they were okay. I wondered what the ransom would be. I had tons of money sunk into real estate and a little bit in stocks, but only two hundred thousand in my two accounts. Jo had access only to the smaller expense account. Aunt Carmen had access to my bigger account, but I worried that news about me being abducted could throw her over the edge. I didn't know if I had enough to get myself out, if it was even possible. It's not like I wanted to hand over all my cash. I preferred that no ransom got paid at all. For that to happen, I'd have to take the matter in my own hands. Eventually, I would figure out how the fuck to get away. I had only dealt with the two apes, plus Ratón and Valita. Valita said that there were forty permanent workers on the grounds at all times. I didn't know how many of them were in on the kidnappings, but I probably wouldn't have to deal with them all. Just Toothless and Fredo. I knew that I could take them in my sleep. The real danger was having no way out of the jungle.

"Do you want out of here?" I asked Valita one night. "I mean, for good?"

"Of course I want out." Her eyes teared. "Ratón will not leave. His family is in the village. He supports them. How can I leave him? He is only a boy."

"Talk him into leaving, Valita. I don't know how, but I will get out of here."

Every night, I dreamed myself home. Every day, I was reminded of the girls in a million ways and wondered if they had gone home, or if they were still in Venezuela. I hoped they had hopped the plane to Miami and then to LA, but I just didn't think they'd do it unless they were going for help. I tried willing them to go, like sending a mental telegram. I knew they must have called the firm, and Oscar and Tom would have sent the girls home.

Maybe the solitary was getting to me. I looked forward to my short conversations with Valita and Ratón. When Valita came in the afternoon, she hardly spoke. Only her beautiful eyes spoke to me. She remained quiet, as if there were someone watching us. I asked her why.

"Night is my cover," she said. "I know where they are at night. I take no chance during the day. Lobo, he is good, but he is just a dog."

The dog, hearing his name, looked up and wagged his tail.

"I understand."

"You're safe enough as long as the Patrón is not here. But any day, Patrón Lario will arrive. Lobo will be stuck in the kennel. I will miss his watchfulness," Valita said.

I had not been keeping track of how many days I'd been here. I wondered how long I had been gone from Caracas and my team. Maybe a couple of weeks.

"Put your clothes on." Toothless spat when he spoke, thanks to the missing front teeth.

They unlocked the padlocks and came inside. They had not done that since the first day, preferring to keep their distance from me. Fredo had his gun out, but Toothless did not. Fredo stood with his back to the door, waving his fucking gun at me. Toothless didn't come too close.

"I see you have a sheet and a pillow. Who is being so nice to you?" Toothless taunted me. "I think I'll take them with me."

"Touch them, and you will regret it," I said, without looking at him. Toothless didn't make a move for the pillow. He watched me while I dressed. He ranted about my face again, about my eyes not healing yet, and pestered me to hurry.

I took off the shorts, and put on the boxers. The fucker was still watching me and getting on my nerves. I knew I should keep my mouth shut and keep a low profile, but I've never been particularly good at turning the other cheek.

"Like what you see, *hijo de puta*?"

"*Cállate, cabron*!" Toothless pulled out his gun and shot a round in the concrete ceiling. The bullet ricocheted.

Fredo ran towards Toothless.

"Pendejo! You could have shot me. The Patrón will be here today. You want to be dead? The Patrón is going to be fucking mad that the bruises are still there. He wants to take pictures. He will say to us 'Luna still looks like he was kicked by a mule.'"

I dressed while they argued, and laughed at them under my breath. They were like a couple of stooges, except they were no Moe, Curly, or Larry, and the bullets were real. I wasn't too worried. They were not going to shoot me unless their patrón told them to. Toothless put his gun away. Fredo kept his out, but at least it was no longer pointing it at me.

The patrón was a no-show.

Some hours later, I put the khaki shorts back on, folded my clothes, and put them back under my cot. I lay down and waited for Valita to come with my coffee and pan dulce, and a few minutes of touching through the bars.

"How do you know when your patrón is coming?"

"He said to have the house ready for him in ten days. It's been longer. We've had clear blue skies, the kind of weather he likes to fly in."

"You have no phones?"

Valita laughed. "No."

I had never heard her really laugh before this.

We kissed in the dark. I felt her hand touch my hard on. I dropped my shorts and she reached for me and pulled me through the bars.

"You are huge," she said.

I looked down.

She was on her knees. Her hair was loose, hanging in curls down her back. She looked up at me, and a waterfall of dark hair cascaded over her shoulder. She was tawny and strong-jawed and sad-eyed. She had a strong face, deeply cut cheekbones, and a slash of dark brows. Her eyes were dark and mysterious and beautiful, and the way she looked at me, I wanted to rip the door off the hinges to reach her.

I felt her lips pulling me in. I wanted her. I stood with both hands gripping the iron door. If it hadn't been there, I'd have collapsed. My joints and muscles melted like ice cream in the heat.

When she left, I barely made it to the cot. I was totally empty, exhausted, and unconscious.

The next day, about noon, I heard the sound of a plane. It seemed to be circling, then it either landed or flew away. I cursed the angle of the door, which limited my view. I could not see the landing strip. I heard Lobo in the distance and waited impatiently, ready to make a move. I was escorted to the john as usual, brought and filled my water jugs as usual, and lingered as long as I could in the shower, as usual. The apes both had their guns out while I was outside. I figured their boss was here.

Ratón brought food. Quietly, he whispered, "They are both here." Less than a minute after Ratón walked away from the gate, he returned and quickly handed me a machete.

"Put it away. Valita and I wish you luck. We hope this helps you."

He was gone before I could thank him. I examined the blade. It was old and well made, a farm implement. I could tell it had recently been sharpened. In my arsenal at home, I had many big swords, balanced precision instruments to work out with, which, as a boy, I had used in karate competitions. I was astounded by the compassion Valita and Ratón had shown me, and at the risk this kid braved to bring this to me. I felt a rush of adrenaline.

The lawyers didn't visit the warehouse right away. An hour later, I was standing at the gate, looking out, and they came into view. I recognized both lawyers I had tried to shake hands with at the funeral. Gustavo was shorter, with lighter hair; Lario had a long face and a dark mustache. Both were wearing Tees and khaki shorts. They weren't in good shape; they had the muscle tone of men who lived in armchairs. They wore big hats to shade their heads.

Though I'd already known they were responsible, now that they were here in the flesh, rage blossomed up, shooting through me. Adrenaline and hormones, fire and brimstone, whatever. I was primed to fight.

They said nothing while Toothless unlocked the padlocks. I considered blocking their entry, but the apes and their waving guns killed that thought. I found it amusing that they all kept such a healthy distance from me as the gate opened.

"Move back," said Lario.

I walked over to my cot.

The four men entered. They were overconfident. The gate remained open.

"So you slimy bastards are behind this." My voice was as calm and level as I could make it.

"Watch your fucking mouth."

"You asked for this. You shouldn't have come to Venezuela to steal from us," Lario said.

I remembered what Ratón had told me. During harvest season, they never brought anyone as prisoner. This was a hell of a sideline to the legal profession. I wondered if they always used it to cut down on the competition. Maybe they did kill their victims in cold blood, burn them, and spread the ashes, as the rumor told it. They were not going to do that to me.

Gustavo showed his yellow teeth and pointed a camera at me. I heard it click a few times.

"How do you figure you are going to get away with this?"

They exchanged looks and laughed.

"Why would we not?"

"You must be really lousy lawyers," I said, "if this is the way you get your clients."

"Shut up and hold still," Gustavo said. He took more pictures.

Lario looked at me with a nasty smile. "If the pictures don't work, we'll start carving you up and sending pieces of you to your girlfriends to convince them to get serious."

I almost laughed in relief. The way he said it meant that the girls were okay. The girls were the conduit they were using to get the ransom. It was a huge load off my mind.

Gustavo thought that cutting me was funny as hell, and he laughed his ass off. He laughed so much he couldn't keep the camera still. Fucker. He didn't have one of those laughs that make you laugh along with. He had the kind of laugh that made you want to punch him in the face, maybe break his jaw. Or maybe that's just me.

"I would have preferred he was not bruised," said Lario. "But he looked a hell of a lot worse ten days ago, Toothless."

Toothless snarled, looking in my direction. He did not like his new nickname, but he didn't have the balls to tell his bosses that. "We have been giving him the frozen meat to apply to his face, and that's why he looks better."

"Imbecile," said Lario. "It is your fault he's hurt in the first place."

"I'm sorry, Patrón."

I got up from my bunk and reached for a quart of water. I swigged from the bottle and sat back down on the cot. I had absolutely no fear. I knew I was going to get through this. I just wondered how many of them I was going to kill in the process. I wished that Ratón had not brought me the machete. It could connect him to me if something went wrong. I didn't need the machete to take these four milquetoast motherfuckers.

Then it felt like an earthquake. The ground was trembling. My cot vibrated. The water in my water jugs vibrated.

"What the fuck is that?"

"It's the devil."

"Sounds like a helicopter."

"Federales!"

"Cops."

I heard gunshots. Either it was the Fourth of July, George C. Scott was going Patton on Field Marshal Erwin Rommel out there, or help had arrived. My captors were distracted. An opportunity like this didn't come around twice. They were all standing with their backs to me within a foot of each other. Like a row of fucking human bowling pins. Nobody had a gun or an eye in my direction. It was irresistible. I took off like a top with a couple of spinning kicks and a roundhouse. Guns went flying, and heads hit concrete. I was moving so fast, even I wasn't so sure what I was doing. That's not really true. I knew. It's just that instinct kicks in.

I swept them. Once. They all pretty much hit the ground, in one fashion or another. I wasn't so much trying to get them all at once as I was trying to disable the guns. It was the guns that were keeping me in check. As I hoped, the guns flew out of the hands holding them. They slid across the floor and ended up against the wall. I grabbed them both, turned on the safeties, and shoved them in my pants. Okay, the safety was an extra few seconds, but I wasn't going to shoot my dick off, thank you very much. And it has been my experience that if you let go of the gun, they always go after it. I didn't have a desk bureau to kick them under.

Now that they were disarmed, I looked for whoever was the closest to getting up. I had swept them to the left. Toothless was on the bottom, then Gustavo. Fredo was just to their right, and Lario was on his hands and knees, about to get up. Lario was pissed off.

"What the fuck are you doing? Get up and get him! Imbeciles!" he yelled.

He roared and came at me. He landed a decent punch, aiming for my healing eyes, but he was soft. He should have stayed in his easy chair.

I hit him fast and hard five or six times in the face. His hands went up, not after me, but to cover his face. I tangled my foot in his legs, and he lost his balance and fell. He did not try to get up a second time, but lay there, whimpering. Gustavo had fallen on top of Toothless, and they were still entangled, so I took out Fredo with a couple punches to the face. Whatever happened later, the apes would be leaving here with matching black eyes. I owed them that much. Toothless shoved Gustavo off. I didn't even hear a 'Sorry, Patrón' or anything.

I saw Toothless coming at me, knee level, and moved aside. He lurched forward and turned around to come at me again. I dodged a punch and hit him in one eye. Dodged another punch and hit him in the other eye. It just made him madder. He tried to score a couple of body blows, but I moved out of the way, made a fist out of both my hands, and slammed the back of his neck, but not hard enough to break it. Three down. Gustavo looked at his partner's swollen eyes, at Fredo flat on his back, and Toothless on his stomach. He put his hands up, like he was waving the white flag. I backed off.

The unlocked gate clanged. Lobo charged in like it was playtime. He looked at me, and something changed in his face. The playful shepherd was gone. I thought, Fuck, he's gone psycho. No time for more. His powerful legs bunched beneath him, and he arched into a leap straight at me, a hundred pounds of muscle and razor teeth.

I dodged to one side, or thought I did. I turned in time to see the glint of a knife. Gustavo came at my back, full throttle. Lobo got in the way, made full body contact, and tore into my attacker. Gustavo buried the knife in him. The tip of Gustavo's blade just caught my forearm. I hate knives and I hate people who hurt dumb animals even more. He jerked the knife loose, but Gustavo was down under the dog, and I gave him a hard chop in the throat. He stayed down, clutching his throat like a balloon with a slow leak. I plucked the knife out of his right hand, and gave him a whack at the base of the skull with the hilt, so he'd take a little nap. I was done with him. I was done with all of them. I was bleeding all over, though it was just a flesh wound, but I gathered up Lobo. Asshole lawyers. Trust Lario to go after my eyes, which were my weakness right now. Trust Gustavo to fake giving up, so he could knife me from behind. Trust Lobo to turn out to be man's best friend. And he wasn't even my dog.

I stood there in the fucking warehouse, the bleeding dog limp in my arms, and wondered what the hell to do. The best plan had been Valita's. She'd suggested to take over the plane. Of course, I can't fly a plane. If I had to go for the jungle, the machete might come in handy after all. But I didn't want to take on the jungle on foot or even a vehicle. That was my instant decision. And another thing. If that gunfire outside wasn't from people on my side, no matter what else, I was up shit creek.

My back was to the door, facing my fallen captors. I was full of adrenaline still. I heard a voice behind me and wheeled around, ready for round two, though what the fuck I thought I would do carrying a dog, I don't know. But it was an unexpected voice.

"Fuck, I could have stayed in Los Angeles."

Oscar walked into the warehouse and found me standing over a heap of bodies. I was covered in blood, holding a dying dog. My knuckles were a little sore and, considering the shorts I was wearing, I was next to naked. I might have been gaping at him with my mouth open. I couldn't believe who I was seeing.

"Hey, man," I said, shifting the dog's weight and managing to free up my thumb up like I was hitchhiking. "Got room for a passenger, Oz?"

Oscar laughed and gave me a big hug. Hugged Lobo, too, who was not protesting.

Behind Oscar were four big men dressed in fatigues with automatic weapons and masks. And there was another surprise. Tom Jones was right behind them. Like Oscar, Tom ignored the elephant in the room, Lobo, and hugged me.

"Good to see you in one piece," Tom said.

"You have no idea how glad I am to see you guys. I heard gunfire and figured it would be a good time to clean house," I said, smiling so hard it hurt. "Resistance when you landed?"

"No resistance. Just warning shots." Oscar was so calm, as if it were an everyday thing to walk around with a military escort and fly around jungle compounds in Venezuela.

"Forty workers are in the compound, but I never saw them. They aren't involved, I don't think."

"We're getting out of here," Oscar said. "Unless you prefer to stay."

"The sooner, the better."

Lario growled, "Fuck you," and lurched upward.

I gave him a sharp kick.

"Get down and stay down, if you know what's good for you," I said.

Lario glared back at me. I was lucky looks can't kill. Gustavo was unconscious. One of the military guys cleared his throat and pointed his Uzi in the middle of the group.

"Excuse me," I said, stepping out of his way. "Don't let me stop you from doing your job."

The soldier glanced at Oscar and nodded curtly.

The apes took a look at the weapons and lay still. I walked to the bunk and kicked aside the corner of the mattress, revealing the machete. Soldiers streamed in, and one of them took possession of the blade I'd revealed. Oscar saw me do this and quirked a curious eyebrow in my direction.

When we were outside, I explained. "There might be consequences to the one who gave it to me," I said. "If the soldier has it, no problem."

"I understand completely."

Tom and Oscar and I headed at a fast clip toward the landing field with the other two soldiers. The ground shook, but this time I could see what it was about. A second chopper was landing ahead of us on the runway. It was black, single engine, and had a military look, with some kind of decal on the back. I guess they were Venezuelan federales. We continued in that direction, toward the other helicopter.

"Two helicopters?"

"You know the military," Oscar said. "Never have just one if two can do the job better."

Tom gave him a quizzical look, which told me that Oscar had made the arrangements. What else was he not saying? Not that I was complaining. I was glad to be out of there in one piece.

As we approached the helicopter, Ratón ran up, his face a tapestry of mixed emotions. Happiness I survived, fear of the blood, pain at the condition of the dog. I lay him down on the ground, and Ratón fell to his knees.

"You're bleeding," he said.

"Not much. It's mostly the dog."

Tom showed Ratón how to stem the bleeding.

I told Ratón, "I'll be right back."

Oscar and I went on toward the chopper, Tom following behind.

"How are the girls?"

Oscar chuckled. "Fine. I promise."

"Where are they? LA, I hope?"

Oscar just smiled.

"They didn't go home," Tom said.

"Let's talk inside," Oscar said as he climbed the steps to the parked helicopter.

It wasn't the same helicopter that I had rented, but it was a huge one, with two engines.

I was so fucking happy to be leaving that I was beside myself. I boarded, and was followed by Tom and two of Oscar's soldiers. The pilots greeted me as I came inside.

There were a pair of seats behind the pilots, facing front. The rest of the seats were lined up along the sides, facing each other. The two military men took seats on one side toward the back. The girls were on the other side toward the front. The girls?

Jo was the first to react. They popped up off their seats and were all over me. My arms went around them, naturally.

"What the fuck. You flew them into danger?" I said with some alarm and surprise in Oscar's direction. I was overwhelmed that they were there and infuriated that Oscar and Tom had risked bringing them into the line of fire.

Jo was first to speak. "Don't be mad at him, boss. Be mad at us. We gave Oscar no choice. He caught us in the middle of renting our own chopper to follow him." She took a breath and let out a moan. "Your eyes, your beautiful eyes." She reached up to my face, touched the contour of my cheek gently with the back of her hand, then snapped at Oz. "We need to get him to a doctor. He's beaten and bleeding." She hesitated for about half a second, then walked up to the pilots and asked them to radio ahead for a medical assist. Or maybe they only do it when you're in Venezuela, in a military helicopter, and Jo takes it on herself to declare some kind of emergency.

Mad as I was, I almost laughed. I could just picture Jo lining up the chopper. Pixie would have probably gotten them matching X-rated commando bikini uniforms straight out of a James Bond movie. Good thing Oscar nipped that in the bud. I was relieved that help had finally arrived.

The door to the black chopper opened, and four masked men exited.

Oscar said, "Excuse me. This will just take a second."

He walked to the steps, pointed in the direction we'd come from, and yelled, "The warehouse, four men."

The soldiers saluted him and went off to the warehouse.

"You all should have waited at the hotel. If you got killed, I'd have to fire you, and punish Oscar and Tom for not taking care of you."

Oscar laughed.

Tom looked a little worried. "It's not like your team will listen to anyone but you," he said.

Pixie, Jo, and Niley were wrapped around me like a bunch of monkey babies hanging onto their mama. I managed to get into a seat without any of them letting go. Fuck it. We could talk later. We were on the way home. I was still shirtless. Pixie kept running her hand over my biceps and abdomen.

"Have you been working out?"

I didn't answer.

I could see through the window when the military guys had disappeared into the warehouse. I had a mental flashback of a kid I'd gone to school with who had gone into the army. When he'd gotten back from boot camp, Pélon and I had saluted him, and because of it, had gotten a thirty-minute lecture on salutes. Every service has its own way of saluting, and there are strict rules about only saluting commanding officers. I wondered if Venezuelan forces were any different. Why were these soldiers saluting Oscar? Who were these soldiers? The fatigues didn't reveal any particular service or country, at least not that I recognized. Not that I am up on things like that.

I asked, "Oscar, are those cops? Are they taking them to jail?"

He shrugged and pointed to his ear and the chopper, like it was too loud to talk. Then he pointed out the window before he took a seat facing forward, beside Tom.

The girls let go of me, and we all looked where he was pointing. I saw Valita and Ratón, both kneeling on the ground.

"Oscar, wait. I have a couple of people I need to thank."

"I thought you were in a hurry to get out of here."

"I am. How much cash do you have?" I asked Oscar.

Jo spoke up, "I have plenty, how much you want?"

"Two thousand."

"I have that," Oscar said.

"It's okay. We got it covered."

Jo was counting. She handed over the bills.

"Do you have a business card?" I asked Jo.

"Of course," she handed the card to me. "I have yours, too."

"Give me one of mine."

I ran down the steps and passed the other helicopter that only had the two pilots inside.

Valita and Ratón looked like they were in shock.

"Your arm," Valita said. I saw she'd already grabbed the sheet and pillow from my cot and brought it out here for the dog. She ripped off a strip and bound my arm, then knelt beside Ratón. She made an effort to put together a makeshift bandage.

"It's not helping," Ratón told her solemnly.

"Your friends are waiting," she said.

She glanced down at the dog, and tears dripped down her face. She looked up at me, looking hopeless. I wondered if she was sad I was leaving.

I am guessing a couple of rescue helicopters and a troop of military guys showing up was not the usual way the kidnappings ended.

I hugged Valita first and pulled Ratón in on the hug. "Come with me, now. I love you both. You saved my life." I gave Ratón a kiss on top of his head, and swept Valita off her feet so I could kiss her old-movie-style. Our lips met.

"You're so hot," I said in English.

She let out a big laugh and responded in broken English. "You hot too, Mister Mario."

"Valita, we have room for you and Ratón. Please."

"I have to stay, mister," said Ratón.

"Lobo got hurt pretty bad. He probably saved my life. Gustavo tried to put a hole in my back, and Lobo stopped him. I owe you both, and I owe him."

Valita grabbed my arm, urgently.

"Take him with you. Maybe you can fix him. He will have a better chance where you are going."

"So would you," I said. But I capitulated. "I will get him back to you," I said.

"You should hurry," Ratón said. "Don't let Lobo die. He is a good dog. I love him, and he is the Patrona's dog, but he really belongs to Valita. She has no one else."

Valita patted his hand, reverted to Spanish, and said, "If Ratón won't go, neither will I. I will run away during harvest. It will start at any time now. Maybe

Ratón will come with me."

Reluctantly, I set her on her feet and handed her the cash. She resisted, but I took her hand and folded her fingers over the bundle of hundred-dollar bills. "I brought this for you. A gift for you and Ratón. I know you will get away. You were able to do it twice before when the lawyers were around. This time the Patróns should be in prison and won't be able to get to you. Here is my card with two telephone numbers," I handed it to Valita. "Call me collect when you get to Caracas. Will you do that?"

"I promise," Valita said. "Go, Mister Mario. *Vaya con dios mi amor.*"

"Gracias. By the way, don't worry about the machete. I gave it to one of the soldiers. I didn't want to leave it because it could connect you to me."

"Go, Mario. They are waiting for you." Valita was tearing up.

I gathered up Lobo, backed towards the helicopter, and, halfway there, stopped to look back. They blew kisses at me. Valita was crying. The chopper engine was roaring, but all I could hear was her soft voice saying she loved me.

When I was back inside, the door closed. I put Lobo down. Niley got on the floor, holding a piece of cloth to Lobo's injury. I took my seat among the girls and looked out of the window. All of the military men were still inside the warehouse. Some of the hands were still going around doing their work as if nothing were out of the ordinary. The jungle looked as bright green and impenetrable as ever. The compound looked like a little coffee plantation out of some other century, except for the helicopters, landing field, and all the generators. Valita and Ratón were not in sight anymore.

"What the fuck was that about?" Pixie asked, kind of kidding, kind of not.

I turned to face my dirty-mouthed girl. "I missed you," I said.

"Oh Mario, what did they do to your eyes?" Pixie started to cry. Pixie seldom cried.

"You think I look bad? You should see the other guys," I said with some satisfaction.

"Who were those people you were talking to?" Niley asked. She was still on the floor, and I saw Lobo was resting his head on her knee.

I didn't feel like talking, but Jo was also curious too. I wanted to get it out of the way.

"They helped me the best they could. I was locked in that warehouse. Valita brought me food and water, and raw beef to put on my black eyes. Ratón, at great risk to himself, snuck me a machete. He's fifteen years old. Just a kid. I offered to bring them with us, but Ratón won't leave his family, and Valita won't leave Ratón. They don't own the dog; but the dog only likes them."

"Maybe we can make them come with us," Jo said as we rose off the ground.

Too late. The blades beat the air, and the motors roared; but the girls and I were silent, huddled together, tears streaming down our faces. I was ready to be gone. As the helicopter lifted, the four of us joined hands. It was good to be together again. We flew over the vast sea of green. The jungle seemed to go on forever. I was very glad I hadn't been forced to hack my way through it.

The chopper landed at the hotel. We took the stairs down to the top floor, then the elevator down two floors to my room. We went to our suite and found a doctor waiting. She made quick work of my cut. Washed it out with a burning solution, numbed me, and sewed it up. She left a stack of bandages and directions for me, and a plastic sleeve to wear over my arm when I bathed.

"Fix him too," I said, pointing to Lobo, who was in the arms of one of the soldiers.

"I'm no vet." The doctor hesitated. Jo gave her a handful of bills, and she took Lobo away. Jo gave her my card.

No sooner had the doctor left then Oscar and Tom joined us. I was exhausted, but stood when they came in.

Oscar said. "I can see you're dead on your feet. I have someone for you to meet, but that can wait. Your assignment for the next twenty-four hours is to rest and relax."

"There's a lot more we can talk about when you're rested," Tom said. "If you have questions about the operation. Planning. Logistics." He looked at Jo, Pixie, and Niley. "The girls."

"I'm sure," I said.

Oscar walked towards the door with Tom behind him. "You get a head start on resting. In the meantime, I'm going to try out that big tub these suites have. You're not allowed to worry about anything. If anyone asks something, refer them to me."

"I guess we skirted some customs regulations here and there." I was kidding.

Oscar laughed, giving away nothing.

Tom said, "Something like that." One reason I like Tom is that he's got a transparent face. He was agreeing, but he looked as uneasy as I felt. "I'm sorry you got banged up like this," Tom said. I saw him looking at the doctor's handiwork, and the bruises left on my face.

I laughed. "What you see right now is nothing." I remembered all the cold beef steaks my eyes had gone through.

"Mama will take care of you," Pixie said, taking my hand.

"Right," Jo said, loftily. In the girls' dynamics, she always took the role of Mama Bear. "I will."

Oscar and Tom exchanged a look. It might have been envy, sympathy, or relief at not having to referee the girls. It was probably a combination of all of those things.

"One last thing," Oscar said. "You don't have to worry about anything here in Venezuela. Nothing else is going to happen." He spoke with complete confidence. He probably had eyes on all of us.

I shuddered. I hadn't even thought of what else could happen. My mind had never gone further than getting out of Gustavo and Lario's clutches.

"All I care about," Niley said, "is that we're going home." She looked up at me. "Together."

Oscar and Tom left for their hotel rooms, and the door shut behind them.

I was surprised that no one knew of the kidnapping, not even the hotel staff. The girls were convinced that someone at the hotel had helped Toothless and Fredo. How else could they have drugged me and exited the hotel undetected? But when I returned, no one seemed particularly surprised to see me. I wasn't going to hear about the kidnapping on the evening news.

"We're going to run a tub for you filled with bubble bath," Niley said.

"Yeah, I need a bath."

My toiletry items were all there where I had left them. I scissored off as much as I could of the beard I'd grown. The tub filled, and the girls gave me privacy. I couldn't wait to wash off the odor of dried blood and dog. I shaved. The hot bath was indescribable, even with the plastic sleeve keeping the bandage dry. After a long stay in the tub, I jumped in the shower. The hot water felt like a miracle after the rigged shower I had been using at my coffee plantation prison.

The phone rang. I turned off the water so I could eavesdrop on Jo talking to the doctor about the dog. They'd stopped the bleeding. If he survived, I didn't know what the hell I would do with him. I didn't need a dog, especially not one that might eat the neighbors.

I came out in clean boxers and a fresh tee. The air conditioning was on full blast, and I could smell food.

Niley was in the hall as I emerged. She cocked her head to one side and said, "I kind of liked the beard." She took another step, looking over my shoulder past me, and smiled. I looked toward the bathroom. I'd used a lot of towels, and they were all over the floor.

I knew what she was smiling about. Once when she and I had flown out on a case, we'd celebrated a little enthusiastically, soaked a Texas bathroom in bubbles, and stolen a bunch of hotel towels to hide the mess.

We grinned at each other.

"I remember," I said.

Niley grabbed my hand and collapsed against my chest for a moment. I held her close and said nothing.

"I missed you so much, so much. I was so afraid." She took a deep breath and stood on her own. "I am so glad you're safe." She opened the door to the dining room. "The food is here," she said, pointing at steaming plates arranged on the dining table.

I took my seat and started on an arepa. It was hot, greasy, and filled with cheese.

"So while I was trapped in the jungle, what were you doing? What happened on our end? I'd have thought—or at least hoped—you went home. Start from the very beginning."

"We got a call that night from some rough-talking asshole who said you were going to be okay as long as a ransom was paid. I took the call," Jo said. "I was warned that we were being watched, and if police showed up or we went to see the police, that you would die."

"So, we waited," Pixie said.

"It was miserable," Niley said. "We argued about what to do."

"We reached a consensus. I did call Tom," Jo said, pushing salad around on her plate. "I left the hotel and called from a pay phone, because nothing's less secure than a hotel switchboard. I explained how we weren't supposed to bring in the cops. I told him that you had money in the bank, but we had no idea yet what the ransom was going to be. He told me to wait for Oscar's call, so I did. Five minutes after I hung up with Tom, Oscar called back. He asked me a bunch of questions about the lawyers that Mario had told Tom about. I gave him their names. A couple hours later, he called us back at the hotel. He told us not to do anything. That he would handle it."

"I fucking didn't buy that," Pixie said. She had been sitting at the table in front of her dinner plate, but remembering got her agitated and she stood up. I watched her walk across the room. She was wearing heels and shorts, and I knew it wasn't by accident. She grabbed a beer from the refrigerator and sat down, conspicuously crossing her legs. She twisted open the beer, took a big swig, and offered it to me.

I shook my head. Pixie took another swig. She reached for a plate of plantains and scooped some onto her plate beside an empanada. She broke the empanada in two and put half on Niley's empty plate. She forked a stack of roast beef on to her plate and dragged half of it to Niley's, too.

"Me neither," Niley said, "but we had no choice. We waited. We stayed in the hotel, didn't go out." She looked down at her plate in surprise.

I saw Jo and Pixie both staring at Niley, waiting for her to take a bite. My guess was that she hadn't been eating. Come to think of it, she did look a little peaked.

"Niley, baby, please eat," I said. "I love you."

Niley's eyes went around the table and dropped to her plate. She took a fork and scooped up a piece of the empanada and took the teeniest nibble off the fork. "I love you too."

Jo continued. "Oscar called in every day, sometimes two and three times. He assured us that he had friends looking into the situation."

"I called Melina and swore her to secrecy," Pixie said. "Phone booth, not from the hotel. Melina said she would get with Oscar to see what was going on."

"I talked to Melina when she called back," Jo said. "She said that Oscar was definitely working it through a former client. Of course, it was like talking in code in case someone was listening. We were talking about her ordering stuff for her Mexican market. It was all very James Bond."

"Melina called us every day. We were afraid of kidnappers and bugs and talked in code so no one knew we were talking about you. 'I will pay whatever shipping fee they ask for' like you were a product she was ordering for her market," Pixie said.

"Oscar said he had it covered no matter what," Jo added. "We waited here, helpless. We had no idea where you were or even if you were alive until the calls started to come in from this loud asshole who said he would be calling with his demands so we best get a lot of money ready. He never said how much. He sent us a terrible picture of you."

"I remember when they took it. I'm glad you didn't see what I looked like before I spent two weeks with raw beef on my face."

"Three days ago, Oscar arrived at the hotel here with Tom. Caught us totally off guard," Niley said. Pixie urged her to take another bite.

"I knew something was happening," Pixie said. "Oscar was real cool about it, but I knew he had something going on."

"We hardly saw him or Tom until this morning," Jo explained. "He was with Tom, and said he was going to fetch you. He told us to sit tight. We told him we were coming too, but he wouldn't have it. I heard him mention a helicopter."

Pixie said, "I told Oscar as calmly as I could that we were going to follow him no matter where he went and that's what we did. Jo had our local chopper guy on the line, and Oscar grabbed the phone and hung up on him. When we were in the helicopter, he said nothing about where we were going."

We finished our meal. The girls piled everything on the cart room service had left and shoved it into the hallway.

"I love you, Mario," Jo said.

I swatted her ass lightly. "I love you too."

"Swat me again, but harder. I need it, boss."

"Hey, we all need it," Pixie complained.

"You got that right," Niley agreed.

"Rain check. You deserve everything you want, but you should have gone home, out of harm's way."

Jo got Melina on the phone for me. "Good news, Cuz," I said. "You don't have to keep calling, looking for that product you wanted. The sales team pulled through. By the way, I'm fine. Oscar did a bang-up job at whatever it was he did, and even Tom Jones is here."

"I am so happy you are okay," she said. "I've been talking Oscar's head off every day so I'm up to speed. If I didn't hear from you today, I had a flight lined up for Venezuela. I was going to come there and kick the whole country's ass."

"I'll be home in a couple days," I said. "I might be bringing home a kennel."

"What?" she said, startled.

"I'll explain when I get there."

"Okay." Melina laughed softly. "I can hear the girls way over here. Tell them to kiss you for me."

That night, it was like I had never been gone, never kidnapped, never rescued. Sometimes between us, we take turns. I always make sure everyone is happy, or equally happy; but that night, the three of them would not let me do anything for them. They were all doing all they could to please me all at the same time. I guess the greatest happiness is being so loved.

In the morning, Juan was there.

"I met with Doctor Manez yesterday, and sat with the dog after they sewed him up," he said. "Then Manez came in while you were all asleep. The dog is going to be laid up for a while. They explained the international quarantine to me, but there are some loopholes."

"Not sure I can have him where I live," I hedged.

Juan brightened. "I always wanted a dog. I can arrange it."

I laughed a little. "Dr. Manez is very pretty, isn't she?"

Juan nodded, grinning.

"Have her send me the bills, and make the arrangements." I said. "The dog is temporarily in your custody. He belongs to Valita at the coffee plantation, but she wants to come to Caracas. She will want him back. Thank you for all the work you did trying to find me," I said. "The girls told me all about it. Very cloak and dagger."

He hugged me. "This is a dangerous country. I am so happy to see you are alive and well."

"Ditto," I said with some laughter. "It *is* a dangerous country. Don't stay too long with the pretty doctor. I'll be in touch."

On our last night in Venezuela, we had dinner in the hotel restaurant. Jo had arranged with the concierge to have coffee and pastries sent to the room.

The girls were casually dressed in shorts and shirts and were taking off the heeled sandals they'd worn to dinner, when there was a knock. I opened the door, and Oscar and Tom entered, accompanied by an unfamiliar middle-aged man. What struck me most as the stranger walked in was a quick glance he exchanged with Oscar. It was a warm, almost intimate exchange between two men who respected each other. It reminded me of moments with Carson, whose mind I knew like the back of my hand. Tom walked in behind them, as if not to interrupt. I took a few seconds to study the stranger. He was several inches shorter than me, and a few pounds heavier. He was Hispanic, with neat dark brows, and the manicured hair of a banker or businessman, iron gray on the top, and a touch of silver along the edges. He had a rough look about him too, like a man not quite comfortable in the clothes he was wearing. His clothes were very fine, and looked expensive. They fit him perfectly. Definitely not off the rack. Next to Oscar, he seemed somehow harder, though he had no sharp edges. He had a jocular, clean-shaven face, cheeks rounded and weathered, a conflict that maybe reflected his personality. This was a man who laughed, and lived life to the fullest. I had a feeling he could handle himself in most situations. Rounded jaw with a bit of a cleft, a suggestion of stubbornness. I turned toward Oscar, not wishing to be caught staring.

"Mario, this is Pepe Camacho, a good friend of mine."

We shook hands. Pepe wore an expensive jacket with a high-collared shirt. No tie. He was wearing jeans with the expensive coat, so I wondered if he'd only put the coat on for my benefit. When he shook my hand, the heavy gold bracelets on his right wrist jangled. He wasn't poor, and he exuded a restless energy. I had a feeling he did not like closed spaces, and he seemed watchful in this closed space. His hands were not as smooth and manicured as Oscar's, and he smelled outdoorsy, not in a rank way, but as if he didn't stay confined in an office.

"Pleasure," I said.

"No, it's my pleasure." Pepe's smile was engaging. His smile was broad and open, but his dark eyes were unsmiling and unreadable. I believed the eyes more than the smile. He was a man I would not want to cross.

"You wouldn't be here right now if not for Pepe," Oscar said.

Pepe said softly, "With a little help from my friend, the general."

The mention of the general brought up questions, but I would ask Oscar later. Now was not the time. I felt rather than saw the girls come up behind me, and I introduced them.

"Jo, Niley, Pixie, this is Pepe, a friend of Oscar's."

I could see my team take on their professional demeanor, in spite of being dressed in shorts, tees and worn-out looking stuffed dogs on their feet. The dog slippers they wore had come from the hotel's gift shop and were Jo's usual solution to walking comfortably on questionably clean hotel carpeting. They were no longer new, emphasizing to me how much time we'd been in Venezuela.

Pepe's hand was out again, and Jo shook it, saying, "*Bienvenido.*"

Niley said, "*Mi Casa es su casa.*"

Pixie said, "*Qué pasa?*"

Pepe responded each time with a big smile, as if he were appreciating each of my girls on her own merits. His gaze lingered for a few seconds on Pixie, who gave off that sassy vibe as she always did.

He turned back to me and said, "Pleased to meet you. Your team is very charming." He glanced at the girls' feet. "And unconventional."

Niley and Jo stood their ground, like they were wearing designer heels. Pixie arched one foot, and glanced down at her sexy appendage from several different angles as if checking out footwear she was about to purchase. The heeled sandals they'd taken off were in plain sight, in a pile by the door.

"Thanks," she said.

I extended my hand out again. Pepe and I repeated the handshake.

"I am indebted to you for life," I said. "Please, sit down."

"Room service," a voice called through the door.

Niley jumped up. "I'll handle," she said.

"Do sit," I suggested.

My guests sat, and waiters brought in the *carajillo* I'd ordered, a coffee drink that was a specialty of the hotel, and a tray of pastries.

They served each of us our drinks and left a full carafe of *carajillo* and a carafe of plain coffee.

Oscar thanked the servers, refusing the *carajillo*. "Straight coffee for me," he said. "No liquor tonight. We're flying out in the morning."

Conversation halted until the servers were gone.

"Finally, I get to meet the great Mario," Pepe said.

"And I finally get to meet you," I responded in kind, though Oscar had never mentioned him by name.

"Oscar was my lawyer in the States when I was facing five hundred years. Your Feds wanted me bad." Pepe chuckled. He patted Oscar on the back, sipped his coffee, and polished off a pastry. "This miracle man got me found not guilty. I came back to Colombia a free man. Oscar is my best friend. For him, I would do anything."

The girls sipped their *carajillo*, and I could see they loved it. They were eyeing the pastries, but not eating them. I expect they were planning to demolish them when our guests were gone.

"I called Pepe soon as I heard from Jo that you had been taken. He took it from there."

Pepe laughed. "It was my pleasure." He gave me his card. "Any friend of Oscar's is a friend of mine."

"I owe you one, man." I'd always known Oscar had a past where he rubbed shoulders with and defended powerful drug lords, a segment of his client roster he used to refer to euphemistically as 'private entrepreneurs.' Up to this moment, he had gone out of his way not to introduce me to any of them. I wasn't up to analyzing what was happening. I'd think about it later. I was free and thankful to be free, and I was grateful enough in that moment that I didn't care if that freedom indebted me to one of Oscar's 'private entrepreneurs.'

We spent a good hour chatting over pastries and coffee, talking about nothing. Pepe opened a leather case, searched through the contents, and withdrew a couple of cards from it. One was a personal card, another the card for his shipping company, New Granada Imports, and another for LAI. "You can always reach me if you need me," he said, handing them to me. Phone numbers had been written in ink on the back of the cards.

We heard the roar of a helicopter approaching the helipad. Niley got up and looked out the window, but said there was nothing to see.

Pepe said, "My ride back home to Colombia."

Oscar looked at his watch and stood.

"Do you know the way up to the top floor?" Pixie asked.

Pepe smiled. "Senorita, I do. Thank you."

"Good to meet you, Pepe," I said. The girls joined in on the goodbyes.

"See you in the morning," Oscar said. "I've arranged a wakeup call."

Oscar followed Pepe to the door, Tom behind them.

Oscar's wakeup call was breakfast delivered by room service on his dime. I went to pay my bill and found the hotel had compensated me for the entire stay, for letting me get attacked and kidnapped while under their roof. An hour later, we boarded Oscar's Learjet. Oscar was all smiles. He and Tom even had hats with captain's bars.

"You guys are piloting us back home?" I asked. Oscar's refusal of the mixed coffee drink last night now made sense.

"You know it. Coffee last night, and a clear head this morning," Oscar said with a big beaming smile. "It will take us fifteen minutes to get ready. Make yourselves comfortable."

"My name is Chastity," a big blonde said. "I'm your flight attendant. I have soft drinks and some great wines. I didn't stock up on too many snacks because we have a fuel stop in Miami, and Captain Oscar says we're eating there."

"I dig the Captain Oscar thing," I said, laughing. I introduced the team to Chastity.

Chastity handed me a cloth-wrapped item. "Before I forget, the captain wanted to make sure you get this."

I uncovered the machete Ratón had given me that I had given the soldier. I guess the soldier had brought it back. I wrapped it back up and slid it under the seat.

"That's quite a trinket you've got there," Jo said, and sank in one of the luxury seats.

"Fuck, I could come just sitting here." Pixie wasted no time putting her seat belt on.

Niley sat and opened her legs as wide as her jeans would allow. "Too bad Oscar is up front or we could do it. I'm so horny."

"Next time," I said, taking a seat. "I dig this jet like you wouldn't believe,"

Oscar was busy with Tom going through a checklist. Chastity served us a glass of wine but not before she checked to make sure our seat belts were on. After that, she sat in a pullout seat and strapped herself in like the flight hostesses on commercial flights. She didn't do the usual stewardess demo.

Captain Oscar did a great job getting us up into the air. It felt like we were shooting straight up without doing a gradual climb. I had never flown with either of them but had confidence in Tom Jones with his years of experience piloting the big planes. I sipped my wine and kept lifting my glass, offering toasts to my beautiful team.

"Checking in, Cuz," I told Melina on the phone from Miami. "We're on a fuel stop and having lunch in a restaurant near the airport with a taxi waiting outside to take us back to the plane."

"I'm so happy you're almost here. So glad you are out of that hell-hole. I hate Venezuela."

"Don't blame Venezuela. It was just a handful of assholes who live there."

I gave the receiver to Tom Jones to confirm where and when we were landing, then he handed me the phone back.

"Johnson is picking you up. Oscar and Tom have their own car coming. I will spring away early and see you at the house. Safe flight, Mario. I love you."

"Love you back," I said. Pixie was tugging my arm.

"Come back to the table and finish eating," she said as I hung up. "Do you really love her?"

We walked arm in arm toward the table, my arm draped over her shoulders. "I love all of you." I kissed the top of her head.

"I can't imagine living without you," Pixie said.

"Ditto, baby."

I carried my suitcase. Johnson carried the machete, still wrapped in the cloth, up to my apartment. The girls' cars were in the Bunker Towers parking lot, but first they went upstairs with me, hung out briefly, smothering me in hugs and kisses and joy before they left for their own family reunions. They had children to go home to. I was alone, but at least I was not alone three thousand six hundred miles from home. Home sweet home.

I found a place for the machete in my weapons cabinet, then went into my bathroom to savor the delights of my own shower. I had just let the water loose when there was a knock on the bathroom door.

"Come in," I said.

Melina stepped in the shower and welcomed me home.

After we were out and dried off, Melina replaced the dressing on my wound. I carried her to the bed and told her about Lobo, from the very beginning to when he was carted off by the Venezuelan doctor. She put her arms around my neck and rested her head on my chest. Her voice was muffled when she started talking. I tilted her head up and saw she was crying.

"I've been so scared that something would happen to you."

I was a little shaken by her emotion. It took a lot to make Melina cry. The last time she'd cried like this had been after an attempt on my life.

"The girls told me you were in touch with them every day. Thank you so much for that. They were scared too, and you were very supportive."

"Please don't thank me."

I kissed her with a passion that I couldn't remember feeling before.

"I have to thank you. Thank you for being there for me," I managed. "Thank you for being in my life. You know I love you."

"I love you, too," she said, laughing shakily. "Along with half the women in the state of California, a good percentage of the girls in Europe, and probably a couple of dozen up in the Arctic circle." She laughed at herself, but I could still see the tracks of her tears. "So, did you have to bury him?"

"Who?"

"Lobo."

The way she said it made it rhyme. I laughed.

"We brought him back to Caracas, and a vet sewed him up. He's laid up anyway, but they arranged for him to recuperate in quarantine in Puerto Rico. Seems like Juan always wanted a German shepherd."

"Maybe. While you were gone, the girls put Juan on the phone, and we spoke. He'd do anything for you."

"Maybe, but I was under the impression he'd do anything for the lady vet."

"Ah," Melina said. "That's a different story."

She came into the bedroom carrying a spoon of peanut butter.

"I ordered Mexican," she said. "Johnson is picking it up."

"Good deal. Hey, Cuz, where's the jar?"

"In the kitchen, where it should be, so it doesn't ruin your appetite."

"Never gonna happen," I said, pouting, but I put the spoon down. I did look forward to some good enchiladas, and felt thankful Johnson was fetching them. I considered Melina, who looked as if she'd completely recovered from her vulnerability. I knew better. "Oscar told me we can't say anything about what happened."

"He told me the same," she confirmed. "I know more than I should about it, so don't worry that I'll ask. I don't want to know what Oscar is into." That was the lawyer in her. She understood right away that Oscar had used other-than-legitimate resources.

Since the outcome was my survival, I couldn't complain.

"Enough about Oscar," she said, "I just want to lie here in bed with you. We don't need to do anything else but hold each other. Baby, your eyes are still all the colors of the rainbow. I can see you're hurting. This cut I just bandaged. It's killing me to see how hurt you are. Sex can wait."

"Tell you a secret, Cuz. The beating, the face, that was weeks ago. It looks bad, but doesn't hurt at all."

"Good to know," she said.

"You should have seen me with blueberry muffins for eyes."

"Absolutely not. I'd have gone after them with my pistol."

I wasn't going to argue with her about getting revenge. It was an argument we'd had before. I put her hand on my growing erection. "However, I hurt here."

"Already?" she said with a watery chuckle. "I thought we already handled that in the shower. Looks like it's popped up again."

Sex waited, but not for long. Johnson brought in the takeout without disturbing us; and after he left, we nibbled enchiladas, and then each other.

Melina did not leave until the following morning. I really loved when she spent the night. Lately, I hated sleeping alone.

I was feeling better, at least until I saw the postmark of a letter atop the huge stack of unread mail: January tenth, 1976. I felt horrible that the girls had missed Christmas with their kids. They never mentioned it, never complained. I got on the phone right away with the girls and apologized, but they assured me that their kids had had a very nice Christmas arranged by phone with the nannies,

Aunt Carmen, and Jo's mom.

I called my aunt.

"I can't believe you didn't even call me for Christmas!"

Aunt Carmen had no idea that I'd been kidnapped. I had no idea that no one had told her. I didn't want to keep secrets, but I couldn't let her worry, either.

"What did you do for your birthday?" she asked in a voice whose sternness masked hurt feelings.

"I'm sorry," is all I could say. "I was stuck in Venezuela. I promise to be over soon to see you. I love you."

"Every time I talked to the girls, you were never around. Always too busy to talk to me."

My aunt went on and on. It was good to hear her voice, even nagging. I loved the girls all the more for keeping her from worrying.

I poured myself a glass of Bordeaux and savored every sip. I was lucky to be alive.

In my head, I prayed. *Thank you, God. I know you're there. I know you're with me. Please look out for Valita and Ratón. Tell me what I have to do to help them.*

Chapter 9
January 12, 1976
Status Quo

Working only aviation cases did not give the girls distraction from their badly concealed anxiety. Aviation cases did not come as constantly as accident cases did, nor did they demand all of their time. While being home and safe gave me time to heal and get back to normal, it also made me remember something that had bothered me ever since Pixie had been hurt in the attack at the hotel in Caracas. It bothered me how helpless the girls were. They needed to be able to defend themselves, and it was time that I did something to change that.

The girls were over early one morning, working on—well, work—as I was working out, and they surprised me with breakfast. Homemade. I walked over to the dinette, and Niley ushered me into a chair.

"What?" I asked.

Jo came out with a platter of scrambled eggs, warmed store-bought tortillas, chopped up avocados with a bit of salsa mixed in, and side bowls of chopped lettuce, *queso blanco,* chopped tomatoes, and a dish of minced fresh jalapenos.

They pushed it in front of me, and stood all around, like they were waiting me to open a present.

"Thank you," I told them. "Is this all for me?"

They joined me. I tore into the tortilla I'd stuffed with dry eggs, flaccid lettuce, old *queso,* rubbery tomatoes, and jalapenos. (There was a reason none of the girls cooked for me.) The girls valiantly ate their share, looking from their own tortillas to my empty plate. No doubt they were wondering if my taste buds weren't operational, or I was just being polite. I didn't mind the distraction of their breakfast, even though I would be chasing it with a spoon of bicarbonate of soda. I had a surprise of my own to announce. I broke my own news as the doorbell rang.

Niley hopped up.

"This is going to be a surprise for you."

"Me?" Niley asked, stopping dead halfway to the door.

"All of you."

"Stand when I do," I told the girls.

"Sure thing, boss," Pixie said.

I stood. They stood. I sat. They sat. I gave them a thumbs up.

Niley opened the door, and in walked Cosmo. Niley led him into the kitchen.

I stood. The girls stood with me. Niley was quick enough to catch on and follow Pixie and Jo's lead. I bowed. The girls bowed with me.

Cosmo looked very much amused, though I am sure the girls saw nothing.

"Cosmo, you've met my team before. Niley, Pixie, Jo."

We all bowed again.

"Would you care for some breakfast, Master Cosmo?"

"Thank you, Mario, but no."

Cosmo was carrying a bundle of Karate *gis*.

"Here is the thing, girls. I did a lot of thinking in that warehouse. I thought about how in that hotel room Pixie got kicked, but hard. She was hurt badly. Every one of you could have been hurt badly. It was great that Jo had some handgun experience, but I have a better solution. Cosmo. Cosmo?"

Cosmo handed a karate workout uniform to each of his three new students.

"Girls, you're taking up karate. I won't take no for an answer." And that's how their workouts began.

The next day, I had the girls come in early, at five. They were moaning and groaning about residual aches and pains from their first lesson, and grouchy because of the time of day I'd had them come in.

I met them at the door.

"Did you bring your gis?"

"Hell no," Pixie said.

"Good. Those are for your weekly class with Cosmo. Yours are in my closet. For the next two weeks, you're going to be here daily at five for your class. I'll work you till you drop."

We had to move some furniture for all of us to have room to work out. I had them run through what Cosmo had them doing, and for an hour straight, made them practice the same moves until they were ready to collapse where they stood. I wasn't adding new moves. Just doing what he did to me, which was work me to the point of exhaustion, repeating the moves until they were instinctive. Because Cosmo also made me lift weights, I had gotten a petite weight set for the girls. As soon as they finished their kata, I would say, "Again." A little faster and sharper each time. Niley was the first to actually drop. That's when I let them off the hook. I helped Niley back up. We put the furniture back in place. I bowed to them. They bowed back, somewhat reluctantly.

I had not broken a sweat. I sat down on my couch, put my arm around Pixie, and looked down at the top of her head. She was tall, but when she was standing, she barely reached my chest.

"We knew we needed to find something to do between accident cases," Jo said, "but..."

"Get up all of you and go take a shower. You're getting sweat on the couch. I'll order out for breakfast." I fed them steak. They ate like stevedores, but now they needed the fuel.

Melina came over with a giant fake ficus tree, Tito trailing behind her carrying a heavy wooden box that looked like the two bottom stairs outside of my aunt's apartment across from Hollenbeck park.

"It's all the rage," she said, showing off the fake tree growing out of fake dirt. "See how real it looks? It's handmade of wood and silk."

I wasn't impressed.

She knew right where she was going. She went straight to the bare white wall beside the big window in the living room. Tito put down the box against the wall where Melina directed, I tipped him, and he left. She perched the fake tree on the step, and I had to admit she was right. It looked like it was meant to be there. I had been home fifteen days.

Ramiro called me from Venezuela.

"The media is putting it out that Lario and Gustavo are drug lords. The federales or the military or somebody raided the coffee plantation and found hundreds of kilos of cocaine. They confiscated the plantation. Lario and Gustavo are in prison waiting for a hearing."

I don't know if I was disappointed they weren't dead, or happy the motherfuckers were alive and rotting in prison, but I was excited. Ramiro read one of the newspaper articles to me, and I was feeling pretty good until I thought about Ratón and Valita.

"What about the people at the plantation?"

"Nothing in the papers about them. Why do you ask?"

"Just curious."

"If anyone had died, the military would've called their deaths resisting arrest."

I didn't want to think of my friends dying in a hail of bullets. Ramiro was still talking. I tried to pay attention to what he was saying.

"...but never mind that. Lario and Gustavo signed fourteen families. They'll be calling me wondering if they can switch to you."

I didn't hesitate. "If they want to switch, okay, but don't pressure them."

"No, I would not pressure them. I don't understand why Lario and Gustavo would be involved in drugs. Both men and their wives come from big money. They own oil concessions worth millions."

"Greedy bastards!" Of course Ramiro and the newspapers readership had no clue that Lario and Gustavo were in the kidnapping business.

We agreed he would call me tomorrow.

I hung up with my mind racing. No kidnapping charges, but drugs? How did that happen? What about Valita and Ratón?

I drove to Oscar's. He met me in the conference room with Tom Jones.

"They're locked up," Oscar said before I could say anything. "It's all over the news in Venezuela and I talked to Pepe on the phone a little while ago."

"The word I got is they were nabbed for drugs, not kidnapping," I said.

"That's good," Oscar said with a straight face. "Kidnapping is hard to prove since they aren't caught in the act. Drug possession is easy. My information is they found sacks filled with cocaine stashed in Lario and Gustavo's personal residences at the plantation. They are hunting for the processing plant."

Oscar was wearing a poker face.

"Oscar's right," Tom said. "Once we got you out, there was no evidence for the court that you were kidnapped. No one saw you being taken from the hotel."

"But the soldiers rescued me with you there."

"No, they walked in. They found four imbeciles lying on the floor of that warehouse knocked out. That's what they would report." Oscar said.

I looked at Oscar as he puffed away on his cigar. "Did Pepe have the drugs planted?"

He looked at me as if he were wounded by the question, but his expression didn't quite match his words. "Pepe and I are tight, but I don't tell him what to do or not to do. Honestly, I would have done anything to get you the hell out of where you were being held. Anything."

Mirroring his nonchalance, I said, "Sorry for the stupid fucking question."

I took a deep breath and noticed his bar cart. I didn't like to drink in front of Tom, but I was feeling unsettled. "Can I have a shot of cognac?" I rarely drank hard liquor, but I felt like I needed something.

Oscar got up from behind his desk and walked to the rolling cart. Tom met him there. Tom poured sparkling water.

"You and I will have a fine shot of Louis XIII." Oscar sniffed his glass, his expression close to blissful.

I'm pretty good about not drinking around Tom, but this time I didn't apologize.

We raised our glasses in a toast.

"I love you, Mario," Oscar said.

I blinked damp eyes and looked at Oscar and Tom. "I love you too. You guys saved my life."

"From my angle, it looked like it was all over before we got there," Oscar said.

"Pepe must be very connected to have found me."

"He's very connected. He brought a friend of his in, a high-ranking general. I believe he's the one that pinned down your location."

"Oz, I need to pay you back whatever you are out. I'm sure you didn't get all these heavies to do this for you without giving them a chunk of bread."

"I paid nothing," Oscar said. "Besides, you are here and that's what is important to me."

We returned to our chairs. Oscar brought up the clients who had signed with Lario and Gustavo, clients in limbo now.

"I agree with what you told Ramiro," Tom said. "If they want to come over, let's get them. How many?"

"Fourteen families."

"Sweet," Oscar said. "How about another cognac?"

The drink left a warm path down my gullet. I was already feeling the golden glow. I glanced at Tom. "Pass on that, but Oscar, I do need a humongous favor."

"Shoot."

"You saw Valita and Ratón. He's just a fifteen-year-old kid, and she was, well, not much more than that. They took chances for me. Ratón slipped me the machete at great risk to himself. We had a half-baked plan. Take over the plane. Get the pilots to fly me to Caracas. We didn't have a plane, but then you showed up and distracted everybody. It was the perfect opportunity, and I took it. But that was then. Now our client Ramiro says the military may have killed everyone at the plantation. I have to know if Valita and Ratón are being held by the federales, or if they were shot. I only know them by their first names. Ratón is a nickname. His actual name is Salazaar. I need to know they are safe."

"I will check and let you know." He made a note of their names. "I will call Pepe. He can check with the general."

My mind was all over the place on the drive home. First, the fuckers had been arrested for trumped-up drug charges and not for their actual crime of kidnapping. Second, Valita and Ratón's whereabouts were unaccounted for. Third, Oscar trusted them but for me, Pepe and the general were unknowns operating in that dangerous arena Venezuela. Unknown elements made me antsy. Fourth, I was a danger magnet, and the girls would be a long time getting up to speed in the self-defense department. At least I'd gotten them started down that path. I'd managed their practices for two weeks. The girls were already getting competitive with each other and challenging each other to longer repetitions on the free-standing weight sets. Cosmo had called after their third lesson to say they were all showing remarkable progress and stamina. Soon, I was going to let them continue their hour-long daily practice on their own, without me.

I hadn't been home thirty minutes when Oscar called me.

"Take this number down," he said.

I grabbed a pen off my desk and scribbled the number on the corner of the *LA Times* classified section I had open.

Oscar said, "I talked to Pepe. He wants to speak with you. Call him soon as we hang up. Careful what you say on the phone. You don't need to draw him a map. He has some questions."

"Got it," I said.

I called Pepe.

"Amigo," he said, "I checked the names that Oscar gave me. The girl Valita is there, and so are several other maids, but no fifteen-year-old named Salazaar."

My pulse surged. "Pepe, what do I need to do to get Valita out of there?"

I heard a low laugh. "Ask me and it's done."

"I'm asking," I said.

I dialed Oscar. "Pepe is going to get her released. I need to borrow your plane. No other way to get there fast enough."

"You got it. I'll call the crew and get back to you in thirty minutes."

I thanked him again. I still didn't know Pepe, but I was about to get to know him a lot better, which made me feel less antsy.

The girls had been watching some aviation films Tom had sent over. Now, they streamed into the office and pulled out the projects they were working on. I realized that two weeks of karate had already made them look more fit.

"You're going to work out on your own for the next few days," I said.

"Cool beans," Niley said.

Jo looked at me with narrowed eyes. So did Pixie.

"Why?"

"I was just getting you into the swing of it," I said.

"Cut the bullshit," Jo said. "Where are you going to be tomorrow morning?"

When they realized I was flying to Caracas, they all went for my jugular. I was in no mood.

"Shut up! I'm going and I'm going alone. You don't have to like it. Final word. Got it? When Oscar calls, I'm leaving."

The girls were mad I that was going into danger, and looked it, but they held their tongues.

Oscar was a trooper, but had a request of his own. "Since you insist on going back to Caracas yourself, while you are there, sign up the clients that want to jump ship from those bastards."

I promised.

When I left my apartment, Jo and Niley were crying, and Pixie was trying to reach Melina by phone. I was out of there before Pixie found what market she was working that day.

I drove myself to Van Nuys Airport. Juan was going to be meeting me in Caracas at the hotel. I needed him to work with Ramiro and round up the families that wanted to leave Lario and Gustavo. Twenty minutes after boarding the plane, I was flying over Los Angeles headed to Caracas. I took my shoes off and slept all the way to Miami, where we stopped to refuel. I wasn't up on how many hours the pilots were supposed to rest, but my only concern was getting to Caracas fast.

The hotel's car picked me up at the airport. By two in the morning, I was in my one-bedroom suite in the familiar hotel. Two hours after I hit the bed, Juan rang to tell me of his arrival.

"Boss, I'm in room 217. Just got in. Going to sleep a little. Call me when you want me to come up."

"Good to hear from you, Juan. I'll call you later."

I was still sleeping at nine in the morning when Pepe called to welcome me to Caracas.

"Thank you. Good morning."

"The jail is a holding place where they keep detainees until they appear before a judge. After the judge passes sentence, the prisoners are sent to a maximum-security prison about fifty miles from Caracas. Before you go to the jail, go to the office of the Comptroller General of the Republic, Av. Andrés Bello, Edificio Las Fundaciones."

I scribbled down the address.

"The general will be meeting you there around noon. The girl Valita will be released when you get to the jail. Everything is arranged, amigo. I'm sorry I couldn't get away to be there with you, but I have many commitments here in Colombia."

"Pepe, I've leaned on you enough. Thank you for handling everything."

Juan and I took a hotel car to the government office. A receptionist gave us VIP passes to clip on to our lapels and said, "You are expected."

A soldier led us past a suite of offices toward a conference room. Just outside the door, a stocky man in a military uniform turned crisply to face us. We would have to pass him and his shorter, thinner companion to enter. I focused on his face, wondering if this was the one Pepe said was meeting us. Roughly six feet tall. Black hair cut short, clean shaven, rounded face, wide spade of a chin below a grim mouth that looked like it rarely smiled. His dark green uniform fit tightly around his narrow shoulders, and tighter around a paunch in his belly. Not a dress uniform. He'd left his medals, if he had any, at home. A thin man in the uniform of a junior officer stepped forward to intercept us. His extremely short hair was lighter than that of the older man, his skin tanned, his shoulders broader, and he looked too young to shave.

"Mario Luna?" he said, looking from Juan to me as we approached.

"And you are?"

"I am Salvatore, assistant to General Maldonado," he said.

The general glanced down at his watch. "Get the car started," he said.

Salvatore saluted the general and scurried out the door.

"General Maldonado," I said. "It is good to meet you."

We shook hands. His was a confident handshake. Juan would have backed off to give us privacy, but Maldonado took his hand too, gave it a single shake, and released.

"Call me Falcon," he said. "Any friend of the Camachos is a friend of mine."

I fell in step beside the general as he entered the conference room. Juan remained outside.

"Sit," he said.

I sat.

"Lieutenant Salvatore will be meeting you at the jail," he said. We exchanged cards. "If there is anything you need, feel free to contact me."

When we got back to the car, I told Juan, "I feel like I just met the King of Caracas."

"Boss," Juan said, "I think you did."

Juan and I took a hotel car to the jail where Valita was being held. The jail was a primitive place, a bulwark of adobe, pitted paint and inescapable misery. It was a few minutes before twelve, and we ran into Lieutenant Salvatore outside. He had arrived in not one but two official vehicles, and was flanked by no fewer than four subordinates, all carrying weapons.

"If this is a holding facility, imagine what the fucking prison must be like," I said to Juan as we fell into step behind our escorts and walked into a deteriorating building that looked like it was still in the last century.

At the entrance to the jail, two uniformed officers sat behind a counter. Behind them, a long corridor stretched into the distance, its unrelieved expanse broken by recessed doors set in arches. One of the officers looked at our entourage and jumped to his feet.

"We are here to pick up Valita," I said.

I noticed that Lieutenant Salvatore took a step back. His four companions had lined up behind him against the wall. They faced the desk, all of them looking ready to pull out their machine guns and blow everyone away. Though he said nothing, I could feel the authority emanating from him, and the rising anxiety of the prison officer behind the desk.

The officer ran his finger down a clipboard page. He was much shorter than I, shorter than Salvatore, and in a uniform the color of dust.

"*Noya,* Valita," he said. "Allow me your passport, please."

I pulled out my passport and handed it to him.

"What business have you here?" the officer asked Juan.

"I'm a friend. Nothing else."

The officer glanced toward the lieutenant, of whom he asked no questions.

He nodded nervously and said, "Sir." He returned my passport and came out from behind the counter.

"Follow me," he said, then raised his hand to stop Juan. "You sit there and wait."

"*Si, como no,*" Juan replied.

The lieutenant did not join us, but stood in place like a statue, his hands folded behind his back.

I followed the guard about halfway down the hall. As we walked, I saw that each of the recessed arches led to short corridors of iron-barred cells. The conditions were horrific. Each small cell held multiple prisoners, most of them half-clothed in the heat. The stink of men in close quarters was reminiscent of the lion's cage at the zoo. I tried not to meet anyone's eyes, and fastened my gaze on the guard's back as he walked ahead of me. When we turned down one of the corridors, prisoners whistled and yelled out at me. Voices rose around us, men and women pleading for cigarettes, for money, for help, and offering sexual favors. I heard cursing, promises, insults, raunchy propositions, and a lot of hate and despair. The noise of catcalls and cacophony rose, echoed in all the other halls, unseen but not unheard. Other halls took up the refrain.

The guard stopped at one of the cells that held four women inside. He used a big key to unlock the door. That's when I made out Valita standing with three other women.

"Oh my God, Mario. What are you doing here? How did you find me?"

The guard drew back his hand and slapped her. Her face jerked with the force of the blow, and I think she would have fallen if not for the women behind her. My natural impulse was to take him down; it took every ounce of control I had not to attack him. Or maybe it was the caution and terror in Valita's face that made me stop.

She raised both hands.

"*Mario, esta bien.*"

"Callate!"

The guard yanked her out of the cell.

Valita looked down at the ground and followed. There were no hugs, no tears, no emotion, nothing. Valita walked beside me, and we both followed the guard towards the entrance. We had passed three or four corridors when I saw Valita flinch. I turned in the direction of her gaze.

Lario, Gustavo, Fredo, and Fraco were pressed against the bars of the first cell down the corridor to the left. I stopped and stared at them. Except for when I left them thrashed on the floor of their warehouse, I had only seen the lawyers in the hotel and at funerals, dressed in their finest. How far the mighty had fallen. They were down to rags and half-naked, as ill-clad as the rest of the prisoners. The condition of their shorts was so bad, I couldn't tell if they were the same ones I'd last seen them in, and like most of the male prisoners, their shirts were gone. It actually took me a few seconds to recognize them in the wild-eyed convicts ranting at me. I walked closer to the entrance to their corridor. They were furiously rattling the bars of their cell.

"I knew it had to be you and that American lawyer who put us in here. *Eres un hijo de puta, lo vas a pagar, cabron!*"[15]

All the cells erupted with another wave of noise fueled by frustration, rage, and powerlessness.

"You should have been more careful who you kidnapped, motherfuckers!" I yelled back. I taunted them. Now they were the ones behind bars facing an unknown future. They had earned their current condition. I hated and pitied them; but I doubted they had learned compassion for their own victims. Compassion. Crazy to think such a thing in terms of Lario and Gustavo, men who kidnapped and killed for ransom. I can't deny that the sight of them resurrected the anger that I had felt when I was locked behind their bars, and that part of me wanted to open the cell door and smash them down till their threats and insults were silenced. I clenched my jaw and found my fists balled at my sides.

---

[15] You are a son of a bitch. You will pay, dumbass!

They continued their ranting, cursing at me and threatening Valita for being ungrateful and a traitor.

"I'm going to peel the skin off your entire body, puta!"

The guard had kept walking, but now he stopped. Valita stopped behind him, still staring at her bare feet. The guard turned around and ordered me to follow him. I had to hold to my objective. I was here to free Valita. Nothing could get in the way of that goal.

Valita said nothing.

We continued to the front counter, but as we walked away, I could still hear the lawyers' threats and curses. Valita was ordered to sign a paper. One of the officers shoved a pen in her hand. She scribbled her name obediently.

The three of us walked out, just like that, led by the lieutenant, our military escorts falling in behind us. We walked past a couple of beige-uniformed officers with machine guns pointed in our direction. It was when we reached the hotel car that I noticed Valita's condition. Her shorts and blouse were torn, dirty, and ragged. She was thinner and bruised. It hurt to think of her free spirit caged in that awful place.

I thanked Lieutenant Salvatore. He gave me a quick smile. He was much younger than I'd realized.

I opened the door for Valita. She climbed in, and I followed. Juan got in behind me, and I scooted to the middle. Once we were inside with the doors closed, Valita sniffed the air and grabbed my arm.

"Mario, the window, please. I've brought the prison with me."

I had the driver open all the windows to let in the fresh air.

"Better," she said, "but I can't wait for a shower and to burn these clothes."

The driver started the vehicle which kicked up dirt and stones as we drove away from the jail. That's when I kissed her.

"I looked for Ratón but could not find him."

"I gave him all the money you gave me. The federales came back. Three helicopters landed filled with soldiers and guns. We knew something serious was happening, but when the soldiers landed, Ratón had already left for his village. He got away."

"Great news," I said.

"Yes, very good news," Juan said.

"Valita, this is Juan. He works with me and is a very good friend."

Juan was on my left, and Valita on my right.

They both leaned forward and smiled at each other. Valita's left palm was resting on my knee. Juan reached over and took her hand. Valita tried pulling away.

"My hands are too dirty. I shake your hand later."

Juan smiled, lifted her hand to his lips, and kissed just above her knuckles. She blushed a little, and withdrew her hand.

When we reached my suite, Valita discovered the two bathrooms.

"Which bathroom can I use for the next two hours?" She smiled brilliantly and looked at one of the tubs as if it were all the holidays rolled into one, dipped in chocolate and covered in sprinkles on a white porcelain plate.

"I love to see that smile on your face. Use whichever one you prefer."

I remembered when I was in Venice and met Fae, I went out shopping while she was in the bathtub. I had taken her clothes and used them for sizing purposes. Fae, when I found her, looked like Cinderella in comparison to Valita. I felt so bad for what she had gone through. I felt responsible, since her arrest was a result of my rescue.

She closed the door. Juan and I shook hands and smiled at having freed Valita. We heard the water run and left her to her own devices as we went to find her something to wear. At a store a few blocks away, the two of us and a friendly young lady found three outfits for our rescued princess, including underwear, shoes, and sandals. Juan guessed at her size. I had no idea.

When we returned with our booty, Valita was still in the bathroom.

I called Jo, who connected me so that I could talk to the trio. They all started talking at once, but I got in control of the situation.

"Just listen. I'm being quick. I have more calls to make. I'm fine. I got Valita out of prison. She's going to be fine. Tomorrow I'll start working on the fourteen families that had signed with the asshole lawyers. I'll go home then. I love you. Got to go."

I had two numbers for Pepe. I left a message for him at the import office, and a message on an answering machine at the other number.

I told the machine, "Thank you. I got her. I owe you big time."

When she came out of the bathroom in a hotel robe, Valita looked almost as I remembered her, except she was a little pale and much thinner. She cleaned up very nicely, and wasn't badly bruised.

I opened the suite's refrigerator for her.

"Pick something to drink. We'll go eat soon as you get dressed."

She took an orange juice can. I opened it for her and handed her a glass.

"I have no clothes," she said. "Maybe I can wash what I have." Her face scrunched in distaste.

Juan laughed. "You have clothes. The main question is if they will fit you."

I handed her three bags.

"Oh, Mario, you've done so much already."

She looked like she was going to cry over a change of clothes. I tried to rush her to keep that from happening.

"Go try them on."

She took the bags and walked back into the bathroom.

It was early in the afternoon. The restaurant was open, but we were the only customers. We sat next to a window overlooking the city.

I ordered large bottles of still and sparkling water, and my favorite local wine.

Valita looked at the menu, then from me to Juan.

"I'm sorry, but I can't read. I know how to spell my name and sign it, but I can't read the menu."

"No problem," I said, "I'll order. Do you feel like eating steak, fish? Anything you want."

She smiled broadly. "You order for me. I am so hungry." She drank a glass of water and poured herself another glass and downed that too. "This water is so... clean."

"Poor baby. I'm sorry you were put through this horrible experience."

"It was horrible. My life at the plantation was in its own way horrible. At least there I had a bed to sleep on, not on the floor like at the jail." She poured a third glass of water, this time from the sparkling carafe. "I keep pinching myself to make sure I am not dreaming. I can't believe I'm here. So unbelievable to me to be here with you."

I turned my gaze from the city view and saw that she was looking at me.

"You are so strong," I said, reaching for her hand. "Don't cry, please."

"Tears of joy," she managed to say. "I thought I would never get out. They said would get fifty years or more."

She vented for a little while. I saw that telling about her experiences gave her some relief.

They brought bread to the table, and we went through the basket as if it were the first time we'd ever seen food. Maybe Juan and I mostly watched. But if it was so, it was because the roll we broke tasted better just because we were watching Valita savor every crumb of bread, every smidgen of butter. The salads came. I ordered more water.

"The patróns have much money. They have not only the coffee business and their law office, but they have been in the oil business for many years. Their wives, they are from very rich Colombian families. The lawyers, they will buy their way out. They won't be in prison long."

"You think so?" asked Juan.

"I know so."

"They got them for drugs. That's serious here," I said.

"The drugs were put there by the soldiers that raided she plantation. I didn't see them do it, but those drugs were not from the residences of Lario and

Gustavo where they were found."

"Let's hope they stay in prison for a long time."

Valita agreed.

"It will be months before they go before a judge for sentencing. We will see what happens."

I remembered them in the cell as I had last seen them and let out a mean laugh. "They certainly didn't look too rich the way they were dressed and crunched up in that cell."

"I hate them," said Valita. She didn't laugh. Her voice quietly carried a wealth of loathing and pain.

We raised our wine glasses. I said, "I toast to you, Valita. May you have no less than two hundred years of life, happiness, and good health."

Our glasses clicked. Valita eyes filled, but she sipped her wine and even smiled through her tears.

"Let me arrange a visa for you to come to the United States."

Without hesitation, she said, "I don't belong there. I practice my English but I don't know the language so good. I prefer to stay in Caracas. I can get a job like I did before. I know cleaning. I can do everything perfect in the most expensive hotel. Lario's maids taught me everything about taking care of expensive houses and things."

"I would feel horrible leaving you here. If they get out as you believe, they will come after you. You heard what they were yelling at us."

"This time they won't find me. I can go somewhere else if I feel threatened."

I was surprised when Juan said, "Do you want to try Puerto Rico? That's where I live. We speak Spanish there."

"I heard about that place. Where is it from here?"

"Very close by plane. It is part of the United States, but you won't know it when you are there. You are welcome to come." Juan looked at me. "If it is okay with the boss."

I laughed and nodded my head.

"Valita has had a patrón all of her life. I am not her patrón. She's as free as a bird. She can do what she wants. All I want is for her to be safe and happy," I said.

"Juan, thank you. Let this night pass, and I let you know." She reached across the table and their hands joined. "You are very kind," she told him.

She never asked him if he was married or what the arrangements would be, but she didn't say no.

Juan walked us to my room. I asked him to call Ramiro from my phone for a status on the families that Lario and Gustavo had signed up.

While Juan was talking, Valita sat down next to me.

"How do you feel?" I asked.

"I feel wonderful. I am so grateful. I owe you my life. I will be at your disposal for as long as I live."

"You owe me nothing," I said.

Juan hung up the phone and turned to me. "Ramiro says the families are ready to sign. He will round them up for a meeting tomorrow afternoon here at the hotel. I will rent a conference room, if it's okay with you."

Juan had a good grip on how this business worked. Without Jo there, he took charge of what the team usually handled. Juan joined us on the sofa, sitting next to Valita.

I couldn't help noticing Juan again, with his movie star looks, especially next to Valita, with her distinctive strong bone structure, high cheekbones, and blast of curls. They looked good together, almost a matched set, like a South American Ken and Barbie, too pretty to be real.

"Good job with Ramiro, Juan. Thank you."

He smiled and said nothing.

"I feel so bad for the other three maids," said Valita. "They did nothing wrong, and they're in jail for life. Every night the jailers bring men to have sex. Many get rough and slap them around."

I felt my heart stop. She had said the other girls. What about her?

"Those were the girls in the cell with you?" I hadn't paid much attention to them, but I remembered that they too had been wearing rags, but they had been young and pretty.

"Yes."

There is no way Valita would not perceive my agitation.

"Were you also forced to have sex with these men they brought?"

"Yes. I never got more than a slap. I know when I'm cornered, so I didn't resist." She looked at me as though Juan wasn't even there. "*Mario, estoy bien, por favor, no te preocupes por lo que ya paso.*"[16]

"I'm sorry I questioned you," I said.

"Don't be sorry. You are my friend. I will answer your questions. I have no right to ask it of you, but if you can help the three girls, I will be your slave for the rest of my life. I feel so bad for them."

"I will see if I can do anything." I made the promise but wondered how many more times I could turn to Pepe. People usually turn to me for help, not the other way around. He was an unknown element. I felt like I was building a pile of obligation to him.

Valita excused herself and went to the bathroom.

I took the opportunity to call New Granada Imports, a division of LAI. A worker there answered and immediately put Pepe on the line. I made the explanation short and asked about the three girls working as maids, still being held wrongfully for the planted drugs.

"Amigo, one day I may need a favor. I will get the maids out," Pepe promised. He was optimistic, and told me to call him back around noon the next day. It was a quick call, and by the time Valita was out, I had already hung up and was pondering the wisdom of asking for so much help from the mysterious and dangerous Colombian.

Juan left. I was alone with Valita. I took off my jacket and hung it over a

---

[16] Mario, I'm fine. Please don't worry about what's already happened

chair. Los Angeles in February is chilly, but the temperature in Caracas was in the eighties.

"Thank you for the clothes," Valita said, and hung on to my shirt like it had lapels.

I smiled and pulled her to her feet. "There's more where that came from," I said. "Let's go shopping."

We shopped the rest of the day. I'm not much for shopping, but I enjoyed walking around Caracas with a pretty girl on my arm. The stores sent clothes back to the hotel, so we didn't walk around with bags. I bought her a suitcase to put everything in. It was dark when we returned. Valita was overwhelmed and grateful.

"Thank you, Mister Mario. I owe you my life, and I will never forget it."

"Let's go back to earlier—just Mario, no mister."

She smiled her pretty smile. "Okay."

"Will you have some wine with me?" I asked Valita, who was sitting beside me. She pulled off my tie, undid the top few buttons of my shirt, and nodded.

"Make it two bottles," I told room service on the phone.

Valita smiled. "Fiesta, si?"

"Si, fiesta," I agreed.

Room service assembled an array of snacks on my dining table, the feast Valita described. We sat facing each other, clicked glasses, ate, and talked.

"I remember this isn't your first time in Caracas."

She nodded. "I tell you how twice before, I come to Caracas in one of the trucks that hauls coffee. First time, the patrón sends his pigs to take me back in his plane. Second time, I get a job in a big hotel like this. The pigs find me and fly me back again. The patrón very upset. He make me work for an entire year with no pay at all."

"I'm sorry," I said.

"I wasn't beaten, but I was a prisoner. When he came without his family, he expected me to service him in every way. He always said I was favorite. I always wish that I not be his favorite so I could get away, and he not send his pigs to take me back."

"Well, I don't know about Venezuelan drug law, but in the US they would lock them up for a very long time."

She stopped eating and looked at me across the table. "Your friend got me out. With money anything is possible here. They have money. They will get out."

I reached for her hand. "I don't know how my friend did it, but he got it done. I'm glad you are here. I am glad Ratón got away."

"Yes, I happy too. Mario, thank you. I know I keep saying. I don't know what else to say."

"No thank you needed." I squeezed her hand gently. "Let's eat."

She lifted her glass. "Eat food, drink wine," she said rather cheerfully. "You have a woman?"

"I'm not married, if that's what you mean. I love women too much to give them all up for just one." A flash of faces went through my head. I thought of my team. "Not one woman. I have three," I said. I thought of Melina. "Four." A minute passed. I thought of Sami. "Five."

Valita put a finger over my lips.

"Six," she said. "Me."

I won't deny I was a little startled, but pleased.

Valita said, "Where I come from, we know our mate, but we can do what we want to do with our bodies. You, Mario, are not my mate. But I can enjoy you, oh boy."

"That's my philosophy. I don't have just one mate, but I do what I want to do, openly."

I was glad we had come to an agreement, but I was impatient. I took her hand, got up, and led her to the bedroom, where we got it on like savages in heat. I fucked her so hard, I was afraid I might hurt her, but when I pulled back, she urged me on. We moved like animals to a furious conclusion.

She nibbled her way down my body to where I had grown soft. Her mouth took me and I quickly recovered. When I sat up, her hands pushed at my chest.

"Take it easy, boy," she said. *"Relajate, chico."* She pushed me back to the bed.

"I remember the iron door," I said.

She smiled at me. "I wanted you so. I wanted to press my *nalgas* against the bars and let you take me, but how could I ask such a thing?" Then she stopped talking, her mouth full of me.

"I remember when you took me like this through the iron door," I whispered.

She pulled away to whisper back, "I, too, remember."

Valita moaned, and her mouth moved hungrily. She pulled away again and got on her knees, looking at me over her shoulder. The bedroom light was dim, but bright enough for me to appreciate her feminine curves. Prison had changed her. She was slim like a reed. Still, her flesh beckoned to me. I remembered the bars that had stood between us and imagined her ass against the bars as I entered her, as she had described. There were no bars between us now. I didn't need to be asked twice.

It was three in the morning. Our bodies had been sated, and we were talking again. Valita had a funny way of slipping in and out of broken English and good Spanish, even more now when she was sleepy.

"You have no family?"

"When I am fourteen, my parents work in a cocaine refinery for a cartel deep in the jungle. One night, the federales land in big helicopters like the one you come in. Everyone in the laboratory is shot dead. No arrests, no prisoners. I am lucky not to be shot, but I am hiding. After that, I work in farms and even two laboratories of cartels. Such jobs don't last. I move on to find another job. When I come to the coffee plantation, it is harvest time. Patrón Lario takes a liking to me. His maid, she teach me to keep house for a big place like Lario's. I very happy to be living in the big house accompanied by the other maid, most times for months without seeing the patrón. Then the patrón comes. I not so happy."

I was sated, but only temporarily. I couldn't keep my eyes and hands off her. In the morning, rather than leave, I ordered room service. The late breakfast that the waiter set up on the dining room table got us out of the bedroom. I watched her finish her orange juice, and poured her more.

"Thank you."

"Eat. Don't be shy."

"After last night, you think I'm shy?" She laughed.

I met Juan and Ramiro at the hotel grill for coffee before we went to a conference room for a group meeting with the families that had signed with Lario and Gustavo. In a conference room that smelled of coffee and cinnamon, I wrote out the retainers myself, just as I had for all those years I signed auto cases. Room service brought lunch for everyone, but it still smelled of coffee. While everyone was eating, I escaped from the meeting and found a secluded phone booth near the elevators off the hotel lobby. I dialed Pepe's warehouse and a machine answered. I didn't leave a message. The first call to his home was a busy signal. On the second call, a woman answered the phone.

"This is Mario. I'd like to talk to Pepe for a moment," I said.

"I'll see if he is around," she said. The woman left. I could hear footsteps walk away. It sounded to my ear like high heels on marble, but I could be wrong. Pepe started talking out of absolute silence. He must have been wearing rubber-soled shoes, or maybe he was barefoot. I did not hear him approach. That was probably how it was with him all the time. No one saw him coming. An ominous thought.

"Good to hear from you so promptly," Pepe said. "You called just in time."

"Somehow, not sure how, I will repay you," I promised.

Then I went back to the meeting and answered questions until there were no questions left. That took six hours, but it wouldn't have mattered to me if it had taken days. It was all a blur to me. I had Valita on the brain. Finally, everyone had signed, our guests had cleared the room, and Juan and I were alone. We gave the conference room key to the desk clerk and took the elevator up. It had been a productive day.

"Good job, Juan. You've picked up this business quite quickly."

"Thanks, boss," he said with a flash of his white teeth.

"Did you mean that about bringing Valita with you to Puerto Rico?"

"Of course I did," Juan said. "She has been in bad trouble. I would not be much of a man if I did not want to help her," he said seriously. "She is very beautiful."

His offer seemed genuine.

"She is that," I said. "I want her to be happy and safe."

"I live alone," he said, "I can give her a place to stay. Maybe a chance to get on her feet."

Juan and I went up to my room. He was walking in front of me, opened the door, and stood there, transfixed. I bumped into him, then looked over his head to see what had stopped him. Valita was facing the door in a very provocative pose. My cock leaped when I saw her. I can only imagine how Juan felt.

"I'm sorry, I didn't know Juan was going to be with you," Valita said. Her breasts were bare and she was in a pair of bikini panties from our shopping. No question that she was hot and I remained hot for her.

She went into the bathroom and emerged in a terry robe.

"Much better," she said with a smile.

No question she was a fox and a flirt. If she hadn't been a flirt, we would never have gotten to know each other when I was stuck in the warehouse. And we would not be here now. She would not be crossing those long legs of hers, wearing a robe that had only a belt holding it secure.

"I talked to my friend. Your three friends will be released tonight or in the morning."

"Oh, my God. Thank you!" She leaned over and gave me a wet kiss, then took a seat between us. She parked one hand on my left knee, and one hand on

Juan's right knee and pushed her way backward, wedged between us.

"I'm finished with my business here," I said. "The crew and the plane that I came in has been waiting for me. I need to get back."

"Of course," said Valita.

"I talked to Juan about Puerto Rico, but you should know that my offer to come to the United States is still open."

"If Juan doesn't mind me around until I can find a job, then I prefer go to Puerto Rico. But I have no papers. Nothing."

I kept a smile on my face, but had a sinking feeling. I did not want to call Pepe again for another favor. Fortunately, Juan spoke right up. Then it didn't feel quite so fortunate.

"I arrange the paperwork in one day here in Caracas. Do not worry about that. If you come with me, consider it done. You will love Puerto Rico. My place is small, but near many hotels, many tourists, many places to find work."

I watched Valita look at Juan. Not sure I liked what I saw. She was ready to accept his invitation. Hell, she already had accepted it.

I wondered if I would get to sleep with her, at least another night. Am I a total asshole or what?

"Do either of you feel like celebrating? We should toast the future," I said.

Juan stood. "Sounds good to me," he said. He opened a bottle of wine and brought it over with three glasses. He put the glasses on the table and poured.

Valita practically leaped off the couch.

"I go with you, Juan. I will be forever grateful."

If Jo had been there, she'd have called me a brat. I felt petty, remembering not too long ago, Valita had offered to be my slave for life. Now I was sitting on the sofa alone, three glasses of wine in front of me, now separated from Valita by a coffee table. I was separated from Juan too, but I didn't want to sleep with him. Valita had turned from me to face Juan. I watched Valita's back and noticed even her pretty feet and ankles beneath the robe were dancing with happiness.

Valita extended her arm to Juan and they shook hands. She tossed off his handshake, moved closer to him and hugged him enthusiastically. Meanwhile, I was seeing my last night with Valita evaporate. I downed one cup of wine and rested one of my legs on the coffee table. Maybe it thumped down on the table pretty hard. Valita, maybe in response to the noise, looked over her shoulder at me, and halted her enthusiastic Juan-hug.

"Mario, you approve of this? If you do not approve, I will stay here in Caracas." Valita pushed Juan aside and sat beside me. I'm no poet, but her eyes were dark pools of longing. I could see how much she wanted to go with Juan. I felt like king of the assholes because I wanted so much to say no.

Juan moved away from her. He parked himself on a wing chair across from where we were sitting. Now we were three points on a triangle, and no one was happy.

"Valita. I am not Lario. I am not your patrón. You are free as a bird. You need to make your own decisions. What you can count on is that I will forever be in debt to you. I'm pretty sure you saved my life. Without you, I'd have forced my way out, and died in some godforsaken jungle. Anything you need, all you need to do is call me. As for Juan, I vouch for him. He's a friend and has never let me down. And he's got your Lobo."

"Thank you, boss, for the kind words," Juan said.

Valita put her head on my chest and started crying. "Mario, thank you so much. I am free thanks to you. How can I ever repay you?"

"You pay me back with your friendship."

I kissed her forehead, then her face, then she moved easily into Juan's arms.

"Your friends came and saved you. Not me, not Ratón."

"You saved my life," I replied.

"Okay, then," Juan said, "Valita goes with me to Puerto Rico. When you want to see her, you fly to Puerto Rico or I bring her to you."

His delivery was easygoing. That's the way Juan was.

Juan got up. No question Juan was damn good looking. No question Valita knew it too.

"I stay with Mario tonight?" she looked at me. "Unless you want me to stay in the other room with Juan."

I smiled at her. "Remember what I just told you?"

She quickly caught on. "Yes, it is my decision. If it is okay with you, I will stay here tonight and move to Juan's room when you leave tomorrow."

Juan winked at me, walked to the door, and let himself out.

There was nothing savage about our lovemaking that night. It was slow, and lingering, and wonderful, and inscribed in my memory a woman I would never forget.

Tom and I sat across from a very happy Oscar at the restaurant at the top of Oscar's building. Because I'd spent most of December and January steeped in shorts and misery, I was acutely aware of how I was dressed. The best, softest shoes on the market, fine wool socks, and exquisitely crafted European suits, finely woven, perfectly fitted. I was aware of everything: the quality of the light from gilded sconces, linen tablecloths, china, silver, sommelier with bottle in hand offering the cork to the table of fusty lawyers next to us. On February seventh, I had returned home with retainers in hand. The clients had all signed substitution of attorney forms. This was Oscar's idea of a little victory brunch. He and Tom were as dressed up as I. Coddled eggs and filets all around. Tom and I had iced tea. I still tried not to drink around Tom. Oscar had a margarita.

I told them in detail about going to the jail facility to pick up Valita, about the conditions there, about the soulless-looking guards and the overcrowding. I brought up seeing the lawyers behind bars and the hostile banter that started up when the four assholes happened to see me when we were walking toward the exit.

"Wonder how much time those assholes will do." I finished off a filet that had been as tender to cut as a stick of butter.

Oz sucked on his cigar, blew the smoke up, looked at me, and then at Tom. He took a sip of the margarita. "I don't know. Maybe life." He laughed.

"They deserve it," Tom said. "It's a shame they couldn't be pinned for the kidnappings."

Oscar said, "Justice is like a rose. By any other name, it is still justice."

"Justice is the letter of the law," Tom said, looking troubled.

My two friends were very different men.

"Something new I learned. In Venezuela, justice is measured by the depth of your pockets," I said.

"Let's go down to the office to see how much deeper I can make your pockets. I owe you for these additional cases."

Oscar paid me three hundred fifty thousand dollars[17] for sixty-five retainers from families of decedents that had perished in the Caracas tragedy. That included cases that we'd snatched from Lario and Gustavo. According to Tom, who was the guy in the office with vast experience in aviation cases, that would be a drop in the bucket compared to what those cases were worth. Nobody was tossing around any specific figures, but Oscar must have had a good idea of what the caseload would be worth when it settled or went to court. I knew that the value of that many car accident death cases would have been a bundle. These cases would be worth more. I hoped. I accepted the money without my usual negotiation. I couldn't overlook the support Oscar had shown in rescuing me from a jungle prison where no one from my world would have found me. No doubt I had used up any reserved favors he had with Pepe. If I had balls, I should have passed on the $350,000, but I wasn't there yet. Someday, maybe I would be strong enough to swing something that big as payback for my life. Jason had taught me that aviation cases required big investments by attorneys who handled this type of case. They needed to have deep pockets. At least Oscar would make his investment back with a huge profit. As for me, three hundred fifty thousand for two months of work was the stuff of dreams. I gave the girls a ten-thousand-dollar bonus each, and that delighted them as well.

---

[17] $350,000.00 in 1975 had the same buying power as $1,595,062.62 in 2017

Chapter 10
May 1, 1976
Coasting

My six hundred units had a very low vacancy factor. The management company took a chunk each month, but the account balances of the rentals kept increasing. I wouldn't have such deep pockets if I hadn't started out buying that first apartment building and continued to keep an eye out for similar deals. The management company got paid a pretty penny to take care of everything. Jo groaned about the expense, kept an eagle eye on the management company, and burned their ears every time they fell below her standards. I kept telling her, everyone has to make a living.

I had pushed the girls to invest in real estate, and my real estate broker, Randy, found small rental properties for Pixie, Jo, and Niley for their initial leap from tenant to landlord. Jo already owned her home, but now she also owned a four-unit building with a small mortgage payment covered by the rental of one of the units. Pixie bought a four-unit building next door from the same seller who sold Jo her units, moved into the larger three-bedroom unit, and was now a landlady for three tenants. Her mortgage was small, and she had cash flow from the rents as long as Jo kept an eye on Pixie's impulse spending. Because of the aviation bonuses, there was plenty of cushion; but Jo had the mad idea she could get Pixie to keep her bank accounts organized. Niley owned the small house I had helped her buy, the one with a garage she'd once had a gift basket business in. She was thinking of selling the house and moving to the six-unit building she'd bought in Monterey Park. My girls were landlords, and I was proud of them.

One of the many nights when we had dinner to celebrate life in general, I raised my glass and toasted, "Who says ambulance chasers are dummies?"

"I won't drink to that," Jo said.

"We're no dummies," Niley said.

"Hell," Pixie said, swallowing the wine in one gulp, "I'll drink to anything."

Not that I would use that phrase around anyone but the girls. Bottoms up. We were happy, and personally I was extremely grateful. Jake, may he rest in peace, had told me more than once, don't talk politics or religion with anyone, especially your friends. No one knows it except maybe my Aunt Carmen, but I do believe in God, and I often have conversations with Him. I have to. I have so much to thank him for. God is Aunt Carmen's good friend. When I was a little kid, I crawled on my knees from the front door of the church all the way to the altar as penance whenever I got caught doing something bad like looking at dirty pictures in magazines or using profanity. If she had a hint of my sexual encounters now, my aunt would have me on my knees in a heartbeat, crawling a furrow into the aisle between the door and the altar. But I guess now that's between me and God.

In the first week of June, I was sitting in Oscar's office. I'd come to talk with him about some small cases we'd signed, a helicopter and a Cessna.

"I talked to Pepe couple days ago," Oscar said.

"How is he?"

"Pepe would say he was okay if he was sitting in a pot of boiling water." Oscar laughed.

"I should call to thank him."

"Do it. He wants to talk to you."

"About what?"

"He didn't say. He's a good contact to have."

Oscar's cigar had gone out in the ashtray. He picked up, moistened the head, and rolled it between his fingers as he held it over the lighter. I'd seen him do this before. He called it toasting. The tip flashed a small flame which went down, and the smoke went straight up. Oscar sucked on one end, and the other glowed red as he puffed. He didn't inhale, just smoked for the mouthful of tobacco flavor. He'd explained it before, but I just didn't get the appeal.

"I will call." I hesitated, staring as the smoke went straight up to a vent in the ceiling. "Is he wanted here by the authorities?"

"Nope." Oscar laughed again. "But you can be sure that Pepe will never enter the United States again. Not for any reason. Not ever. No matter what."

Right or wrong, I pieced together my own profile of Pepe. I'd been considering him for a while. I reflected on what he'd done to get me out of that plantation, then Valita, and then the maids. He was powerful. Connected. I didn't know exactly what his bit was. I'd never asked Oscar directly what it was about Pepe's occupation that made him so shady. It was enough knowing he was popped for cocaine-related charges carrying a century-long sentence. But I knew the law would sometimes pull a sleight of hand and use one charge they could nail in lieu of one they couldn't, like they'd done to the lawyers in Venezuela. Oscar was all hush-hush about it, so there was much more involved. Pepe had given me that business card for an import company. He had a company where I called him. Whatever else he did, I didn't need to know about. It was no different than my childhood friend Pélon, who was still in prison for murder. Pélon was always into bad business, and I never asked. It's how Pélon was, and instinct told me it was how Pepe was too.

I visited a cluster of pay phones in downtown Pasadena which were like old friends. I must have called from that corner a thousand times, running down car crashes back when that was what I chased. Nothing new about coins and pay phones, except that local calls were a dime. I had three rolls of quarters.

With any luck, he wouldn't be at the two numbers I had for him. I might get away with just leaving a message that I returned his call. The phone rang at the first number. No one answered. I dialed it a second time. Still no answer. I felt like my luck was holding. The coins fell into their niche, and I picked them up again. I was relieved and nearly dropped them in my pocket. But no. Pepe had stepped up for me. If not for his involvement, I might be missing ears and fingers, still in the remote coffee warehouse, or ashes in a Venezuelan jungle. I got pissed at myself for being a jackass. I tried the second number. A girl answered. Minutes later, Pepe and I were chatting in Spanish.

"Amigo, everything is well with you?"

"Thanks to you, everything is well," I said. "How are you, Pepe?"

"Life is beautiful," he said. I thought about the boiling water that Oscar had mentioned to me.

"Wonderful," I said. "Things are good here too. Oscar gave me your message. What can I do for you, Pepe? I'm here for you."

There was a pause.

"Amigo, thank you for saying this."

"I mean it."

"I only wanted to say hello. Oscar tells me you travel a lot. Let me know when you go abroad. We can go party."

I was relieved by what I heard. Pepe wasn't looking for payback. I had imagined all sorts of things he might want me to do, but not a party. "Of course."

"I have a small fleet of planes. I go to Rome often, and many other countries."

I wanted to say 'but not the states,' but held my tongue.

I drove home confused but relieved that Pepe wanted nothing from me. Reading Oscar's mood, I'd thought there might be more.

It was hot in the way Los Angeles does July, though the temperature in my apartment was perfectly cool. I was alone when I answered the phone.

"Amigo, how are you?"

Chapter 11
July 1976
Pepe and Camila

I recognized Pepe's voice. It had been a month since I'd last talked to him, and he'd slipped into the back of my mind. I wondered about his calling me at home when I hadn't given him my home line. Few people know that my home and office lines are at the same location. Of course, he knew Oscar, so there was my answer.

"I'm going to Rome for a few days. Want to come along? I have a beautiful pad there. We can fill it up with ladies, eh?" His Spanish was fast.

"I'm in," I heard myself say.

"I can pick you up in Tijuana. Tomorrow at noon your time."

He gave me details of where to find him. I wrote out his plane's tail number and the airport details for someone who could direct me to the plane.

When Melina came over after work that night, I already had a duffel bag packed.

She went to my wine rack and picked out a bottle.

"That's expensive stuff," I said. "It's gonna cost you."

"Cost me what, big spender?"

I looked her over. She was wearing one of her designer numbers, classy looking. A million tiny buttons.

"It'll cost you that dress."

She tilted her head as if she were considering it.

"Only if that goes for you too." She leaned forward from her perch on the couch. I was facing her on the ottoman. She almost kissed me, but slinked past, walked behind me, and pulled my jacket down halfway down my back, essentially trapping my arms at my sides. It took some tugging on her part, and I let her do it. I started laughing because my arms really were kind of pinned. I wouldn't have let anyone in the world do that to me but Melina.

"How long have you been planning this little maneuver?" I laughed.

"Weeks and weeks," she said. She stuck her hands inside my shirt and subjected my ribs to a tickle. She got me laughing so hard I couldn't get loose.

"Okay, okay," I said. "I won't wear a dress."

"Not what I meant," she said, and tickled some more.

I wrenched my arms free and tossed aside my jacket, shirt, and pants. If she'd had good sense, she'd have run. But no. She faced me. She stood there, and watched me, her eyes dark and challenging, with a hint of laughter.

I hooked one hand in her dress. Hooked the second hand in. It was a pretty dress, sleeveless, navy blue with white dots. No sleeves and a little collar. A triple row of tiny white buttons marched down the frail summer fabric of the front, collar to hem, and the hem ended well above her knee. It was thin cotton, or maybe silk. I gave a hard jerk. The fabric gave with a ripping sound as the fabric tore down the front, and buttons rained down on us like chunky snow. Practically in slow motion, I walked behind her and slid the dress down to her elbows, not as if it could pin her in its sleeveless state, but it's the thought that counts. She shrugged, and the dress wafted to the ground. The bits of lace she was wearing could hardly be called underwear. I sniffed the curve of her neck, and behind her ear. She smelled delicious, of fruity warm shampoo, and honeysuckle, and clove. Maybe Chloe.

"Better," I said, and got up to pour the first glass of wine.

Melina settled on the couch, crossing her long legs in a move that was sheer poetry. She was still in dark pantyhose. For a second, I mourned the demise of stockings and garters.

She might be looking like a centerfold, but it was the lawyer talking.

"From everything you've said, this guy is a criminal. Why are you going to socialize with him?"

"I never said he was a criminal." Although I might not have said it, Melina was right that I believed Pepe bent, bought, or broke whatever laws he needed to. The unavoidable truth was that I had a debt to him that I could not overlook. "I owe that man my life. He found me when I was buried out there in the Venezuelan jungle."

"I can't like this." She looked at my duffel with concern. "I'm sorry. I got a bad feeling. I'm afraid this is the first step of a bad road."

I poured us wine and set the two glasses on the coffee table by my couch. "Cuz, I'm not going to get involved with anything that can get me locked up. I grew up with criminals. I know how to handle myself. There's a fine line to walk, and I know where it is."

"You're talking about Pélon. Pélon, whom I still would pay to get rid of my father's killer, if you would let me. I still have nightmares of when he's going to get out of jail and kill me."

"You know you can't do that. Pélon will get his hooks in your wallet and never let go. You'd be paying hush money for the rest of your life."

She shrugged. "At least I'd have a life, and wouldn't have to worry about that murderer coming after me. So?"

We had slipped easily into that old argument. I slid the lace strap over her shoulder and nuzzled her neck again until I could tell her concerns about Pepe moved to the back of her mind, or at least out of her mouth.

I kissed her ear. "So what? Let's go in the bedroom, and I'll give you a nightcap," I suggested.

She downed the wine and held up the empty glass. "That was the nightcap," she said, kicking off her hose. She put the goblet on the table upside down. She stared at my glass until I emptied it in a gulp, and put it next to hers. "No need for the bedroom," she said. "Fuck me here."

She walked to the picture window overlooking the city and hit the light switch. The lights outside were so bright that the room didn't get completely dark, but the focus changed. She planted her stiletto on the fake potted plant and shoved the ficus off its perch. It fell with a thud, but the heavy china pot didn't break. She stepped up and took her place on its perch, which brought her to the perfect height. I laughed quietly. I should have guessed there was a reason why she'd gotten this particular plant stand. The city lights glittered against Melina's nearly naked body. The edges and peaks were frosted in light. She extended her arms and hands above her head against the wall, awaiting me. I reached her, and her face was at my eye level. I was torn between holding her hands in place and making her hold them there, but the dilemma was easily solved by trying it both ways.

A moment later, I was deep inside. "You're so wet," I said. That woman always inspires me to new heights. She convulsed in my arms right away, and at least twice more. I might be leaving against Melina's wishes, but at least I was leaving her satisfied.

I let Jo know I would be gone for a few days. She gave me an earful till I cut it short.

"You guys can stay home until I get back, or come here and work the newspapers."

"Promise to keep in touch?" Jo said.

"Of course, baby. Kiss and hug Pixie and Niley for me. I got to go."

I arrived at the airport in Tijuana an hour early, parked my car on the US side in San Ysidro, and walked across the border into Mexico. A taxi delivered me to the airport.

I called the number Pepe gave me and was told the plane had not yet landed. Thirty minutes later, I was paged to the front desk and directed to a waiting area. A well-dressed young man introduced himself as Paulo. "I work for Pepe. We are five minutes from the plane."

Paulo knew his way around the airport. We left the building and emerged on the tarmac away from the big jets. Pepe's plane made Oscar's cool Lear look like a midget. By now I knew my planes pretty well. I didn't recognize the vintage, but it was a burgundy McDonnell Douglas DC-9. No name. Just the tail numbers in black. I followed Paulo up the steps. Pepe greeted me at the doorway.

"Amigo, welcome aboard."

We hugged like old friends.

I didn't want to look stupid, but it was tough not to appear dazzled. I entered a plane the likes of which I had only seen in magazine shoots of the Playboy plane. He showed me the two bedrooms. The beds would never be long enough for me, but they kicked ass. The bedrooms and main cabin had television sets. In addition to TV, I saw at a glance plenty of entertainment aboard, like piped-in stereo, a movie screen, and three arcade machines.

"Do you like it?"

"I'm speechless."

"I copied lots of things from the Playboy plane. It's the same model as this one. Did you know Hefner sold it to a Venezuelan airline company earlier this year?"

"I didn't know."

"I was in his plane before I designed mine."

I was introduced to the crew: two pilots and a backup, and three gorgeous flight attendants wearing practically nothing. They looked like Vegas showgirls without the big hats. Paulo was aboard. I didn't know his exact role, but he appeared to be Pepe's assistant, or right-hand man, possibly one of many.

Pepe and I took seats facing each other in wide, beige leather chairs. There was a full aisle between my seat and Pepe's. If my team had been here, and Pixie set her eyes on this whole shebang, she would be saying she was coming. I chuckled at the thought.

"More power to you. I am very happy for you."

"Amigo, thank you. You will love this trip, I promise you."

I wondered why Pepe was courting me. I'd seen Oscar do something similar with a client he wanted to sign. I felt like something was up, and maybe Melina's instincts were on to something. One of the showgirls—I mean, stewardesses—handed me a glass of red wine, and my spark of worry was doused. Pepe drank a Chivas water.

We toasted. Over the speaker, the pilot told us we'd be airborne in five minutes.

Before we hit the flying bedrooms, Pepe talked a little about his trucking company headquartered in Colombia and Venezuela, and his commuter service that operated in Brazil between Sao Paulo and Rio de Janeiro. The plane we were in was one of a fleet of six, but there were other planes he owned that were for family use only. Though I already knew he had homes in Bogotá, Rome, and Rio, I still had no clue what his import company could be exporting or importing. Whatever it was, it was profitable.

The limo that picked us up at the airport followed a path that wound like a corkscrew around a hill that had a view of the Vatican.

"Here we are," Pepe said.

"Unbelievable." I was knocked for a loop at the first glimpse of the Roman villa Pepe called home. It was late in the afternoon when we arrived, and it was spectacular. The red tile roof and the stucco building fit perfectly into the landscape, as if it had been there for a hundred years. From a distance, I could tell it was huge. The building was a perfect rectangle, two stories high, and an optical illusion. It doubled in size as we pulled up the drive. It could have been a public building, museum, or tourist stop. Stucco and gates on either side of the house were grown with vines, hiding what lay beyond. If I'd been a kid, I would have snuck in just to see what was there.

"Mario, you like it?"

"You must come to Rome a lot."

"Two, three times a year. I have many homes. Property is a good investment."

I thought about my apartments, but I remained silent. This was an investment of a whole other level.

At the huge front doors, Pepe was greeted by six maids uniformed in different colors and styles.

"My cleaning staff lives here year round," he explained.

They did their job well. The house was spotless. I didn't have to inquire about the men posted around the house, because Pepe explained their purpose.

"They are security guards. I don't need as many when I'm not here, but when I visit I take no chances. Let me show you to your room," Pepe said.

I insisted on carrying my duffle bag myself and followed Pepe up a winding staircase.

"*Mi casa es tu casa,*" Pepe said, opening the door. The bedroom he revealed was out of sight, bigger than Sami's bedroom in London, and four times the size of my bedroom at home. The drapes were open. I walked past Pepe straight to the window where I stared in shock.

"Shit, man," I said, at the view of a stunning back garden where two colonnades branched off the house and framed a pool that reminded me of the reflecting pool outside of the Lincoln Memorial in DC. It was more like a hotel than a house. When we'd driven up, I seen no clue that the villa stretched out like that, or that the garden was there. I wanted to go down and take a look.

Pepe laughed at my reaction. I wasn't embarrassed, but I didn't want to seem like a yokel. I turned to look at the bed, a huge antique in front of the massive window. I knew from my experience with Melina's shopping that the fabric of the pleated, open drapery was top of the line. A wardrobe took up an entire wall. Even with the padded chest at the foot of the bed and a sitting area, enough free space remained that I would have had room to work out. The attached bathroom with a vintage claw-footed tub was not at all modern, but it was the same tone as the wall-to-wall marble and had a fireplace of its own. I'd never seen or imagined a bathroom with a fireplace.

"I should be giving you something. I'm the one who owes you, remember?"

He laughed. "I hope we can be good friends. Just because I refuse to set foot in the US after my last experience there doesn't mean I can't have American friends."

"We are friends," I said. Pepe was about five foot eleven, so I actually looked down on him. My being tall makes things awkward sometimes, but the height difference didn't seem to bug Pepe.

"Gracias, Mario."

"*Al contrario,*" I said. "Thank you for all this attention and generosity."

"I have made no plans till about midnight," Pepe said. "I'll have them wake you up to see if you want to join me in the disco downstairs. I plan to have some interesting company for us."

Pepe was smiling from ear to ear. It was eerie that he reminded me of Pélon and Carson rolled up into one, but maybe that's what made me feel like I'd known him for a very long time. I couldn't wait to see a disco inside someone's house.

"I would like to check out the grounds," I said, "I did sleep on your amazing plane, but maybe I could use a few hours of sleep later. Jet lag," I said.

"Do check out the gardens around the house if you want. If you are hungry, dial 0 and the cook will answer. Order anything you want. You must be hungry." He pointed out the phone.

"Thanks."

"Enough thanks," Pepe walked to the open door. "I'm going to get some rest."

I took a bath in the claw-footed tub. It was small, and my knees were around my ears, but hot water is hot water. I put on jeans. I found a back staircase, and one of the house staff told me it was just for the help. She showed me a back exit that led into a patio. I ran into a gardener watering plants in pots, and he gave me a tour of the highly landscaped garden with bird baths, vined trellises, a maze, shrubs sculpted to look like creatures, little koi ponds with bridges arching over them, and marble statuary of fauns and nymphs that the gardener introduced by name. Pepe could have charged for tickets. There's nine hours' difference between Rome and LA, and I was starting to feel it. I thanked the gardener, went up to my room, and dialed the cook. At four Rome-time, a covered plate with a steak and a baked potato was delivered to my door by one of the very pretty house ladies. I thanked her as she set up a place setting for me. She turned the television to something familiar. I found myself watching an episode of *Happy Days* dubbed in Italian, which was hysterical. I wanted to call the girls and share it with them. I polished off a tray of Italian delicacies at a small café table beside a window in my room. The nine-hour time difference kicked me in the ass since I'd only slept for a couple of hours. I crawled into the strange bed and dropped right off to sleep.

It seemed only a moment had passed, but it was six hours later and pitch black outside when a maid knocked on my door. While I'd slept, the table had been cleared of my dinner. My body was confused, but my watch told me it was four p.m. LA time.

"Come in."

"*Señor, el jefe* is in the disco if you care to join him."

I thanked her, used the tub for the second time, and put on another pair of jeans and tee. My clothing options were limited. I don't know what I was thinking when I packed a duffle bag, but at the time, I just hadn't wanted to seem too fussy. I had not packed to impress him, but Pepe would be thinking I have no wardrobe. I wasn't expecting he would have a place like this one. Why the hell not? He had a whole fleet of planes. I was in a mansion with a guy I'd never seen in anything but top-notch designers, and all I'd brought were freaking Levis. A fat lot of good my fantastic wardrobe was doing me back home in my closet.

The maid led me through the house to his disco room. It was in his basement, a room startlingly big to find in a personal residence, outfitted with a dance floor, disco lights, mirrored ceiling, and disco ball. One wall was painted black with the Studio 54 logo. Two other walls were painted black, with the bars of the Studio 54 bridge set into one wall and a go-go dancer's cage inset in the wall on the other. The fourth wall had a graffiti-type painting of the studio 54 crowd directly on the wall. I'm pretty sure I saw the signature of Andy Warhol on it. I was relieved to see that Pepe had on jeans and a casual long-sleeved shirt. The lights were on, so I could see the black couch and a couple of black tables and chairs around the edges of the dance floor. The black walls were pretty much invisible, making the room seem to go on and on, especially in the disco lighting.

Pepe was already drunk. He'd obviously started well before midnight. I sat down on the couch across from him. He was in a talkative mood, and chatted as I had never heard him before. He made veiled references to several businesses, but nothing specific.

"The girls will be here soon. Any minute." He looked at his watch. "They went up to change clothes."

"The girls?" I asked.

"That Hugh Hefner, he really knows how to live. I have lots of girls here in Rome. They're a wild bunch," he said. "But you should see the ones I got in Spain."

I didn't quite have time to digest that thought, because like magic, the party girls streamed in.

"Mario, let me present a few dolls that came over to party with us. Dolls, this is Mario. Mario, these are my dolls."

I grinned as we started a cycle, kissing all the girls' cheeks, European style. I was reminded of my experiences with European models. It was practically déjà vu.

"Pleased to meet you."

A fine-looking waitress in a multicolored wig offered me a drink. I ordered wine.

"Feel like dancing?" Pepe asked me.

"Why not?" I asked, standing up.

One of the girls put her hand on my bicep.

"Wow," she said, sounding like she was creaming her jeans. "I love the way these sleeves show off your muscles. Can I dance with you first?"

So we danced.

I've never really been a dancer. Most times I pass, but tonight I felt different and I didn't think how my height sometimes made me self-conscious on a dance floor. I was a little embarrassed, but she was hot. "Anything for you, Doll." I felt like asking her name but didn't. Pepe hadn't mentioned any names.

"Girls, hit the lights." Pepe said, laughing. He was fit and confident, not like a guy who worked out of an office. More disco lights streamed into play.

I heard one of the girls say, "*Jefe*, we are here to serve you."

Most of the girls were on the floor dancing with each other, and several were surrounding Pepe. When the music stopped, one girl who had not been dancing climbed the stairs to the dancer's cage and shut the gate. She shook off the tie-died short kimono she was wearing. Underneath, she had on a dance-dress covered with rows of fringes that shivered when she moved. The music started up again, and she moved a lot. Pretty mesmerizing.

I walked with another girl to the floor. Pepe went to the dance floor too, immediately surrounded by dancing girls. There was one dim light by the couch. When that one went out, I suddenly got the full effect. In the dark, the black walls completely disappeared. The sound system was killer. The room turned into Studio 54. The wall with the bridge inset looked real. The go-go dancer outfit was shimmering with rows of swinging fringe, and the cage's backside was mirrored so it looked like there were two of her, dancing butt to butt. She had on shiny panties, also with shiny, swinging fringe.

It was a fast dance, a song I'd never heard before, but with a fast disco beat, and sung in Italian. The girl I was dancing with was grinding all over me, as if it were a slow dance. She reminded me a little of Pixie.

I caught that Pepe was called *jefe* the way that most people I knew were calling me boss.

The girls were tipsy. My host was tipsy. No one was evaluating how good or how bad I danced, so I danced and laughed a lot. The girls and Pepe slowed down and sat down with sweaty faces and damp armpits. I wasn't even warmed up, since this dancing was not nearly as consuming as a stretch before one of my workouts. I excused myself and went to a bathroom to get rid of a lot of wine. When I came back, the girls were kneeling and sitting on carpet and floor pillows crowded around the black coffee table with round mirrors in front of them.

One of the girls had flipped a switch. A warm, dim, ambient light came on in addition to the strobes, enabling me to see Paulo put down a small crystal bowl filled with something white. He put a careful scoop of white powder on each mirror and five one-hundred-dollar bills, one alongside each of five single-edge razor blades. Pepe was sitting on a wing chair. I parked myself in the twin of his chair just to his left, feet from the girls. The doll who had been the last to dance with me made three lines and rolled a hundred-dollar bill. She looked at me and patted the pillow beside her. No one had told me her name, but I heard another one of the girls call her Maggie.

"Come on, Mario. Let's party. This is the best stuff ever," she said.

"Go for it," I told the girl. "I pass."

"You don't use coke?" asked Pepe.

"I'm a wine guy," I said. "Maybe a little pot once in a while." I eyed the bowl on the table. That much cocaine would easily get a body fifty years in prison. It was the first time that I had been this close to cocaine. At my age, you'd think I'd have been around it. But the truth is, when Pélon was fooling around with drugs, I kept my distance. Besides, where I came from, cocaine was not the drug of choice.

"I'll get you some weed." Pepe waved at Paulo. "Roll some joints."

"*Sí, jefe.*"

"I don't use coke either," Pepe said. "I drink too much, but I don't mess with coke or any drugs, not even marijuana."

"Pepe, Paulo, no joint, please. I'm happy with the wine. Really."

Watching the girls do the coke was an experience. I could recall seeing drugs in movies, but never up close and in person, with the girls reeling when they felt the drug hit.

"*Provecho*," Pepe said, lifting his Chivas as though toasting me. I toasted him back with my glass, and I passed on the joint that Paulo tried to give me.

"Seriously, man," I told Paulo. "The wine is good."

"Mario, I'm glad you are not into drugs. All my friends are in the business of selling drugs, and they use. It's too bad."

I sipped my wine and considered his words. Paulo kept filling my glass so that it was never empty. That was the most Pepe had opened up, referring to his friends, dealing. It seemed a confirmation that Pepe was a big-time drug lord, one serious enough to be critical of dealers who use their own product. He stood, staggering a little. He was definitely boozed up. There were a couple joints going around. I wondered if this was some kind of test.

"Mario, take any girl you want, or as many as you want," he yelled over the music. "I have more."

"You are too good to me," I said, moving down on the floor behind Maggie on the pillow she'd invited me to share. She was deeply involved with the coke as I nuzzled her ear. As soon as I moved, I could tell I was drunk on my ass, but I didn't care. The room was pretty thick in smoke, and my senses sharpened. I wondered if I was getting a contact high. Maggie smelled so good. I was sure by their cleanliness, manners, and the way they were dressed that she and the other call girls had a high-end clientele of wealthy men like Pepe. Maggie looked away from the cocaine as someone handed her a joint. She took it and inhaled deeply, but did not exhale. She turned the joint around in her mouth, put her lips to my mouth, and exhaled her smoke through the joint between her lips. I'd turned down the joint and had just been expecting a kiss. The smoke went straight into my lungs, a powerhouse of a shotgun, and my head went spinning off into another dimension. I took the joint from her, flipped it around and returned the favor without losing any of the smoke. It was an intimate kiss that we kept going till the joint was too small to use. We did a pretty good job of keeping all the smoke. Maggie giggled. I giggled, and felt proud we'd managed to shotgun the whole joint. More joints were circulating. I remembered I'd refused Paulo's, but Maggie had been very persuasive. It didn't matter. No one was keeping score and I was far beyond being high. My mouth tasted like the dry floor of a cab, so I finished off my wine, and Paulo refilled it. Half of the wine missed my glass, and Pepe and I found it hilarious. I had no idea how many glasses I'd downed. Pepe had a chick on his lap, his hand clearly up her skirt. From the position I had on the floor, I could see he was dipping his hand in the bowl of coke that Paulo held for him and fingering the girl with the drug. The girl was going crazy.

Maggie turned around and put her arms around my neck and brought me close.

"Take me right here, if you dare," she said, giggling. She lay on the carpet and raised her short skirt.

"Bedroom," I said.

When I woke, I woke alone, and my head was still spinning. My room was dark with only a sliver of daylight showing between the closed drapes. I had no clue of the time or day. I remembered telling Maggie we were coming to the bedroom, but nothing after that. I smelled of wine and pot smoke. I opened the curtain just enough to let in the sun. The sunlight on my skin reminded me of home and felt delicious. I stood there for a long time, just soaking up the sun on my bare skin.

I picked up the phone and ordered coffee. By the time I came out of the shower, a silver platter had been delivered to the coffee table along with a huge basket of breads, with dishes of butter, honey, and jam.

My watch, still on LA time, said three. That meant three in the morning, making it noon here in Rome. I was in my boxers and a tee, drinking my second cup of coffee, when there was a knock on the door.

"*Pase*," I said.

Pepe walked in with a big smile and a beautiful girl on his arm.

"Let me put my pants on," I said, getting up fast.

Pepe and the girl laughed.

"Boxers are fine," Pepe said. "I have to run for a little while. I want you to meet my sister."

I dragged my jeans on in record time and rushed over to join them. I was very glad they'd arrived after I washed last night off my skin.

"Pardon me for keeping you waiting," I said. I took her hand, shook it, then kissed it, much as Juan had done to Valita in the taxi when we had just gotten her out of prison.

"How nice is that?" she said. "No one has kissed my hand in many moons. Can't even remember how long ago."

"Pleased to meet you. And your name is…"

"Camila," she said with a brilliant smile.

First impression? Waves of sun-streaked dark hair, provocative and promising eyes. Fashionably put together, like Sami and Melina. Perfect makeup. Scarlet lips. A hungry mouth. Pepe was in his forties, and she was much younger, a couple inches shorter than her brother, and slim where he was muscular. In her red and white patterned A-line skirt and hat, she looked like a stick of dynamite about to explode. I think I just stared at her, and hung on to her hand until Pepe brought me to my senses. I could tell that I was still high from the night before. I dropped her hand.

"Mario, if you fuck my little sister, you will have to marry her. So be careful." He was laughing.

"Pay no attention to my brother, the bully," Camila said. "I fuck whoever I wish, whenever and wherever I wish."

Pepe ignored her. "Camila surprised me this morning dropping in for a visit. She woke me up way too early and plans to stay here for a few days."

"You have a beautiful sister," I said.

"I'm right here," she said, challenging me.

"Touching, but no fucking," Pepe continued, laughing. I didn't know how seriously to take it. If I had a sister, I'd probably be carrying a shotgun. But I'd hate to have to corral a sister with my sexual appetite. There's not enough time in the day.

"I have to go check some properties. I'll be back." Pepe left us standing near the door of my room.

"Pay him no mind," she said. "He's overprotective."

"This is his house, and you are his lovely sister. No way I blame him for being protective."

She brushed up against me as she peered at the table in my room. "I see you had coffee. Let's go out by the pool and I'll get you a late breakfast."

My body instantly responded. I took a step back and didn't look down to see if it showed.

She extended her hand.

"I'll put my shoes on."

"Come as you are. No shoes needed. You could have kept your boxers on. Are you shy or something?"

"Not at all," I said.

I took her hand and walked beside her through the hall, and down the winding staircase.

Pepe dropped me and my duffel bag off in Tijuana. I thanked him again. He hugged me like I was an old friend.

"*Vaya con Dios, Mario.* Let's do this often. You are great company. We will be good friends."

"Gracias, Pepe. *Fue fenonemo, otra vez te debo.*"[18]

"If you're going to keep thanking me, get off my plane."

I smiled since I was disembarking anyway, gave him a light punch on the

---

[18] Thank you, Pepe. It was phenomenal, again, I owe you

shoulder, and took the stairs to the tarmac. I followed Paulo to the terminal, caught a taxi to the border, crossed on foot, and got my car from the parking lot where I had left it four days before.

It was late when I got back from Tijuana. The drive home, with me being jet-lagged and alone, was not fun. At one in the morning, Melina came over. I had fallen asleep right after a shower, but I heard her come in. My bedroom was dark.

"Don't play like you're asleep. I can feel when you're awake," she said as she slipped into the bed.

I glanced at the clock. I'd been home for two hours. I extended my arms and Melina came into them. We were face to face in the dark. I could feel her naked skin slide like silk against me.

"Baby, I missed you," I said. "You feel like home."

"Yeah, right. Not even a phone call."

"I wouldn't have known what market to call you at."

"Asshole."

"I'm so tired," I said.

"Tough shit. So am I." She rubbed against me. I might still be asleep, but my package was raring to go.

"Let me get a little of that fine ass," I said, feeling her.

"That's more like it, stud."

I turned her to her side and was there in seconds.

"I love fucking you," I said. She lit like a bottle rocket at the first touch.

"I'm starved," she said, panting. She wanted more, and I gave it to her.

Afterward, we laid there in the dark and talked. I told her everything from the time I arrived at the airport. Melina was quiet up until I told her about the coke.

"That's some bad shit, Mario."

"I know it's bad shit. No worries, baby. You know that's not me. And maybe it was a test to see what I'd do."

Then I told her about Pepe's sister, Camila.

"How old is she?"

"Thirty."

"Perfect, Cuz. She's only two years older than you. Not ten years like me. Did you fuck her?"

"Not a chance. I told you what Pepe told about fucking her. I'd have to marry her." It was my turn to laugh, but I wasn't so sure how serious he was.

"That fucker is a gangster. Can't figure out what he wants. How old is he?"

"Camila said he's forty-seven, single, never been married. She said he probably has a dozen bastards he planted here, there, and everywhere."

"Why is he paying so much attention to you?"

"Camila said that he told her I was special. I think we have Oscar to thank for that. Oscar talked Pepe into getting me rescued. He must have talked me up. Camila thinks her brother is just bored with his rich Colombian and Venezuelan friends, and he wants to expand his horizons with new people like myself."

"Maybe he's looking for surrogates to do his business here for him. The fucker has got to be loaded."

"Got to be. You wouldn't believe his house in Rome."

"Is Camila married?"

"It was a close call twice, and something happened to prevent it."

"Her brother probably had them killed."

I laughed. "You never know."

"Be careful, please. You don't need to be a regular with either of them. I'm not just saying that because you say she's beautiful and available. Remember that shooter who killed Tanis and shot you; the asshole who tried to brain you with a baseball bat when you were asleep in bed; Hugo, who shot you; and the goons who kidnapped you. Next time, you might not have a window to toss them out of, or a helicopter to come pick you up."

"No more next time. No more dark thoughts," I said. "I can take care of myself. I'm a big boy."

"I know you can take care of yourself," Melina said, with a hot shiver in her voice. "And you sure as hell are the biggest boy I know."

I kissed Melina on the lips. The only light was the clock radio that I had turned away so that its dim light reflected on the wall. I could not see her in the pitch black room, but I could feel and smell her. I loved the smell of her. I loved her breath in my mouth.

"I know you mean well, baby."

We whispered together, face to face, lip to lip.

She grabbed my growing cock.

"I don't want to lose this. Don't get killed."

I laughed. "What a bitch."

"Horny bitch," she corrected me. "What else happened there?"

"Camila told me about her business, exporting and importing goods from Colombia, same as her brother. Get this: she has her own plane. She has her own fucking Learjet."

"Fuck! She's in the cocaine business."

"No, I don't think so. I don't think he'd let his sister do that. He seems protective."

"You didn't even finger her like Pepe did that girl in the disco?"

"I spent two days with her. I had more time with her than Pepe. She showed me around Rome. Gave me an insider's tour, better than the last time I was there. Talking. Laughing. No fucking. Truth is, I'm not even sure I did it with Maggie the call girl, or any other doll that Pepe kept around until we left Rome. I drank too much wine, and I smoked a shitload of weed. You know I don't do that."

"Cuz, smoking pot once in a while isn't so bad. Every day to the point you can't even remember? That's not like you."

"It's not, and neither is hanging out with fancy-ass working girls wasted out of their gourds, free for the taking, all smoking pot and snorting cocaine. The smoke was just one night."

"And Pepe has his sister around for all of this?"

"She just showed up. I don't know how Pepe feels about that. Camila doesn't do coke, but she smokes weed like some people smoke Marlboro."

"Fuck," Melina said, shaking her head.

The only thing I didn't tell Melina was how fond Pepe was when we parted. That fond goodbye was a promise of things to come. Melina would only worry about that. And though she probably guessed it, maybe I didn't talk to her about the fantasies of fucking Camila that bounced around in my head. After meeting Camila, whenever I fucked Melina or any of my team, I often thought of Camila without any guilt at all. Fantasy is private business anyway. I had the hots for her. So what?

Chapter 12
November 1976
Figueroa Winding Down

By the time November 1976 rolled around, we had picked up clients in airline crashes in Greece, Egypt, and Morocco. It wasn't so much that owning apartment buildings became an obsession, but that I needed work to keep me busy between crashes; and the buying of real estate became that work. I didn't buy just anything that came along, so I looked at a lot of property. Randy was a young guy, stocky, close to my own age, and hungry in the way I like my associates to be. At least three times a week, Randy and I met for lunch near some property we were visiting. I made note of all the particulars, like number of units, state of repair, current vacancy factor, and income bracket of the neighborhood. I was careful and bid low, no matter what my broker advised. He called me painfully careful with a real estate dollar. If a building was selling for four hundred thousand, I offered two hundred seventy-five thousand[19]. I didn't always get what I asked for, but I didn't pay full price, either.

My real estate assets grew. I was okay with my economic progress, except when I compared my success to Pepe's. What I had was dwarfed in comparison to his assets. His plane, the house in Rome—all of that was far out of my reach. I don't know why he became such a fixture in my brain, except he had some shiny,

---

[19] $275,000.00 in 1976 had the same buying power as $1,196,284.68 in 2017

unbreakable mystique thanks to Oscar's attitude toward him, his rescuing me, and the sheer magnitude of his pull and money. I barely knew the guy. He lived in a world that I'd never realized existed, but it was a world I found quite enticing. Though Oscar had advised me against it, Pepe called me on my home phone whenever he wanted, and I went along with it. I had no business with him, so there was never any dangerous business to discuss.

When I told the girls about the trip, they were interested in the plane, the house, and Pepe in general. Pixie and Niley begged to go on my next trip.

"We met him in Caracas, so it's not like he doesn't know us," Pixie said.

"She's right," Niley said. "I want to see that plane that has beds. I can't believe it. I need to see it with my own eyes."

"Oh stop it," Jo said. "I know you've seen pictures of Hefner's plane and his bedroom, so you've seen a plane with a bed."

"Yes, mother," Pixie snarked.

Jo was handling Niley and Pixie, but she had her own concerns. She waited till the girls were distracted. We were all snacking on ice cream, and she took me aside.

"I know I have no business telling you what you can and cannot do. But, boss, you gotta promise us you will never mess with coke."

"No promise needed. Not a chance I'm doing that," I said with finality. "Next subject."

I was spared from her next gripe by a timely call from Valita. Juan worked every case we handled, which gave me an opportunity to talk to Valita, but those weren't the only times Valita and I talked.

"Juan tells me you're happy."

"We are. We laugh. We do stuff in Puerto together. He takes me places I never been. You know they have coffee plantations here? They have tours." She laughed heartily over the thought of someone wanting to visit a coffee plantation. "I have housekeeping work at a hotel. Juan gets some investigations locally."

"I'm glad."

"He looks forward to jobs you give him. It's more money, and he gets to travel. And he gets to come home to me." She giggled. I'd never heard her sound so happy.

"Where is home now? Juan gave Jo a new mailing address."

"His apartment too small for Lobo and me. We have little house with a yard. Nothing for Lobo to do but chase cats. He happy too."

My calls with Sami were not so full of domestic bliss, just demands for me to visit. I talked with Jason two or three times more than with Sami. There wasn't a crash anywhere in the world he didn't know about. He really knew his stuff.

Between May and November, Pepe had called me several times at home. Short, friendly conversations. Camila had called more frequently, two, sometimes three times a month. I learned she was on her plane a lot and presently working with contractors on new high-rise projects in the United States and Mexico. She sold American contractors marble and granite from Rome, and used an ocean freight broker to ship it. Each call, I invited her to come visit.

"Be sure you let me know when you come to the States."

"I plan to," she said on our most recent call. "I haven't been to Los Angeles since we met. Right now, I have two big projects in New York."

"Do you fly over in your plane?"

"Of course."

"Entrance in the US isn't a problem?"

"I was born in Miami. Pepe could get a visa, but he's never going back to the US."

"I'm dying to see you again," I said.

"I'm very busy right now, or I'd hop over there and surprise you. We'd be safe, since Pepe won't go back there." She laughed softly.

I said nothing about her comment, but I mulled it over. To me, she sounded like Pixie, who had a penchant for breaking rules just because they were there. Pepe's protectiveness had put the kibosh on any plans I might have had of sex with Camila.

"You come and I promise to behave," I said.

"Speak for yourself."

I liked that soft laugh of hers. "I can't get over how great you speak English."

"That's another story I need to tell you." Laugh. "We have lots to talk about. I want to hear more about this business Pepe says you are in with plane crashes."

"That's me. I'm all over the place on plane crashes."

During lunch at PDC, Oscar told me, "Pepe called me a couple of days back and said the lawyers got sixty-five years, and their henchmen got twenty each."

"Sixty-five years. Not as good as life, but good. Why didn't you tell me?" I asked, annoyed that Oscar wasn't keeping me in the loop.

"I just did," he said, being a wiseass. "Besides, I just found out. I figured I'd tell you in person. I doubt they will be serving their full sentence. If they have the money I think they do, they'll get out in a few years."

"That's what Valita's scared of."

"Money buys anything down there."

"What else did Pepe say?"

"That the government confiscates property where drugs are found, but this time, the government failed. Tried and failed. Pepe thinks the wives paid someone off. Do you talk to Pepe?"

"He calls me but not often."

"Use the pay phone."

"We don't talk about anything. He calls to see how I'm doing. I haven't seen him since the trip to Rome."

"You should still use the pay phone. A person like him is always being watched," Oscar said. "He's not a wanted man anywhere, but the authorities aren't stupid. They know what he's into. They keep tabs. They watch and listen."

It was my turn to be a wiseass. "They can watch and listen all they want. There's nothing going on with us."

"I know that. Pay phone is better, but they bug those, too, especially if you use the same ones. Just be careful. You don't want to get your name muddied up by being a known associate."

"I know nothing about his business and don't want to know." I remembered the bowl of cocaine in Rome. I really did not want to know.

"Good boy," Oscar said.

As close as I was with Oscar, he never talked about Pepe's business beyond what was public record. He had represented him here in Los Angeles in a case where Pepe had stayed in jail for a year waiting to go to trial. He was released after Oscar got him a not-guilty verdict. If I really wanted to know more about Pepe, would Oscar tell me? I wasn't going to ask.

"I hope those assholes don't get out for a very long time," I said.

I know from experience that greasing certain palms with cash makes things happen. Been doing it myself since I was a kid. But to think these motherfuckers could bribe a life sentence down to a couple years seemed a gross miscarriage of justice. Sooner or later, I'd have to deal with them.

When I called Juan, Valita was home. She picked up the extension, and I talked to both of them. I told them about the lawyers' sixty-five year sentence.

"They will be out in short time," Valita predicted.

"That's what Oscar says. Anyway, I wanted you to know."

"Okay," Juan said. "We keep our ears to the ground so we know when they get out. I don't think it will be tomorrow."

Valita laughed and asked in Spanish, "Why would you put your ears to the ground?"

I sat for a moment as Juan explained the English idiom. "I agree. Ears to the ground. Do me a favor, Juan. Call our client Ramiro. Keep tabs on him. See if he's got news about anything. Don't mention the sentence."

"I do that," Juan said.

Juan called back to say Ramiro only had old news. Nothing new had gone public.

The girls had their own opinions.

"Let's hope for a change. If they do the sixty-five years, we don't have to worry about them," Jo said.

"If there is nothing in the newspapers about the sentence, a big-ass someone is keeping it hush-hush so they can let those motherfuckers out and keep it on the down low," Pixie said.

"If they are as powerful as I hear, they'll be pulling strings behind bars," I said. "Fuck them. As long as I see it coming, I can handle whatever they dish out."

Pixie did a high kick against a wall. "I'm going to be ready for them."

"Show off," Niley said. "Don't let the karate go to your head. We ain't there yet."

"Not there yet," Jo said. "But we are on the way."

My team. Ten months of workouts and they were masters in training, at least in their own minds. They made me laugh, but not so much that I gave them a break. We all did an extra hour of practice.

Jo lit candles and hid the peanut butter. Pixie turned the TV on with the sound off. Niley put out the new wineglasses Melina had bought me, and I poured the wine. The centerpiece was a platter of cheese, grapes, limes, avocados, and dried apricots, a canister of red pepper flakes, and a dozen types of crackers with two different jams that were out of this world. Jo and Pixie had hit Melina's market to put together the big platter.

"The problem, if it is a problem, about the aviation business like we are in is that there is too much down time. At least it's been good for our training." Niley stabbed an apricot with her fork and began nibbling at it like a popsicle.

"If not for the workouts, with the extra food we been putting away, we'd be fat." Pixie made a face.

"We drink too much," Jo said.

"We can work that off too," Niley said.

"Or become alcoholics." Jo finished off her glass and held it out for a refill. I refilled it. We laughed.

"I'll never be an alcoholic," Pixie said, eating away at the jalapeno cheese and holding out her wine glass for a refill. "But you better not talk about being bored, because he'll put us through workout hell."

"I haven't heard the word bored in a long time," Jo said.

"Sorry, boss," Niley said. "We took a class together this morning at seven, and I had to go home and take a nap right after." Niley was getting tipsy. One glass made her happy. "I brought some good weed. We don't have to smoke it, but I put it in Jo's big purse."

"Gee, thanks for telling me," Jo said. "What if I got pulled over, Miss Rolling Stone?"

Niley shrugged and gave her a sheepish grin. We all looked at each other.

"Get it," I said, a bit loud. "I hope it's not as badass as the shit I smoked in Rome."

"I can't believe you said that," Pixie said. "You want it good so you get that kick."

"I can't even remember half of what I did during that visit, and I know it wasn't the wine."

"Sweet," Niley said.

"Not sweet," I said. "I still don't remember if I fucked anyone while I was in Rome."

Niley rolled a joint, and we passed it around. One minute we were inhaling the delicacies; the next, the platter was bare. Nothing was left except the jam, and Pixie brought that into the bedroom with us. We were naked and sticky and rolling around on each other on my bed, passing another joint around.

We all showered together, and then dressed, which meant that all of us were more or less naked, since we were wearing my growing collection of hotel robes. Niley and Jo argued about which robes were best. Niley preferred the one from the Hilton. Jo argued for the one from the Marriot. I remembered the robe Sami had which trumped them all, decided to call it a draw, sent Jo off to get the brand name from Sami, and had her order me four just like hers. We finished off the peanut butter while watching the laundry machine turn as it washed the jam out of the linens and our clothes. Pixie's tie-dyed shirt turned everything pink as we were all curled up on the floor, staring at the rolling sea of pink.

"Should it be that color?" Niley asked, handing me the spoon and the dregs of the peanut butter.

"Dunno. It's not as bright as the color on the Tide box. Maybe we need to add more," I said, passing the jar to Jo.

"I ordered the robes, but I think Sami is sending some too." Jo took her bite and passed the jar and spoon on to Pixie.

"Can't have too many robes," I said. I was feeling expansive. Plus, I had lots of closet space.

"Mario," Pixie giggled, "We need to change the channel."

"Seat saved," Jo said. She jumped up. Niley scooted next to me and took her place. Jo switched on the stereo.

"Better," Pixie said. "I like this channel better." She was still focused on the laundry channel. She hit the bottom of the peanut butter, but kept on scraping at it.

Jo came back from turning on the stereo. "You took my spot, Niley."

"You snooze, you lose," Niley said.

Jo grabbed a new jar of peanut butter and switched it out for Pixie's empty.

Pixie dipped her spoon into the new, full jar.

Jo told Niley, "I said, 'Seat saved.'"

"Jo did do that. She said, 'Seat saved,'" Pixie said earnestly to Niley. One side of her robe had fallen off and her scarlet hair had dried standing up instead of down. Not like the hairdresser had intended, but it was Pixie, after all. She took the right sleeve in one hand and the wrong end of the belt in the other, and stared at them for a minute, then tied them together around her waist. She tried to pull it up to cover her exposed boob and shoulder, but gave up. She was more on the robe than in it. She handed the jar to Niley.

Jo was still standing with her arms crossed. She'd placed a pitcher of iced tea with four glasses full of ice, just out of reach. We all looked at the tea and smacked our dry, peanutbuttery mouths.

Jo, still standing, finished off a glass and poured herself another. It looked so refreshing. She said, "Who wants another joint?"

"Me," Niley said, jumping up. "I'll roll it."

Jo was like some kind of acrobat, as she sat down on the spot next to me that Niley had just vacated. She was carrying three glasses of tea and didn't spill a drop.

"No more weed for me, thanks, but you can knock yourself out," Jo said.

I laughed at the way Jo had maneuvered Niley and gave her a hug with my left arm. Jo gave me a big glass of sweet iced tea and passed one to Pixie.

"I see what you did," I said to Jo.

Niley came back with the joint she rolled, got the remaining glass of tea, and saw she'd lost her stolen spot. Her face fell. Jo laughed aloud and scooted over about six inches, patting the spot she'd left open between her and me. Niley squeezed in, more on my lap than on the floor, and kissed Jo somewhere between the top of her head and her right ear.

Pixie shook her head. "Not right, Niley. You didn't say, 'Seat saved.'" She picked up her spoon, which she had managed to get stuck in the knot of the robe. "Who's got the peanut butter?"

-

I didn't have end bonuses coming from Oscar, but I still worried he might be biting off more than he could chew. Jason told me how some of these cases took years to settle. We'd just brought in families of victims in three airline crashes. Oscar paid me immediately and always asked me to get more. Carson was doing really well, so that had to be costing Oscar another pretty penny. I would never want to be a lawyer, much less a lawyer with what I believed was Oscar's overhead.

Every time I shared my worry that Oscar might get cash strapped, Jason told me, "Your job is to bring in the cases. It's Oscar's responsibility thereafter. Don't worry about him."

I did worry because I was getting paid more money than I had ever dreamed. I wanted the gravy train to last.

"Sami misses you. Come see her. It's only a plane ride."

"Of course, I'm going to do that. I miss both of you."

I called Sami.

"I miss your American ass." Sami was emphatic and pretending jealousy. "You call Jason more than you call me."

"Not true," I lied. "I call you, but you're never home."

"What a liar!"

"Baby, I miss you. I'll be there when you least expect it."

"Are you avoiding me because I asked you to move in?"

"I remain flattered."

"Flattered my English ass," Sami said. "I want to spend time with you. Are you waiting for me to get old and ugly?"

"You'll never get old and ugly."

"I am devastated about the kidnapping. I need to touch you. I need to see you. I need to see that you are all right as you claim. I haven't seen you in a year!"

We had talked a dozen times since the kidnapping, and she still said this every time I called her. I was totally over it.

"Baby, I'm fine, my dick is fine, and I'm working out like never before. You won't be able to keep me off you."

"Never mind the sex. I just want to see you."

"I'll be there right after Thanksgiving."

Aunt Carmen was so glad to see me at Thanksgiving that she didn't even scold me about not visiting or calling. We met in a huge hug in the middle of the house I'd bought her when I'd been a kid. I was glad she didn't feel frail in my arms. She'd been in her twenties when her little sister died giving birth to me, so she's younger than I give her credit for.

"Thank you for inviting me," Melina said to my aunt, giving her a hug and kiss.

"Look how lovely you are." Aunt Carmen touched her cheek. "Just precious."

Pixie and Lainey had come over earlier to help prepare the feast.

"Hey, Auntie, how come you never tell me I'm precious?" Pixie moved close for Aunt Carmen to squeeze her cheeks, which Aunt Carmen did, then laughed, snapped her with a kitchen towel, and told her to finish plating the fruit salad.

"She calls me precious all the time," Lainey said.

Melina joined Pixie in the kitchen to help set up. Lainey got credit for setting the table.

My aunt put orange aprons on Melina, Pixie, and Lainey.

"Gotta to get a picture of this," I said, reaching for my aunt's camera sitting on the coffee table.

It was Thanksgiving, and not the time for it, but just looking at Melina and Pixie, I got so very hot. It was cold outside, and very comfortable inside, but my internal heater was on overdrive. This is what happens when you aren't very busy, and you happen to be Mario Luna. I'm a sex freak, but not as much when I'm busy working on a case. Not that I would be wishing for a crash. It had been a busy year, but not so much, now.

As they had last year, Jo and Niley were doing their own thing, except Thanksgiving night last year, the team brought their suitcases to my apartment in preparation for the Caracas trip. Time flies. It had been almost a year since my kidnapping, and I still felt bad that the girls missed Christmas with their families because they were cooped up in Caracas in the hotel waiting for the kidnappers' demand.

Aunt Carmen said grace while we all held hands around and across the dining room table, and then we ate. Melina surprised me, tried everything, and had white meat and gravy twice. Pixie and Lainey stayed to help clean up. Four hours after we arrived, I drove Melina home. After all the years they lived at my aunt's house, Pixie and Lainey were the only ones my aunt allowed in her kitchen. And now Melina.

When Melina and I got home, we went directly to my apartment where we had a little port as a digestif. I'm not much for port, but I had it in my bar. Melina's idea.

"I had a good time. I am so impressed. Your aunt is a great cook and quite a character. She's younger than I expected. I asked her about your mom, but she was so good at diverting me, I never got any answers."

"Yeah," I agreed. "She's that way with me, too. Sometimes I wonder what she's not saying."

"Thank you for sharing today with me."

We were sitting in the living room. My arm was around her. I pulled her close and kissed her. "I love having you with me," I said.

She punched my shoulder. It was playful and painless, but there was emotion behind it. "You have so many women around you all the time, and now you got this millionairess after your ass."

"You mean Camila." I laughed a little.

"You know I mean Camila, you oaf."

"I love you, Melina."

"I know you can't keep your dick in your pants, and I understand. This Camila—I don't know."

"Are you jealous?" I kidded. I shouldn't have. Melina was taking this to heart, and instead of lifting the mood, it made it worse.

"I could be."

"If…"

"If she turns out to be a threat."

"A threat?"

Melina eyes met mine. I could see she was troubled. "Yes, a threat. You could end up in her web. I don't want to lose you."

"I'm not in danger of being caught up in anyone's web. You will never lose me. Not ever." I did my best to reassure her. I looked deeply in her eyes. I pulled her into my arms and held her with her head resting against my chest. I carried her into the bedroom and made love to her, as if our bodies could speak a language beyond words. But later, it came up again.

"Mario, I love you so much."

"In that case, let's get married." As much as I loved her, she knew I didn't want to get married. It was just something I threw at her every time we got serious.

Melina came back with that open smile. "We are not getting married. Why should we? We're already tighter than any married couple. Someday when I get old, if you still want me, we'll talk then."

"Oh, the age thing again."

"Fuck me and shut up."

I stretched out on the sofa behind her and pulled her cashmere pants down to her knees. She kicked them off, and they went flying across the room, ending up on top of the TV. We spooned, and she pushed back against me. I slid deep inside.

"Baby, I can't believe you went to my aunt's house wearing no panties." I pushed my mouth against her hair. She looked and smelled like queen of the flowers. She smelled fucking great. I pushed deep. She pushed back. We caught a rhythm, opposing, yielding, opposing again. I heard her begging for more. We rocked the couch, and she kept begging, harder, louder, ending in a wordless scream. I did my best. I moved my mouth to her ears, her face, the tender junction of her neck.

"Happy Thanksgiving," I said.

"Thanks to you and your horn of plenty." It took a while for our hearts to slow down to normal speed, but when they did, she said, "Now you know why I had them make this sofa ten feet long and a hundred and twenty inches deep. I wanted to be sure you fit."

"We fit all right, but it was a tight squeeze." I laughed, and dodged her punch at my shoulder. "You never told me that."

"Your last sofa was only eighty-four inches wide."

We chased our Thanksgiving with ice cream and a repetition of the festivities until my horn of plenty was plentied out.

I didn't have a car as big as Melina's limousine, but I was in the market for a car, one that was big enough for my purposes. I love little sports cars, but I just don't fit. I hemmed and hawed over my choices until Melina was fed up. As much as I wanted a sports car, it wasn't practical. Melina had enough and dragged me to the Rolls dealership. "Buy the damn car already!"

I did.

I announced I was going to London. Pixie drove all of us to the airport in my new Rolls. Ah, the sweet scent of leather upholstery and new car carpeting.

"You can all stay home unless something comes up. I'll call Jo and she can use the contraption to conference us."

"How long will you be gone?" Niley asked.

"Ten days. Fewer if we get a case. More if something comes up."

"We can manage it until you get back even if we get a case," Niley said from my left.

"Sounds like you want me to take my time."

"She doesn't mean that at all." Jo, on my right, leaned up to glare at Niley. "I don't see why you need to go."

"I couldn't just keep ignoring Sami's invitation to visit."

"If you hire a driver, the three of us can ride in the back with you," Pixie said, turning around to look at us.

"Eyes on the road," Jo said.

Pixie turned back to face the road. I could see her pout in the rearview mirror.

"It's bad enough I bought this show-off car. I'm not getting a driver."

"Here you go again," Niley said, just like Melina. "It's just a car. A big dude like you needs a big car."

I turned and kissed Niley. "Love you, baby."

"Maybe you'll get a Learjet like Oscar," Pixie said, turning around to look at us again.

"Why buy one? We use the hell out of his for nothing," I reminded her.

"It's groovy to fly around in that thing."

"Groovier if we could fly Pepe's plane with the two bedrooms and all the toys like the Playboy plane," Niley said.

"Playboy plane is history." I had already told them about Hefner's money issues and how he sold the plane to a Venezuelan operator.

"Okay, already," Niley said. "Pepe hasn't given up his, and that's the plane I want in on."

"Shut up, Niley," Jo said impatiently. "Eyes on the road, Pixie. You're about to hit the airport."

Pixie faced front and got the car back on the asphalt.

Here I was again. Two days after Thanksgiving and off to London again. I was flying and so was time. We'd signed the Caracas case last year, closed the year with the kidnapping, but began the new one with my rescue. This year we'd signed three airline cases. The year had been fast and busy.

"Are you worried at all about taking that supersonic plane?" Niley asked.

"That has to be so bitching!" Pixie interrupted. "I'd come all the way. Three hours to London from New York."

I finally got a word in. "Something like that. No, I'm not worried. I'm more moved by the cost of the ticket."

"Way too much," Jo said.

"Fuck it. I'll let you know if it was worth it."

"Oh, boss, please be safe," Niley said. "That fucker is fast."

"Just say it. You are worried it could crash."

They all chimed, "No."

Jo grabbed my arm. "I just wish you had waited a few months so British Air had time to find and fix any glitches. They just put the thing in service."

"Don't worry. It's just a plane ride."

I loved Sami and Jason, and I wanted to spend time with them. I loved life in London. I didn't love the terror over there, but at times felt no safer at home or traveling to other countries. Look what had happened in Venezuela. After Venezuela, London was nothing to fear.

I had no alcohol on the plane because I was saving myself. Once I got around Sami, there would be a lot of drinking. I anticipated the excitement ahead, but the boner I got was from dozing off and reliving the encounter with Melina on my living room sofa after Thanksgiving dinner.

Sami was grumpy as hell that I refused her offer to come and get me herself or send a car. In London, it was so easy to jump in a taxi. I hailed what they call a hackney carriage, and it brought me from the airport to Sami's. I didn't want to keep the driver waiting to get paid while Sami and I were busy necking, so I looked at the meter and paid the driver as we pulled up. Sami met me curbside where the cab dropped me off. She was a striking figure, the long sable mink coat setting off her pink cheeks, her bright hair whipping around in the wind.

"How was that supersonic ride?"

"Fast."

It wasn't until we stepped in the elevator that I realized why she had come down. In order to get to her floor, it now took a key when you touched 'Penthouse' in the elevator.

"I made a few changes. Just a little remodeling."

When the elevator door opened, instead of getting off in a hallway, we stepped into her penthouse.

"Impressive. You got this done in nothing flat."

"It took months. Do you like it?"

"Nice," I said. The former hall had been incorporated as a foyer. Marble, of course. "Where are Ginger and Crispin?"

"Troops are busy. I've got you all to myself. Come on."

She led me down the familiar wide hallway, which was unchanged. I took a left into the bedroom I used and dropped my bag on the floor, then let her drag me across the way to the master bedroom.

"Sit for a little bit," she said. "Let me look at you. I missed you so much."

"Do I look like I was kidnapped?"

When I realized that her eyes were watering, I picked her right out of her chair and kissed her. The drama ended as quickly as it had begun. Sami didn't play up the drama as Pixie would have. Sami is very British in that way.

"Can I shower first?"

"Shower, later. Sex now," she ordered.

We fell on her bed. Clothes went flying.

I couldn't remember Sami crying before. It touched me. Sami was not in love with me. We were friends, but strangers too. I knew nothing of her real life, just as she knew nothing of mine. Being separated by an ocean most of the time kept us from getting too close. We each had our own realities to return to. Sami was predictable, but not boring. Even if I knew what she would do next, I loved being around her. She said the same about me. I often had to remind myself that Sami was a doctor. I always figured that doctors were stiffs, but the last thing Sami was was a stiff. If Sami had adult patients or actually went to work every day like most doctors I know, would she be so wild? I guess that's like asking if my sex life would be different if I punched a clock like other guys.

I had been there twenty-four hours before Ginger and Crispin emerged to say hello and deliver a great lunch. Our sleeping and sexual exploits had left a mess, so they served us on the table in my room while they went over the master bedroom. I ate the English breakfast but skipped the beans. They never felt like breakfast to me unless they were in a tortilla. I skipped the tea and had coffee. I was planning some things to do while here, like get another English-tailored suit or two, and pick up something for the girls. On my last visit, I'd curtailed shopping.

"Are they still blowing up things?"

"Unfortunately, yes. You just need to be careful where you party or shop."

"Does it frighten you?" I asked.

Her words matched the flush in her face. "It angers me. That's all." A good English answer.

"You won't be bored," she promised.

"I'm never bored here," I said.

She was standing against the black-out curtains in some kind of black lingerie concoction that cupped her breasts but left them bare. Her nipples were pink and erect. Looking at them, I didn't mind the chill in the air.

Jason showed up for dinner two nights after I arrived. The memory of him sitting in that chair next to the bed when I was having sex with Sami didn't bother me. I didn't fear it, but didn't look forward to it happening again, either.

Jason and I talked over dinner, as usual.

"Are you handling any small aircraft cases?"

"Is there money in it? I've had one or two, still pending. Not sure about value."

"Don't ignore helicopters. Single engine and dual engine crash all the time right there in the States. Some of them are financed by hospitals. Medical evacuations."

"Jason, you have such great ideas." I wondered if he was encouraging me to keep my business close to home, or just trying to widen the field of Oscar's potential clients.

"You have to hope that the cause is product liability, or that the client paid to be on the aircraft."

"I will look into it more closely."

Jason smiled. "While you're waiting for the big ones, it will keep you busy. They are not all going to be good, but all you need is one or two."

"Jason, you're so brilliant. I have to ask why don't you have a practice of your own?"

"I like doing what I'm doing. I don't want the pressure of having my own firm. Like Sami, I've been blessed since birth. I have substantial income from a family trust. I don't need to work. However, I went to school, spent all those years getting a diploma, then my license. I figure I have to do something. And if I ever choose to father an heir, he or she will inherit more than I did."

"I see," I said. I should have guessed that Jason was rich. Maybe that's one reason Sami and he got along so well. Each had their own fortune. Maybe they'd even traveled in the same circle all their lives. Almost like Pixie and me, at the opposite end of the spectrum. Except that Pixie and I left our origins behind us.

While Jason was still there, I talked to Oscar and Tom by phone about handling smaller aircraft cases. They were excited by the notion. I could tell they wanted to get started on it right away. I got no arguments from them.

"I'll get the hunt started," I said.

I called Jo at home, and after she cross-connected Pixie and Niley on a conference call, I told the girls about helicopters and small plane crashes.

"Subscribe to newspapers outside Los Angeles and of course keep reading the *LA Times* and *Herald* every day. Look for this type of case."

"We get the Sunday *New York Times*, but I'll order the rest of the week," Niley said.

"Good idea," Pixie said. "I'll make a list of cities and start calling to sign up to their publications."

Niley said, "I see little crashes all the time but don't pay any attention because I've been looking for big international stuff."

Sami and I shared meals with Jason on six occasions. The bond got tighter between all of us. If Sami had asked me, I would have done it, but I was not again asked to make love to Sami while Jason watched. I guess she just liked to push the envelope.

I talked to my team daily. They were making good progress on going through new subscriptions for potential cases. I was so excited over the new business, I almost cut the London visit short. I told them to hang on to them till I got home; then Jo said that Camila had left a number for me. I took the phone number down with no clue what city or country it was from. I asked Ginger to figure it out with the long-distance operator. A few minutes later I was on the line.

"Am I speaking to the most beautiful Learjet owner on all seven continents? I heard you left me a message?"

I heard Pepe clear his throat. "Si, all the ladies say that to me."

"I thought I was calling Camila," I said. "Pepe, I mean no offense, but you're not my type."

Pepe laughed, and kept laughing.

I felt stupid. "Sorry, Pepe. It's always a pleasure to speak with you."

"Camila is right here with me in Mexico City on business. She heard you were in London. I told you to let me know when you go out of the country so we can meet."

"You did say that. We could have had a blast here in London." I spent a few minutes telling Pepe about my London friends, and that I would be leaving in two days.

"I got an idea," Pepe said. "Camila can leave her plane here in Mexico City. We can come get you in London and fly to Rio for a few days. I want to show off my house there."

Ginger had left me alone in the parlor and it was a good thing because I was twisting in my chair with anxiety. I did not like to give up control, and it felt like that was what Pepe was doing to me. I'm not a wishy-washy man, but I hemmed and hawed. "That's a long way to come and get me. I can fly to Los Angeles, then we can do it, no?"

"Mario, do you have time? A few days to visit Rio with us?"

"Yes, I have time."

"Do you want to go—yes or no?" I could hear impatience in his voice.

"Yes, I want to go. I need to touch base with my team on business, but I can do that over the phone."

"Good." The irritation was gone, and his good humor was back. "Here is Camila. Talk to her while I speak to my pilot on the other phone."

I told Sami I was being picked up by friends and going to Rio for a couple days.

"Rio. I'm jealous," Sami said.

"You are not jealous," I said, picking her up. "You can go to Rio any time you want. You could charter a plane, go to Rio or anywhere, right?"

"I can do that."

Just after noon, I called Jo. I woke her up at half past three, just before I left for the airport. I told her about the change in plans, to let the girls know I called, and to reach Melina as early as decently possible to explain Pepe had arrived a day earlier than expected. I had no time to call her before I got on the plane with Pepe. Jo must have been asleep, because she gave me no lip other than wishing me safe travels.

When Ginger drove me to the airport, it was to Gatwick Airport instead of Heathrow, where I would have departed from had Pepe not changed my plans.

Paulo and Camila were waiting at Gatwick's information desk. I kissed Camila, gave Paulo a slap on the chest, and he gave me one back. Paulo took my three bags: two with the usual travel baggage, one with nothing but gifts for the girls and new Savile Row clothes.

I counted seven workers carrying various kinds of cleaning paraphernalia and dressed in canvas coveralls emerging from Pepe's plane.

"Cleaning crew," Camila explained, her arm around mine.

The crew was made up of five pilots, two in the cockpit and three in seats outside the cabin, and three female flight attendants. This plane was configured differently from the last Camacho plane I flew in. There were partitions that didn't go all the way to the ceiling but gave a feeling of separation from the cabin and the business end of the cockpit. The public area was better than his other plane, with two seats facing two seats across from each other, but like Pepe's other plane, it reeked of luxury. I'm pretty sure the seats were leather. The plane was scented with lavender, or something great. Light, not perfumy.

One of the stewardesses handed me a glass of wine right after I hugged Pepe. He kissed me European-style. My right cheek and then my left cheek. I did the same to him, and we took our seats.

"You must be pooped out," I said.

"I never hear that word before," Pepe said, in English.

"He's kidding," Camila said, laughing. "Pepe, quit giving Mario a hard time. We both slept. You know, we thought about staying over in London, but we didn't want to disrupt your schedule too much. We want to get you to Rio. You'll love it there."

Chapter 13
December 1976
Bunker Towers Goodbye

"Hang on," I said into the receiver. Pixie and Jo were wound up over the holiday and trying to get me to go shopping with them. I opened my wallet and handed Pixie one small stack of bills, and Jo another.

"You get a tree. You get the decorations. When I come out, I want to see it in my den." The girls headed off to do what they love to do.

That had been nearly four hours ago. Since then, I had been closeted in my office on the phone with Oscar and Tom. They both had sticky family situations that had blown an office meeting off the schedule and moved it to the phone line. Oscar's relatives were in town and parked at his house. He kept escaping the festivities and grabbing minutes here and there. Tom was squeezing in time with his ex-step children, which involved careful arrangements dodging resentful ex-wives who apparently kept showing up and ruining plans. From my end, it looked very complicated, and I was glad I had no such problems. Their topic was one of the plane crash cases that looked like it was going to court. I was just the sympathetic ear, but I was learning a lot.

I heard the girls come in, and muffled conversations about whatever they were doing. I heard Tito's voice, and then some thumps and bumps and falling things that made me wonder what was going on in my living room. When I tried opening the door, they freaked and blocked me.

"Tito, don't let them break my house! What's happening out there?"

"No problem, boss," he said, then the girls made him quit talking, so I was still in the dark.

"You can't find out till it's done!"

Pixie shoved a plate of sandwiches at me. "That should hold you a while."

Jo ran and got the peanut butter, a can of soda, and a glass of ice. "Yell if you need anything," she said.

The apartment smelled of pine. And I could hear them arguing off and on about the placement of every single shred of tinsel. Eventually they let me out.

"I love it," I said, embracing them in our usual huddle. "And I love you."

"Boss, we love you, too. Without the tree, it was dead in here," Pixie said.

It was certainly not dead now. It's amazing how much a nine-foot tree can transfigure a room. Fronds surrounding a silver star brushed the ceiling. It had to be at least seven feet wide at the base, smelling like a whole forest. A metal frame was hidden by a cloth underneath that was already covered with gaily wrapped boxes. The silver star presided like moon over branches bright and thick, covered in shining glass and tinsel, silver strings, reflective globes of many sizes and colors, and glittering strands of lights of all colors.

Pixie was right. The tree added Christmas to my living room, not only the aroma of pine, warmth, festivity, and color, but also the passion and love that went into the decoration of it.

"We got the tree at Melina's market. She had it delivered and refused to charge," Jo said. "So we put the whole budget on decorations. Tito put it on the stand."

I looked at the boxes underneath and quirked an eye at them.

"Oh, those," Pixie said. "We've had those in the closet for weeks and weeks."

"C'mon in the kitchen," Jo called Pixie. "We have enough branches from the top I think we can make a wreath for the door."

I shared breakfast on my dinette, in the shadow and scent of Christmas pine. Melina provided tortillas, eggs, and chorizo. I provided coffee, dishes, mugs, silverware, and Aunt Carmen's jalapeño jelly. The tree made me think of gingerbread and egg nog.

Out of the blue, Melina said, "Real estate is money. I'm tired of wasting rent that could be equity. Look at all the apartments you have. I'm looking at a house. You can come with, or not."

I stared at her. I'd been thinking how well the cream-colored lingerie suited her tawny skin, and imagined escorting her into one of her markets dressed as she was now. Those troublesome managers of hers would snap to attention, I bet.

"What?"

She sipped her coffee and put it down on the table. "Where are you, Mario? I just said I'm tired of the apartment. I want a place to stretch out when I'm home. I'm investing in a house. Coming?"

"Investing? Look at all the markets you have." Libido was still running things, and my brain was still catching up. I poured cream in my coffee.

Melina grabbed the jelly jar and channeled her irritation as she tapped the lid hard on the floor to loosen it. She spooned some jelly on her plate and pointed the jelly-covered spoon at me to punctuate what she was saying.

"I want to show you the house before I decide."

"Only if you promise that I can have the entire day and night with you."

"Deal, but you have to promise the same thing."

We sealed the agreement with a kiss.

After breakfast, Johnson drove us in the big Mercedes. Melina's real estate agent Carl was meeting us at the house she said she loved.

"You have to be kidding," I said as Johnson drove down a very long driveway. It was on several acres of lush grounds. Then the house became visible. "It's a fucking mansion. You're going to live here? Alone?"

"Fuck yes. I have a gun, and I'll hire help. I'll need a live-in or two. It is a big house. It's old, but it's been completely redone. I can't wait till I decorate it."

I recalled Pepe's house in Rio with the most fantastic view of the ocean one could imagine, and his mansion in Rome, and the curbside appeal I always checked for when I bought an apartment building. You couldn't see it from the curb, but Melina had picked a winner, equal to Pepe's Rome pad. Maybe not quite so big, but what was?

I could tell that the house had been redone, and not only because it was spotless. The master bathroom was bigger than Bunker Towers' master bedrooms. In fact, the master bedroom was three times the size of the master bedroom in the apartments. The ceiling was high enough to fit a whole other house under there.

"Sixteen thousand square feet of house," she teased. "Think it will be big enough?"

"It's big enough for the LA Dodgers. How much?"

"A fucking steal. A million bucks! Asking price is more, but I'm shooting for a million."

I knew zero about houses, but I knew about apartments. This was a lot of house. On the land where it sat, I could build five hundred apartments. A million bucks was cheap.

"Buy it."

"Mario, do you really love it?" She took my arm.

"I love it."

Melina's eyes sparked. She really wanted the house. I saw that the price was right, and that she loved it. I didn't want to tell her the truth, which was that I did not want her to move. I could see that moving was going to change our relationship. We would lose our cozy down-the-hall breakfasts, and the drop-in sex nights, and the comfort nights, and those times we ran into each other that led to something else. A spouse, or a relative, or the other half of a committed couple would have a say. As a friend, I could only encourage her to do what she wanted to do. Interjecting my feelings into her decision was not part of our deal. But I could only admit to myself that it would be strange, maybe even a little lonely, living where I lived and knowing that Melina was not there anymore. She was the reason I'd been attracted to Bunker Towers in the first place. Now that our work was not a constant day-to-day routine, the girls had their own lives. I was coming to depend on Melina's presence. I would miss her morning visits. I would miss the midnight liaisons.

"It's going to cost a bundle to furnish this place, but what fun I'll have doing it."

"Will you have the time?"

"I'll make time. I'm the boss, remember?"

"No question about that."

We toured the grounds. We saw every room, walked through the attic, looked out of every window, and opened every closet and bathroom door. We even stood in the showers and bathtubs. We had made our way back to the white marble of the front foyer. Melina looked at her watch. I figured we were ready to leave.

Melina took the agent aside, and told him, "Carl, I'm ready to make an offer, but I need to take a look upstairs again."

"By all means, go. I'll be down here reading the paper."

I looked toward the folded newspaper. Carl parked himself on a small sofa and picked up the front section. I was wondering if the classifieds were intact. I hadn't read them yet today, but Melina pulled me toward the stairs. She let go of my hand and broke into a run. She wanted to play a little cat and mouse. I didn't mind being the cat. I followed her as she dashed up the long, winding staircase. She didn't stop when she got to the second floor, but wheeled around the corner. I still followed, thundering after her and determined to catch up. I walked through the door of the master bedroom, and she tackled me. A moment later, we were rolling around, wrestling on the plush carpet of the master bedroom. In a split second, I had pulled her panties off and wrestled her into her favorite position on top of me.

"I love you, Mario."

She moaned as she moved on me and leaned forward. Our tongues battled. She flexed and moved. We caught a furious rhythm that was very like dancing, almost, but the beat was inside us, teasing us, driving us higher and deeper. She moaned. I growled. She grabbed my nipples. I nibbled hers. She bit my neck, moved her mouth to my ear. I could feel her on every inch of my skin.

"I love you, Melina."

It just slipped out, but I didn't mind. I tell everyone I love them, but this was different and we both knew it. Our mouths pressed together, and we rolled around until I was on top of her, her legs wrapped around me.

"I've always loved you," she spoke into my mouth.

"Even when I told you I no longer wanted to be your partner and you bought me out from the market deal?"

"Even then." She was breathing heavily. "You fucker!"

"I think I've always loved you too."

She was back on top of me, and was the first to notice Carl standing in the door, slack-jawed with shock. She stopped moving and started laughing.

"Carl, come back in here. Haven't you ever seen two people fuck before?" She yelled down the hallway, but he had vamoosed out of there. He didn't come back in, and was red as a ripe tomato when we returned to where we had left him on the first floor, calmly reading the paper. Except for the color of his face, he was totally cool.

"Prepare an offer," Melina said. "One million. [20] As is. No contingencies. I can close escrow as quickly as they want."

"I really think the one point two is firm."

"Bring the offer by tomorrow. I'll be in Montebello. One million. No contingencies should go a long way. If I must have an inspection on this place, no telling what it will find."

"I'll prepare the offer," he said, still scarlet to his earlobes.

We had a late lunch at Pacific Dining Car. All the way there, I was thinking

---

[20] $1,000,000.00 in 1976 had the same buying power as $4,350,126.13 in 2017.

about our exchange. We had not had a single drink. We weren't rebounding. I did not know if this was this for real or just a crazy impulse. We had always kept it cool, called it a "cousin" connection, and guarded our freedom fiercely. Of course, we were not cousins at all, but there was something more between us that we had never named.

"So now what?" I asked. "I'm afraid if we mess with our...relationship... it will break. It's working now. We change things, it might not work."

She sat across from me and toyed with the mushroom on top of her steak.

"Let's live together, Cuz" she said. "I'll buy the house. I'll furnish it. No strings. If it works, we take it a step further."

I put down my fork.

"I had an offer for something like that from Sami in London. The difference is she didn't want me to work. She wanted to support me."

I picked up the fork and started working on my steak again. It was almost strange that we could speak of such private things in such a public space, but we were all in our little privacy bubbles. I might guess, but I had no real idea what was going on at any of the booths or tables around me. People all around us were going about their everyday lives. Waiters were walking around with plates, taking orders, talking and joking amongst themselves and with the customers. The strangers around us were eating—breakfasts and dinners, but mostly lunch specials—and we were all watching the spectacle of chefs dashing around the kitchen with deliciously chaotic efficiency, walking around in a steam of coffee and bacon and other delicious fragrances.

"What a cunt. I'm jealous."

I teased her. "No way is baby jealous."

"Wants to support you. Are you serious?"

"Cuz, I'm not going anywhere."

"Asshole, you better not."

She kissed me, bit my tongue, and then my lip. Not too hard but enough for me to say ouch.

"And what else did the Cuntress offer?"

I smothered a laugh. Sami did have a title, but I'm pretty sure it wasn't Cuntress.

"That's it. Isn't that enough?"

She got a twinkle in her eye, and I could see her negotiating cap go on her head. The wheels were spinning, and she gestured at me with her fork. I grabbed her hand, adjusted the angle, and ate her mushroom. She laughed, lowered the fork to her plate, and negotiated her deal. "I'm not going to support you, but I'll pay all the house expenses."

"You just want control."

"Sure, it's my house." She paused, but didn't meet my eyes. "Maybe our house. We could buy it fifty-fifty."

"You're just saying that. You want the house, a hundred percent. No way," I said. "I think we both are too independent. Partners with you will ruin everything we have. We both want our lives, a hundred percent."

"You're right."

I stopped eating. I put down my fork again.

"I'd marry you."

She put her fork down too, and extended her hand across the table. She took my right hand. "I'd marry you too, but what's the rush? What's the hurry? A man like you. You got to get the play out of your system. Down the road, I'd get pissed off at you over some meaningless fuck with some chippie."

"You play too. What about your system?"

"Exactly. You're right. I like to fuck around."

She started on her steak. So did I.

"By the way, I've missed my period. I could be pregnant."

I looked up. She met my eyes evenly.

"You're on the pill. I've seen you taking it."

"I am, but I get so fucking busy, I miss sometimes. The house is not about a baby or a biological clock."

"Is it mine?"

How many times had we done it in the past two months? A whole lot.

"Could be. If he's dark-skinned, it could be one of my butchers that I invite up to my office from time to time when I'm in Echo Park. If he's black, I only fuck one, so that one will be easy. If he's Asian, it will be a problem because I haven't fucked an Asian yet."

She laughed a little more with each possible father. I was getting irritated with her.

Melina laughed really hard, so hard it broke through our personal bubble, and some of the other diners chuckled to hear her. I knew Melina. She was playing. I grinned.

"I'm kidding, asshole," she whispered across the table. "I'm not fucking pregnant. I saw you on the edge of panic. Babies aren't about burdens. They're about joy. Didn't anyone tell you that?"

I hadn't had that experience. I just felt a weight lift from my shoulders. "Aunt Carmen delivered so many of them that I'm immune. If you were pregnant and it wasn't mine, I would still love you." I knew it was true. That had happened with Pixie, and I still loved her. But I'm not denying that I was relieved.

"Ha," she said. "You think you're immune. Just wait. Someday someone is going to come along and make a little Mario for you, and you are going to fucking adore the kid. I'm not sure a kid would make either of us faithful."

"You could be right," I said. "We are sex freaks. We'd have to have one of those open marriages."

"Yeah," she said. "Now tell me about the trip to Rio. All you talk about is Sami in London but not a word about this chick, Camila. Well?"

"I'll tell you the whole story in detail, but let's go back to the apartment. I need you right now."

"I'll take you up on that."

We kissed all the way to Bunker Towers.

She came straight to my apartment. We undressed, showered together, and crashed in the den. The TV was muted. Bukis played low on the stereo.

As we had done in the old days, we talked and talked. I steered the conversation to Sami and Jason, and let her know I had told Sami about Camila as well.

"So, you're really tight with the Cuntress Sami."

"You'll love her."

She shrugged. "Probably. Will you fuck me and talk dirty to me like you do Sami?"

"I shouldn't have said a thing to you about Sami."

"Aw, baby, you can't keep a secret from your Cuz."

"Cuz. What do you mean, Cuz?"

"You think you're being slick."

"Slick?"

"You think I haven't noticed that you still haven't told me about your Rio trip? Talk!"

"I didn't fuck Camila, and my kisses were on the cheek, if that's what you want to know."

"Cuz, stop playing the dummy. What motivated them to go all the way to London to pick you up, then go all the way to Rio, then to Mexico City where you hopped on to Camila's plane and she flew you back home?"

I grinned. "Baby, you practically have the entire story, you just told it to me. As for motivation, I have no clue. They are both jetsetters. They like me. I guess they like me." I had nothing to offer those two friends.

"You are avoiding the juicy parts. Where are the details? I want to hear everything starting with when you got on Pepe's plane in London."

"The house in Rio is on a bluff overlooking the ocean. It is fucking magnificent, but no better than the house you are planning to buy, minus the view. It's a big fucking place. All his houses have discos and big staffs to take care of the houses. He has maids and guys he calls assistants that are like butlers, all there to serve his guests."

"How does Camila fit in all this?"

I shrugged. "One night Pepe had six bitching chicks over. Camila was a happy camper. She sat alone watching the activity, smoking a joint and sipping wine with a big smile on her face. Pepe dished out mega coke to the chicks. Camila didn't touch it. Neither did Pepe. He won't even smoke a joint. He smokes cigarettes like a chimney, drinks like a fish, and throws around coke like it's sugar candy, but he doesn't use. The chicks love the shit."

"He's a fucking asshole to make it available. I'm sure he pays the girls. They are going to whore without the coke. Why does he fuck with their heads?"

"Good point. Don't have the answer."

"Did you get wasted, Cuz?"

"I did, but just on wine. At least in Rio, I clearly remember who I fucked."

Melina laughed. "Cuz, you are a prick."

"I am a prick."

Melina stayed the night. She was there when I woke up. It was a change, but a good one and I loved it. Maybe I'm just fucking lonely. Maybe it is more than that. There was something good and solid about beginning the day together, about the routine, and knowing who gets the coffee, and who makes the toast. And with Melina there were always odd little things thrown in. This morning, I made the coffee; she ran to her apartment to bring back a box of cream samples. She set them down on the table.

"Taste test," she said. "We're thinking about trying a couple new dairies. What do you think?"

"I think I better make more coffee." I looked over the array of half pints of milk, light and heavy cream, and half and half; I pulled out all of my coffee cups and mugs and poured into each a small bit of coffee. I made a second pot.

"Do we label these or what?" I said. "I've never done this."

"Could have fooled me. Next time we have a focus group, I'll put you in charge."

She laughed and put in spoons of cream and stirred. We sipped with no sugar so that we would be more sensitive to the taste of the cream. Thirty minutes and a coffee cream orgy later, we'd decided on a dairy and were chewing on tortillas to clear our palates.

"Mario, our relationship is special. I don't want moving or a ring to fuck it up. Let's give it time. Keep doing what you do, and I'll do what I do, but just know that I do love you. I'm just not ready. And one other thing truly bothers me. I'm so much older than you."

I kissed her. I loved the taste of coffee in her morning mouth.

"Age doesn't matter to me." Sami was also worried about her age, but now was not the time to bring it up to Melina.

She shook her head sadly. "You can say that now. But it won't be so nice when you're stuck with some *vieja loca corajuda*[21] and your roving eye kicks in."

I shook my head. "You know this too: I do love you, *mi viejita*. I'm just not ready."

Our kiss was tremendous.

"You have to do something for me," she said.

"Try me."

"Find a house. I have to be close to you. It's time you get out of this fucking place."

"I'll think about it," I said. "I'll ask my broker to get me something to look at."

"I'll write down the address of the place I'm buying. Yours has to be nearby. The houses are fabulous, and I can feel like we're still close."

"I could move into your house," I said, not meaning it.

"You're lying, Mario. You'd never move in."

"I would if we were married."

I played with the possibility in my head. I visualized it. It wasn't a bad picture. Was that where we were heading? I didn't know.

"Let's give it time. I want to keep opening markets. I want to keep fucking

---

[21] crazy old lady

anyone I want on impulse. You can keep buying up apartment buildings and fuck-ing your team and the parade of broads who would love to get a piece of you. One of these days, you will have conquered Camila, and there will be others, like in Rio. We're not ready. I just want you to know how special you are to me. You're all the family I have."

I nibbled her ear.

"How many times a day do you fuck others on impulse?"

"Fucker, you got nerve to ask me that. You walk around with a hard on all day."

"And you walk around with a wet pussy all day."

"You're so nasty." She licked her lips. "Come get my wet pussy again."

We spent the day together, and that night. Two days and two nights in a row. I think it was a record.

I got up at five and started my workout. Minutes later, she peeked in and blew me a kiss.

"I'll be back with coffee in a couple hours. Carl waited for me yesterday. I forgot he was supposed to bring me the offer."

"Hey," I said.

She turned around.

"You got a fine ass. You are so hot!"

"Asshole. You tell that to everyone."

"I love you, *mi viejita*," I said. I didn't say that to everyone.

"Ouch, that hurt," she said, and she was gone.

I paid my Christmas calls early to a couple of people, including, of course, Aunt Carmen. On Christmas Eve, Melina and I ate heartily, food that Melina had catered from her Echo Park Market. She had her enormous antique buffet carpeted in food, easily enough for thirty people. It was just the two of us, and she didn't eat all that much. I think the centerpiece of the dinner was a whole roast turkey, or maybe it was the ham, or the standing rib roast.

"I couldn't decide," Melina said. "You can take a couple of these home if you want."

"We can keep the mess in your kitchen," I said. I couldn't decide either.

I filled up a plate with sliced meats. I saw four kinds of salad, counted a dozen savory vegetable casseroles, not counting three kinds of stuffing, six kinds of pie, and five different kinds of bread. Everything hot was served in silver chafing dishes. The cold stuff was in decorative platters chilling over blocks of ice. We put away several glasses of wine and spent a long time eating, drinking, and getting messy.

"I'm full," I said, getting up to carry a plate to the kitchen.

"Stop," she said. "Leave it." She dialed her maid, Soledad, and promised her double time and a half plus the ham if she would drop in and handle it.

We left the mess and spent the rest of the night at my apartment. The Christmas tree glittered as though it knew it was on special duty. We polished off two bottles of great Merlot. Like in the old days, we talked about everything that came to mind.

The phone rang off the hook. The girls, then Camila, then Pepe called to wish me a Merry Christmas. Pepe was still in Rio; Camila was in Chile.

On Christmas Day, I drove Melina to Aunt Carmen's. Pixie and her daughter were there. It was difficult to eat because we had stuffed ourselves the night before, and even after Melina had given away the ham, we stuffed ourselves again and still had a ton of leftovers. Just before sundown, Melina and I returned home to Bunker Towers. Melina did not stay with me that night. She slept in her own bed. I slept in mine. I went to sleep thinking about my phone conversation with Camila, the part that Melina could not hear. "*Yo sé que tienes alguien contigo, no digas nada. Quiero culiar, Amor, tú y yo.*"[22]

Jason was correct; small aircraft could be good cases too. We were getting

---

[22] I know you have someone there with you, don't say anything. I want to fuck, Amor, you and me

busier with these small crashes. I had no idea as to the end value of these cases, but Tom Jones wanted them. That meant Oscar wanted them. That meant a payday all around. Tom Jones had great brochures printed outlining his experience and presenting a list of crashes he had handled in the past and present. There were pictures and histories. The brochure was a proven door opener.

Juan had already been in Miami for a week. Juan had these brochures and had used them to open doors. I sent Pixie and Jo to join him on the month-old Learjet crash. The husband of a victim wanted to talk. The wife had chartered the Learjet to travel to New York on a business trip, but it had crashed. Ten minutes after taking off, it went down in the ocean. The wife's body had been recovered. The funeral was two weeks after the crash. Whatever the cause, we had a case against the charter company. If Tom Jones found product liability, all the better.

Niley and I were working a twin-engine Cessna that had crashed in Monterey, Mexico. The official government report blamed the accident on the failure of both engines. Niley and I flew to Mexico City where the families of the passengers lived. The crash had been a year ago, but the pain we saw in the family members was as fresh and raw as if it had just happened. A deep-pockets service company in Laredo, Texas did the regular service on the plane and had recently worked on the engines. That company was our target.

Niley and I met with the two widows, Eloisa and Natalia. Their husbands, partners in a construction company that built highways, had been going to check out an upcoming project that they had been asked to bid on.

The widows' lawyer, Raul Mendez, accompanied them to our meeting.

"I'm sure you can handle this case yourself, Raul, but you don't practice in the United States. My lawyers will go after that service company. They will be ready for war. If the service company won't settle out of court, we will file a lawsuit without delay."

"He's right," Raul said. "This firm has the experience. The retainer agreement clearly states that if they don't collect, you pay nothing." Raul and the widows were looking over copies of Oscar's law firm brochure. The widows looked interested.

"And just so it's all transparent, since Raul is your attorney, we will associate him in the case. He will be paid to help us get what we need from the Mexico side."

Raul gave me a thumbs up.

Niley said, "No amount of money in this world will ever be enough to bring back your loved ones. We know this. The lawyers know this. Raul here knows this." The widows had both been teary when they arrived, but Niley stopped when they both began crying. Niley had been sitting, but then she took a page from Pixie's book. She got up and stood between them, holding hands with both. "Eloisa. Natalia. We can't get them back for you, but we can do everything possible to maximize the compensation you receive for this tragedy. I'm sure your husbands would want that, not only for you, but also for your children."

The widows agreed.

Five hours later, Niley and I were on a plane heading back to Los Angeles. Niley had the retainers in her briefcase. "Let me ask you something," I said. "Do you feel it when you hold hands with a client like you did today? I mean no disrespect, baby, I'm just asking."

Niley's eyes watered instantly. "I don't put on. I'm not an actress. Of course I feel."

I took her hand, brought it up to my lips, kissed her fingers, and then the palm of her hand. "I'm sorry," I said. "I love you, Niley." I still sorely missed her sister Tanis, when I allowed myself to remember. I'd seen that pain in Niley about her loss. "You are awesome, baby."

A few minutes passed. Niley had calmed down. The tears were gone. The ride was getting a little bumpy, but instead of focusing on the turbulence, we concentrated on each other.

"How about you, Mario? Do you feel it with the families? Even though, over and over again, you go through it so often?"

"I've always felt it. I identify. When I see tears, I am right there with them, feeling it. It's not drama. It's emotion."

"You are such a big man. You're like a Superman, but I've seen you cry with the families so many times."

"Yeah, I can be a crybaby all right. Super Crybabyman."

"I love you, boss." We smiled at each other, ignoring the bumps. "I love you, Mario."

Niley and I had come to the airport in separate cars, and we left that way. It had been a fast, intense trip, and we were both drained. Dealing with grieving families is very stressful. She went home, and I went home. I hadn't even gotten unpacked when my phone rang.

"Boss, we signed the case!" Pixie always got excited when she came through.

"Jo, what do you think? Can Tom make a case out of it?"

"I talked to him several times. You know how he is. All he said was 'Sign it up.'"

I gave them my own news. "Hey, by the way, Niley and I signed the Mexico City case."

In the background, Pixie was cheering. Then they were both talking at once.

"Fuck, we're on a roll."

"We've been on a roll."

"When are we not on a roll?"

"Great work, babies. Come home. Safe travels."

"Miss, you, boss," Pixie said.

Jo said, "See you tomorrow, boss."

Melina returned to visiting me every morning for coffee on the way to work and after she got off work, which was late. She seemed to be living in both the apartment and her new place. One evening, she had me over for dinner in her huge new house. She had a project underway that she was dying to show me.

Melina led me to her basement lounge, which was still in the process of being decorated, and opened a door I'd never noticed.

"What is this?"

I flicked the switch, heard a hum, and saw a flicker. It was a few moments before long florescent bulbs set in the low ceiling came to life. Some of them weren't fully lit, but they proved just enough to illuminate a rectangular room with a wooden floor, and a far wall so distant I couldn't imagine the length of the room. I bet it ran under the whole house, and maybe even beyond.

"This used to be a bowling alley," she said. "The last owners used it for storage. I had it cleaned out. Guess what it's going to be now?"

"A hotel," I said, making random guesses that made her laugh. "An underground stable for miniature horses and ostriches. Oh, I know, a twenty-four-hour market so you can get to one of your stores without getting out of your pajamas. An incredibly awkward garage. A track. A home office."

"That last one sounds like a good idea," she laughed, "but wrong on all counts."

The only piece of furniture visible was a beat-up worktable made of unfinished wood. Several paper tubes rested on its surface. To the left against one wall was a floor-to-ceiling stack of two-by-fours, tools, tarps covering a pile of supplies, a pallet stacked with recessed lighting modules, and evidence that a carpenter had been there recently—sawdust and the scent of raw wood. The tubes above us flickered unpleasantly and buzzed.

"Changing the lights is the first thing," she said, scowling at the florescent bulb and unrolling a sheet of architect's paper. We held it open with four blocks of wood. I looked at the plans and then realized what I was seeing.

"You're building a shooting range? Under your house?"

"Practicing. I want to stay sharp and want to try out other firearms."

"You're still worried about the guy who shot your father," I said.

"What if he gets out of prison?" she said, looking up at me, worry written in her eyes and forehead.

I pulled her in my arms. "No way."

"I've already talked to the girls about it," she said. "I'm inviting them to practice shooting with me. I've got us a shooting coach lined up. Retired cop, very distinguished, a safety nut. Pixie will love him. He's built like a brick shithouse. Former body builder, too."

"Well…" I considered who we were talking about. I admit I hoped retired meant white-haired. "Jo's already a sharpshooter. Pixie will be more likely to practice if her teacher's a ten."

"He's a ten, all right," Melina said. "Retired after twenty years, so he's just in his forties." I had heard more than enough about the hunky coach. Melina had the good sense to switch topics. "The shooting gallery has its own entrance. I'm getting keys made for the girls."

"That's a good idea; a great idea," I said. After our recent experiences, I'd been wanting the girls to learn how to defend themselves. This seemed like a good start, in spite of Captain Hunk. "Woman, sometimes, I swear you read my mind."

Saturday night, it was back to my apartment for dinner. The routine was new and old. It felt familiar and strange, reminding me this was the last of the days when the only distance between us is a hallway.

My broker was great at getting me apartment buildings, but slow to find me a house near Melina.

"If you don't perform, I'm going to get Melina's broker to find me a house," I told Randy.

He wrinkled his little stub of a nose and shook his head. "Don't. I have to split the commission as it is. I'll have to split with the listing agent."

"I don't want to hear it. Find me a house."

Pasadena was his turf and Carl had the advantage. Really my mistake, since I'd given Randy all of Pasadena to choose from, but Carl was working on the proximity to Melina's behemoth of a house. I just hadn't wanted them bumping heads. On a Sunday when I was in town and Melina was free, Carl showed us two homes. Melina was with me when I took a look. Both houses were occupied and way too big for me, but one had the magic ticket advantage of being across the street from Melina's new property. From the street, all you could see of either one was the driveway gate.

"Carl, I'll buy this house for $900,000, and you need to give my broker a cut of the commission."

"Two problems. Asking is 1.4, and the listing broker is in for half already."

"Make a deal. Each gets a third of the commission, and the price is $900,000."

Carl smiled. I didn't know if it was with me or at me, but I didn't care.

Carl presented the offer that day. While I waited impatiently for his response, I considered buying the furnishings.

I told Melina, "I like the way they had it set up. Maybe I should buy their furniture too."

Melina nixed that. "We start from scratch."

"Not entirely from scratch. We both have lots of furniture." It was not enough to furnish more than a couple of rooms.

"They dropped the price," Carl told me on the phone.

Chapter 14
February 1977
Pasadena-Bound

"Yes," I said.

The sellers came back with an offer of their own, dropping the price from 1.4 to 1.1 million. [23] I could have held out longer, but I wanted the house. Even after we sealed the deal, the closing would take even more time. I caved. Truth is, I felt the house was worth the asking price.

I told Melina, "This house has three acres. Yours has two. This house is seventeen thousand square feet, and yours is sixteen thousand square feet. I figured it's worth the extra money."

"It's a great buy," Melina said. "And we're across the street from each other. That's a miracle. It's exactly what I hoped would happen. Close the deal fast so you can move. Fix it up while you are there." So that's what I did.

The girls had their own opinions, but they were anxious. I knew they'd love the house. My plans were to make it a truly fun place where we could spend time together between events, and each would have her own room for whenever she wanted. As cool as my apartment was, by comparison, this house would be paradise. Location hardly mattered. All the work we were doing was a plane ride away.

---

[23] $1,100,000.00 in 1976 had the same buying power as $4,785,138.74 in 2017

Melina's house was in move-in condition. Except for a single sofa and an end table that belonged to Carl's real estate agency, it was empty. She hired movers, and in one day, she was gone. Bunker Towers was instantly dry and soulless. After the fact, there was activity in the hall; I peeked in and saw the apartment manager, Flo, had already called in the troops. Tito was the janitor now. He had brought up a floor machine that was waiting in the corner, and the walls had already been taped off for painting. A couple of painters were busy with rollers and a spray gun. I went back to my place. Physically, my apartment hadn't changed, but because I knew Melina wasn't at the Bunker Towers anymore, I felt like the life had gone out of the building.

I talked to Sami often and Jason even more. If I didn't call for a while, Pepe or Camila called me to keep in touch. They were curious about the house I'd bought in Pasadena. Camila had too many remodeling suggestions about a house she'd never seen, one that I already had too many people renovating.

"Pepe, you inspired me to get out of that apartment. My new home is a matchbox next to yours, but for me, it's a mansion."

Pepe laughed. "You are way too modest, Amigo. Oscar told me all about the house you purchased in that city famous for that parade on New Year's!"

Camila wanted to see my house. But mostly she complained that she hadn't seen enough of me. Enough as in all of me. "I've known you more than a year and we've never done it."

"Remember what your brother said." I chuckled.

"I'm not a nun. Amor, he knows that I fuck. And who I fuck is none of his damn business!"

The move to Pasadena brought me closer to Aunt Carmen and the girls. Three months after I moved to Pasadena, it was April, and I was still dishing out money fixing, repairing, and remodeling. The good thing is that business was good. I didn't have to use my rental income. Expenses weren't just decorating; they included moving walls, removing carpeting, sanding and refinishing hardwood floors, stripping wall coverings, painting endlessly by a troupe of twenty painters, and a huge overhaul of the whole house to include air conditioning. And finally, buying furniture. My new phone system had an intercom button to call any phone in the house, or I could press 1-1-7 and be heard at once on every phone. I had phones in every room, several in the office, and a Nutone Intercom System to talk between rooms.

The last owner had old golf carts for his help. I replaced them with three new ones so that the live-ins would be able to commute from their quarters, a building that was out of sight of the main house. It was a long way.

I found myself walking around the big empty building talking to myself— whole two-sided conversations, with me saying both sides aloud.

"Hey, what do you do for a living that you can afford this mansion?"

"I'm an ambulance chaser. Yes, you heard right. I'm an ambulance chaser. No, I don't sell drugs, and I'm not a fence for hot goods. All my money is legit."

I loved my life, but sometimes I wish the jerkoff judge who'd sent me to the Terminal Island pokey when I was a kid could see me now. The first thing I did was get the plaque built into the gates proclaiming it my new residence. Now the house with the long driveway had a name: Casa Luna. It was written on the left gate on the driver's side so it was easy to see as you entered, and it was stylized in stone as a casa under a full moon centered at the apex of a granite arch you drove under. I guess when you have a house with a name of its own, you can feel like you've arrived.

"No wonder I got a deal on this house. It needed rebuilding."

"You got a fabulous deal. This house will be worth 3 million in no time flat."

"By the time I'm done, I will just be breaking even."

"You love it. Stop exaggerating. You aren't spending millions."

"I do love it."

Thank God I had Melina. She worked countless hours at her markets but found the time to deal with her and my sub-contractors and furniture wholesalers. She was pushy but directed it at sales people and workers, never me. She'd started first and finished her house before mine. There were rooms in my house I hadn't even been in more than once, even after I'd been there for a number of months. She insisted that they be part of the overhaul.

In some ways, it was like being married. Back when we'd met, Melina and I would talk for hours and hours. We've had our ups and downs, but our relationship was back to close communication now. Sometimes when we were talking, I'd picture or hear Sami. I felt guilty thinking of Sami when I was around Melina, but it was a fact that they were so much alike. We still did what we wanted on our own, but she ran the construction and decoration of my house with my money. I told Melina I already had a good alarm system, but when they installed her alarm system, Melina said mine was obsolete. I ended up with new, state-of-the-art alarms.

My old bedroom furnishings were installed in the help's quarters, but the first re-done thing that was complete in my house was my all-new master bedroom. The centerpiece was a bed, eight feet long and seven feet across with a beautiful, massive headboard. Crown molding to match the rest of the room's woodwork held a beveled mirror directly over the bed. Everything had to be custom-made, since no one mass produces mattresses, linens, and pillows that size. As for Jo, Pixie, and Niley, they could not believe the size of the bed. They jumped on it for hours on end. Who needed kids when I had them?

I bragged to Sami, "You will never believe the size of my bed. I had it made to order."

"Send me a picture," Sami said. "Maybe I can have one made for here."

Camila wanted to see it in person.

I was bragging to multi-millionaires. I know they could afford anything they wanted. But I was proud of what Melina and I were putting together. Fuck it.

As the house came together, it reminded me increasingly of Sami's penthouse, with all those unoccupied bedrooms. Pepe's houses had the same feel, lots of spare rooms to lounge around in. I knew Sami had more than one estate in England, and couldn't help but wonder whether she or Pepe had more money. I bet she could sell that diamond she wore all the time and buy a plane with it.

Melina had never looked as happy as she was now. She was in her element. I couldn't help but think that I was one of the reasons behind her smile.

At every opportunity, I told her, "You're the best designer in the world."

"I'm not bad at designing," she said, laughing, "for a grocery clerk."

Sundays were good for Melina and me. We had breakfast either at her house or mine. She had a cook and three housekeepers, so I ate a lot of dinners at her house. Johnson was still her driver and all-around assistant, always available. Her former maid, Soledad, had graduated to head housekeeper, a fit thing because she was a nurturing little woman. She watched over Melina like a mother hen.

I hired two live-in couples: Chete and Caro Garza, and Memo and Yoli Munoz. They stayed in the original carriage house that had been converted by previous owners into quarters for their staff. Four single-bedroom units were all upstairs, furnished, and each had a private bathroom. I felt they were big for bedrooms, but small for living quarters for two. The two housekeepers, Caro and Yoli, divided the indoor housework between themselves. Chete was the gardener. Memo did the heavy work inside, including brass polishing and chandeliers.

My accountant handled expenses out of my business account, and we treated it as a business expense. Melina told me she did the same. We treated a lot of things as business expenses. If I ever got audited, at least every penny was correctly documented. I'd pay whatever was due. I wouldn't go to jail out of ignorance as I had before.

"If you needed a million dollars tomorrow, would you have it in the bank?" I asked Melina. "I'm just curious."

"Barely," she said. "I have over ten million in equity in the markets,[24] so my credit line is hefty."

"I was just thinking the other day that I have six hundred apartments, the big house, and a couple of cars. I worry that all I keep in my checking accounts is about two hundred thousand. I seldom get above that."

---

[24] $10,000,000.00 in 1977 had the same buying power as $41,483,161.51 in 2017

"You can't have it both ways," Melina said. "You got equity, right?"

I nodded, thinking of how little my commercial mortgages were, and four buildings that were free and clear. "Yeah, I have a lot of equity, but if I had needed a million bucks to pay ransom to get out of that fucking hole in Venezuela, I wouldn't have had the money. Unlike you, I have no credit lines."

"I had you covered. I have a credit line for a lot more than a million dollars. I would have come up with the money no matter how much it was."

I felt a rush of love and gratitude. Our eyes met.

"I would have done the same for you, even if it took everything I have."

She looked at the clock and stretched. Her bed wasn't eight feet by seven feet, but it was pretty big, and plenty comfortable. She had silk sheets, and they draped over her flesh in a way no sculptor could have matched. I peeked under the sheets.

She tapped me on the shoulder, and I looked up.

"Want a Sunday morning fuck, or you want to go out?"

"I'm all yours," I said. "Sunday belongs to my baby Melina."

We stayed in bed all day. Her cook stayed in the kitchen, and her other live-in played room service. We hid naked under the sheets when she served us. We took a break for wine and cheese and crackers, then returned to bed.

I'm not sure what she'd said that had gotten my mind back to bank balances, but there I was again. "Come to think of it, I'm not counting my rental accounts where the management company deposits the rents they collect."

"There you are, worrywart. You have—what is it?—six hundred apartments? You got a ton of money coming in each month. You're Daddy-Fucking-Warbucks."

I lived and operated from the money I made with Oscar, but my CPA told me that after mortgage payments, insurance, utilities, and maintenance, there was a robust monthly cash flow from my apartments directly into my personal saving account.

"I think I'm going to start saving from what I do in aviation. I want a reserve like you have. A million."

"That's not a reserve," she corrected me. "You asked if I needed a million tomorrow and I said barely. You are worrying too much about cash and ransoms."

She swatted me on the ass.

I glanced in her direction. Her hair was tousled from all of our rough-housing. She might have slipped into her bathroom at some point and put on a hint of makeup that enhanced her dark eyes, but the excited flush in her cheeks was all her. She sat up slightly propped on her elbows, and the silk sheet slid down, revealing her breast. She posed provocatively, tugging the sheet down with the movement of her leg.

"Stop thinking about money and get on me."

I didn't need any more encouragement than that. A second later I was on top. Melina and I are matching sex freaks. Come to think of it, my entire team are sex freaks, not that it's part of the job.

About all I missed from Bunker Towers was the doorman, although all I needed to do here was pull up to the front or back of my house and walk in. I could have any of four people act as doorman or chauffeur, and probably would do so if I ever had a party. A dozen cars easily fit around the house's circular drive, and the garage could house eight cars. As much as I love cars, I wasn't going to be collecting and storing vintage cars like my predecessor. It's silly, in my opinion, to collect them just to park them in a garage. But then, he'd had a herd of offspring. Of course, if my team brought all their cars inside, we'd all put a good dent in that space.

Cosmo helped me plan a masterpiece on paper: the gym in the basement. I call it the basement, but it's not subterranean. It was big enough for competitions if I went that direction. At the gym's completion, Cosmo returned to check it out and got weepy and sentimental.

I pulled out a bottle of wine and shared it with him.

"I am so proud of you. I remember when you showed up at my door looking for work. You were a baby," he said.

"I was ten," I corrected him.

"You were living in the alley behind my studio," he said. "And you were so skinny I thought you might be starving. So I got doughnuts from next door and shared them with you."

"I remember," I said. "I wasn't living in the alley, though. Pélon and I had a clubhouse back there, a big wooden packing box. Aunt Carmen was off delivering a baby, and I got locked out. So instead of spending the night at Carson's where Carson peed in the bed, or at Pélon's where I was liable to come home with fleas and a black eye, I slept in the clubhouse. I remember that night. It was a bad night. Carson told me my aunt was arrested. I was looking for work to bail her out of jail."

"You were a ballsy little kid," Cosmo said. "Standing there, telling me you'd get me customers. I barely had enough karate students to keep my doors open. I figured what the hell. I'd give you a chance. I thought you'd try and fail and burn out in a week."

"I wouldn't be here now if you hadn't hired me."

"I wouldn't be here either. You're the only thing that kept that business going. You took me from the brink of bankruptcy and made me one of the busiest studios in town. I'm still teaching the kids of the kids you brought me."

That was a strange thought. My peers were old enough to have karate kids. Time was passing faster than it felt. I wasn't sure where I was in my life, but I couldn't imagine kids in it.

"And now I'm working for a lawyer, all because you introduced me to Harry when I was fourteen. You made it all possible."

I made a sweeping gesture at the room around us. I was feeling justifiably proud. The wine cellar tucked behind us was hidden behind a solid hand-crafted wooden door that felt like it might have been protecting wines for the last six hundred years, instead of having been installed last week during a remodel of the cellar cooling system. We were sitting in an elegant wine tasting area, a table and six coordinating but not matching chairs, all of which could have been plucked from the fanciest restaurant in Europe. This was my favorite table, chiefly because of the deep, comfortable chairs. This was going to be my play room; I expected to come down here after work to relax with Melina or the girls. It felt perfect. The cellar and wine-tasting area shared the basement with the gym.

"Hell of a gym," Cosmo said.

The gym felt open, maybe because there were mirrors and light, or maybe because it wasn't really a basement. Cosmo and I were drinking the one bottle I'd brought down from the kitchen just for him. When I'd first seen the cellar, it had been packed with thousands of dollars' worth of wine, but the seller had taken every bottle. To fill it, I might have to make a deal and buy out some little wine shop. Adjacent to the wine cellar was my cold spa, then the hot spa that included a big steam room and sauna. You've never seen so much granite. This was the perfect feature of the house that needed nothing at all. If Sami would ever make it here, she'd be jealous of my spa with four granite slabs to get scrubbed or massaged on.

We didn't drink the whole bottle. After a glass, Cosmo wiped his eyes. We hugged, he with tears in his eyes and me with tears in mine.

"You were my good luck," Cosmo said.

But after he left, I knew it was the other way around. He had been my good luck charm. And it wasn't just me. The good fortune he'd brought me extended to my Aunt Carmen first, then to Jo, Pixie, and Niley. It didn't end there. The good extended to the hundreds of clients who would have received less compensation if they hadn't trusted me to bring them to Harry or Jake or Jeff or Oscar or Tom's capable hands. That was very important to me, especially now that I was working with clients outside of the United States, clients who I would likely never see again after the case was finished. Without a good lawyer, a middle-class family living in Guatemala or Venezuela would be stepped on like a cockroach by insurance carriers' attorneys. In a perfect world, everyone connected to a case I signed would benefit, all thanks to Cosmo setting me on my path.

It was June third when Camila called me.

"Guess where I am?"

"Tell me you're in LA?"

"I'm at Van Nuys Airport."

"Come on over."

"I can't. I was in Tijuana and decided to surprise you. There's a catch. You have to come to me."

Camila was in one of Pepe's bigger planes. She'd flown early out of Colombia especially to Van Nuys to see me; then she was heading to Miami, where she had a dinner meeting later that night. I got to the airport, and the plane was fueled and ready to leave. I walked across the tarmac and ran into a steady line of her crew heading the opposite direction. They were leaving as I was just getting there. At eleven when I arrived, she stood smiling, framed in the open door. I ran up the steps to her.

"Been much too long," I said, bending to embrace her, lifting her up just a little.

Though it was stationary on the ground, the air-conditioning and lights were on in the DC9, much like a commercial plane. One attendant, Polly, remained. Camila told her she, too, could go.

"Have I been on this plane before?"

"I don't think so. I prefer my Lear, but this trip is too long for it. Come."

I followed Camila to a stateroom. The bed was bigger than the one I had slept in when I traveled with Pepe to Rome, and when I traveled with Pepe and Camila to Rio.

Camila closed the door. She had no makeup and she was beautiful. She kicked off her shoes, got on top of the bed, and hugged me.

"I've waited much too long for this," she said, kissing me. "I want you right now. They won't be back until one. We have that long to make up for lost time."

We tossed our clothes. I was already hard. Our bodies met and engaged with no foreplay, nothing but fury and a hunger that had been building for eleven months since our meeting in Rome. The wine Polly had left us went untouched as we burned off the hunger. Our bodies were ecstatic in completion.

Just after one, I got in my Rolls and set off for home where Pixie, Niley, and Jo were waiting.

"Boss, are you okay?" Niley asked.

"Of course, why?"

"You looked flushed. Maybe the heat out there got to you." Jo ran to get me an iced drink.

I chuckled. "Yeah, maybe. I'll go jump in the shower, then we can eat. How about that?"

"Boss, where were you? You just took off without saying anything." Pixie wanted to know.

"I went to the store." I lifted the paper bag I was holding and pulled out a large jar of peanut butter.

Later that night, after her dinner meeting, Camila called from her Miami hotel room.

"Was so good to see you, Amor."

"That's for sure."

"I'm sorry I didn't get to see your house. I wanted to."

"There will be other visits. I think we had a pretty fulfilling meeting, even without a visit to my house."

"Yes, Amor."

Two days after the phone call, I met Camila on her plane at the airport. I saw no crew, only Camila, about to make her way to Guatemala, then Colombia.

"I can't get enough of you," she said as I entered her.

"Ditto."

That made her laugh, but her laughter didn't interrupt our bodies' reunion. My mind raced. This was not Melina, not Sami. Not Pixie, Jo, or Niley. It was my wild, passionate Colombian jewel. After our fires burned out, there was a moment for chat between us. We drank the best red Colombian wine I've ever had, not in seats but on the bed, our backs against the headboard.

"How was business in Miami?"

"It was good. I am buying a house there. I met with the owner."

"I've never had a plane crash there." I was surprised at the business of buying a house in Miami. Another house. Why have so many houses? You can only be in one place at a time.

"Miami is beautiful. Have you been there?"

"Only as a fuel stop."

"Next time, we go together."

"Great."

"Great if the seller agrees to my terms."

I laughed.

"What's so funny?"

"My friend Melina is like that. She likes to haggle. She likes to win."

It was Camila's turn to laugh. "I'm not negotiating to get the price lowered, just for the seller to agree to accepting cash."

"You mean like green cash?"

She nodded. "Yes, dollar green."

Not everyone wants to mess with cash. Camila had a lot of it, for sure.

"I'm sure you'll get the house."

"I hope so. I gave him three days to think about it. He's going to call."

I turned to face her. "You'll come by here again if he says yes."

I saw Camila look at the clock. I got up and began pulling on my clothes. She stretched out on the bed like a cat, tossing off the sheets. I stopped dressing to admire her body and felt a stirring of the old appetite.

"Count on it, Amor. And if you ever need a partner in your apartment buildings or anything else, you'll let me know."

"Something to think about," I said.

"*Amor, si*." She wore a big smile and pulled a robe over her body. "We can do anything you want. The sky is the limit."

Two months later, in August, the phone rang in my home office. The team was poring through newspapers and magazines at the conference room table a few feet away. Jo made a move to pick up the phone.

"I've got this," I said.

The girls had missed the early morning workout and had changed into *gis* to make it up before lunch. I answered.

"*Como estas, Amor?*"

"Camila," I said, "what a pleasure to hear your voice. It's been so long. I thought you forgot about me."

"*Amor,* forget you? Never. Are you crazy?" Her voice was always upbeat.

"Where are you?"

"I'm at the Beverly Hills Hotel. Just landed a couple of hours ago. I want to see your new house!"

"Should I come get you?"

"No, I have a hotel car. Give me your address and tell me what time to come."

After I hung up, I looked up to find myself the center of Jo, Pixie, and Niley's attention.

"Aren't you supposed to be working?" I asked.

"Are you gonna fuck her this time?" Pixie leaned in my direction, the magazine she was going through falling forgotten to the table.

"Not a chance."

"Can I watch?" Niley asked.

"You want us to leave, boss?" Jo asked.

"It's not even noon. You can go if you want, but not because Camila is coming over in two hours."

Jo stood. "Two hours. We'd best get karate out of the way." She led my troupe down. I didn't join them, but the drill must have been abbreviated, because in under an hour, they were back in the office with damp, showered hair, and dressed to kill.

"What's all this?" I asked, seeing designer suits instead of their usual shorts and tees. I recognized the outfits I'd picked up for them on one of my Italy trips.

"These were in the closets," Niley said defensively.

"No argument," I said. "You look good. All of you."

"Back to work," Jo commanded. "It's not a pageant."

I chuckled under my breath. It was going to be a pageant for Camila's benefit, but I was proud. I knew that none of the staff in Pepe's houses worked with him the way my team did with me. And my girls looked like the winning professionals they are. The suits were made of light cotton for summer, in pastel colors. Pixie's had a bolero jacket with matador shoulders. Niley looked like a sunflower. Jo had a short jacket with a white cummerbund that made her waist look about three inches wide. They were all in stilettos that matched their dresses instead of the silly, comfortable house shoes they usually wore.

I could have waited in the office and had Camila escorted in, but I put the staff on alert. I headed for the front door when Caro signaled me that a car had been buzzed through the gate. I opened the door myself.

Camila was standing there in some kind of leather corset and a floor-length brown skirt that looked like she'd snatched it off some gypsy from 1792.

"Wow," I said. "You look fantastic." We did the European double-cheek-kiss thing. The corset top had a stunning effect on Camila's figure. I was telling the truth about that. Can't say that I cared for the skirt. Someone, probably Pixie, thumped me on the back, and I got out of the way to introduce my team.

They stayed and behaved themselves. There was a spate of background noise from workers somewhere in the house, and our conversation proceeded in the gaps.

"I'm sorry about the racket. I'm infested with the contractors for the foreseeable future. Let's sit in the living room. It's done."

"I love the house," Camila said, though she had seen very little of it.

I walked beside her from the entry, the girls behind us.

"Coming from a jetsetter like you, that's a huge compliment. We can take the full tour in a few minutes if you want."

My team got us wine, a bowl of mixed nuts, chips, and salsa. We sat on the two custom suede sofas, on opposite sides of the gorgeous glass and iron table that Melina had bought for me. My team sat in the wing chairs. All of us stood to toast the first time around, then sat.

"Can I smoke here?" Camila asked.

"Of course."

Niley went to one of the end tables and moved an ash tray within Camila's reach.

She opened her purse and took out a joint.

I glanced at the girls who were sitting primly with their hands in their laps and their legs crossed. They said nothing. Niley would have yelled 'Hurrah!' if she hadn't been watching her manners, and Pixie would have screamed she was coming.

"What beautiful company you have," Camila said, lighting up and looking at the girls. "*Lindas, pero muy lindas!*"

"Yes, they are beautiful. Though it is not company. This is my team."

The odor of the joint flavored the air. Camila offered the joint to Jo, who took a short drag then tried to give it back.

"No, share it," she told Jo. "I have more."

"Tell me, do you sleep with these gorgeous women?"

Pixie had several good drags in her by now, so she was fueled and ready to do something embarrassing. "Not sure how much sleep we get," she said, giggling. The pot had liberated her.

"I love your bustier," she said. "Who's it by?"

"Yves Saint Laurent," Camila said.

"Mario hates the skirt," Pixie volunteered. "He prefers legs. As bare as possible."

"Pixie!" I snapped at her and tried to stop her with a glare, but she was immune.

For a moment, I thought Camila was offended. As soon as my guest left, I was going to throttle Pixie. I gave her another glare. Pixie didn't even have the good sense to look worried.

Camila stood, shook out the paisley skirt, and sat again, shifting her torso slightly so that she could cross her legs. The dress fell away, baring her from thigh to ankle, a set of slim angles that were sheer poetry.

"I do not hate the dress," I said.

Camila smiled, a little smugly.

"I hated it too," she confided. "I had my tailor add the slit up the side."

"Good move," I said, taking a hit off my wine.

Jo made a strangled noise and got up to refill the wine so she could whisper in my ear. "What would you do if Pixie scissored up a thousand-dollar skirt?"

"It's her dime. She has her own fucking plane and her own fucking tailor. She can afford to use it for Kleenex if that's what she wants to do," I whispered back. "Besides, look at her."

After the joint, Camila wanted a tour. The whole herd of us obliged, walking her through the house, the grounds, all the way to the staff quarters. Camila refused the ride in the golf cart and copied the way the girls kicked off their heels. My gardener had golf course experience and kept the lawn like a putting green. We left the shoes in a pile by the front steps.

"I love this house and the neighborhood. I'd love to buy a house here."

"That would be nice if you lived nearby."

"Let me know if anything comes on the market."

"Count on it."

It was still daylight when my team and I walked Camila to the front entrance where the hotel car and driver waited.

"Such a short visit," I said. "When I visit you guys, I stay for days."

Barefoot, Camila was taller than any of my team. She put her arms around me and kissed me on the mouth. It was a first public kiss for us.

"You are not rid of me yet, *Amor*. I'm going to be here for a few days. Come to the hotel and we can have lunch tomorrow?"

"Sounds like a plan."

Camila hugged and kissed Jo, Pixie, then Niley. She gave Pixie a little pinch on the cheek.

"You and I have to talk sometime."

Pixie beamed like she'd been handed the key to the city by the Queen of the Rose Bowl Parade. I forgave her for her mouth. She was, after all, just being Pixie. As I watched the hotel car drive away, I wasn't too sure how much I wanted that little tête-à-tête between Camila and Pixie.

We wandered inside to the unfinished kitchen. "I am so hungry," I said. I rummaged through the pantry. There wasn't much there, but I found a jar of peanut butter.

"So, what did you think?"

Niley snatched the jar out of my hands.

"I think we should go out to eat, boss," Niley said.

"Hey, you can't take my peanut butter."

"Yeah, she can," Pixie said. "You'd eat that stuff till you got scurvy or the bends. Let's go find a restaurant where we can talk about Camila. I'll drive."

"I don't think you can get the bends from food," Jo said. "But I wouldn't mind going to the old neighborhood."

"I'm not going to ELA right now," I said.

"Downtown," Jo said. "How about PDC?"

I nodded. And we were off.

When I arrived at the Beverly Hills Hotel for lunch, Camila answered the door in a silk button-down blouse that was longer than her shorts. I could tell by her rosy-gold color and flushed cheeks that she'd been out by the pool, and she carried the lingering scent of chlorine, plus some kind of expensive fruity-smelling perfume. I was glad that I resisted the girls' advice and had followed my instinct not to dress up. I knew they'd been star-struck by Camila's designer outfit from yesterday. My jeans, a blue shirt that I wore tucked in, and a white blazer with white loafers were good enough. I wasn't putting on airs for anybody.

"You are such a fox," Camila said as she let me in. I kissed her on each cheek.

"You are so beautiful."

"I'm not beautiful. I'm just a girl with a so-so face and a body that I work very hard to keep the way it is."

"You are beautiful," I insisted. I followed her in and saw the staircase. "I didn't know they had two-story suites here. Cool crash pad."

"There's a reason this is my favorite hotel. I hope you don't mind that I took the liberty of ordering. We have steak, chicken, and the swordfish that room service recommended."

On the balcony, sheltered by a colorful awning, a big round table with two place settings awaited. With the Beverly Hills Hotel pool below us and palm trees in the distance, it was very different from London, but it reminded me of the balcony where I'd spent so much time with Sami. I took off my coat and tossed it over the back of the couch before I stepped out of the air conditioning.

We settled in. The chairs were deep and comfortable. We talked until two waiters arrived with the food and the wine steward arrived with a good red wine.

"This is good," I told Camila.

"I remembered what you were drinking at Pepe's last get-together and told them to hold the champagne."

We ate steadily for at least an hour. I did my damage to the beef, and Camila did justice to the fish. Neither of us touched the greens. Then she ordered two sundaes with a selection of ice cream, chocolate, and heaps of whipped cream served in a huge bowl. The dessert was spectacular enough that I wanted to take a picture to show the girls. I saw a two-hour workout in my future.

"How do you keep that fine figure eating like this?"

She reached and pinched my abs.

"The question is how do you do it?"

We scooped spoonfuls and fed each other heaping mouthfuls of ice cream dripping with chocolate fudge, chasing the ice cream with sips of red wine. We watched the comings and goings at the pool below. There wasn't an empty place that we could spot. The shade did not protect the ice cream from the Beverly Hills heat, not that much of it was left when we were done. A thin, tanned girl was swimming laps, and a muscular man was showing off his diving skills to an admiring girl in a bikini. Some kids were playing in the shallow end of the pool. The rest of the people were buttering themselves up and roasting in the sun.

Camila fanned herself vigorously. Sweat had broken out on her forehead. "I'm feeling about to melt, like that ice cream," she said.

We went in the living room with the wine and our glasses. The air-conditioning hit us with a welcoming blast, full-on with the balcony doors still open. Camila unbuttoned some of her top buttons, and then opened up some of mine to keep it even.

The waiters cleaned up. The steward brought a new bottle of red. Camila opened her purse and paid the bill with hundreds, then handed the waiters and wine steward two hundred as a tip.

I wondered why she paid cash. It's so easy for taxes and recordkeeping to sign the bill. But that was none of my business. I didn't ask.

Our wine glasses clicked more times than I could count. No joints. I didn't ask, but I counted Camila smart not to smoke weed in a hotel room. She sat next to me on the sofa, her legs crossed. I wanted to bury my head in there.

She asked about my family.

"There's just my Aunt Carmen, who raised me."

"And then there are your girls," Camila said.

"My team."

"I take it they're not housekeepers."

"My housekeepers are housekeepers," I said. "Caro and Yoli. And you can thank Chete for the quality of the grass in my yard. He's the gardener. Memo does everything else."

"I want to know about Jo, and Pixie, and Niley," she said. "The girls I met. They're real characters. I can tell."

"That's my team," I said. I explained the girls' job. I mentioned some of the big crash cases they'd played a big role in, and some smaller cases they handled on their own. They played a big role in my business, and I hoped that my explanation did them justice. Camila was a good listener, nodding as I spoke.

"You've done well," she said, moving closer. "Your aunt must be proud of you."

"Except for when I got arrested," I said.

"Arrested? You?"

I told her about my arrest. Maybe it was because she was such a good listener, or maybe it was the wine. I'm not ashamed of my history. I realized that I still knew nothing about Camila.

"I've been talking for an hour. How about you?"

"Get me some more wine, and I'll tell you."

I filled her glass. Every glass we drank, she unbuttoned a button. Her shirt was just barely hanging on her body. There was some lacy lingerie underneath. She reached over and undid the last button on my shirt, and chugged half of her glass.

"Wine is fine, but I wish I could fire up a joint. It would bring the cops." She laughed.

I said nothing. It was her turn to speak.

"My father was a Colombian drug dealer. A big drug dealer. I think my mother was involved in the business, but I have never known for sure. She's been dead for years. I never asked her." She hesitated. "Did I shock you?"

"Not at all."

She shook her head.

"I don't want to scare you away. It's a bad story."

"You don't need to tell me if it makes you feel bad."

"I want you to know. When I was eighteen, my mother and my father left me at home and went out to dinner. My mother drove them into a head-on colli-sion that killed my father."

"I'm so sorry," I said.

"That's not the worst of it," Camila continued. "She killed him on purpose. She'd just found out that he'd been molesting me since I was twelve."

I hardly knew what to say to that, but I didn't have to think of anything, because she was still talking.

"It was a wreck, and she didn't go to jail. But a year later, she died of a heart attack. Are you shocked?" she asked again. She wasn't smiling, but she was in good spirits.

"No," I said. "My best friend is in prison for murder." What is worse? Mur-der or molesting your daughter?

I noticed that it had gotten dark outside.

She put her head on my lap. Her hands wrapped around my waist.

"So, it's just your brother and you?"

"Just Pepe, me, and my little sister. I trust you, but don't tell him I told you about our parents."

"Don't worry." I wondered why she'd told me. This wasn't a secret I wanted to know.

"My brother is powerful. He's very rich."

I knew about his planes, the two houses, and had heard talk of many more houses.

"I'm sure he is."

"He likes you."

"He doesn't know me, but he's been good to me. He sure saved my ass in Venezuela."

"He didn't know you when Oscar asked for a favor, but he knows you now."

"I owe Oscar big time, too."

"My brother thinks the world of Oscar. I don't think there is anything he wouldn't do for him. And from what I hear, Oscar thinks the world of you."

I felt Camila's mouth, hot and wet through my jeans. My body remembered the two afternoons when we met on her plane at Van Nuys Airport.

"We're going to be good friends," she said. The way she said good, I knew she meant sex.

"I may not be around long enough for a long friendship," I said. I wasn't afraid. I counted Pepe my friend. I was feeling the moment. My mind had checked out on how I could just fuck his sister after he had told me not to.

"Pepe doesn't run my life," she said. "You didn't say that the two times we met on my plane in Van Nuys." She gave a soft laugh. "How many times did we do it in those few hours?"

"Not enough," I admitted.

"I was ready the day I met you." She reached out and grabbed both my hands, trying to pull me off the sofa. I let her pull me to my feet. "And I've been dying to have you again since we met the last time. My legs are shaking."

I kissed her.

There was no fanfare. We left our unbuttoned shirts on the winding stairway and stood in the bedroom for a few minutes with the bed between us. This was different than the cabin on a plane. We certainly could be feeling shy, or maybe we were just enjoying each other, but there we were, naked, staring, and longing. My dick was at full mast.

This was not the first time with Camila, but it was still new. It's always different with someone new. With Melina, it had been like meeting my other half. With Valita, it had been savage. With Niley, it had been cathartic, like purging Tanis. With Camila, it was just erotic. It felt like everything was moving in grueling slow motion. I drank wine off of her body, and she off of mine. She was slick with sweat. Me, not so much.

"If Pepe finds out, then what?" I figured if we kept doing it, he would find out.

"Then nothing."

"He is protective of you."

"He is, but not about who I sleep with."

She'd said her father molested her. Not a good thought when you're in the middle of an erotic encounter. Knowing what he'd done to her made my libido flag. But now, she showed no signs of being torn by it. What did I expect to see?

I stayed the night. In the morning, I left a message for Jo that I was taking the day off, visited the men's clothing store downstairs, and bought a change of clothes. Room service catered to us. We went down to the pool, swam, sat around in the sun. I even did some dives to show off my skills.

On the third day, Camila had me invite the girls over.

"Are you sure?"

"Of course. I like them."

"They like you, too."

I hit the men's store again for dinner wear, with some help from the concierge to buy off the rack in my size. I'd warned the girls to come in formal wear. Camila was dressed to the nines. We had dinner at the most exclusive restaurant in the hotel. We were certainly the hottest table there. A couple of out-of-towners even came by to ask us for autographs. The wait staff could not have been more accommodating. We drank 1961 Chateau Mouton until we closed the restaurant. None of us were feeling any pain when we went to Camila's suite.

"Are you into group sex?" Pixie said with a winey giggle.

"Sorry," I said, "Pixie had too much wine. She kind of swings both ways."

"Pixie isn't drunk," Camila said, and moved close and kissed Pixie on the lips.

This was, so far, a girl thing. I was moved but uninvited. It was okay. Nothing wrong with the view.

"I'm in," Niley said.

"Me, too," I heard Jo say.

The girls were huddled, standing, arms around each other, kissing.

It took a few minutes for them to remember me. They all looked in my direction at once.

"*Amor*, are you in?" Camila asked, looking like she was already on the verge.

"I'm in."

None of us had a shy bone in our combined bodies. On that king-sized bed, we had a night for the record books.

Then Camila was off, winging off to Colombia. We were off to work, as usual, filling the months with small crashes, flying all over the country. Oscar was delighted, and the girls were happy to be so busy. They were competitive with each other, so that kept the searches pretty intense.

And then, in August, Jason called.

Chapter 15
August 1977
Father Goose in Mexico City

"A plane with a hundred and forty people aboard crashed during a landing," Jason said.

I put the phone on speaker, and the girls listened in.

The following Sunday, in the middle of August, I missed breakfast at Melina's because I was back in Mexico City with the girls. The airline company had gotten there ahead of us, so the families were locked up in two hotels to keep lawyers out. The media got in and reported the sad day-to-day life of the families grouped together. Everyone aboard had died. Most of the passengers traveling from New York were residents of Mexico. We didn't rely on Juan to come and open doors for us, but started working first and didn't call Juan for several days. The bodies had been recovered. Every day, the coroner released newly identified remains to family members.

The families accepted the partial payments that the airline gave them to pay for the funerals. They accepted the food tickets. They accepted that they got to stay in a hotel mourning with other families. What they didn't accept was the lack of information from the airline on what had caused the plane to crash in perfect weather in broad daylight. The tail of the plane had struck the perimeter fence of the airport more than two hundred feet short of the runway.

The families wanted answers. Their complaints to the media were aired in newspapers, on radio, and television. Families wanting answers were nothing new. I had never worked a case that had a fast official report of what caused the tragedy. Tom Jones said it sometimes took years. The official reports by the government agencies were efforts to prevent a tragic reoccurrence, but the investigations took time. This wasn't something the families in Mexico City were ready to hear.

Twice daily, I talked to Tom Jones on the phone.

"It's too soon for the airline to have anything to tell them."

I wasn't a mechanical expert, and even though that made sense to me, even if there weren't definitive answers yet, the families needed to know whatever there was to know. And if there was nothing more to know yet, they needed to understand why. Maybe the families wanted to talk about what may have caused the disaster. I asked Tom Jones to help us on this one. He flew to Mexico City. I wouldn't say the hotel where the airline was putting the families up was a fleabag, but I arranged a meeting at the Alameda Hotel, which was, at least by comparison, deluxe.

Jo, Pixie, and Niley passed the word along to the workers inside the hotels where the families were staying. I had told them to stay in the background, so they didn't even try to get inside. They stood outside near the employee entrances and paid off savvy-looking hotel staff to quietly let the families know that an unofficial family meeting would be taking place at the Alameda Hotel, and at that meeting, one or more pilots familiar with the type of plane that had crashed would talk to the families about what might have occurred.

I was in my suite at the Alameda looking over notes when Juan arrived with the newspaper reporter he had found. Jaime was young and shaggy, fast-talking, and carried a little tape recorder like the one I used to make notes to myself when I was driving so I didn't have to stop to write things down. He liked Americans and introduced himself to me as Jimmy.

"I'm not looking for publicity yet, but I want to get the word to the families to walk over here, to the Alameda. We are providing snacks and drinks and a pilot experienced in flying a plane like the one that crashed. The families will be able to ask questions."

"But how can they answer questions before the investigation?"

"Good question," I told him. "That's exactly the kind of question we'll be answering."

I asked him to spread the word and handed Jimmy two hundred dollars American. He took it with the flash of a grin and a fling of his head, which tossed back his long bangs.

I don't know which strategy worked best, but the turnout was fabulous.

We were all gathered in the nice conference room we'd rented, set up similarly to how we'd been set up before. My team and speakers were at the head of the room. The people we were speaking to were at tables to facilitate their ability to partake of the tapas and dessert buffet we were offering. I spoke first, before Tom, and I was glad that I had grown up speaking Spanish.

I assured them first that we had not come to solicit them, then got to the heart of the topic.

"Newspaper, radio, and television tell me how you, the families of the victims, are upset that you haven't been told what caused this crash. The lead attorney I represent came at my urging. He's not only a lawyer. He's been a pilot in the US Air Force and has flown bigger and smaller planes, as well as the same kind of aircraft as the plane that took your loved ones away. Also joining us are two retired pilots who have hundreds of hours flying the same model plane. I know you are filled with questions. You will be able to ask your questions. Talking is healing. Let's talk."

Tom had found our two pilots. One flew in from Texas and the other from Chicago to help us out. Of course, they were being paid for their expertise. The girls and I sat with the pilots and did not answer questions.

Tom Jones spoke enough Spanish to introduce himself, then an interpreter stood beside him and translated.

"Please understand that everything I tell you today is conjecture. It has to be, because it is too soon for even a preliminary report to be released by the government. I have studied the facts as we know them now, and I want to share with you the most likely scenarios."

Tom described a possible radar failure and a possible altimeter failure. "If this turns out to be at least part of what caused this tragedy, the manufacturer of these instruments will have to answer to the charges of their failed products. It may turn out that the pilots came in too low and possibly too slow."

Once the families understood that his explanations were just conjecture, he talked for half an hour and then took questions for ten minutes; then he stopped to introduce one of the two pilots that had traveled to talk to the families.

I had not invited the press, but probably thanks to our cub reporter, Jimmy, they were there. Tom Jones and the two pilots spoke with experience and honesty. They made it clear that they were speculating as to the causes of the crash, and that no one would know what happened until the official investigation had a full report. The report would take a year or more, and everyone knew how hard it would be for the families to wait that long to understand what happened. They made it clear that they were just giving the families the benefit of their personal experience before they had their say, and then they answered questions. The families had a lot of questions. They kept the pilots busy coming up with answers for almost two hours.

As the meeting continued, the families warmed up to the pilots and eventually to me. When a question was asked, one of the pilots would answer. Sometimes the pilot would stand up and draw on one of the two blackboards that were behind us facing the families.

Tom drew a picture of the failed plane and marked the spot on the aircraft that he believed hit the fence before crashing onto the airport property, far from the beginning of the runway where the plane was supposed to land. Reporters took pictures of many of the illustrations.

None of us handed out a business card. The families knew where I was staying, and I wasn't going anywhere.

The evening news that night had coverage of the meeting, supplemented by at least two interviews with official spokesmen of the airline. One official said that everything was conjecture, and until the preliminary report was released by the federal government, we would not know for sure what happened. A family member was interviewed, and they spliced in that the families had learned that fact at the meeting. He also expressed great gratitude to us for providing the meeting, because otherwise, they'd all been in the dark about the details of what might have happened. Another told a reporter, "If the families got some relief attending the meeting, good for them."

There were favorable consequences to the meeting. Several family members, self-appointed leaders of the families, arranged with the airline security to allow us entry to the two hotels.

Tom Jones had flown to Mexico City in Oscar's plane, and he headed back to Los Angeles minutes after the meeting. His being there was just walking on the wire. Some jealous attorney could cry foul and say it was soliciting.

In the course of our daily routine, we ran into some attorneys from the United States. We made friends and had dinner with them twice. They were friendly guys from Chicago. We shared restaurant tips and travel tips, and they flirted with my team. We never talked about how many cases we had. I knew they went home with retainers, but had no idea how many. We exchanged business cards and promised to stay in touch.

"What do you think?" I asked the girls when we were back to our hotel suite. They had conflicting opinions.

"In touch, no way," Jo said. "That's the competition."

"Good answer." I was pleased. "And the correct one. But who knows. Someday, we might work a case together."

Carson had called twice in as many days, offering to help out. He wanted in the aviation business. At least he is consistent. I chewed him out and reminded him that he had a ton of contacts sending him business and to keep his focus on where the money was coming from for him.

It was Sunday, and we didn't have any meetings. She and the girls had finished two hundred sit-ups nonstop, reminding me of Tanis. Then they changed into bathing suits to lie out by the pool. I was especially proud of Jo, almost ten years older than me and she kicked ass like the youngsters like Pixie. I also liked the abs they had developed.

On the phone, I told Oscar, "I should have handled it with just the two pilots and not involved Tom at all."

"It's fine. Tom's a big boy. I'm sure he handled it right. Go get them signed up," he said.

"You're going to need a whole lot of money on this one, Oz."

I could picture Oz. He was probably at that enormous desk of his, probably smoking a cigar. I'm glad he couldn't see me, wet from a shower and not wearing a stitch. I'd been in a suit all day. August in Mexico is hot weather to be wearing suits, and the one I'd had on was already making its fourth or fifth visit to the hotel's dry cleaner. No question.

"My checkbook is ready."

I had promised to let Pepe know when I was out of the country, so I let him know where I was, and that I'd been there for more than a week. "It's too bad I don't have a house in Mexico," he said. "I'd invite you to stay there. Camila and I do a lot of business there, but I don't trust the government, so I don't buy real estate."

I was relieved that Pepe was busy and couldn't come visit. He was in Germany. I figured he'd be a distraction from what I was there to do. I enjoyed his company and no doubt I'd stray with him here.

Camila was in Athens on business. She said she would let me know if she could stop by on her way back. Secretly, I wished she didn't stop by and blur my focus on this case.

"*Te estrano, Amor*,"[25] she said.

"I miss you, too."

"I left Los Angeles daydreaming of the days I spent with you at the hotel, and that last night with you and the girls. It was fantastico!"

"*Me pones duro hablando así*,"[26] I said. Camila often shifted into Spanish, and I followed her lead.

"*Quiero que me cojas con esa verga gigante que tienes*."[27]

We were in the hotel's conference room with a number of families that had requested a question-and-answer session. It was catered by the hotel who had provided us a pricey hourly rate for the room, but with free drinks, chips and salsa, and pastries. I ran through my speech, mostly adlibbing, then took a few questions. We'd started with the coffee and drinks. The salsa and chips were placed in large communal bowls on the tables. We were holding the pastries till we were done. Everything was going well.

A hefty woman stood up. "You said only family members are eligible. What about a common-law wife?"

A second woman on a different row hopped out of her seat. "Adelita, you aren't a common-law wife, you heifer."

A third woman at the front table didn't bother to get up, but put her two *centavos* in. "Neither are you, Abella."

The first two women snapped back, "Shut up, Justina."

From that point, not much of what they said was distinguishable. The three of them broke out into a loud squabbling match that could have been the fight warm-up on Saturday morning wrestling. The room exploded into arguments, with a number of people from other families jumping in to keep the women apart, and others yelling about their own questions that were still unanswered. I

---

[25] I miss you, my love

[26] You make me hard talking like that

[27] I want you to fuck me with that giant penis of yours

didn't try to raise my voice over theirs, but it was clear something had to be done before actual fisticuffs broke out.

I stuck my thumb and forefinger in my mouth and blew a whistle that could have cracked glass.

The room went silent.

"Ladies, let's talk about this privately, please?" I waved Jo over and had the girls take the women outside, in separate areas, to talk about their situations, but mostly to schedule them at a later meeting. Juan went out to switch places with Jo, then Jo and I finished up and signed the remaining families.

It turned out that Juaquin Munoz was the problem the distressed women shared. He was one of the victims who had perished in the tragedy, and from the look of it, he'd left behind a knotty mess that was going to be a challenge to untangle. As soon as our bigger meeting cleared and those families signed, we took the complicated situation in a private room with the three squabbling mothers, Abella, Adelita, and Justina.

Pixie handed me a fresh black coffee when I walked in and took a seat at the head of the conference table.

"Ladies, please help yourselves," I said, waving my hand to indicate sodas, coffee, and a variety of cookies.

The ladies were still riled up from their near-fight. They did not get up to accept refreshments. That's always bad. The road to a retainer, like any sale, is paved with little yeses.

"Here is what I know," Justina said. "Juaquin married no one. I have five children from Juaquin. I don't care about these other women here and their claims."

Abella stood up, her posture furious. I could see her hands were already knotted into fists. I was still hoping I could prevent a fistfight.

Abella said, "Juaquin fathered three children that I have at home. They don't count?"

"I have four of his children!" Adelita yelled. With her loud voice, she didn't need to get up to command attention. She also had a hundred kilos over the other two mothers.

"I'm not putting up with this if I have to put up with them!" Abella shoved out of her chair and headed for the door. "Juaquin was *hijo de puta sin vergüenza; que bueno que esta muerto!*"[28]

Pixie headed her off at the door and embraced her.

"You don't mean it. You aren't glad he's dead. Come back. Please stay. For the sake of your kids, listen to what Mario has to say. Please, Abella."

By the time Pixie finished her sentence, Niley was also hugging Abella. The three of them stood hugging in plain view of everyone at the conference table. Abella was crying uncontrollably.

Adelita and Justina's eyes watered sympathetically as they heard Abella's sobs. However they all regarded each other, they had all lost a mate, and they were all suffering. For their sakes, I really hoped that Juaquin had had a good job with a significant income. Pixie and Niley maneuvered Abella into her chair and sat on either side, like matching buffers. When all was calm, I began again.

"All of you have a claim. It does not matter that none of you were married to Juaquin. Each child he fathered has a claim in this matter. I will accept retainers on their behalf from the three of you. The attorney will probably let you know that you personally do not have a claim. Your children do."

I had already covered this in the bigger conference room. Now, finally, they seemed to be listening. In twenty minutes, Niley was serving them the coffee and cookies they'd refused earlier. Over these refreshments, they engaged in a session of sharing all of Juaquin's secrets, which included, among other things, a propensity for undressing when he walked in the door, a predilection for beer, and a habit of eating dinner in his underwear in front of the television. Another thirty minutes later, they shared a pen, signing the retainers that named the children.

As they left, I reminded them, "Remember, ladies, without a birth certificate that names Juaquin as the father, the case for that child will be very difficult."

---

[28] Juaquin was the son of a whore, without shame; it's good he's dead

Abella, Adelita, and Justina hugged me and did the same to my team.

When they were out the door, I gave Juan the assignment of collecting the birth certificates of the children. If the mothers did not have them, he would fetch the records. One mother lived in Mexico City. The others lived in the outskirts. All of the children were close in age. Juaquin must have been a very busy man.

"I thought it was a lost cause, but you signed all the kids of Father Goose," Jo said after they left. She finished off the last of her coffee and put the retainers into a neat stack.

"Not a chance that it was a lost cause," I said, standing up. "You know better than that. But considering the decedent's history, there might be more heirs out there."

The girls looked so alarmed that I nearly laughed out loud. If Juaquin had more offspring, these women weren't likely to bring them up and divide his estate even more. "You got everything?"

Pixie surveyed the table and picked up the pen. "That's everything." She looked in my direction, waggling the pen at me. "Boss, you are good," Pixie said. She folded the remainder of the cookies into a napkin and dropped them in her pocket.

"Eat all those and you'll end up like Adelita," Niley said. She picked up a wadded paper napkin from the table and dumped it in the trash before she turned to me. "I keep learning from you." Niley followed Pixie, Jo, and me to the door.

"Stop the kiss-ass. Let's go sign some more."

I glanced into the empty room, flicked off the light, and gave the desk manager the meeting room key.

Roberta, the mother of decedent Eliseo Martinez, wanted to talk to me in private. We met in the executive lounge of my hotel. I knew from my notes that Roberta was sixty-one, but as she walked up, I realized she looked older. I wondered if it was the burden of the crash that had aged her. I greeted her, and we walked toward a corner of the room. She walked slowly, possibly painfully. She was a tiny woman in a black paisley dress. I took her arm carefully and walked beside her as she selected an upholstered chair with padded arms. I saw a tall bentwood chair that would fit my frame and pulled it so that we sat, shoulder to shoulder, at right angles, with an end table nearby. It was close enough to be intimate, but not face to face, so it was non-confrontational. My seat faced the door. Hers faced a view of Mexico City. It was an effort for me to sit quietly, because I saw she was highly emotional; but the smart thing to do was to let her take the lead.

"Everyone I talk to says you are a compassionate young man. We believe you that the attorney who will handle our case in the United States is a warrior in the courts."

I knew that wasn't what she wanted to talk about. I reached for her hand. "Thank you, Roberta, for the kind words. What is the problem?"

"My son's wife Elisa does not deserve anything from my son's death."

"She is his wife," I said.

"She is a *puta*. Everyone in our small town knows it. There is not a man there who she has not had relations with."

Her lip quivered, and she made a pained noise deep in her throat. Tears ran down her face. She was still grieving her son, and would be crying about his loss for a long time.

"Don't cry, Roberta. Your son must have let it pass and stayed with her for a reason. He could have divorced her, but he didn't. Whether we like it or not, she is the wife and rightful heir. Without children, she's the primary beneficiary. I told you when you signed the retainer that it is likely the attorney will get you compensation because you depended on your son for partial support."

Roberta nodded her head. She seemed to be hearing me but was still not accepting the facts. All she could do was feel the injustice of the unfaithful wife surviving to collect benefits. She left calmer than when we started, but I had the feeling that nothing would ever change her mind that her son's wife was not deserving of a single penny for the wrongful death.

"I trust you, *hijo*," she said. I bent down and gave her a careful hug, mindful of her frailty. She put her skinny arms around me and squeezed and sobbed.

"I will always be available to you," I promised.

It was a difficult moment, and one that made me think. Maybe I should make a will. I had no one to survive me except my aunt. But my aunt was not frail, like this woman. She was fierce, down to her bones, a thing I had never realized growing up. I went straight from the lounge to my suite and gave Aunt Carmen a call, just to say hello.

The families left the hotel after almost three weeks of being housed there. All bodies had been recovered, and funerals had taken place. It was time for the families to go back home, wherever that might be. More than half of them lived in Mexico City or very close, and the rest lived in other areas of Mexico.

When our work was done, Juan took a commercial flight back to Puerto Rico and Valita. Oscar sent his plane for us.

If you've never had sex on a plane, you've been missing out. There's a reason that the mile-high club has a following. The Lear is small, but the seats are just wide enough and comfortable. There is enough room on the carpeted floor for some squeeze-sex. We made the best of it. The only problem is that Mexico City to the Van Nuys Airport is just a little over three hours. Jo, Pixie, Niley and I made it work at thirty-five thousand feet, but just when things were getting really interesting, it was time to land. The flight attendant, our friend, the tall blonde named Chastity, was a good sport. She didn't participate, but she kept our wine glasses filled, except for Pixie, who had a one-drink limit because she was driving from the airport. The pilots didn't know or played it like they were unaware of what was going on while we were cruising, and during the turbulence when we should have had our seat belts on. When it came time to exit, Pixie kissed the two pilots and the stewardess and shared some free advice.

"Air the plane out before Oz takes his next trip," she said.

Jo nudged her. "Don't be so nasty."

Pixie stopped right outside the plane.

"You have *cajones,* calling me nasty. Just minutes ago, we were all naked, fucking, and sucking while Chastity faked reading and pretending not to hear, and the pilots pretended like they knew nothing was going on. You call me nasty because I suggest they air out the plane?"

Jo said, "Yeah. Everyone was being very cool, pretending they were deaf and blind while you were having your screaming orgasms. You didn't have to go call attention to it. They aren't stupid. They were pretending, but their noses weren't blind. You were stating the obvious."

Niley was red-faced. Jo patted her hand. "Don't worry, kiddo. You didn't scream. I'm pretty sure your moans didn't reach the cockpit over the engines and music. But hell, they probably heard Pixie down in Mexico City while we were flying overhead."

There was no denying it. Pixie was loud. I laughed. I couldn't help it, even though Pixie was giving me the glare of death. It wasn't long before Jo, Niley, and even Pixie were laughing too.

"I love you," I told my team.

When we climbed in my Rolls in the Van Nuys Airport parking lot, Pixie complained about having to get in the front seat by herself.

"You should have had Johnson drive us."

"You're much prettier than Johnson."

"And the boss' car was here where we left it," reminded Jo.

"It needs washing," I said. We'd been gone a long time.

Pixie was never down for long. "I loved our all being together for three whole weeks. I mean, I missed Lainey, but I loved us."

"I loved us too," Niley said, grabbing me between the legs, "Even though you limited the sex. Compared to before, it was like church camp."

"I don't know what kind of church camp you went to," Jo said, rolling her eyes. "Were we on the same flight back?"

"We'll make it up, right, boss?" Pixie asked.

"Of course. What we just did on the plane was a preview," I said.

"Why do I always have to drive?"

As always, Pixie drove with one eye on the back seat and one eye on the road.

At two in the morning, we arrived at Casa Luna. The girls would have normally slept with me, but we were all tired. They'd crashed here before, but they were looking forward to their bedrooms at the new house. I went to the master bedroom, and they went into their rooms. They'd each contributed to the design and decoration of their favorite bedroom and staked their claim, not just with personal time spent there during working days, but also with some of their things hanging in the closets, and their favorite toiletries in the attached bathrooms. After they scampered off, I took a short shower and crashed, glad to be in my own bed.

Melina woke me with a passionate kiss. She had a head start, because she was already naked and in my bed.

"Baby, I missed you," I said, sitting up. "Please tell me you walked over here naked."

"I missed you more," she said. "But no, I didn't come here naked. I was dressed and ready for work. Came here with a thermos of coffee, but when I saw you lying there, how could I resist? I don't have a whole lot of time, but the sun's not up yet."

I lifted the sheet and she slid in next to me, her skin like hot silk. I don't know how long I'd been sleeping. Not long, but long enough to rev up for an instant morning quickie with Melina. I don't care if I was half asleep. It was a hell of a siesta, and I'm surprised we didn't wake anyone up. When Melina ran into the bathroom for a three-minute shower, I almost called her back. She came out half-dry, with a towel on her hair. I watched her dress and brush her wet hair as we talked. I knew she was going and I wanted her to stay.

"Are the girls here?"

"Yeah. We got in late."

"How come they're not in your bed?"

"We got in late." I didn't mention the plane or the ride back from the airport, but I had a feeling Melina already had a pretty good idea about that.

She shook her head in mock despair. "What a waste. Gotta run, but I'll be back tonight if you want."

"I want."

By the time we finished talking, Melina had gone from centerfold to the executive that she was.

"Which of your five markets are you working today?"

"All of them," she said. "Long day. I'm hiring."

"Next time, make them come to you."

She laughed. "You're good. It's why you get the big bucks. Next time I will."

"I'll be waiting," I said. "Want some coffee?" I held up the thermos she'd brought. I was playing with the idea of giving her another distraction, but she gave me a wicked look that showed she knew exactly what I was thinking and dodged my embrace. I could have convinced her, but I knew she needed to get to work.

"I wish. I'm late."

She went out my bedroom door, then she came back and stood in the doorway.

"I love you, Mario. And I did miss you."

I blew her a kiss. "Ditto, baby."

I went back to sleep. I was in bed till after dawn, then I had a furious workout. I let them sleep. They were exhausted. By noon, the girls were up and dressed in clothes they kept at Casa Luna for days like this. We had a brunch lunch and talked about our plans for the next few days before they sped off to surprise their kids when they got home from school around three.

We returned to Los Angeles with retainers for a hundred and one decedents and nineteen association agreements with five Mexican attorneys. Two additional attorneys had cut a deal with me to let me bring their cases to Oscar's firm. The papers were already in Jo's briefcase.

"Jo, you take the retainers to Tom Jones, then split for home." I kissed her. "I love you, baby."

"I love you more, boss."

"Pixie, you go straight home. Drive safe. Watch where you're going." I hugged her tight and picked her up. She liked that. It always made her giggle.

"Niley, go spend time with the kiddos."

Niley bit my lip, but lightly.

"You all did a fantastic job," I said to the three of them. "Your bonuses will reflect how happy and proud of you I am."

Chapter 16
September 1977
Casa Luna, Pasadena

I watched them get in their cars and stood there until they had driven off. I walked out to the end of the driveway and looked at my Casa Luna plaque, and the moon and house etched in the arch over the driveway. I could not deny the rush of pride I felt. I thanked God for being so generous with me. I went inside the house, maybe feeling a little sad that the girls had gone. I was alone but not really alone. The housekeepers were always there, and the gardener, and the handyman. I thought about Melina and her words of love. I pictured Sami in London, and remembered the time I had spent with Camila in Beverly Hills. But I had no one to be with. I was alone.

I walked to my home office and thought about a second workout but skipped it.

I've always thought of myself as a simple guy, but maybe I'm not so simple. As much as I hate being alone, I get a chill when I think of commitment to one girl. I don't know what the problem is. Was I ready to give up playing the field? Was I ready to get tied down, even if it was to Melina, who would let me keep playing the field? My aunt always said that if I didn't know for certain that I was ready to settle down that I wasn't ready. All I knew is that I loved the girls and Melina. They were my life.

In the afternoon, Oscar and Tom called me together on a line. They were delighted with the retainers they'd been hearing about by telephone, but that is nothing like having the originals. I wasn't a lawyer, but I knew the feeling.

Tom hung up, leaving Oscar and me on the line.

"Are you sure you don't want a bonus at the end of this one?"

"I'm sure."

"Okay by me. I don't know what you want, but we're going to work it out. You could be missing out on a lot more money than you are getting up front."

I believed Oscar. I know he wanted to keep me happy. Happy means loyal.

"Oz, you don't have to pay me all at one time. I just want to know exactly what I'm getting and when."

"Mario, I'm not worried about the money. Come over when you're ready to work it out."

When we hung up, I considered the past and future. Jake was my past. I had lost a million, maybe more, when he died, because of a legally unenforceable bonus agreement, and although I'd promised myself not to get caught in that situation again, the idea of bonus money was as seductive as ever. The girls and I had signed ninety percent of the families, an unbelievable number. When I told Jason the retainer count, he was thrilled.

"You are incredible," he said.

Money is seductive, but not as seductive as Melina, and certainly never as direct. Melina had promised to come over that night, but she called to tell me that she couldn't make it. The next night was the same. Midweek, she called me and did not mince words.

"Did you miss my tight pussy?"

"Did they teach you that kind of talk in law school?"

"Fuck yes. That's where I learned it."

We laughed.

"I miss your tight pussy," I said.

"I miss your big cock. I'm sorry I keep hanging you up, but you know I'm crazy busy till late."

"If you're horny, why not just come over like right now? Or after work. You live across the street; or did you forget?"

"I have meetings, and I still have three more markets to go to. Baby, I won't be over tonight, but I promise we'll spend all of Sunday together. Unless you take off to some foreign land again."

"I'm not going to a foreign country in the next three days. I'll be here Sunday."

"You were gone for three weeks. You owe me three make-up Sundays during the week. Plan on it."

"And you're gone every single day for hours and hours," I said. "You give me the place and time, and I'm there."

"It's a deal," she said. "I love you. Tell me you love me. Don't tell me ditto."

"I love you, Melina. You're my baby."

"I love it when you say that," she said haltingly. I could practically hear her wheels turn. "You call all the girls you're in lust with baby, too... but it's okay." She said it was okay, but it obviously wasn't.

"Hey, light-weight. You're my only baby." I teased her. We were always walking the precipice of some deeper relationship that neither of us knew how to handle. I don't think either of us had a clue what we were afraid of. I said it again, less teasingly, and more like I meant it. "You're my only baby, baby. The team is the team, but you're you."

She sat quietly on her end of the line, so quietly and so long that I wasn't sure she was still there.

"Asshole!"

I don't know if it was funny, but we both laughed.

With no one around, I figured I should get to that second workout. I was going to start jumping rope. I had the rope in hand when the phone rang. Lucky me. I tossed down the rope.

"Mario, this is Betty. Remember me?"

I knew many Bettys. I could remember at least three of them who used to send me car crash cases.

"Of course I remember you." I paused for about ten seconds. "Which Betty?"

"I worked for Oscar. I was the receptionist. The one you always ignored." I heard a little giggle.

I pictured the pretty girl that Oscar had told me several times had broken up with her boyfriend or fiancée.

"Sure, I remember you. I asked Oscar where you went, and he said you'd gone back to school or something."

"It was between real estate school and massage school. I picked massage."

"Good. And how are you doing? Do you have a parlor?"

"No, I travel to residences or businesses. I'm all licensed and everything. Carson tells me you're doing great. He gave me your number. I just wanted to say hello and give you my number just in case you want some relaxation."

She would know Carson from Oscar's office. "You read my mind," I said. "What's your schedule like right now?"

"I can do it. Tell me where and when."

"I live in Pasadena."

"No problem. Give me the address."

She took my address and said, "I bring a massage table, linens, towels, music, and a wide variety of oils."

"You got it together," I said. "Bring oils. I have the rest."

It was dusk when the housekeeper pressed the button to open the big gates for Betty to drive in. I was standing at the door when she pulled up in a red Camaro. As she walked towards me carrying a big bag, I could see she was in awe over my house. I was in awe over her face and body. I kissed her lightly on the lips and took her by the hand. As we walked in, I felt grateful to Melina for having picked out everything that was gorgeous about my furnishings. In the entry, the chandeliers all lit up, hung with crystals that looked like diamonds and glittered festively. All the surfaces were gleaming. I was almost embarrassed at the over-the-top grandiosity of it: towering ceilings, floor-to-ceiling windows, curved banisters, polished granite floors. But I loved it for its beauty. I was bursting with pride to know it was mine.

"This is a mansion. I saw the name, too, all lit up and everything. Casa Luna. Beautiful name. I can't think of when I went to someone's house that had a name. Not even Oscar's house has a name."

"You've been to Oscar's?"

"Once a week I massage his wife, and when he happens to be home, I get to do him too. He says it's a shame I was ever wasting myself in his reception area."

"How long have you been doing this kind of work?"

"I got licensed six months ago. Getting steady customers isn't easy, but I'm trying."

"Can I get you a drink or something?"

"I'm good. Thanks."

"Let's go down to the spa. That's where the massage tables are."

"Oscar has a huge house, but what I've seen of this place is spectacular."

We walked down stairs and I opened the door.

"I've never seen anything like this," she said, following me down to the lower floor. She was nearly speechless at her first glimpse of the spa.

"Look at all the marble. This place is amazing, Mario."

"The slabs are polished granite," I said. "But thanks. Let me shower really quickly while you set up."

"I see four tables. Do you have a favorite?"

"Take your pick."

Ten minutes later, I was clean, dry, and wrapped in a towel. I walked to the table where she was waiting. On her own, she'd already found a cushion for the table.

"Do you want me to keep a towel on you?" she asked.

"Only if you're shy."

"Not shy."

"In that case..." I dropped the towel and lay down, face up.

Betty cleared her throat. She was looking below my waist.

"What on earth does it look like when it's at attention?"

I laughed without a reply.

"Let's start with your back," she suggested.

The stereo was broadcasting Neil Diamond at a low volume. The lights were dimmed and three scented candles burned close enough to the table to make it cozy.

"Want to check the oils I brought?"

"You pick. I'm cool with whatever you recommend."

She started with my neck and shoulders. She was stronger than she looked, but I guess that's part of the job.

"Carson says you travel all over the world working airplane crashes."

"Not all over the world, but I do clock some heavy miles when we're busy."

"Exciting."

"Sad, too."

I explained a little about the families of victims.

"You have good hands. Good touch," I said. "I needed this."

"Your neck is tense," she said, working her hands expertly. "Tell me if I work you too hard."

My head was to the right, and I could see her miniskirt was just long enough to cover her panties. That wasn't anything new. Girls dressed that way in September in Los Angeles.

"I hope you don't mind my looking, but there's not much else to see from this angle," I said. "Nice miniskirt. Nice legs."

She laughed. "Thanks. They're culottes."

That explained why the panties never showed up. What was new was Betty. I stared for about twenty minutes at her slim ankles and pink tennis shoes.

They had rainbow-colored laces. About thirty minutes into the massage, I knew I loved it. I'd had a lot of massages, including good massages by Pixie, but Betty was better than good. She'd had training.

"How long shall I do this?" she asked.

"How long is it normally?"

"An hour? Two hours? Anything in between?" she offered when I turned over on my back.

"Can you do two hours?"

"With pleasure."

"Betty, there's a refrigerator across the way." I pointed. "Help yourself. Get something to drink. There's juice, sodas, and cold fruit."

"Want something?"

"I'll take a grape juice." I sat up. "Let's take a ten-minute break before you start this side."

"Are you tired?"

"Tired? I could go hours."

"That's nice, Mario. I can go hours too. But a cold drink will be perfect."

I remembered her voice from when she was receptionist for Oscar. She had a husky voice that was seductive. The Latin women I've known don't have that voice, but Niley has something close. Tanis had it.

"Anyone ever tell you that you have a turn-on voice?"

"Nah, it's just my voice. My mother used to tell me that I must have never gotten over the bronchitis I got once."

"Maybe."

I was sitting on the table when she handed me the can of juice. I took a good look at her. Even in candlelight, I could see her clearly. She was pretty up close. Her dark hair was short and straight. I remembered it being longer and pulled into a bun. She looked better without the glasses she used to wear at Oscar's office.

I decided to take a chance. If you don't ask, you never know.

"Seems only fair that the masseuse matches the client dress code."

Betty smiled. "Mario, it's your two hours."

She stepped out of her shoes. The culottes dropped to the floor, revealing slim hips and tawny legs. She tugged the tee over her head. She wasn't wearing a bra, and she didn't need one. Her breasts were small and perfect, and her nipples were pale but prominent. The tan lines revealed that she wore a tiny bikini over very pale skin. She probably five-eight or nine, certainly not tall and lanky, but her breasts and body reminded me of Zara and Bella. Maybe she was cold. She'd slipped out of her clothes in under a minute. Her breasts were very appealing, and her pale nipples were unusual to me. I could imagine their texture against my tongue.

"Is this better?" she asked in a voice that would get any man's attention.

"You're missing something," I said, my eyes drawn to the plain white bikini panties.

She dropped the panties. She bent over, in the process, giving me a flawless moon. Not just a moon, but one with a little shimmy, like a dance move that was over in an instant. She scooped up the clothes, draping them over a bar stool. That wasn't a jeans ass. It was a bikini ass.

"Perfect," I said.

It took self-control for me to keep from reaching for her naked body or to move her hands onto my dick that was at the ready for most of the massage when I was facing up. The two hours were up way too fast. I took another shower, put on a terry robe. She was waiting for me, clothed. As we walked out of the spa, I tried to be a host.

"Would you like wine? A drink? Something to eat? Ice cream? Peanut butter?"

"Peanut butter?" She laughed.

"I eat a lot of peanut butter."

"Is that why you have those hard abs and biceps?"

"Yep, that's the secret."

In the living room, I poured her a glass of red. We sat across from each other, a heavy granite table between the sofas.

"I cannot get over this house. Who decorated?"

"Her name is Melina. She's not a decorator, but she's the best. She lives across the street."

"Bitching. You'll have to give me a tour someday."

"I'll give you a tour right now if you want."

"I'd love to, but I have an appointment back in Hollywood in an hour. I have to plan for the traffic."

"How much do I owe you?"

"Twenty an hour, if that's okay."

I walked over to my desk and came back with a hundred-dollar bill.[29]

"Are you serious?"

"Not enough?" I asked.

"So generous. Thank you."

"You are great at this," I said. "I needed a massage. Just didn't know it."

"You're so sweet." She drank the rest of her wine quickly, got up, and walked over to lean forward and kiss me on the lips. "Thank you, Mario."

I walked her to the front door, where she kissed me again.

"Can I come back?"

"I'm a regular from now on. Put me on the schedule. Once a week to start. And I'll be getting you some new customers."

"Promise?" She clasped her hands and gave a little jump.

"Cross my heart."

She walked to her Camaro and waved as she drove away.

I went straight to bed. It was early for me, but the massage wiped me out. I slept straight through until five in the morning. I worked out hard and thought about Betty.

The Mexico City case had been brain boggling. After it, on my insistence,

---

[29] $100.00 in 1977 had the same buying power as $414.83 in 2017

the girls had stayed away for a week. A week off was barely enough time to even out, to handle jet lag, and to catch up on home things that had been neglected. Today was their first day back, and it was supposed to be a fun day, but I had the blahs. We were in the billiard room shooting eight-ball, but it was a lazy kind of day. Two pool tables to choose from, and four pinball machines. *Space Invaders* had been delivered while we were in Mexico City. I also had an arcade room set up with a wide variety of machines and games.

We abandoned the billiard room for the wine cellar and sat around my favorite table with the deep, comfortable chairs.

"It's going to cost me a fortune to stock this cellar."

I had already started looking for wines to put in it.

"Fun," Pixie said. "You and Melina will get into that."

"I know my wines now. I don't need Melina for everything." But I'm not denying we'd had some fun vino weekends tasting at local vineyards. The first time, I hadn't gotten the point of spitting out the wine, but that had been a long time ago, before I'd gone to Europe where wine was safer to drink than water.

"Yeah, right," Jo said.

Jo opened a bottle of Chateau Mouton and poured it in a decanter so it could breathe faster.

I passed out envelopes with their bonus checks from Mexico.

"Awesome," Pixie said taking the envelope.

"Totally awesome," Niley added.

"You are so generous, boss. We love you," Jo said.

"I have a toast," I said.

Glasses went up. I looked at the smiles sitting around the table.

"Here's for the love I have for the three of you. Without you, I'd be totally lost. Life would be so fucking boring. I wouldn't be able to bear it."

We got up from the deep chairs so we could click glasses.

"I love you, boss," they chimed.

"Not as much as I love you."

"Wrong," Jo said. "We love you more."

On the second bottle, conversation shifted from business.

"If you marry Melina, which house will you two live in?" asked Jo.

"Good question," I said. "I have a spa, barber shop, billiard room, arcade, and the gym."

"So you'd live here," Pixie said.

Melina liked her control, but she was not my boss. "We talk about marriage often, but never seriously. When she's ready, I'm not. When I'm ready, she's not. The only thing we're in sync about is that we're not in sync, so I can't answer that question. We might live in both, or get another place entirely."

"Boss, if you get married, what about us?" Niley asked.

At her words, I pictured myself walking down the aisle surrounded by my team, and when Melina stepped next to me, instead of handing me over, the girls stayed. Melina was marrying us all.

I laughed, but didn't explain what I was laughing at. "You'll be right with me for as long as your heart desires."

They didn't confess what was going on in their heads, but I knew one thing. I wasn't going to make the mistake I had in the past of telling them to go out and get boyfriends or husbands. I didn't want them to do that anyway. I wanted them for business, and on a more personal note, I wanted them for myself. Melina was right when she said I was a greedy asshole.

It was back to work as usual. The phone rang. I was in the office at my desk and answered it. The girls looked up, listening to my end of my conversation with Betty.

"Did you enjoy the massage? Are you really going to be a regular for me?"

"Yes, Betty," I replied. "I promised."

"Will you call me, or should I call you?"

"When you don't hear from me, you call me. If I'm away, don't give up. I can always use a massage. You have great hands." I wanted to say something about her tongue and teeth, but Pixie and Niley and Jo were giving me the eye.

"Thank you, Mario."

The girls were pantomiming going through newspapers at the conference table, but everything had stopped. I could hear their questions before they asked them.

I told them about Betty.

"We need to use her when any of us want a massage. She is good."

"Did you do it?" Pixie asked.

"No."

"Okay, so you didn't fuck, but did you get off?" Niley asked.

"It was just a great massage. My dick was hard as steel and she didn't touch it. End of story."

"We believe you, boss," Jo said with finality.

"Right," Pixie said. "If something happened, you'd be bragging about it."

"Pixie, you are so bad."

"So are you, boss. And you love me the way I am."

I turned to Jo and Niley.

"You will like this girl. She's licensed. She's legit."

"Did she show you her license?" asked Pixie.

"Stop it," I said. "If you guys don't want to get massages, don't get them. But weren't you doing something?"

They went back to their projects. Niley had started scrapbooking newsprint articles of all accidents we found in little binders. At Tom's suggestion, each binder was dedicated to a specific type of aircraft. Sometimes he would call and ask details of one type of vehicle or another, but I think it was really his way of teaching the girls about different kinds of planes. The scissoring and note-taking were moving at a snail's pace. This was stuff we only did between cases.

"Betty is anxious to come back?" asked Niley.

"She was just checking in. I told her I would be a regular."

Pixie said, "How convenient." A bit of sarcasm.

I walked up to Pixie, picked her up, and swung her around. "You aren't getting jealous, are you?"

Pixie giggled.

"Do that to me, too, boss," Niley said, batting her eyes. "I'm jealous."

"Me too," Jo said.

"I don't believe it for a second," I said, but swung each of them around in her own turn.

Pasadena had plenty of restaurants, but nothing to compare with the breakfast restaurants like the Pantry or Pacific Dining Car that I was so accustomed to in downtown Los Angeles, a ten-minute drive from Bunker Towers. Pasadena is just a short eleven-mile drive to downtown Los Angeles, but traffic makes it seem much farther. I was tired of driving out for breakfast or having to make do with peanut butter.

I brought the issue up to Melina on Sunday. I'd spent Saturday night over there. We'd had an early breakfast in her room, and around three, we were having a late lunch. I knew she'd had a long list of applicants at the markets, which was how she found the cook she'd hired for her own kitchen. I surveyed the spread steaming in chafing dishes on her buffet: pancakes, fruit compote to top the pancakes, and scrambled eggs, fried potatoes, chorizo, rice, beans, and tortillas to roll it all up in. I passed on the pancakes, but I was up for everything else. They looked and smelled like hot and toasty ambrosia, but if I added the pancakes to my already-full plate, I'd have to work out twice. Her choice of a cook was a good one, expert with more than just Mexican food. He was a real chef and looked it. Leave it to Melina to have him in work in whites, including the chef hat.

I pulled a seat out and sat at a right angle to Melina in her very formal dining room, all shining antique dining table and chairs, as well as a matching buffet and two hutches full of sets of beautiful china. I dug into the steaming breakfast on my warmed plate. Melina had a much cozier breakfast nook with big beautiful windows with a view of her rock garden. It was a room that I think we both preferred, but we weren't there because, at this time of day, we had to pull down shades because of the angle of the sun.

"I have a room open for a live-in cook too," I said, digging into the pile of spicy fried potatoes. "I spend too much time at home not to have the kitchen covered. I had peanut butter for dinner three times last week." The peanut butter dinners were true. Of course on all three occasions, I'd had huge late lunches, though if a meal had magically appeared for me, I'd have eaten it. The thought of having a live-in chef got me excited, and that meant I was talking too fast.

"I have enough kitchen to run a restaurant and no one in there to use it. Help me."

"You are looking a little skinny," Melina said. "Maybe you are working too hard." She put her hand on my bicep. "Not too skinny," she said, sighing. She took one pancake and topped it with a single spoon of cherry compote. She took a bite. "Pancakes are just a way to have dessert for breakfast." She ate half of a pancake slowly, savoring every bite, and pushed her plate aside. "I know a chef that needs a job badly, but there's a slight problem. He comes with a companion. He was my first choice, but I didn't have room for the girl. I met them both. They are willing to live in, six days on and one day off. I can get the pair for you, cheap."

"But what will the girl do?"

Melina shrugged. "Let the housekeepers tell her what to do. She can do housework, I guess. She has a license to drive. Find out if she has any skills. You're writing it all off anyway."

"Okay. Send them over. Let me talk to them."

"You'll like her. She's a real cutie."

I chuckled. "Just what I really need. A cutie with a boyfriend. I don't want to kill anyone else in this lifetime."

"Right away you connect sex to everything. Her name is Letty. I don't think she and the chef are connected that way." She took a sip of water and looked at me out of the side of her eye. "She eats pussy like you wouldn't believe."

There was a story there. I wondered how she would know that, and probably would have asked, except that it reminded me of something. "I got a surprise for you."

"What?"

"If I tell you, it won't be a surprise."

"Asshole. Tell me."

"What a nasty mouth. Geez."

"Tell me."

"I have Betty coming over to give you a massage."

"Who is Betty?"

I explained.

"She's that good?"

"You will have her over regularly. Just you wait and see."

Betty set up her massage table in Melina's bedroom. Melina wasn't primed or ready, but she was naked on the table except for a towel. I kissed her on the back of the neck and noticed Betty had on her pink tennis shoes. The rainbow laces were looking frayed.

"Massage is on me, Cuz. I already paid Betty for two hours."

"Two hours," Melina said, as far from relaxed as anyone could be. "I can't take two hours off for a massage."

"It's my Sunday, and I say you have time for this. Two hours. Trust me."

I winked at Betty who was wearing a mini—or culottes. She had her hair pinned back. As before, she was wearing a tee. This time I could tell she was bra-less.

I pushed Melina back down on the table. "Massage now. Talk later."

"I love you," Melina called out as I was walking to the door.

"I love you too," I said.

I went home to make my appointment with Miguel and Letty. Melina was thrilled with her massage. After Betty left, she had a second wind and called me to come back over.

The next morning, with my own eyes, I saw Melina was right that Letty was cute. She was wearing hot pants, boots, and had great legs. Miguel was in jeans and the kind of sleeveless tee my aunt called a "wife beater." They were wearing matching earrings, which was something I'd never seen before. Melina hadn't mentioned Miguel looked like a *Powerlifter* magazine cover. Have I mentioned how much Melina reminds me of Sami? This pair reminded me of a Hispanic version of Crispin and Ginger, though Letty didn't have red hair. Less than twenty minutes later, I hired them.

"Miss Melina already discussed pay. We are fine with her proposal," Miguel said. Letty nodded.

The carriage house had four one-bedroom apartments on the second floor, of which two were in use. Each bedroom was furnished and had a TV and its own bathroom. The first floor had once housed a carriage, and later a workshop, but when I remodeled, I had it floored and carpeted and made into a great-room common area: a communal kitchen and big den with lots of seating, supplemented with the big television from my old apartment. The common area looked very trendy, with tall ceilings, beams with bare brick walls, and a huge sliding glass window where there had once been a garage door. I had Caro, the downstairs housekeeper, show them the living quarters and told them that if that was acceptable to them, they could start as soon as possible. They walked through, picked the corner apartment, and took the job.

Miguel asked, "Mr. Mario, who does the shopping?"

"Take my car," I said.

"Thank you, but I have a car. I just need a little money."

I handed him five hundred dollars. "Is this enough?"

"It will get us started," he said, folding the bills and stashing them in his wallet. "I'll take Letty if it is okay with you, so she can help."

"Sure."

The next morning, after my workout and shower, I walked in the kitchen.

Miguel had the big stove fired up. The griddle in the center of my stove was hot. Miguel was pinching off balls of dough and rolling them in preparation for tortillas. I don't think I've really watched anyone do that since I was a kid watching my aunt. She could roll out a stack of tortillas so fast I swear her roller made sparks from the friction, but Miguel was running a close second.

"Hey, boss," he said, "I left a notepad on the table so you can jot down your favorite dishes and what you like to have for meals. I took the liberty of putting up a little corkboard calendar inside the pantry door for when you want a special dinner and we can develop a rotation of your favorites. I also took the liberty of this breakfast." He waved his hand to indicate his work in progress.

"A chef and a mind reader," I said.

He laughed. "I wish. Miss Melina mentioned you favor Mexican food."

I noticed he had a fast rhythm going as he rolled and turned tortillas, and his conversation did not in the least interrupt his routine. Covered pots were simmering, giving off a scent of chilies and tomatoes. Something enticing and cinnamony was baking. I saw some strips of thinly sliced raw meat marinating and waiting to be tossed on the grill. He deftly tossed the hot tortillas on a warming plate and covered them. I could see he was happy. The kitchen was his element. He was eager for me to sit down and try his wares. I inhaled deeply. My kitchen finally smelled like a kitchen.

"You have an absolutely beautiful kitchen. Everything new—wonderful."

"If I'm missing anything, let me know and I'll get it." I doubted that I was missing anything. Melina had my kitchen totally gutted and put back in grand form with appliances that rocked by their looks. She had redone a walk-in refrigerator and freezer, which I figured were dead weight because I also had a huge double-door refrigerator and a matching double-door freezer. She had argued that you don't take out a walk-in if you already have it. I would be taking away from the value.

"Letty can work around the house when she's not helping you," I said. "Let me know if there's something she really wants to do. You take charge of the kitchen, pantry, and dining room. You can also turn on the walk-ins. I have no problem if we start using them. Most days it is just me, but I never know when my team of three will be eating."

"Sure, boss," Miguel said. "I use everything here. Right now, Letty's actually organizing the butler's pantry. If you want, she can serve you this morning."

"Fine with me. Who told you to call me boss?"

"Miss Melina's driver, Johnson."

I laughed.

"And Miss Melina seconded it."

"She was here?"

"No. She asked me to call her twice a day. Morning and night, for instructions. I hope that's okay."

"I have no problem with it." Melina, my guardian angel. I love that woman.

The tortillas were all finished. His knife flashed. He demolished an onion into thin slices and squashed some cloves of garlic. His spatula swept across the grill. He reached for a cleaver of sliced aromatics and hesitated.

"I'm not starting this until I know you're already sitting in front of a plate. Will you be eating right away?"

"Yes," I said.

Miguel flashed his set of white teeth. He dashed some oil on the grill. It sizzled, and he tossed onions and garlic. His spatula swept across the grill. The vegetables danced and sputtered in the hot oil and gave off a cloud of onion gas. My eyes teared up from the onions, and I took a couple of steps toward the door.

"Sorry, boss." Miguel flicked a switch on the vent hood and the motor kicked in. "Miss Melina, she got very upset that I went shopping at Ralphs and didn't tell her so I could get what I needed from one of her markets."

"We can make arrangements for your grocery shopping at her markets," I said. "I'm sure I can run a tab there."

He nodded. "Yes, boss." He added some spice to a dish and turned to me.

"Are you planning on hiring more people?"

"Not really," I said. It was still a little bit of a shock to me to be employing three couples for the house.

"If you're not hiring anyone else, I was wondering if you'd mind if Letty has the empty room. But not if you object. She has a lot of clothes, and so do I."

He looked a little worried over how I was going to respond, so I answered quickly.

"That's fine with me." I turned toward the food, but my eyes were still watering from the onions.

"Looks fantastic. Smells unbelievable. Can't wait," I said. I went into the breakfast room off the kitchen and saw through the window that the table overlooking the pool had a place setting. The *LA Times* was folded and ready for me. I took the hint. I grinned and went outside. Why had it taken me so long for this? All the more incentive to keep working my ass off. I felt like a king.

I sat down and picked up the newspaper. Letty came out with a covered tray. Tortillas, fajitas, eggs, bacon, rice, and beans.

"Miss Melina mentioned you favored meat," Letty said. She poured me coffee from a carafe already on the table. Just as I picked up a crispy bacon strip, I heard the door chime.

"Three more for breakfast," I told Letty.

She smiled. "And we were worried you wouldn't have anything for us to do." She rushed inside to tell Miguel and came back out with placemats, plates, silverware, and mugs.

It took a few minutes for the girls to find me, and by the time they made it to the pool, their places were set. Pixie had already changed into one of the bathing suits I'd gotten for the girls on the Mexican trip. I wondered which of the three couples now working for me pointed out my location, or if they figured it out on their own.

"Just in time," I said as they kissed me good morning. Pixie did a cannonball and got everyone wet, then came out and gave me a post-pool kiss, making sure to get me as wet as possible.

"Brat," I said.

"Sure as fuck beats managing apartments." She laughed and sat down, pushing her chair a foot away from the table so she'd be in full sun. It was September, but no one had told the sun that. Niley and Jo were in shorts and sleeveless cotton shirts, and they stayed in the shade of the umbrella.

Letty emerged with two full carafes of coffee, a pitcher of cream, and a bowl of sugar cubes. She poured coffee for everyone, emptying the first carafe and leaving the full one with us.

"I love sugar cubes," Pixie said, sticking one between her teeth and sipping coffee through it. After it dissolved, she said, "Nana always drank coffee like this. I think she said it was how the Russians did it."

"Nana didn't have any teeth left," I reminded her.

"I'll brush, I promise," she said.

Letty was making a second pass of the table. She brought serving dishes heaped with fried potatoes, fajitas and onions, fluffy scrambled eggs, cilantro salsa, and bacon. She filled the tortilla warmer.

"Letty, these girls are my office wives: Jo, Pixie, and Niley. Letty here is Miguel's assistant and his sweetheart, I think."

"Letty, you are gorgeous," Pixie said.

Letty didn't even blush. "You too," she said to Pixie with a smile. I remembered what Melina had said about her proclivities and thought she might be flirting with Pixie.

Pixie took a few bites; she loved the food but had never been a morning eater. She went in to thank the chef, shower, and change.

Letty cleared. We drank coffee. Pixie returned smelling of toothpaste and wearing short shorts and a shirt. Her hair was blonde this week, still wet, and now slicked back into a tiny ponytail. She thanked Letty for the coffee. Letty touched Pixie on the shoulder as she left.

"Good coffee," Pixie said. She did not suck her coffee through a sugar cube this time, though it was heavily creamed and sugared.

"I love my life," I said, surveying the girls, the pool, the house, and, well, everything.

Pixie waited for Letty to leave, then whispered so we could all hear. "Miguel is gay. No way are they a couple."

"Shhh," Jo said.

"How do you know?" asked Niley.

I looked at Pixie. No question. Pixie would know.

"I know. And I think Letty goes either way. Maybe he does too, but I wouldn't bet money on it."

I didn't care about their proclivities, as long as they handled their jobs.

We moved to the home office. It had once been a den, but I'd had library shelves installed all along one wall. The girls' desks from the apartment were there, along with the conference table we were now strategically located around. We read through a week's worth of papers from New York, Florida, Northern California, and San Diego. There was a backlog from when we'd been out of town. We also had stacks of monthly magazines.

"Here's a crop duster that crashed in Fresno. Killed the pilot," Jo read aloud.

"Something had to fail. No passengers," I said.

"It says here the motor stopped. Pilot tried to land, but it caught fire on impact."

"So where is the evidence?"

"I'll call Tom," Pixie said.

"Good idea," Niley agreed.

"Hey, we don't even know we can get the case," I said, laughing.

"Wrong," Pixie said, giving me the finger as she dialed. "We can get any case."

"Hey, you can't be giving me the finger like that. I'm the boss."

"Sorry, boss," Pixie said softly, probably because the phone was ringing Tom's office. She gave me the finger again, and then Tom picked up. They talked for a few minutes. She covered the receiver and told us, "Tom said sign it."

"Tom always says sign it," I said. "Do you even know who it is?"

"We can get that from the fire department," Niley said.

"Coroner is better," Jo said. "Coroner's public press release will have more information than this article."

Pixie hung up the phone. "So, boss, are you coming to Fresno?"

"You and Niley go."

"What about Jo?"

"She can stay here and keep me company."

Jo gave me a thumbs up.

"Not fair," Niley said.

"Totally unfair," Pixie said.

"Keep the room service down to a hundred dollars," Jo said.

I looked at her.

"What?" Jo said. "They can have steak for breakfast, lunch, and dinner for three days running for a hundred dollars." She whispered in my ear, "If I say nothing, Niley won't eat once on the whole trip, and Pixie will order everything from the menu."

"True." I agreed, but I said, "Spend whatever you need to spend. Don't worry about it."

It wasn't three days. In two days, Pixie and Niley returned.

"Widow signed. The plane had just had an overhaul on the engine in Oakland."

Pixie handed me the retainer. Niley handed me the receipt for the overhaul. I put the papers on my desk in a folder that was going to Tom and headed to the basement. I stopped, looked behind me, and quirked my finger.

"Oh, no," Pixie groaned. "Not another workout. You and Cosmo are going to kill me."

"Beat you to the gym," Jo said, running past Pixie out the door and down the hall and snatching her *gi* out of the closet she used. She slammed the door behind her as she buzzed past me, tossing off her clothes as she ran. Niley and Pixie shoved me out of the way and came barreling after at a run. I stepped over their clothes, laughing. I would have to change downstairs, since I'd left a couple of my *gis* down there.

After the workout and the wet area, we were off to the living room.

"You gals are getting better. Cosmo says you're making good progress. You're his best late bloomers."

"Faint praise," Jo said, heading ahead of us where she collapsed on a couch. She was wearing a towel.

"You didn't start as five-year-olds," I said. "Good thing I have the workout area in the basement for you to practice in."

"I don't see why you call that level a basement," Jo said. "It's not a basement."

"It feels like a basement to me," I said. "It doesn't have the windows like the rest of the house."

"It's not a basement," Pixie complained. "It's a freaking dungeon."

I laughed.

I put my arms over Niley and Pixie's shoulders, and they put their arms around my waist on either side. We walked in tandem to the den. Niley switched the TV on with the sound off. Pixie turned on the music. I took a seat in the middle of the sofa.

"Where did Jo go?" Pixie asked.

I pointed out where she was snoring on the other couch.

"Just how hard did you work her while we were gone?"

I grinned and didn't answer, but got up and covered Jo with an afghan.

I returned to my seat. Pixie bounced on the couch, landing on her knees and ending up with her head on my lap, one hand grasping my crotch.

I laughed. "Pretty hard, but she worked with a smile on her face. Now, you two are dynamite. Landing that case. Niley, come to Papa," I said, patting the cushion next to me.

"I can tell you about our adventures with room service," Niley said. "I have pictures."

She dropped a Polaroid in my lap. I picked it up. It showed Pixie sitting cross-legged on a bed with a bowl of whipped cream. I saw Niley's shoulder behind her on the hotel's double bed.

"What did you do, snap this with your feet?"

Pixie laughed. "The Polaroid has a timer on it."

After they had gone home, I went to bed early. The girls had worn me out, and I was out like a light by seven. Thanks to the spa accommodations at home and the girls working out with me later in the day, I had become dedicated again to the regular workout. My five o'clock workout came early.

It was after midnight when I woke up. The girls had my security codes, but they had gone home. Melina was in San Francisco. That only left the staff. I don't know what it was that woke me, but I smelled a combination of bakery goods and flowers, and saw her shadow in the doorway to my bedroom. I recognized the scent. It had to be Letty. I did not move when she slid in my bed naked and embraced me from behind.

"This is a surprise, Letty," I said.

"I thought you'd be asleep. You did me righteous giving me my own room."

"I was under the impression that you prefer girls and Miguel prefers boys. You and Miguel must have an interesting relationship." `

I felt her hand on me under the covers.

"Do you mind?" She moved her hand on my growing shaft.

"Mind? But whatever for?'

"If you don't know what this is for, I will be glad to show you." She slid her hand up and down. "I knew you were this big. I imagined it."

Just a short while ago, I had been exhausted. Now I was raring to go.

She got dressed in the dark, if a tee and hot pants count as being dressed. She sat on the side of the bed and whispered, "Did you dig it?"

"Fuck yes, I dug it."

"Don't fire me. I wanted to thank you."

"I'm not going to fire you. Why would I? But what about Miguel?"

"What about Miguel? He has nothing to do or say about what I do."

"Okay. I get it." I didn't really, but figured I'd understand soon enough.

"How about the office wives? Are they jealous?"

"Not at all."

"Maybe we can do it all together. Let me know."

I wondered how much Melina had talked about what I would expect Letty to do. "So, you are game for anything?"

"Try me. Just don't fire me. Please."

"Fucking is not part of the job. But this is not an office where the help can't fuck around with the brass."

"I totally dig that. I love fucking around with the brass," she said, with a sultry timbre that made me shiver with sex. "Breaking the rules and all that shit."

Except for Melina, I tend to get to know people backwards of the normal order. First the intimate stuff, then later I really get to know them.

"Tell me about yourself," I said.

"I'm three years younger than you," Letty said.

That made her three years younger than Pixie.

"That's a start," I said. "What else?"

"I guess I have a wild streak."

"I see." I couldn't disagree. How could I forget she had just slipped into my bed?

"I never finished high school. I did eight months in juvie for going after my stepfather with a knife."

"Did he deserve it?"

"Yes," she said. I could tell by the finality in her voice that he did.

"As long as he deserved it. What happened after juvie?"

"Miguel stepped in. He's my cousin. He took custody of me. He apprenticed, and was working as a sous chef when I turned eighteen, and I stuck with him. He did his best, but there was never much money. I never did get a decent job, so it was all on his shoulders. One time his car was going to be repossessed, and Miguel went in a liquor store while I sat in the driver seat of the getaway car. I've never been so scared. We were living in a tiny studio apartment. When we got home and sat on the bed and counted it out, there was just enough to make the car payment with a hundred twenty dollars left over. We were so scared. Both of us, sitting there crying. We both couldn't sleep for weeks, and we saw cops around every corner."

"You're not planning on doing that again?"

"No." She shuddered. "It was horrible, and no way was it worth it."

"I dig your honesty," I said. "How is Miguel going to feel about your telling me?"

She shrugged. "If I didn't tell you, he'd tell you himself."

I kissed her and she was gone. I had just learned a whole lot about her in a very few minutes. She'd been direct, with none of Pixie's drama, Jo's righteousness, or Niley's shyness.

In the morning, the girls complained that Cosmo had gone overboard. They were wiped out and it wasn't even noon. I gave Betty a call.

"Massage emergency," I said on the phone. "This could take all day."

"Be there in a flash."

The girls were surprised by her arrival. She massaged Jo, Pixie, and Niley for an hour each.

"That bitch is bitching," Pixie said. "I feel so good."

The others agreed that Betty was great. Plus, when I paid her, Betty was as happy as a person can be.

During my massage, Betty mentioned that Melina had called to schedule a very late massage two days before.

"She works late and gets home tired as can be. She wanted to try a massage at that hour."

"How did it go?"

"She went to sleep three times, but she kept waking up. She said she loved it, though. Gave me a great tip and told me to pencil her in for a regular slot starting this week."

Not only had Betty become a regular for me, it looked like she was winning Melina over too.

"She will call," I said. "Be sure you let Melina do all the talking, or no talk if you see she's quiet."

"Got it," said Betty. "I'll remember. Thanks."

Betty's massage was a regular massage during the first hour, then a body massage for the second hour. It was a total first for me, and I'd had a lot of massages. The turn-on was the oiled bodies of two people embracing the entire body as a sexual organ. Betty moved her body on mine. Every part of her, her legs, feet, arms, and hands were all tuned in.

I told the girls about it.

"We do that all the time, but without the oil," Jo said.

"Try it with Betty," I told the girls.

Pixie was the first to talk about it.

"Fuck, that girl rocks. I couldn't believe what she did to me with her toes and bottom of her feet."

Betty was happy with the business and told me so. "You have helped me so very much. You, and your crew, and Melina are my new best friends. I'm grateful like you wouldn't believe. I love you, and I owe you"

I hugged her. "I love you too, but you owe me nothing," I said. I took a whiff of her hair. "You always smell great."

"You've never asked for a happy ending. I want you to know it's not off limits. Fucking is okay, too."

"You are a total turn-on," I said.

Her words gave me a hard on, and I had come close to having an orgasm when she did the body massage, but I let her drive away. I liked the relationship the way it was.

When she left me alone, I was rattling around my big house. I called Camila using a phone number that answered 24/7. The lady answering would either connect me to Camila or give me a phone number where I could reach her. Today, she connected me.

"Where are you, *Bella*?"

"*Me gusta cuando me llamas Bella*,"[30] Camila said with that soft laugh.

"I call you that because you're beautiful."

"Tell me that again. I'm lying in bed. Maybe I'll come if you keep telling me."

"I wish I was there. Where are you?"

"Back in Athens. These *pendejos* here are giving me trouble about a granite purchase I've been trying to finalize."

"I can fly over and kick their ass."

Camila laughed. "I prefer you come to make love to me. You do it so good, Mario."

In my head, I had a perfect picture of her lying naked in hotel sheets.

I walked up the stairs, hearing my footsteps echo. I owned my privacy and independence, but I hated the emptiness when the girls were all gone. I guess I really don't like to be alone with myself.

I didn't have to be alone, at least that night, because Letty was a mind reader. From the staff quarters, far from the main house to my bedroom, she knew when I was alone and in need of company. She showed up in my bedroom in her usual tee and hot pants.

"I can give you massages like Betty does," she offered.

I don't know how long we lay facing each other, naked. We hugged and

---

[30] I like it when you call me beautiful

lay body to body. Before long, her hands were all over me. She sucked on my fingers, one hand at a time—something only she did. She got me steaming and one thing led to another. For a while, I was too busy to feel lonely.

Chapter 17
November 1977
Pasadena Thanksgiving

All the indoor remodeling was done. The noise and dust were gone. I had a chef. Early in November, I made the decision that this year would be different. I was equipped to host my first Thanksgiving Day ever, at my home. I borrowed Johnson and Melina's limo to deliver my aunt to my house for a lobster dinner, something she loved but would never cook. Miguel set up a salad and several vegetables on the sideboard and dazzled her with the lobster, with drawn butter on the side.

I told Aunt Carmen that on Thanksgiving, she wasn't going to have to slave in a hot kitchen all day. Instead, she could put her feet up, and we would be waiting on her, hand and foot. She didn't really want to get with that program. I saw bullishness show up in her face the instant I mentioned it; I think Thanksgiving was her chance to pull out all the dishes she'd learned from her mother, and to show off her own specialties. We argued, but maybe the lobster was the strongest part of the argument, and my winning salvo. She agreed, on one condition.

"I'm bringing a turkey and my special stuffing."

"A must, Auntie. Without your turkey, it won't be Thanksgiving. I don't know how many people will be coming, but when we know, maybe you can talk to Miguel and give him the benefit of your advice?"

Aunt Carmen wasn't stupid. She knew she was being handled.

"Too smart for your own good," she told me before heading off into the kitchen to talk menus with Miguel. When Johnson drove her home to Monterey Park, she had a sack full of leftovers. I got off easy. The real verbal scuffle concerning Thanksgiving Dinner was between Melina and me.

She wanted to have the dinner at her house. I wanted to serve it at mine. She finally conceded and let me have my way. My one concession was that her chef would be on hand to work with Miguel. I was going to have to give Miguel a bonus, if he was going to have to deal with Melina, Melina's temperamental chef, and my demanding aunt.

My dining room was a prize, with twin chandeliers posed over the table that had been made to my specifications. The long table had enough leaves to accommodate twenty. I especially liked the wall covering in that room that looked like grass cloth, but it was actually silk. It reflected light differently at different times of the day.

Most years, I was working and only considered Thanksgiving a chance for a nice meal and obligatory hug with my aunt. But this year, I felt more thankful than usual. It wasn't just having lived through attempts on my life, getting shot, darted, and kidnapped. It wasn't just spending so much of my time relating to victims and suffering families. It was maybe a combination of everything. The thing is, I constantly rub shoulders with people from all walks of life. My day-to-day contacts were people from the top of the food chain and those at the bottom, too. Maybe others overlooked where I came from, but I never did. I take nothing for granted. The luxury and grandeur of my life were the fruits of my hard work. I couldn't lay my success at the foot of my real estate investments. I never touched that revenue.

Oscar introduced me as his client-development consultant. As much as I hate the label of my profession, the truth is that it all my assets stem from being an ambulance chaser.

Fuck it. Doesn't matter. I do what I do, and I'm good at it.

Betty came over every week, sometimes two or three times a week. I was getting addicted to massage. It was becoming part of my routine of getting up at five to work out. I regularly shared her services with my team, especially when I worked their asses off.

Afterwards, she always asked, "You want me to finish you off?"

"I'm good, baby."

I'd discovered I could manage to keep my hands off at least one girl who was a total turn-on for me. I don't know what it was proving, but it was a first.

Betty would leave, and I would return to work.

I joined the girls in the office and settled down at my desk, going through my inbox. Jo flashed her half-finished to-do list so I could see how far she'd gotten in the past two hours. Niley was bent over the conference table, the most recent issue of the *New York Times* spread out before her. She had a highlighter in her hand, and her dark hair fell over her shoulder as she read. Pixie was curled up in a chair going through magazines. She had a pair of scissors in hand. Her hair was black again, and snipped short and wispy. Jo had what she called her Dorothy Hamill hair. It was short with bangs, deceptively staid, but it moved like crazy when we worked out.

"We're having Thanksgiving here," I said. "You and your families are all invited."

Announcements like that always brought work to a standstill.

"Boss, thank you," Niley said. "I'll bring Nanny Delores to help with cleanup and to help corral the kids."

"I can't believe you got Auntie Carmen to agree to have it here," Pixie said.

"She's bringing a turkey and her stuffing."

"Cool," Pixie said.

"I can't wait to show off this place to my mom and the kids. I'll also bring my housekeeper to help with cleanup."

"Jo, Cosmo and Oscar and Tom Jones will probably be having Thanksgiving with their own families, but invite Tom Jones here for Thanksgiving. He's divorced. And invite Betty." I turned to Pixie. "Before you get started back on that magazine, Pixie, would you call Carson and invite him, plus?"

"Plus what?"

"Plus whoever he is bringing."

Pixie dialed. She put her hand over the receiver and whispered at me, "Girlfriend, sisters, and mom." I gave her the thumbs up. She aimed the phone in my direction.

I yelled across the room, "See you soon, dude. I got room." She was still chatting when I headed for the kitchen to give Miguel the numbers and my thoughts on the food. Since Miguel had been here, the kitchen always smelled great. He was partially responsible for my renewed interest in karate. It took a lot of working out to burn off so much deliciousness. As I stepped in, I saw a big bowl of fresh fruit on the counter looking like something off a magazine cover. Something spicy and mouthwatering was simmering slowly in a crockpot.

"I just fixed a fresh pot of coffee," Miguel said. He poured me a mug and pushed the sugar and cream pitcher in my direction. It was some exotic blend from Melina's store, and I decided to drink it black.

"I've just invited half the city for Thanksgiving."

"Boss, no worry, we got it covered."

"I want more than enough food, I want too much food. I want an embarrassment of food." I rattled off everything I could think of. I started going off on bakery goods, and Miguel stopped me.

"I've already met Señora Luna and Miss Melina's chef. Senora Luna is bringing her turkey. I will prepare three turkeys and twelve ten-pound turkey breasts. I have some recipes for some of Senora Luna's pies. Miss Melina's chef Roscoe Pepper will be bringing biscuits, olive bread, cheese bread, and a list of other bakery items."

Both chefs had gone shopping mad. Melina sent a delivery truck full of their selections—enough produce and raw materials to feed an army. We finally had a reason to use the walk-in.

"Fuck, this is more fun than sex," I said to the team.

"Nothing is more fun than sex," Pixie said.

"You're twisted," Niley said.

"I'll remind you when my tongue is working you."

"Pix, remind me now," Niley said, laughing.

"Girls, take it easy. The help is going to hear."

"So what?" Pixie said, then hit the intercom and called all the help in the house.

"Boss, make her stop," Niley begged as she buried her head in her folded arms.

Pixie was geared up to make some kind of nasty announcement, but when everybody showed up, I gave them each fifty dollars. "No reason," I said, "and you're all getting smoked turkeys for Thanksgiving."

The girls came up with a helicopter crash in Utah and two small plane crashes, one in Northern California and one in Tucson, Arizona. I took a plane to Tucson, spent two days there, and signed the case, although it would not be an easy case. The family deserved a shot at going after Cessna for a possible defect. Niley went alone to Northern California and met with two families. She didn't push to get signatures, because they wanted to think about it. Jo handled Utah. In three days, she signed three families of three decedents.

She came back and flexed. "I'm the best."

Potential clients always asked, "What kind of experience does the lawyer have about this type of case?" In answer, we could pull out the case book. It answered all the questions. Oscar's growing case book continued to be the door opener and life saver. On the cover, Oscar was pictured in a three-piece suit with an antique chain that looped between his right and left vest pockets. A wall of law books was the background, and his desk was in the foreground, a cigar in Oscar's right hand. Each case we signed was included in the growing book. No private details were made public, but we included a picture of the aircraft in its prime, and a factual account of the circumstances of the event. The book was impressive, and it had been my idea.

When I got back from Tucson, it was late. It had been a successful trip businesswise, but the temperature had dropped unexpectedly. I was cold. I didn't waste time shopping for warmer wear. I was chilled when I got in the plane and didn't warm up, in spite of the stewardess bringing me two blankets. I left the airport with the flimsy blankets wrapped around my shoulders. I turned the car's heat on full blast and finally warmed up. I wondered if I might be coming down with something.

As I drove through LA at night and the chill fell away, I looked outside. The landscape looked as cold and inhospitable as I had felt earlier. I got stuck at a light, waiting two minutes for the light to change; but it was stuck on red. I tapped my foot impatiently, played with the radio dial, and then happened to look to the right. There was movement there. A bus bench. It wasn't one of those plain, barren benches. This one had a frame over it, with a collection of movie posters—*Close Encounters of the Third Kind*. I hadn't seen it yet, and the poster was just a barren road leading to a distant light, with stars in the sky. The streetlight partially lit the bench, and as I looked, something moved again.

I was still stuck at the light, with no car in sight. I don't know why, but I opened the door and walked around to the bench. Some old guy, maybe someone's grandfather, was lying on that hard wood bench, with nothing to warm him but a pile of crumpled newspaper. I didn't get too close, but he smelled like old beer, urine, mildew, and sweat. I walked back to my car, grabbed the airline blankets, and put them over the old guy. He never woke up, but he heaved a breathy, alcoholic sigh. I returned to the car, ran the light, which still hadn't changed, and went home. I had crazy homeless dreams all night.

In the morning, I gave Pixie and Letty a project.

"I want you to give Thanksgiving to six people who need it. Get them a nice change of clothes. Take them to a hotel in Pasadena to get showered and dressed, and we'll have a couple of taxis bring them here at four to join us for Thanksgiving."

"Why not just bring them the way they are?" Pixie asked.

"They should feel good about themselves when they get here. Be dressed nice. Feel like people."

"Sorry for asking such a fucked question, boss."

Letty stopped dead, frowning. "Miguel and I would be homeless or in prison without you."

Pixie thumped her on the top of the head and then gave her a hug. Letty looked so startled that Pixie explained. "If not for Mario and Aunt Carmen getting me off the street when I was a pregnant teenager, I'd still be a hooker."

"That's all behind you," I said. "And stop giving me so much credit. You changed your own lives. You get the credit."

Inside the house, the chefs were busy before dawn. The helpers the girls had brought were busy arranging things and directing traffic until four in the afternoon when the festivities were set to begin. Melina had hired two bartenders and three girls as waitresses. Pasadena Taxi was on notice we might be calling them.

As soon as they arrived, one by one, everyone wanted to tour the house. I left that to Jo, Pixie, and Niley. The guests all sorted themselves out where they wanted to be. Letty was working in the kitchen, bossing around the extra kitchen help. It was too cold to swim, but the game room filled up. It was set up like an arcade. The billiard room was also busy, and we'd put out a couple of ping-pong tables on the screened-in porch.

Carson was feeling no pain when he put his arm around me.

"You really know how to throw a party, *ese*. I'm real proud of you." He gave me a big hug. From a distance, my Aunt Carmen and Carson's mom and Pélon's mom, Ida, watched us and beamed, happy that we had mended our fences. The girl on Carson's arm that he introduced as his fiancé, Rita, looked like a miniature Farrah Fawcett, with such a big head of streaky blonde Farrah hair that the rest of her looked too small in comparison. She was in beautician school. When she got drunk, she started offering to do everyone's hair and nails. She was deep in conversation with Melina when Carson turned to me. He was a little drunk.

"*Ese*, I got bills, man."

"Don't we all?" I responded, laughing.

He beckoned me closer with his hand and slung his right arm over my shoulder. "*Ese*, it would be nice if you could include me on your aviation team. Let's you and me earn some real money."

"You have a good thing going with Oscar. I gave Oscar my whole client list. I know for a fact that you're doing okay."

"*Ese*, you know I'm good with people. Use me."

I put my left arm around him. "I know you are good at what you do. I have no slots open. If I did, I would consider you."

Carson gave me a strange look.

I continued, "We are better friends if we don't work together. But maybe I can throw something your way sometimes."

He gave me a dark look but flashed that winning smile of his. I remembered when he used to practice that smile in front of a mirror.

"*Ese*, you probably right," Carson said. "Not enough money for two bosses. I'll be fine."

I smiled back. "You're already fine and you'll get better. Anything else I can do for you, hit me up. No problem."

Rita turned to us and saw Carson and me standing shoulder to shoulder, arms looped. "I wish I had a camera," she said a little loudly, taking a pretend picture of the two of us with her hands. "I see you really are best friends, like Carson said. I didn't believe it, but now I see it with my own eyes. And I want whatever you're having."

Unlike Rita, Melina wasn't drunk. Like Sami, Melina was drinking Cristal, before and after dinner. The room was abuzz with conversation. The girls were at the other end of the table, chattering about something with one of the homeless people the girls had found. Carson was arguing with the other. The girls' kids were with the homeless kids at the table in the breakfast room with Nanny Delores. At the grown-up table, my aunt sat on my right and Melina on my left. When everyone was busy eating, Melina pulled me so my ear was an inch from her lips. "I want to fuck you."

I smiled. I whispered back. "I'm going to eat your pussy."

Melina giggled.

I don't know what there was about that laugh, but the room fell suddenly silent. All eyes turned in our direction.

"Sorry," I said. "I just told a joke, but it's not suitable for the kiddos."

Everyone returned to their plates.

Letty was still in the kitchen. She wasn't great at serving. Tended to lose track of food delivery and got caught up in conversation. Melina gave a girl one look, and the three servers she'd hired sprang into action and started circulating bowls of food, family style, beginning at my left and going around the table, ending at my right. Corn on the cob, sweet peas, fried mushrooms, mashed potatoes, gravy, sweet potatoes, all the salads, mac and cheese, and multiple small trays of sliced ham, turkey, and smoked turkey. When a serving bowl got low a third of the way around the table, it was replaced with another one full of steaming goodness. Rather than interrupting conversation, the circulating food became the topic. A second waitress handled drink refills, and the third was making sure the kids were being provided for. It was a long time before everyone was finished, and the desserts were laid out on the sideboard. I could have started a bakery or pie shop, at the very least.

"Having the homeless family here tonight wins the prize," Melina said.

I didn't have all the details, but I knew enough to assuage Melina's curiosity. "Pixie and Niley found a husband and wife and five kids. The Sandovals. He lost his job. They got evicted. Sheriff locked them out of their home and put their stuff on the street. And the second couple over there, the Abels. I don't know anything about them, but they are older and kind of pathetic. He has no teeth, and she smokes like a chimney. I think they have a son in the military."

"That's the pits," Melina said. "About the Sandovals, I mean. Do you do that? Evict people?"

"The management company handles everything. I'm not sure what they do when someone doesn't pay. I guess they evict the tenant." I told Melina the story about how Pixie got one tenant to pay when they were running the apartments. No one could tell the story better than Pixie, but Melina laughed.

"I'll have Jo check and see how we handle evictions. There should never be an eviction on a holiday like Thanksgiving or Christmas."

"Do it, Cuz. You should know every single thing there is to know about your apartments and what the management company does. There is nothing I don't know about my markets and the operation."

I smiled at my baby. "That's because you are special and smart."

"You were smart enough to buy what you have," she shot back.

"Okay, I got it."

"I'll remind you," she promised, rather sternly. "So, what are you going to do with them?"

"Help them get jobs. It shouldn't be too hard to help them find work, maybe give them a first month free on an apartment."

I'd been in the house for almost a year, and this was the first time I'd tried entertaining. It felt good. I felt good about the house bringing everyone together to eat, drink, and be merry. Being able to share all this was like a reward for all that work I've done.

Betty left with the girls well before midnight.

"Thank you for inviting me and sharing your lovely home." She kissed me on the lips.

Melina and I did a walk-through. The help the girls had brought had been busy; the house was already bearing no evidence of the party, except for the kitchen. And even there, all the dishes had been washed and dried, but they were all sitting out, waiting till morning to be put away.

"I think one of the homeless couples had sticky fingers," Melina said. "Some of the knickknacks on that bookcase are gone. That set of Russian nesting dolls. One of the Fabergé eggs. Probably the older couple. They didn't stay seated for long, and I had the feeling the wife was shopping in your house. She had eyes like a cash register. And I saw him looking at the eggs."

"Maybe that's why they left before Jo got them set up in their apartment." I laughed it off. "Maybe it was Carson." I laughed again.

"This was fun," Melina said. "But I am pooped. That was Thanksgiving enough for two years. You've inspired me to be generous. I'm going to find out what I can do to help the homeless. Downtown skid row is filled with homeless." She got on the phone right away and called the manager of the store closest to skid row and told him to set up a street buffet for tomorrow, starting with a truckload half-full of turkeys she'd had no room for.

I went into the shower, and when I came into my bedroom, there was Melina asleep on my bed, her hair braided and damp from a shower of her own. I was pooped too, but not too much to take advantage of the situation. I hit the lights and went to town. Melina woke up halfway through me fulfilling the promise I'd made during dinner.

I might have gone to bed at midnight, but by one or so in the morning, Melina and I were just warming up.

The phone rang. It was the loud ring, and when I looked, it was the third button that was flashing, the one we called the hot line. The calls that had to be picked up, no matter what. It might be Oscar or Tom, or one of the girls with an emergency.

I reached for the phone and selected line three.

Chapter 18
December 1977
Puerto Rico Blaze

"Boss, the Palomar Hotel is burning," Juan said.

"The Palomar? The one where I stayed in Puerto Rico?"

"That's the one. It looks bad."

"Bad like people dying?"

"Yes, boss. It's on the news."

I turned the TV on and flipped through the channels, but nothing was on at this hour.

Melina looked at me with a question in her eyes.

"Turn the radio on. Get the news. KFWB or something. A big hotel is burning in Puerto Rico," I told her.

"Juan, If the hotel is owned by a US firm, it could be a good case. I need to ask Oscar, but first things first. Call me in four or five hours."

I was going to call the girls, but by now they would be digesting or asleep. The work would start soon enough. I let them rest for the time being.

There was nothing on the radio yet, but by seven, every TV channel had an estimate of over a hundred casualties. The fire department didn't have the ladders to get beyond five floors. Many of the trapped tourists had been so desperate, they jumped out of windows.

I called Oscar, and he told me before I could ask.

"Damn right, it's a good case. Go for it. Sign them up!"

We were working under certain disadvantages. Tom had stepped out of his aviation comfort zone to provide us retainers. Though Oscar had a general brochure, we had no brochure for this kind of case. My advantage was Juan. His home was Puerto Rico. His connections dug up the list of all decedents and the injured, including the addresses used when they registered at the hotel. Even though the Palomar appeared to be a total loss, it was not completely unsalvageable.

I explained what to do, then Juan worked the hospitals just as the girls and I had worked the hospitals when we were doing personal injury. He was a fast learner. He understood the objective and the limitations he had to work within. We wanted cases but couldn't outright solicit a family or a victim. He was good at being cool, making connections, biding his time.

We arrived on November thirtieth. Our advance team, Juan and Valita, met us at the airport. They were dressed in jeans. Everyone was wearing jeans everywhere these days, but on Valita the denim looked like something else entirely. The denim was worn to the softness of cashmere, and it clung to her curves like it loved being there. Juan spiffed his white shirt up with a light blazer. I was business as usual until Valita said my name.

"Mister," she said. That was all.

Her voice conjured up the night in Venezuela, the dark of the warehouse, her mouth through the iron bars. I swear I could smell the jungle, feel the trickle of sweat down my back in the humidity, hear the night birds, and feel her mouth on me. I wrenched myself into the present.

"Valita," I said. My voice sounded normal, but my body instantly was bathed in sweat. As soon as we broke the handshake, I gathered Pixie under one arm and Niley under the other, and we moved on to the car. It took me longer to get my body under control. Her voice instantly transported me into sexual heat.

I know two days does not sound like biding time with the families, but the case was all a matter of timing and respect; and it was really more than two days, thanks to Juan's advance work. Before forty-eight hours passed, we signed eleven injured individuals that Juan had already won over.

Valita shifted around her housekeeper schedule at the hotel where she worked so she could accompany Juan when he talked to families.

The families of victims were put up in a hotel, just as it happens in airline cases. Juan had not stopped with the eleven injured. He made a connection with three more families who were waiting for body identifications and urged me to talk to them.

"Way too soon," I said. "They aren't ready. We don't talk to families who haven't buried their loved ones, or haven't been given the body to ship home. It's pushy, and shows disrespect for their vulnerability. "

"Bossman, these families are in a category of their own. They are Puerto Rican, but they live in Miami. Sure, they are vulnerable. But they are also pissed off. They don't want to wait. They want a lawyer."

"Mister, Juan is right. These families want you now," Valita said.

There was no denying it. Valita was Juan's girl. He knew it, she knew it, and I knew it, but when I looked at her, my body had a mind of its own. I took care not to show what was happening to me when she was in the vicinity. I know she said that her people believed they could have casual sex; but she'd made a point to choose Juan. She had drawn the lines, and I was doing my best to respect her choice. She still called me "Mister."

The girls and I met with Juan's three families together like they requested. I sent a hotel shuttle to drive them to my hotel from where the Palomar's owners were putting them up. The three families we were meeting had lost seven people. Without a brochure to brag about handling fire cases, we were operating without one of our great door openers. I took it as a lesson that we had to be ready for anything big outside of aviation, and put it on my to-do list to get Oscar to get a brochure bragging about other areas of practice, which included all types of wrongful death cases such as bus crashes, train crashes, and other types.

We bluffed it without brochures, thanks to the gift of gab—mine and the girls'—that won us the trust needed for a family to sign a retainer. The door openers, Juan and Valita, had done a great job and continued to do so.

In plane crashes, we rarely heard the victims' stories. Not so here. Some used sheets and towels to get free of their burning rooms on the lower floors. On the higher floors, the fabric was not long enough to reach the ground. A few were long enough to reach a fireman on a ladder to bring them down to safety, but for many, their ersatz ropes were preludes to a faster death. Many people survived their frantic leap to safety, only to die later of infection, smoke, broken bones, broken everything. From these survivors, or near survivors, we were faced with horrifying stories.

We met Margaret, a woman that Juan had already signed. We joined her in her hospital room. As Juan opened the door to her room, he said, "Margaret leapt out of her window on the third floor trying to land in the pool below. She didn't quite make it to the water."

"I hear you're the high-dive artist," Pixie said.

Margaret gave a little laugh, which must have killed her ribs, and groaned. Pixie sat down beside her and introduced herself before Juan had a chance to. She took one of Margaret's hands, which was one of her few uncovered body parts. She was in the hospital with a broken leg and fractured ribs. As Pixie sat beside her, the sheet fell back, revealing arms purple with bruises.

"It's a miracle your arms and hands aren't broken," Pixie said.

Margaret whispered something into Pixie's ear. We all talked to her and answered some of her questions. When we were back in the hall, I asked what she'd said.

"That her fall would have been worse if not for that umbrella table she bounced off." Pixie gave a little laugh, but she looked more horrified than amused.

Down the hall, we talked to Lupita. She was thirty-two. She was loud and brash and angry.

"I'm from Dallas, Texas, and I don't care who knows it."

"Tell us what happened."

"Oh, I'll tell you," she said. "I came down here on vacation, and woke up halfway to being barbecue. Don't matter none how much them fuckers pay me, it ain't never going to be enough for the scare of my life. You try waking up with your fancy-ass bed on fire and your room so full of smoke you can't tell your ass from a hole in the ground. I want to sue the bastard owners and sue the fucking city fire department! Sue the fucking King of Puerto Rico."

"Oh, we got a lawyer for you," Niley said, beating Pixie to the punch. "If he don't squeeze everybody responsible, I'll take off my belt and give him what-for." With little coaxing, Lupita told us in detail about waking up and finding her room full of fire. She'd had time to grab her sheets and get them wet in the bathroom. She'd been on the third floor, and the wet sheets she'd knotted together came undone while she was hanging on them, dumping her on an awning she ripped straight through to land on concrete below.

"That sidewalk was fucking hard," she said. "Sidewalks should be made of rubber." She had a salty mouth, and even in her rough condition, she gave the girls as good as she got. We left with her retainer.

Juan, Valita, Jo, Pixie, and Niley worked at the hospitals. As the bodies were turned over, I became more involved and met with families staying at the hotel. For once, I kept an eye on the calendar. We'd been there since a couple of days after Thanksgiving. On December twentieth, I sent the girls back home to spend Christmas week with their kids. It was not easy to get their asses on a plane.

"You missed Christmas two years ago thanks to the kidnapping," I said. "It sits heavily on my conscience. Get packed, pronto." I ignored their protests, even thought about going back with them, but in the end, I was too engaged with the families. There was a lot of competition on this one, but during this week, the competitors all thinned out. When they went home, it opened up the field. I'm not one to overlook the greater opportunity; and, without poaching, I took advantage of it. I sponsored a non-denominational Christmas memorial for the victims at the biggest local church and made sure that all our families knew of the event. They shared it with the rest of the families. I provided tall candles for all the family members, smaller candles for everyone else, a crate of local doves to be released, and began a fund for a memorial to be built, but did not speak. It was attended by several local religious leaders, two of whom came only because I'd made generous donations to their personal causes. I hired carolers (locally known as *parrandas, asaltos,* and *trullas*), and they filled the night with joyful songs, then later showed up at the families' houses for more of the same. Juan was not religiously very demonstrative, but since his family did have a local church they had attended for years, we provided for a memorial there, too, for anyone who wanted a specifically Catholic service. It was a lovely little building, stucco, tile, and timber, lovingly maintained. The pews inside were hard and uncomfortable, but hand-carved and lovely. Each pew seated two unless you were squeezed in, with a wide aisle in the middle leading to the altar. The red clay tile floor had a high gloss and was probably a hundred years old. The crowd that showed up for our Catholic memorial was too big for the church, and we ended up on the church grounds with candles on a starry night. It was very moving.

I did like the little church. When standing in the center aisle, I could reach up and touch the ancient beam arching over my head. Juan and Valita made sure I joined them at the church's "*Misa de Gallo*," a local Christmas mass held at midnight. It was intimate and quaint rather than showy and spectacular, as it was back in LA. Aunt Carmen would have been proud of me, except that I entertained myself with fantasies of Valita that I kept in my head. I didn't let them leak into reality, which was a new one for me. I developed a liking for Spanish apple cider and for "*turrón*," a hard, white almond nougat which was very good, even if it had no peanut butter in it. Both were local holiday foods. I returned to the room with a goodie bag of Christmas treats. No one was there, and I found myself on the phone with Melina, talking all night.

On December twenty-sixth at about midnight, I was just dozing off alone in the hotel bed when I heard a knock. The girls were not due back yet, so I wondered who it could be. I opened the door and found myself looking at Camila in all her beauty. She'd had her hair layered and frosted Farrah-style. She made no move to walk in, so I picked her up and raised her to my lips.

"*Amor*!" Her arms lifted around me.

"Merry Christmas, *Bella*. What a wonderful surprise. I like my present." I held her at arm's length, looking her over and turning her around and around like a gift I was inspecting. "I can't wait to unwrap you. And here I was thinking that Santa had forgotten me. I guess he knew I have been a really good boy this year."

"Anyone sleeping here?"

"Nobody but me."

"Lovely," she said. "I rented a suite three doors down."

"You rascal. You don't need a room. I'm here."

"We can make love in both rooms."

Room service delivered wine. By the time we had our first glass, Camila and I had gone through half a joint.

A glass of wine later, Camila pulled out a small gift from her purse.

"*Feliz Navidad,*" she said, handing me the little box.

"Baby, not fair. I thought you were the gift. I got you nothing."

"Don't worry about a gift for me. Open it."

As she sat impatiently, I tore away the red foil wrapping to reveal a yellow-gold Rolex with a diamond-filled bezel.

I admired the watch, gushed over it a little, and kissed her.

"*Gracias, Bella. Te debo.*"

"You owe me nothing," she said, then her tongue was in my mouth. We tore up my bed, then tore up the suite, then tore up my bed again. After more wine and another joint, Camila was foxed to the gills, but she mumbled something about jet lag and passed out lying across the foot of my bed. Dawn was just cracking across the sky when I picked up pillows and cushions and tossed them back on the couch.

I called Juan and made my excuses. I asked him to handle everything for me and took myself out of commission for a couple of days. I looked at all the sheets and blankets strewn everywhere and collapsed next to Camila, only to be wakened by housekeeping some time later. I did a double-take at the thrashed room, pulled a twenty from my wallet, and stuck it on my bedroom mirror with a thank-you note to housekeeping. We took the remainder of a bottle of wine to her suite. I ordered a breakfast for us, but not much of it was eaten. Her bed worked as well as mine.

Twenty-four hours after Camila arrived, a tawny brunette babe walked in to claim her. We had retreated to the living room, and Camila stretched herself across me like I was part of the loveseat. At least we were wearing the hotel bathrobes. The brunette was wearing a wispy, beachy cotton thing that emphasized a smooth tan and legs that went up to her neck. Her long hair was pulled back in a ponytail, her face carefully and expensively made up. She had dark eyes and a stubborn chin with a dent in the middle of it.

"Pleasure," I said, looking her over. Hard to tell her age, maybe a little younger than Camila. "And you are...?"

"She's Olga. Don't get any ideas." Camila laughed. "Olga is like a sister I got as a birthday present. She's family, and grew up in my father's house. Her father worked for my father until he died."

"I am sorry for your loss," I said. "You speak English?"

Olga had expressive eyes, but she hadn't spoken yet. Camila was still speaking for her.

"Olga speaks five languages," Camila said.

"Do you speak? Or is Camila pulling my leg?"

Camila laughed and grabbed my leg, tugging on it. Leisurely, she got to her feet.

"I do speak."

"Condolences on your loss," I said again.

"Thank you but my father died a lifetime ago. Pepe and Camila are my family now." Olga looked from me to Camila and said, "Time to go soon."

"I'll be ready, Amor."

So Olga called her that, too.

Olga started for the door, then turned and said in perfect English, "Pleasure meeting you, Mario."

I watched her leave. Tall, slim, barefoot, with an air of mystery. Some of the electricity in the room left with her.

"Where have you been keeping her?" I said. "She's stunning."

"We keep her busy," Camila said. "She has her own room."

"What does she do for you?"

"A number of things," she said vaguely. "We normally don't travel together, but when we do, she's like an assistant. She's family, so I can't be mean to her. I can see you like Olga."

I turned my attention to Camila, realizing how rude I'd just been. Leering at her sister. That behavior was probably not correct in any culture. "I don't know Olga, but I will probably enjoy getting to know her. As for Camila...I like Camila."

A few minutes later, Olga let herself back in without knocking. Apparently, she had gone to her room to retrieve a carry-on bag and purse and high-heeled sandals that emphasized her legs. I noticed that cleft in Olga's chin as she walked past me into Camila's bedroom. She came out a few moments later with Camila's suitcase, which she had packed with lightning speed. I don't know if it was her long hair or something else about her that made her seem such a novelty. I readied myself to be the gentleman and carry their luggage, but a bellhop arrived and then they were gone.

I returned to my room, which was fresh again, and slid between the clean sheets to sleep off Camila. To my great luck, Camila and now the mystery of Olga proved to be an adequate distraction from my obsession with Valita. I gave Juan a call and told him I was back on schedule, then crashed. Once I was in bed, I fantasized about that night in Beverly Hills when Camila had gotten to know my team intimately. I admit that I added Olga in the scene in my head.

In the morning, Juan was back before room service provided breakfast, returning me to the sad business of dealing with victims of this terrible fire and the families of victims who had perished. I called for two plates. We strategized over *huevos revueltos, jamon, tostadas, toronja,* and *mango,* and some excellent coffee. I did feel the loneliness after Camila was gone. I am not good at handling being alone. I made some calls to fill the night hours. Several nights, like kids, Melina and I stayed on the phone from midnight till the sun came up, giggling, talking of everything and nothing and erasing the distance between us.

On December thirtieth, the girls returned.

The girls clustered around me. It was good having them back. Christmas would have been lonely for me if I hadn't focused the days on working and making connections with the families. Those hours with Camila after Christmas Day had been a welcome distraction. I had been invited to family gatherings all over Puerto Rico. I declined most of them. It's not like I could travel all over the territory and attend them all. The few I attended made me feel such solitude. I chastised myself for any loneliness I might have felt. It was nothing compared to the depth of their losses. How could I allow myself to feel lonely when I was with people gathering in a church or around a tree, all mourning the people who would not be around to open their presents or hear this year's Christmas mass? At least when I got home, the people I missed would be there in person.

December thirtieth is a day before my birthday.

"So there went the party," Pixie said, making a sad face.

"I can do it next year. What's the big deal about me turning three decades old?"

"Boss, you make it sound like you're ancient," Niley said.

"No way. I'm just getting started," I said, taking a squeeze of her ass. They were all clustered around me. With them back, I wasn't feeling lonely any more.

"Do that again, boss."

"Me first," Pixie said, moving her ass close. So did Jo.

"No," I said. "First is Jo."

"About time," Jo said with a mock sad face. "I feel like I'm out of touch."

I cupped her ass with both hands and kissed her on the lips. Pixie and Niley applauded.

I told my team about Camila's visit and the introduction to the mysterious Olga.

"So now we have two Colombians to compete with," Pixie said.

Niley and Jo looked restive. I pulled them all together on my lap.

"Olga is hot. She's just not you. No worries, babies."

Pretty soon, we were rolling around on the bed. It wasn't sex, though, just pursuit of the television remote control, and then a few minutes later over the room service menu. But then Juan called, inviting us out to his favorite local restaurant. We had a banquet and caused a big stir. I handled the bill with enough generosity that Juan would be dining well there for a couple of years.

Juan and Valita were at the airport to see us off. I hugged Juan and handed him an envelope with five thousand dollars.[31] It was his biggest paycheck yet with me. I knew he would be happy. I handed Valita an envelope with one thousand, a bonus since I had already paid Juan. The girls were in a manic mood, triumphant over our successful trip, and they had me spinning them in circles.

"Me too," Valita said.

When I did, her laughter rang out. Juan, Jo, Pixie, and Niley clapped like it was a big production.

Valita was learning English. She was happy with her life now. Even through the shade of jealousy I was feeling, I was happy for her.

We got back from Puerto Rico on January tenth. We signed forty-five injured and thirty-one families of decedents. I was happy with our results, and Oscar was happy. I wasn't sure what to charge.

"Throw a number at me," I said.

---

[31] $5,000.00 in 1978 had the same buying power as $19,438.97 in 2017

Chapter 19
January 1978
A New Year

"How about a hundred, and I give you another fifty for your expenses?" Oscar said.

I had spent a lot on that memorial.

"Oscar, there are thirty-one dead. Give me another number."

This fire case was not my typical aviation case. Oscar seemed excited over the case, but he was being cautious in how much he had to front. I understood his possible caution, but I needed to get a fair deal for all the work we put in and the results I brought him.

He gave me two hundred twenty thousand.[32] As in the past, I sang all the way to the bank.

Melina and I grew closer, but no closer to marriage. I had been home only a week when Melina had a grand opening for a new market. I think it was number six. I closed escrows on three more apartment buildings that were pending when I'd left for Puerto Rico. I now had seven hundred and thirty apartment units. The mortgages on some of the buildings were bigger than what I wanted, but that was thanks mostly to Uncle Sam and the State of California kicking my ass with taxes, leaving me with less cash for down payments.

---

[32] $220,000.00 in 1978 had the same buying power as $855,314.65 in 2017

"How do you manage to keep opening markets if you pay so much in taxes?"

"Same way you keep buying apartment buildings. I borrow the money."

"Are we doing it right?" I asked.

"We are doing it right. Stop bitching about money. You're swimming in rental income. Oscar is paying you bigtime and up front. You got it made."

"You're right, baby."

The phone rang while my team and I were eating, and I motioned to Letty. She answered it and I took it on the breakfast-room phone. The call made Pixie laugh. She still thought it was hysterical that I had phones in every room. Yes, even the bathrooms.

"Guess what?" Carson said. "I rented an apartment in the high-rise where you used to live."

"There goes the neighborhood," I said.

He laughed.

"Cool," I said. "How you doing? Keeping my old contacts happy and paid?"

"I'd still be homeless if I wasn't doing that. But, *ese*, you should let me help you on the big aviation cases where the real money is."

I deliberately ignored his aviation comment. "If you need me for anything, don't hesitate to call."

"Okay, I hear you loud and clear, *ese*. When I get settled in, I want you to come over and have dinner with my fiancée and me. We're trying out living together."

"Same girl you brought to Thanksgiving? Still dating Farrah the beautician?"

"Her name was Rita, but nah. New girl, really hot. Name's Ana Paula, but I call her Paulie. We actually got engaged, ring and all. Very Catholic. Auntie would love her."

He sounded more mature. His words made me wonder which of my girls my aunt preferred. She'd never said. I mean, I knew she wanted me to settle down and have a house full of good Catholic babies, but she'd never encouraged me to get hitched to any one girl in particular.

"Congratulations, *ese*."

"Thanks. Think about the aviation, man. Don't shine me on."

"I'm not shining you. Like I told you, we're better friends not working together. Besides, the girls and I have it covered."

"Don't be like that. At least think about it."

"Part of Oscar's success is your work, Carson. I'm proud of the way you are taking care of business for the clients, and for yourself. I've heard some good things about you."

I felt a little guilty when I remembered how, not that long ago, I'd dreamed of all sorts of ways to kill him for grievances he had not committed. "I seriously doubt that Oscar would want you in aviation, because the business you are sending to him would take a big hit."

"Think about it? Later, *ese*."

"How's Carson?" Pixie asked.

"He's got a new fiancée, not the one we met at Thanksgiving. He's moving into Bunker Towers. Every time he calls, he asks me to let him in aviation with us."

"No way," Pixie said.

"That's your old building," Niley said.

"Right, the building Melina and I lived in. I think it's great he's moving up. He's bringing a lot of business to Oscar. I'm happy for him."

"Fucker always did want to follow in your footsteps," Pixie said. "Don't let him in. I see the writing on the wall. You two would be at each other's throats again in no time."

"I don't think Oscar would want to lose the volume he gets from our old contacts," Jo said.

"I told him that. I'm happy for him." I'd hated him so much for so long. The last thing I wanted now was to think badly of him.

"Glad you buried the hatchet without any bloodshed, boss," Jo said. "I agree there is no room for him with us."

"For sure," I said.

Pixie and I were both eyeing the last taco shell. She made a dive for it and laughed when she got it. I sighed a little, watching as she packed it expertly and snapped it in half. She reached over and put half on my plate. The bigger half.

"Not quite," Jo said, picking up some shreds of lettuce that hit the table during the exchange. She dropped them on her plate.

Letty came into replenish our drinks and pick up the empty dishes.

"Cleaned your plates," Letty said. "You want another round?"

"Better not. I think I—" Pixie sighed in a way that meant she wanted more but wasn't going to ask. I felt a rush of love for her. She'd had her heart set on that whole taco, but she'd given me half.

"What she means to say is yes, bring her one more taco," I interrupted. Pixie gave me a thumbs up. "How about you, Jo?"

"I'm stuffed. Thanks."

"Nothing more for Jo," I said. I glanced at Niley. She wasn't much on meals, but she would eat snacks, and she loved milkshakes. I'd ask for a chocolate shake for her later.

"When is Miguel getting back?" Pixie asked. "Because if it's not till tomorrow, I'd love your tapas tonight."

Letty looked in my direction. I nodded.

"Tapas it is," Letty promised. "Miguel always stays gone a day and a night, so he won't be feeding you till the morning."

"How come you don't leave like that?" Pixie asked. "On your day off, you hang out around the pool whether it's nice or not."

"So do you," Letty said to Pixie.

"So I do." Pixie laughed. Letty and Pixie high-fived each other. Letty sneaked a chip from a dish in the center of the table. Pixie patted the seat next to her. "Here, you finish them."

Letty looked at me. I nodded.

"I will, as soon as I get back." She disappeared for an instant into the kitchen and returned to attack the chips and guacamole like she hadn't eaten in a week.

Caro came out with a tray loaded with enough ingredients for five more tacos and placed it in the center of the table. Everyone grabbed one and started loading them up, even Jo.

"You know us too well," I said, munching away.

"Have you lost weight?" Caro looked Pixie over. "Not that you were ever fat, but you look different."

Pixie responded in her *Laverne and Shirley* voice. I was never sure if it was supposed to be Laverne or Shirley, but what it lacked in accuracy, it had in entertainment value. "Mario has us working out every morning like gangbusters. Five a.m.. Can you imagine? I have to get up at four and drive over here in sweats. Sure as fuck wakes me up though. He gets us all dripping in sweat, then we run and jump in the freezing-ass pool."

Niley said, "Then we get the big reward. That steam room and sauna. Worth every bit of pain and sweat."

"This is the big reward," Jo said, standing up and showing off her waist. "I'm in better shape now than I was at eighteen."

"That's not the big reward," I said. "The big reward is that now you can defend yourselves. No punk-ass *matón*[33] is going to take advantage of you without getting his ass kicked."

The girls did a high-five.

"How come you don't go to a show or get out?" I asked Letty.

"If there's a good flick, I'm there. You just don't notice."

"How about dating?"

---

[33] bully

"I don't know anyone out here, and I don't want to go back to where I do. I'm fine. I'm in heaven in this house."

Again, the girls high-fived. I gave them a little toast with my iced tea. I felt lucky Letty was there for me after everyone left. Letty was an underused resource. I had confidence that she could do more. She hadn't yet messed up anything I threw at her to do. As Jo had been working with her, she would be the expert on Letty's progress. I waited till Letty finished her bonus taco and was out of earshot before I whispered, "How is she doing?"

"She's smart," Jo said. "She's smart enough to handle it. I've tuned her in on what we do and how we do it. She just needs hands-on training. She's not shy. She's a people person. She's going to be better at what we do than she is at what she's doing now."

I nodded. "Okay, slackers," I said. "Find a case."

That night I was alone and kicked myself in the ass, thinking I should get in the fucking car and go clubbing instead of wandering around my big house.

At one point, I went down to the wine room and opened something good and expensive. I just sat there in the dark with the open wine bottle and empty glass.

"Mario."

I felt a hand on my shoulder, jostling me. It was dark, not pitch black, but too dim to see who it was. But I smelled her. Melina. Lavender and freesia. I was slumped in a comfy chair in my wine bar.

Melina walked a few feet. Light flickered as she lit a few candles, putting one of them in the center of the table. The flame flared, making the dark darker. She came close, so I pulled her into my lap. I felt her hands in my hair. She held me, then reached out and poured glasses for both of us.

It was always good when Melina came over instead of waiting for a Sunday, a day when she actually didn't go to the markets. Sunday was a busy day, often busier than Saturday. It was a day some whole families came in to shop for the week.

"So nice when you surprise me like this." I kissed her.

"If we were married, we'd be fighting over my late arrivals from work, and I'd be bitching about you trotting the globe for weeks and sometimes months at a time on a case."

"You're probably right. We're fucked."

"We're not fucked, but if we throw marriage in, then we're fucked."

"You believe that, huh?"

She was sitting on my lap. "It's a fact," she replied.

Melina stayed the night.

I don't know if it was fantasy or not, but sometimes I believed it would be nice to have the girls living in the house with me. I understood why men in the Middle East had a bunch of wives. I bet those women don't get along like my girls do, though. I daydreamed about it. I knew the girls had their own homes and their own lives. Maybe the problem was having too much time on my hands, always having to be on standby for a plane crash or an interesting small aircraft crash. The routine, or maybe it was lack of routine, was getting to me. I even complained to myself that my workouts were too routine, even when the girls joined me to work out together. Maybe I was just getting old. I had hit the big three-oh already. Still, my testosterone was overflowing. Most times, I walked around with a hard on.

None of the girls seemed inclined to be interested in developing a relationship with another man. Jo, Pixie, and Niley adored their children, and they had built an extended family so the kids didn't suffer when they had to be away. I knew Pixie had flings whenever she felt like it. It was not only not a secret, but she went out of her way to entertain us with her antics. She had men friends of all sorts. Regular guys, playboys, crossdressers, bi men, gay men. She was always out for whatever was fun. She'd fly off like a butterfly, then come back and ground herself with us. It would have been fine if she missed a day or took a week to go off somewhere, but that never happened. Pixie was a great team player who could always be counted on. We were her family. Sometimes I wonder what would have become of her if I had not brought her home with me, when we'd been teenagers and she'd been pregnant and alone.

Every so often there would come a window when I would ask where they stood, if they had given up on looking for a permanent relationship with someone. It was always during some intense moment during a case when someone had made a decision to sign or not to sign. When people are so broken, it is impossible to be around and not open your heart to them. A moment would come when a wife or husband lost the other half of their soul; and I would have to say something to Jo, or Pixie, or Niley, wondering if they felt like their other half was out there in the world, somewhere lost without them. Jo would speak of Tanis and say that, like me, she had buried her heart. I know she was referring to 'Nando as the lost love of her life. It was a romantic thing to say, but even I didn't know if Tanis had been the love of my life. Pixie was a butterfly who could not even comprehend settling down to one person. More than once, she told me how she felt. "When I was on the street, I must have fucked and sucked a thousand dudes. No right guy is going to want me, and I don't care." I would ask Niley, and she would say there was no man she would trust. Like Tanis, she'd had a bad relationship, that had burned her out on all hope of love.

As for Melina, she just never gave herself a chance. She believed that as soon as you put up a fence like marriage, the grass got greener on the wrong side. More important than that, she didn't want to be controlled by a man—or anyone, for that matter. A man, a husband, would want to take control. Even men she dated more than once tried to control her. She'd grown up in a home that wasn't quite broken. All she remembered of her mother was sadness. Her father had affairs. He didn't hide them. She hung on to her freedom. Melina was a whirlwind with the opposite sex. If she had a notion to have sex and we weren't together, she'd do it, then go about her business.

The girls all swore they were happy the way things were. I only hoped they were not depriving themselves. I know I wasn't.

Carson would joke that I had a cult going with my team. I hated the meaning of the word cult. There was no cult. The girls were my friends. We hunted cases together. We did our best to sign up those that want to come with us. The girls returned to their families. My house was just where I had the office. We would work, then we would wait. Sometimes we waited while drinking together, eating together, working out together, and living life, and—yes—having sex together.

Letty joined the karate lessons. The team was way ahead of her, but Letty was an aggressive learner. Twice a week she would drive to Cosmo's early in the morning for a lesson with him, the same as the other girls. We were still looking for a way for her to fit in. She became my driver, much to Pixie's delight. When she wasn't hauling people in the Rolls, she was hauling purchases in the Ford station wagon I'd gotten for that purpose. Miguel was picky about everything in the kitchen, but he wasn't much for shopping. Letty shopped for everything we needed in the house, for housekeeping and to keep Miguel's pantry happy.

To ease my loneliness, maybe I needed to buy a dog. Or a dozen cats. It was late and I was restless and feeling alone. I was feeling that way frequently. It was almost eleven at night when the intercom in the kitchen came on. It was Letty.

"Are you alone? Do you need company?"

"I'm having peanut butter. Next, I'm going to have ice cream, or open a bottle of wine. I'm not the least bit tired."

"You didn't answer my question, boss."

"I'm alone, and yes, it would be lovely to have you here."

I heard the alarm reset, then arm. Letty was in the house. I was still in the kitchen, listening to her approaching footsteps.

"You got here fast. Took a cart?"

"Ran all the way."

She kissed my cheek. In order for her to do that, I had to lean forward.

"So, what's it going to be, wine or ice cream?"

"Boss, it's your call. Do you have the blahs?"

"I'm bored. I should be out in a bar or a club. Did I tell you I got my key to the Playboy Club?"

I sat down.

"You told all of us. I'll drive you there if you want. Should be open till two."

"It's all the way in Century City. Hardly worth the drive," I said. I took a good look at her. She was wearing Daisy Dukes and a blouse tied so that her belly button showed. Tiny waist. Fine ass.

"You're beautiful, Letty. What do those Playboy girls have that you don't?"

"Bunny ears?" She laughed. She moved behind my chair, put her arms over my shoulder, and squeezed my nipples through my tee.

"Ouch."

"Sorry, boss. Want me to suck you or fuck you, or anything else?"

"By anything, you mean read me a book, or what?"

"Boss, I can do anything. Just name it. Let's go to the bedroom. I will make you feel better."

"Promise?"

"Promise. Boss, I'm going to get you high with what I plan to do."

"I just got hard," I told her, winding my way up the stairs. I stepped out of my shoes and left them there, one on the fourth step, one on the fifth. The marble was cold even through my socks.

"That will come in handy." She smirked. The corners of her mouth turned up.

"How about some wine?"

"You don't need wine."

It didn't diminish the hard on, but I felt guilty walking up the steps. All I had to do was crook my finger, and I could be satisfied. Some nights Pixie or Niley would drive all the way to my apartment. Letty was convenient; maybe too convenient.

"You don't have to do this. This is not your job."

"Boss, I rang you on the intercom. I had this feeling you needed cheering up."

Before I was on the bed, Letty was pulling my boxers off. My tee was behind me on the stairs with my socks and slippers.

"Give me a minute to light the fireplace and candles."

"They should put the fireplace on when they do my turn-down in the evening," I said.

"I'll pass the word along."

I wasn't tired, but I lay there like I was totally out of it. I closed my eyes.

I felt her lips on my stomach. Not just her lips. I felt a lot of smooth skin. She was rubbing her naked body on me.

"Your abs are such a turn-on. And your arms," she said, running her hand over my biceps. I think it was her hands. "I know Betty does this to you. Tell me if I'm getting the hang of it. She's done it to me twice. I want to practice on you."

"What, a body massage?"

"Yeah."

I wasn't complaining. A body massage is like dancing with a strange woman, like making love with all the touching and moving and feeling each other's bodies while not actually having intercourse. It is provocative, intense, and makes it impossible to be still. It is tough for a guy like me to give up control and not just take over. Every time I tried, Letty took my hands and put them back at my sides.

"I'm running the show, boss," she said. How perverse am I? The more excited and frustrated I got, the better I felt. By the time her mouth went from my abs to below the belt, I was shimmering with excitement and hard as a bat.

Chapter 20
February 2 1978
Bahamas

"*Amor*, I'm going to the Bahamas," Camila said on the phone. "I would love you to come with me."

"You expect me to drop my business and everything I'm doing, just like that?"

"*Si, Amor*, just like that."

"All right," I said. I was always glad to hear from her.

"Good," she said. "Because I'm already at the airport."

"Van Nuys?"

"Yes."

I did drop everything. Just like that.

An hour later, I was following Olga up the airstairs into the DC9 where Camila was waiting.

"*Amor*, thank you for coming. I'm so excited."

We kissed passionately. Olga disappeared into a cabin with my suitcase.

"You're kidding, right? You went out of your way to take me with you to paradise. I have to thank you, not the other way around."

The spontaneity of this trip made it feel like an adventure. As frequently as I travel, that's unusual.

"We're taking off in about fifteen minutes. Want to use the cabin? Or should we sit out here until we're flying?"

"I'm easy, *Bella*. You lead."

We sat facing each other on two wide, comfortable seats. I looked out of my window, and Camila looked out of hers. We were still on the tarmac.

Olga came out of the cabin where she'd left my suitcase.

"Let me guess." Olga put a finger to her chin with a big smile. "Mario, you want a Red Bordeaux, and Camila, Cristal?"

"Perfect, thank you," I said.

Camila gave her a thumbs up. I always remembered Sami when Camila drank Cristal, and vice versa.

"I know I keep thanking you, but I am so looking forward to this. I've been working so much. I get caught up. So... thank you."

"You're so welcome, *Amor*." We leaned forward just far enough to click our glasses.

The captain's voice came over a speaker, telling us to put the seatbelts on. The plane began to move.

Our eyes met. We sipped from our glasses.

"You're fucking lovely, *Bella*."

"I love the fucking lovely." She smiled.

The engines were roaring now. We sprang down the runway. She was facing me and leaned forward slightly. G-force pushed me deep in the seat as we sped faster and lifted off. There's always that rush of a moment when you leave the ground. I like that feeling, and I could see Camila liked it, too.

"What's in the Bahamas?"

There was the smile again. "You will love this house. It was built in the fifties when Nassau was all about luxury, class, and sophistication."

"You have a house there?"

"It was my parents' house. After they died, Pepe had it renovated."

I guess we hit cruising speed. We flew above the bumpiness of the clouds, and the plane leveled. Our seatbelts came off. Camila moved to my lap. We clicked glasses, sipped, and kissed.

"That's cool."

"We also have a boat. Pepe got it in payment of a debt."

"Tell me about it."

"It's a big one, about 150 feet. We have a crew on standby, but we've only used it a couple times. Pepe seldom comes to the Bahamas anymore. Perhaps some bad memories. I have never asked him. I have stayed overnight on the boat, but I've never taken it out."

"We got to try that."

"Of course, *Amor*, we will do it all. I only have a half day of business, then I'm free. We can stay as long as you like."

"Dig that. Nice," I said. "You are much too good to me."

She rubbed her hand over my raging hard on. "Your *vergota*[34] is good to me. What can I do but give something back?"

I picked her up and carried her into the bedroom. We kissed, and more. Camila had left the Cristal behind and was now drinking wine. Olga came in and out a few times without knocking to keep our glasses filled, though it seemed to me that she could have left the bottle. Still, Olga was a feast for my eyes, and incentive for my dick that was busy working Camila. The mattress was big but had some pointy metal parts in the center to avoid. A part of my mind was always keeping track of our placement on the mattress.

I was absorbed in our activity, but then I felt a change in altitude and turbulence.

"What's that?" I asked. Camila didn't have to respond. Olga came in.

"We are landing to refuel, and we'll be on our way in less than thirty minutes."

Olga assisted us in putting on the seat belts built into the bed. We lay on our backs, and Olga snapped us in. The mattress was really two, and the sheets

---

[34] huge cock

had snaps coming through, which is what I had been avoiding because they could be painful. The snaps, sheets, seat belts, and interruption of Olga failed to separate us. Our hands were busy on each other. Olga shut the door when she left.

The bed in the house in the Bahamas was small, but perfect for us. It was a king, half the size of my custom-made bed. But everything else was bigger than my house. The master bedroom was twice as big as my huge master bedroom. Walking the full tour of the house felt like a hike—two floors of bedrooms, each with its own bath and shower, so many I didn't count them. A deck wound around, so that each bedroom on both floors had its own lanai. The pool was built into the deck, surrounded by deck chairs and patio seating and dining and bistro and lounge furniture and a couple of free-standing bars, fully stocked. We came and went through the back door facing the street, a door which was nothing special, except it opened into a hall wider than some houses. The front of the house faced the water. The back door gave a clear view, straight like a shotgun to the ocean view. What looked like the front of the house faced the water.

Three huge seating areas were strung along the water-side of the house. As you faced the ocean, the dining room table was on your left hand. It was placed next to a huge kitchen that faced a breezeway to the building next door, where the servants lived. Our arrival sent all the help scurrying. Camila barely acknowledged them, but I got a chance to see Olga in action, running the household.

There were so many maids and uniformed people that I could not imagine what their jobs were. They were all locals with long hair, dark skins, and lilting accents. They kept apart from us as if we were lepers. I would not have tolerated that in Los Angeles. My house crew is part of my family. But Camila explained there was a sharp and uneasy divide in the Bahamas. Olga sent some of them to shop, some of them to clean, others of them to do who knows what. She had people spinning like plates in a Vegas magic act. Everyone was busy. All the activity put Camila off.

"Let's go to the yacht," she said.

"I'll take care of dinner," Olga said. Presumably, she left the house to confer with the yacht's chef, or maybe he came to see her. I don't know.

We hit the beach and showered outside on the stairs leading to the house, then walked down to the convenient marina where the yacht was docked on a long floating pier.

The boat was right out of a 007 movie. There were three hospitality-related men on board that I knew of: a waiter, a chef, and a chef's assistant. I am pretty sure that the two men armed with machine guns who were walking the gangplank had purposes that were unrelated to hospitality. A man Camila introduced as the skipper gave us a tour. We went through a living room that would have pleased Melina with all of its antique chairs and couches and whatnot, and lots of polished wood. Living space filled both the two lower decks, and the interior was outfitted with wood, and glass, and stylish public seating areas. The master bedroom had a mirror over the bed and dressers built into the wooden paneling. The portholes weren't what I expected; they were much bigger, enough to let in lots of light. The skipper pointed out two doors behind the master bedroom's headboard. One led to a bathroom with a tub, and the other a shower. Both had full sinks, toilets, and bidets. Another bedroom had twin beds, and another had a queen; they shared a black marble bathroom with a shower. There might have been a couple more bedrooms. I quit counting. The kitchen was dolled up in granite, almost as fancy as my kitchen at home. And really, why granite? It doesn't float. A circular stairway led to an upstairs office, a hall that had couches, recliners, a bar with nautical-themed stools, a game table, and plenty of views of the sea. At one end was another eating area, open to the outdoors on three sides, but ceilinged by the topmost deck. I was certainly dazzled by the luxury and unreality of it. How could my friends own something like this and not use it? It was like having a personal floating Hilton hotel.

I hadn't digested the tour yet, but Camila cut the skipper off and led me to one of the eating areas. Dinner was served in the fancy wood-paneled dining room.

"Do you want to go back to the house and change?" I was leery of sitting on the furniture. We were wearing bathing suits that had dried in the eighty-degree sunlight, but they were still bathing suits.

"No need," Camila said. "Who are we trying to impress?" She found us a couple of plain white Tees to wear in the air conditioning. I don't know if they belonged to Pepe or the chefs, but they were new. Camila placed me at the head of the table and sat at my right shoulder. The remaining twelve chairs at the table were empty. We had not seen Olga much through the day, but she came down from the house for dinner and helped the waiter.

"Lobster thermidor," Olga announced. The waiter brought out the biggest lobster tails I had ever seen. I tasted brandy and butter in the lobster, and I don't know what else, but it was amazing. We took our time eating, and then Olga announced the steaks. There were a lot of sides I wasn't familiar with. Camila pointed out fried plantains and dishes with rice and peas. At least I recognized the potatoes. There were several fish concoctions, whole roasted grouper with mushrooms and chilis, snapper, and sole. We were full halfway through the steak, but tasted every dish to keep from insulting the chef. Crisp, chilled white wine from Argentina accompanied the fish, and it was as fabulous as everything else.

Olga sat at a chair but didn't eat. She kept running back and forth to the galley with the waiter.

I could not imagine the cost of keeping the yacht in the water, keeping it with a crew who kept everything sparkling. I'd never priced boats or boat maintenance, but it was, for sure, way above my touch.

Later, we walked the deck and went up and down stairs wherever we found any to work off the huge dinner.

"There's one thing you need on this boat."

"What, *Amor*?"

"A gym."

She looked thoughtful. "Good idea. I'll look in to it."

"I'm kidding," I said.

"No, you're not kidding. It's a good idea."

We walked back across the deck to where the skipper had left us. She pointed out more stairs. I went up ahead of her and froze when I got to the top. I was not expecting yet another whole living space on the very top of the boat: a bar, sitting area, and certainly not the hot tub reflecting the colors of the setting sun.

"Now I've seen everything," I said.

"You haven't seen the pilothouse yet." Camila laughed.

"I have seen enough."

After a bout in the hot tub under the stars, we ended up in the master cabin. I was as exhausted as only beaches can make you, and I fell into a deep sleep, barely feeling the movement of the water.

We had breakfast on the deck. I looked across the marina, scarcely believing it was real. When people talk about blue, they barely scratch the surface of the color of the water in the Bahamas. Not to mention the sky, which was cloudless. February at home is cold and miserable, but here, it was in the eighties, and the breeze off the water offered the perfect degree of cooling.

I could not face food after last night's dinner, and I was satisfied with iced juice.

"*Bella*, you fit the setting. Gorgeous," I said. She was wearing some kind of wrap made of brightly colored cloth. The wind had brought a blush to her cheeks, or maybe it was makeup. I don't know.

"*Amor*, you always look gorgeous." It could have been a honeymoon.

Camila was eating biscuits. She noticed how I watched Olga as she walked away from our table after refilling my juice glass. She was wearing short shorts that had no secrets. They hugged her naked, obviously brazil-waxed bottom.

"You like Olga, *Amor*?"

"I'm sorry." I grinned. "I'm still growing up. I can't help looking."

Camila smiled back, mischief in her face. "*Amor*, it's okay to look, and anything else to make you happy."

I took her hand. "I have my hands full with you, *Bella*, and I love it."

After two nights on the boat, Camila announced, "Alas, it is time to work. Today is my half-day of business."

We returned to the house. My things had been relocated from the master suite to a guest room much bigger than any of my guest rooms at home. The move reminded me of Sami when Jason was around for the night. I wasn't making any judgements, but I was either being thrown out, or Camila was telling the truth that she needed to get ready for her afternoon meeting.

I took a swim in the surf, and then in the pool, came back to my room, showered for the second time that day, and got back into my sundried bathing trunks. The servant who had moved me here had packed my suitcase for me, and I didn't feel like unpacking it. I was okay in the suit. I lay on the bed and played with the television stations. Not much to choose from on Bahaman television. I left it on *I Love Lucy* reruns. I missed my earphones and my music. I was certain that somewhere in this house I had seen a stereo, but I wasn't sure where. I toyed with the idea of going around to look for it. My watch had been on the end table in the master bedroom. Someone had moved it to the mirrored tray on the dresser in this room. I set it to London time, then Bahama time, and put it on, then lay on the bed killing time, which seemed funny after blowing an hour playing with my watch. I decided to look for the music. I was in bathing trunks and socks, dressed enough not to alarm any of the help, but it seemed like they were all gone.

No one was around. Maybe they took a siesta. I didn't know the local culture. My stocking feet slipped around on the slick floors as I made my way into the wide hall upstairs whose end overlooked the water. I heard a man's voice. I couldn't make out the words. I heard another man, distinctly deeper; a bass. I guessed from their voices that one sounded white, and the other Calypso. They sounded angry. Camila chimed in in furious Spanish, cussing someone at the top of her lungs. I followed the hall toward where the shouting was coming from, downstairs. One of the sitting areas. I could see part of the room from the landing. Camila had her finger pointed first at the white man, then at the black one. They were all yelling in each other's faces, all of their features distorted in rage. Something was escalating. I ran down the stairs. As I reached the bottom step, I heard a gunshot then another and another. I heard the thuds of bodies hitting the floor.

Camila!

Afraid I would be too late, I ran in and slid to a stop. The men were down. One black, one white, both on the oriental carpet, looking dead. Nothing but silence now, and the scent of gunpowder. I stared at the bodies. Heard a noise. Looked up. Standing next to Camila was one of the guards. Maybe I had seen him on the yacht. I'd seen him somewhere. He was holding a pistol angled toward the dead men. At least it wasn't a machine gun. I was feeling a degree of shock at seeing him, but not as much shock as when I was looking at those bodies lying at my feet. As for those bodies, they weren't feeling anything, ever again.

Camila made a small, unintelligible noise. One second she was across the room, the next she had leaped into my arms.

"*Amor*, I'm sorry, I'm sorry."

"What are you sorry about?" I asked. She mumbled something and started crying, big hard sobs. I looked over her head at the guard. A muscular, swarthy fellow. He returned his pistol to his holster. He wasn't looking at me or at Camila. I followed his line of sight and saw Olga standing in the portal, a gun in her hand. I'm guessing the shouting had summoned her, as it had brought me.

Camila was clutching me, sounding hysterical, but when I was able to get a clear view, I saw no tears. The guard was looking calm. Olga was looking pretty cool under the circumstances, her gun still out, pointed at the bodies. Her hand was steady. I didn't know which of them had done the shooting. I stood there for Camila as she clung to me, wailing. My eyes wandered from the bodies to the table at my left. A briefcase was open, filled with neat bundles of hundred-dollar bills.

"Let's go to the plane right now," Olga said.

"Give me a second to run up and get my suitcase." I didn't want to leave anything of mine behind, just in case. Of course there were plenty of my fingerprints everywhere, but I couldn't do anything about that.

Olga put her hands on Camila's shoulders and disengaged her from me. Camila's face still showed no sign of tears. Olga seemed unsurprised at Camila's mental state, whatever it was. I wondered what all the sobbing and clinging was about. Olga pointed Camila toward the guard who had had his gun out. Belatedly, my ears registered what Olga had said. I dashed to the bedroom, and pulled on my sweats, and tennis shoes. I think I shoved my trunks in the suitcase before I grabbed it. By the time I was back—and it was only a moment—the bodies were gone. Olga had left the room. Camila hugged the guard and kissed him on each cheek. Olga returned with two large men in tow. I didn't know if they were guards or house staff. It didn't matter. They were Pepe's.

"Don't worry, Miss Camacho," the guard said. "Everything will be taken care of." He looked down. Every one of us looked at the fine carpet, marred by two red splotches, the only evidence that those men had ever been here. I wondered what they had done with the bodies, but that was one question I would never ask. One of the servants and I had a little tug of war before I realized what he was doing. I released my suitcase. He walked with it ahead of me, double-quick. By the time I was outside, I felt the vibration of a helicopter. It had gotten here fast. Process of elimination told me it was probably Olga who had called. She had been running things the whole time we were here, and she was still directing traffic. The noise reminded me of Venezuela, of my rescue, of when I'd rented the helicopter to take families to see the killing field where their loved ones had died. I could tell I was shaken. My mind was flitting everywhere. This wasn't Venezuela. This was the Bahamas, and we were at Pepe's heliport right outside his mansion where two men had just been shot. The helicopter zipped Camila, Olga, and me to the airport. As we landed, I saw the DC9 waiting, the airstairs ready for boarding. I could even see the pilots in the cockpit.

I looked at my watch. I had been expecting a delay at the airport. I don't know how many hours of my life I have spent waiting for planes. For sure, it has been a lot. But it had only been thirty minutes ago that I'd heard the gunshots. At home, I would have called the police and waited for their interviews. Heck, the

LA police wouldn't even have been there within half an hour. In that span of time, we had already taken a helicopter, landed at the airport, disembarked, and boarded the flight home.

We took our seats, where we faced each other. I was unsure how we had gotten here so fast, or even why we were running, but asked no questions. Olga ran to the galley and came back opening a bottle of wine. She handed over two glasses and filled them like a character in a fast-motion picture, then dropped into the perpendicular seat stretching across the wide aisle.

The captain's voice came on the loud speaker.

"Welcome aboard, Miss Camila and guest. Please fasten your seat belts. We will be airborne in under ten minutes."

Camila put her glass of wine on a side table next to the window and lit up a joint. She took a big hit, then handed it to me.

I took a deep drag. I felt the hit crash into my brain. Camila smiled for the first time since we left the house. She was impeccable. No sign that a single tear had been shed. I handed her back the joint and drank my wine. Olga met my gaze. I lifted my glass to her. She smiled.

"*Salud*," she said.

Camila blew Olga a kiss.

I had a list of questions I would like to have answered, but I didn't ask. I was calm, cool, and collected, or maybe I was just high from the two drags I had taken from the joint.

Death was nothing new to me. I had killed the man who had shot Tanis, and two men who had broken into my Bunker Hill apartment. At least I wasn't doing the killing in the Bahamas. I looked at the two women who were acting as if nothing had happened. How were they taking it so easily in stride? It did not seem a normal reaction to violent death, unless it was something, perhaps, they had seen before. The events of the last hour added to the mystique of Camila and Olga, at least in my head. Olga was drinking from a bottle of Coca-Cola. She'd parked herself across the cabin, and every so often she looked our way to see if we needed refills. Is that what Olga's job was? To cope with everything as Camila did whatever she wanted? Or was she Camila's caregiver? The more I saw of them, the less I understood. So many unanswered questions.

The jets became a whisper. I saw nothing but endless black skies out the window. I knew the clouds were out there, but I couldn't see them. Olga squeezed in beside Camila, two fine asses in one seat. Olga relit the joint and handed it over to Camila.

"You have questions." Camila took a drag of the joint. Olga held Camila's wine glass.

"It's none of my business."

"You ran in the room. You could have been hurt."

I shrugged. "I was coming to make sure you were okay."

Olga said, "I have heard how you fight."

"If you were in danger, I would have taken them out. Your guard took care of them first."

I chugged what was left in my wine glass. Olga jumped up and gave me a refill.

"I don't need to know anything else," I said with simplicity.

"It was them or me," Camila said.

Olga returned to the seat with Camila. She had no drink. She wasn't smoking.

"I believe you." It might have been the joint talking, but at least in that moment, I believed her. The one thing that bothered me was when she pretended to cry.

"Where are we headed?"

"Anywhere you want, *Amor*."

I felt the power her words carried. She had this huge airliner, and she wasn't kidding.

"At some point we have to refuel," I said.

"We are scheduled to refuel in Washington, DC," Olga said, "but flight plans are easy to change."

I don't know if what I felt was because of what had happened, but I was excited. I wanted her. I wanted both of them.

Washington was snowed in. All runways were shut down. We were rerouted to New York.

"Can we make it that far?"

"We have plenty of fuel," Camila said, "just not enough to make it to Los Angeles. I have a feeling that's where you want to go."

I drank some wine and nodded. "Rain check on anywhere."

"Si, *Amor*, I love being with you." She exchanged a glance with Olga. Leaned a little bit and kissed her on the lips. "We both love being with you."

I knew I was being handled. I didn't know why I was being handled and it didn't matter. I loved it.

New York City was embroiled in a snowstorm. For a guy from LA, from the air, it looked unreal, like a giant snow globe. All airports were on standby. We ended up landing in upstate New York north of the Catskills, in the Adirondacks. We climbed down the stairs into the bitter cold and crossed the tarmac to the private airport deep in snow. Evergreens and mountains around us and the lateness of the hour made the location seem exotic. A sign on one of the hangers said "Mechanic on duty 24 hrs." Driverless, the tractor of a plow was rumbling, bouncing, and belching out nasty fumes and steam, sitting beside the perfectly swept runway which we had landed on, a runway as clear as if it had been summer. Walls of shoveled snow lined the unpaved portion of the airfield. Camila was in a full-length fur, and I was wearing fur that belonged to Pepe. The hem hit me between the knees and ankles. Who the hell keeps a fur coat in a plane, just to have it? It had a fur hat that buttoned down. It made me feel silly, costumed like some Cossack transported from Siberia, but it was warm. It was tough to face this much winter when only hours ago, we'd been soaking up Bahaman sunshine. My memory of happy sunshine was blocked off by the grim aspect of those bodies, but something dangerous in the experience perversely turned me on.

The private airport had a diner that never closed. Signs indicated the airport had heated and unheated hangars for rent, and looked like it took in a lot of business. Once we were inside, it reminded me more of a bus station than an airport. There were more people around than I would have expected, but then there were snowstorms all around us, and it seemed that plenty of pilots were roosting here, waiting out weather somewhere else.

"Look," Camila said. "Nanook of the North."

She pointed at a big man in the restaurant. We had a brief conversation with him. He turned out to be the plow driver, a heavyset man who was unwrapping himself as he greeted us. Two long scarves, three sweaters, and one big jacket later, he was down to normal proportions, sitting at the counter, nursing a tall silver thermos, warming his hands on the cup, his ice-encrusted gloves defrosting into a puddle on an empty stool. He was actually quite thin, with a long, bony neck and narrow chest. His face and hands were badly windburned. I did not envy him his job, but I thanked him for how well he did it. Olga joined us at the booth and sat across from me. We got coffee and pie, and I gave the waitress a fifty to give Nanook of the North whatever he wanted. I doubted I would ever return to this airport, but out of habit, I gave him my card and a hundred dollars. Camila returned after calling Pepe. I didn't hear what she told him, but when I called Jo, she got the team on the line. All I said was that I was on the way home.

Camila left her coat draped over the booth and went to the restroom, leaving Olga and me alone.

"Are you feeling okay?" I asked.

She shrugged. "Of course. I'm fine." She sipped her coffee. The silence dragged on. "It was self-defense."

"What?" I had been wondering what was keeping Camila.

"I said that it was self-defense." Olga stirred cream into her coffee and sipped again.

"Like I said before, it's none of my business."

"Now you know."

She was all in white, long-sleeved turtleneck to sneakers. She'd braved the weather in no coat but only a soft-looking sweater, maybe cashmere. She looked like a winter flower, maybe edelweiss.

"Don't you have a coat?"

"It's back in the plane. I've got on lots of layers. I'm fine."

"Yes, you are," I said. "You have beautiful eyes."

A smile curved Olga's lips.

Camila walked up. She looked from me to Olga. "Making plans?"

"I just told Mario that it was self-defense."

Camila sighed and looked at me. "I told you on the plane, it was either me or them."

"I heard you, and I believed you."

"Let's board so we can get a smoke," Camila said. She wasn't talking about tobacco.

By the time we touched down at Van Nuys Airport, the sun was rising. Camila's plane was being refueled again. I recall thinking that her pilots must have had caffeine for blood, or maybe she had a spare crew hiding in the cargo bay. I had not slept. I guess the dead guys had made more of an impression than I allowed myself to consider. My eyelids weighed a ton. I only paid partial attention to our goodbyes. At least half of my brain was already asleep.

"We're off to Colombia," she said. "Pepe is there. He's not going to be happy."

"I guess not," I said, thinking of the bodies.

"Not why you're thinking," Camila said. "They were selling us two parcels of land we need for a construction project. Now we will have to rethink everything."

"Will there be a problem with Pepe?"

"Of course not. Two heads are better than one. Never a problem. He's my brother, but he's also a business partner. I have as much to lose in this deal as he does."

I did not ask for details of the deal. I kissed Olga on both cheeks, then she hugged me. She had taken off some of those layers. The scarf and sweater were gone and I could feel her body beneath the clothes. There was something about that hug. When I was away from the airstairs, I turned around. The door was shut. Olga and Camila were blowing me kisses through the window. I blew a few kisses back, goggled over the size of the plane, and staggered off to my car. I was so tired I am certain I dozed off at least twice on the way home. I have no clue how I made it to bed.

Chapter 21
February 1978
After the Bahamas

Camila and I got tighter after that trip to the Bahamas. Once I was home, she called me daily, always from a different place. We talked about everything. Everything, that is, except the Bahamas. It was like it had never happened. It was invisible, like glue.

She called from over the globe. Whenever I asked about Olga, she said, "She's flying around on her own, doing errands for us."

"But she's okay?"

"*Amor*, of course she is okay. I think you like her maybe more than me?"

"*Bella*, no way. You're the queen."

"*Si, Amor, soy la Reina.*"[35] She laughed softly.

I wasn't in love with Camila or Olga, but, no question, I was infatuated by them. Melina and my team were my homegirls. I adored them. They were part of my daily life. My Colombian friends were filed in a different part of my brain.

I came home after handling issues stemming from a small crash—a chopper performing fire rescue. An investigator I'd worked with before was distantly related to one of the victims. He had called me around dawn from a pay phone

---

[35] Yes, Love, I'm the Queen

feet from the tarmac. He believed the helicopter had faulty propeller parts and faulty maintenance. It was too early to tell, but it might well turn out to be big, so I'd arranged a meeting of the investigator, Tom, and Oscar. I hadn't been at the office, though. We were in the field helping at the emergency site. The girls were still at the Red Cross evacuation center doling out a truck of supplies I'd brought in. I'd helped unload it and then came home for a much-needed shower. I was walking into my bedroom, scrubbing at my hair with a towel, when I picked up the phone. Before anyone spoke, I knew from the echoes that it was from out of the country.

"Mario, it's Olga. How are you?"

"What a surprise. I'm good. How are you?"

"Camila says that you always ask about me. How nice."

I tossed my towel and grabbed the bedspread, pulling it back so I could sit. I had the phone balanced between my shoulder and my ear as I pulled on the shorts I was changing into.

"Just checking if you are okay."

"I'm fine. Thank you for caring," she said. "Guess what?"

"Tell me," I said, settling back on the bed and stretching. I'd unloaded two semi-trailers before I started on the truck I brought in. I'd really needed that shower, and I wasn't going to be needing a workout in the morning, either.

"I'm on the plane's radio phone. I'm in Van Nuys."

I laughed aloud. She was Camila all over again. "Fantastic. How long are you staying?" I looked at my watch. It was nearly noon.

"I'm here eight hours while the pilots sleep. That's it."

"I'll take you to lunch or something," I offered. My dick was already hard, planning the 'or something.' My brain was already sending me dirty layover jokes starring Olga that my body was preparing to commit to action.

"Is that what you really want to do?" she asked.

No, it wasn't all. I wanted to know what they did about those dead guys. That was unfinished business. Somewhere in my head, I knew it had only been a short little while since the Bahamas shooting. A part of me was waiting for some kind of discussion or update on what was going on there; but I was starting to suspect that they were never going to mention it again. I guess I was just supposed to relax and let them handle it, and I was just supposed to shove it under the rug and pretend the murders never happened. Pretending doesn't make the bad stuff go away, but what's done is done. All I could think of was that Olga wanted me.

My dick pulsed. My mind raced. This was too good to be true. Maybe Camila was setting me up. But why would she do that? Every time I looked at Olga, Camila told me she wasn't the jealous type. I hadn't responded to Olga. I glanced down at my hard self. I hadn't responded in words, anyway. I could hear her breathing on the phone.

"Mario?"

"Lunch is okay, but I'd rather just see you."

"In that case, get your ass over here. The clock is eating up time."

"I'm hitting the road now."

With a big grin, Olga met me in the lounge of the executive jet charter company that rented short- and long-term space at the airport. The long mink she wore revealed bare ankles and a pair of slippers. I had arrived with my imagination already stuck in overdrive, so as soon as I saw it, I instantly pictured her naked under that coat.

"It did not take much time for you to strike the road," she said.

I laughed, then hugged her. We kissed cheeks, European-style. We walked together out to the tarmac and up the airstairs of the Boeing 727. I'd never been on this one before.

"Who is with us?" I asked as I followed.

"Just us."

"No Camila?" I asked. I never heard an answer.

We had just cleared the entrance. I shut the door. As I turned to face Olga, the mink slid off her bare shoulders and dropped to the carpet. My busy imagination was gratified to be correct. She raised her arms up toward me. I leaned so she could hug my neck, cupped her ass, and lifted her. We were still standing, the kiss dragging into something else. Then I was the only one standing as Olga's legs wrapped around my waist. I looked toward the cabin, planning my steps to the bed awaiting us, and there in the portal was Camila, naked.

"Surprise!"

Camila, laughing, ran toward us. Olga slid off me, and the two of them escorted me toward the bed, helping me out of my clothes as we walked. The plane was gorgeously outfitted for an executive; two cabins, twelve seats. Seats in the cabin were fixed in a circle around the bed, plus there was also a fixed round table with four seats. But it wasn't the plane I was excited about, and I was really excited.

A Louis Vuitton suitcase sat on the table, Vachetta leather trim with the distinctive Vuitton fleur de lis pattern, brass hardware, gold plating. I recognized it right away because I'd given Melina a full set. It cost a pretty penny, so it was probably Camila's rather than Olga's.

Naked, we clicked glasses and drank Dom Pérignon.

"*Amor*, be happy, I want you to be happy."

"So fucking happy. Please pinch me." I extended one arm to Camila and another to Olga. "I want to be sure this is happening."

"It's happening," Olga said.

She did not pinch. She did slide onto my lap. Camila was at my back, holding me and nuzzling my neck. From that point on, for the next five hours, everything was a blur of fantasy come to life. I think we did everything possible, and some things that I wouldn't have thought were possible.

Olga hung up the radio phone.

"The pilots are on their way," she said.

I was already dressed, prepared to leave, and as empty-handed as I had been when I arrived. The pilots were my cue to leave. I headed toward the airstairs when Camila touched my shoulder. As I turned to face her, she handed me the suitcase that had been in the cabin. I accepted it, curiously.

"What is this?" I asked.

"*Amor*, I want to buy a house in Pasadena. Please hold onto this until I find something. I know I will probably need more. This is a start."

Camila and Olga were both still the way they entered this world. I felt uncomfortable being the only one with clothes on.

"Do you mind, *Amor*?"

"I don't mind, *Bella*. How much is it?"

"Two million."

I did a slow whistle. "I don't know where I'll put it, but okay."

"Just put it at home somewhere. I'm not worried."

I kissed her. "It will be me that worries."

Olga took my hand and squeezed it. "You don't have to worry; the risk is on Camacho."

When I got home, the team was gone. I made it to my office. Sixty seconds behind me, Letty showed up.

"Boss, hi, are you hungry?"

"Starved."

"How about a porterhouse and baked potato?"

After I said it, I realized I was starving. "Yes."

Maybe I was a little emphatic about that steak. Letty looked surprised, then amused. She tried to hide a little laugh as she said, "I'll let Miguel know."

After she left, I opened the suitcase on top of my desk. Neat bills like the ones I had seen in the Bahamas. This suitcase was not that briefcase. What I had noticed on the plane was correct. This was Louis Vuitton. The Vachetta leather was still new and hadn't developed the patina, but the little brass fittings all had the signature fleur de lis pattern stamped on each one. The pattern was not to my taste, but it was very expensive.

I had two safes. The five-foot safe that was supposed to be burglar-proof was located adjacent to my office in what we used as a file room and supply room. The safe was very heavy, strapped to the floor and not on wheels. I only kept my good watches and my cash socks that I no longer stashed with my boxers. In the same room, I also had a rifle safe with the racks removed. I used it to stack bulky files like those from the close of escrow. I probably didn't need all that old paperwork, but I kept it anyway, just in case. That safe was also combination but easy for two strong men to roll away.

I took the open suitcase to the supply room and stacked the two million in the five-footer. There was still room for more, but I hoped this was it. I didn't like the responsibility of having someone else's cash, but what were the chances someone would get to it? Slim and none. I wasn't even sure why I wasn't anxious about it. Maybe the sight of two dead bodies over a Camacho money deal made me less sensitive to money dangers. I stashed the empty suitcase on a top shelf.

I jumped in the shower to wash off five hours of sex with two athletic women. By the time I had dressed, Letty announced that dinner was ready.

"Join me," I said to Letty. I picked her up like a bride. Her arms went around my neck and I did a fast walk from my bathroom, down the stairs, and all the way to the dinette where the table was set up for me to eat. She giggled all the way. I could smell the hot biscuits that Miguel kept making even after I complained how fattening they were. I wasn't happy to see the one place setting.

"No plate for Letty?" I asked Miguel.

"I'll just keep you company. I ate earlier." She sat beside me. "What are you thinking about, boss? Did you have a good afternoon?"

I thought of the way I was tricked to think that only Olga would be there, surprised that Camila was also there, but not very surprised. The hours I spent with Camila and Olga had been the kind of sex guys dream about. I brushed away any concerns I had over the dead bodies in the Bahamas and the two million in my safe. I was feeling good. Though as the exhilaration wore off, my brain was kicking in.

"I had a great afternoon. How about you?"

My mouth was full. I accepted the biscuit she handed me, melted butter oozing out one side, and placed it on my full plate. The steak was perfect, and I did not leave a bite. I mangled the biscuit but didn't really eat it.

I figured that Camila and Olga had set up the afternoon to bedazzle me into holding two million cash for them. I saw it. I'm no dummy. Maybe I should have been disturbed, but I wasn't. I wouldn't have taken it from Carson or Pélon, back when that was their racket. If the money is drug money and they find it here, would I be back in federal prison? How would I know where the money came from? She handed me that two million like it was nothing. Man. I was still reeling from it. Unbelievable. It almost trumped the memory of those bloody bodies.

"It was good. Did lots of shopping for Miguel."

Letty and I ended up in the wine room. She loved to play the jukebox. She picked out some songs, then moved behind my chair to massage my shoulders.

"Do you want anything? Do you need anything?" I asked her.

"I'm good," she said simply. "Happy."

"Come, sit on my lap and let me smell you," I said. "I like the scent of happiness." I buried my nose in her hair. She smelled like a familiar spring garden. Letty was far from being innocent. None of my girls were innocents. But they didn't arm themselves with secret agendas. In that way, they *were* innocent. Even Pixie. Olga and Camila had their secret agendas.

I'd had Olga sitting on my lap today before we got in bed. Olga and Camila were drawing me to them, deliberately. I could feel it as they wove the web. It was painless, and I was entertained, but I knew it was there.

Letty clicked glasses with me, and we drank. I glanced at her smooth face, as lovely in her way as Camila and Olga, but also guileless. I was glad to be home.

Jason called about the airline crash in Amsterdam an hour after it happened, long before the news media let us know about it in Los Angeles. The flight had been headed to Libya, but it crashed five minutes after takeoff.

"Is this where they have legalized pot?"

Jason laughed. "That's a touchy subject in Amsterdam. I understand coffee shops sell it, and they are not shut down, but the growers can't grow it legally."

"Sounds like a mess."

"It is a mess," Jason said. "But Amsterdam is beautiful."

The plane was manufactured in France by Airbus, which provided no angle for US court involvement, but I called Oscar and Tom anyway. We had a phone meeting on speaker.

"Go for it," Tom said. "Not sure if a treaty is involved. I'll check it out. I'll handle my end. You sign them up."

That's all I needed to hear. This would be different from cases where the aircraft was manufactured in the United States. When US-built planes were involved, local lawyers and family members of victims often responded to the pitch that their case could get into a US courtroom, where compensation tended to be higher than anywhere on the globe.

"You make it sound so easy."

Oscar was loud and cheerful. "It's easy. You're the best there is."

I wasn't sure if I should thank him. The best ambulance chaser? I let it pass.

Jo normally handled bookings, but there was a lot of prep work to do. I had Oscar's travel agent book the flight for the team and me. Tom was buried in ongoing cases, so the team and I assisted in preparing the retainers applicable to this case and arranging the proper updates to the aviation public relations booklet that introduced Oscar's firm.

Juan said he'd be on a plane the next day.

"Once you are there, hire a private investigator to help you out. I don't know how the people are in Amsterdam. You should have a local with you. But do not bother the families. It's too soon."

"Okay, boss. I find someone. Don't worry. I know about respect to the families."

Three days later, Juan had arrived in Amsterdam, but we were still in Los Angeles.

On the speakerphone, Jason told me details not yet released to the public.

"There are sixty-seven decedents from Amsterdam and the surrounding areas. Sixteen from Libya, thirty-one from Russia, three from France, and one from Italy. One hundred eighteen plus eight crew.

"Jason, you are my hero. Thank you."

"I sent you the manifest with all details on each family this morning, express. You will have it day after tomorrow."

"Perfect. We'll have it a day before we leave."

Melina agreed to have dinner with me that night. I was surprised because it meant she had to leave her office at six in the afternoon instead of eleven p.m.. I kidded her about it as we took our seats.

"My aunt would be looking for reasons why you accepted the invitation for dinner," I said. "Whenever I do something out of the ordinary for her, she jumps on it like Baretta."

"Down, boy. You can put Baretta away. I was hungry."

"And not hungry the last hundred times I invited you?"

She poked me in the shoulder. Not a gentle move. She looked fantastic in some kind of shiny beaded thing—black cloth, but the beads sewn on it shimmered even in the dimmed light. She had ditched her comfortable work shoes and had stilettos on. It wasn't a mini, but from about mini-length, the beads hung down in a fringe, swinging when she walked and falling aside when she crossed her legs. They made a clinking noise. It was a dress made for dancing. Maybe I would see if she wanted to dance after dinner, if she was in the mood to say yes and there was room on the dancefloor. It was my first time at the Coconut Grove Restaurant downtown at the Ambassador Hotel on Wilshire, convenient to Melina's Echo Park Market.

Coconut trees were placed strategically along the aisles. We passed them and walked downstairs into a low area near where musicians were playing big band music. Everyone was beautifully dressed. I felt sure there were stars in the crowd, but I didn't want to seem like a tourist and look for them.

"What a fantastic place!"

"I knew you'd like it," she said.

We started with Chateau Lafite-Rothschild 1961, a favorite of ours. It took fifteen minutes to let it breathe before the wine steward poured our glasses.

"So you're off to Amsterdam. I went there when I escaped to Europe," she said.

"I've never been."

"You can get laid everywhere, and you can smoke pot legally. Almost legally."

"I'm going over there on a crash. There's not too much fucking around during these trips. We work our asses off." I smiled, knowing she would not believe me. But it was true.

"Asshole. Lies."

We clicked glasses. The band finished a song, and everyone clapped. We clapped too. The lamp's base was a coconut stalk topped with the leaves of a coconut tree, on which the candle and miniature lampshade were nested. I moved the candle from the side into the center of the table, reached over, and took her hand.

"Baby, you are beautiful," I said. "Even that salty mouth of yours."

"I've been working since six this morning. How can I be beautiful?"

"You are beautiful, and you know it, smart ass."

"I'm going to miss you. We hardly fuck anymore."

"We do on Sundays."

"I love our Sundays." She made a funny face. "We are so fucked and weird."

"I know."

"If we don't get married, I have a feeling that Colombian is going to take you away."

It was my turn to make a face. "Please. Camila is a friend." I thought about how I'd been manipulated. "Believe me, you have nothing to worry about."

"Yeah, right."

"Baby, if I married Camila, it would certainly end in divorce and no doubt end my life because her brother would have me killed. I prefer marrying you."

"You mean someday, right?"

I laughed. "Yeah, baby, you and I aren't ready."

"I love you, Mario. Does that make sense?"

The candle at our table cast a golden glow over her features. Her lips were curved in a smile so incandescent that it was like she was the one giving off the light. The glow danced in her eyes, skimmed the lustrous contours of her skin, and broke into a million little shimmers on her dress. The candlelight loved her as much as I did.

"I love you, Melina. Yes, it makes sense to us, right?"

"Right." She drank from her glass. "Fucking great wine."

"Always is, no matter where they serve it."

We looked over the menu. When the waiter arrived, simultaneously we asked for Louisiana jumbo shrimp cocktails, roast prime rib of beef, baked potatoes, and cheesecake. I considered ordering the filet in butter sauce, just to be different.

"Same preferences in bed. Same taste in food. Same taste in wine." I laughed.

"We're so close, we could have been twins."

I laughed. "I don't think I'd do that dress justice." I reached out and took her hand. "Baby. Brother and sister we're not."

Her laugh was like bubbles in champagne. "Right, Cuz."

The shrimp, huge pink and white prawns, came hooked in massive bowls of crushed ice. We dipped them in cocktail sauce and fed them to each other. I nipped her finger just as the waiter arrived with the rare and succulent prime rib. She told the waiter he saved her from being eaten alive.

"That comes later," I said, as wickedly as I was able.

It was a great dinner. I was disappointed when we parted in the parking lot. I tried convincing her to come with me.

"I'm going back to the market. I left a mess," Melina said. "I changed and left my clothes all over the office. If you need a ride, Johnson can take you home."

After two bottles of wine, I was in no shape to drive. I saw Johnson had Melina taken care of.

"Letty brought me," I said, "Letty can take me home."

Melina and I hugged and kissed. I felt like we were both on the edge of asking each other to spend the night, but neither of us took that step that might end in rejection.

"Okay," she said. I wasn't sure what was okay, and was too buzzed to figure it out.

We separated and headed to our separate cars. I was a little drunk, a little hard, a little grouchy, and after that great preamble of a dinner, more than a little disappointed not to be ending up in Melina's bed. I stepped in the back of my car and slammed the door. I think I woke Letty up. She'd been waiting a long time.

"Letty, I'm so fucking sorry you had to wait on me like you did."

She yawned and stretched, then started the car. Unlike Pixie, she talks without looking back.

"Boss, it was no big deal. I made friends with the valet people. I was hit on at least ten times by customers coming to the restaurant. It was kind of fun till I fell asleep."

"I'm an asshole," I said. That's all I remember until she shook me awake in front of Casa Luna.

I got out of the car, still drunk but suddenly wide awake, picked her up, and carried her to the master bedroom. Maybe I was staggering more than walking.

"You are so hot, Letty. So good to me," I said. I left my clothes all over the room, fell on the mattress, and was soon asleep, alone in the bed when Melina let herself in.

"You came," I said, delighted to see her as she slipped between my sheets wrapped in a tiny silk camisole like a Christmas gift.

"Not yet." She laughed softly and snuggled next to me. It was a night for cuddling, and I hugged her close. "I didn't think I'd find you alone. I thought Letty would be here."

"I think she was."

Melina laughed at me. "You're funny when you're tanked, mister. Go to sleep."

"Later. Got some things to do first."

She stopped laughing. "Mmm."

Our flight to Amsterdam stopped in New York and Luxenberg, which wasted hours of flight time. Too much time wasted doing nothing. Not enough time to leave the airport to do something. We had made it to the first-class lounge at Luxenberg Airport waiting to board the last leg of our trip—fortunately a short flight. I couldn't help thinking of the time we'd save if we had flown on one of Pepe's big planes. We filled the time with talk of strategy.

The Amstel Hotel we checked into fronted the Amstel river's east bank and was thirty minutes from the three hotels where the airline had put the families. The rooms were posh in an old-style way, with lots of toile wallpaper, with real wood where there would be Formica back home. Adjoining rooms.

"What a waste of money," Pixie complained. "Why do we each need a room?"

"You need to get your rest every day. You know the drill. This is not a vacation in Acapulco," Jo snapped, so I didn't have to.

Fewer rooms would have been cheaper, but we might be here awhile. At least this way there was a bathroom for each of us, and our own beds to sleep in. With enough room to move around in, we wouldn't get on each other's nerves if we got pressured. The eating and meetings would be in my suite, as usual. We all had the river view, but the suite had tall ceilings and floor-to-ceiling windows. Prints of famous Dutch painters hung in all the suites, all very realistic and precise. The bed had floor-to-ceiling drapes that made me feel like I was in a cocoon.

Juan met us at the hotel and introduced us to Andy, a local private investigator who spoke so-so English. He was young, and I could tell he was hungry. Jo gave Juan a copy of the manifest that included the families' contact information.

"Do you have a lawyer you plan to contact?" Juan asked.

"Jason didn't have anyone he could refer, so we're on our own."

"I have lawyers that send me business," Andy said, "but I don't believe they handle aviation cases."

Tom had impressed on me when we first started in international aviation that it was best to connect with a local lawyer.

"I don't care if they are experienced aviation attorneys. I just need them to help us get the families to hire them, and they associate with us or the other way around."

"I will find a lawyer," Juan said. "Andy will help. We have the details of where the bodies are being taken for identification, and other information that may help us once you start going to the hotels where the families are."

"Great," I said. No question that Juan knew the business by now.

"I have a strange feeling about Amsterdam. It's not a Latin country. I wonder if we will bond with the families as we have with other families in other countries."

Andy nodded. "Our people are very suspicious of foreigners and anyone that offers to help them."

I nodded in agreement as if I knew this already. I didn't know it, but it was exactly what I feared.

"Maybe I'll just have to resort to my old ways," Pixie said with a shimmy of her hips. "To collect signatures."

"Don't be so crude. These families are suffering," Niley said. "They are no joke."

"Kidding."

"You weren't kidding," Jo said.

It reminded me of Tanis. I'd never known if she was kidding when she said something like that, either.

Andy and Juan found me three attorneys who seemed interested at first, but were so fucking square they turned me down. No matter how I explained it, they believed having meetings, whether group or one-on-one with the family members, was a form of soliciting. They wouldn't do it.

"Hypocrites."

I reported my meeting failures. My team was sympathetic and encouraging. "Lawyers refuse to help families who need our help, but they don't have a qualm about smoking a joint in a café or walking the red zone to find a paid sex partner to get laid or sucked off."

"Boss, I love the way you put that," Pixie said.

"Is Juan working on finding more attorney prospects?" Niley asked.

"He is," Jo said.

"Tomorrow is another day," Niley said.

While I was with the lawyers, the girls had checked out the three hotels.

"How did your day go?" I waited for them to report. They had done a walk-through to see if family members were visible.

"They have badges like in other cases," Jo confirmed. "They are easy to spot."

"The badge gets them free food and all that," Niley said.

We'd eaten dinner, but it was too early to turn in. Failure had pushed my sex drive into overdrive. The girls collected the comforters and blankets from their beds and placed them on the expensive tapestry carpeting in the living room. We lay on it like a giant bed, lined up side by side like sardines in a can, flat on our backs, staring at the painted frescoed ceiling. Pixie was so excited, she was shimmering.

She said, "Now this is fucking cool. I expected another no-sex trip, again. We're going to have a blast." She giggled that hoarse, sexy giggle I loved so much.

"We're just going to lay here," I said. "No one said anything about sex."

Everyone was quiet for about ten seconds. But the girls rolled over, one by one, and stared at me like I'd grown an extra head.

"What?" I asked, keeping a straight face, and looking from one impish face to the next.

The girls took their pillows and started beating me up with them. They had long experience single-, double-, and triple-teaming me in pillow fights. Their teamwork was intricate and practiced, and they cheated with their growing knowledge of karate. When I saw this playful side of them, I think I fell in love with them all over again. I could have taken charge, but instead I covered my face and let them have the upper hand. I was laughing so hard that all I could do was laugh more and hold my stomach. We laughed until we cried tears, rolling around helplessly, and whenever it seemed like it was over, one of them started it up again, until there was a knock at our door.

"Room service."

Niley hopped up, but she was bent over, still laughing.

"It's the wine I ordered earlier," she gasped. "And a whole bunch of snacks. That joint I had at the café gave me a crazy case of the munchies."

Not a timely interruption. I remembered two things simultaneously, the red wine the room service supervisor recommended so highly, and the time that the Colombian goons knocked on the door.

Everyone was still laughing, but at the knock, they looked at me. I dashed into one of the other bedrooms and peeked down the hall at a couple of hotel-uniformed teenagers pushing a cart full of food. I ran back.

"No worries, babies," I said in a stage whisper. "We're not in Venezuela."

Pixie was laughing so hard she couldn't stand up. She crawled a few feet, pulled up on my bedroom door, and said, "C'mon in here, you guys. We probably shouldn't shock the Amsterdamians too much."

"Amsterdamians? Amsterdamites?" Jo laughed.

"Amsterbedamned," Pixie said.

We staggered, tumbled, and rolled out, and left the makeshift bed on the living room floor as Niley put on a hotel robe and opened the door for room service. We waited, listening, as the feast was laid out, then Niley opened the door, laughing at us.

"You should have seen the expression on his face," Niley told us after he left.

We returned to play on our giant floor-bed. Although it was two in the morning before we dismantled it and found our own beds, by eight, we were showered, dressed, and eating breakfast in my suite, ready for another day.

Juan arrived alone and sat down to drink coffee with us. "I have another attorney," he said. "Your appointment is at ten. She doesn't sound too convinced."

"We shall see about that," I said with a positive tone like I would work magic, though I still had that feeling of doom. "Jo, you take one of the hotels. Pixie and Niley take the other two. Walk around, make friends. You know what to do."

"Got it, boss."

I reminded them. "Do not pass out business cards."

"Boss, please," Pixie shot back like I had just insulted her.

"Snotty bitch," Niley said.

"I'd bitch slap you, only you ate me so good last night, I'll let it slide."

"Let's get serious," I said, watching Juan turning red. Maybe I was making a mistake cutting sex way back on these business trips. We were all in a great mood this morning.

The attorney, Anika Vos, was a middle-aged, good-sized woman, blonde with straight hair, no makeup, and no fuss.

"Mr. Luna. Pleased to meet you. Do have a seat." She shook hands with me, then Juan. "I met Mr. Reyes yesterday afternoon."

"The pleasure is mine. Your English is great."

"Everyone in Amsterdam speaks English, Mr. Luna."

"I just got here to Amsterdam. My first trip here. I didn't realize it, but that's great." I felt like such a fucking dummy. Juan should have told me. Instead he'd made it sound like we needed interpreters for Dutch and West Frisian, the official languages.

I handed Anika a brochure of Oscar's law firm.

"Mr. Reyes gave me a brochure yesterday, and I reviewed it. Impressive. The firm has handled many plane crashes around the world. What exactly are you looking to do here?"

"We want to represent families of victims against the insurance carriers of the airline operator."

An assistant served us coffee and pastries. Anika was pleasant enough, but she just wasn't interested. She was calm, not rushed. She asked questions and patiently listened to my answers.

"Mr. Luna, I can't approach families that live here in Holland unless they call and ask me to meet with them. We don't do consulting that way." It was the same story I'd gotten the day before from the three lawyers I met.

A few minutes later, we left. I was not used to striking out. Four strikes in less than two days. It wasn't even noon. I was frustrated, but not giving up.

"Let's take a taxi to one of the hotels," I told Juan.

"Andy is over there. We can catch up to him. He's just testing the water, same as the girls."

I entered the Holiday Inn, one of the three hotels where the airline had placed the families. I didn't know which of the girls was at this hotel and had no way to find out because our pagers only worked in the Los Angeles area. The hotel lobby was chilly, and most of the people I saw were in sweaters, coats, and jackets. I felt wrongly dressed in my three-piece suit. I sent Juan to find more lawyers, and to get rid of Andy if he wasn't producing. As I walked around, I saw badges on a number of men, women, and some older children sitting here and there.

I took a taxi back to the hotel, changed to jeans, a great Versace shirt, an Armani shearling three-quarter-length jacket, and Vans tennis shoes. I felt and looked relaxed. When I returned to the hotel, I spotted Pixie talking to a young man and girl, older than teens, maybe a young couple. Both had badges. She spotted then ignored me. No telling what she was up to, but it was obvious she didn't need my help.

At home, the typical Holiday Inn is one self-contained unit. This hotel had multiple buildings, two full-service bars in the lobby, lots of seating, and at least three restaurants. In the hotel tobacco shop, I purchased a London newspaper, sat down in the lobby on a comfortable leather chair, and a waiter served me a glass of red wine. I was in no hurry. I would do this every day until my face became familiar. If all the families were in one hotel, it would have been easier, but you don't always get what you wish for. My team would handle the other hotels, doing something similar.

I finished my wine, paid the bill, and resumed my walk around the hotel. I didn't want to appear to be disrespectful of the tragedy, but I'm a people person and showed it, saying hello to anyone that met my gaze or crossed my path. I passed by where I had last seen Pixie, but she was nowhere around, and I didn't see the couple either. At three in the afternoon, I took a cab to our hotel, beating everyone home. I put on a hotel robe and found the spa, where I took a sauna, steam, shower, and a ninety-minute massage. No comparison to Betty's hands, but it was good. I made my attendant feel like she was the best ever, and showed my appreciation by giving her a fifty for a tip.

Pixie was the only one there when I got back to my suite. Housekeeping had come and gone, and it was spotless. She was excited.

"Boss, I think I'm going to sign those two you saw me with."

"Great. Why did you shine me on?"

"I was just getting to know them. They're college students. We connected right away."

"Pixie, that's great. Sit down. Tell me about it."

She sat, but once she got started talking, she popped up again. She had on some clothing layers that she shed as she was walking. Jacket. Scarf. She sat down to toss aside her heels and went back to pacing, talking the whole time, describing every minute of the encounter.

"They lost their brother, an unmarried doctor who was paying their way through college."

I stopped her now that she'd come to important details. "Any other heirs?"

"No other family. Martino and Angela Urbano, twenty-one and twenty-two. From Milan."

"Jason said there was one Italian."

"That's him. Alessandro Urbano, the decedent."

Pixie memorized anything she thought was important, which I found impressive. She no longer used a tape recorder anymore and seldom took the notes that Jo wanted her to.

"So now what?"

"So now you fuck me."

"Baby, come on. What's the plan?"

"Tomorrow I'm going to meet them for lunch. Their English is good. They have the booklets on the firm. I'm telling you, boss, we hit it off. They like me."

I put my arm around her. "Can you blame them?" I kissed her cheek, then her lips. She put her arms around me.

"Boss, I miss the one-on-ones we used to have."

"Baby, I'm always here for you."

That might have gone somewhere, but then Niley announced herself walking from her room through the other connecting rooms.

"Anyone home?"

"We're in the suite."

Jo followed a little while later. Everyone reported a good day, but the best news was Pixie being on the verge of signing the brother and sister. Juan reported that he fired Andy and made an appointment for me the next day at eleven with a lawyer who might just be interested. I had my fingers crossed.

I told Tom about our lawyer issues. "It's not like we need a local lawyer, but as you always say, it's best we have one. I just don't think it's going to happen. I've met four so far, and they all have the same attitude."

Tom said, "Let's play it by ear. We really don't need local counsel."

"English is one of the official languages, so at least language is not a barrier."

The next morning, we all carried retainers. I don't like the team carrying briefcases unless we have meetings set up in advance with family members. We were still just getting started.

"When I get home tonight, I will have at least one retainer," Pixie announced. We showed our support with a high-five for Pixie.

In my three-piece suit, I met the attorney as scheduled; but after thirty minutes, I knew it was going to be an uphill climb with no end in sight. Point blank, he was not interested in associating with a US attorney and balked at the idea of meeting clients who had not requested his services in advance. I was getting used to this. The lawyers here were turning out to be a total letdown. I put my overcoat back on and headed out into the cold of Amsterdam. Amsterdam was a frigid bitch in more ways than one.

Juan was disappointed, but he went off determined to find an interested lawyer. I made an appearance at the Holiday Inn, then took a cab to the Hyatt, one of the other hotels where family members were staying. I did not see Niley, who was at this hotel. The lobby was warm, and I checked my coat at the desk. I spotted a few family members with their badges. Some were in groups, talking. I saw several who were distraught, quietly crying with each other. I kept walking, then took a seat in the lobby, ordered a Coca-Cola and picked up an English newspaper from the newspaper table. As I started to read the first page, I looked up and saw a dark-skinned woman about my age.

"I'm sorry to disturb. Are you a lawyer?"

I stood. "No, I'm not a lawyer." I extended my hand and introduced myself. The lady had a firm handshake. She introduced herself as Aya.

"Can I help you in any way?"

"I think I need a lawyer. You are so dressed up. I thought you were one."

"I'm a consultant for a law firm in the United States."

I wished that I had not left my booklets in the pocket of my coat.

"I don't think I need a lawyer in the United States. The crash is here."

I told her how we handle cases all over the world, and the experience the law firm had with insurance carriers that insured airlines such as the one that crashed here in Amsterdam.

"Can I get you something to drink?" I lifted my cola in her direction.

She shivered and said, "Thank you. Hot tea would be lovely."

Aya was from Libya. She stirred a bit of sugar in her tea, sipped it, and made a face.

"Very weak," she said.

I was a little surprised when she reached in her purse and pulled out a packet of airline peanuts and poured them in her tea. Judging by her expression, I guessed that must be some kind of Libyan comfort food.

She talked. She told me how her mother had died in the crash. As in almost every case we ever had, the airline had brought her from Libya to join the other families of the tragedy. She told me how her father was too heartbroken to come.

"My mother was fifty-six."

"I'm so very sorry about your loss, Aya."

Tears ran down her face. She swiped at her eye with a paper napkin. I pulled out a fresh handkerchief, and she used it and handed it back. I let her keep it. I had a stack of them.

"My mother had a jewelry business. She always came to Europe to buy for her shop."

After we talked for a long time, we walked to the desk. I retrieved my coat and gave her the booklet. As we stood there, she thumbed through it, looking at pictures of planes from previous cases. She glanced at the summaries of the cases. I could see how the booklet reassured her.

"How do I reach you if I want to talk to you again?"

I wrote my hotel number on the back of the brochure.

Without ever seeing Niley, I left the hotel. Back at the Amstel, I followed my new routine: sauna, steam, and massage. This time I got a pretty young blonde in spandex who positioned herself on my back while she worked on my neck and shoulders. She wasn't naked, but it felt like she was. I got turned on.

When I returned from the spa, no one was back yet.

Niley and Jo arrived empty-handed. I gave them some encouragement. Truth is, I felt positive about the day, even if wasn't sure I would get Aya to sign a retainer. After the nay-saying lawyers here, it felt good that I'd had an opportunity to talk to a family member about what we do. Normally I wouldn't have just done so, cold, but it had been my good luck that Aya had walked up to me.

"I think we're rushing. That's not how we do it. It's only been days since the crash. We need to just walk around and get to know the families. It may take days—weeks, even."

Jo and Niley nodded in agreement.

Pixie was the last one to get back, and she walked in beaming and waving a retainer over her head. I wondered if Pixie had had sex to get that retainer from the Urbano brother. It was entirely possible.

She did a grito that was likely to have the hotel sending someone to see if we were okay and danced around like a cross between a flamenco dancer and Suzi Quatro. She tore off her layers, flinging them wildly, including her shoes. Jo followed behind, picking up, and Pixie stuck her tongue out at her.

"The ice is broken! I got one signed!" She got on the couch and started jumping up and down like a happy kid. Jo put down the clothes in a neat pile, and she and Niley joined her. Getting that first signature is what it's all about. It's the lever, the game-changer, the connection. They're all like skiing downhill after that first one. There was a good chance that our having signed a client or two would seduce some lawyer for us. I was as happy about it as the girls, but if I jumped on the couch, my head would end up stuck through the ceiling like one of the three stooges. I sat back on the sofa they weren't abusing and enjoyed the show.

"Come here, baby. Let me see that retainer."

"Not until I get a fuck."

"What a mouth," Jo growled. She must not have been too bothered, because she didn't stop jumping.

"Okay, come over here," I said. "I'll fuck you."

One minute, Pixie was wearing leggings, and the next, they were on two opposite sides of the suite. The short skirt she was wearing went flying off in one direction. The coat fell behind the couch. She tossed off the scarf, and it landed over my bedroom door. The panties went flying somewhere. She practically jumped to where I was seated and was on me in a heartbeat, still unfastening her top. She tugged it over her head. Apparently she'd worked today without a bra.

Jo and Niley were wide-eyed. I was conveniently still in my hotel robe, so clothing was no impediment. She gave me her back and sat on me, facing the girls, her hips gyrating and moving faster and faster.

"Fucking aerobics," Niley said.

"Next time, keep the leggings on," Jo said. She started counting off like a coach. "And one, and two—"

"Fuck you both. You're just jealous."

Pixie is quick. She was so fast that I was mentally prepared for them all to line up for the same treatment, but probably lucky that was just a fantasy I could finish in my head at my convenience.

The next afternoon, Aya signed. When I came back to the hotel, no one was there, but I was all smiles. You'd think it was my first case.

Pixie showed with a retainer signed by Angela Urbano. She made no demands, just bragged about how she was the best ambulance chaser of all time, conceding second place to me. I picked her up, kissed her, then rocked her like a baby in my arms.

"Proud of you, baby."

Pixie had been responsible for more signed retainers than I could count, but these first cases were a big break, creating an opening for us in Amsterdam where I couldn't get a lawyer to work with us.

Two days later, the body of their brother was released to our two Italian clients. The team and I attended a solemn service held at the crematorium in a room hung with purple curtains and windows hung with purple sheers. Foot-tall candles surrounding the casket mounted on six silver waist-high candlesticks were lit during the ceremony. All was incomprehensible in Dutch and Italian, but it was moving anyway. We were all brought to tears. A riser in the room's center first held a casket, then the urn with the ashes. There were sixteen of us attending, all seated in yellow armchairs, all facing the riser, all looking like they had been plucked from someone's modern den. I had plenty of time to memorize the look of the small chapel while the body was cremated. Floor-to-ceiling windows, slate tile floors, twelve recessed ceiling lights, low ceilings. Really, the only people in attendance were my team, me, and our clients. The other nine were family members who had befriended our clients, and who would soon be having their own cremations. Pixie and I sat on either side of Martino and Angela, holding hands for an hour straight. Niley and Pixie sat across the way with the other mourners, listening to sad stories. It ended with the Dutch priest handing the urn with Alessandro Urbano's ashes to Martino and Angela. Pixie and I were in a car with the Urbanos, but I had a moment in passing with Jo, who had visited the bathroom to fix makeup smeared by tears.

"You look like you could use a hug," I told her.

She nodded.

"These services always kill me. It's like burying 'Nando all over again." She hung on for only an instant, then pushed away. I could see she had pulled herself together and was ready to rejoin the families she was connecting with.

"For me, it's Tanis," I said. "I missed that service." I'd been in the hospital, out of it at the time, not knowing if Tanis had made it or not.

"Me too." She gave me a wobbly smile and went to join her group in the other car.

I took everyone, including the other families at the cremation, to lunch at our hotel. Alessandro Urbano's brother and sister were charming, easygoing, and vulnerable. I could tell why Pixie found them so likable and had connected with them. It was a subdued meal where we all listened as the families remembered their loved ones. Several days later, we signed three of them. We'd only known them a few days, but they felt like old friends.

Jo signed a Parisian mom who lost a daughter and son. Niley brought in three retainers signed by a widow who had lost teenaged sons in addition to her husband. Pixie's young college friends helped her get to five more families they had gotten to know at the hotel.

"I got all five signed." She beamed. "And you don't need to fuck me until you want me."

After nearly a month in Amsterdam, I paid Juan. He returned to Valita in

Puerto Rico. I still remembered Valita and how we did it through the iron door when I was locked up in that warehouse.

On our last day, I called Pepe and left a message that I would call him from Los Angeles. I reached Camila, who was not happy with me.

"*Amor*, you were in Amsterdam a month and never bothered to call. I left you so many messages in Los Angeles. *Eres tan malo*."[36]

"I was busy on this one. Forgive me. You aren't really mad at me, are you?"

She paused, making me wait for the answer, and then said, "*Amor*, I could never be mad at you."

"Thanks, baby. Where are you?"

"Geneva."

"Ouch. Cold?"

"Yes, it's cold."

"I hope you and Olga are keeping warm."

"She's plenty warm in Madrid."

"Someday you'll have to tell me why you travel around so much."

As soon as I said it, I wanted to pull the words back inside, to make the words unsaid. I wondered why that had come out of my mouth.

"*Amor*, of course, I have no secrets from you."

That, I didn't believe.

The whole case in Amsterdam had been a slow process, but I was happy. A single case would have covered thirty days of the expenses we encountered. We called it quits after twenty-seven days and forty-three retainers. Only two were from Holland. It was puzzling, frustrating, and unbelievable how we struck out with the Dutch families. I blamed myself. My negative thinking. Maybe it began even before when I asked Juan to find a local private investigator. I wanted to pin down the exact problem, but I would never know. The girls and I talked about it in three different lounges, in three different airports, and it was the main topic of

---

[36] You're so mean

conversation on the way home.

"Boss, we did good. Don't beat yourself up," Jo said.

"I agree, baby. I'm not beating myself up." Even after I assured her, I still puzzled over it.

The trip with its three layovers felt like forever to get home. I kept thinking of the cabin with a big bed and realized the first-class seat I was in just wasn't good enough. Oscar spoiled me with his Learjet, Camila spoiled me with her big jets, and now that's what I wanted. It was like Pixie when she discovered lobster, when she swore she was going to quit wasting her eating on anything else. Of course, that resolution only lasted till the next course, when she had her first taste of fried ice cream. I dozed off now and again, and each time during the trip I dreamed I was in my own big jet. The drive to have my own jet is going to be harder to shake than Pixie's taste for lobster. And the price tag for owning and maintaining one was a hell of a lot more than lobster and fried iced cream. When I dreamed about owning big jets, I did not dream about paying for their crews, gas, and daily up-keep.

Melina sent Johnson to pick us up. He delivered me to Pasadena, then took Jo, Pixie, and Niley to their homes. Our suitcases filled the trunk and the passenger seat. I didn't realize we had done that much shopping.

Letty was like a happy wife. She greeted me at the door and hugged and kissed me.

"I missed you, boss, so fucking much."

"I missed you too, Pixie."

"Boss, I'm Letty."

"I know, but you talk like Pixie."

"Does it really bother you?" A look of concern lifted her eyebrows and tilted the corners of her eyes. She put her left hand over her mouth. It was like a shadow fell over her bright face. I wanted to see that smile of hers again.

I kissed her. "It doesn't bother me."

We ran all the way to the spa. I turned on the sauna, the steam bath, the hot spa, and the ice spa. Behind me, candles flickered to life everywhere. Letty turned down the lights and blew out the candle she'd used. We stepped into a shower and played with the soap. I was glad that Letty was here to greet me. If Letty weren't here, I'd feel how alone I am. Sure, I had Miguel, my chef, Chete and Caro Garza, and Memo and Yoli Munoz, but Miguel, the Garzas, and the Munozes were help. They did nothing to ease my loneliness. Letty's being there for me filled up the empty places.

Sunday, I spent the day at Melina's. Right off, she let me know. "I'm so hot and horny."

We spent two hours in the bedroom before we hit the brunch her chef prepared for us. Normally, we ate, then retired to the bedroom.

Afterward, I said, "Tell me you haven't had sex since I last saw you."

She gave me the finger and a smile. "Betty takes care of me. Now you tell me."

I grinned. "You know, I get mine."

"Asshole. I thought you said no fucking on business trips."

I sighed like a comedian, with sound effects. "I lied."

"Asshole."

"Truth is, we haven't, not since I don't know when. I'm not one to kiss and tell. But there were a couple times in Amsterdam when those vixens had their way with me." I shifted the subject to her exploits. "No question, Betty is good. I got a massage yesterday. The massages in Amsterdam were nothing by comparison."

"Does Betty give you happy endings? Do you fuck her?"

"I've told you before, no sex with Betty."

"Lies."

She crossed her arms and pouted at me. I leaned over and bit her lower lip. Not too hard. But it was looking very bitable.

"You should have been a movie star with all the drama. Like you really care."

Melina stuck out her tongue.

"I do care."

It was my turn to say "Lies."

Over brunch, I was more serious. We were on a balcony overlooking the outdoors, sitting shoulder to shoulder so we both had the view. I tried to advance the subject with her. "Good thing I have Letty. I come home to an empty house. It's hard. I have days when I really feel lonely."

"Get out more. You never go out."

"I could, and I do. You don't know it because you're at the market working late. It's not about going out. It's about coming home to no one."

She met my eyes squarely. "You've been gone a month. That's more than four Sundays of coming home to no one. And that includes every other day of the month, too."

I was quiet. I put down my fork. I stopped eating and faced her instead of my plate. "You're right. It's just that I keep picturing us as one. You and me. Crazy, but I do."

"But the feeling is only short lived, right?" She forced out a little laugh but didn't sound amused.

"Yeah, you got that right. It ends when I walk into my empty house and lie down in my empty bed, when I have to call in a woman I don't love; not like that, anyway."

"I'm the same," she said. "I lie down on this bed alone. It is so empty. The only thing that fills it is knowing you're there, even if you are out of sight. Even if I don't come to you. Even knowing Letty is in your arms. At least we have our Sundays now. What's to say if we married that we would even have that much? And we'd argue. I just know it."

"We never really argue."

"That's because we're not married, Cuz."

"I think I'll get seconds." I got up. I saw she was out of frozen fruit salad and decided I'd grab some for her. "You're right, baby."

"And you better not marry anyone else," she warned. "Not without fair warning."

I returned to the table. She noticed my plate.

"I thought you said that fruit concoction was too sweet?"

"It is," I said. "This is for you."

I doled it onto her plate.

For myself, I had gotten seconds of a spicy casserole her chef specialized in, even though I'd used up the salsa I liked with it. Then one of her kitchen staff knocked on the door, delivering more of that sauce. She must have ordered it when I wasn't paying attention. She looked from our dishes to me, her eyes deep and brown and unfathomable. I could see the glimmer of tears, and the corners of her mouth curling into a smile. We were both trying to make each other happy, even in the little things.

I thought of my team. They were my extended family. If I had to choose a wife who was not Melina, who would I choose? My first thought was Camila. Then Olga floated past my mind's eye. But that's just dreaming. I know my infatuations. I wasn't wanting to tie myself to mysterious women with secret agendas. My dream girls are to travel with, to have fun with, and then I return home. There is a difference, I'm certain, between love and infatuation. Love means lives that are lived together, and woven together by shared history that is sacred and unbreakable.

Chapter 23
March 1978
Easter

I was never big on Easter. For Jo, Pixie, and Niley, it was like Christmas. They spent it with their kids and family. Pixie and Lainey spent Easter at my aunt's. Aunt Carmen always hoped I'd show up, but she settled quietly for my absence when I told her I was going to church. For sure, I hated to lie to my aunt, but I had so much church as a kid that it was enough for the rest of my life. I believe in God, but I'm pretty sure God has better things to do than follow me around, measuring me with my own personal yardstick.

I accepted an invitation to spend Easter with Camila in Rome. Pepe wasn't sure where he'd be, but he encouraged me to spend a few days there. He'd never mentioned the Bahamas to me, and that was good.

Pixie wasn't happy that I was going on a vacation without her and the team, but I gave them a week's notice. By the time my trip was three days away, Pixie was resigned to being at my aunt's without my being there. I knew she'd go for Lainey's sake.

The night before I left, I had a little talk with Letty.

"Take off somewhere. Get on a plane. Go to Frisco or anywhere. My treat."

"Boss, I got practically all the money you've paid me since I started in the bank." She giggled. "I've got it covered. But if it's okay with you, I'll just stay here and housesit till you get back. I adore this house. I don't need to go anywhere."

Letty drove me to Van Nuys Airport. I was there at eleven on the dot, as planned.

"Love you," I said after kissing her.

"Love you more, boss," she replied. A Jo line.

No one greeted me at Van Nuys. I went right through the lounge to the tarmac. There was the DC9, a big hose between the wing of the plane and a fuel truck. I ran up the airstairs, poked my head in the open door, and walked in. The temperature in the plane was perfect.

"Anyone home?"

"Hey, stranger," Olga's happy voice rang out. She emerged from the rear galley, running towards me wearing fitted black silk pajamas and matching comfy slippers. She was a vision straight out of *Playboy* or a lingerie ad, with her long, straight hair, slim waist, and lithe figure.

"Hey back," I said, opening my arms to catch her. We were past European kisses on the cheeks, but we started with those and rapidly progressed to more interesting varieties. She kissed with gusto, reminding me of when we'd both been in bed with Camila.

"So where's Camila?"

"Waiting for you in Rome."

"I thought she'd be here."

Olga tried to take my suitcase, but I resisted and heaved it to an overhead compartment.

"I'll take good care of you until we get to Rome," she promised. She took my hand and led me to a seat a few feet away. The configuration on this plane was similar, with a seat in front of where she parked me and a window on either side of the seats. "This is a different plane?"

"*Si*, this is the plane I use when I'm doing errands."

"I didn't know you had your own plane."

"I only wish it was my plane. You'll love the bed linen."

"Promise?"

"Yes, I promise. Let me get you a drink. Wine?"

"Sure, I'll have a glass."

She took off for the galley. As soon as she left, a girl showed up, startling me. I'd really thought Olga and I were alone on the plane, except for the pilots. She was young, and pretty, and the belted bright blue uniform she was wearing was closer to a shirt than a dress. She reached up and secured the compartment that held my suitcase. I saw bright blue matching shorts underneath. I tried to recover my cool from the surprise of her appearance.

"My name is Luciana, and you are Mr. Luna. Pleased to meet you." Her English had a lovely Italian accent. Part of me melted, and another part got hard. I got up and shook hands.

"Mr. Luna was my stepfather. My name is Mario."

"Nice to meet you, Mario." She handed me a pair of pajamas identical to Olga's. And slippers. "We had a dozen made just for you."

"How nice. Thank you."

Olga emerged from the galley with two glasses and a bottle of wine.

"Good. You two met. Luciana has been assisting me for the last two weeks during this trip. She will be with us to Rome."

"Excuse me," Luciana said, disappearing into the front of the plane. The airstairs were disengaged. Five minutes later, Olga and I were seated, seat belts on, each with a glass of wine in hand. I leaned forward as did she. Our glasses clicked.

A man's voice came on the PA system. "Miss Olga and guest, we will be pulling back now. Please fasten your seat belts."

I was still holding the pajamas.

"Going to put those on?" Olga asked.

I held the pajama bottoms in front of me, surprised how they fell to the proper length. I was out of my clothes in a flash. I stepped into the bottoms, and they fit perfectly. Had to be made to order. The slippers too.

"I knew they would be a perfect fit," she said, already buckled up.

As I sat down, Luciana hustled to pick up my clothes, boxers, and shoes. I couldn't help comparing this to being in first class. Couldn't quite imagine standing in the open on a commercial plane and stripping down. I have a good imagination, but couldn't picture the commercial stewardess picking up my underwear from the floor while wearing a smile and a bright blue uniform that barely covered her frilly blue ass.

"I just got back from Amsterdam. Hated it. Flew first class. I've always loved first class."

Olga gave me a knowing smile. "You are spoiled now. You like that big bed on these Camacho jets."

I nodded and raised my glass as she did.

"I am spoiled." I admit it. And I like it.

"I like being with you, Mario. I missed you."

"I think of you all the time," I said.

"Me or Camila?"

"Both of you. I think of you as my dream girls."

"I'm jealous," she said.

"Of what?"

"I want to be your dream girl."

"Believe me, you are."

I'd never had so much time with Olga before.

She told me all about herself. Without revealing what role he played in the cartel business, she said her father had worked for Camila's dad. Whatever he did for them was important enough that when his death left Olga an orphan at fourteen, she moved into the big house in Bogota with the Camacho family, where she was treated as a second daughter, though never formally adopted. She was two and a half years younger than Camila, which made her a few months older than me. Since her father died, Olga had lived in the Camacho family home, and she grew up with Camila as a little sister. Pepe put Olga through college studying international business. Two years in London, two in New York. When she was done, she was fluent in four languages in addition to Spanish. She returned to Bogota to put her education to work with Pepe and Camila.

"Camila never made me feel unwanted or unloved. I promised that I would never leave them. They saved me by taking me in. I will be forever grateful."

I could never repeat any of this, though I wondered if Camila wanted me to know and asked Olga to tell me. Or maybe Olga just trusted me. After all, we had already been there when two people were killed in the Bahamas. It wasn't like we weren't already sharing secrets.

We talked across the US, all the way to the fueling stop in New York. She had shared a lot of answers to questions I hadn't been asking, but I suppose Camila had told her it was okay to talk to me. Or maybe it was because I was keeping her glass filled. I'd never really seen her doing much drinking before. It was proving to be a very revealing flight.

"So you know about international business," I said. "It must help your work."

She nodded. "Camacho businesses have many banks worldwide. When I travel alone, I'm headed to a bank somewhere to make a deposit or attend to some other banking business. Usually when I travel with Camila, we're headed to close a deal she's already arranged. I deliver the money to close the deal."

I nodded without revealing my feelings. I had two million sitting in my safe. Banks tracked that kind of cash. Camacho business didn't include working with banks that refused or tracked cash deposits. I got the picture.

"Sounds like fun," I said. I poured her another glass of wine. "You're the banker, kind of."

She looked up, glass in hand, drained it, and held it out for me to fill again. "It keeps me busy. I love the international travel and control I have over the plane. I love buzzing around South America and Europe. I treasure the trust the Camachos have in me. It's like it energizes me."

"South America and Europe. Not the United States?"

"The US has a silly requirement that if you deposit ten thousand dollars or more in cash, the person making the deposit has to fill out a form to the Internal Revenue Office. You can guess how Pepe feels about that."

"Yes, I know," I said, but the truth was that, personally, I didn't know. Personally, I didn't deposit actual cash in my accounts. The management company handled my rental income, and Oscar, of course, pays me by check.

"Some banks outside the United States are getting a little stricter. We don't visit those as often, not more than once a month or even longer."

"You'd think banks would love the money rolling in."

She waved her glass expressively. "If I owned a bank, I would welcome all the money a person wanted to bring me. It used to be that way when Camila's father was alive. The managers we deal with are game, and they get paid very well." For emphasis, she tapped her glass against mine with each word after 'game.'

Though I wouldn't be surprised if Camila had told her to tell me all this, I didn't want to hear more. I felt bad about the wine and put a quick stop to the conversation.

I stood up. "Excuse me. I have to get rid of some of this vino," I said. I made for the lavatory.

Olga giggled. "Okie dokie. English is so funny. Dokie okie." She giggled again.

Luciana appeared for the first time since we had taken off. I took my seat.

"Olga, Mario, we're going to land in New York in about fifteen minutes."

"Thank you," Olga said, collecting her dignity, a mirror image of Camila talking to Olga. "We are fine for now."

I watched Luciana leave. She was attractive, but not on the level of Olga. Olga was a stone-cold fox.

"You like Luciana? I think you like all pretty girls."

"Guilty as charged," I said. I dropped my voice to a whisper. "She's not bad, but she doesn't measure up to you. You're a stone-cold fox."

She grinned. "I agree," she whispered. "She doesn't measure up to you, either. You're a stone-cold fox yourself."

After we took off from New York, Olga and I made our way to the main cabin to check out the bedding that I was supposed to like. Silk sheets and duvet, black like our PJs.

"Can we do this without Camila?" I asked, undressing.

"We're adults and can do anything we please, yes?"

"Yes, we're adults." I wondered if Camila was not jealous. We'd had a threesome, but now, it was just Olga and me and the Atlantic Ocean. No Camila.

Olga reached for a button.

"No," I said, "let me."

Her kiss was wet, unique. We lay down facing each other. I unbuttoned each button with great care, exploring her body as it was revealed.

"You're moving the wrong way," she said. I laughed against the smooth skin of her waist.

The dip between her hip bones.

Her navel.

Her slim torso.

Her perky breasts.

Each stop was a revelation to me, firing my enthusiasm to great heights. I teased her as long as she could stand it before moving from one button to the next. By the time I got to the top, she jerked the pajama blouse open, and the button went flying off to clatter against the wall. It was a moment that would have gotten laughter at home, but Olga was deadly serious. She was ravenous. She pulled me on top of her. I tried holding myself so I wouldn't press against her, but she pulled me down, wanted to feel the weight of my chest. I entered her and she urged me deeper, her legs around my waist.

There was a moment or maybe several moments when I would have married Olga right there and then. Maybe it was the wine, but I don't think so. And it wasn't weed, because there was no joint lit.

Olga disappeared into the palatial Camacho residence in Rome. A servant I did not know carried my suitcase and escorted me to a huge bedroom, newer, larger, and nicer than the one I'd been given before.

"Dinner will be at eight fifteen," he said.

I checked my watch. It was already eight, but the Camachos dined late; Italian hours. I barely had time to shower and change before being escorted to the dining room where Camila greeted me enthusiastically. I waited for her to ask about Olga. She did ask questions, didn't mention Olga, and the questions she did ask threw me for a loop.

"Are you religious?"

"I believe in God," I replied.

"Are you Catholic?"

"I was baptized Catholic and had my first communion like all good Catholic kids. Yes, I'm Catholic. I'm just not a good Catholic."

"Me neither," she said, "but we have two very special seats for Easter Sunday mass at the Vatican. Will you go with me?"

It was the last thing I was expecting. My first thought was that Aunt Carmen was going to be thrilled.

"Absolutely. Thank you."

Two days later, Camila and I were ushered to a second-row seat at Saint Peter's Square for a papal mass by John Paul VI. Three hundred thousand people were standing and sitting behind us.

Easter Sunday mass at the Vatican touched me. I felt everything deeply. The fusion of hymns and harmonies, the familiar litany, the tangible devotion of everyone in attendance, but especially the sermon of a very sick Pope who really held his own throughout the long mass.

On our way home, we were both uncharacteristically quiet.

"Camila, thank you very much for bringing me."

"It's my third time. I know how you feel. We leave here, and we are moved by something, yes?"

I nodded. "Yes."

At her house, it was a feast day. Easter in excess, Roman style. I found it fascinating. Eating, drinking, and then doing it again and again. I spent the time between meals in Camila's gym and spa, trying to sweat out the calories. She had three masseuses on duty, all Italian, none of them measuring up to Betty.

Olga turned up at lunch, the first time I'd seen her since we'd arrived. She'd been around and busy. She did have lunch and dinner with us, but she settled into her daily grind of keeping the personnel of the big houses buzzing. My feelings had shifted. I suddenly had a great deal of affection for Olga. I felt close to Olga, closer than to Camila. But the Vatican trip still increased my infatuation with all things Camacho.

I stayed in Rome a week. Late during Easter Sunday, Pepe called, and after he spoke with Camila, I talked to him. Camila, Olga, and I spent an entire day at the Spanish Steps, then went shopping. It was next to impossible for me to find clothes that fit right off the rack, but shoes were easy. Rome has some fantastic shoemakers, putting me in buying mode.

Camila went into a jewelry store where two clerks greeted her by name. While she and Olga were busy looking at a section of the merchandise, I got busy with another clerk at the opposite side of the shop. I'd seen that Camila and Olga always wore watches, but I'd never noticed whether they each wore only one, or if they rotated different watches. It didn't matter. I needed to give them something, and their favorite brand of timepiece was a better selection than menswear. I selected two Rolexes, one for Camila, one for Olga, paid, and brought the boxes with me.

Camila was looking at diamond rings. Time and again, she'd select something, put it on, but once she put it on her finger, she didn't like it any more.

"No luck?" I asked.

"Nothing is just right," she said. "*Es un pecado comprar mas joyas cuando tengo una caja fuerte llena.*"[37]

I handed my dream girls each the unwrapped box with their watches, each with a different shape, model, and band.

"*Amor.*" Camila opened the box. "It's lovely. Are you sure?"

I kissed the back of her cheek. "It's a gift that is tiny in comparison to all you give me."

She took it out of the box and put it on. "No," she said.

I couldn't see what was wrong with it. The clerk beside her offered to size it, solving the problem.

Olga didn't make such a fuss. She opened her box, removed the watch, looked up at me, winked, and smiled.

"*Gracias. Muchas gracias*, Mario." She kissed me.

While the jeweler was busy sizing the gold bands, I went back to my clerk to select six more watches, each a little different, for my aunt, Melina, Jo, Pixie, Niley, and Letty. While their watches were being boxed, Camila and Olga walked over to see what I was doing.

"Picking out gifts for my aunt and team."

Olga turned to the clerk and said, rapid-fire, "What kind of a discount did you give him?"

The clerk was a little alarmed. He stuttered something, attracting the attention of the jeweler, who came over.

"Rolex is a fair-trade item all over the world. If we discount it, we can lose the license to sell the brand."

Camila poked him with her elbow. "Would you prefer losing me as a customer?"

Instead of paying $2,500 US each—what I had paid for the first two watches—I got all six watches for $11,000. I pulled out my credit card, but Olga shoved it aside. She opened her purse and pulled out a stack of hundreds.

"What are you doing?" I asked.

---

[37] It's a sin to buy more jewelry when I have a safe full

"Camila wants to give your team and aunt a gift."

Camila, who was looking at more watches in the display case, nodded in agreement.

"No way."

"*Amor*, don't be stubborn. The owner here likes cash. That's why we get the discount."

"*Bella*, tell me I can pay you back. I can write you a check, I have checks in my suitcase."

When we were in the car on the way back home, I pushed and pushed.

Camila was in a happy-go-lucky mood and relented. "Okay, write me a check."

At the wheel of the Range Rover, Olga was shaking her head. "Let's see, what word am I looking for?" Olga asked. "You are a hen."

"Chicken," I said. "Why am I chicken?"

"For not accepting my gift," Camila said.

"Another time, okay?"

That night before dinner, I wrote a check for $11,000, left the payee blank, and gave it to Camila, who gave it to Olga.

"Thank you," I repeated for the hundredth time.

That night, Olga joined us in bed. When I woke up, Olga was gone. She was not around for breakfast or when we boarded the helicopter that took Camila and me to the airport. Camila explained our plans.

"*Amor*, the plane will drop me off in New York when they refuel and will take you to Los Angeles. I have two days of business in New York."

"I can catch a commercial flight from New York."

She kissed me until I stopped talking.

As we boarded the Camacho jet, the pilot welcomed us aboard and handed us customs forms to fill out. Somewhere over the Atlantic, I asked Camila about plane inspections by customs officers. My direct dealings with customs had only been to show passports.

"For the plane to land in the US, it either has to land at an international airport to go through customs or we request a customs officer at a private airport at our expense. I've never had a problem. If they check, there is nothing but a few joints that I carry in my purse."

"What about cash?"

"We have receipts that the cash was withdrawn from a bank in Colombia." She smiled. "You're curious, *Amor*?"

"Curious, but it's none of my business."

"Look, you go to a bank anywhere in the world where you have money." She raised her hand. "Not the United States. Olga or I write a check for one million or two million dollars and request US currency, cash. The cash is put into a suitcase or briefcase and we are given a receipt."

"Why would you take out cash then deposit it again in the bank somewhere else?"

"*Amor*, no. The withdrawal in cash is to get the receipt and have it on the plane where we carry cash. If they ask where it came from, we show them the receipt. It doesn't matter how old the receipt is. It shows where the money came from."

"I got it."

"*Amor*." She smiled. "Now you know."

I really didn't know. The mystery was where the cash was from. She hadn't said where it was coming from, and I wasn't asking. I'm not naïve. I knew there was something secret going on, something not completely innocent. They were going to great lengths to move that cash around.

"I know you are curious, *Amor*. We have many businesses that generate cash. Take the forty-thousand-seat sports stadium we own in Germany. A tremendous amount of cash is generated each month from there. Bankers believe that if it is cash, the money is dirty, so we must pay them to accept it. A number of our businesses generate cash."

I believed her, but I knew that sports stadium could not be the source of all their cash. She was presenting me a bogus explanation as a distraction. There was too much of it and too many places. Where there were sports stadiums, there was gambling. I'm not a betting man, but I'd bet some of that money was from gambling. All their money, including the two million I had in my safe, was in hundred-dollar bills. It wasn't German money, and it wasn't in common increments. It didn't matter. She'd told me more than enough to get the basic idea of what was going on.

"Baby, I don't need to know."

She smiled, her eyes on mine. "Did you have a good time in Rome?"

"No. I had a good time being with you." Our seat belts were on through a bit of turbulence. She leaned forward and I did the same so our lips met.

"Are you ever going to get married?" she asked.

Took a few seconds for me to reply. "Are you?"

She sighed. "I hope so."

I remembered Pepe. "A beautiful woman like you must have a ton of guys wanting you."

She laughed. "*Amor*, you are so sweet. I am never in one place long enough to build a relationship. You still haven't answered me."

"I have thought about marrying Melina. We're both married to our work."

"You have such lovely women working with you every day. They don't interest you?"

"I adore them. I don't think I would marry any one of them. I'm not grown up enough to appreciate and take care of a wife like one should. That's the biggest problem."

"It's difficult to be monogamous. Is that what you mean?"

I took a drink from my glass and nodded. "That's it exactly."

"Like last night, you had two of us in bed."

I nodded again. "Yes. It was delightful. But what would it be if I was married?"

"We are much alike, Mario." For once, she didn't call me *Amor*.

We stared at each other for what seemed a long time. The ride was still a bit bumpy. I broke the silence. "If I was married to Melina, I'm sure—absolutely sure—that I would still picture you in my mind and want you. And if it not you, I'd think of Olga. Or one of my team. I don't think me getting married would work for my wife at all."

"I love you more for being so honest."

"Camila, you are so beautiful."

Our eyes met and stuck. Communication happened. She unfastened her seat belt. We balanced ourselves through the turbulence, walking to the cabin, and lay on the bed facing each other. Our arrival in New York was much too soon. She dressed and prepared to disembark. I considered dressing, but stayed in my black pajamas.

Someone pushed the airstairs against the plane, and one of the pilots opened the door. A customs officer boarded and spent three seconds looking at Camila's passport and bags. A redcap collected her two suitcases.

I had the suitcase I had left home with, plus one that I bought in Rome, filled with new clothes. I showed him my bags and handed him the form that the pilot had given me.

"I'm getting off in California," I said.

"I'm going to waive the duty on these things you bought there. It's too late to deal with it right now."

"Officer, thank you."

He stamped my passport and left.

Camila lingered for a moment. "My driver will be waiting in passenger pickup curbside. You might as well go back to bed. Get some sleep," she urged. "I love being with you, *Amor*."

"Ditto," I said.

That brought a smile to her face.

"I will be at the Waldorf for two nights. Call me."

"I sure will."

The plane landed at Van Nuys airport. It was the first week of April and still cold. I rolled up the pajamas and stashed them in my old suitcase. The truth is, I usually sleep in my birthday suit, but these were comfortable.

I took a cab from Van Nuys. When I paid the cab outside my gates, it was three in the morning. I let myself in and walked the long driveway to my front door. I was tired. Looking forward to my bed. Trudged up the steps. Set down suitcases. Pulled keys out of pocket. Yawned. Pointed key toward the lock. Lock moved before I got the key in. Door opened. Robe. Bare feet with pink painted toenails. Letty smiled up at me. Beaming. The whole house was smiling, because I wasn't coming home to emptiness. I picked her up and kissed her.

So happy to be home.

In the two days she was in New York, I talked to Camila three times, and once to Pepe in Colombia to thank him for the trip. Camila had invited me, but Pepe was behind the scenes somewhere.

I told Camila I had reached Pepe. She wanted to know what he had said.

"How wonderful it would be if you and I got married."

Camila laughed. "And how did you respond to that?"

"I said you are too good for me. He agreed."

Camila was still laughing. "You must believe I'm an angel. I'm not."

I said. "Pretty sure an angel would be booted out of heaven for that last night with you and me and Olga. Or that time on the plane."

Olga and I had made a deal that she would stay in touch with me. She wasn't as easy to locate as Camila and Pepe.

"Do you miss me?" she asked when she called from somewhere in Europe.

"How did you know?"

My team was delighted with their watches. Over the next few days, I filled them in on Rome. I dropped in to see my aunt and gave her the watch. She was very excited over it, but not half as excited as she was to hear I spent my Easter Sunday at the Vatican. My visit was cut short when four couples showed up at her door for their Wednesday Lamaze class. She took them into Pixie's old room that she had redecorated as her classroom. It was filled with floor mats and a wall of pictures of babies she'd delivered. The sunroom was now the birthing room. My room was exactly as I had left it.

I had the back of Melina's Rolex engraved: "To my Cuz, Love Mario." I think she was more excited over the engraving than the watch.

On Sunday, I went straight to the stairs, thinking we were having the usual lazy bedroom Sunday, but she beckoned me into the dining room, handed me a plate, and we did the usual pickings from her chef's spread. Usually we ate upstairs out on a balcony overlooking her estate, a few feet from the bed. This Sunday's food was laid out on the buffet in silver chafing dishes. Melina led me from the dining room to a nook close to the kitchen, far from her bedroom. The help retreated after serving our drinks. I didn't think much about the change in routine. The little table where we sat was a fragile-looking antique. I wondered if it would even hold our plates, but the 'L' shaped bench around it was deeply padded and luxurious. I remember when Melina had designed it. She'd measured it to my height.

"I get this feeling that you and Camila are getting serious."

"Are you jealous?" I was kidding and eating.

"I'm not jealous. I'm serious. I'm worried. I don't know her or her family, and neither do you. I'm scared that she might be connected to something that could pull you down."

"She can't pull me down, because I'm never going to do anything illegal."

"People around you can influence what law enforcement believes. You can go down for association."

"Baby, you sound like a criminal lawyer. You and I know you never practiced law, not even for a day."

Melina looked up from the piece of broccoli she was mincing into tiny bits. She looked shocked. "Asshole. I've represented you when you were being questioned how many times?"

I felt horrible. "Sorry. You're right. Yes, you have. But you have Camila all wrong." I tried to keep it light. Usually when she called me asshole, it was like a joke. Now I felt the part.

Melina looked down again, focused on her plate. She ate slowly, each bite a work of four minutes of painstaking attention. She toyed with her fork and knife. Not much actually went into her mouth.

"I received your insurance policies for the house and the last two apartment buildings you purchased. Jo wasn't around, so I went over to your house to put them in the safe." It would have been the big safe where all my rental files were located.

"Thank you for that. I'd be totally lost without you on matters like insurance. And all that."

"While I was there, I opened the small safe."

It took a few seconds to hit me. I was cool about it. After all, both combinations were set to her birthdate. "So?"

"You know I'm nosy. It's not like I was going to hit the money in your socks."

I laughed, but I knew what was coming. My heart was pumping. "You've always been nosy. That's okay. I have nothing to hide from you."

She finally looked up. She wasn't crying, but her eyes were reddened and sad.

"What is all that fucking money doing in your safe?"

I stopped eating. "It's not what you think."

"What do I think?"

"Maybe you think that I'm pushing drugs. Did you count it?"

Melina slammed her hand on the table. The orange glasses almost tipped over.

"Fuck no, I didn't count the fucking money. But I knew instantly that it was Camila."

I did not try to deny it. "So what?"

"So what? What straight person has that kind of money lying around? There has to be a million or more. Why would she give it to you? There is no good reason." A few tears rolled down her cheek. She wiped them away with her hand.

"You want to know what the money is for? I'll tell you what it's for. She plans to buy a house in Pasadena or in Los Angeles. It's two million. I didn't count it either."

"You idiot! She's going to pay for the house in cash?"

I took a long drink of water. I put the glass down. "Yes, she's going to pay cash." I got up, leaned over to her, and tried to kiss her.

She slapped me. Slapped me hard.

"Didn't getting sent to prison teach you anything? You could have done two years for that simple chicken-shit case. This kind of money means serious jail time."

"You're assuming the money is dirty. You are assuming that some cop who is nosy as you is going to find the fucking money in my safe and send me away because of possession of cash? Is that what you are saying?" I was getting pissed. I couldn't remember being pissed at her since her escapade with Carson, when she wanted to persuade him to get Pélon to knock off the surviving shooter that had killed her father.

"I'm saying that whatever you are into with her has to be illegal."

"I'm not in to anything with her." I hated to sound like I was pleading. I hated this whole blow up. What was her beef, anyway? "The money is hers. She only asked me to hold it."

"You tell me everything. Why not this?"

"Just look at yourself, that's why."

I kissed the top of her head, hoping this would blow over. My face was still burning from her slap. I was still standing beside her chair. Just when I thought she was calm, she got up, lifted the side of the table, and tipped it over where I had been sitting. Everything toppled to the floor. Shattered plates, food, glasses. I was holding my water glass. One of the housekeepers came running in, the chef right behind her.

Melina stormed out of the nook.

"What are you, seven?" I yelled after her before finding myself face to face with the help. They stared blankly at me. I stared back. I shoved my glass between the housekeeper's fingers. I spread my arms and hands and shook my head, exhaled a burst of air, and got out.

In three minutes flat, I was in my gym stripped to my boxers. I threw myself into a workout. I was so agitated, I couldn't think. I was pissed that she had opened the fucking safe, pissed off at being accused that I was into something with Camila when I wasn't. I was pissed, pissed, pissed. Letty came in and asked me why I wasn't at Melina's. I didn't reply; I kept working out. She took a good look at my face and got the hell out.

An hour later, I was still sweating out the venom, and Betty walked in.

"Letty says you need a massage."

I stopped what I was doing and looked at her. I nodded.

I jumped in the shower. The water was brisk, but it failed to cool me down. Betty assisted me with a towel. I lay back on the massage table, naked as always. She slipped out of her sweats. She never undressed unless I asked, and I had not asked. She worked on me using her body as part of the massage. After an hour, she leaned over me. I put my hand on her arm. That's all it took. She licked her lips. There was no questioning what she wanted and I needed. I got to my feet and stepped behind her. I barely looked at her lean athletic frame that I had been feeling and glimpsing. I pushed her forward till her hands rested on the massage table. I pressed myself inside. She sighed. I groaned. It took less than a minute for me to explode. Sex with Betty. A first. But it was hardly anything to be proud of.

"I'll make it up to you," I promised.

"I came too," she said softly.

That made me feel a little less like an ass, but only slightly.

She worked on me another hour. I lay there, calm at first, then the tension returned.

"I need to pee."

I excused myself, and when I got back, I heard Betty's stomach growl.

"Hungry?"

"I could use a bite," she said.

I only had a few bites at Melina's.

"Let's see what Miguel can cook up."

We got dressed and strolled up to the kitchen, where Letty was baking pies and who knows what else with Miguel.

"I'm starving," I announced. "Food, please."

We snacked from a platter of beef sopes with all the trimmings—delicious finger food. We drank red wine. That afternoon, after being fed, I found tranquility with Letty and Betty in a threesome, another first. We'd certainly been talking about it long enough. I closed my eyes and I was fucking Olga. Kissing Camila. The anger rush was gone. Betty surprised me when she lit a joint, took a drag, and blew the smoke into my mouth. I took the smoke and blew it through the joint into Letty's mouth. Letty took that smoke and blew it into Betty. Then Betty came to me again. We returned to the bedroom and sprawled around the fireplace on pillows.

Thanks to Letty, Betty, and Mary Jane, I felt happy. I saw them kissing each other, then they kissed me. It was so fucking hot. My mind was wrapped in sensation. The Melina argument this morning and the money in my safe was shoved to the corners of my brain, piled under a stack of pillows and blankets and rosy lips.

The next morning, I woke with a terrible headache. Jo, Pixie, and Niley stood around my bed, arms crossed, looking as if we'd done something wrong.

Letty, who never stayed in my bed all night, sat up, held her head, and whispered, "What?"

I wondered what happened to Betty. I sat up too. "Want breakfast or do you want to fuck?" I asked the girls.

"Fuck you," Pixie said, looking from me to Letty. "Breakfast," she said, and went storming out of my bedroom. The others followed, leaving Letty and me alone.

An hour later, we sat down for a ten a.m. feast. The shower had revived me.

A sightseeing helicopter from Las Vegas went down over the Grand Canyon with seven people, all one family. The girls hadn't gotten over whatever hit them that morning, but I was over their shit. I wasn't in the mood to tolerate nagging or bad moods. Pixie found the crash article in the *Los Angeles Times*, and I got the lead from the article.

"I'll handle it," I said, taking the cutout.

She glared at me but said nothing as I dialed long-distance information to get the names of some Las Vegas PIs. She gave me three names and numbers. I had to ask for the supervisor to come on the line to get a few more. I called them all, got answering machines on all of them, and left messages and my phone number. Nothing else to do at that point but wait until they called back.

"I'm handling this case," I told the girls.

"Why?" Pixie asked sharply.

"Because I want to," I snapped.

"I think that bitch Camila and Olga are controlling you with a witch," Pixie accused.

Melina accused me, and now Pixie. Enough already.

I barked back, "Fuck you, Pix."

"Want to fuck me here right now or in the bedroom?" No giggle. Only Pixie would dare talk to me like that. It had to do with the long-lasting friendship.

"I wouldn't fuck you with Carson's dick," I said. "Fuck off. And Pixie—"

"What?" she snapped back.

"You have a dirty mouth."

Jo's face froze in shock. Niley fled. Pixie stood there and looked at me like I'd slammed her with a Mack truck. I stayed behind my desk.

"Call me names. Cuss me out. Anything you want, Mario," Pixie said. "Don't get nasty with me, not on the real side, not right now."

"Or what?"

"Or else." She started crying and ran out.

Chapter 24
April 1978
Las Vegas
Tricia

I had three PIs call back, but only one seemed hungry enough to accept my promise that I would pay as I got to Vegas. I liked her voice. She was calm, quiet. She'd never yell "fuck you" at me.

"What hotel?"

Tricia recommended either the Dunes or Caesars Palace.

"What's your favorite?"

"The Dunes," she said.

I hired her to find the relatives of the decedents in the helicopter crash and, more importantly, to find out if the relatives were being transported to Las Vegas to identify the bodies and claim them. I could have stayed at home as Tricia worked the assignment, but I couldn't wait to get away. The team was gone. Letty was keeping her distance. I passed her in the hall.

"Are you okay?"

"Sure, boss." She eyed me over warily, "Just giving you space."

I kissed her lightly. "I'm off to Vegas on this case."

"Sure, boss; be careful."

I headed for the front door with my suitcase. I left the house at two p.m. to drive to Las Vegas.

I often wondered why I continued paying for the car phone service. I could never reach an operator to make a call out. Receiving a call was one in a hundred rolls of the dice.

The phone rang. I couldn't believe it.

"This is me," Pixie said. "I quit."

I was calm now. "I tell you off, and that's enough to get you to quit?"

"You said you wouldn't fuck me with Carson's dick!"

"Oh, that bothered you enough to make this call?"

"Fucking A!"

There was a long pause. With mobile phones, you have to limit your calls to three minutes. The mobile operator cut the call long before the three-minute mark for profanity being used on a live line.

"Fuck it!" I yelled. It was April, great weather, and I drove with the window open. I yelled "fuck it" from the outskirts of LA till I saw the 'WELCOME TO VEGAS' sign. Till I was hoarse. I was pissed. Let them all quit. I regretted that I had not brought Letty, though.

I dumped my suitcase on the hotel bed, called Tricia to say I'd arrived, and went down to the lobby to meet her. Sometimes a voice tells you nothing about a person. In Tricia's case, the voice matched the calm, quiet young lady dressed in jeans, a button-down shirt, flight jacket, and a scarf around her neck. Her hair was cut short with long bangs. Streaky blonde. Blue eyes. Self-assured. A little bit tough. She reminded me of Jodie Foster, but dialed down very low on the excitability factor. That was fine with me. I knew too many temperamental women, anyway.

"How old are you?"

"Old enough. Older than I look."

She looked about twelve years old. We moved to the bar, where she tossed down a resume half an inch thick and a whiskey, straight. I was a little impressed, maybe even intimidated. The light was too dim to read a resume.

In the elevator, she pulled out her ID and showed me her Private Investigator License issued by the State of Nevada. She was twenty-seven.

I let her in my suite.

"You must be a gambler," she said.

"No."

'Only gamblers get comped suites like this."

"The house wins. I don't like those odds. I rented the suite."

I sat down and looked at her resume. She didn't pace. She faced me, head on, expressionless, stiff like a stick was up her ass. No shit about the military experience. She had the military bearing down pat. She had all kinds of medals for shooting, bravery, and a list of missions I didn't know they let women get into.

I looked up from her military history. Fuck. I had hired G.I. Jane. To be honest, that got me a little excited.

I knew how to play poker, but didn't play for stakes.

"So how are we going on the investigation?" Might as well find out what she could do.

"The guy who rents the helicopters gave me the low-down on the relatives. From Wisconsin. Heading to Las Vegas. Probably here tomorrow."

"Great work, Tricia."

"The employee of the helicopter company cost two hundred."

"Anything else?"

"The tour company reserved three rooms for the family at the Sahara. I'll get you the details in the morning."

"How about a drink or something?"

"You owe me seven hours at $25 and $300 expenses."

I reached in my pocket and counted out one thousand in hundreds. "Take what I owe you from this."

She tried handing me five hundred in change. "Take this, and I'll get you twenty-five out of my wallet."

"No," I said. "That's yours. Credit me against the $25 per hour. Twenty-one hours unless there are expenses."

"I knew you were the real deal," she said.

I was on the sofa admiring the view. She was on a side chair. She looked great. Not at all like an ex-marine.

So many lights. Caesars Palace glittered like an adult wet dream. The whole street was candy, liquor, and sex wrapped up in light. Gambling too, but any gambling I do is in life, not a casino.

"I knew you were real, too."

She had a nice smile. I thought she was refusing the drink, but she didn't. I thought she'd refuse a bottle of wine, and she didn't. I had just about concluded she was gay, but after a bottle of wine, we ended up in bed. Tricia left when we were done. I got out and played tourist until five, then slept until eleven a.m. when Tricia returned.

"I'm here for seconds."

I picked her up and carried her to bed and started to undress her, beginning with her scarf and jacket.

"Wait, I was jiving you." She laughed. "I brought you the names of the family. They get in today."

"Later," I said. "Let me get a little of that fine ass."

Over lunch, because it was too late to call it breakfast, I learned that Tricia was divorced. She'd been a Navy brat moving all over the world and became a marine sniper on graduating from high school in 1969. She didn't get a good re-signup package, so she left after her six years and let the government get her a degree in criminal justice. She'd met her husband in the military, but after an injury, he got hooked on dope. She'd thrown him out of the house four times, and he kept coming back. The divorce didn't stop him. After she got her license, she was allowed to have a concealed weapon. Only then did the ex stop bothering her. "I put the gun in his mouth. I was ready to kill him. He's never been back."

I told Tricia about my work. I explained how it goes with soliciting, how I can't solicit and don't, not even outside the country.

"Let me get this straight. We are waiting for the family to do what exactly before you introduce yourself?"

"I never know in advance."

"I don't get it."

I told her how I handle a lot of international cases, pretty big ones. "I want to develop some business in the US. Here it is mostly small-craft stuff. I have no one here to find the families. I have a guy I use out of the country. I've flown him here before."

"I can always use the work," she said.

I started hanging out at the Sahara Hotel where the family was. Tricia got a bellman to get us the room number, but I wasn't about to go to the room and knock on the door of a grieving family.

Judging by the hours she put in hanging out with me, waiting for the right moment, it was obvious she had no other cases active. She drove me back to the Dunes, and I invited her for dinner. We ate Italian in the hotel restaurant and finished off two bottles of fine Bordeaux.

We snuggled together on the sofa.

She whispered, "Fuck me like you did this morning, and I won't charge you for my hours today."

"Are you serious?"

"As a heart attack."

We did it for hours, and then lathered each other up in the oversized shower attached to the suite. She had a great body, and up to that moment, I'd hardly noticed it. Sure, in bed she looked good, but up close under soapy hands, I felt her sleekly muscled torso.

"Do you work out?"

"I do."

"I can tell."

She rubbed my abs, then cupped my biceps, one arm at a time.

"I can tell, too." We kissed.

We talked half the night.

"This is the best gig I've ever had. I get to hang out in this palace and get paid for it. And tomorrow, I'll watch the family closely. I'll take pictures, check out how they dress. That will tell us if they are a family of means or so-so. If they are so-so, they will be easier to talk to."

"Exactly, Tricia."

I heard her get up, and I stirred a little but went back to sleep. This case, only two hundred and eighty miles from home, was a vacation from all the bullshit troubling me. I slept like a baby.

In the morning, I called Letty and told her where I was. "Have the girls been around?"

"Not Pixie. Jo wants you to call, and so does Niley. They've been here." She hesitated. "Boss, you all right?"

"I'm fine. Miss you. I got out on the road and almost came back to get you."

"Boss, miss you too."

From the newspapers, I already knew and Tricia had confirmed that the decedents were a mother and father and their three young children. There was also a newlywed couple on their honeymoon. I was showered, dressed, and ready for anything by one in the afternoon, when Tricia showed up full of news.

"These people are down and out. Mario, this is one whole family that got wiped out. The older Boyds, Fannie and Robert Jr., and their three kids, and Robert's nephew, Bill Boyd Jr., and his new wife Virgie. I talked to the parents of both couples. Mr. and Mrs. Bob Boyd senior, and Mr. and Mrs. Bill Boyd senior." She handed me a Polaroid so I wouldn't get confused and pointed out which were the grandparents. "I didn't solicit them. I just approached at breakfast this morning. Showed them my ID and told them I knew someone who consulted for a Los Angeles law firm specializing in this type of case. One thing led to another. Lots of crying. They are waiting for the bodies to be released. They want to meet you."

Suddenly I got charged up. I leapt off the furniture and swung her around.

"Tricia, I fucking love you." I put her down, then lifted her off her feet and swing around again a couple of times for good measure.

"You're a strong mother," she said, laughing.

I met the family. There were whole lot of Boyds. In addition to the parents of the couples, the deceased adults had adult siblings. That night at my hotel, there were fifteen of them when I took them to dinner, and that's not counting Tricia and me. I was dressed in a three-piece suit, accessorized by one of my Rolex watches, and the gift of gab that God gave me, which has been keeping me fed since I was ten years old.

The tour company had brought them out all expenses paid, but they had no money. They could barely afford to eat in the hotel. The tour company kept the families close, attempting to manage them so they would be eager to settle without hiring lawyers.

When the bodies were released, I was there. I advanced the money to the mortuary to prepare the bodies and put them in caskets for transportation back home. I paid the airline to transport the bodies. The clients had their return tickets covered by the tour company. I advanced the parents of both couples each $2,500.[38] I advanced the brothers and sisters $300 each.[39] I sent Tricia to Los Angeles to fetch retainers. She was met at the airport by a clerk from Oscar's office. The Boyds signed the retainers, and I shipped them back home.

I returned to the Dunes to pack.

"Okay, baby, what do I owe you?"

"Should I deduct the sex like I promised?" She was all smiles.

"No way. No deductions. It was the best sex ever, and you are the best company I could have ever have away from home."

I paid Tricia.

She walked me to the parking lot. We were deep in conversation, talking about the possibilities of future cases. We reached my Rolls and I opened the door.

---

[38] $2,500.00 in 1978 had the same buying power as $9,719.48 in 2017

[39] $300.00 in 1978 had the same buying power as $1,166.34 in 2017

She whistled. "Man, I didn't know you had wheels like this. You been hanging with me in a beat-up '65 Camaro." She bent over at the waist and wrapped her head in her arms, then stood back up, blushing. "I didn't even clean the 7-11 cups out of the back seat."

"I been running with a hot freckled PI in a Camaro." I tapped the freckles on her nose with my finger, grabbed a last kiss, and ruffled her short fair hair. She knocked my hand away. Tough girl.

"Gonna miss you, Mario."

"Ditto," I said, getting in my car. "But we're going to reconnect soon. I promise."

I got home a little after three in the afternoon. I handed my suitcase to Caro and went to my office. Jo and Niley were reading newspapers spread out on the conference table. "Hey, you," I said, putting my briefcase down on top of my desk.

"Hey, yourself," Jo said.

"Was that a friendly 'Hey, yourself,' or what?"

"You're the boss," Jo replied.

"Niley, good afternoon."

"Good one to you, too, boss."

They were working. They were smiling. But something was off. I hated when they made me probe for what was wrong, but it was just the "everything's okay" scenario when everything is not okay.

"What's wrong?" I asked, pulling out the retainers and my notes from the case I signed in Vegas.

"Pixie is what's wrong. How could you let her quit?"

"Bullshit. She's not going to quit for long."

"That's what you think," Niley said.

I walked over to the conference table and put the retainers and notes in front of Jo. "Look these over. Run them over to Tom. Tell him to call the clients.

Family's in Wisconsin. Big case, seven deaths."

She got up. "Sure, boss."

"Are you going to go over everything?"

"No. I'm sure it's perfect."

"Okay, wise-ass. You can go straight home from there."

"Got it." A second later, she was out my office door.

"What is it, Niley?"

She stopped with the newspapers, I sat next to her, and we faced each other.

"You changed since you started running with Camila and her assistant."

"I didn't just meet her. Are you saying I changed over a year ago, and you are just now telling me my change is affecting how you feel?"

She hesitated. "No holds barred?"

"There never are. Spill it."

"You changed in the last couple of months. You're not yourself. You're even mean. You've never been mean. Pixie would do anything for you, and you hung up on her when she called you in the car." Niley started to cry.

"I didn't hang up on her. The mobile operator probably disconnected the call because Pixie was cussing at me."

Niley looked up at me. "She thinks you hung up on her. That made her feel like you didn't care if she quit."

"I haven't changed. The three of you have changed. What is it? Are you guys jealous because I go off to do things I've never done before, like get on a private plane and head to another country on the spur of the moment?"

Niley wiped her eyes. "Maybe. Maybe we are just jealous."

"You don't feel that way about Melina, and that's a woman I was thinking of marrying."

"We all heard what happened. We know about the cash in the safe."

"Fuck! Who told you?"

"Melina told us. We called her about Pixie, and she was kind of broken up. It just came out."

Letty walked in. "Welcome home, boss. Are you hungry?" She stayed by the door.

"Baby, bring me a bottle of wine and three glasses."

"Back in a second."

"I don't want to drink," Niley said, getting up. "I don't feel good. If it's okay, I'm going home."

I looked up, but she wasn't looking at me. She was heading for the door. What the fuck was going on?

Letty poured a glass of wine for both of us, but I was the only one drinking.

"I called Betty to come and give you a massage."

I was still at the conference table, and she sat where Niley was sitting before. I lifted her chin and smiled at her. She smiled back.

"Are you mad at me, too?"

She leaned against my chest without getting up. "No, I'll never be mad at you."

"What did the girls say all this time I've been away?"

"For the first couple days, they shined me on. Jo said I shouldn't stay in your bedroom, that I should leave after you go to sleep."

"What the fuck business is it of hers?"

"Boss, I do that anyway. Only reason I didn't the other day with Betty was because I was out of it. I didn't wake up in time. When they came in, there I was."

"Fuck Jo."

"Don't say that, please. They got over it. Everything is okay. Pixie called three times to check if you had called. She wanted to know if you were all right."

I smiled and took a drink. "So she's pissed at me, but still worries about me."

"For sure."

Folded neatly on the conference table, the newsprint page that Pixie had cut the article from caught my eye. I unfolded it, held it up, and saw what it was. I peered at Letty through the neatly cut square. "I did good. I got the case, seven deaths. Terrible tragedy, but the families will be happy the way Oscar will take care of their case." I balled it up and tossed the newsprint in the trash. A copy of the article was with the retainers, and the original was in my files.

"Good job, boss."

We moved from the conference table to my desk. Letty sat across me. I picked up the phone and dialed Pixie. She answered on the first ring.

"Pix, I'm sorry."

Long silence. I could hear her crying, and Lainey in the background. A few minutes passed without a word. I stared at Letty. I could tell she was wondering what was going on.

"I needed that," Pixie said. "I love you, Mario. I've always loved you. I would die for you."

"Pix, I want you here tomorrow. I need you."

"Thank you, boss. I've been crazy. You know how I get when it's that time of the month, and I spoke up about nothing. I'm the one who's sorry."

"Pix, I'm sorry. It's been a bit crazy lately. I'm in a fog running around with Camila and Olga. When I'm there, I feel like I belong there, so I lose it when I get home. I know I did that day, and I'm sorry. I love you."

"And I love you."

Letty was crying as she listened to my end of the conversation. I don't know if she could hear Pixie, or was imagining what Pixie was saying, or what.

We agreed that we'd have a breakfast meeting at ten. Pixie would let Jo and Niley know to be here.

I called three markets before locating Melina.

"Baby, it's me; I'm sorry about the other day." I heard a click.

"Melina hung up on me," I told Letty.

"She'll get over it, boss. She loves you, too."

I stood up and felt a little dizzy. I put down the wine glass and told Letty to put up the bottle. I headed to the spa to steam the Vegas out of me. The successful trip had done me a great deal of good. I had taken a case from scratch and brought it home. I didn't do it alone, but I engineered it from start to finish. Sometimes I needed to do the job to confirm I still had my mojo.

Betty was in great form. She did not mention our last massage. I wasn't ready to bring it up, either. Normally I don't talk too much when I'm getting a massage, but when I lay down, Letty sat on the table next to me and peppered me with questions. I told them both about my trip and about Tricia.

Letty was back to normal, her mood bright. Calling Pixie was a good start at getting things back to normal.

She asked, "Boss, do you fuck all the pretty girls everywhere you go?"

Betty answered for me. "He does. I've never been with him on a trip, but he does." She slapped my dick playfully.

"Careful, you'll get it hard."

"Get it hard," Letty said. "We can do it like the other night."

"Right on. Want me too, boss?" Betty asked.

I'm told that it's testosterone that keeps a man sexually active. Don't ask me about it, because I have no clue how testosterone works or how our bodies produce it, or about pheromones, for that matter. I mean, I liked the smell of Letty's clean hair, but it didn't make me climb the walls. If it is pheromones and testosterone that attract me to the opposite sex and keeps me ready to go at all times of the day and night, I must have a fucking bunch of both.

"Yes, Betty, I'm ready for anything."

In the morning, though no one walked in to find me that way, I woke up alone.

I didn't want to think about Melina hanging up on me. I had called to apologize, not even knowing what I was apologizing for. The only thing I figured I had done was not to tell her I got the money from Camila to hold. But what the fuck. I'd gone to enough confessions as a kid.

I came out of the shower after a late workout and Pixie was sitting on the edge of my bed, looking up at me. Our smiles bounced off each other. One second she was sitting, the next she was airborne. The instant I caught her, her legs went around my waist and her arms around my neck. I kissed her with all the passion in my soul.

"I love you, Pix. Don't ever quit me again."

"I love you, too. I promise. I won't quit you."

Jo, Letty and Niley walked in. They caught us twirling and kissing and giggling and tickling, and they applauded.

"Should we fuck or eat breakfast?" Pixie asked the girls.

"Eat, please," Letty said. "Miguel has been upset over all the drama, so he's been cooking since five in the morning. Looks like a Hilton Grand Buffet down there. And I'm starving."

Jo asked everybody one by one. The consensus was that we were all hungry, so we went downstairs to eat. Miguel had fixed four kinds of muffins, three kinds of bacon, three kinds of potatoes, biscuits, and a week's worth of tortillas. There was also a fresh fruit salad and a side of sliced tomatoes marinating in something savory, the tall silver salt shaker and pepper grinder, a cut glass jelly dispenser with six kinds of fruit jelly, plus little pots of fresh cilantro, salsa, and grated Cotija. Miguel was holding off on the eggs because he liked to bring them in straight from the pan.

All our plates were full, and we were parked at the dinette table in my breakfast room. Letty turned to go in the kitchen, and I told her to get a plate and join us. It only took a few moments for Miguel to deliver everyone's individual eggs, and we were eating away. A stack of tortillas under a cloche was the only serving dish on the table. Everything else was on the sideboard. We spent a good five minutes eating before I broached the subject of money. They knew about the money, so I felt like I had to talk about it. I told them what I had told Melina.

"Camila wants to buy a house here. The money is for a house."

"What's the big deal about that?" Letty asked.

I didn't answer right away, and no one else chimed in. I didn't mention what Olga does for Camacho or get into the cash business. My not answering made me feel like I was putting on Melina's shoes for a second. I could see her perspective only when I was not letting Letty in on what the big deal was. I didn't like that I was hiding something.

"The big deal is that I didn't tell her they gave me the cash to hold. And she thinks the cash is illegal, drug money or something. But I'm thinking it must be legal. If they were drug people, they would be low key. They wouldn't be flying around in Boeings and Learjets. They wouldn't have houses all over the world or own stadiums in Germany and other countries. You know every time we fly back into the country, customs agents come aboard and joke around. The big DC9 comes into Van Nuys, and that's a big deal for Van Nuys. They special order customs people so they can fly in. These people are not sneaking around. They have nothing to hide. One thing is for sure. I will never do anything illegal that could put me in prison and or endanger any of you."

"I see it like that," Pixie said. "Just because they have tons of money doesn't mean they are dope peddlers."

"I agree about the obvious," Niley said. "If they were hiding, they wouldn't be prancing all over the globe in multi-million-dollar planes and living in a bunch of multi-million-dollar houses."

Trust Jo to be the grown-up. She was last in offering her input, and after all, she had been the one who talked to Melina.

"Melina has a point. She loves you and doesn't want anything to happen that will take you down. She saw the money. She panicked. She felt all along that the man who freed you from the kidnappers was a heavy drug lord with big connections. She reminded me that Valita said there had never been any drugs at the plantation. The soldiers found sacks filled with cocaine. Pepe wanted them prosecuted for something that would stick, like drugs."

Melina had not said all this to me. At least not recently.

"Look, it sounds good. It's all speculation. We didn't see Pepe's people plant anything. Valita could be wrong. Anyway, that's history." I raised my voice. "I love Camila and her assistant Olga, and I owe Pepe my life."

Everyone stopped eating. They all looked at me. I failed to swallow the bite I had just taken. A blob of egg stuck in my throat and felt like a fucking boulder. I gulped some water and choked it down. "Look, babies, I don't love them like I love you. You're my family. I come home to you." I looked at Jo, Niley, Pixie, and Letty. Eye contact. One by one. "Do you get it?"

They nodded slowly.

Letty looked down at her plate. Her hair was up in a ponytail, with dark strands falling down in her eyes. She shook them back with a careless jerk of her head.

"Letty, you will soon be traveling with us. Jo's always been in charge of training, and since she has been working with you and says you can do it, you will be part of this team. As far as I'm concerned, you already are."

She grinned at me, then looked nervously around the table. The smile vanished.

"I don't like when you guys are mad at me," she said.

Pixie turned to Letty, who was sitting beside her. She put one hand on each of Letty's shoulders. "Letty, I'm jealous because you get to stay here with the boss. I'm sorry for that. I know you are good company for him. Without you here, he'd be going out every night to get wasted at some club." She released Letty and raised her orange juice glass. "Thank you, Letty."

The other girls raised their glasses.

"It's true," Jo said. "I thank you, too."

"Me too," Niley said.

Letty wiped away some tears. "Thanks, bitch." She let out a grito.

"Bitches, you cunt!" yelled Pixie, giggling. She had apparently swallowed all of her bad feelings along with her orange juice.

Niley threw a biscuit, missed Letty, and hit me.

"Hey," I said, "I know you don't want to start a biscuit fight with me."

Miguel's light, crumbly biscuits were flying, raining crumbs. The crumbly mess got everywhere on us, the table, in the pile of the carpet, and everywhere else. Once the biscuit platter was empty, we recovered the pieces and launched them till the projectiles got smaller and smaller. We were each on our own, no holds barred, at least until we all noticed Caro and Miguel staring at us from the kitchen door. I stood, showering crumbs everywhere. Caro had her arms crossed, her eyes narrowed, and her foot tapping. Miguel just looked shocked.

"The biscuits were delicious," I said. "Really, everything was. You outdid yourself."

The girls looked like they'd been caught by a stern babysitter, but in a second they were hiding giggles. We headed out for the pool for a spontaneous swim.

Letty said, "I'll get this."

I heard Miguel behind me say, "Go play, *chica*, and be happy."

Letty giggled and rushed out to the pool.

I heard Caro said, "It is good seeing everyone all smiles again."

I made a mental note to give Miguel and Caro a little something extra this week.

We all enjoyed each other's company that day. No newspapers to look over. No business talk. No more discussion of my recent trip to Rome or Las Vegas. It was just us. After the dunk in the pool, we worked out for a while in the afternoon. Betty came over and gave everyone a massage. We did it all.

Life at Casa Luna was back to normal. Almost.

Chapter 25
April 1978
Making Up with Melina

May was right around the corner. On the first Sunday, I rang the bell at Melina's gate instead of using my key.

"Please let Melina know I'm here for Sunday brunch," I told the intercom. A maid responded. The wait was so long, I almost turned around to walk back home. Eventually, the gate opened.

As I walked the long driveway, a stream of memories flowed through my head.

Shopping for some of the statuary and shrubs now growing around me.

Lying on a quilt under the stars by the arbor.

Hanging on for dear life as she dashed around in the knee-cracking sports car now sitting outside of the garage. None of these things would have been the same without her.

When the pavement curved to reveal a view of the house, Melina was there in the open door. At the sight of her, I felt a great rush of emotion that I might call relief. The silk robe she wore stood out like a banner, bright white, its only decoration a tiny pattern which, as I got closer, I could make out to be oriental writing. It brushed the floor and rippled in the soft breeze. In the house, she was above me; but the closer I got, the more we leveled. A few steps up to the entry and we were even. At the door, I looked down. She looked up at me.

"I miss you, Melina."

She stepped aside to let me in. Closed the door. My heart raced. I could see a vein in her wrist pulsing. Since our falling out, we had been distant, and now I was beside her. Too many words to stay. They were stuck inside.

Her arms went around my waist, her cheek to my chest.

"I miss you, too," she said. "I can hear the beat of your heart like this."

"I was afraid you wouldn't let me in."

"I've waited for you for two Sundays."

"You hung up on me."

"I did. I treated you like a juvenile delinquent. Judging you because I found the money. When do I not listen to you? I always listen to you. I am just afraid when you don't listen to me. I'm sorry."

I picked her up, cradled her in my arms, and kissed her. We hadn't moved. We were still in the foyer.

I was surprised to see the buffet already set up, a feast as usual. We sat at the same table she had taken her temper out on when I was here last time. It seemed none the worse for wear. The chef brought in a chafing dish and smiled and greeted me, as did her housekeepers. She now had three couples.

We both dug in like hungry wolves, but the food, good as it was, was just a distraction from things we needed to talk about. We had to clear the air.

"I want only the best for you,"

"That's a ditto."

She frowned over the ditto.

"I mean, I want the same for you. Melina, I love you. I love you more than you can imagine. You are part of my anatomy. I've been in a daze ever since we've been on the outs."

She extended her arm across the table and touched my hand. "I've been out of it, too."

"It's behind us."

"Yes, it's behind us."

"Look, it's possible that cash is dirty, whatever dirty means. I realize your concern. I just try not to think of it. I really don't know where the cash came from. It's just they don't act like they have anything to hide." As the words came out of my mouth, I felt a little sick. I remembered the bodies in the Bahamas. They did have something to hide, plenty more than I knew about. But there was no reason to alarm Melina. I hated having a lie between us. Lies have a tendency to take root and grow. But this one was necessary.

She nodded.

"Look, they don't hide their planes, or their mansions, or all their businesses. And speaking of business, I have no business with them. I have invested nothing, and they're not paying me. We're only friends, not business associates. "

"Why did you agree to hold the money? It sounds like you know better."

"I guess I could say I'm indebted to that family for my life. You have no idea where I was out there in the jungle. I was days, maybe hours from killing my way out of there when they showed up. They saved me from committing murder, and possibly from dying in a Venezuelan jungle. So when they pushed the money on me, I didn't feel I could say no."

There was some understanding showing in Melina's face.

"Yes, I remember he was part of that rescue."

"He *was* the rescue. He physically wasn't there, but his men were. Oscar asked for Pepe's help. Somehow Pepe found me. Pepe sent the helicopters filled with soldiers to free me, and that was before we had even met. He even got the military involved. And now that I know them, I have to tell you, I like them. They aren't angels, but I believe they are genuine. There is no free lunch, but I'm awake, eyes wide open. I'm not a sucker, baby. Never have been."

Melina was nodding. "I hope not."

"I love you, Melina."

"And I love you, Mario." She looked deeply in my eyes. "I've fucked three different men and had sex with Betty four times since we had that argument. Can you stomach that?"

I felt a flash of jealousy, but I was so cool. I laughed. "That Betty does get around," I said.

"You and Betty, finally," she said, laughing. "It was bound to happen."

"Betty and Letty, as it so happens," I corrected.

Her smile dimmed a little. "So how is your stomach?"

"I can stomach it. I'm no better. I'd have to do a count. I had a private investigator in Las Vegas that I hired on a case. Can you stomach that?"

"Yes. I don't know how I feel about that kind of open marriage. You know I have employees, couples who swap wives and husbands on weekends, just for kicks. It seems very tawdry."

"No judgement. More power to them," I said.

"Ditto," Melina said. "Their lives. Their rules."

"Hey, that's my word."

She laughed. "It is, and I hate it. I want to say one thing more about the money."

"Go for it."

"Oscar is Pepe's lawyer—or was. They are close. If they weren't close, why would Pepe have sprung you from those bastards?"

"Is that the question?"

"Only a rhetorical one. The question is whether you asked Oscar about the law, the money, what you did, and what you can do. That fucker owes you."

I shook my head no.

"All the business you give him. Don't you trust him?"

"Yes, I trust him." I sipped my coffee. "If I tell Oscar about this, I'm snitching. I can't do it."

"Then what about another lawyer?"

"Same."

"Maybe I should hit the books, then."

"Baby, leave it be."

We spent the day in her bed.

"I'd like to wake up to you every day," I said.

"Me too. Would we feel the same after a year? After two? Would the fire still be there? I don't want to lose it."

"I have no crystal ball, and no warranty, but I don't think the fire's gonna burn out."

Melina smiled at me.

Betty was due for a standing appointment. I kissed Melina and went home.

Letty was watching television in the main den. I walked in, glad to find her there.

"How was the day, boss? Is it all cool over there?"

"How did you know I was there?"

Her little laugh was hoarse enough to be sexy. "Word gets around."

I sat next to her and took a drink from her Coke bottle.

"Yeah, it's cool. We're good now."

I put my arm around her, and she snuggled in. I kissed the side of her head. "Thanks for being here."

That little laugh again. "Boss, that's so silly. I told you, I love it here. Thank you for letting me stay like I do."

And then the only sound came from the television.

When I looked at all the mail delivered to the door or the mailbox every day, sometimes I thought I had a subscription to every newspaper in every major city across the United States. Letty had started going through the papers with us. That was our daily grind, taking up time between the cases we found. In late May, we found a helicopter crash that had occurred a week before in Wyoming. Tourists checking out Yellowstone. Including the pilots, there were eight decedents in total.

"I'll call Juan," Jo said.

"Wait, Jo," I said. Juan hadn't done that great in the Netherlands. Amsterdam had been hard. I wondered if maybe I shouldn't save him for Spanish-speaking countries. It's true he had done well in New Orleans, Florida, and Texas, but most of those cases involved Spanish. I didn't even know the nationality of the Wyoming tourists. Something from one of the articles the girls had dug up made me think they were American. I could ship him about three thousand miles to Wyoming or use someone practically next door. Las Vegas was less than six hundred and fifty miles away. Okay, maybe I'm rationalizing a little. I would not mind working with Tricia again.

"Let's try someone closer," I said. "I'll call Tricia in Las Vegas and see if she's hungry enough to get on a plane and get us the details on the families."

I called Tricia. "Wanna do some work?"

"Hey, Mario. You mean, you fuck me and I work for it outside the bedroom stuff? What's with you? You don't even say, 'Hello. How you been?'"

"Tricia, how are you? How have you been?"

"I'm good, and you?"

"Can I give you the scoop now?"

"Sure," she said, "I'm done playing it cool. Shoot."

"I got a crash in Wyoming that needs investigating, and maybe a foot in the door."

"Fuck yes. I'll go to Wyoming. I'm down to less than a hundred bucks. Can you wire me?"

"We can do that right away. I'll give the phone to Jo. She's on my team. Give her the details."

Jo took over. She took the phone with her and walked a room away to her pad and pen. All my phones have long cords.

"Was she really a good fuck?" asked Pixie.

"Not as good as you and Niley."

"Don't play us," Pixie said. They both gave me one of those fuck-you looks.

"You tell me if she does her job."

"Deal," Pixie said, with narrowed eyes.

We made no effort toward the pilots, and the other two families weren't interested. I stuck it out at home while the girls traveled to Arkansas where the family resided.

"I want you on that team before the end of the year," I told Letty.

"Boss, I'm ready."

Fifteen days after I called Tricia, my team signed a family that lost four. When they returned from Arkansas on June fifteenth, they were as elated as usual about signing the case. The reviews I received about Tricia were great, even from Pixie.

"That bitch knows her stuff. She tracked that family from the mortuary in West Yellowstone all the way to some little dunghill town in Podunk Hollow, Arkansas. By the time we got to the family, they knew all about the firm. She performed. They were not just ready. They were expecting us."

"Jo, do you know how much we owe her?"

"She counts hours. Eighty hours is $2,000. I gotta tell you, boss, she worked her ass off. Her expenses were $1,103.62. Minus the wire, we owe her $2,100."[40]

"Send her $2,500, soon as possible."

I talked to Sami often, and every time, she invited me to London. Jason invited me, too. My English friends. I loved them. I wondered what Sami would think if she knew as much as Melina did about Camila and Pepe.

"I promise to be there before the end of the year," I told Sami. "And I promise to call you no less than once a week."

"It's so nice having you here. Hurry up."

· I could not talk about the money. I couldn't tell anyone about the Ba-

---

[40] $3,500.00 in 1978 had the same buying power as $13,607.28 in 2017 *Full amount Mario paid

hamas shooting, not Sami, not my team, and for sure not Melina.

When Olga checked in as promised, she brought up something I'd just as soon forget. "You and Camila were dancing."

"Dancing?" I could not think of any time we went out dancing. It's not something I do much, even when I go clubbing. "Where?"

"On the way to New York over the Atlantic."

"Oh, that." It was true. "I hardly call what I did dancing," I admitted to Olga. "Bee Gees. Camila insisted."

"You and I will dance from now on when we fly together."

"You will change your mind if you are around my dancing in person," I said.

"Camila and I are going to meet in New York next week, then head out together to Los Angeles for two days on way back to Colombia. Will you be in town in June?"

"I'm here, unless a plane crash occurs."

"I can't wait to see you," she said.

"Ditto."

"You're the only person I know that says ditto."

"You don't like it?"

"I like it if you like it."

On the day of their arrival, Camila called to change plans. "*Amor*, I am engaged in something. Olga will be in Los Angeles without me. I'm sorry."

"I'm sorry, too."

"You will have fun with Olga, I'm sure."

"You are okay with that?" As much as I wanted to see Camila, I was totally excited about being alone with Olga.

"It's all in the family."

Camila surprised me with that response. "*Bella*, you are over the top. I love you," I said.

"*Amor*, and I love you, too."

"Shall I prepare a guest room?"

"She can stay at hotel, is better, but she goes to see you. Don't worry."

Melina knew about Camila and Olga arriving. I updated her on the change to just Olga.

"Cuz, you know my schedule during the week sucks. Say hello for me."

In downtown Los Angeles, Olga checked in at the Bonaventura Hotel, a great hotel with towers and elevators that you could see outside the hotel. I had eaten at one of their restaurants but had never been to a room or suite. Downtown was easier to get to than Beverly Hills.

"Come for a late lunch," I invited. "I want you to meet my team. Want me to pick you up?"

"I'll take a hotel car."

The girls had started off upstairs in designer clothes as they had dressed for Camila, but there had been a lot of water under that bridge. Pixie had had enough. "I'm not dressing up for anybody," she said. "I don't care if it's the queen of England." She tossed what she was wearing aside and pulled on a pair of ragged blue-jean short shorts that had seen better days. The next thing I knew, they were all in shorts and camisole tops, all tanned and rosy-cheeked with summer-streaked hair and looking as adorable as I had ever seen them.

We were all waiting for her at the door to Casa Luna when the hotel limo pulled up.

Pixie saw her, and I heard her swear under her breath. "Fuck. She's fucking Farrah Fucking Fawcett. You didn't say she was Farrah Fawcett. Fuck. I should have kept the fucking dress on."

I looked in Olga's direction. Brown hair. Brown eyes. I didn't see Farrah at all, not even the hair.

"She's not Farrah. She's perfect. You're perfect. Deal with it," I told them all. "You're going to be best friends."

Olga arrived dressed like a banker, stunning in a suit. Most bankers were men, and she was dressed to be their equal, but stunning. I did the Euro kiss on both cheeks. What I wanted to do was grab her and take her upstairs to my bedroom. She carried a purse and a Louis Vuitton carry-on suitcase that I just knew was filled with cash.

"Camila told me so much about you," she told Jo, Pixie, Niley, and Letty. "And now I have the honor of meeting you." She kissed all of them on the cheek.

Pixie, who misses nothing, whispered in my ear. "She has an overnight bag. Is she staying here?"

I shrugged. "I don't know."

"Maybe it's more money," Pixie said.

I shrugged again. "I have no clue." I would have preferred Pixie not noticing the bag, but there was nothing I could do about it except to play it cool.

The weather was pretty good for June. A big round table with a huge umbrella was set up near the pool. The sun was out but not blaring. The girls had put Olga across from me and between Jo and Pixie. Niley and Letty were on either side of me. I was glad Olga was across from me, because when I gazed at her, I didn't have to turn my head. It wasn't noticeable.

Everyone had soft drinks. No one had wanted wine. The girls carried the conversation. I could tell that my team liked her. I hoped Olga felt the same way, but I couldn't read her like I do Jo, Pixie, Niley, and Letty. Mostly, Olga asked about work. She wanted to know what they did when we went out on a plane crash. I listened, never adding anything to the conversation. The girls took turns explaining. Even Letty, who had only been helping going through newspapers, and who had never been out with us, knew enough to add her own input.

"Mario has never explained his business to me other than he works airplane crashes as a consultant to Oscar. It's a sad job you have."

"But we get to travel," Niley said.

"It sounds like you've been to many places."

Pixie said, "We just signed a helicopter crash that happened in Wyoming. Do you know Yellowstone Park?"

"I've never been there, but yes."

"There was a helicopter crash there. Eight people died."

Pixie told her what the team had done to bring that case home.

"And you did this without Mario?" Olga looked at me.

I shrugged. "They're good. Don't need me."

"Oh, boss, we need you. You're the very best," Niley said.

I took a drink of my Coke and leaned back. "I had forgotten that Oscar introduced us to Pepe, and you would of course know Oscar."

"I know him for many years."

"I don't want you to think wrong of me for what I'm about to say," Pixie said.

A statement like that out of Pixie's mouth is alarming. We all half-stood in our chairs.

Pixie continued. "...Olga, you are even more beautiful than what boss said."

We all sat down again.

Olga smiled at Pixie then looked at me. "Very kind, boss," she said.

"I'm far from being your boss," I said.

"Everyone here calls you boss. I call you boss, too."

It wasn't a fast LA lunch. It was European. It took several hours of slow conversation and slower eating before we were done with food, and then we went inside. Olga and I went to my office. Soon as I shut the door, she was in my arms. We kissed passionately. I was drawn to this woman.

"Camila asked me if you could please hold the two million in the bag that I left in the foyer."

"I need to ask why."

"She wants to buy a house here."

"For four million?"

"Sure. Maybe more."

"Olga, I will do it, but you need to tell me I have nothing to worry about."

I was looking right at her. I focused on her eyes, on her breathing, on the pulse I could see in her neck. I wanted assurances that she was telling the truth.

"I promise, you have nothing to worry about. I would never put you in harm's way, and neither will Camila." I waited for her to mention Pepe. She did not.

"Okay, baby, I'll get the suitcase before you go. I may have to put it in another safe."

"Just put it on closet shelf. Who will know, yes?"

"You're so easy-going about this."

She laughed. "Of course. It's just two million."

The first two million had caused me enough trouble already. I hope this didn't cause more.

"I'm going to leave. You will get away and come to the hotel tonight? Please."

My hug was the reply. "Only if you have a big suite with a great view."

"I do, I promise."

"I was kidding."

"I wasn't. Floor-to-ceiling. All of LA at our feet. Night lights and mountains."

She said her goodbyes, and then the limo that had brought her carried her away.

"Camila thought it would be nice if I breezed by and picked up your team," Olga said a week after her whirlwind visit. "How about I take them with me to Honolulu for a few days?"

"Just like that?"

"Just like that."

"I'll run it past them. Call you back."

Jo, Pixie, Niley, and Letty met me in the wine room. It had been a productive day, and they'd each found small local US cases to keep me hopping if they left. I was game if they were.

"Clear your schedule Thursday to Sunday afternoon. All of you." I looked at Letty. "Olga has invited you to Hawaii, and I am recommending you take a vacation. I'll get the ball rolling on the cases you found today while you go sit in the sunshine."

Letty's jaw dropped. Her eyes were shining. "Hawaii? Really?"

"How strange," Niley said. "Why would she do that?"

"She likes all of you. It's probably her idea, but she claimed Camila thought of it. She thinks it will help you get to know each other. When they buy the house in Pasadena, you'd be the only friends they know other than me."

Pixie giggled. "I think I speak for all of us when I say..." then she made a sound there are no words to describe. I'll call it a whoop. Whatever you call it, it was definitely a yes. They were all on their feet, jumping, squealing, hugging, and talking over each other.

The girls went home to make arrangements. They were walking on air, bubbling over, and excited over the sudden vacation. I watched them get into their cars. Letty disappeared to somewhere in the house. Their departure left behind a silence. I called Olga back. "You got the team."

"Wonderful." She sounded excited. Not as excited as Pixie, but definitely charged up.

"Which plane will you be in?"

"Normally, it would be the Lear, but I'm in the big plane from here to there."

"This will be a tremendous expense."

"Mario, don't worry about the expense. It's nothing. Really. What is money for, anyway, if not making our friends happy?"

"It's a grand gesture, a great thing you're doing. I just feel like I owe you something."

"Fine," she said. "Let's just say you owe me a banging."

"A banging?"

"Yeah, a deep banging."

I had been pacing. Letty bounced in from telling Miguel of her good fortune and was following my end of the conversation.

"I have to sit down. I just got hard."

Letty made a funny face and stuck her tongue out at me.

I was glad the girls were going. I wanted them get a taste like I got. It sticks.

Thursday morning, when the girls piled their suitcases into the station wagon, when I took the wheel, I felt I was dropping them off for summer camp. I'd never gone to summer camp, and never dropped off anyone that was going, but I had heard the girls talk about it when they sent their kids. I felt like the parent, even though Jo is older than I am. I listened to their excited chatter nonstop to Van Nuys Airport.

"That's a lot of luggage for hanging out in bathing suits," I said. "But I'm not judging."

"I talked to Olga and got the rundown on what to take: one evening dress and bathing suits." Jo said. "Did you know they have a house in Honolulu?"

"I had no clue, but I'm not surprised." I laughed. Not over the Hawaii house. Their excitement was infectious.

"Olga says we'll love the house. It's right on the beach. They have a chef and housekeepers, and a pool, and boats." Jo paused for a breath. She was looking out the window. We were getting close to the airport.

Pixie, Niley, and Letty squealed.

"I understand they have houses all over, and they keep them fully staffed. If it's anything like their places in Rio or Rome..." I left the sentence hanging, knowing whatever their destination would be, they would have to see it to believe it.

I walked them through the airport, where a couple of attendants took charge of the luggage. We followed them out to the tarmac. I pointed at the huge plane.

"That's your ride," I said, waiting for the girls' reactions.

"I'm coming," Pixie said as she shut her eyes and made appropriate noises. That girl. I can never tell when she's kidding.

"I already did," Niley said.

Jo and Letty were speechless.

I herded them up the airstairs when they stopped to sightsee. In silk black pajamas, Olga appeared on the landing, greeting everyone, Camila behind her.

"What a great surprise." I laughed with gusto, hugging Camila first, then Olga. "Now I wish I was going," I said.

"We can make room," Olga said.

"No way. I know a ladies' day out when I see it. Besides, I have work scheduled all this week."

I said hello to the pilots and kissed everyone goodbye.

When I got home, I reached Melina and gave her the news.

"What the fuck are those cunts up to?"

"This is a great experience for the girls. They travel on cases with me and even vacations, but this is different for them."

"I'm sorry, Cuz. I just see ulterior motives everywhere I look. I know you think I'm paranoid about them."

"You are," I agreed.

"Asshole," she said. "You know this means I have you to myself this week."

"For sure," I said, not expecting anything out of the ordinary. Melina is a real workaholic. Betty began a two-hour massage thirty minutes after I returned from the airport, hung around for Miguel's great dinner, and stayed until almost midnight, when it was time for her regular meetup with Melina, who would just be getting home from work.

"I can come back and spend the night. It might be late, but I'll do it."

I kissed her. "You're always welcome, but I'll be out of it by then."

I had just shut her out, but she kissed me back before she left. I headed up to bed. As I walked through the door, the phone rang. It was Pixie.

"Fuck, you would not believe this place!" Her excitement came through the phone. Not just hers. I could hear the girls around her going off like a high school cheering squad.

"Where are Camila and Olga?"

"We're on speaker, boss. Camila and Olga are cool. No wonder you love them. They say 'Hi.' They're getting ready to go dancing," Niley said.

"They really know the meaning of the red carpet, boss," Jo said. "Everywhere we go, it's like we're royalty or something."

"How was your ride?"

"Smooth, boss. Man, this plane is something else. Can we get one? Next we're going out to dance in shorts and tees. Are you okay?" Letty asked.

"About to hit the hay, kiddos."

"Aw, poor baby going to bed alone. Sleep tight, boss," Jo said.

It was an unusual week. With the girls gone, I woke up each morning in bed with Melina. We alternated houses, starting with Friday morning, which came as a complete surprise to me. She came over as soon as Betty left her, and I can vouch that Melina could not have gotten any sleep at all. She called to tell her managers she had a project she was working on at home, and was putting in minimal work hours. Minimal for her is max for anyone else. I had all day free to work, and the six hours a night she was not at her markets, she spent in my bed. I was in heaven.

Chapter 26
August 1978
Spain

A Boeing 707 lost power five minutes after takeoff and crashed in a commercial area, taking out two buildings in Madrid. A hundred and two died. Four on the ground were seriously injured. The number of victims would have been larger if it hadn't been Sunday.

I wanted to take Letty with us, but she was waiting on her passport.

"Next time, baby, next time."

When we arrived in Madrid, I went to see a lawyer that Jason hadn't met but recommended, though I could not tell Ricardo Munoz that Jason had given me his name and contact information. Meeting him, I knew a couple things right away: Munoz was sharp. Given the opportunity, he'd be a tough competitor. I'd rather be ahead of the game and get him on our team than face him in the field.

I called for an appointment and, bingo, a few hours later I was dressed in a three-piece suit and sitting in Munoz's very modern office, stark and minimal and metal, but decorated with a bunch of crazy Salvador Dali paintings I found really perplexing. Ricardo Munoz was no Oscar, but he looked and talked like a lawyer. He had several of his staff answering his phones. While I was there, I heard Spanish, of course, but also French, German, Italian, and something Middle Eastern, possibly Arabic. He was prepared for a cosmopolitan clientele.

When we shook hands, I looked him over. His hair was the kind of black no one mistakes for brown, almost blue in its blackness, worn longer than Oscar's, and he was deeply tanned, with burned-in lines around his eyes and mouth. He probably played tennis or golf—something that took him outdoors. I saw a pale line on his hand where a ring used to be. Eyes light brown, heavy brows, lashes invisible. He didn't shake tough, like he had something to prove, but firm enough. He was on the slim side, lightly built.

"To what do I owe the pleasure?" he asked. "I presume you are a lawyer, or are looking for representation."

"I'm not a lawyer. I'm here looking into the Boeing tragedy; and I'm a consultant for this firm." I handed over my card and an updated bilingual book of Oscar's firm. "As you can see, they are experts in aviation. We have heard a lot about your expertise. I wanted to see if we could work together."

He seemed friendly enough so far. I observed him across the desk.

He put his elbows and forearms on the table. He was curious, but seemed open to negotiations. On the other hand, I'd heard he was a skilled negotiator, so he might be just playing with me.

"Mr. Luna, why do I need to work with a lawyer in the United States?"

"I can give you one reason: the aircraft was manufactured in the United States. That doesn't guarantee that we'll get a judge in the United States to let us try a case there against an airline operator whose headquarters is in Spain, but it's worth a chance. If the investigation reveals there is product liability, we get a shot at keeping the case in the United States."

He nodded his head. "Go on. I'm still listening." He tilted his head as he listened and tapped the desk with one finger.

"I'm here to talk with families of the decedents. I know from experience that it would be nice if we did it together. By nice, I also mean that we will both be more effective. I'm sure we can come to an understanding about a fee split between your firm and the Cooke firm in Los Angeles."

Tom Jones had prepped me well. I could tell I had his attention. But it was too soon to know.

"I can give you another reason. The firm in Los Angeles is really good at settling aviation cases without a trial. We have had so many cases, the insurers know the firm does not mess around. No bluffs. We file lawsuits. We bury them in paperwork. We mean business, and they know it."

"You have time for lunch?"

I showed him a smile. "I have time, and I'm hungry."

He ordered a salad and black coffee. I would have been happy with a sandwich, but I followed his lead.

"Ditto," I told the waiter. "*Idem.*"

At the table, he asked questions about Oscar and his firm, the kind of questions that showed a keen appetite for business. I could tell the prospect of working with Oscar was beginning to grow on him.

The next morning, I had another appointment with him. By now, we were on a first-name basis.

"Since Mr. Cooke's firm will be doing most of the work, we will agree to a split of twenty percent of the attorney fees. You have agreed that if we encounter expenses, Cooke will reimburse me."

"Correct," I said. "Speaking of expenses..." I pulled out an envelope from my inside coat pocket and placed it on his desk. "Five thousand American[41] on account."

"Mario, you're the real thing." He was grinning, his smile splitting deep grooves in his cheeks.

"I'm nobody. But Oscar Cooke and Tom Jones are the real thing." I tapped Oscar's book on his desk with Oscar on the cover.

"You are too modest, Mario. I will agree to this, but I must have access to you. You speak my language. As far as I'm concerned, I will hold you accountable that the contract I sign with Cooke encounters no difficulties."

"You got it."

---

[41] $5,000.00 in 1978 had the same buying power as $19,438.97 in 2017

Ricardo was well connected and had gotten the word out. When we showed up for the first family meeting at the hotel auditorium, there were more than a hundred people there. Ricardo had newspaper and television as well as the families' word of mouth. On the second meeting, we had many repeat families, plus another hundred people. Ricardo was impressed that I had it catered with soft drinks, juice, coffee, and sandwiches. Jo, Pixie, and Niley mingled. They signed families who didn't want to wait, and who had arrived with their minds made up.

As we had done before, we also had small group presentations. Ricardo presented at every meeting we had. He was good. He knew aviation and was able to answer his share of questions. He told our audiences he teamed up with us because two experienced firms working as a team are better than one, but I know he looked forward to doing half the work instead of all. I knew he was optimistic about the long-shot possibility that the case would be filed and kept in a United States court, where the awards for cases like this were known to be much higher than elsewhere in the world. He felt confident enough to joke about being able to do only a fraction of the work.

When it was time for me to speak, I tried to keep it short and simple. I told the families, "We don't know what caused the power failure, but no matter the reason, you are entitled to compensation from the airline operator. If the investigation reports there was a failure in some system, we will sue the manufacturer of that system." My team, as usual, sat lined up behind me, either against the wall or on the podium, ready to answer questions and look supportive.

I kept in touch with Jason to let him know how we were progressing, thanking him for the lead to Miguel.

"You're so close to London. Come see us. Sami would love it."

"Soon as I get back, I promise I'll do a U-turn and head to London. I owe you big time, Jason."

"No you don't. You owe me nothing. We're friends."

Chapter 27
September 1978
Pit Stop

After landing, we slept for a few hours at my place, then went to Oscar's office, where we were escorted to a large conference room to meet with Oscar and Tom. I had never taken the team like this to deliver the retainers after a trip. It was a first.

When we walked in, I tried to see the office through the girls' eyes. We walked past the desk in reception where Betty used to sit, which made me smile. Jo, of course, had been here before. I introduced Niley and Pixie to all the familiar faces, people they might have contact with if they ever came in on a case for me. The office was spacious and expensive. Lots of marble, windows, and busy legal people. A long, wide hall led to many offices with secretaries, paralegals, financial officers, administrators, support personnel, assistants, and law clerks. While we were there, a court runner came through with papers needing signatures.

"How did you do?" Oscar asked after dispensing with the court runner. After all the daily calls, he already knew the answer.

I nodded for the girls to go ahead. Jo presented Oscar with thirty retainers. Pixie handed him thirty, Niley handed him thirty, and I handed him five.

"Are we good or what?" I asked. We had been in Spain for three days shy of a month.

Oz balanced his cigar in the ashtray. His eyes teared up. I thought he was going to cry.

"I'm speechless," Oz said. He said complimentary things to each of the girls.

"Thank you, Team Luna." Tom hugged us. Oscar came around the table and hugged and kissed the girls, and even kissed me on each cheek. The girls went home for a well-deserved rest.

I hung around longer than I intended. Oscar's practice was thriving with eleven lawyers, including five of whom who worked aviation with Tom. Oscar still had a criminal practice that other lawyers handled. These days, Oscar personally handled only the big-money cases. I got chills of anxiety every time I imagined how much his overhead must be, and then on top of it all, there was me. It was an ongoing outlay, but Oscar never complained.

I was happy to see Melina when she came over that night, late as usual. She found me asleep in the spa and kissed me awake. Her workaholic hours at the markets were crazy, no crazier than mine, but at least I had breaks between crashes. She allowed herself no breaks. I felt like I'd worked every minute of twenty-eight days straight. I was wiped out and jetlagged. She devoured me with kisses.

"You need some shut-eye," she said.

"I know, Cuz. We barely napped when we got in at two a.m., and early on, we got wrapped up in business at Oscar's. I stayed there way too long—till six. Oscar bought lunch and would have bought dinner, but I convinced him I had to go home. It was seven when I got here, barely awake for the meal Miguel fixed. I knew you were coming, so I tried to keep my eyes open with a workout and hit the spa."

"Which is why I found your naked ass passed out on that cold table," she said. "I guess I'm lucky I didn't find you asleep on the shower floor."

"The table felt good after the steam room."

It had long since stopped being comfortable. While we were downstairs,

I took a quick shower that woke me up a little and pulled on some sweat pants. Okay, and maybe I didn't shower alone.

We walked up the stairs to my bedroom. Melina stopped at the door. Her hair was wet, and she was wearing a pair of the new sweatpants I'd had Letty put a supply of in the spa. She didn't step inside. I thought about it but didn't have the energy to coax her.

As she was walking away, I said, "I want to fuck you bad, baby."

"Ditto," she said. "Want me to call Betty to come give you a massage?"

"Thanks, baby, but I'm over and out."

I didn't really want her to go, but talking took too much energy. Thinking took too much energy.

She looked at me. I gave her a big smile. The next thing I knew, I was falling asleep in my bed, spooning Melina. The sweats were draped over the back of a chair. I slept until three in the afternoon and awoke alone, wondering when Melina had left. I hit the shower, then pushed the intercom's kitchen button.

"Miguel."

"Boss?"

"Coffee. Food. I'm starved."

If my bedroom wasn't soundproof, I would have heard Letty run up the stairs. She burst through the door, waving an envelope like a banner and jumping around like she was walking on hot coals. I was sitting at the end of my bed, wearing boxers, still jetlagged. Deciding whether or not to dress felt like a big decision, but the day just got a lot brighter. I smiled.

"Boss, I got my passport!"

"Congratulations," I said. It was hard to resist her enthusiasm.

"Boss, I've been waiting for you to wake up. I hardly saw you yesterday, and before that, not for a whole month."

I put off dressing for a while.

"Come here, baby," I said, beckoning, my arms open. "I missed you too."

She handed me the passport to look over. The camera had caught her making a very serious face. She'd probably gone to a beauty shop and had her hair done. Her bangs were feathered. I held the passport up and adjusted her hair till she matched. "There you are," I said.

She giggled.

"You're in, then. Great news!"

"I'm so happy for the chance to make good. Thank you!"

I ate and worked out alone in a lazy fashion, with the wrong music playing. I showered and watched the clock for Betty's arrival. I'd gotten used to three Betty-massages a week, and I'd missed a whole month's worth. I collapsed on the table and let her beat the jet lag out of me.

"Hey, chief, I missed you. Welcome home."

"I'm chief now? Everyone else calls me boss. Chief is okay. I like chief."

She blushed a little. "Sorry, it just slipped out. My father was a sergeant for LAPD. Everybody called him chief. It just slipped out."

"Oh, so I remind you of dad?" Not something any healthy red-blooded man wants to hear, especially from a beautiful young woman whose got her hands on him. I was no exception.

"Not at all. I'm sorry, I'll call you boss."

"I'm sorry about your dad, I was just kidding. Call me anything you want, Mario, boss, chief, I'm game. Melina calls me asshole half the time. Not too crazy about that one."

Her pink shoes were looking a little threadbare. She never complained about money, but I had a feeling she needed every dollar I paid her. I sent Betty as much business as I could. When she was done with me, I used the intercom to call Letty in.

"Betty is going to give you a one-hour special."

"Cool," Letty said. "Are we going to do another threesome?

"My legs still tremble when I think about when we did it," Betty said.

"I don't tremble. I come." Letty grinned.

"It's in my memory book for sure," I said. "For sure in the top ten of my hit parade."

Betty began Letty's massage. I walked out of the bedroom and went back to my desk.

On Sunday morning, as I got out of the shower, Melina was waiting for me, just standing there in my dressing room with a giant, soft towel. She helped me dry off and walked me toward the bed.

"I told Miguel we're doing brunch here today."

"Yes, ma'am. Boss. Miss Melina." I was grinning ear to ear.

Melina looked at her watch. "We have twenty minutes before Miguel sends up our starters. Just enough time to get off once or twice."

"Speak for yourself."

"I am." She grinned.

Sixty seconds later, I was deep inside her, and I felt her explode.

"Make that three or four times," she gasped.

She kissed me passionately. By now I was on top. Melina had her legs wrapped around me and was in a wild frenzy. I heard the door but didn't turn to see who walked in.

When we took a break, we found the balcony table set up, everything covered to stay warm.

"I missed you," I said.

"You run away to work with your trio and expect me to believe that?"

"We seldom do it on business trips, Cuz."

"But you hit the ground running when you get home to play catch-up."

I nibbled her right earlobe. "What can I say? You know we do it. And I know you do it, too."

Melina leaned toward my nibbling. "Yeah." She sighed. "We're freaks."

"Our whole generation is made up of freaks. Drive by Echo Park. Naked bodies bouncing around on the grass."

Melina rolled her eyes at me. One of her markets is across the street from the park. The weekend traffic in that park is insane: wall-to-wall vehicles from one end to the other as young people showed off their cars, but certainly the traffic meant business. She'd had an artist make perky, friendly signs: "No shirt, no shoes, no service," and kept flip-flops on hand so the hippies in training could actually put them on their grass-stained feet and not interrupt their urge to spend money at her store. She whacked my arm with an open hand. "They are not naked on the green, fruitcake."

In robes, we sat on the balcony that overlooked the grounds and the distant pool. We ate in a leisurely fashion and headed back to bed. While we napped, the table was cleared.

Letty knocked and came in with a big smile on her face that didn't break when she saw Melina lying next to me. If anything, she smiled even bigger.

"Boss, what would you and Madam like to eat for dinner?"

Melina sat up in indignation. The sheet fell, revealing one plump breast.

"Melina is good enough. What's this 'madam' thing? I don't run a bordello, and I'm not a grandma."

Letty rephrased her question.

"Surprise us," Melina said. "And congratulations, Miss Priss. The boss says you are going to join the team. We'll have to go clothes shopping. Next time I get a minute off, I'll call you to meet me at Fiorucci's on Beverly Drive."

Letty beamed like the headlights on a Porsche 911.

We ate in the dining room two hours later.

"Betty is coming over at nine to give me a massage," Melina said. "You were right. She's a prize."

"She is. I can't get enough."

"Me neither. Are you fucking her?"

"The day you beat me up about the money, I came home in a fury, got a massage, then I furiously fucked her."

"Keep going."

"We had lunch, then another first. Betty and Letty and me; I even smoked pot. I was running away from the hurt. You were so pissed at me. The team came in and found Letty and me, and then they were pissed at me too. It was a bad day all round. Betty was good, though."

"Betty is good at taking care of my needs, too."

"Do you fuck her?"

"I don't have a dick, asshole."

At eight in the evening, I walked Melina down my long driveway, out my gate, across the tree-lined street, through her gate, and up a long driveway to her front door. We embraced. We kissed as though we'd been a couple of teenagers out on a date and I was delivering her home.

"I love you, Mario Luna."

I started to say ditto but caught myself.

"I love you, Melina Marron."

She was standing at her door with it halfway open. "If you love me and I love you, why do we sleep around?"

A topic of conversation almost every time we met.

"You tell me," I said, giving her a kiss on the lips.

"Who the fuck knows. We're freaks. We're the sex, drugs, and rock and roll generation, except you and I don't do the drugs or rock and roll, and we make up for it with more sex."

"Doesn't matter. I do love you, Miss Marron."

She looked up at me seriously and said, "I do love you too, Mr. Luna."

I went directly to my spa, where I took a hot steam and shower. My bedroom, when I returned to it, was pristine, my bed made with fresh linens. The forced air was providing a perfect temperature. Outside, it was the hottest September I could remember. The bed was turned down and ready. I sat on the sofa, turned on the television, put on my headphones, and listened to Neil Diamond.

I didn't hear the knock on my door, but I looked up to Letty walking in. She lit candles around the room and turned on the bedside lamps with their pinkish glow. I didn't take off my headphones but waved her over.

She sat next to me and wriggled her right hand and arm behind my back to hug my waist. I pulled on one side of my headphones so she could hear what I was hearing. She grabbed another pair of headphones, hooked up, and joined me. I was pretty relaxed.

"Letty, I'd be so lonely without you."

"I'm happy to be here."

We got on the bed. We turned to our sides and faced each other. It was becoming a popular position on my bed.

"There's something I'm not sure you realize," I said in a low, serious voice.

"What, boss?" She sounded a little worried.

"You are getting prettier and prettier."

She kissed me. "So are you."

Afterwards, we returned to the couch to listen to music.

Maybe I dozed off. I didn't hear the phone, but Letty did. I opened my eyes and watched her answering it. I read her lips. Emergency.

I took the headphones off. Letty turned off the TV, put the headphones away, returned to my side with the phone, and handed it over.

Jo said, "There's been a helicopter crash in Puerto Rico. Juan says he's been calling, but it keeps going to the exchange."

"Sorry," I said. "Did you get details?"

Letty stood, looking uncertain. I tapped the seat beside me, and she sat.

"A Bell Tour helicopter. Nine tourists on board. All dead."

"When did it happen?"

"Two days ago."

"Okay. I'm thinking of going to London, but I won't if you want me to go with you."

"We can handle it, boss. Juan already reached out to three families that live in Puerto Rico. The others are from other places. No details yet."

"Let's get what we can get. But you have to be jetlagged," I said.

"We'll be fine. We'll leave in the next day or so. Be in touch tomorrow."

"Jo, thank you for taking care of business like you do."

"That's my job, boss. No thanks needed."

"Love you," I said.

"Love you more."

As soon as I put the phone down, it rang. It was Pixie, also calling to tell me about the Puerto Rico crash.

"Baby, I just talked to Jo. You kids are handling. Letty is going with you. I'm taking off on one of my London trips."

Letty heard this and started jumping up and down, clapping her hands.

I needed to let Oscar know. I was giving him so much business. I knew it had to be costing him dearly. I remembered when I used to worry about Jake's expenses from bus and train crashes. If there was a problem, I hoped that Oscar would say something.

It felt later than it was. Not too late for a phone call. I called Oscar instead of Tom.

"I'm sending the girls to sign one in Puerto Rico. Oz, I don't want to smother you. Is this all business that you can cover without any problem?"

Oscar laughed hard. "Are you worried I'll run out of money?"

I hesitated before answering. "I'm not worried that you can't pay me. I'm worried you may be biting off more than you can chew. I sit around guessing about the enormous overhead you have, so I worry about you. I'm not worried about me, believe me."

"Kid, keep them coming."

I couldn't remember him calling me kid before. Jake used to call me kid. Some kid. I was pushing thirty-one. He hung up, and I replaced the phone in its cradle.

"Do you want to rest? I can leave," Letty said.

"Are you tired?" I asked.

"Never."

"Then why would I want you to leave?"

We put our headphones on. Twenty minutes later, I poured us each a glass of red. Letty nursed hers, but she was still excited about going on her first case. I'd been drinking off and on all day with Melina, but the buzz had worn off.

"Next month will be our one-year anniversary. Can you believe we have been working for you that long?"

I kissed her. Letty had become an addiction that I depended on when the team went home.

"When are you leaving for London?"

"I haven't made reservations yet. Soon. It will be a short trip."

"I wish you were going on this case, too. Boss, why London so much?"

"It's the coats. I'm crazy for the coats. If I wore my long coats here, people would be thinking I had lost it."

Letty laughed and poked me in the side. "Seriously."

"I love London. I like shopping there. I like clubbing with Sami. I like hanging out. Sami's got a cool place, but it has nothing to do with that. I just like London. Seriously. If you scratched off the LA in me, you'd find a Londoner underneath."

"I get it, boss. Sounds bitching. Maybe the team can go with you sometime."

"For sure."

The phone rang.

"Please get it," I asked Letty. I watched her get up and answer the phone. The candles in the room reflected off the sheen of her hair and the soft tan of her creamy skin. She had a perfect profile, a bit of a Roman nose, and a little cleft in her chin. Her hair was board-straight and hung down her back almost to her waist, without a streak in it. She must have sprayed a ton of hairspray on it to make her bangs look like they did in her passport photo. I liked how she wore it loose, not so much how she put it in a ponytail at night. It could see how it could get in the way of her getting a good night's sleep.

"It's Betty." A stream of hair caught the light, cascading like a waterfall over her shoulder as she handed me the phone.

"I heard you were giving Melina a massage tonight."

"I just finished. Want me to come over?"

"Letty is under my covers."

"Not a biggie at all. I'll do both of you."

I laughed. "You'll do both of us, huh?"

"Sure, you know I will."

"Come over."

I conferred with Juan about the helicopter case. He had things on his end well in hand.

"You want me to arrange rooms?"

"I think Jo is handling. I'll be in London, so it will be just you and the girls."

"Enjoy London, boss. Don't worry about a thing. We'll get the families signed."

"I'm not at all worried."

Tom Jones showed up at the house with retainers filled out for that particular crash and a box of the firm's updated aviation brochures for the girls to take with them. Juan had already secured invitations to speak with the families, but every little bit helps.

The girls arrived dressed for travel. Letty had set the table for four, but they were too excited for a meal. Pixie wanted to sit by the pool, but she had such a tendency to jump in, Jo wouldn't let her, for fear of her making them late. They gulped down coffee and talked about their plans to eat later on the plane. They loved eating on planes. The surprise of what would be there. The neat dining tools. The pull-down table. Their luggage had already been stashed in the limo. Their cars were staying in my garage till they flew back.

"Did your passport come yet?" Pixie asked.

Letty said, "It did. I told Mario. Sorry I didn't tell you." She was clearing the dishes.

"It's just Puerto Rico," I said, and cleared my throat.

Letty stopped what she was doing to see what I wanted. She was wearing a little shift with an apron that she thought made her look like a housekeeper. It didn't. She looked like a little girl playing dress-up. Her arms were full of dishes.

"Put down the dishes," I said. "I told you yesterday that you were on the team. Go. Pack. Pronto."

We were on the move, heading toward the back exit.

"Never mind packing," Jo said. "She won't have the right clothes. I can buy her stuff over there."

"I have lots of clothes," Letty said. "I got it covered."

"Okay, let's go see."

Letty shrieked and started dancing around, even though she'd known since last night that she was going. Maybe she hadn't believed it. My girls were not kids, but sometimes it was hard to tell if they were adults.

Jo had already commandeered one of the golf carts.

"You can walk if you want," Jo said, taking off for Letty's quarters. Pixie and Niley caught up and jumped aboard. "Do you have a suitcase?"

"Yes," Letty yelled after them.

Not a minute later, Letty was sprinting after the golf cart. I stood outside the main house back entrance, watching Letty's fine ass. What a fucking turn-on my life was.

My foursome took a flight to Miami, Florida, where they would catch the plane to Puerto Rico. After a call to Aunt Carmen, I was on my way to New York, where I had a two-hour layover for the direct flight to London. Every time I flew to London, I remembered this was the flight where I had met Sami. I never would have imagined that this woman and I would become such intimate friends, and that her friend Jason would be my mentor in aviation, a client development business that was making me rich. How far I had come.

From the beginning, body shops had sent me business because I put green in their pockets, whether or not I landed the cases they sent. I wanted to compensate Jason too, but worried that cash might put him off. I knew that he collected fine wine, so I'd been adding to his wine collection. Problem is, he matched me by giving me wine back, so I never felt I'd caught up comping him. I'd heard he was as rich as Sami, and had a feeling he would interpret payment as an insult. Sami didn't send me business, but she sent me Jason. She wouldn't take money, but she was a London perk, no lie.

Sami was beautiful and single by choice. Like Melina and me, she was a woman of her time, and just liked being free and doing what she wanted. She delighted in our freewheeling relationship. She had a fierce sexual appetite, and I had the feeling that when I wasn't around, she led Jason on quite a chase. Jason appeared to be a staid run-of-the-mill sort, but there was a whole lot going on under the hood. I really didn't know (or care) if he or she was the kinky one, or if it was both of them. If Jason wanted to watch us fuck again, I'd do it in a heartbeat. I have my kinky side too.

Chapter 28
September 1978
Last Hurrah

On the layover, I called from New York, telling Sami I'd take a taxi from the airport to her penthouse. She wouldn't hear of it. I had no agenda, no other plans in London, no extra baggage, so I conceded. When I cleared customs and walked the ramp from the terminal, I saw that beautiful face of Sami's. It would have been hard to miss her in that waistless, sleeveless turtleneck mini dress she was wearing, patterned in gold bricks with purple mortar, with bright purple hose, tall, clunky shoes, and, oh, those never-ending legs.

The airport was abuzz with noise. All around were families coming together, greetings, exchanges in different languages, drivers with signs naming people they were picking up. Sami had a sign too: "Mario Luna" in huge purple letters, the color of the day. I wonder if someone had told her recently that redheads can't wear purple. It would be just the kind of rule it would delight Sami to defy. She ran at me in a blur of purple, and I caught her up. Her sign and my carry-on hit the ground as we kissed, deeply and passionately. The shocked, dead quiet brought me out of it. I looked around and found all eyes on us and Sami's legs wrapped around me. When I put her down, the silence filled with applause and laughter. I took a bow, then took Sami's arm. I heard a few random comments.

"Who are they? Are they movie stars?"

We were bathed in flashing lights, cameras going off like mad. I blinked.

Sami waved and posed for a second, then grabbed my arm.

"Let's go."

I picked up my suitcase, and we ran for the exit where Ginger was waiting in the Rolls. When she saw us, she jumped out and opened the door. In passing, I kissed her lips.

"Good to see you, Ginger."

She waved and closed the partition, leaving Sami and me with the feeling of a little privacy.

"Mario, thank you for coming to visit. I love having you over. I love having you."

We had turned to face each other. Our mouths pressed together, lips moving when we spoke, still kissing.

"Please don't thank me. I love London."

She was already rummaging in my pants as if she thought I'd left mine at home.

"Yes, I brought it with me."

She found my growing hard on. I had no idea why in the world I had become special to her. For her, special didn't mean exclusive. That was okay in my book. Sami did a pretty good job of making me feel special.

"I'm getting older," she said. "You better get it before I grow old and ugly."

"Baby, you are beautiful."

Sami had perfect skin. Her body was as firm and trim as the girls'. I wasn't sure what Sami did to stay toned; maybe meds. She was a doctor, after all. We never discussed it. I had never seen her work out. Maybe she worked out when I wasn't there taking up her time.

London was beautiful. Though September was about to end, cold weather had not set in. Three days after my arrival, we stepped outside our routine and hit Harrods. That night, we went clubbing. Everywhere we went, they were playing music from *Grease*. We hit a casino and went back to Sami's place.

As a good host, Sami always had options during the day. Often there was a male masseur for her and a female masseuse for me, waiting for hours to see if we opted for a massage. I was always game, but sometimes Sami passed. Sometimes we shopped at home. Louis Vuitton, where Sami shopped, sent over four models. Versace sent models, including two men. They all had merchandise for us before it was in the store. Once, they all arrived at the same time, and stared at each other uncomfortably from either side of the den. They walked the hall as if it were a runway. The models were cutthroat competitive. Sami thought it was a blast.

"I want those ties," I whispered to Sami, "but I must pay for them."

"Stop worrying about the small things," she told me. Big smile. "It all goes on my tab."

At least once every trip, Sami hosted some kind of charity benefit for kids somewhere. These were huge events at big hotels, with hundreds of people eating from benefit plates they'd paid for, or buffets with auctions. They were always to benefit some poor country that Sami would be flying to in order to do some kind of essential surgery for impoverished children. That was usually a night when I was free to play tourist, and Jason escorted her. This time, I went myself and saw everything in person.

It was exciting for me at this benefit, especially when she left the table and walked up the stairs to talk earnestly to the audience about whatever the charity was about. She looked beautiful up there, and showed me a side of her I'd never seen before. She never talked about work or about her patients. I wonder how she managed to leave that kind of emotional work at the office.

The night of the benefit, I had a fantasy of Sami that included the audience.

One night, Ginger drove Sami and me to a huge mansion. Ginger giggled as we drove up, and she stayed in the car. I walked in expecting a stuffy cocktail party. The entrance hall was manned by a butler who was practically invisible. After he and Sami conferred quietly, money changed hands. We exited the foyer into a smaller room. She turned her back to me and asked me to undo her dress, a strapless, tight, red-sequined number that went to the floor with a peekaboo slit up to her right armpit. It was a sexy dress. A couple of filmy straps on the right side always threatened to give way and bare all. She was practically sewn into that thing, and I had to unfasten each of the straps from her under her arm all the way down to her hip. I did as she wished, and she squirmed the rest of the way out. Without her in it, the dress shrank to half its size. She hung it on a hanger, kicked off her red, strappy stiletto heels, and stood there completely naked, looking at me impatiently.

"No underwear?" I asked her.

"Saves time," she said.

I looked at that huge diamond ring she had on.

"You taking that doorknob off your finger?"

"Honey, it's fifteen carats. You should know I never take it off."

"Better be careful. You could take someone's eye out with that thing."

She laughed.

I followed her lead and hung up my custom-made Italian suit in one of several wardrobes, all full of evening wear. I shoved my boxers into a trouser pocket, and socks into my shoes. We exited the dressing (or should I call it undressing) room into a scene out of Playboy fantasy fiction. The lights were dim, but I could see we'd walked into an orgy. Writhing bodies were everywhere. All kinds of bodies, too. Young, old, sexy, not so sexy. Candles were on every surface, and so were couples. There wasn't any other lighting.

"If you don't like what you see in one room, you just move to another," Sami explained. Apart from having to pay, being bare-ass naked was the ticket to move around the mansion full of writhing strangers.

Their bar was endless. The liquor they served was anything you asked for. I asked for a bunch of different things just to see if they were there: Arak, which tasted like licorice and turned cloudy when we added water. Needed the water. Absinthe, which they had, and was awful. Cachaça, which I'd had once in Brazil. Soju, which was from South Korea, and as far as I am concerned can stay there in the sweet potatoes they make it from. Sami pulled me from the bar and we had Cristal and walked around with a glass in hand, checking out the goings-on. I would be lying if I said I wasn't turned on. I was hard to the point that it was difficult to walk—and naked, there is no hiding it.

"I didn't know you were into orgies," I said.

Sami took my hand. "London has a middle name. Orgies."

I had talked about orgies with Melina and Pixie, but I didn't want to admit to Sami that I had never been to one.

We lay on a bear rug, and Sami moved on top of me. It was just the two of us, but people were circulating and watching. I barely noticed them, but Sami was so excited, she was trembling.

"You're so hot!" I said. I whistled.

Sami laughed. "You do say that a lot, don't you? I bet you say that to all the girls."

"Only when they're so hot," I said.

We laughed.

"I'm not bad for thirty-eight," she said.

"You're hot, period," I said. She could have been in her twenties. Hell, she could have been eighteen.

Another group of people walked through, watching us. Sami went as wild as she'd been the night that Jason was watching. Now I didn't know if he was a voyeur, but I was sure getting the benefits of Sami being an exhibitionist. I wondered if she and Jason had been here before, or if they came here regularly, but I didn't ask. I don't know how long it went on. I got lost in the moment, drunk on sex, drunk on Sami. Sami was on top of me, and soon there were other bodies around. Sami was a treasure for sure, but how my mind wandered. Pixie, Jo, Niley, Melina, Letty, and oh, Valita. The one that got away. My brain focused on Camila naked, but I pictured Camila where Sami was. Crazy in the midst of all this sex and all these strangers, I was bringing my girls into it, in my head. But that's fantasy for you.

I had never seen Sami so turned on.

My first-ever orgy. I learned at a mile a minute that night, caught up in enjoying what I was doing and what was being done to me. I absorbed it with all my senses. I was ever so hard, and the last thing on my mind was to have an orgasm anytime soon. Ginger drove us home and we were still so excited that we tore at each other in a frenzy of passion and love making. I couldn't get enough of her or her of me.

I had already stayed longer than planned. Whenever I was in London, it was always difficult making the decision to leave. Once I made the decision to go home, Sami always went all out to change my mind. The orgy visit was one of Sami's delay tactics. The next night, we stopped at a pub that could not have been any more different from the rich ambiance of the orgy mansion. The pub was noisy, sweaty, communal, packed, and nowhere nearly as nice as others we'd visited. Compared to the mansion, it was downright shabby.

"You like slumming?"

"Slumming is good, sometimes."

We had a table for two in the back. I wanted the wall seat, but Sami insisted.

"This time, I get the view." She whistled through her fingers, a thing I had never known she could do. She put her hand up with two fingers, signaling two beers.

"Mine is the better view," I said. The wall behind Sami was concrete blocks painted green, a perfect frame for her pretty face.

Within minutes, two draft beers were slammed in front of us by a waiter at a run. Sami waved at the bartender, a burly guy with big teeth, slightly crooked in that British way. He waved back and gave her an intimate smile.

"They know you."

"They remember anyone who tips well."

She clicked my glass and sipped the beer. Warm draft was a long way from the Cristal we had with dinner, but I got caught up in the ambiance of the place, her mood, and the friendly roar of everyone talking and laughing.

Halfway through her beer, Sami talked into my ear. It was either that or yell.

"I've actually picked up men here. I've taken them home and showed them the door in the morning."

"Really?"

I glanced at the bartender. His eyes followed her. Instinct told me he was one of her pick-ups. I wondered why she would do that, but I wasn't shocked. Didn't I do the same thing when the mood struck?

"This place has a good reputation for studs hanging out. Sometimes I send Ginger, but I don't always like what she brings back."

I smiled. "You don't need to tell me."

"I know. I'm not ashamed. Jason knows. He doesn't look down on me. Actually, he likes me to tell him about it."

I might like hearing about her conquests, too. I was no better. I remembered a hundred girls. I'd been with many girls in cramped cars parked behind Los Angeles night clubs. I remembered Valita taking me in her mouth while I stood there behind that iron door. I'd fuck anyone that I became attracted to. I remembered when Melina fucked Carson as a way for her to get his connections to off someone in prison, and the story she told me about the chief of police who gave her the gun permit in exchange for sexual favors. My eyes were on Sami the whole time I was thinking.

"Mario, did I space you out?"

"Not at all. To be honest, you made me think of girls whose names I've forgotten. Maybe we're not unalike."

I kissed her, a wet kiss, and passionate. I wanted to take her, then and there. We parted, sat down, and gazed at each other, smiling.

A tremendous explosion shook the walls, and then another. A loud bang, and a whoosh. Fire erupted. I don't know what happened to Sami, but I was ejected from my chair, airborne, flying across the room until I crashed halfway through a window, taking down tables and people and getting showered with glass. I shook it off and managed to find my feet. There was smoke. The diners were pushing for open doorways. I tried to move toward where I'd been sitting with Sami, but the table was gone. I looked for her, but couldn't see for all the smoke. I pushed through the mad rush of injured and bloody people, falling over, tripping on bodies lying on the floor.

"Get out!"

Someone was screaming. Many were screaming.

The pub was afire. Sirens were going off like mad. People were talking, crying, yelling, screaming. A chaos of noise, voices like a meaningless tower of babble. I made sense of nothing except the fire eating the walls. This place was in the process of burning to the ground. Heat scorched my skin, and I shook blood out of my eyes. Picked myself off the floor. Something hit the back of my head, or maybe that was me hitting the floor. My face was wet. Made out the floor tiles again, at least that was clear. Smoke hovered, floating a couple of inches over the clear air hugging the ground. Sami's purse was toppled on its side. I got to my knees, looking through the smoke, and made out Sami, some twenty feet away. How did she get so far? No, I was the one who had moved. She had been knocked against the wall. Burning tears poured from my eyes, and I coughed hard, lurched forward and down. Air by the floor I could almost breathe. I tottered ahead, picked her up, gulped some hot, bad air, and powered through the crowd to the exit. I knocked someone down, a girl, but didn't stop. I saw her dark eyes flash in terror, a tiny thing, big dark eyes, and then she was behind me. Fire engines and ambulances were arriving. Bobbies were everywhere. Bobbies manned the crowd, the cars, the pedestrians, and helped the injured get away from the building. An arriving ambulance squealed in front of me.

"You need to take care of her right now."

I placed her ever so gently on the gurney before they'd even gotten it set up all the way. Sami's eyes were open, but I knew she could not see. She was clutching my hand. Blood had dripped on her face, but it was mine. I could see her chest move in and out. I was talking, but my ears were ringing. I couldn't hear myself. The medical tech was saying something, but I couldn't hear him. I saw blood on Sami's mouth and wiped it away. My ear hurt, and it was wet. My head was spinning. I felt a surge of nausea and nearly threw up. Then I did hack up the beer and the dinner I'd eaten, feeling better and worse. Acid vomit burned my lungs. I coughed it out and gulped air that was cool and fresh and tasted like smoke. I had on one of my new Harrods chambray shirts and an undershirt beneath. Both were drenched in blood. I jerked off the chambray and wiped the blood off my face with it.

"Fix her," I told the guy with the gurney.

"Wait," he said. I could make out that much. He kept talking, but I couldn't comprehend his words. My head rang with sirens and some voices, but my ears were still hearing an explosion. I coughed, finished wiping, and tossed away the ruined shirt. All I could think of was the girl I had knocked down when I was getting Sami out. I turned to the building, the entrance pouring smoke and a slow stream of damaged patrons. One of the bobbies said something to me. He grabbed my arm and tried to get me to go the other way. I shook him off, maybe flipping him, not sure. I managed to get steps closer to the pub entrance. Guilt poured over me. In my head, I saw those eyes, pleading. I plowed through a stream of people fleeing for their lives. I took a last breath, dived into the smoke, and blindly made my way through. It wasn't far. I found the girl flat on the ground, face down, not far from where I'd left her. Not far to the door. I grabbed her arms, couldn't pick her up. Jerked, and managed to get her over my shoulder. Something above me cracked. A rush of sparks showered through the smoke, stinking, stinging, burning. Holding my breath. I wasn't inhaling the noxious gray smoke, and my lungs were screaming for air. Lurched out, bumping into a fireman invisible in the thick haze. Something cracked again, and a weight knocked me down. I collapsed flat, slamming my head for the second time. I felt the ground move beneath me, then everything went black.

"Wake up, man!" I heard voices. British voices.

I opened my eyes. I was drenched in sweat. Looked around. I wasn't at the pub. I was moving. Inside an ambulance. Heard a siren. My body hurt. My head. I shut my eyes, then opened them again.

"You're having a nightmare." Some stranger was standing over me. I was in a hospital bed with an IV in my arm. Disjointed images.

"Tanis," I said. I remembered the shooting. Closed my eyes again.

I looked up and saw a face.

"Sami, it's you."

She smiled at me, a little sad.

"You know, I really liked you, Mario."

We were both sitting on the hospital bed, side by side. I was wearing a clean chambray shirt, and she had on some bright gown I hadn't seen before. Around us, medical techs were working furiously. The lights faded. Sami was gone. I felt very alone, tethered down in tubes, surrounded by white fabric walls. Low ceiling. An ugly industrial table lamp lit the space I was in. Fabric partitions. I started coughing, horrible coughing. I was surrounded by people, strangers. Someone pulled out a needle.

"Where did Sami go?" My voice sounded strange. The needle burned. I closed my eyes and found Sami there, waiting.

Someone in white, a nurse, shook me awake. Over her shoulder, I saw Melina backed up against a hospital curtain, looking small and frightened.

"You must have been having a dream." The nurse spoke in sharp British tones and sounded very far away.

"Nightmare," I said. I closed my eyes for a moment. I reached out to her.

"I'm soaked. I'm freezing." My voice cracked, and I started coughing. My mouth tasted of smoke.

The nurse pushed tubes into my face. Oxygen, I guess. The nurse kept talking. I couldn't hear her, but she put her finger over her mouth. Pantomiming. *Shhh.* I didn't feel soothed. Coughing. More IV. More sleep.

Someone piled blankets over me. I was shaking. Someone took them off. I couldn't open my eyes. I heard voices. More British voices. No one I knew.

"The hotter he gets, the colder he'll feel."

I was freezing and burning up at the same time. Headache. Earache. Everything ache. Felt no clothing but a wet sheet. Then I was steaming hot. I was in the coils of a horrible nightmare and couldn't get my eyes open; then I did. Dizzying, freefalling, spinning through space, through time. Flashing lights, exploding, ground rushing up to meet me. I woke to a hospital, then falling again, endlessly, and kept waking there. I tried to wake into Sami's apartment, to no avail.

In my line of work, I've known many people who have come back from the dead, or believed they have. I've heard more stories than I can count from clients who survived. "I saw green pastures; the sun was brilliant like a shining star," one woman had told me. And another: "I was flying in a blue sky among hundreds of doves, guided by a brilliant light." Others had told me how they saw long-lost relatives and moved into a light. I had no such revelation.

I opened my eyes and tried to focus. Everything was blurry. I blinked—once, twice, many times. I heard a voice like a dissonant radio station, saw faces as jumbled and static as the sound. Gradually, I made out a face of a black woman. White coat. Concern in her eyes. I could see her lips moving and match them to what she was saying. It took longer to make out the meaning, but I understood her well enough. Behind her, Melina, in a chair, passive as I have never seen her, white-faced, terrified. Our eyes met. She didn't look like herself. She was head-to-toe in black. Long sleeves. Pants. It was cold out. We were in London. Why was Melina here?

"Mr. Luna, welcome back. I'm your neurologist, Dr. Young. Can you hear me?" I felt a hand on mine. "Nod or squeeze my hand, and tell me if you can see me."

I nodded and squeezed.

I heard myself ask for water. The frown lines crossing Doctor Young's face flattened. She gestured to a person out of my range. Someone, I guess a nurse, held a glass. I sipped water through a straw. My mouth was still dry. Throat raw. Wherever I'd been, I was back.

"Where am I?"

"London Hospital."

I had more questions than I could ask, but I suppose the doctor recognized that. "Your prognosis is good. You will fully recover."

"How long?" I asked, but I guess I was pretty inarticulate. I got no reply, just directions.

"Move your fingers. Open and close your hands if you can." There were more instructions, more talk, more medication introduced into my IV. I stepped into a cycle of waking and sleeping, but at least I knew where I was.

I wasn't alone. Melina was always there. I felt her kiss on my cheek. She spooned food into my mouth. Nurses propped me on pillows. Time was a crazy thing, moving sideways in fits and starts.

"Baby," I heard myself say. "Everything will be okay."

I blinked. The disjointed images told me time had passed. The room lighting had shifted from day to night. No idea how much time went by. Melina's chair was empty. I saw Jo and Pixie.

"Remember us?" It was Letty. Her eyes were so close to mine that she was out of focus. Then Jo spoke. They were holding my hands, both hands, holding hands with other hands. I drew comfort from the touch, sucked it in like a dry sponge finding water for the first time, before I went out again. My team. My girls. My family.

I heard a familiar rattle. Someone was pushing a food cart. I smelled hospital, with undertones of chicken. A girl in a red-striped uniform brought in a tray and set it down beside the bed. The doctor was standing over me.

"Doctor Young," I said.

"Mr. Luna, you remember my name." The doctor seemed surprised, maybe even relieved.

"Of course."

She went into a routine that felt familiar. Having me squeeze her fingers, nod, cough. Coughing was the worst. It felt like it rattled my brain. The room seemed too bright. I winced and shut my eyes.

Eyes still shut, I asked, "What is happening?"

"In order to protect your brain, we induced a coma."

That sounded drastic. I remembered bits and pieces. The doctor was still talking. I squinted to see her face, trying to focus on her words.

"...and the best news is that all your X-rays show that the swelling has diminished."

"How long was I under?"

"Seventeen days. Eighteen since the bombing."

She was still holding my hand after her tests. I squeezed it gently. "Am I missing any parts? Is my body intact?"

It's hard to explain, but I felt like a puzzle with missing pieces. I tried moving my toes. The sheet over me moved. Cotton brushed cool and coarse against my skin. Toes accounted for.

"You are intact, young man. We will be giving you some hearing tests, but it appears even your ear seems to be functioning normally. Keep making progress as you have been, and you'll be out in a week."

"I'll do my best." I squeezed her hand again, reluctant to let go. I looked at the tray the candy striper had left.

"Doctor, I think I'm hungry."

"You can eat," she laughed. "It's good to hear you say that. You will have help with your tray in just a moment. I had to chase your cousin out of here to examine you. She's been here nonstop. I think she'll be glad to know the tray is for you and not her."

"That's Melina, for sure," I said. But it was hard to picture Melina settling for a tray of hospital cooking. Or skipping work, for that matter.

"You have a room full of family waiting here. They've been here for days."

I was glad to know that the memories of Melina and my team were not hallucinations. I had not noticed a nurse in the room, but she was there. She did something at the foot and side of the bed to bring me to a seated position. For a moment, the room spun.

"Are you okay?"

"I'll be fine when the room stops moving, Doc." Then, "Better."

"Do you feel up to answering some questions?"

"Okay." I said. My voice sounded harsh, and my mouth was a desert. I coughed a little and tried to hold my head still. The nurse reached for the water and held it to my mouth. I sipped gratefully and thanked her.

"Do you remember what happened?"

"Explosions, smoke." The words triggered the memory. It was all live in my head. "Oh, my God. Sami. What happened to Sami?"

"She was here. Now she's at the London Memorial Hospital."

"How is she?" I stared at the doctor, but her face gave away nothing.

"I haven't heard."

"Why did they move her?" Maybe that was a hospital where she had privileges. I didn't know. I wish I'd asked more about her practice. I knew nothing except that she worked in pediatrics.

"London Memorial is a good hospital. It opened just last year. Her family had her moved two weeks ago."

"You must know something more?"

"Mr. Luna, one step at a time. Your friend has her own doctors."

Dr. Young nodded at the nurse, who left for a moment and returned with Melina.

"Your cousin has been living in that chair for days and nights," the nurse said.

Melina took the chair, but only after a hug and a passionate, if uncharacteristically careful gentle greeting. I don't know how she managed to smell like flowers, even in a hospital.

"Thank you for being here, Cuz." I felt tears in my eyes.

"You're all I've got," she said. She cleared her throat. "Everyone is here. Aunt Carmen has been here since the beginning. She and the girls are based at the Mandarin since they are only allowed here during visiting hours. Who do you want to see first?" She dug a spoon into the tray of bland hospital food. It looked like potatoes, peas, and some kind of fowl with gravy. It looked and tasted like baby food, but I was ravenous. I made faces at the taste and ignored the clatter of noise going on outside of my curtains. Swallowing was difficult. I might not have been aware of all of the last couple of weeks, but the noise of the ward sounded familiar.

"Dr. Young promised to get you off the bland diet soon. She even gave Letty permission to bring you peanut butter."

Melina spooned the food into my mouth, and even that seemed familiar to me. Two guests were the limit for everyone else, and though Melina had worked it out with the head nurse to let in up to four visitors at a time, she hadn't managed to negotiate bypassing hospital visiting hours. She told me about the Hyde Park Hotel, and about the girls, Oscar, and Tom.

The ward was never quiet. I couldn't see beyond the fabric, but I could hear when the people around me suffered some kind of trauma, or when new arrivals were installed, or when they left. All too frequently it was the new arrivals who left, their monitors screaming alarms and an alarming flat line tone calling in a team of doctors. It always seemed to happen late at night. Melina and I would be silent witnesses. The tone, the noise of the medical team working frantically, talking urgently among themselves in terms I didn't know and didn't want to know. One man arrived and died within hours. Then it was a woman who'd been in a headlong collision. Once they brought in a child. There was some discussion of putting her in pediatrics.

I was sitting in the dark, Melina in her chair.

"Do you hear this?" I whispered.

"Yes," Melina said.

A doctor, not Doctor Young, was arguing that this was the best place for the child since she was in a coma. Another doctor, also not Doctor Young, said she would have better care in a pediatric hospital. Her monitor went crazy, but only because they were moving her. When they put her in a bed, the rhythmic beat settled. Two pairs of feet approached and passed my curtain and stopped a couple of beds over.

"Oh, my baby," a woman said. She was crying so hard most of her words were unintelligible. All I heard was that the child's name was Mary. Something had happened in a winter swimming pool. A nurse, then two, joined her. One checked the child, and the other had forms and comfort for the mother. It was small comfort, though. A list of rules for the ward. Directions. Suggestions for the mother.

"We shouldn't be hearing this," I said.

"It's no different than when you first got here," Melina said. "I sounded just as bad. And the girls. Your aunt, though, she believed you would shake it off. And so you have. I think her belief in you really helped." She turned in my direction and took my hand. "Let's believe in the little girl?"

I was glad it was Melina who was with me.

I rolled on my side. It bothered my monitor. One of the nurses left the little girl and pulled back the fabric to peek in. I'm guessing she saw Melina and me with our eyes shut. She walked to the machine making the noise, did something to it that calmed its frantic clatter, and then took my pulse. Just as silently, she left, so quietly she could have been floating on a gust of air.

"Come on, Mary," I said. "You can do it."

Melina squeezed my hand. I could see the red flannel nightgown she'd changed into. In the half-light, the pattern looked like it was moving. Sleep did not come. We did not hear the girl wake, but a day later, we heard the noise and bustle as she was moved somewhere else. I wanted to think she woke in the pediatric ward and went home. The curtains were there, but they provided little privacy in the ward. I heard the other patients and all their people. I could only wonder what everyone here heard and thought about all of mine.

Aunt Carmen arrived in style, in new clothes, new hair, and with a tremulous smile. She took the chair on the side of my bed opposite Melina. A third chair was at the foot, stacked with blankets, folded sheets, and a pillow.

"I am so glad you are better," Auntie said.

My Aunt Carmen is an absolute rock. Not quite sixty, she looked young for her age, but I could tell that this vigil over me had been hard on her.

"Tell me how you've been?" I asked. "I can't believe you're here in London."

"I was in the waiting room. I didn't want to leave for a minute, but they chase us out at night. And as soon as Doctor Young told us you were going to be all right, Jo insisted on dragging me out for shopping and a makeover." She stood up and did a model-type spin. Her enthusiasm made me laugh, but then I grabbed my head to keep it from moving. The exuberance deflated right out of her. Instantly she was bent over me, asking what she could do, wanting to call the doctor back. I could only imagine what shape she must have been in, and felt a rush of love for my girls for seeing to my aunt.

Jo, Pixie, Niley, and Letty came in together. They were all in turtlenecks, long pants, and sweaters, layers on layers, more warmth than fashion. I had flashes of memory of their being here. They seemed boisterous and full of energy, but I could tell they were putting on a strong front on my behalf. They were never good at holding back their emotions. First it was Jo who teared up, then the others let go.

"Hey, I'm not dead." Those four words resulted in more sobs from my team. "I can't handle the crying, babies, please." My eyes were moist again.

"Boss, you look terrible." They argued with each other about how bad I looked, about the shadows under my eyes, and they promised to stuff me with food when I got home. They joked of peanut withdrawal. That reminded Letty of what she had, and she pulled out a jar of peanut butter. She opened it with the same kind of flourish you see at a restaurant when the waiter offers the pepper grinder, or a sommelier offers wine. She took the hospital spoon from the tray, stabbed it into the jar, and held it out to me. I let her put it on the table by the bed. I made happy noises, not letting on how the sight of it made me queasy. I was still digesting a tray full of bland.

I made them promise to take my aunt out to play tourist.

Melina poked her head in. She must have gone outside, because her cheeks were red from the cold, and she'd pulled on a sheepskin jacket over her long-sleeved knit top. Jeans tucked into boots. She didn't have leggings on, but the girls did.

"Okay, kids, out. There is a queue for Mario forming out there."

I got five full minutes of kisses and goodbyes before my girls left, leaving Melina and me alone for a few minutes. She straightened out my bed covers and the pillow behind my head. She called for more pillows and put one under my knees. A backache I didn't know I'd had suddenly eased. A nurse came in, and did some routine prodding and poking, then Melina had the girls return.

"When Jo heard you were injured, one of the people she called was Oscar. Oscar told Pepe you were in the hospital. Pepe sent a jet to bring us all to London."

"I feel special," I said softly, overwhelmed, just realizing how close I'd been to dying. "Did they fly here with you guys?"

"No, Pepe got here a day or so later, and Camila hours after that. And that night, Olga showed. I think they came and went in separate planes. They must be made of money."

"Did you hear about Pepe sending that big plane to fetch us from LA and bring us here?"

"Melina told me."

It felt good to have my team around me. I asked them something that had been on my mind.

"How is Sami doing?"

The girls looked back at me with blank faces. I didn't know if they were uninformed or hiding something.

"No idea," Letty said. "I don't even know who to ask."

"Me neither," Niley said. She changed the subject, "So, girls, dish. What do you think of that Pepe?"

"That man is way over the top," Jo said, reaching into her purse and producing another jar of peanut butter. She handed it to Niley.

"That's for sure, and he's single," Niley said, grabbing the jar and putting it beside my bed.

"You wouldn't marry Pepe, would you?" Letty asked Niley. Niley opened the older jar of peanut butter, saw it was empty, and tossed it in the trash. Letty produced a spoon and put it on the table beside the jar.

"No one will marry me," Niley said. "With four kids, I'm a package deal. No matter. I'm happy. And what brought marriage up? Are you thinking of marriage or something?

"You're beautiful," Jo said. "How are you thinking no one will marry you?"

Niley shrugged. "You don't see me crying, do you?"

"I'm not thinking of getting married, period," Letty told Niley. "You have to wonder how it would be to fly all over the world in your own jets."

Jo eyed the spoon Letty had left for the peanut butter. "Hospital spoon?"

Letty shook her head, grinning. "Hyde Park Hotel, room service. They have plenty more where that one came from."

"I'd fuck Pepe," Pixie said. "He's a good-looking guy. Reminds me of a gangster like in the movies. And then, there's all that money he must have. What's he worth, anyway? Bundles and bundles."

"Stop," I protested, realizing I might be sounding jealous, but I didn't have a jealous bone in my body—I knew that. Their cross-talking chatter was normal. "Is sex all you guys talk about?"

"Fuck yes," Letty said. "Money too. Money and men."

The girls laughed. I started to, but laughing bounced my brain in my skull like popcorn in a popper. I settled for a smile, but it had to be wavy around the edges.

"Pepe sprung me from the kidnappers. Boy, do I owe that man. Do they know I'm back among the living?"

Jo nodded. "I called Pepe, and then I called Camila. Pepe is in Milan. Camila in Paris. They know you're conscious. Olga too."

"Good," I said. "Did they say anything?"

"Camila and Olga were worried right along with all us. Olga had to run errands, but said she'd be back. I gave her the hospital number and our hotel number. She's called every day since she left, and she catches me here or at the hotel."

Melina returned with a milkshake. The girls had gone. When she handed it over, I took it gladly. At least that was something I could feed myself, once I was propped up. She rearranged the pillows for me. I looked at her sidelong, wondering if she would get an answer for me.

"Please find out about Sami. How is she? No one will tell me anything."

"I don't know," Melina said honestly. "What if all I find out is bad? Doc Young said no bad news for you."

I didn't care if it was bad or good. Wondering was killing me. "Bad or not, I have to know. All I have heard is that she's alive. There's some reason she's at that new hos—" I broke off my sentence in surprise as Tom and Oscar came in. Tom had a stack of magazines, and Oscar was carrying a huge box of chocolates. I felt the urge to get out of bed to shake their hands.

Melina put a hand on my shoulder.

"Behave," she said to me, as if I were able to get up. I was almost flattered. I could barely sit up, much less walk.

"Glad to see you awake, man," Tom said.

"We tried to get you a private room," Oscar said. "But the bomb filled up the hospital. Socialized medicine. Look at this curtained area you're in. You gotta be kidding. Can you believe they call this their critical care unit? My cat's veterinarian is better equipped. You have to be half dead or royalty to get a private room.

I'm glad that Doc Young of yours knows her stuff. I was ready to have you shipped home."

"Oz, they did something right. I'm alive."

Oscar nodded.

"We considered changing hospitals, but your doctor impressed Melina. We agreed you were in good hands, even if you were behind a curtain instead of a private room." Tom always sounded calm. Maybe it was the pilot in him.

Theoretically, I knew I'd been in a coma for seventeen days. I remembered something from that time, but not seventeen days' worth. It was a confusing jumble of images. The bombing felt like it had been yesterday, and yet it also felt like it had been years. I guess that's what a coma does to you.

Melina stood, offering her chair to Oscar.

"If you promise not to stress him out, I have something I have to check on," Melina said, giving me a look that promised she would bring me news of Sami. Whatever it was.

I don't know if it was because I'd gotten better, or rooms had come available, or someone had been throwing money around, or if the ward was just sick of my constant stream of loud visitors, but I was moved to a room with a door. Its advantages, on top of having a door, were that now I had four chairs, and Melina had room for a recliner chair that turned into a bed. The hospital still maintained strict visiting hours with the exception of one constant family member. Everyone said goodnight and went to the Hyde Park Hotel. When Melina returned, Oscar and Tom were long gone, and Pixie had gone to sleep on the hospital bed, squeezing between the tubes and gadgets latched onto me. I still felt half-gone at times. Having Pixie's body next to me was comforting, even if she was in sweats. Melina had traded her old-fashioned red flannel nightgown and now had on some kind of soft-looking lounge wear that bared her midriff. Glow-in-the-dark pink and orange with huge bell bottoms.

Melina reclined. "I checked the waiting room and the hotel. Where did

Oscar and Tom go?"

"I told them I'm going to be fine and asked them to go home. They've been here too long. The cases will suffer."

Melina smiled. "They really stuck it out."

"What have you heard?" I whispered, trying not to wake Pixie.

Melina put her finger over her lips and wafted one of her sheets over Pixie and me. She was lugging some kind of massive purse. I wondered if Jo had picked it out for her. If Letty had stocked it, it would be full of peanut butter. She stashed the purse. I heard its substantial weight hit the ground. She clicked off the bedside lamp. Light in the room dimmed. I waited impatiently. Melina sat on her recliner and lay back.

"Tell me about Sami."

"She sustained damage to her lungs. She never had the brain trauma you did, but she's not..." Whatever she was going to say, she broke it off and changed direction. "I talked to Jason. He's been with her nonstop since the bombing, except for when he came by to check on you. He's coming by tomorrow to give you details. He knows more than I do, and he wants to tell you himself." She hesitated again. "And the young girl you got out of the fire. She's already home with her family. They hadn't told me you tried to play hero. If you hadn't gone back in for her, you'd have been able to skip this whole hospital thing."

Pixie snored softly, fitting herself closer to my right side.

From her makeshift bed, Melina reached for my hand. Her voice sounded thick, as if she was crying, but I didn't turn on the light to see.

"Baby, the stores. Who is taking care of business with you gone so long?"

I heard a sniff. "Fuck the stores."

I knew she had managers, and that she always micromanaged them, but I was thankful she was here. I fell asleep wondering why she'd been crying. Tomorrow I'd push for her to sleep at the hotel or even consider going back. I knew I'd be fine.

The breakfast tray arrived unreasonably early. It was still dark. When I sat up and fed myself, it felt like an accomplishment, although I had some obstruction from Pixie, who was still in the bed. She smothered me with kisses. Not that I was complaining.

"Baby, you will get me excited. I'm not sure I can handle it," I said, but not really wanting her to stop.

"I had to fight to keep her in that bed," Melina said. "All the nurses complained. I got the doctor to approve it."

"Thanks," I said.

Of course, eating was easier as Melina's bag held a plastic bag of homemade tortillas. She rolled up the hospital eggs in the tortillas along with some salsa that emerged from the big purse.

"Where did you get these?" I waved the tortilla around and took another bite. It was the first time I'd been able to eat more than a bite or two without feeling queasy. "These are great tortillas, as good as Aunt Carmen's."

"They are Aunt Carmen's. I like London," Melina said. "But I can't find any of the products I market back home. No tortillas. This all started because your aunt wanted to fix you tortillas. I thought we could buy them. I looked everywhere. Well, the girls looked everywhere. I talked to the concierge at the Hyde Park Hotel who got me to the head chef in the kitchen. I slipped him some British pounds and he let your aunt mix and roll out these flour tortillas. He was fascinated, by the way, at Aunt Carmen's technique. She rolls those things out like a machine."

I didn't answer right away, chewing away at the taste of home till my jaw hurt.

"Maybe you should open a market in London. From the sound of it, you won't have any competition."-

She looked at me like I had grown a third head.

Everyone left for the hotel to shower and change clothes.

"Don't do anything I wouldn't do," Melina said on her way out. I knew I was getting better because this was the first time Melina left me with no one on watch.

"That means I can fuck the nurse," I called after them.

"You got all of us. You don't need the nurse," Pixie said, last out of the door, blowing me a kiss.

When Camila walked in, I felt a slight rise between my legs.

"*Amor, Amor, Amor*, I was so worried. Now they tell me you will be out of here soon. I'm so happy to have good news."

She leaned in, hugging me. Hugging is not easy when you are lying in bed with all kinds of tubes all over you, but her touch turned me on. A good sign, for sure. The machine I was hooked to went nuts whenever I moved.

"Hug me tighter. I can handle it."

She didn't hug me tighter, but she did stay there leaning over me, her lips all over my face.

One of the day nurses came in and glared at Camila. When I looked up, there was Pepe behind the nurse. Neither I nor Camila heard him come in. Camila disentangled.

The nurse checked me over. She wiggled her finger at Camila.

"It's bad enough he has his cousin sleeping with him during the night."

She told Camila not to excite me and stormed out.

"Ignore her," I said. "She does that all the time. This is the biggest gift ever, to see you guys."

I didn't know if the flush on Camila's face was embarrassment or excitement. I hoped it was excitement. It has to be excitement, I was getting to know her better, and I doubted that Pepe had anything over her, any real control over her personal life. I don't think much would embarrass Camila. She was pretty much impulsive and vivacious and did not hold anything back, as far as I knew.

"*Amigo*, good to see you conscious. I never doubted for a minute that you would wake up."

Camila stepped out of the way, and I extended my hand to meet his firm grip.

"I owe you so much, Pepe. I heard you visited when I was out of it. *Gracias.* And thanks for sending the plane. My aunt, my team, Melina. It means a lot. I treasure your friendship. I can't tell you how much I owe you. Thank you."

"Please don't thank me. We are friends. There is nothing I wouldn't have done to get you well."

Pepe got a quick kiss from his sister.

"My brother is the sweetest person in this world," she said.

"No question," I agreed.

He made small talk for a while, then said, "I am going back to Colombia. Camila is headed to New York. We will be checking on you every day. Melina and Oscar know how to reach us if something comes up. Promise you will not be shy."

"I promise," I said.

Pepe smiled. Camila linked arms with his and smiled too.

"Oscar and Tom are flying back with me," Camila said. "The pilot will drop me off in New York. They will continue to Los Angeles."

"You are way too generous." I looked at her, then at Pepe. "Thank you for coming. I love you both. I feel like I've known you all my life."

Camila kissed me on the lips, ignoring her brother. "Maybe we met in another life," she said.

Pepe let out one of his boisterous laughs. "Anything is possible."

"*Amor, te quiero mucho.*"[42]

"*Y yo a ti,*" I said. "*Los quiero a los dos, muchisimo.*"[43]

"Olga is worried. She will be here to see you tomorrow."

I was glad they took my advice and headed for home.

Olga came by and sat with me. She didn't have much to say. She looked worried.

"I went by the hotel where everyone is staying," she said. "Camila and Pepe had me pay the bill. Some deals I don't always like when they send me to pay, but

---

[42] Love, I love you very much

[43] I love you, too. I love you both a bunch

I liked paying everyone's bill at the Mandarin. Your aunt is lovely. Melina is beautiful. Someone named Juan was very charming to me. You have many people who care for you," she said. "Including me."

When I woke up, she was gone.

The bobbies came by the hospital with questions. They'd been there before when I was unconscious. Now I told them everything I remembered. The bombs going off. The fire. The ambulances.

Then Jason was there around lunch, giving me a hearty welcome that did not ring true. It was very British of him to act as if everything were normal. At least, he started out that way. But I could see the worry in his face. He looked exhausted, deep shadows under his eyes, new worry lines creasing his face. His clothes were rumpled as if he'd slept in them. Maybe the stoic look was just the British in him. He gave me a hearty handshake, acting very unlike himself. I knew something was up.

"Sami sends her best wishes.

"Is she going to be okay? Did she really send her best wishes?"

"Yes, she is conscious. Her brain functions are fine." His face was tight. He was holding back.

"What are you not telling me?"

His face broke. He blurted, "That it's a miracle she's lived this long."

"What are you telling me, Jason?" I pictured the last time I saw her. Picking her up. Getting through the smoke. Getting her to the ambulance. She had been breathing. Nothing broken that I could recall.

Jason teared up. He was standing by my bed, his eyes on mine. "It's not good, Mario. It's not good."

He looked like he was going to fall down. "Sit," I said.

Jason sat like his feet had been knocked out from under him.

"If she's made it this long, how can they not fix whatever is wrong? This is 1978. We've been to the moon. How can they not cure her?" I heard the panic in my voice. I tried to push off from the bed. The monitor I was hooked to started going crazy.

"She has the best medical care available. Five doctors working together. Two of them attend the royal family. Everyone knows Sami, not only because of her family name, but also her generosity to so many charities. This is payback time. They are coming together to look for a solution."

"What kind of solution?"

"It's not good, Mario. No matter how many doctors. It's not good." He choked up.

I felt sympathetic tears roll down my face. I tried sitting up, putting my legs over the edge. My monitors were screeching.

"One of her lungs," Jason said. "They call it blast lung." His face had melted into grief. All his British reserve was gone, and he was crying as if his heart were broken. Maybe it was. After all, he'd known Sami his whole life.

A nurse knocked and poked her head in. She rushed to my machine hookups and checked me over, trying to settle me down. She turned to Jason, but once she saw his complete meltdown, she held back whatever she was going to say to him.

"Lie down," she told me, as she had dozens of times before. "Use the button if you need something."

I waited till the nurse left.

"I've got to see her," I said. I didn't care that I still had tubes attached to my body and wasn't sure I could walk farther than the toilet three feet away, where I was finally able to go on my own, with tubes hanging, pulling the drip tower with me.

"Stay positive. Melina says if all goes well, you'll be out next week."

We both stopped crying. I tried to take heart in what he'd said. I was determined to be out in a week. Sami would be there next week.

"I will make it my life mission to spring out of here faster than fast," I said. "I need to see Sami."

"She will be happy to see you. She knows how critical she is." His face was grim, but he tried to smile.

Of course she knew her condition. She was a physician.

"How is she taking it?"

"Sami is a tough gal, but only she knows what is going on inside her mind." He looked toward my window, and then back at me. "She just signed 'Do not resuscitate' forms. Instructions that she does not want to be revived if she slips away."

"I can't believe this." I wanted to jump up and pace the room. I held myself still, trying to keep the machine noise attached to me at a minimum, though my heart was racing. It was hard, but it was a distraction from this sudden ton of grief I was feeling. I'd known they were hiding the truth from me, but I hadn't thought this was the truth.

"Let me tell you something, Mario. She has been worried sick about you. When I told her you were out of the coma and alert, she insisted I get my ass over here. I had already told Melina I'd be here today."

"On an earlier trip, back in '75," I said, "there had been an explosion close to a restaurant we were in. There was some chaos, some traffic. We got in the car and Ginger drove us back to her place. We hardly even discussed it. It should have been a warning. A fucking warning to stay out of pubs and public events and department stores."

"The IRA bombings are public knowledge," Jason said heavily.

I told Jason how the police had been around, and I repeated all I had told them and asked him to fill the blanks.

"This is what I know," he said. "Ginger rode in the ambulance with Sami. She talked to the police on the scene and saw you put into another ambulance. That's how you ended up—initially, anyway—here at the same hospital. Ginger called Sami's father and me. Sami's father was here less than ten hours after getting the call. He's been with her since he arrived. We both have. When Ginger tried to reach your family, she got the exchange, and they connected her to Jo, who had just returned from Puerto Rico. Jo contacted everyone on your end. I met your Melina in the waiting room. She's a cheeky little number, isn't she? You know, she doesn't half remind me of Sami."

"I've often thought that myself," I said. "They are so much alike."

"I ran into another friend of yours last week in the emergency room. Pepe. From Colombia," he said.

"He just left," I said. "You just missed him. He's going home."

"He must be quite a character," Jason said. "He flew all of your people out here in a private plane, and the group checked into the Hyde Park."

"He's like that," I said. "I owe him a whole lot."

"Too bad Sami has not had a chance to meet him," Jason said. "Sami wanted to own a plane big enough that she could go anywhere." He was pensive. "She never bought one. Too attached to the hospital, to her life here in London, not out there in the family estate that her mother left her."

"She asked me to come live with her, and we could travel the world," I remembered aloud.

"She wasn't kidding. She thinks the world of you."

"The timing is fucked, but I need to ask. Why didn't you two get married? You're so close."

Jason nodded slowly, a sad smile. "We talked about it, but we didn't want to ruin what we had."

I couldn't believe my ears. That was exactly what Melina and I told each other when marriage came up.

"I need to wake up. Tell me this is a nightmare. All of this," I said, closing my eyes.

"It's no dream, Mario. It's real."

I had a flashback of Tanis and me outside the motel room when that hooded bastard shot us, killing my Tanis and almost killing me. I had been spared then, and this time I was spared again. Sami wasn't dead like Tanis had been. Sami could have a chance to make it. I needed to get out of here. I needed to talk to her. I needed to get her to hang in there, not give up.

By the time I'd been delivered another bad hospital meal, the girls were back. Melina had relayed to them the doctor's okay to talk about work, so they reported how they had signed the Puerto Rico families in the helicopter crash and already delivered the retainers to Oscar before they'd left for London.

"Tom said it's a great case," Letty said.

"Hey," I said, "you have your first bonus coming."

"I love being out with the team. I love you all for letting me be part of your mission," Letty said.

"You make it sound like we're doing you a favor."

The girls left. My aunt came by with some more food she'd prepared in the hotel kitchen, then Melina came in with me for the rest of the day. She had brought a salad from the hotel, which she ate while I fed myself the sad hospital blandness that passed for dinner.

"You can feed me," I told her. "Take off your clothes, and I can pour some of this..." I sniffed to be sure, "...gravy somewhere interesting, and let me lick it off."

The monitor started registering my increased heart rate. We both laughed.

"Behave yourself before that nurse comes back to yell at me," Melina said, but she was still laughing. "One of the day nurses said you've been getting too worked up."

"Maybe that's the one that walked in when Camila kissed me." I grinned. "You should have seen her face. The nurse, I mean. You'd have thought she caught us fucking."

"I'm glad you're getting better," Melina said. "That's really the only thing I care about."

Four was the limit, but I had all five of my girls in the room, except my aunt, who was napping at the hotel. I told them about Sami.

Tears formed and pooled on Melina's lashes.

"Jason never said how serious it was."

"Mario, I'm so sorry," Jo said. Everyone was crying. Pixie and Niley rested their heads on my chest. Letty embraced them, standing and leaning behind them. I could feel what they wanted to say without having to hear it. I'm known as a big tough guy that can kick ass, take on anyone that fucks with me. Today I was falling apart.

At last, after my being conscious for ten days, Doctor Young released me. She gave Pixie three huge envelopes with copies of my records. I'd gotten instructions from her on how to ease back into karate. I was to be extra careful, in case there might be nerve damage. I promised not to push myself too far and to obey if my body was alerting me that I was in pain, instructions that went completely against everything Cosmo taught. Cosmo was the type who believed most of the time that if it didn't hurt, I wasn't working hard enough. But I was to watch in case my brain failed to deliver pain signals. She suggested I wear a helmet when working out with someone else, or to consider giving up karate altogether. I trusted that I'd heal. No way I was wearing a helmet. No more karate for me till the doctors stopped threatening me with a helmet.

I went to the hotel. I spent a few hours with everyone, which gave me a glimpse of how they'd all been bonding with each other here ever since they'd arrived. Jo had collected all my things and they were packed up in her room. I got up from the sofa in my aunt's suite and looked down Hyde Park toward Sami's place. The whole group was absorbed in making dinner plans, but Melina got up and joined me at the window.

"No one will be offended if you go see her," Melina said. "The only reason I would stand in your way is to keep you from being hurt. It's going to hurt to see her, but you will feel worse if you don't and… you lose the chance."

I kissed Melina on the forehead. In that minute, I think I loved her more than ever. She called for a hotel car to take me to Sami's. I rode over there alone, remembering that not long ago I had a cab from the airport to find Sami was outside on the sidewalk waiting for my arrival. This time it was Jason. I felt a knot in my throat.

"She will be so glad to see you," he said. "We've made a few changes in the flat. We had to make it a hospital in order for her doctors to approve the move."

"I assume this is what she wanted," I said as we got in the familiar elevator.

"She said she wanted to die here and not in a hospital."

I shook my head. My heart twisted in anguish. I felt myself crying again.

"I'm just being straight with you," Jason said, his own hurt written all over his words.

"Please, keep it that way. I need to know. How is her father?" We ignored the tears streaming down both our faces.

"Devastated. Hard to tell when you speak with him. He refuses to accept that Sami is going to…" He was keeping it real, but he couldn't finish the sentence. His voice broke.

"I won't accept that either," I said.

Ginger appeared and gave me a hug.

"So happy you are out and about. So worried about you, Mr. Mario."

"Cut the Mister." I kissed her left and right cheek.

"Have you seen her yet?" she asked softly.

"No," I said.

Ginger's face crumbled, just as Jason's had done. In a low, worried voice, she introduced me to two off-duty nurses, but I wasn't paying attention to their names. The nurses were all sharing one of the guest rooms that had twin beds. I knew the room well. Sami and I had once had sex on both of those beds. It seemed to have been very long ago. I was eager to see Sami, but also dreading it. I think just about any image would be better than my last sight of her on that gurney, with my blood on her face. I had to stop and gather myself. I forced back the tears. I pushed the anguish down in me, but my throat was full of it. If I made even a sound, nothing but pain was going to come out. How does pain do that, live in your throat like that, swelling your vocal cords till you are strangling in your own grief? But I did not want to break down in front of her. I felt somehow that if I could convince her to be okay, she would be.

I didn't see the flat's changes until I walked into the first bedroom. It was no longer just a bedroom. It was straight out of a hospital, but the most luxurious hospital you could imagine. She had a hospital bed, but it was king-sized, set inside some antique frame, and made with the most luxurious linens. The carpeting had been taken up, so that the bed rested on shiny wooden flooring, probably something exotic. The third nurse was sitting in the room with Sami, along with a man who was introduced to me as Doctor Roberts, a pulmonary specialist who was staying in one of the bedrooms. I'd have recognized them as medical professionals by their white uniforms even without introductions. There were other additions: a table full of remote controls, a television, radio, a record player, and a stack of books. The blackout curtains were open, revealing the great view. And there in the midst of it all was Sami, entirely unchanged. But changed forever. She was the first thing I'd seen, still the center stage of any room she was in. Her glowing fair skin marred with bruises tore at my heartstrings, and she could not be more pale. Her hair was bright as ever, impossibly red now that she was so pale and bruised. She was smaller, too. How could she have gotten so small and frail in only a few weeks, when I was in the same explosion and already on my feet? It was not fair.

She smiled when she saw me, suddenly her old self. I could see Sami inside this shadow of herself, beaming. But then she began to cough. The cough went on and on. The nurse got up and halted me with an upraised palm. She pulled down an oxygen mask from a resting place on the bedframe and fastened it to Sami's face. Minutes passed. The nurse let me sit beside Sami and take her hand. I don't know how long I was there, because I lost track of time. Eventually Sami took off the mask.

"Mario," she said with her biggest grin. "I am so glad to see you." She opened her arms wide and gave me a hug. I could hear her breathing, harsh with effort. Her shoulders were frail, her shoulder blades like butterfly wings. It was obvious how hard breathing was for her. I fought to tamp down my emotional response. "I hope you forgive me for choosing that pub that night. I can't forgive myself."

"I would forgive you anything, but this was not your fault. You're not allowed to feel guilty. Promise you won't," I insisted.

She nodded. Her eyes gleamed, full of emotion she had no breath to express.

"No one knew how you were," I said. "They've been lying to me."

She smiled, beaming. I could see how important it was that I forgave her. She coughed again. "They told me the same. You look wonderful."

I could say nothing. I was full of the unfairness. It was not fair that I could already be back on my feet while she was fighting for every breath.

"Give me a second to take some of this oxygen. It helps." She held the mask up to her face on her own for a few minutes, then she removed it.

I'd never seen her so pale and wan. "You gotta shake this off so we can go out and party."

"Doing my best," she said, but it came out as kind of a wheeze. She gave me a thumbs up. I leaned down from my chair by her bed, and she gave me another hug. It was like getting a hug from a butterfly. It felt like she was barely there. I was terrified I was going to crush her with my big, clumsy self. My stomach turned. I fought to control it. Shock. Anxiety. She wheezed again and lifted her arm away. I backed off gently, holding my rigid mask of a smile. My throat was full of tears I could not shed. I saw Jason in the doorway looking in.

"Mario, I enjoyed every single minute we spent together," Sami said. "You are my very good friend. I worry about you. Your volatile life. All the things that have happened to you. If I knew you'd move to London, I would gift you this house."

"Baby, please don't talk like that, please."

She placed the mask on her face and waved at the nurse. It must have been a prearranged signal, because the nurse stepped outside.

Her father came in, by accident, timing, or because the nurse had gotten him.

She removed the mask. "Daddy, this is my friend, Mario." She smiled. She was breathtaking. I wondered how that smile of hers could still telegraph so much joy.

I shook hands with her father. He was six inches shorter than me, but a healthy-looking man. I remembered she'd told me that he was a lawyer. He looked like a lawyer. We shook hands.

"Daddy, I've given Jason my favorite ring to give to Mario. Maybe someday he can give it to his bride."

"Don't give up, Sami," her father said. "Please."

I agreed wholeheartedly. "Don't talk like that," I said. "You've got to believe in yourself."

Her father glanced at me from the opposite side of her bed. He had her light eyes and fair skin, but his hair, if it had been bright once, had faded. I could see his pain, and his approval of me. We both waited to speak. She pulled her hands free to use the mask again. She took our hands again as she breathed, eyes closed, terrifyingly pale against the pillow and her bright hair. Terrible patience. The clock ticked. I tried to will every bit of my strength into her, through my hand, while she was here, breathing. The oxygen tank made a soft whooshing sound. Clocks ticked and ticked.

She shook her hands free and pulled off the mask. "I'm a doctor. I know exactly what is wrong with me. I don't know how I've lasted this long." She smiled. Incandescent. "Probably to make sure I saw you," she said to me.

Her right hand moved to hold up the mask. Her father's eyes filled with tears. He turned away so she didn't see him break down, and he stepped outside. He grabbed Jason in the door, and they hugged. I could see her father's shoulders shaking with the force of his grief before he tore himself away to recover in the hall. Jason took her hand across from me. She whispered something to him, and she looked at me again. I was fighting my sympathetic response to her father. My own grief was building up.

All I could see was her beautiful eyes. Her beautiful eyes, focused on mine, blinking the seconds away.

I leaned over to kiss her, felt the tears spill.

"I'm sorry," I said. I don't know what I was apologizing for—for the tears, for not being strong in front of her, for not insisting to sit by the wall, for her injuries, for her having to bear this terrible fate. I wanted desperately to pull back time from what was to what could have been. She pulled her left hand free and touched my head. She ran her fingers through my hair. I knew that touch so well. I picked up the oxygen mask and held it to her face.

The doctor walked in, an unwelcome presence. I wanted to chase him from the room. Foolish emotion. I knew he was keeping her alive, but he felt like death.

"You need to step outside for a bit. Give her a chance to breathe the oxygen."

I hugged her as best I could, but she was so frail. She pulled me to her with both hands and whispered in my ear, "I love you. Thank you for sharing yourself with me."

"I love you, too." I wanted to say more, but what else was there that I could say?

The doctor hustled Jason and me from the room. A fatigue hit me like I'd never known.

I sat with Jason and her father in the room off of the balcony. I could not think of how many times I'd been here. The weekends I'd stolen away, played hooky from my routine to taste life with Sami. And now she was struggling to breathe, just a few feet away. I could not bear it.

We were each wrapped up in our own thoughts. Ginger came around and saw us sitting like statues. She brought out the glasses and poured us each a brandy.

"To Sami," Jason said, his voice ravaged.

The three of us clicked glasses and drained our snifters. The drink was nothing. Just a prop. We took comfort in each other, a vigil that lasted all night. I looked at my watch just before dawn.

I stood.

"I have to go," I said.

"Take this." Jason rummaged in a drawer and pulled out a box and an envelope. I pocketed them both without looking. They made me sad. I looked in on Sami, but she was asleep. It was hard to leave, knowing this would be the last time I would see her alive.

Ginger took me to Heathrow in the wee hours.

Pepe's plane was waiting to take us to New York and Los Angeles. Everyone was already aboard. My aunt was asleep in one of the beds, and the girls were piled in the other two, asleep. Only Melina was in the main area with me. The others were lucky. They'd escaped my terrible mood.

"Why wasn't it me?" I raged until I was exhausted. Melina faced me head on, or as much as she could seated next to me in the main cabin area, tricked out like a living room. The steward had already removed the partition between our seats.

"Bad luck of the draw," Melina said. "She was a little closer to the blast. She's small and frail, and look at you. It was like your karate thing, rolling with the punches or taking the full brunt. She got the full brunt. You rolled."

"We were both there. It should have been me."

"Of all the pubs in London, how did you end up in that pub? It didn't seem to be anything special."

"I had never been there before. Sami knew the place."

"I see. So she took you there. Maybe it's her fault."

"Don't think that way, please."

"I'll stop if you stop with the 'it should have been me' business."

I brushed it off with silence. Being belted into the seat didn't help. We had flown into turbulence. If I could have been pacing the aisle, maybe I would be handling this better. I wasn't handling my inner turbulence. The plane's violence just felt like an extension of my emotion anyway.

"You went opposite directions. She was knocked into a wall that didn't collapse, toward confined space. You were thrown the opposite way, toward the glass and doors. She sustained more impact."

"Melina, stop it already."

I was furious, trapped in that chair, my hands balled into fists. I needed to punch something. "She wanted to sit by the wall. I always do that. I should have insisted." I must have said this a hundred times already.

Melina's face was unmoved, but I saw her dash away a tear. I realized at long last that she was trying to put on a brave front for me. Maybe she knew I had to yell it out. I don't know. I don't know if she was shielding the girls, or letting me vent, or what the hell she was doing, but I was pissed off, and she was the only one there.

"You've known about this from the beginning," I accused.

"Doctor Young advised us to let you find out for yourself so you could heal. I talked to the police bomb expert, to Sami's doctors, to the hospital staff who said she was going home to die, to Jason, who sometimes said she was dying and sometimes said she was better. The worst thing was not being able to tell you, and being afraid that your knowing would cause some kind of a relapse. Now you know. But three weeks ago, we were grieving over you. Not Sami. You." She grabbed me with both arms and hugged, hard. Then she let go. "You're alive. I don't care how pissed off you are. You're still here."

Melina suddenly changed course. "I'm tired," she said, shutting her eyes.

Fuck. Now I was pissed off at the world *and* myself. I loosened my seatbelt and pulled Melina against me. She grabbed my lapel, and I felt her lean against me.

I could not sleep. When I shut my eyes, I saw Sami, pale, weak, struggling to breathe. The turbulence had passed, and I got up to splash water on my face. I found in my pocket the box Jason had given me and opened it.

It was the huge rock she always wore. The stone was a 15-carat emerald-cut white diamond. I looked over the certificate that had come with it, but mostly I stared at the beautiful piece, remembering Sami. She'd always had the ring on. If only it could talk, think of all the Sami stories it could tell. I put the ring in the box and returned to my seat. I handed the box and certificate to Melina.

"This could be worth a million dollars. It's a perfect stone," Melina said. "You must have meant a lot to her." She patted the seat next to her. "Sit down. Try to sleep."

I complied. Melina handed the ring back to me, and I cradled it as if it were Sami herself. Like Sami, it was valuable and one of a kind. I'd have gladly given it back somehow, if it meant she could have a future.

When I got home, a message from Jason was waiting. I knew what it was before I heard it: news of her death. Still, I listened, and my heart sank when I heard the words aloud. I cried alone, for I don't know how long. I put the small box on top of my desk. I opened it, stared at the ring, and remembered the woman who had worn it. It took all my guts to make the call to Jason. Emotionally, I was in bad shape, but not as bad as Jason had been when we'd parted at Sami's place after Doctor Roberts had told us he didn't think she was going to wake up. We had already said our goodbyes. As much as I was hurting, I knew he was hurting more. I owed him all the support I could give, so I sucked it up and made the call.

"I cannot hug you over the phone. Is there anything I can do for you?"

"You did everything you could. You forgave her for taking you to the pub. You don't know how much that was bothering her. All that matters is that she's not suffering anymore." He assured me he was doing the best that could be expected. He said he'd keep in touch. After he hung up, I just stared at the ring and breathed. My lungs felt no pain, but my heart was another story. It would take me a long time to deal with her disappearance from my life. Maybe I would never get over her. I'd never really gotten over Tanis, either, and all we'd had were hours stolen from Tanis' grueling emergency room schedule. Sami and I had spent so much time together since we'd met in 1975. We lived together for blocks of time, almost every minute of three years' worth of frequent London trips. I felt her loss deeply, and wondered how I could ever face London again.

Epilogue

Two weeks after I got home, I wasn't even close to hitting my morning workouts, but I was walking and hearing well, and I was feeling better, at least physically. Emotionally is another thing altogether. I talked to Jason daily, and for a while, with Sami's dad. He stayed in London for another month before heading back to his home in New York City. I did not think I could face London without Sami in it. Jason and I cried on each other's shoulders, or as much as you can do that on a phone line. Sami's death felt like an ending to me. An end to innocence, maybe, except that I don't think I was ever innocent. Beauty and passion should not die so harsh a death. How was it possible that such a brilliant light be cut off in its prime? It seemed that though she was gone, my infatuation for her was still a living thing. It was hard to think of the world without her, because she so expanded my perspective. Sami opened my eyes to a different life. Sure, she and Pepe and Jason were wealthy beyond any normal expectations, but it was more than that. They were people who were larger than life, and they lived that way. Sami had called me a deal maker. Maybe one day, my drive and ambition could take me far, but not now, not when grief left my spirit so crushed that I could barely cross a room, much less navigate the currents of making even the simplest deal. I was trapped in the black room of grief, where it is impossible for life to go on normally.

I trusted I would find my footing again, but it would take time.

Author's Notes

I know it was quirky of me to add the footnotes for money values, but I believe it is essential to understand how much more currency was valued when Mario was getting started. I know that as the years pass, the footnotes might need to be updated, or I might take them out. At one point, I was considering a Spanish glossary at the end, but footnotes worked best for that as well.

In spite of harvest gold kitchen appliances, sweater vests, body suits, polyester clothing, wide lapels, and fashion disasters in general best forgotten, the seventies had a lot to recommend it. It was a time before AIDS, and young peoples' attitudes toward sexuality were very different from those of their parents generation.

About the Author

George Hatcher is an entrepreneur with a gift for business and storytelling. Whether he's traveling the globe as a consultant/strategist for lawyers in high pro- file wrongful death cases, running one of his many enterprises, or at home with Molly amid the birds and cats in California, he's always got his eye on the next project. He does a whole lot more than what is mentioned here.

A longer bio is on his website at: www.georgehatcher.com/bio/bio.html